DANGER
ZONES

DANGER ZONES

Sally Beauman

FAWCETT COLUMBINE
NEW YORK

A Fawcett Columbine Book
Published by Ballantine Books

http://www.randomhouse.com

Library of Congress Cataloging-in-Publication Data
Beauman, Sally.
Danger zones / Sally Beauman.—1st ed.
p.   cm.
ISBN 0-449-90881-X
1. Fashion—Fiction.   I. Title.
PR6052.E223D28   1996
823'.914—dc20   95-52461

TEXT DESIGN BY DEBBY JAY

Manufactured in the United States of America
First Edition: July 1996
10   9   8   7   6   5   4   3   2   1

To Lovell, with love

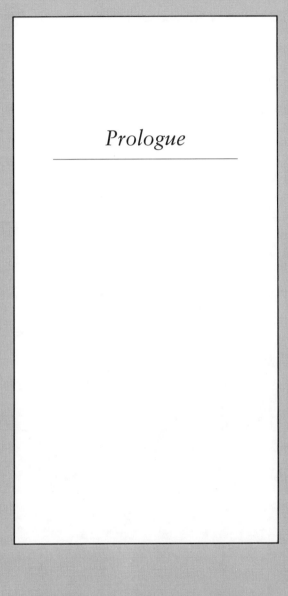

Prologue

The young executive in the black overcoat was nervous, but he had no trouble when crossing the borders. He left Amsterdam at six on a cold January morning, driving one of the fleet of Cazarès Mercedes. The temperature outside was below freezing, and inside the car he kept the climate control at sixty degrees Fahrenheit: no warmer, for he wished to stay alert. Fearful of black ice, of even the most minor accident, or any run-in with the police, he drove with precision and care, keeping five miles below the speed limit.

He tensed as he reached the border with Belgium, but the traffic was increasing by then. He was just one of many similar businessmen, in similar sedans, heading for Antwerp, Brussels, or Paris. Besides, EC regulations had dispensed with most border formalities: unless there was a major security alert, it was rare to be stopped.

He made good progress south on the fast, flat Belgian highways. Before ten, he was crossing into France on the autoroute, with his destination—Paris—no more than a steady hour's drive to his south.

Once in France, he began to relax—an error, he thought later. He switched on his CD player, allowed himself a much-needed cigarette. Feeling a rising elation, for his mission was almost accomplished, he also allowed his speed to creep up.

The Mercedes responded to the least touch on the accelerator. Coming up fast behind a lumbering truck, he pulled out to overtake, shot past with a contemptuous look—and saw the police car that had been concealed in front of it five seconds too late.

He felt a thump of adrenaline, an immediate drying of the mouth, but he drove on, gradually reducing his speed, signaled, and pulled back into the middle lane. He told himself the police would overlook his actions. If he had been driving a flashier car, a Porsche for instance; if he had not been wearing such irreproachable clothes, a Hermès overcoat and a custom-made Savile Row suit, they might flag him down. As it was, he looked the very picture of affluence and respectability. Surely he was safe.

As he thought this, he realized the police car was right up on his tail, and its lights and sirens had started up.

Keep calm, he said to himself. A warning, at worst a fine; he could handle this situation. He gave a polite gesture of acknowledgment, and pulled over onto the hard shoulder. He had about fifteen seconds while the police car pulled in behind and the officers got out. He glanced down at the black attaché case next to him on the passenger seat. Such cases were issued to all senior Cazarès personnel. This one bore his name, Christian Bertrand, and a discreet monogrammed tag attached to the handle, embossed with the letters JL. This indicated that Bertrand was one of six senior aides who reported directly to Jean Lazare himself.

For one long, painful second, he stared at the briefcase. His every instinct was to cover it with his overcoat or a newspaper, to conceal it under the seat. But the first policeman was already approaching, and any action that drew attention to the briefcase was a mistake. He checked his own reflection in the rearview mirror—he looked pale but composed. Then he opened his door. By the time the first policeman reached his side, he had his documents in his hand; he was polite, respectful—and ready with his excuse.

His apologies, of course; a momentary lapse of concentration. He paused, thinking—*don't mention Amsterdam*—then continued smoothly. His mind had been on the details of his breakfast business meeting in Brussels, and the report he would make to Monsieur Lazare when he reached Cazarès headquarters later that morning. He waited, allowing time for these names, of magical significance to any Frenchman, to take effect. They registered—Bertrand could see that.

The policeman did not show deference at once, but his manner thawed somewhat. He remarked that an important business meeting and a momentary lapse of concentration could excuse many things, but not hitting a speed of one hundred and thirty kilometers per hour in a ninety-kilometer-per-hour zone.

Bertrand murmured additional apologies. Handing over his documents, he remarked in a casual way that this was, of course, a very pressured time for anyone associated with Cazarès—as the officer would

certainly know, the Cazarès spring collection would be shown the following week.

The policeman absorbed this information. He gave Bertrand a slow,
assessing look. His eyes took in the cashmere coat, the expensive suit,
shirt, and tie, the conservative Elysée-style haircut, the tinted tortoiseshell-framed spectacles. Bertrand prayed silently that his sobriety of
dress would prove his salvation. The Sorbonne, Oxford, an MBA from
Harvard Business School—he silently recited this litany of achievements
to himself. Let the cop be a reasonable man, he prayed, and not an
overofficious busybody, the way some of them were; let him see that he
was now dealing with a well-educated, well-connected businessman
whose efforts on behalf of Cazarès were of international importance,
and added greatly to the luster and prestige of France.

Let him be patriotic; let him be goddamn well impressed, the young
man thought wildly, then he froze. While the first policeman was examining his documents with intolerable slowness, his partner was making a
measured pass around the Mercedes. He bent over its license plate,
touched a rear light, moved around to the front, examined the windshield wipers with minute and terrible attention. Then he opened the
passenger door. Bertrand watched him covertly. He leaned into the car;
he examined its dashboard, its instrumentation, its CD controls, its
hand-stitched black leather seats. Reaching forward, he opened the
glove compartment, then shut it again. Bertrand averted his eyes. He
thrust his hands into his overcoat pockets, hoping neither policeman
would notice that they had started to shake.

The second cop was looking at the attaché case now, Bertrand could
sense it. He risked one glance around, and he was right: the man had
moved the case, and was inspecting the monogrammed tag. Bertrand felt
fear clench his stomach; he began to feel sick and light-headed. He
thought, *I have to distract them. . . .*

Then, suddenly, it was over. The second policeman slammed the passenger door; the first folded up the documents and handed them back.

"Under the circumstances . . ."

He left the sentence unfinished, but Bertrand understood; he felt a
dizzying relief. They were letting him off—not even a fine! He was safe.
The second officer was already returning to his car. The first was also
turning away, then stopped.

"Cazarès . . ." he said.

Bertrand tensed.

"You've worked there long?"

"Four years."

There was a pause. Bertrand stared at the policeman uncertainly, trying to read his expression. It looked less officious now, almost reverential, he judged.

"Then you must have met her—Cazarès herself?"

Certainly reverential now, even awed. Bertrand relaxed.

He was off the hook. This question was familiar enough. He encountered it at dinners, at parties, at business meetings in Paris, in London, in Rome, in New York. It had its uses, working for a legend: little ripples of the glamour associated with Cazarès spread outward, touching all those who worked for her, whether executives or seamstresses. He smiled. He said that he had seen Cazarès, of course, on those celebrated occasions twice a year when she came out of seclusion to take her applause at the end of her couture shows. He paused, lowering his tone to one more confidential: and, he added, he had had the privilege of meeting her. He had been introduced, two years before, at a reception in her honor, by Jean Lazare himself.

"You mean you actually spoke to her?"

"A brief exchange, yes. Mademoiselle Cazarès is very shy, as you know, very sensitive. She didn't remain for that reception, of course, so I was exceptionally fortunate. A woman who dreads her own fame—an artist—so beautiful. An encounter I'll never forget . . ."

The lies tripped from his tongue; they were well rehearsed, for they were company policy, and he had given this same answer, or variations upon it, on many occasions before. It had to be made known that while Cazarès was shrouded in mystery, she did function, she did continue to design. Other senior Cazarès personnel might choose to stress her appearance, or her charm, or her degree of inspiration: Bertrand, who had never spoken to Cazarès, had always found that tortured artistry went down best.

"An extraordinary woman," the policeman said now, and shook his head.

Bertrand solemnly agreed, but offered no further information, since the more extraordinary aspects of Maria Cazarès—and he knew of them only by deduction in any case—could be imparted to no one, not even his own wife.

The incident was over. The police car departed. Bertrand, still shaken, returned to his Mercedes, smoked a cigarette to calm himself, and decided that he would not, under the circumstances, mention this little incident to Monsieur Lazare.

By the time he reached the courtyard of the beautiful seventeenth-century *hôtel particulier* which Lazare had purchased for the Cazarès business headquarters fifteen years before, he was nervous again. Lazare's dislike of being kept waiting, and his temper when delayed, were notorious. He prepared himself for the tongue-lashing that would certainly come. He pushed past the doorman, waved the elevator attendant aside, made for the stairs, and broke into a run as soon as he was out of sight.

Lazare's suite of offices was on the top floor of the building. His lair was guarded by a succession of secretaries and assistants and minions stationed in a sequence of hushed rooms. Since Bertrand was anticipated, no one made any motion to stop him, though Lazare's most senior secretary, a woman, lifted her eyes to an exquisite clock set into the paneling opposite her mahogany desk. She gave a tiny gesture of warning: *"Calmez-vous,"* she said.

Bertrand straightened his tie, tightened his grip on that attaché case, and opened the far door. He walked through an anteroom, along an enfilade flanked by mirrors and by tall windows overlooking the rue St. Honoré. It was one of the most beautiful, and one of the most expensive, views in the world—or so Bertrand liked to boast to his wife.

The door to Lazare's office was thickly padded with black leather to absorb sound. Bertrand paused, cleared his throat, then entered. He knew his arrival had already been announced, and—as always—he gave himself a few seconds in the doorway, so his eyes could accustom themselves to the gloom in which Lazare preferred to work.

He crossed the parquet floor to the desk and chair that constituted this office's only furniture. He stood looking down at Lazare, gave a respectful half-bow, and braced himself for the onslaught.

There was silence. The onslaught never came. Lazare slowly raised his head. He looked at the attaché case rather than Bertrand. Then with one long-fingered hand he swept the documents in front of him to the side of his desk.

"No difficulties?" he asked.

"No, sir, none. The traffic was very bad on the autoroute. I apologize for being late."

"You have the new product?"

"Yes, sir. As arranged."

"We have enough time?"

"Yes, sir. They advise a four-day monitoring period, to establish tolerance. One tablet daily, first thing in the morning, with food . . ." Bertrand hesitated.

"Continue," Lazare said.

"Food intake is advised, sir. Water intake must be ensured, before and after dosage. They stressed that point."

"Side effects?"

Bertrand hesitated again. Lazare moved, leaning forward so the pool of light from his desk lamp lit his features. "You heard me. Side effects? Yes or no?"

"Well, obviously, sir, the testing of the product has been limited so far, but they claim no adverse reactions. In a few cases an accelerated pulse rate, but that lasts only a few hours. Sleeplessness has been known, but only in cases where dosage has been increased, or administered too late in the day—"

Lazare cut him off with a curt gesture of the hand. He motioned Bertrand to place the attaché case on his desk, then looked at it in silence for a while. These silences on Lazare's part were famous, designed to intimidate, Bertrand had once thought. Now, more used to his ways, he saw Lazare's silences as less theatrical, a product of his extraordinary and unsettling concentration. To all intents and purposes, Bertrand knew, he had just ceased to exist.

He stood quietly, looking down at Lazare, whose fine hands now rested on the briefcase. He had worked for him since 1991, yet he understood him no better than on the day of his arrival. In four years Lazare had permitted no intimacies or insights, had conveyed not one single personal fact. Bertrand knew only that Lazare was around fifty, that he was probably not French by origin, that he spoke five languages fluently, that he worked long, slept little, and was rumored to live alone—although Lazare kept several properties in and around Paris, as well as others abroad, so even that rumor might not be correct. Of Lazare's famous business acumen and ferocity, Bertrand had firsthand experience; of his dedication to Cazarès as a business empire, there was no question. Bertrand remained uncertain whether it was true, as whispered, that this dedication and devotion extended to Maria Cazarès herself.

The silence continued. Looking down at the disconcerting and ascetic man who employed him, Bertrand, who did not like Lazare but respected him, felt admiration and fear mix with pity. It was not in Lazare's proud nature to admit weakness, and yet evidence of weakness—a weakness he would never have suspected—now lay between them on Lazare's desk. If this was what it took to get Lazare through the days leading up to the collection, then the strain upon him recently must have been greater than Bertrand had thought. Examining Lazare now, he realized he could detect evidence of that strain, and that he should have noticed it earlier. Lazare looked fatigued and bleak; when he raised his dark eyes, Bertrand was shocked by their expression.

"Open the case," Lazare said.

Bertrand did so. Inside were a number of tiny packages, each pains-takingly wrapped by Bertrand in his Amsterdam hotel room the night be-fore, according to Lazare's precise instructions. Each package consisted of a white box, two inches square, and each contained one tablet folded inside a piece of heavy gold *faille*. Each box had as its outer wrapping the heavy white raw silk that was one of Cazarès's signature textiles; each box was fastened with Cazarès's silver silk cord. The packages glimmered in the light from the desk lamp. They looked tiny, tempting, as if they contained something rare and sumptuous, a precious stone, some intri-cately worked jewel, or a minute phial of rare scent. It had been Lazare's idea that they were best disguised as gifts. There were six of the boxes in all. Lazare moved them so that four lay next to his left hand, and two to his right. He looked up once more. The lamplight accentuated the sharp jut of his features, and the dark, impenetrable quality of his stare.

"A four-day monitoring period. That takes me to the day before the collection. Then?"

Bertrand swallowed.

"On the actual day of the collection, sir, two tablets may be administered."

"I double the dosage?"

"Yes, sir. The level of tolerance will have built by then."

"And the results?"

"An intense sensation of well-being and optimism, sir. Elation. Confidence."

"How good to know one can purchase such things."

"Together with a marked physical improvement, sir. The effect is temporary, but the renewed energy is visible. Radiance is imparted to the skin and . . ."

"The eyes?"

"Just very slight contraction of the pupils, sir. Nothing too marked, and perceptible only at close range."

"Speech? Movement?"

"Unimpaired, sir."

"You tested the product yourself?"

"Yes, sir, as instructed."

Bertrand kept his eyes fixed on Lazare's, as he found it prudent to do whenever he lied to this man. "I took one tablet yesterday morning."

"One whole tablet?"

"Yes, Monsieur Lazare." He had in fact taken half. "I took the med-ication at ten A.M., after a meal in my hotel room. The effects were al-most instantaneous, and startling—"

"I don't require detail. The desired result was achieved?"

"Yes, sir. Dramatically so. There was an immediate release from all tension and anxiety. A sensation of calm and confidence. A heightened spatial awareness. Colors and sounds became extraordinarily intense, and . . ."

"Could you *rest?*"

Lazare posed the question with sudden intensity. Bertrand stopped short.

"Rest? Well, yes, eventually. I went to sleep around midnight—"

"You slept well? No dreams?"

"Only pleasant ones, sir." Bertrand risked a smile. "They were the kind of dreams I'd welcome any night . . ."

"I don't understand you."

"All five senses are stimulated, Monsieur Lazare. The effects are erotic. I did notice, shall we say, a marked and immediate increase in libido. Had I not been alone, I . . ."

"You may go."

The dismissal was curt. Bertrand, who had thought even Lazare might be amused by his last remarks, realized he had misjudged his tone badly. A closed, forbidding expression now masked Lazare's face. He bent his head to examine the boxes once again. Bertrand looked at the sleek gleam of his black hair in the lamplight. He began to back away from the desk. Overfamiliarity was something Lazare did not tolerate: with luck, he thought, he might just make it to the door before Lazare's temper snapped. He had been fortunate earlier, when his lateness went unrebuked. He could scarcely expect to be spared twice. Moving toward the door, he braced himself for the dressing-down, the icy sarcasm. One of the most fearsome aspects of Lazare's temper was its coldness: he could reduce a man to zero without ever raising his voice.

"Wait," Lazare said.

Bertrand paled, and turned to face him.

"Tell me . . ." Lazare was still examining the parcels. He was holding one of them, turning it this way and that.

"These little miracle pills—have they christened them? Have they given them a name yet?"

Bertrand, almost overcome with relief, confirmed that indeed, the little miracles had been christened. Their creator, the young Dutch chemist, had been in favor of a hard-edged, aggressive name, something that would give his new product immediate street cachet. His long-haired, spaced-out American partner had dissuaded him. What they needed, he argued, was a name that conveyed both the initial rush and the sensation of deep feathered calm that succeeded it.

"Once it hits the streets," he had said, "the kids will rename it anyway, they always do. Meantime—it makes you fly, man, then it wraps you up in this cozy little nest, then . . ."

"What's their *name*?" Lazare said again.

Bertrand, now recovered, came to the point. He told Lazare that the miracle pills, which were small, untinted, and sweet-tasting, were known as White Doves.

The name seemed to touch some chord in Lazare, who repeated it, as if to himself. He looked up at Bertrand again. His final question was sharp: "And they're safe?"

Bertrand, eager to escape, decided that now was not the moment to go into further detail. He decided not to mention any of the Dutch chemist's more crude remarks, or the American's incoherent warnings. He certainly had no intention of admitting to Lazare the full effects only half a tablet had had on him the previous night. Bertrand, a married man and straitlaced on most occasions, was not used to such loss of control. Lazare was in for some surprises, he thought, not without a certain malice.

"Powerful, sir," he replied. "But yes, completely safe."

Part One

ENGLAND

CHAPTER 1

The meeting with Rowland McGuire was scheduled for ten o'clock in his office in the features department, not in Lindsay's in fashion. Lindsay agreed to this venue, then realized it gave McGuire a territorial advantage. Irritated, she had begun planning at once. She did not like McGuire; she was disposed to loathe McGuire, who, in the two short months he had been at the newspaper, had already bested her more than once. It was becoming urgent to deal with McGuire; Lindsay had decided that at this meeting there would be no more feinting: she would—somehow—deliver a knockout punch.

She arrived at her desk that morning, as usual, at eight. She had gone to bed the previous night at twelve, and had risen at six. Before she left home, there had been the usual domestic imbroglios—leaking pipe, no milk, cat sick. Attacking her in-tray, she tried to persuade herself that she was ready for this bout with McGuire, resolve and energy intact.

By nine she had approved that week's fashion pages, lined up three future shoots, acted as unpaid analyst for her favorite photographer, Steve Markov—most of her photographers were neurotics, but Markov, whose latest boyfriend had just decamped to Barbados, was a maestro of temperament—and had finalized all the arrangements for the *Correspondent*'s coverage of the spring Paris couture collections, which would begin the following week.

At nine-thirty she retreated to her private office and shut the door on the shrilling telephones, the scurrying assistants. She drank her third black coffee of the morning, and began making lists—always a bad sign.

The lists grew. On the one headed WORK was a screed of numbers for models and assistants and accessorizers and fixers, all of whom, if soothed and bullied and cajoled and flattered in the right way, might ensure that she covered the spring collections efficiently, and without Markov threatening to slit his throat at ten-minute intervals. The other list, headed URGENT, made her spirits sink. It said things like *chicken?* and *toilet paper!* and *get petrol/call Gini/talk plumber*/wholemeal *bread/ tell Tom return vid tapes.*

It was now Friday; she was going away for the weekend. Neither her mother nor her son could be relied upon to remember to buy food, or to call plumbers when pipes leaked. How was she supposed to perfect her plans for McGuire when she was constantly distracted by trivia like this?

Straightening her back, and gazing icily at the view of leaden January sky from her window, Lindsay sat practicing *froideur* for a few minutes. The way to deal with the McGuires of this world, she had decided, was with an arctic and powerful disdain. She tried to recall the demeanor and techniques of the grandes dames who had still dominated the fashion world when she first began her own career, fifteen years before.

As a breed, these Vreelands were now almost extinct: vestiges of their chilly elegance, of their effortless tyranny, could be detected in certain of their descendants, but such qualities did not come naturally to Lindsay herself. As far as she could remember, of course, these women had been insulated from anything resembling real life. They presumably had bevies of drivers, maids, housekeepers, and cooks; their husbands had been nonexistent or invisible; none, as far as Lindsay could remember, had had children, and if they did, the children were exemplary and had long since left the nest.

I am fashion editor of a prestigious newspaper, Lindsay said to herself. I hold down a much-envied job, which is widely if erroneously perceived as glamorous—whatever that means. I am an independent working woman. I can be a grande dame anytime I feel like it. I am off to the Paris collections on Monday. Watch out, Rowland McGuire, because I also understand office politics, and I am about to grind you underfoot.

Lindsay looked down at the feet in question, on which she usually wore blessedly comfortable black canvas high-top sneakers. Today they were clad in sleek Manolo Blahnik black pumps with three-inch heels. The shoes, eye-stoppingly elegant and heart-stoppingly expensive, pinched her toes. Her son Tom called them her executive tart shoes.

Lindsay practiced another blood-freezing glance at the window, screwed up the lists, lobbed them hard at the wastepaper basket, and missed. The truth of it was, she was not cut out to be a grande dame. First, small and boyish-looking, she had the wrong physique. Second, there was no disregarding the facts of her life: she was a thirty-eight-year-old single parent who lived in a chaotic West London apartment with a mother who was born impossible and a seventeen-year-old son who was about, she hoped, to emerge from the hormone storm of adolescence: both mother and son trusted her implicitly to pay all the bills and solve every crisis in life.

Tom was fiendishly clever, but taciturn. For the past three years his normal mode of conversation had been a grunt. Since autumn, however, he had in rapid succession acquired a girlfriend, had the flu, and discovered Dostoevsky. The combination of love, literature, and the recent 102-degree fever had restored his voice. Lindsay was now harangued about ethics as she tried hastily to dust or cook. Louise, her mother, who drifted through life on a cloud of purposeful optimism, said this was a breakthrough; Lindsay was less certain.

"Tom's emerging from the chrysalis, darling," Louise had said the night before. "Now you'll be able to cement your relationship. Lots of splendid wise motherly *talks*."

"He can talk to his girlfriend," Lindsay said through gritted teeth as she stirred canned spaghetti sauce very fast. "That's her function. Boys Tom's age don't want to talk to their mothers."

"Nonsense, darling," Louise said airily, pouring herself some wine and lighting up a cigarette. "He doesn't want to talk to the girlfriend. Her function is sex."

Lindsay closed her eyes. The guilty voice at the back of her mind, always hyperactive, was now starting to jabber about contraceptives, AIDS statistics, and unwanted pregnancies, when she needed to concentrate on McGuire. She looked at her watch, swore, rose, applied some extremely red lipstick, and squirted herself with a super-powerful and unsubtle American scent. She stalked through to her outer office. There, Pixie, her assistant, who was looking forward to this moment, waited until precisely five past ten, then dialed McGuire's office. She explained in tones of dulcet insolence that Ms. Drummond was in conference, and would be delayed: Lindsay stood over her, making faces, while she did this.

Pixie was nineteen and ambitious. Talented too; her intention was to be editing English *Vogue* by the time she was thirty, and to take New York by

storm by the age of thirty-three. Pixie, a nouveau punk, could always be relied upon to dress originally. This morning she had a diamond in her nose;
she was wearing bondage trousers, an African necklace, and a Gaultier top
that appeared to be made of shrink-wrap. She had a strong Liverpudlian
accent, and she was streetwise. Lindsay used to pretend she had hired her
for this last quality; in reality, she had hired her because she liked her, and
because Pixie reminded her of her own younger, blithely confident self.
Pixie, who often made Lindsay feel old, giggled as she hung up.

"Poor McGuire," she said. "He's about to be gutted."

"Good."

"Why don't you like him?" Pixie eyed her. "I think he's gorgeous
myself."

"He's a *man*. An interfering, arrogant man. Watch and learn, Pixie,
all right?"

"He can interfere with me anytime. I wish he would."

"Pixie. Pay attention. Do I look intimidating? How about the suit?"

"The suit's totally brilliant. Really keen. You want to test me?"

"All right. I'll give you a clue. It cost five months' salary. It required a
mortgage. A loan from the World Bank."

"It's a Cazarès, obviously." Pixie frowned. "Give me a second. Last
year? Spring? Autumn? Yeah—autumn, 'ninety-four. Not the ready-to-
wear line . . . It's saying 'couture' to me. . . ."

"Let's hope it says the same to McGuire."

"—but it couldn't be couture. Not unless you met a millionaire
recently . . ."

"I wish."

"So it's the ready-to-wear, but top of the line. I'm looking at the buttons—*love* the buttons, and the cut of the jacket, on the bias, and the
fabric. Cashmere?"

"And silk. What else?"

"The collar?" Pixie began to smile. "The way the collar sort of curves
around the neck?"

"Good. Getting warm."

"Got it. Autumn 'ninety-four. The Signature line. Kate Moss modeled
it, in beige, not black. It came out number forty-two."

"Forty-three. Very good, Pixie. So—am I late enough now? What
d'you think?"

Pixie grinned, and consulted her watch.

"Twenty minutes. Give it another five maybe? I mean, if you're going
to be rude, be really rude, right?"

"Exactly." Lindsay returned the grin.

She gave it ten.

"Have some coffee." Rowland McGuire lifted his feet off his desk and rose to his full six feet five inches. Lindsay gave him a look of calculated ice, its effects slightly marred by the necessity of looking up.

"If you have time," she said. "As you know—I'm running late."

McGuire let this pass with only a brief glance at his watch. "Sit down," he said over his shoulder. "Sorry about the mess. Just kick those books out of the way. Review copies. All junk."

Lindsay glared at his broad-shouldered back. She saw that unlike every other man in the building, McGuire seemed capable of making coffee for himself. Another of his ruses, she decided—and one designed to impress. She was certain that had she not been there, a female secretary would have been summoned, one of the clutch of assistants, all new, who sat outside McGuire's office and trembled at his approach.

Without comment she threaded her way to his desk. Her progress was impeded by stacks of papers, piles of books. In two months McGuire had transformed this department, and its efficiency. Pre-McGuire, the features department had been an amiable place, populated by talented young men who avoided strenuous activity and spent much of the day when not lunching with contacts congratulating themselves on the fact that they had avoided the demands of the newsroom where people were actually required to work. Since the advent of McGuire, these loafers had departed. They had been replaced, Lindsay had noted sourly, by a large number of attractive young women, all of whom were rumored to be ambitious, frighteningly bright—and in love with Rowland McGuire. That morning Lindsay had run the gauntlet of their assessing stares; she had been extremely glad to be wearing the Cazarès suit.

McGuire's office was equally transformed. Formerly a place of humming modernistic display, all chrome and black wood, it now resembled a scholar's bolthole circa 1906. McGuire's state-of-the-art IBM computer was there, it was true, but it was virtually invisible; every surface in the room was piled with papers, magazines, and books. Sitting down by the desk, Lindsay squinted at the titles and was annoyed to see that the pile nearest her consisted of government white papers surmounted by a dog-eared, clearly much-consulted edition of Proust. In French.

She leaned forward and inspected the papers McGuire had been reading when she came in; she could see a large green file, a pile of faxes, and that morning's edition of the *Times*, folded back at the crossword. McGuire, it was whispered, completed these crosswords in fifteen minutes flat; she now saw that the insufferable man filled in the answers in ink.

"You must be the only man in London," she said, "who fills in the *Times*'s crossword in fountain pen. What happens if you make a mistake?"

"I don't. Usually," McGuire said, handing her a cup of coffee. "I've always found crosswords quite easy. Even the *Times*. It's a quirk. A sort of knack."

Lindsay gave him a sharp glance. His tone was modest enough. Two months before, when McGuire was first appointed, she might have been deceived by that tone: now she was not. Having given the impression that he was startlingly handsome, pleasant, and too good-natured to last long in this job, McGuire had started firing people. In between felling the dead wood, he had overruled Lindsay's decisions twice in his first month. To do so once was forgivable. To do so twice was not. Lindsay had wasted no further time in arguments with McGuire, whom she realized she should have distrusted on sight. She went straight over his head, to the editor of the *Correspondent*, an old friend, Max Flanders.

In Max's office, over a large whiskey at the end of the day, she had made a further discovery. McGuire, who had seemed so uninterested in power plays, had gotten there first.

"Look, Max," she had said. "Who's running the fashion department here? I thought it was me. It says it's me on my contract. Now I discover it's an Adonis with attitude. Do something, Max. I turn to you in desperation. Get this man off my back."

"Strong words," said Max, and lit a cigarette.

"Max, he knows nothing about fashion at all. Why in hell is he interfering? Since when did I have to answer to features? Is he empire-building, or what?"

"Certainly not. Rowland doesn't operate that way. Though I have to admit, I sometimes think he's being groomed for my job."

Max, once a wild young man, and one whose ascent to editorial power had occurred at vertiginous speed, now cultivated a bland manner. He wore conservative three-piece suits, as befitted the editor of a powerful conservative newspaper. He had recently acquired spectacles Lindsay was certain he did not need. Max was thirty-six, masquerading as fifty-six, when on duty at least. He now suppressed a smile, adjusted the superfluous horn-rims, and gave Lindsay an owlish look.

"Max—am I getting through to you? This man pulled some Steve Markov pictures it took me three months to set up. This man didn't like the model, didn't like the pictures, didn't like the clothes. The same man who did these things, Max, has never heard of Christian Lacroix. He admitted it, for God's sake! I doubt he's ever heard of Saint Laurent."

"That's what Rowland said? That he'd never heard of Lacroix?"

"He didn't even blush."

Max sighed. He lowered his eyes to his desk. "You don't want to believe everything Rowland says, Lindsay. He likes teasing people. I expect he was sending you up."

The remark did not improve Lindsay's temper.

"He's a clown," she said. "A damned devious one too, I'm beginning to think."

"Not exactly. Not really," Max replied in a mild way. "He has a starred First from Balliol. Devious, on the other hand—well, he's extremely determined, so there you could be right."

"Fine. And his Oxford degree was in fashion, was it?"

"Come on, Lindsay. This is boring. Classics."

"Okay. I'm impressed. He can read Latin and Greek in the original. The fact remains, he knows less about fashion than my cat. So who's running the fashion department, Max? Me, or some Oxford pedant with a power complex?"

"Wrong on three counts." Max gave her a smug look. "You shouldn't associate him just with Oxford. He's half Irish, a farmer's son. He isn't a pedant, he's fun. He's a very experienced and much-sought-after journalist whom I brought onto this paper to clean up the features department. Which he's done, in under two months. And he doesn't have a power complex. He just likes getting things done his way. As do you, of course."

"Oh my God. I'm beginning to understand. How old is he?"

"Thirty-fiveish."

"Your age, more or less. You're contemporaries, in other words. Did you know him at Oxford, Max?"

"Yes," Max said, still mildly. "I did, actually. We shared digs our second year. We shared a motorbike. We admired the same woman, only Rowland cut me out. We—"

"Give me strength." Lindsay finished her whiskey in one gulp. She could see how much Max was enjoying this. She stood up.

"Right. I won't mention old boy networks, Max. . . ."

"Far too cheap."

"I won't even mention male bonding. I get the message."

"I didn't like those Markov pictures either. Or the model. She looked half-starved. I don't like these waifs."

"I was overruled, and I stay overruled, right? That devious bastard's lobbied you. I've been screwed."

"Just in these two instances. Let's say I listened to McGuire's arguments. He thinks we could improve our fashion coverage if we took a stronger, more journalistic stance. Lindsay, he's very bright, you know. He's also bloody good. His views prevailed. Next time . . ."

"Next time his views prevail, Max, I resign. It's the collections this month. I won't have McGuire interfering. I won't work like this."

Max beamed at this threat. "Nonsense," he replied. "You'd never resign. You love this job. You love this newspaper. You love me—I'm a good friend, and an exceptionally good editor. . . ."

"You were once."

"And you'll love Rowland McGuire, given time. Ask around, Lindsay. Everyone loves him. Except the people he's fired, of course."

Not me, Lindsay thought now as McGuire returned to his desk. Had she disliked him and distrusted him less, she might have been prepared to admit that Pixie's description of him was apt. McGuire had the kind of looks that stopped traffic—and Lindsay had to admit that whatever other faults he had, vanity was not one of them; McGuire seemed genuinely unaware of his good looks. He certainly did nothing to enhance them. He had a lean, muscular build that even the aged and crumpled tweed suits he tended to wear could not entirely disguise. He had wild black hair, worn slightly long, and badly cut. He had green eyes, an amused, lazy, and faintly mocking expression: he was rumored to have the temper of a fiend, but Lindsay had never witnessed this.

Had she not known him as she now did, she might have imagined him striding across fields through Celtic mist. She could have seen him being capable in an outdoors sort of way, performing vaguely rural masculine acts such as ministering to a sick animal or chopping wood. She could see him being brave; she could imagine him being fearless on a mountainside; she could envisage him as a soldier or a poet or vet: what she could not see was a man who would function effectively in a modern newspaper office—yet clearly he did so, so this was her mistake.

Now she looked at him narrowly. The apparent kindness, the occasional gentleness of manner: they were deceptive, she thought, deliberately designed to disarm and charm: they merely ensured that McGuire, in the competitive world of newspapers, disabled his opponents and got to the finish line first.

"You're going down to the country today, I hear?" McGuire now said. "You're staying the weekend with Max?"

Lindsay jumped. Lost in contemplation of McGuire's ruthlessness, possible and already proved, she was forgetting the grande dame gambit. She straightened, and gave him a polar look.

"Yes, I am."

"Give my love to Mrs. Max. And all the mini-Maxes." He smiled. "Four children. I used to think it was excessive. Now I think—it's nice. I gather there's a fifth on the way."

"Yes. It's due in two months."

"Maybe it'll be a girl this time. Max would like that."

"No doubt," Lindsay replied, ignoring the almost imperceptible Irish lilt that had crept into his voice. Both it and the smile were attractive—and McGuire knew it.

"Look, can we make a start?" She leaned forward. "I have a lot of work to do before I leave. I'm finalizing the arrangements for Paris. Did you see the outline I sent you?"

McGuire shifted papers on his desk. "You're going down to Max's with a friend, I think Max said. . . ."

"Yes. Gini. Genevieve Hunter. You know her?"

"No. Before my time here . . ." He continued to sift papers in a distracted way. "I'm familiar with her work though. And her reports from Bosnia last year, of course. They were excellent. As good, in their way, as Pascal Lamartine's photographs . . . They'd worked together before, I believe?"

"Yes."

"They made a good team. I said so to Max. Where did I put that damn outline? It was here a second ago. . . . Why didn't she stay out there and continue working with him?"

"I really wouldn't know."

"Someone mentioned . . . She's been ill, I gather?"

"Not really. No. She's fine now anyway."

"Oh, I must have misunderstood. Max said . . ." He did not complete the sentence. Lindsay ignored the prompt. McGuire was well informed; if he knew about Gini's illness—and few people did—then Max had been gossiping. Clearly he and Max were far closer friends than she had realized.

It was then, when she was trying to figure out what in hell else Max might have told him, that McGuire sprang his surprise. He finally found the outline and tossed it back across his desk.

"Fine," he said.

Lindsay stared at him. "Fine? You mean you're happy with it?"

"You're the fashion editor." He shrugged. "If you have to use that damn Markov, use him. Feature the shows you select. If you could bring yourself to put the knife in just occasionally—that would be nice."

"You have no suggestions? I'm surprised."

"No. The collections are your domain. I wouldn't dream of interfering. After all, I can't tell a Lacroix from a Saint Laurent."

Damn Max, Lindsay thought, catching the glint of amusement in McGuire's green eyes. Her conversation had been reported back.

"I'm glad you've learned your limitations." Lindsay pushed back her chair, intent on a fast exit.

"There is just one other thing," McGuire said.

Lindsay turned back in surprise. McGuire had picked up that green file, she saw, a heavy green file, tied with tape.

"That suit you're wearing—it's a Cazarès isn't it?"

Lindsay gave him a venomous look. "Yes, as it happens. It is."

"Have you met Cazarès ever? Interviewed her?"

Lindsay looked at him uncertainly. She was unsure if the question sprang from ignorance or guile.

"No," she replied. "I haven't. And as you probably know, no journalist has. Cazarès doesn't appear in public, except at the close of her shows. And she doesn't give interviews, ever, to anyone. She's virtually a recluse."

"A beautiful recluse, I gather."

"She's certainly that."

"But Jean Lazare, on the other hand—he does talk to the press?"

"To safe journalists. Friends of his. People who won't ask awkward questions about Cazarès, yes, he does. I wouldn't describe the process as an interview, but he does give an audience occasionally."

"Could you swing an audience with him?"

"If I wanted one, which I don't. Probably. Yes."

"Try. See if you can get to him while you're in Paris."

Lindsay gave McGuire a puzzled look.

"Why? It's pointless. If he did see me, I wouldn't get anything usable. Sure, I'd like to know if the rumors are true—wouldn't we all? I'd like to know if Maria Cazarès really did start cracking up five years ago. I'd *love* to know how much of the collection she actually designs these days. Everyone would like the answers to those questions. . . ."

"So ask them. Ask Lazare. Why not?"

"Several reasons," Lindsay snapped. "In the first place, I wouldn't dare—and if I did, my feet wouldn't touch the floor, I'd be banned from all Cazarès shows so fast. Secondly, I told you—it's pointless. Lazare has a set text for interviews: Maria Cazarès is a genius. His function is to protect her from the intrusions of the herd. That's it."

"And to run a multimillion-dollar company. Let's not forget that."

"Sure. Which he does with ruthless efficiency. He'd talk about that quite willingly. He'd discuss their ready-to-wear lines, their cosmetics, their perfumes. He'd talk statistics and turn on the charm. Waste of time. I already know the statistics. Cazarès has the best PR department of any Paris couture house. I've heard it all before, all right?"

"Have you? Are you sure?"

Lindsay was about to make a tart reply, then paused. McGuire's emerald-green eyes were regarding her sharply, and there was a sudden edge in his voice. She hesitated, sensed unspoken reprimand, then shrugged.

"Okay. I exaggerate. I haven't heard it all—nor has anyone else. There are mysteries about Lazare, and Cazarès, obviously. They go way back. . . ."

"I'd say so, yes." McGuire glanced down at the folder. "Speaking as a non-expert, that is. Where they came from, how they met, how Lazare made his first fortune, the exact nature of their relationship now, why Lazare was trying to unload the company last year—"

"Was *rumored* to be trying to unload," Lindsay interjected.

"Why, this year, Lazare has changed his mind, is sitting tight. Just a few minor things like that. Nothing to concern the fashion rat-pack too seriously . . ." McGuire gave her a small green glance.

"Of course," he continued, "fashion editors don't function like other journalists, do they? I'm learning that. They don't ask awkward questions. They don't investigate the industry they're reporting. They attend the collections, coo at their friends, shut down the small sections of their brains still capable of operating, ooh and aah over hemlines, and experience ecstasy. Over a skirt. Or a jacket. Or a hat . . ."

"Just a minute," Lindsay said.

"What they're looking at," McGuire went on imperturbably, "bears no relationship to the lives of ninety-nine percent of ordinary women. It won't even affect the way those women dress. It's frivolous, obscenely, expensively insulting to the female sex. . . ."

"Could I speak?"

". . . But their reports provide, of course, free publicity twice a year for a highly profitable industry. And the fashion journalists go right along with that. They help promote the product no matter how crass, how foolish, how damned *unwearable* that product is. That used to puzzle me. Why lie? Why extol this nonsense year after year? I'm learning, of course. They can't criticize. They don't *dare* to criticize. If they did, they'd risk losing their precious invitations, their prestigious seats in the front row. Do you sit in the front row, by any chance, Lindsay?"

He turned his cool green gaze in her direction. Lindsay dug her nails deep in her palms.

"Yes," she said. "I do. It took me ten damn years to get there, and I report what I see a whole lot better than I would from ten rows back."

"I'm sure you do," McGuire said. "Where I grew up, they used to say that if you supped with the devil, you should use a long spoon. But I'm sure that wouldn't apply in this case. After all, if you wrote what you actually thought—if you pointed out, for instance, that the Cazarès collections had become uninspired, lackluster, what would it achieve? You'd be banned."

He quoted her words back at her with the most charming of smiles. Lindsay, who had once possessed a fierce temper but had learned to control it, counted to ten and inhaled calming, counted yoga breaths. Bog-Irish idiot, she said to herself. Prig. Preacher. Insufferable, smug, overbearing, rude . . . She hesitated. She was honest enough to admit there was considerable truth in what he said, and furious enough to have no intention of admitting that fact.

"Perhaps it would help, Rowland," she began finally, her tone excessively polite, "if I explained to you some of the realities of my job. I go to the collections to report clothes. To report *trends*. I look at cut and color and fabric and line. I'm expert at that. It helps that clothes interest me. I like clothes. So do the hundreds of thousands of women who read my pages every week. The female readers this paper needs. The ones who gladden the hearts of the ad agencies, Rowland, the agencies that buy space in this paper, and help pay your salary as well as mine."

"I'm aware of the economics of this industry, thank you," McGuire put in.

Lindsay fought down a rising urge to lean across his desk and slap him.

"Oh, come on," she said. "Take a look at your features output, Rowland, before you preach. Last Saturday, for instance. You ran a long piece on Chechnya, and a piece on the Clintons. . . ."

"So?"

"You *also* ran a report in the car column on the new Aston-Martin, a piece on an exclusive Thai beach resort under travel, and a comparison of fifteen brands of virgin olive oil in the food column, the first *sentence* of which was so damn pompous and pretentious, it made me choke. You allowed that ghastly girl who reviews restaurants for you—a ghastly girl *you* brought on to this paper—to devote an entire column to some damn fancy restaurant outside Oxford, where she and her latest boyfriend had just blown nearly two hundred pounds of your department's budget. On lunch. That's not frivolous? That's not obscene? Come on, Rowland. Don't give me this shit."

There was a silence. Grandes dames, Lindsay thought, would not have used that last epithet. Too bad, she thought. She now felt much better. No regrets. McGuire, she noted, had colored. But if her remarks had struck home, he recovered quickly. He gave her a brief glinting glance, then—to her annoyance—laughed.

"A hit," he said. "A palpable hit. However"—he leaned across the desk—"the ghastly girl retained her critical faculties. She gave the béarnaise sauce the thumbs-down."

"Big deal."

". . . And our motoring correspondent got tough over the Aston's instrumentation design—"

"Give me a break. He drooled over that damn Aston."

"The olive oil article, however—now, there I'm with you. Appalling. Unreadable. Precious beyond belief."

"And you've done something about that, have you? In your capacity as features editor?"

"Sure I have." He met her gaze levelly. "You hadn't heard? I fired that columnist this week."

There was another silence, longer this time. Lindsay sat very still. She looked at the green eyes and the tweed jacket and the piles of books. She thought briefly of school fees and mortgage payments and leaking pipes.

"Is that a threat?" she said eventually, enunciating the words clearly in her calmest voice.

McGuire seemed astonished. He gave her a blank look, ran his hands through his hair, then began to speak rapidly.

Lindsay was not listening. She rose. She felt as if she were trapped in some cold, icy place, where the air was too thin, so it was hard to breathe.

". . . Because if it was a threat," she went on in that calm, flat voice, "I'd better call Gini and delay my appointment with her. I should be meeting her in about an hour, and, of course, I'll be late."

"Late? Late? What are you talking about?"

"Gini will have to wait. If it's of any interest to you, which it probably isn't, so will my mother, and my son, and the shopping and the plumber—"

"Plumber? What plumber?"

"So will the garage and the damn shop where they might, just *might*, have one last pair of the size twelve football cleats my son Tom says he desperately *has* to have. So will all the many tedious, trivial matters I have to deal with in addition to my work, which—in case you're wondering—is finalized for this week. They'll all have to wait, Rowland, because I'll still be upstairs, in this building. I'll be talking to Max. I won't work like this."

Lindsay, pleased with the controlled sarcasm and dignity of this speech, moved to the door. She felt she was timing the exit well; McGuire coughed.

"Soccer or rugby?" he said.

Lindsay stopped. She turned and gave him her most withering look.

"The football cleats," he repeated. "Soccer or rugby?"

"Soccer. And don't try to ingratiate yourself with me. It's too late."

"Size twelve? He must be tall."

"He's six feet two. He's seventeen. Does that help your calculations?"

"I wasn't calculating, but I am surprised. I thought you were around thirty. Thirty-one, maybe."

"Too late for flattery," Lindsay, who was secretly gratified, said. "Too late to extricate yourself. I—"

"It wasn't a threat," McGuire interrupted, now speaking rapidly and rising to his feet. "I've approached this wrongly. I didn't ask you up here to threaten you, or criticize you. I don't like fashion. I don't pretend to understand fashion. . . ." He suddenly gave her a broad smile of great brilliance, and took her arm. "I don't like Aston-Martins much either. Or two-hundred-pound lunches. I'm compromised. I admit that."

Lindsay stood still. She looked down at McGuire's hand, which was large, tanned, and beautifully shaped. She wondered distantly if she was experiencing arrhythmia, if the peculiar flutterings beneath her Cazarès carapace were the result of overwork, anxiety, poor diet, and stress. She was later to wonder if it was at this point in her relationship with McGuire that she made her first, and crucial, mistake. She could, after all, have detached his hand and continued her brave exit, but she did not. Instead, she met that amused glance, and she started to relent.

"Why did you ask me up here, then?" she asked, and allowed McGuire to lead her back to his desk.

He picked up the green file again, undid its ties, and handed it to her.

"Because I need your help," he said, "with this."

The directness and simplicity of the appeal surprised Lindsay. She searched his face for further signs of duplicity and guile, but failed to see them. It occurred to her that McGuire, when not in the ascendant, might conceivably be a man she could like.

She looked down at the folder, which was thick, heavy, and unlabeled.

"Is this a fashion story?"

"No. Only indirectly. It's bigger—and nastier—than that."

"Are you going to explain?"

"I can't explain fully, no. Not yet."

"It's confidential?"

"You could call it that."

Lindsay opened the file. A familiar face stared up at her, a famous face. The photograph, one of the very few in existence that had been posed, not snatched, had been taken by Cecil Beaton. It dated from the seventies, and once seen was not easily forgotten. Maria Cazarès was captured at the height of her beauty. Black-haired, black-eyed, she was laughing, her hand half lifted, as if about to shield her face. Her hair was cropped; she looked, as Beaton had famously said, like the most beautiful boy in the world; she wore a small gold crucifix around her neck.

Lindsay frowned, and began to flick through the file. It was composed of press clippings; all concerned Cazarès and Lazare. They spanned almost three decades. The file was four inches thick.

"I want you to read through it," McGuire said. "Everything my researchers could find is in there. The American clippings, the British, the Italian, the French. Could you do it this weekend?"

"It's that urgent?"

"Yes. It is. I thought . . . I thought you might fit it in at Max's. After dinner, maybe. In bed . . ."

He gave her another greenish glance. To her surprise, Lindsay realized that McGuire had other talents she would not have suspected; when it suited his purposes, he could flirt.

"It might help," she said, "if I knew what I was looking for."

"Gaps."

"There'll be hundreds of gaps. You mentioned a few of the obvious ones yourself, earlier. This whole file will be supposition. Rumor and counter-rumor. Legend. Myth."

"Never mind. Anything you know, or have heard, no matter how unlikely, how unsubstantiated—if it isn't in that file, I want to know about it."

"Even gossip?"

"Especially gossip."

"Report back Monday?"

"Er—yes." He glanced away. "Before you leave for Paris? If you have time, if you'll let me, I'll buy you a thank-you lunch."

"Maybe."

McGuire looked injured. "Haven't we made peace?"

"No. Not yet." Lindsay met his gaze. "I still think you're manipulative. Devious. I don't trust you an inch."

"But you will help me?"

"You're marginally more bearable when you ask favors. So—yes."

Lindsay rose, and turned to the door. McGuire, in a surge of gallantry, also rose and opened it for her. In the doorway he asked one final question. Had Jean Lazare any known connection with Amsterdam?

"No. Why would he?" Lindsay asked, puzzled. "Whatever nationality he really is, it isn't Dutch. And Holland hardly features on the international fashion circuit."

"No," said Rowland, whose telephone was ringing. "No. I thought that . . ."

He picked up the telephone; Lindsay lingered in the doorway. She could just hear a female voice from the receiver, speaking rapidly. Rowland frowned.

"I'll see you Monday, then, Rowland . . ."

"Monday?" He gave her a blank look.

"Our *lunch*, Rowland. Your *apology* lunch."

"Oh, yes. Of course. Monday. Sure."

Lindsay glanced back as she left. Rowland's female caller was still speaking—indeed, had continued speaking all this while, without pause. Rowland, believing himself unobserved, gave a sigh. He placed the receiver gently on his desk, picked up the volume of Proust, and began reading. As Lindsay closed the door, Rowland's caller gave a cry of apparent anguish. Rowland, unmoved, turned a page.

At one, just when Lindsay was finally ready to leave, Markov called. He had called twice during her meeting with Rowland. He was more than capable, Lindsay thought wearily, of calling every five minutes for the rest of the day and night. Markov was like that.

"So, sweetling," he said as she picked up the phone. "Give me the lowdown. Did you plunge in the knife?"

"You bet," Lindsay replied mendaciously.

"Darling, well *done*. Straight through the aorta, or was it a more lingering death?"

"Lingering. Now, go *away*, Markov. I'll give you the details in Paris, all right?"

"Can't wait. I've been picturing the scene, beloved, all morning. This McGuire—describe him. He's short? Fat? Receding hair? No testicles to speak of?"

"As a matter of fact, he's six feet five. Black hair. Mean green eyes. Leaks testosterone . . ."

"Darling! Why didn't you say? He sounds *exactly* my type."

"Not a prayer, Markov."

"You're sure?"

"One hundred percent."

"Ah, well. Life's a bitch. Introduce me sometime anyway. Oops, call on my other line. Maybe it's Barbados. *À tout à l'heure,* my museling," Markov added in a very bad accent, and hung up.

At one-fifteen Rowland McGuire moved to the windows of his editor's twelfth floor office, checked his watch, and looked out at the Thames, the buildings of Canary Wharf, and the parking lot below.

"Right on schedule," Rowland said.

Max Flanders, munching one of his favorite cheese and pickle sandwiches, put down the file Rowland had brought him and joined him at the window.

Both men watched as a small, slender woman emerged from the building and threaded her way between parked vehicles to a new, gleaming Volkswagen Golf. The woman's hair, short, curly, and unruly, was as black and shiny as the paintwork of her car. She was wearing black high tops, black leggings, a black sweater, and a voluminous black coat. She was carrying a briefcase, a canvas tote, a bundle of books, and a large green file sealed with tape. She was having difficulty balancing these articles, and as she reached the car, several fell. The woman gave the canvas tote a hefty kick. She glared up at the sky. Her lips shaped a succinct expletive, interpretable from twelve stories above. Rowland smiled.

"What a shame," he said. "She's changed out of that suit. And it was such a splendid suit too."

"Not the Cazarès?" Max grinned. "She wore that for your meeting? In that case, it's definitely war, Rowland. You haven't a prayer."

"You're wrong. She's off to collect Genevieve Hunter now. Everything's going according to plan."

"She didn't suspect?"

"Of course not. I told you. I charmed her. I made her coffee. I complimented her on that suit. It'll be a piece of cake, Max."

"You hope. You don't understand women, Rowland. You never did."

"Have faith." Rowland ignored Max's remark. He watched the black Volkswagen accelerate to the exit, where, signaling right, it turned left.

It narrowly avoided a large truck, whose brakes screeched. Max closed his eyes.

"Just never drive with Lindsay," he said. "That's my only advice, Rowland. Whatever damn fool plans you may have—avoid that. It's dicing with death. Especially when she's in a temper."

"She isn't in a temper." Rowland turned away from the window. "I told you. Two days ago it was war. Now it's détente. It's easy to win a woman like Lindsay over, once you set your mind to it."

He picked up one of Max's sandwiches and began to nibble on it in a contemplative way. Max, repressing a smile, lit a cigarette.

There was a brief companionable silence during which Rowland, whose mind never left work for very long, flicked through the contents of the file he had brought Max, and Max, watching his friend—his extraordinarily handsome friend, who had never understood his own effect on women—had plenty of time to savor the latest development in the ongoing tragicomedy of Rowland McGuire's life.

"Listen, Rowland," he began, deciding on a word of warning, "about Lindsay. She isn't nearly as invulnerable as she pretends, and Charlotte and I are both very fond of her. I know how important this story is to you, and I understand why her help could be useful. . . ."

Rowland was not listening. He was rereading the latest report from his U.S. Drug Enforcement Agency contact in Amsterdam, submitted to Max a short while before. Max did not know the name of this contact, and was unlikely to be given it: that was the way Rowland worked.

"Sure, sure," he said, closing the file and waving Max's remarks to one side. "Stop fussing, for God's sake, Max. Next you'll be asking me what my intentions are."

"Unlikely. You wouldn't tell me if I did."

"Work," Rowland said in an impatient tone, picking up a sheaf of photographic prints from Max's desk and leafing through them. "My intention is to work. To get this whole story tied up. Lindsay's peripheral. If she'll condescend to help, fine. If she won't—too bad. I'll continue the charm offensive—"

"Give me strength."

"These pictures . . ." Rowland laid them back on the desk. "They're the latest from Pascal Lamartine?"

"Yes." Max picked them up. "I want to use one tomorrow. Page one. Photo editor wants this one."

"He's wrong." Rowland indicated the photograph in Max's left hand. "You should use that one. People are getting complacent about Bosnia. Shock them out of it, Max."

"Maybe," Max replied, knowing that Rowland was right. He looked down at the picture Rowland had recommended. A group of mourning women were clustered around the body of a boy; the boy's right hand still grasped a Kalashnikov; his left lay, outflung, in a pool of blood. The boy's face, mercifully, was hidden, but the faces of the women were not. Lamartine would have had less than thirty seconds in which to capture this grief; this was his great gift, Max thought, the gift that put him in a class by himself: technical brilliance, informed by compassion. The photograph had haunted Max all morning. If one of my own children were to die, he thought, that is how I would feel, that is how my wife would look.

He glanced up, met the understanding in Rowland's eyes, nodded, and pushed the photograph to one side.

"How much longer is Lamartine staying out there?" Rowland asked, rising and beginning to prowl Max's office. "I thought he was coming back with Genevieve Hunter?"

"That was the original plan." Max shrugged. "When he's ready, I assume. Lamartine's a law unto himself."

Rowland made no comment. He returned to his chair and sat down.

"So. Shall we get on with it, Max?" He glanced at his watch. "You were going to fill me in on Genevieve Hunter."

"Was I?" A slightly evasive look crossed Max's face.

"Yes. You were. As you well know. Come on, Max. We've got ten minutes before your meeting. I want the details. *All* the details. A to Z."

"Rowland, we've been over this. You know most of it already."

Rowland's expression became obstinate and concentrated. He leaned forward.

"Possibly. Tell me again," he said.

CHAPTER 2

In the mornings now, Genevieve Hunter walked. Sometimes she walked for one hour, sometimes two, and always at random. Walking was beneficial: it occupied her body, lulled her mind, and made the day shrink. If she stayed in her apartment, she felt obliged to try to write, but the words that came up on her computer screen refused to cohere or make sense. If she stayed in her apartment, she felt the absence of Pascal too acutely. This was the first home they had ever shared: they had found it together, furnished it together; it was a place that proclaimed their love—and they had lived in it together for less than five months.

It was on the fringes of Notting Hill, on the top floor of a huge, extravagantly turreted house designed for his pre-Raphaelite artist friends by an architect whose work was regarded as radical in 1868. Though Rossetti had once had one of the studios in the building and Ruskin had been a frequent visitor there, Gini could not sense her building's past life. For her, its existence only truly began the moment she and Pascal first saw it: after weeks of searching, of losing heart, of viewing one overpriced gimcrack conversion after another, suddenly, like a miracle, they had come upon this.

There was one vast studio room, as tall, as spacious, as the interior of a church. A spiral staircase led up to a gallery bedroom lined with shelves for books. One entire wall was window, a tall, arched north-facing window. Light flooded through its panes and moved upon the walls. It was a spring day, a glorious spring day, a day in which regeneration sang out in the air, and that window let spring into the room. From it, the city was invisible: still transfixed in the doorway, they looked out at a pale azure sky, at small high clouds that raced, at the branches of plane trees just green with new leaf; the brilliance of the sunlight dazzled their eyes. "It's ours," Pascal said after a long silence. "It was intended for us. It has to be ours—yes?"

After that they had both tried very hard to be pragmatic. Hand in hand, they explored. They searched for defects. Solemnly, Pascal tapped walls, inspected wiring and plumbing; equally solemnly, Gini examined a kitchen she knew she loved at first sight. They discovered there was a second bedroom, on the studio level, a small, romantic turret bedroom, a domain Rackham might have drawn for some fairy-tale princess. It was a room made for a child with imagination. Gini could see Pascal, thinking of his daughter.

She said, "Marianne could come to stay, Pascal."

"She could," he said. "She would *love* this room."

For a while after that, neither of them quite dared to speak. They returned to the huge studio room, and stood holding hands in front of that tall, glorious window. Pascal jangled the keys the agent had given him. They looked at each other; Pascal's gray eyes lit with amusement. He knew that she was about to voice the unspoken. Before she could do so, he lifted his hand and rested his fingers lightly against her lips.

"No. Wait," he said. "You're about to be sensible. Before you're sensible, I have to do this."

He lifted her long, pale hair away from her face. He looked into her eyes, then, drawing her toward him, bent and kissed her on the lips.

The embrace was long, and it left her shaken, her mind in disarray; he had, she thought, intended this. She drew away from him at last, with a smile and a shake of the head. She laced her fingers in his and examined his face from a safer distance, arm's length. She watched the sunlight move across the darkness of his hair, across the planes of his face. She loved the line of his brows; she loved every aspect of his face, every inflection in his voice, every variation in his touch. Finely attuned to him, she knew precisely what he was thinking. It was there in every lineament, in the set of his mouth and in the glint of amusement that still lit his eyes. Nonetheless, the unspoken had to be voiced sooner or later.

"It's too expensive," she said, "we have to face facts."

Pascal, the most determined man she had ever known, a man who could always contrive to get himself to the back of beyond, by yesterday, when there were no flights, gave a shrug. He began to pace the room. Gini, familiar with his refusal ever to accept defeat, watched him with quiet affection. She had seen him like this before, when he worked. Pascal, who could argue or charm his way past any barricade or impediment, Pascal, who, failing to get in some front entrance, would always contrive a way in through the side or the back, Pascal, who went into war zones and brought back the pictures no one else could get.

Gini tried to concentrate. She added up, again, the money she could expect from the sale of her own London apartment; the money Pascal thought could be raised from the sale of his Paris atelier; the figures the mortgage companies had mentioned. No matter how she added up those figures, the discrepancy was huge. She gave a sigh; Pascal, undaunted as always, returned to her at once. He put his arm around her waist.

"My car," said Pascal, who drove fast in a classic, old, and much-loved Porsche. "I'll sell my car. I'll get a dull car. That would help."

"I'll sell mine too." She smiled. Gini drove an ancient Volkswagen Beetle. Pascal, who did not admire this vehicle, gave her a serious look.

"A sacrifice I couldn't permit. Besides, we'd have to pay someone to take it off our hands."

"We could live on vegetables."

"We could." He drew her closer to him. "Turnips. Parsnips."

"No new clothes for the next ten years."

"A better idea. I prefer you without clothes, in any case."

"I could change careers. Stop being a journalist. Become a merchant banker. A corporate lawyer. An advertising whiz kid . . ."

"I think not. That would be a waste. Look at me, Gini."

She turned to face him; his arms encircled her waist.

"Do we want this, Gini?"

"Yes. We do."

"Then let's get it," said Pascal.

From that moment onward he was as she most loved him—very energetic, very charming, very steely, and very French. First the owners of the apartment, then their agents, then the bank, began to give way under his onslaught: the price, it seemed, might after all be a little negotiable; the mortgage might be, after all, increased. Returning to Gini's apartment, with its forlorn For Sale sign, he found her a buyer within a week. At night, when to his annoyance and chagrin—for Pascal himself did not observe office hours and despised those who did—the bank or real estate agents could not be reached, he covered hundreds of sheets of paper with calculations. Sum after sum, all the sevens neatly crossed. He added up their expenses, his child support payments to his ex-wife for Marianne, the mortgage payments, the cost of heating and travel and—Gini saw to her amused delight—wine and bread.

"Wine?" she said, leaning over his shoulder. "That's a luxury. Cross that off."

"To you, my darling American, it may be a luxury. To me it is a necessity."

"You've left out electricity."

"Candles?" He looked at her with a smile.

"Insurance?"

"Damn. I'll have to call Max."

He called Max there and then, as—Gini suspected—he had intended to do from the first. He told Max that he was enjoying being wooed by the *Correspondent* very much, but if Max wished courtship to lead to marriage, the dowry would have to be increased.

"I have been doing sums," Pascal said. "I had allowed for wine but not electricity. A foolish oversight . . . When you come to dinner with us, you see, Max, in this wonderful place we mean to have, it would be useful to be able to cook for you— Oh, really? A ball park figure? What is that?"

There was a pause while Pascal, who understood the term very well, listened intently. He then named a sum of money. Gini paled; Max said yes.

And so it had become theirs, all this wonderful space. Pascal went to see an antiques-dealer friend with a warehouse on King's Road. After an excellent lunch, and several hours of fierce Gallic bargaining, he acquired a bed. It was a high, wide, glorious four-poster, once the property of a king's mistress—or so the dealer claimed. It had pillars carved with vines, and its original hangings of worn scarlet silk. He kept the purchase secret, and had the bed installed on a day when Gini was out interviewing a very dull and self-satisfied Cabinet minister. When she came home that spring evening, there it was.

They climbed into it together at once. It was like being aboard a sailing ship. From its pillows, they looked out across the gallery balustrade to the magnificent window, to the tops of trees, to a scudding sky, to the lights and sounds of the invisible city that thrummed five floors below. They drank wine there, then ate supper there, then made love there, then slept.

"I am content," Pascal said, gathering her into his arms the next morning, "I have never been so content."

Gini was also content. She liked the word, which seemed to link them in its embrace. She thought of all the years since she had first met Pascal, and realized with a shock that they comprised almost half her life. She thought of the weeks when she had first known him, and first loved him, in Beirut. She thought of their years apart, and their reunion. She thought: I want for nothing. Everything I love and value and esteem is here. Oh, yes, I am content.

She felt no unease, not the least premonition, not even a prick of superstition that the beneficent gods who dispense bounty to humans have a grim habit of giving with the right hand, then immediately taking back with the left. Five months after moving into that apartment, she was granted what had always been her other wish: she was sent to Sarajevo, to cover the war in Bosnia. She went with Pascal, and worked there with Pascal. He had operated from war zones before, many times; she had not.

Six months later, she returned alone. Pascal, unaware of the extent of the change in her, agreed that her return to London was the best course. He would remain in Bosnia for a brief period—at most three weeks, a month. He had now been there, alone, for nine weeks, and the date of his return was still not fixed. At first, although Gini was careful not to tell Pascal this, she was glad of the delay. She thought it would give her time—time to cure herself of the aftermath of Bosnia and what she saw there, time to cure the nightmares, the sleeplessness, time to cure herself.

Wars could be exorcised, she told herself as the weeks went by. It must, somehow, be possible—not to forget, she would have despised herself had she ever forgotten—to distance herself. But death—the sound, taste, sight, and smell of death—pursued her. It prevented rest, jerked her awake with a cry of fear in the lonely morning hours; it seeped into this lovely apartment and soiled its contentment; it pursued her out into the ordinary streets.

She had, as had many of the reporters out there, been physically wounded while in Bosnia. One evening, in a small village set high in a mountain pass, on her way with Pascal to Mostar (and above all she feared to think of Mostar) they had been caught in a mortar attack. A piece of shrapnel had lodged in her upper arm. It was a minor injury of which she was almost ashamed, given the maimings she had witnessed; it was quickly, and with reasonable efficiency, patched up.

Now, nine weeks after leaving that country, the wound had almost healed: her mind had not. Pascal, long acquainted with modern warfare and its hideous results, had tried to warn her. And she, not being a fool, had listened to those warnings, of course. Quietly, with reluctance, he had shown her, before they left for Bosnia, some of the pictures he had taken in the past, pictures taken as documentation only, never intended for publication, pictures no magazine or newspaper could ever reproduce.

"You have to be prepared." He laid out the black and white rectangles in front of her. "You will see this, Gini. And worse."

He waited, in silence, as she looked down at the photographs.

"That's the threshold," he said eventually. "Are you sure, Gini—absolutely sure—that it's one you want to cross?"

Shaken, nauseated, fighting the physical symptoms of her distress, she had turned away, unable to face him. Their journey to Bosnia was still one week away; he had timed this, she thought, so that it was possible for her, even then, to back out.

"It wouldn't be cowardice," he went on gently. "You mustn't think that. It would simply be a choice. There *is* a difference, Gini, between the sexes. It is harder for a woman to look at this, to live with this—"

"*Why?*" She swung around to face him again, sensing he might be right. "*Why*, Pascal? These things happen. These atrocities *exist*. Why should women be shielded from them? That can't be right. I think that's weak—and I don't want to be weak."

"It isn't necessarily weakness. I don't think of it that way. These incidents you see here"—he gestured at the photographs—"they are perpetrated by men. So they are something all men have to confront. But if a woman turns away from them, if you turn away, Gini, might that not be a sign of strength?"

She had been moved then by the concern and the gentleness in his face. It was very characteristic of Pascal, she thought, not only to offer her an escape route, but to do so with grace.

The offer had been quietly made, and quietly she refused it. But once they reached Bosnia, Pascal did attempt to shield her at first. There were dangers he, if alone, might have risked, to which he would not expose her. He was careful what she saw, and tried to ensure that, like a plant susceptible to frost damage, she was gradually hardened off.

It took Gini less than a week to understand that this process, which he never admitted but observed meticulously, was hampering their work. And so, almost from the first, it became necessary for her to act. She, who had had no secrets from Pascal, now had many: if he had suspected her true reactions, he would have insisted she return to London at once.

She could disguise fear and fatigue well enough. It was harder to disguise the tears, and hardest of all to hide the pain and mounting incomprehension that lay behind the tears. Day by day she would discover new devices to deceive him—and they had to be rigorously employed, day and night (no weakening when she lay in his arms and could not sleep), for Pascal was quick, sensitive, and attuned to her. Just one glance, one wrong inflection, one gesture, and he would begin to see the truth.

So, day by day, she perfected herself; she put her heart on ice; she made herself numb, turned herself into an efficient walking-talking automaton, an automaton who looked at ruined buildings and ruined bodies and ruined lives, and got on with the job. To do so, she found, was to un-sex herself. It was as if something fluent and fluid in her body began to dry up; made her dry-eyed, bloodless, without appetite for food. When Pascal embraced her now, there was no immediate rush of response; she felt like a husk, a dried, withered thing. It came as no surprise to her, although she was on the pill, when her periods stopped: women bled—but she was no longer a woman, she was a robot.

Some of these symptoms, of course, no lover could mistake. She could see that Pascal was hurt by them, and redoubled her efforts at once. She began to fake her orgasms, and Pascal quietly allowed her to do this for two weeks. At the end of that time he took her in his arms, waited for the confession that did not come, and then said:

"Gini. Never do that again. I won't have you lie to me. And above all, I won't have you lie to me in bed."

She could hear pain, and regret, and anxiety in his voice—also a certain sternness. On that occasion she did briefly weep, and Pascal held her while she did so. After that he questioned her, and tried to persuade her to speak, but when she avoided his questions or denied any reason for concern, he ceased to press her. He made a private decision to accept her reticence, she saw, and said nothing, though she knew that this scrupulousness, both verbal and physical, cost him dearly.

Professionally, impressed by the coolness she showed, he did gradually accede to her requests. Ratchet by ratchet, he increased the risks. He allowed her to bear witness; he took her on the necessary stations: the rape victims, the dead, the dying, and the mutilations of death. She thought he could see what she found the hardest—after Mostar, he was certainly in no doubt; he could see that while she had learned to look at dismemberment, the grief of parents and the injury to children remained hard for her. The tears would spring to her eyes, and her hands would shake. He tried to avoid places and situations where such encounters were unavoidable, but even Pascal could not entirely succeed in this. In that country, predictions and plans could never be sure: mortar fire would suddenly open up in a remote and apparently deserted mountain pass; death could be across the next street.

The proximity of death, the skull beneath the skin, the abomination around the corner, that was, for Gini, the essence of Bosnia. And it returned with her to London, although writing to Pascal, and telephoning Pascal, she never mentioned this.

"You are sleeping, darling? You're eating properly?" He would ask, and she would say yes, of course, her appetite was back to normal, she'd slept for ten hours straight the previous night.

"And you are going out, darling? You are seeing people? Your arm—you're sure it's healed?"

Yes, she would lie, she'd been to the theater, the movies, she had seen Lindsay, her arm was fine now that the stitches were out. How well she could act on the telephone! How well she could deceive when she wrote! The last thing she should do now, she knew, was burden Pascal with worries on her behalf, and so she would inject warmth, amusement, conviction into her voice. He was surprised, she suspected, but he was gradually convinced. He was lulled into postponing his return, when that return was the thing she most desired in life. Yes, she acted well, but she had had six months in Bosnia to practice—and she knew it was easier to convince someone who was himself working under great stress.

Some of what she said was true: her arm had healed; but Gini, walking the London streets, knew her mind had not. How long did it take for a mind to cure itself, she wondered. Six months, a year, a decade?

Nine weeks had achieved very little. The normality of London made it worse. Here, not surprisingly, people continued with their day-to-day lives, and Gini, trying to communicate with them, remained locked in some other private place. There she was, on the other side of a glass panel, gesticulating, trying to speak, trying to fight her way out of her mental war zone—and failing. Days passed: weeks passed: friends became impatient with her, and her sense of dislocation increased.

Now, alone in their lovely apartment, alone in their lovely bed, she was beset with fears. She would begin weeping for children she wanted to save, and whom she knew were months dead. She would hear bombs and mortar fire, think of snipers, and remember that Pascal, said to lead a charmed life, could become a statistic like anyone else. There could be a telephone call, a somber visit from a stranger: Pascal might never come back.

Fearing for his safety, she would open the closets and touch his clothes, take down his books from the bookshelves. She would read his letters, then reread them, until she knew them by heart, all these reassurances of his love. She would write, careful words that hid her despair, and she would make sure that no tears ever fell on the ink. At Christmas—she had been sure he would return for Christmas—she began to hope again. It would be their first Christmas together. She rushed out, bought a tree and tinsel and stars to decorate it. She bought him presents, and—rationing her joy—wrapped one present only each night so her happiness and excitement might last for an entire week.

But Pascal did not return as planned; the opportunity suddenly came for him to get through to a zone in the north to which no journalists had had access in months. "You must take it—you must go," Gini said on the telephone—and after some persuasion, he did.

That was when the new fear gripped her. She had gone into the bathroom, switched on all the lights, and made herself confront the image in the glass. She could see, she made herself see, the physical effects of lack of appetite and sleep. She looked at the pale face in the mirror in front of her: she knew that Pascal found her beautiful, for he told her so often enough. She turned her face this way and that, searching for some sign of the woman he described, the woman he loved.

She could not see her. She felt a flurry of panic then. This woman he would scarcely recognize, and surely could not love. She had a thin, tense, secretive look; her eyes were secretive, shifting away from her own glance. One secret above all, of course; one confession that should have been made in Mostar, but was not. That secret she still nursed. If Pascal had walked into the room now, she would have longed to voice it, but feared to do so: the words would stick in her throat.

She spent a sleepless night; the next morning, febrile with new resolve, she did the sensible, the obvious thing. She consulted a doctor. It was a necessary step—and one she had been avoiding for two months.

The doctor was a stranger. His office had been closed over Christmas, and there was a backlog of patients. Gini sat in the crowded waiting room, an unread magazine on her knee. She tried to block out the sounds of fractious children and squalling babies. She was trying to decide how much to tell the doctor, and how to make her explanation brief.

She thought: I must be clear and concise. I must tell him I was in Bosnia. I must mention the hours we worked. I must explain that I thought I could cope, and I tried to cope, but I found it very hard to look at—death. Yes, she thought, that was the word. Just death. No need to be more specific than that. She jumped; her name was being called for the third time by an irritable receptionist. Clutching her purse, she rose to her feet.

She found the doctor in a room the size of a small cubicle, a young man of about her own age, with a harassed air, who said without preamble, "What's the problem?"

Outside, telephones rang; a child shrieked. Gini fixed her eyes on an antismoking poster. It was immediately clear to her that she could not mention Bosnia to this man; she could not mention Bosnia in this place. It would be too long, too complicated; it would be too cheap.

The doctor was staring at her, tapping his pen.

"Symptoms?" he asked. "What symptoms are troubling you?"

"I—can't sleep," Gini replied. She was starting to sweat. The room felt airless; the pen tapped. "I'm having nightmares. I've been under— some stress. I'm not eating too well. I've lost weight—about fourteen pounds, I guess. . . ."

The doctor was scribbling notes. He did not appear sympathetic. Gini was unsure whether that was because he viewed unmarried women with sleep problems as neurotic pests, or because his ballpoint was refusing to work properly. He shook it irritably.

"I—cry sometimes," she went on, "for no reason at all. I'll be in a grocery store, or just walking along the street, and—I can't seem to control it. It just happens. I can't stop."

"How long has this been going on?"

"Around two months."

"What triggered it?"

"I'm sorry?"

"Bereavement? Divorce? You lost your job?"

"No. I'm not married. I—"

She stopped. Bereavement: she tried the word in her mind. Perhaps that was the word she should use. Except no, bereavement implied the loss of someone you knew and loved—a mother, a father, perhaps. Could the deaths of strangers be described as bereavement? No, she decided, she could not use that word; she did not have the right.

"The weight loss is rapid. Anything else? Vomiting?"

"No."

"Periods normal?"

"No. I haven't had a period in four months. I've been—abroad, and they stopped while I was out there. But that can happen to me, it has be-fore. If I'm working hard, if I've been under stress, and—"

"Abroad? Abroad where? Not India, Africa, anywhere like that?"

"No. I was in Eastern Europe."

He lost interest at once. He was writing again. He wrote a "4," and drew a circle around it. Over and over, above the noise of children and telephones, Gini could hear the rattle of machine-gun fire, the soft crunch of masonry falling. This happened sometimes, and it had to be controlled, because if it was not, those sounds would take her back to Mostar, back to that hospital ward, and back to a certain young boy there. She would remember his eyes. She gripped the arms of her chair tightly. She spelled out the words on the poster, letter by letter.

"You've been tested presumably?" The doctor glanced up.

"Tested?"

"You've had a pregnancy test?" He shot her a cold look, as if her stu-pidity irritated him. "I would assume you have, since you haven't had a period in four months."

"Yes, I have. While I was away—I had a test out there. . . . " She hes-itated, coloring. "As soon as I missed the first time, I went to a doctor, and—"

"That would be too soon. Didn't you know that?"

"Yes. I suppose I did. It was just—I was eager to know, and . . . And anyway, I've tested myself since. Last month. This month. I bought those kits. In a pharmacy—"

She broke off. She could hear how odd and breathless her voice sounded. The room felt insufferably hot. The pen was still tapping. He looked at his watch.

"They were negative. I knew they would be. I'm not pregnant. I'm on the pill. At least—I was on the pill. I stopped taking it when I returned to London."

"Why?"

"Because I—well, I'm not sleeping with anyone in London. . . ."

"That could change, presumably."

His tone was dismissive. The femaleness of this was beginning to an-noy him, she could sense.

"In any case"—he made another note—"those pregnancy testing kits can be unreliable unless you follow the directions on the package exactly."

"Look, I can read instructions on a kit, all right? A five-year-old child could understand those instructions. I just—"

"Of course. Of course."

Her voice had risen; her tone had been a mistake. He became instantly soothing, a veneer of calm over a deepening lack of sympathy.

"Well, I very much doubt that there's anything seriously wrong. You've been overdoing things, I expect. We'll take our own sample, however, so we can rule out pregnancy for certain. I'll run a blood test too. I don't like the weight loss. See the nurse now and come back in three days. I'll see you then."

Gini returned three days later. She saw a different doctor, the first being out on emergency call. The second, a woman, was cheerful and brisk. The pregnancy test was negative. The blood test was normal. She diagnosed stress. She prescribed a short course of Valium. Gini collected the pills, took them home.

They made her violently angry. She tipped them down the sink.

Confront the demons: that's what Pascal would have said. Her stepmother, Mary, her friends—they might have given the same advice. But Mary, to whom she was so close, was away on a three-month trip to the States, and Gini did not ask her friends, not even Lindsay. To confront demons properly, she believed, you had to do it alone.

She tried to work, and failed; she tried to sleep and mostly failed. And, in the mornings, to make the day move, time pass, she walked.

No set pattern. That Friday, the Friday she was due to meet Lindsay, she walked north to Portobello, then south to Holland Park, then west to Shepherd's Bush, then back along the main road to Notting Hill Gate. It was raining, a fine, thin rain, and cars hissed by on the streets. All the shops and restaurants seemed to buzz with a peculiar disjointed, distant life. Normal, normal, normal, Gini said to herself. *This* is normal—people shopping, friends meeting. It will be a normal weekend. I shall be my normal self. I'll talk to people and function properly. I'll stop sleepwalking through my life.

"A weekend in the country," Lindsay had said. "Do you good, Gini. You like Charlotte. You like Max. You like their kids. You're turning into a bloody hermit, a recluse. You're coming. I'm driving you. No argument. That's it."

Gini *had* argued. She said a country weekend was just another kind of Valium. She said she wasn't turning into a hermit, or some dotty recluse, she just liked to be alone, and she needed time to think.

"Bullshit," Lindsay said. "You think too damn much. You always did. Pascal will be home soon. . . ."

"It might be soon. It might not."

". . . And when he gets back, what's he going to find? A wreck. You've lost too much weight, you look ill and sad. You're not working, not writing, not going out. You're getting peculiar. So stop."

"All right," Gini said obligingly, anything to make Lindsay stop nagging. "I'll come. I won't shame you. I'll talk. I'll eat. I won't twitch."

"You don't twitch," Lindsay replied fondly. "Not yet anyway. But you have to reform. Twitching's next."

She had arrived, Gini saw now, at Lindsay's house, although she had no recollection of aiming for it, or turning into the right street. She mounted the steps and rang the bell, and after a long delay it was answered by Tom.

"Oh, hi," Tom said, leaving the door wide, and sprinting for the stairs. "Come on up. I'm alone. Gran's out. Mum phoned. She said to make you a sandwich, she's going to be late. I said I would make a sandwich, but there wasn't any bread. She said there was a shop on the corner, and she hung up. She sounded mildly premenstrual, but then, she often does. I had a temperature of 102 two days ago, did Mum tell you? Extreme, huh? I mean, four more degrees and your brains boil. Did you know that?"

"Not consciously," said Gini, reaching the top floor and the kitchen. "But it makes sense."

She looked at Tom, whom she had not seen since leaving for Sarajevo. He had grown a ponytail since she last saw him, and he seemed to have acquired new powers of speech. He was wearing a torn sweater, torn jeans, and he had nothing on his feet. He was about to be a man, and about to be handsome, Gini thought, but he had not yet acquired a man's social duplicity. He was staring at her; then he blushed and his eyes slid away from her face.

"I know," she said. "Didn't Lindsay tell you? I've lost weight."

"I'll make some coffee. . . ."

He was already turning away in embarrassment, trying to fill the kettle at a sink overflowing with unwashed dishes. "Shit," he muttered. "Maybe I'd better clear up a bit, before Mum gets back. It's Gran's turn—we have assignments now, Mum's latest ploy to keep chaos at bay. Gran skives off though. She doesn't like washing dishes. She says the detergent gives her a rash."

"Convenient," said Gini, who knew Louise of old.

"Yeah. That's what I said."

"I'll help. If I wash and you dry, it won't take long. What time is Lindsay getting here?"

"She said one-thirty. Maybe two. She's in a flap because she's off to

Paris Monday. Away this weekend with you. The social whirl." He grinned. "That makes her guilty. When she's guilty she gets, like *seriously* premenstrual. Plus there's some creep at her office and they're at war, about to go nuclear, and this creep held her up."

"Concise," Gini said, running hot water. "Perhaps a little crude on the female psychology, but I get the picture. You didn't want to join us at Max's, then?"

"Not my scene."

"It was once."

"Not anymore. Too many babies. Charlotte's pregnant again, and— What's the matter?"

"Nothing. I just scalded myself, that's all. This water's a bit hot."

"Anyway, there's a Bergman retrospective at the NFT this weekend. Twelve hours' solid viewing. Immaculate art." He gave her a sidelong glance. "Bergman. Antonioni. Fellini. Godard. Not your American directors. Not anymore."

"You used to like my American directors. *Mean Streets. Taxi Driver. The Godfather.* We saw *The Godfather* three times at least, Tom."

"Yeah. Well, *early* Coppola's okay. And Scorsese is great. Did you see *Goodfellas*? Oh, and Tarantino, of course. I mean, Tarantino is seriously amazing. You've seen *Reservoir Dogs? Pulp Fiction?*"

"No."

"The two greatest American films ever made. Bar none. Postmodern cinema. They're violent, of course."

"So I hear. I'm not in the mood for violence right now. I'll catch up with them eventually, I guess. . . ."

"You must. There's this scene in *Pulp Fiction*—I don't want to spoil it for you, because he plays these narrative games, of course, but there's these college kids, and you know they're about to get shot, and Travolta gets out his gun, but he doesn't point it at them or anything. He's just standing behind them, and then—" Tom stopped.

"Hey, look. I'm sorry. I shouldn't have started in on that. Mum warned me. She said—"

"It's fine, Tom. Really. Don't worry about it. I'm okay. Just pass me that saucepan, would you?"

Tom passed it across. He stood beside her, wielding his dish towel ineffectively, occasionally glancing in her direction.

"I would like to know—" He hesitated. "I mean, what happened to you in Sarajevo? Do you talk about it? Mum says you don't talk about it. Not to her, not to anyone. Why?"

"You used not to talk," Gini countered. "Tom, for three years, four years, you scarcely spoke at all. It drove Lindsay wild with anxiety and guilt. I'm sure you had thoughts, ideas, feelings, that you could have chosen to communicate. You decided, for reasons of your own, not to do so. And I don't think I badgered you, Tom, at the time. . . ."

"No. You didn't. You were cool." He paused. "That's okay. I can read that. People talk too much anyway. In this family they talk all the time. Mum never draws breath. Gran never draws breath. I just needed a bit of space. A bit of silence for a while."

"Yes, well, sometimes that can help." Gini looked away.

"Sure. No sweat. You used to talk, that's all. I liked talking to you—you remember that? We'd go out, you'd treat me to a movie, grab a hamburger. It was fun."

"Yes. I remember. I enjoyed it too."

"So I can't help wondering . . . what brought this on." He hesitated again. "Mum says it's post-traumatic stress disorder—did she tell you?"

"No, she didn't. And it's nothing so grand."

"Too many dead bodies, Mum says. I said—Pascal can handle all that, he's covered hundreds of wars, so why can't Gini? Mum says it's different for women, because they feel things more, but I don't buy that. I think . . ." He weighed his words. "I think you'll get *inured* to it in time. And it had to be hard for you, because it was your first war, and it meant a whole lot to you because that was always your ambition, right? To cover wars?"

"Yes, it was. Once. Why don't we change the subject?"

"Sure."

There was a brief silence. Tom dried a saucepan and some plates while Gini grimly scrubbed and rinsed. She would be fine, she told herself, if she could just concentrate on this small, menial task. Then Tom did the one thing she would never have expected, the one thing she could not deal with at all.

Blushing again, and with a gauche clumsiness that reminded her of him as a much younger boy, he put his arm around her shoulders and apologized. He said he knew it was crass, and he shouldn't have raised the subject, and he was sorry he had, but someone—well, his girlfriend, actually—had told him he had to get in touch with other people's feelings, so he had been making an effort, and it seemed to be working, kind of, and he hadn't meant to be intrusive, but Gini did look so different that he felt he had to say something. . . .

She began to cry. She could see that her tears distressed Tom, but she was powerless to stop them. Tom drew her to the table. He brought her a handful of Kleenex. When she saw how agitated he had become, she battled the tears, and finally controlled them. Seeing her grow calmer, Tom grew kinder still. He made her some coffee, then he sat down beside her and took her hand.

"Tell me," he said. "You can tell me. I won't tell anyone else, I promise. I understand. What made you cry?"

"It wasn't you, Tom." Gini squeezed his hand, then released it. "Please don't blame yourself. You were very kind. It's just—in Bosnia I couldn't cry. I couldn't let myself. So it's as if the tears stored themselves up. They waited till I got home—and now I suddenly remember something, and they begin, and I can't stop them. That's all."

"What do you remember?" He looked at her gravely, and Gini was touched. She could see that, half-boy, half-adult, he was trying to act as he considered proper for a man.

"Ugly things I saw. People dying. Wounds. You watch the news on TV, Tom. You can imagine. I'd seen those programs too, before I went, obviously. I'd seen Pascal's photographs. I knew what I'd find. I thought I was prepared. Only when you see it, stand by it, for months at a time—when you know that nothing you do, and nothing you write, is going to alter it . . ." She bent her head.

He frowned. "Why did you want to go there, Gini? Why cover wars? Was it because your father did? Because he won that Pulitzer Prize thing? Or Pascal, maybe? So you could work with him, be together?"

"All of those things, I guess, Tom." She sighed. "I don't *know* anymore. All I know is—I couldn't go back to Bosnia. I'll never write about another war."

"I expect you will," Tom said in an encouraging tone. "I read those pieces you wrote. They were really moving. When Mum read that one from Mostar, she cried, and—"

"Don't, Tom. Let's not talk about it anymore. Okay?"

"You miss Pascal." Tom rose. "Mum says that's half the problem, and I agree. She says you'll be okay when he gets back. In fact, she's pretty mad at him for staying away so long. She said the other night, if she had his number, she'd call him, give him a piece of her mind."

"What?" Gini also rose. She looked at him in consternation. "Tom—she didn't mean that, did she? She mustn't do that. She has no right to interfere."

"It's okay. She won't. She just gets these ideas." He paused, his face changing. "Oh, I see. I understand. You haven't told him, have you? He doesn't know you're ill—"

"I'm not ill. Can we stop this?"

"Because if he knew, Mum's right, he'd be on the next plane."

"Tom, will you just stop this?"

"No. I won't!" Tom, she realized suddenly, was also angry. His face had paled. He shot her a glance fierce with adolescent purity. "You're *lying* to Pascal. You shouldn't lie, not to someone who loves you—"

"I am *not* lying." Gini rounded on him furiously. "There may be certain things I prefer not to tell him, but there are reasons for that. He has to *work*, Tom."

"It's still a lie. It's a lie by omission, that's all. *I* don't lie. I wouldn't lie to my girlfriend. I haven't told one lie, not since November ninth last year. Not even a single white lie—"

"So I see. Well, you should learn, Tom. Sometimes the truth causes pain. Sometimes lies can be helpful. Or merciful. When you're older, you'll understand."

The final remark was fatal, she knew instantly. Blood rushed up into his neck and face.

"Couples shouldn't lie *especially*," he burst out. "That really makes me sick. Wives lying to their husbands. Husbands lying to their wives. My dad does that. When he's here, which is once every century, he just fucking lies all the time."

Gini could now hear the mounting distress, could feel his sudden rage. The turn in the conversation, and the speed of his unforeseen reaction, took her by surprise.

"Tom, *don't*," she began, holding out her hand. "I'm sorry I said that. And you mustn't think that way. Lindsay doesn't lie. Lindsay is one of the most truthful people I know. And your parents aren't together. They haven't been for years. You mustn't make judgments about them like that."

"Why not? It's true. I know the facts. They were married. For ten minutes. They had a wedding. They made all those vows. I was born. Then they split. They made a promise, and they never kept it. And you— you're just as bad. . . . "

"Tom, I don't think you mean that. You don't understand."

"I thought you were different, you and Pascal." His voice rose. "I should have known—"

He broke off. From below, a door slammed. They both listened to his mother's footsteps climbing the stairs. Tom's face worked. Gini stared at him helplessly. She had little experience of children, no knowledge of how you spoke to someone who was half-adult, half-child. She was only twelve years older than he was, not yet thirty, but she watched him now from across a huge divide. Her own inadequacy silenced her. Her hand was still extended toward him, and Tom was still ignoring it. His mother had reached the first landing below. He gave a sudden angry gesture, began to speak, stopped, then stalked from the room and slammed the door.

The door of his own room thundered shut a few seconds later; almost immediately, a blast of rock music rent the air. Lindsay entered, looking ebullient, and secretly pleased with herself. As if on cue, the second she entered, the telephone began to ring. Lindsay picked it up and listened in silence.

"Markov," she said eventually. "I don't want to hear this now. I don't *need* to hear this. It's the *weekend*, okay? Now, piss off, Markov, and leave me alone." She replaced the receiver, turned to the door, and raised her voice. "Tom," she shouted, "down a few decibels, *please* . . . "

The boom of drums reduced.

"What happened?" She turned to Gini. "A row?"

"Sort of. I'm not sure. Tom was being very good to me. We were talking. Then the conversation took this sudden swerve. Then . . . "

"Fission?"

"Yes. Oh, Lindsay—I think I failed him in some way."

"Don't worry. That's what adults are there for. I fail Tom around five times a day. Teenagers!" She flashed a smile. "Let's get going. I'll call Charlotte, then we're on our way. I have a million things to tell you. . . ."

Heading west toward Oxford, Lindsay drove at top speed, and without sign of skill. Gini, who had forgotten just how appalling a driver she was, eventually closed her eyes while Lindsay steered and talked. She talked all the way to Oxford; she talked *in* Oxford, where having missed the turnoff, she lost the way. She talked on the country roads beyond Oxford, and she did not, it seemed to Gini, have a million topics to discuss, despite her claim.

She had one topic, and variations upon it. Her subject was a man Gini had never met, and in whom Gini was not interested. His name was Rowland McGuire—and Lindsay could not stand him. Or so she said.

CHAPTER 3

Charlotte Flanders had been making pastry, and her hands were still floury and white. Her youngest son, Daniel, was seated at the table at the far end of the large country kitchen, happily, if messily, engaged with finger paints.

Tubs of slurpy paint in brilliant colors surrounded Danny and herself. He had deposited paint on his hands, face, elbows, and clothes; there was paint on the floor and the table. So far, he had drawn a red tree, a square house, a blue bristly dog, and a fat orange Charlotte with a fuzz of pink hair. The large, untidy, comforting room smelled of yeast; a clock ticked. Charlotte knew that she should feel tranquil, and in this situation usually did; but this afternoon she was anxious and tranquillity remained elusive. She looked down at Danny's portrait of herself. Why is my hair pink, she wondered, and found she suddenly wanted to cry.

She hugged Danny impulsively and rested her face against his hair. The scent of his hair and skin, a scent peculiar to babies and young children, affected Charlotte deeply. It tugged at her heart. She kissed Danny, then withdrew, because he was wriggling in that maternal embrace, eager to get on with his art.

Shortly after three, still preoccupied, thinking about the weekend to come and the arrival of her guests, she left the house to take the four dogs—two fat Labradors and two violent Jack Russells—for their afternoon walk. She left Daniel with Jess, a neighborhood girl who'd come to help in the preparations for the weekend. Both were now engaged in making little sponge cakes for tea. In the garden Charlotte paused and looked back through the bright rectangle of the kitchen window, the dogs woofing and circling at her heels.

Jess was beating up sugar and butter; Daniel was assembling the cake decorations he loved, the crystallized violets, brightly colored sweets, and silver balls. Daniel liked cakes only with acid-pink icing and lots of decorations. For his fourth birthday next month, they were going to make one in the shape of his favorite animal, a hedgehog. It was to be a pink hedgehog, with chocolate-flake quills.

It was a beautiful cold, clear afternoon; the air smelled of damp earth and woodsmoke. By the time Charlotte had reached the end of her driveway, she felt calmer and soothed. Her natural serenity—the quality in her that Max most loved—was beginning to reassert itself. She tightened the bright red headscarf over her untidy hair, clasped her old coat tighter around her stomach, whistled to the dogs, and set off on her usual circuit. She would walk down to the river, past the church, and then back across the hills. By the time she reached home again, it would be almost time for Gini and Lindsay to arrive. She would just have time to shut the hens in the henhouse before it grew dark—and she must remember to do that, for there was a dog-fox hunting the area. Then, once Jess had returned to her own family, and her own older sons had returned from school, they would make tea. Toast on the fire, Charlotte thought; Danny's acid-pink iced sponge cakes. It would be fun. She was looking forward to seeing Lindsay. In fact, Charlotte thought with a smile, she had plans for Lindsay. Her husband, Max, might have his doubts about those plans, but Charlotte, a born matchmaker, believed they might work.

Lindsay was warmhearted, independent, and strong. But Lindsay's life, unlike her own, was difficult. She had a son who desperately needed a father figure. His own father, Lindsay's ex-husband, whom Charlotte had met once and instantly loathed, was a handsome, weak-willed deadbeat, last heard of in Canada, who contacted Lindsay rarely and Tom never, and who put in an appearance only when short of cash, or abandoned by the latest in a long line of girls.

Lindsay deserved better than a man who had walked out on her six months after Tom's birth. She deserved better than to spend the rest of her life supporting her supremely selfish mother—and that, once Tom left home, was a possible fate, Charlotte feared. Every man with whom Lindsay had ever been seriously involved since her divorce had been chased off by Louise, whose instinct for self-preservation was acute. Lindsay needed a man capable of freeing her from her mother's clasp. Charlotte, much to her husband's surprise, even had a candidate for this role; a gallant knight who would rescue her friend.

Of course, Lindsay might well feel she did not want, or need, rescuing. Well, Lindsay was wrong. Lindsay needed rescuing from herself as well as from her mother. She had to learn to trust, to perceive that pain and abandonment were not always and inevitably attendant on love. She had to be made to see that some men could be trusted, and that the right man could transform a woman's life, just as Charlotte's life had been transformed by Max, and—to take another triumphant example—as Gini's life had been transformed by Pascal.

She had reached the river; Charlotte stopped. She clipped on the dogs' leashes, walked along the narrow road, and paused on the bridge. Thinking about marital contentment and tranquillity, she watched a fish move through the reeds. Then, seeing the hills were now mauve, and the light was beginning to fade, she hustled the dogs together, stepped back into the road, and began making for the fieldgate just beyond the bend. Before she could reach it, and at a point where the road narrowed, she heard the car. It was on her in seconds, swerving on the bend, being driven far too fast. It cut in close, a large, brand-new silver BMW. She felt its slipstream clutch at her coat; its rapid passage sprayed her with mud. Charlotte shouted angrily after it, but its driver, a man, neither acknowledged her nor slowed. Charlotte watched the car turn into a track farther on, and begin to bump its way up the steep gradient to the beech woods beyond.

Feeling shaken, wrapping her old coat more tightly around her stomach and her unborn child, Charlotte walked on. She encountered no one on this stage of her walk, and glimpsed only one other pedestrian, a man, walking along the river road below, with what looked like a lurcher dog. He paused at the bridge, as she had done. The wind gusted. Charlotte shivered, and whistled to her own dogs. They had had their romp: it was time to return.

She made her way back through the village, past the graveyard, the Norman church, the almshouses, and the tall drystone wall that bordered the manor gardens. Lights now shone from the windows of the cottages she passed, and Charlotte's heart lifted. Her despondency and unease faded. She wanted to be at home with her sons, and her friends, and her husband; she wanted afternoon to ease toward evening, and the evening to lengthen companionably as they sat together by the fire.

She passed two people only on this, the last stage of her walk: two girls, in school uniform, making their way back to the manor. One was Cassandra Morley, a pretty fifteen-year-old who sometimes baby-sat for her, and whose mother—a brittle divorcee—Charlotte disliked. Her companion looked like Mina Landis, who had moved to the area recently, whose father was the commanding officer of the nearby U.S. air force base. Charlotte had invited Mina's parents for drinks that evening, along with a few other local friends.

She called a greeting to both girls, but to her surprise they seemed determined not to see or hear her. They made no acknowledgment; Cassandra, the taller of the two, broke into a run; Mina hastened after her. Charlotte heard laughter as they reached the manor gates.

How odd and ill-mannered, Charlotte thought. Rudeness from Cassandra was not unknown, but Mina, quiet little Mina, had always struck Charlotte as well brought up. She shrugged and walked on, then quickened her pace. As she approached her driveway, a small black car skidded to a halt, reversed, then roared into the drive, only narrowly missing the gateposts. By the time Charlotte had shooed the hens to safety for the night and made her way back through the orchard, Lindsay and Gini were already settled in the kitchen, which now smelled of newly baked bread.

Lindsay had Daniel in her arms, and was deep in conversation with the departing Jess. Gini—and it took Charlotte an instant to realize that it was indeed Gini—was seated at the kitchen table. Charlotte stopped short in consternation, and stared.

Lindsay had warned her to expect an alteration, but Charlotte, who had not seen Gini since she left for Sarajevo, was still insufficiently prepared. Charlotte had once considered Gini one of the most beautiful women she knew. Now she was painfully thin, and her face was without animation or color; her extraordinary silvery-blond hair, once long, had been inexpertly, even savagely, cropped.

Charlotte heard herself give an involuntary exclamation, then controlled herself as she caught Lindsay's warning glance. Forcing herself to smile, she hurried forward. Gini rose, and Charlotte took her warmly in her arms, overwhelmed with sudden pity and distress. Gini returned the embrace, then quietly disengaged herself. As she drew back, Charlotte caught the glitter of tears in her eyes, and Gini—proud and deeply reticent by nature—at once turned her face away. Presently, with a muttered excuse, she left the room and went upstairs with her suitcase.

Charlotte turned to Lindsay, her kind face dismayed; her immediate question was what might have caused this transformation in their friend—but Lindsay, she found, was curiously reluctant to answer, and became evasive at once.

"Was that Charlotte Flanders?" Mina said as the door of the manor slammed behind them.

Cassandra was busy deactivating the expensive alarm her mother had installed: eventually, the beeping stopped.

"Four vile dogs? Pregnant yet again? Yes, it was."

"Oh, Cass." Mina took off her coat and hung it up neatly. "We should have spoken to her. She's nice. She's been really good to my mother, trying to help her fit in. . . ."

"Sure, sure—she's nice." Cassandra sounded impatient. "And she *talks*. Mina, we don't have the time. Also, she's always asking questions—like, how's my mother? *Where's* my mother? Why lie more than we need, right?"

"I don't know." Mina's small pale face contracted. "I feel guilty, I guess. My parents are going there for drinks this evening. What if she mentions she saw us?"

"So what if she does? They know you're coming here."

"Not this early. If she mentions the time, my mother will know something's wrong. She'll know we played hooky—"

"Oh, forget it," Cassandra said carelessly. "She won't even remember. If your mother does ask questions tomorrow, make something up. Say one of the teachers was ill. Who cares? It won't matter by then."

"What if my mother calls tonight?"

"She'll get the answering machine. We're going to the theater, remember? In Bath. With my mother. It's a long drive, we're meeting friends for dinner afterward, then my mother's driving us back. We won't be home until after midnight. . . . Come on, Mina, it's a perfect alibi. Not even your mother can crack it."

"What if someone at Charlotte Flanders's mentions your mother's away? What if she told someone in the village that she was going to New York?"

"No way," Cassandra said with a shrug. "She doesn't bother with people in the village. She calls them the peasants. Anyway, it was a last-minute thing—she just took off. Just *relax*, Mina, let's make this place look occupied. Then we'll eat, all right?"

Cassandra ran up the wide staircase that led up from the hall and turned off to her right. Mina followed more slowly. She tried to persuade herself that she was not having second thoughts about this scheme of Cassandra's. After all, Cassandra had been to raves before, and she said they were amazing, just great. The one at Glastonbury last summer; the one outside Cheltenham just before Christmas, and now the one tonight.

Cassandra had told her all about it, what it would be like: a huge barn up in the fields, miles from the nearest house; hundreds of cars, buses, trailers bringing kids and new-age travelers from all around. Music and dancing and stars so bright and seeming so close you could reach out and touch them. And the man called Star. Cassandra had told her all about Star.

Mina mounted the stairs and turned left. She entered a succession of opulent, overfurnished bedrooms, all advertisements for Cassandra's mother's skills as an interior decorator. Mina switched on lights and drew chintz curtains as Cassandra had instructed her to do. Cassandra's mother was so careless; just taking off like that for New York, leaving Cass alone in a large house. Her own mother seemed to forget that Mina, too, would be sixteen in a few months. She continued to treat Mina as if she were ten: she worried about everything—men, parties, cars, smoking, drinking. She saw the world as a dangerous place filled with pits ready to entrap her daughter, but the nature of these traps embarrassed her. She would try to discuss them with Mina, and then she would become flushed and confused. Sex and drugs were the two things she most feared, but she could never quite bring herself to use those terms, so she would talk about "boys" or "pot," or clip little scare stories from the newspapers about unwanted pregnancies or heroin addiction and leave them on Mina's desk. The transparent subterfuge made Mina angry. She would ball up the clippings and throw them away unread.

Until her father was posted to England, until Mina began attending the Cheltenham Academy, until Cassandra became her friend, Mina had for the most part accepted her mother's fussing: she loved her mother and could see the protectiveness was well meant. Then, a few weeks before, during the Christmas holidays, when she and her mother were alone in their house, Mina had picked up the telephone extension in her room, intending to call Cassandra. She had interrupted a conversation between her mother and an Englishman whose voice she did not recognize. She was about to replace the receiver, then stopped.

"Darling," Mina heard her mother say urgently, "darling, I'm desperate to see you too. But I can't. Mina's here—we'll have to wait until next week."

Mina felt herself go very cold, then very hot; the blood rushed into her neck. She stood there, unable to move, still clutching the receiver.

She heard it all, the whispered questions, the reassurances of love, the details that spelled out lies and adultery. Then she replaced the receiver very quietly, went into her bathroom, and was sick. Lies, lies, lies, she thought to herself: the lies made her miserable and furious, and her thoughts tangled and hot. After that she was much more prepared to listen to Cassandra, and much more prepared to emulate her: so what if it involved lying to her mother? Lying didn't matter now that Mina knew her mother was a cheat.

In the last of the opulent bedrooms, Mina stopped. She had caught sight of her own reflection in a cheval glass; she looked herself up and down with a cold and critical eye: a small, thin girl in a drab school uniform skirt and sweater. How she hated her red hair, her pale complexion, her freckles, her flat chest. *I look twelve,* Mina thought, and wished for the thousandth time that she resembled Cassandra, who was tall, golden-haired, careless, and daring, Cassandra, whom God had blessed with breasts.

It was still not too late to change her mind, she told herself. It was possible her mother didn't really have a lover, and the conversation she had overheard was innocent. It was possible that this whole painful past month was some horrible mistake.

But Mina knew that it was not. She felt the tears well behind her eyes, and blinked them back. She let the anger swell and rip. Anger was preferable to tears, because it gave her courage. She thought: I *will* go, and serve her right. Then she turned and ran back downstairs to the kitchen. There Cassandra was staring with disgust into an empty refrigerator.

"Can you *believe* that?" she said on an indignant note. "I mean you'd think she'd have left *some* food. There's a few tins of baked beans, some bread, and that's it . . ." She slammed the door, then, recovering her temper, gave Mina a quick smile.

"Look what I bought," she said, reaching for a tote bag and tipping its contents onto the table. "Hair gel, makeup, some of those water-transfer tattoos—check them out, Mina, aren't they great?"

Mina looked at the fake tattoos doubtfully. There was a black scorpion, and a hawk and a dragon, and some letters that spelled HATE.

"We'll fix our hair and our faces—you can borrow some of my old clothes, I think they'll fit. . . . How much money did you bring?"

"Ten pounds."

"Shit. That's not enough. We want to score, right?"

"I guess so."

"Whizz, tracers, maybe some E's. A little Ecstasy—you wait, Mina, it's fantastic. It makes you feel really sexy. Hey, techno music—I hope they play the Prodigy. Maybe Liquid Death. I'm going to dance all night. . . . Hang on. There must be some money here somewhere."

Mina watched Cassandra open kitchen jars and canisters. She wondered sometimes if Cassandra was hurt by her parents' indifference. Cassandra always spoke of it as an advantage, but Mina wasn't always sure she spoke the truth. Once, when she came back from a weekend with her father, who was forty, and her new stepmother, who was twenty-six, Cassandra had cried. But that was nearly a year ago; now Cass never spoke of her father, and rarely saw him. Mina hadn't seen her cry since.

In the fifth container, Cassandra found some money. She tossed it down on the kitchen table with a little smile of triumph.

"I *knew* it. Forty quid. Great. We need plenty. Just wait, Mina! This is going to be great."

Cassandra began rolling a neat joint. She lit it, inhaled deeply, then passed it across. Mina drew the sweet smoke down into her lungs; after a few minutes she began to feel lightness and lift. It made her feel calm and floaty and safe. It drove all the anger and muddle away, so she forgot about her mother and the telephone call that changed her life.

"Will Star be there?" she asked, breathing out.

Cassandra's face became dreamy and soft.

"Sure he will. I told you. Just wait till you meet him, Mina. He's, like, truly amazing. Wild. When he touches you . . ."

"What happens when he touches you?"

"I don't know. I can't describe it. But he just takes your hand, maybe, or touches your arm—and you can feel this *power*, and it's passing from him to you, and it's just—filling you up . . ."

They went upstairs and changed, and molded their hair into Medusa-like snakes; they painted their eyelids gold and their lips black. They applied the fake tattoos last of all. Mina fixed the black hawk to her left cheekbone. Cassandra pasted the scorpion to her forehead, the dragon to her throat, then she held out her left hand, and Mina helped her apply the four letters that spelled HATE.

"We look brilliant," Cassandra declared as they inspected themselves in the bathroom mirror.

"Great," said Mina. She still felt floaty. "We look great."

Cassandra gave her a hug.

"I'll introduce you to Star, promise," she said. "You'll really like him. And he's bringing some new stuff. It's amazing, he says. The best ever. He brought it back from his friends in Amsterdam the other night."

CHAPTER 4

Across the valley from the manor, the thin young man with the lurcher, whom Charlotte had glimpsed earlier, continued his walk. He turned off the river road onto a track, and headed uphill to the beech trees. He walked at a leisurely pace, scenting the evening air: he could smell damp grass, woodsmoke, the residue of exhaust fumes, and—nearing the wood—the stink of fox.

He paused to look back across the alley to the curve of the river, and the village beyond. He noted the church tower, the graceful façade of the manor, the lights in the cottage windows. It was a famous view, one that had changed little in four hundred years, and—the epitome of a certain Englishness—one much featured in Cotswolds guidebooks. The young man looked at it with loathing: safe, smug, complacent, rich. Star hated the English countryside; he preferred the textures, smells, and dangers of city streets.

Star—it was not his real name, but it was now the only tag he answered to—rolled saliva in his mouth, then spat. His dog cowered at his heels. Star jerked the length of string that served as a leash, and walked on. He entered a clearing on the edge of the beech wood. There, parked discreetly behind a wall, its lights cut, was a brand-new 5 series silver BMW.

"Yours?" said Star to the plump, smartly dressed young man who was standing next to it, blowing on his fingers and stamping his feet.

"Christ. You made me jump." The young man swung around. "Why do you have to creep up on people like that? This place gives me the willies. You're late."

"Your car?" Star repeated. The young man recovered himself. He gave a tight grin, and made a seesawing gesture of the hand.

"In a manner of speaking. Classy, isn't it?"

Star gave him a look of bilious contempt. He did not like the man, whose name was Mitchell, and who worked in the City money markets; he did not like his car. He shrugged.

"German shit. If you're going to buy German, get a Mercedes, they're best."

"Who said anything about buying?" Mitchell grinned again. He edged away from Star, who had not washed recently, and who smelled richly of sweat.

"All fixed for tonight?" he went on, again stamping his feet. "Christ, it's cold. I've driven all the way from London. I've got the usual friends joining me, so I damn well hope it's fixed."

Star was wearing a huge, torn, tweed overcoat. From one of its pockets he produced a small and very expensive mobile telephone. Mitchell regarded this object without surprise, though it was greatly at odds with Star's gypsyish dress. Star punched in a number.

"One more call," he said. "And, yes, it's fixed."

"Sweet?" Mitchell said on an interrogative note. Mitchell's taste was for speed and teenage girls, if possible in combination. Star's task was to provide both, so he understood the question at once. He pushed back his long black hair, let the number ring, and smiled. Star was blessed—or cursed—with startling good looks, and the smile, practiced before many mirrors, was intended to disarm. Mitchell, who knew Star of old, was not disarmed. He noticed now, as he had noticed on occasions before, that Star's blue-black eyes had a nasty glint in them, a not-quite-sane might-do-anything worship-me-Charles-Manson sort of glint. In the fading light Star's eyes and teeth gleamed. Mitchell took one step farther back.

Star spoke briefly into the mobile phone, then disconnected, and snapped it shut.

He finally answered Mitchell's question.

"Sweet?" he said. "There'll be three hundred people. Three hundred *minimum*. And the pigs don't have a sniff of it. Feel the power in the airwaves, man—that's sweet if you like. The tribes are gathering. I've got music, fire eaters, jugglers, lots of gullible little rich kids." He laughed. "One big fucking stairway to heaven, man—I can promise you that. Trust in Star. Have I ever let you down?"

"Yes," said Mitchell, recovering his nerve. "You have."

"Example?"

"Last summer, *for example*. Ground-up fucking aspirin. Ground-up fucking dogs' worming tablets. Twenty quid a tab for crap. My friends weren't pleased. I wasn't pleased. More like a grave than a rave that was—I was throwing up for two days afterward. That little Dutch bitch you fixed me up with gave me the clap—" He paused. Star was not listening.

"What happened to that little bitch, by the way?"

"She's dead."

"My condolences. The fact remains. You let me down. As such occasions go, that one was shit."

"It rained."

"It was amateurs-ville."

"It was a tryout. Tonight will be different. You wait. This time, my friends came through. I've got some serious stuff."

Mitchell began to look more interested. "Samples?"

"No free samples."

"Look, I have to be sure this time, all right? I've come a fucking long way. I've got friends coming from Birmingham—I waste their time, I look like a schmuck. . . ."

Star shrugged and did not move. There was a silence, a tussle of wills. Eventually, Mitchell produced a fat wallet. He peeled off a twenty-pound note and handed it across. Star ignored it.

"You've got to be fucking joking."

"I never joke."

There was another pause, then Mitchell peeled off another note. Star took the money and handed him a small packet. Mitchell opened it, examined the pill inside, then swallowed it. He waited, paced a bit, lit a cigarette. Some time passed. Star watched, arms folded. Mitchell talked on. Then, abruptly, he threw the cigarette down. He closed his eyes, swayed against his car, and clutched his chest. Several more minutes passed. Star continued to watch him in silence. Eventually, Mitchell opened his eyes again.

"Christ," he said. "Jesus Christ."

"Some rush, huh?"

"Express—and I'm still traveling. Wow. This time you've really come through. Where in hell did you get that stuff?"

"Amsterdam."

"God bless the Dutch. What's it called?"

"It's a White Dove."

Mitchell closed his eyes once more.

Star turned. "See you later tonight, then," he said. "With your friends—oh, and, by the way. You got a discount. For them the price goes up."

Mitchell sighed. "Start time?" he said.

"Eight. Nine. Ten. Time has no meaning to free men."

"Don't give me that hippie shit." Mitchell opened his eyes. "You like money the same way I do. Also girls. This is Mitchell you're talking to, remember? I saw you, last summer, with that Dutch kid. And that French girl the year before. One word from me in the right quarter—"

He broke off and caught his breath. Some new chemical reaction was fizzing inside his skull. He paled, then trembled, then swore. When his vision cleared again, he saw that Star was now very close to him, the blue-black eyes just inches from his own. He flinched.

"You saw?" Star said. "Tell me what you saw."

"Nothing. I saw nothing. I was just—Jesus, Star, it's this stuff. I can't think straight. Come on, we know each other, right? No hassle, we're . . ."

"Oh, sure, we know each other." Star moved closer and gripped Mitchell's lapels. "You know me really well. Like, inside out. You know what makes me tick. Tick-tock. Tick-tock. What does make me tick, exactly, Mitchell? Is it money, pills, little girls, like you? Or is it more?"

Mitchell began to struggle violently. "Let go of me," he began, his voice rising. "Let fucking go of me, okay?"

"I think it's more, Mitchell. I think it's this—*appetite*—I have for more. More of everything. More sex, more money, more pills, more thrills, more *excess*. What should I do with you, Mitchell, now that you know me so well? Should I kiss you? Should I kill you?"

Mitchell gave a moan. Star was strong, and he was lifting him up now so his feet dangled above the ground. His wide mouth and even, white teeth were now half an inch from Mitchell's own.

"*Sweet* . . ." Star said, dragging the word out so it sounded like an incantation. He bent forward, then he bit Mitchell's nose.

Mitchell gave a howl of pain. Star laughed, and dropped him.

"Just a love bite," he said.

Mitchell fumbled for a handkerchief and mopped his face. His nose was bleeding, and his hands were shaking; the tides of chemicals were still ebbing back and forth in his brain. "You fucking maniac . . ." He stared at the bloody handkerchief. He looked around him blankly. In the gathering dusk, Star had disappeared. He shook his head, breathed deeply, closed his eyes, then opened them. This time he could see Star. He was standing right in front of him, unaffected by these events, looking much as before. A down-and-out with diabolic eyes. Mitchell shivered, then swore.

"Who the fuck *are* you?" he began. "*What* are you? Why in hell . . ."

Star ignored the question; he gave a sweet, wolfish smile. "You know the place? See you tonight, then."

He did not wait for any reply from his client. Mitchell's gaze was now glazed, his eyes closing again. Star watched him for a few moments more, coolly and dispassionately, the way a scientist might watch the result of laboratory tests on mice or rats. Then he gave his thin dog a caress and turned.

Mitchell, coming to his senses a short while afterward, searched the clearing, then checked the track. Star's capacity to materialize and dematerialize alarmed him. Mitchell felt a bit twitchy, a bit paranoid; no more than a minute or two had passed—Star had to be in sight.

He stared down the straight track to the road below. Shadows and shapes moved in his brain; the track undulated like a switchback, it had a life of its own. Mitchell watched it snake and coil. Slowly he began to understand: the track was deserted; the road was deserted. Star should have been visible, but was not; the air had assimilated him. Star was gone.

Charlotte, a wonderful cook, always provided magnificent teas. Faced with an array of little sandwiches, with toast and honey, with gingerbread and Danny's iced cakes, Lindsay always vowed to show restraint—and never did. Guiltily aware that Tom had rarely if ever been provided with such a tea as this, and that his custom on returning home from school was to graze on chocolate bars or potato chips, reminding herself that each of Danny's delicious little cakes contained five hundred calories at least, but feeling that she had to make up for Gini, who scarcely touched the food, Lindsay consumed an inordinate quantity. To please Danny, who was watching her with the solemnity of a three-star Michelin chef, she compounded her own felony by eating two of his cakes—the one made in her honor, with an "L" in silver balls on the top, and also the one with a "G," destined for Gini, which Gini had quietly refused. Lindsay was peeved at her for this. It was then she noticed that of the cakes remaining, one was iced with the initial "D" for Daddy, and was clearly intended for Max, and the other bore the initial "R." No one in this household had a name beginning with that letter.

"Who's this one for, Danny?" Lindsay asked.

To her surprise, Danny instantly blushed a deep and fiery red. He looked at the floor, then he looked at his mother. He looked at his three older brothers, as if desperate for their help, but Alex, Ben, and Colin were leaning over the fire, making toast.

"Maybe it's a 'B,' " Lindsay said. " 'B' for Ben, is that it, Danny? How silly of me—I can't see too well from here."

"It's an 'R,' " Danny said on a sudden fierce note. "It *is* an 'R.' It doesn't look like a 'B' at all. It's an 'R' for—"

"For Ripper!" Charlotte cried quickly, hauling herself to her feet and pouring tea. "You know, Lindsay. Ripper, the Jack Russell. Jack the Ripper—one of Max's ghastly jokes. The one who ate your slippers the last time you came. The one who eats everything in sight."

Lindsay looked down at the dog in question, who, for once, was quiet, lying snoring at her feet. She wondered why he was the only one of four dogs to be awarded this treat, and why—if that were the case—it had not already been given to him. To her certain knowledge, this tiny and malevolent animal had already consumed three shortbread cookies, the braid from a cushion, one piece of Lego, and four pieces of toast. She was about to remark on this, then thought better of it. Danny, darting small, surreptitious glances at his mother, was still round-eyed with some inexplicable distress.

Still, small children could be like that, Lindsay thought, sinking back in her chair. Perhaps it was some specific ritual Danny had. Perhaps Ripper received his cake when, and only when, his master returned from London—which would be soon, she realized, glancing at her watch. Heavens, it was past five-thirty; they'd been sitting there for ages; Max ought to arrive at about six o'clock.

The rich food and the warmth of the wood fire were making her sleepy. She settled still deeper in her chair. How she loved this house, she thought, and this room. How unlike London, how nice this was!

Across from her, Charlotte and Gini sat side by side on a huge battered sofa. The older boys, bored with toastmaking, were departing upstairs to play; Danny had picked up a picture book. Charlotte was persevering with Gini. She was coaxing her beyond monosyllables, and had begun to succeed, it seemed, in persuading Gini to talk.

Not about Bosnia—Charlotte was too intelligent to risk that subject—but first about neutral things, then Gini and Pascal's apartment—Charlotte longed to see it, begged Gini to describe it—and then, finally, Pascal himself.

"I miss him," Charlotte said with her customary warmth. "Do you remember that dinner we all had to celebrate your joining the paper? In

that tiny French restaurant Pascal found? I still dream about the food—
it was just so good. When he gets back we must all go there again. And I
want you to bring him here, of course. Would he be bored in the country? No, I don't think he would."

"No. He's never bored. He—I'm sure he'd like that very much. And
he likes the country. He grew up in the country. In a village in
Provence."

"Provence? I never realized that. I think of him as so—high-powered, I
suppose. International. Always catching planes, speeding off to the next
job, taking those extraordinary photographs. They've broken my heart,
some of his photographs. It must cost him so much to do that, year after
year—and yet, when you meet him—I expected him to be somber,
haunted by what he's seen. Yet he seems so"—Charlotte frowned as she
sought the right word—"so filled with energy and ideas. And so happy
too. But then, I first met him with you. And everyone's happy when
they're that much in love."

It was a compliment, and an overture, Lindsay thought, listening. She
watched as painful color washed into Gini's cheeks. For an instant, gratitude and reassurance flooded her face, then she tensed and looked
away, as if afraid that Charlotte, having made her overture, would follow it with questions.

Charlotte, who could be subtle, did not do so immediately. She talked
on for a while, and Lindsay felt her thoughts begin to drift. She closed her
eyes. Charlotte, living in the country, had met Pascal on only a few occasions, and knew him less well than Lindsay. She knew none of the background to this romance, was not aware, as Lindsay was, of the strange
circumstances of Pascal's original meeting with Gini. Charlotte had not
witnessed, as Lindsay had, the force of Gini's reaction when they met
again after years apart. It might be difficult to imagine now, while Gini
was such a ghost of her former self, but Gini was a passionate woman,
and Pascal—as Charlotte had been attempting to convey—was a passionate man. Passion alarmed Lindsay, and occasionally embarrassed her; she
shrank from its manifestations, and she shrank from the word. Yet a passion that went far deeper than the electrically obvious sexual attraction
between them could be felt whenever Pascal and Gini were together. It
sparked across a room; it charged the air around a dinner table—and it
had, on occasion, made Lindsay deeply envious. Pascal Lamartine had a
beautiful, fiercely expressive face: to watch him watching Gini, to observe
his unwavering loyalty, and concern, his constant attunement to her, and
hers to him, had been, for Lindsay, a painful experience. She was hon-

est: she knew she was witnessing something she herself had never felt, or inspired.

The most passionate love Lindsay had ever felt was reserved for her son; his welfare, well-being, and future happiness were her dominant concerns—and in some ways she was glad of this. Such love was unalterable; passion between a man and a woman, different in nature, and combustible, was less sure.

"So, tell me, Gini," she heard as she drifted on the edge of somnolence. "How do you manage—can you call him?"

"Yes. And he tries to call me every day. Sometimes the lines are bad. And we write, of course."

"Often?"

"Oh—every day if we can. Pascal writes wonderful letters. I can hear his voice when I read them. Sometimes, if we're lucky, they get through very fast. Sometimes they take weeks to arrive. I haven't heard from him this week, but that will mean he's been somewhere remote. He's not always in Sarajevo. He constantly moves around."

Lindsay, listening more closely now, paid silent tribute to Charlotte, who had prized this much information from Gini—more specific information than she herself had obtained in two months. She hoped that Gini was telling the truth, and was deluding neither Charlotte nor herself. But Lindsay was no longer sure that this communication did continue as reliably as Gini claimed. Since Christmas, watching the deterioration in Gini, she had begun to believe that some quarrel, perhaps a final quarrel, had taken place in Bosnia, and that the affair, originally begun in a war zone, had now ended in one, as suddenly concluded as it had suddenly begun. Nothing else, she was beginning to believe, could account for Gini's continuing unhappiness, and her continuing unshakable reserve. It would be very characteristic of Gini to refuse to admit it, should the affair be over. Gini rarely took people into her confidence, and by nature she was proud.

She would mention the possibility to Charlotte later, Lindsay thought; Charlotte might be able to elicit the truth before this weekend was over. Or not. Gini had just turned the conversation back to more neutral topics, she noted. She was now prompting Charlotte to talk about her family, this village, the Cotswolds, her questions as forced as those of some nervous stranger at a cocktail party.

Poor Gini: she was trying so hard. Lindsay glanced again at her own watch, caught Charlotte doing exactly the same thing in a furtive manner, and roused herself at once. Coming to Charlotte's aid, and giving

Gini the opportunity to be silent, which she obviously sought, Lindsay began to chatter away. She discussed, in quick succession, the traffic they had endured on the trip down, the inadvertent detour they had made through the hell of Oxford's one-way streets, the excellence of Charlotte's baking, and then—finding the subject suddenly popped into her head—Rowland McGuire, the character of Rowland McGuire, and the many defects of Rowland McGuire.

She warmed to her theme. She said several times that it would be very pleasant indeed to spend an entire two days away from Rowland McGuire, in a place where she never need hear his name mentioned— and then she stopped.

Just as she was remembering—too late—that the wretched McGuire was presumably a friend of Charlotte's as well as Max's, in which case her remarks were doubly untactful, Gini said in a dry voice: "If you want to forget him, Lindsay, why mention him? No one else did. You harped on him the whole way down in the car."

"I did not!"

"I've never even met the man, and I already know more than I need. I could describe his appearance, the sound of his voice—"

"Yes. Well." Charlotte was rearranging cushions energetically. "Lindsay doesn't know Rowland very well. I do. And he's—" she hesitated oddly. "He's very nice. Not devious at all."

Lindsay was about to expostulate—"nice," in Charlotte's book, was high praise, though in Lindsay's view Charlotte's benevolent nature awarded the term too often and too easily. She opened her mouth to speak, then shut it again. A car had just passed, on the road beyond, and Lindsay saw that Charlotte, having heard it, had instantly tensed. How odd, Lindsay thought, and then it struck her that Charlotte, always so serene, was on edge. Anxiety about Max on the highway, Lindsay thought. Rising, and moving to the windows, she looked out.

It was dark outside, and the moon was already rising. Lindsay pressed her face to the glass. Behind her, Charlotte was fussing with the tea things, and wondering whether, when he arrived, Max would want tea or a stiff drink.

Lindsay looked out at the garden and tried to construct familiar patterns from the shift of moonlight and shadow. She could feel an early evening sadness, an inexplicable and vague regret, creeping in on her. There was the yew hedge, she told herself, and that pale blur was an urn, and that was the curve of the drive that divided, one arm leading around to the front of the house, and a second leading to the stables and garages at the back. There was the drive, and there—suddenly—were lights. She glimpsed the familiar outline of Max's car as he paused where the driveway forked.

"Max is home," she began, and then frowned. "And I think he's brought someone with him, Charlotte. Were you expecting that? I'm sure I saw someone in the passenger seat."

"Oh?" Charlotte had risen to her feet. She was looking about her in apparent consternation.

"Whoever could that be?" she said.

"Rowland! I don't believe it! What a lovely surprise!" Charlotte swung around as Rowland and Max entered, and embraced McGuire with fervor. It did not escape Rowland's notice—or, he thought, Lindsay's—that Charlotte was crimson in the face: clearly, she was privy to this "surprise." Rowland, in response to a fierce nudge from Max, hung back. Lindsay was standing by the window, hands tightly clenched. On the sofa next to her, and directly facing Rowland, was a woman who had to be Genevieve Hunter. As he entered, she raised a pair of clear gray eyes to look at him. That inspection, acute, he would have said, but without interest, disconcerted him. As Max began speaking, she looked away toward the fire. Firelight moved against her hair. Her hands, long-fingered and ringless, were folded in her lap.

"Yes. Well. I was just leaving the office," Max said. "And I ran into Rowland by chance. In the lobby. Then the idea came to me—on the spur of the moment. Why doesn't Rowland join us, I thought? After all, he's been working flat out. A weekend in the country, I thought. It could be just what Rowland needs. He could relax. He could . . ."

Max's explanation died away. Lindsay's eyes were fixed on him with a basilisk stare. Her lips were pursed, and two bright flags of color had appeared in her cheeks.

"How very providential," she said. "How nice for everybody, Max."

"Yes. Indeed yes." Max averted his eyes. "And luckily, Rowland had no plans for this weekend. Well, he did have, of course, much in demand and all that, but he was able to cancel them."

"And at such short notice too. I'd never realized how impulsive Rowland was. I'd have said he was a man who always planned things very carefully."

At this, Genevieve Hunter looked up. Rowland thought she might have sensed the tension in the room—it would not have been difficult, it was even subduing the dogs. If so, it did not appear to affect her. She glanced at Max, then at Rowland, then leaned back against the cushions. She had the look of people on airplanes, Rowland thought, the look you saw on people's faces when they were listening to music on headphones, following the intricacies of some melody inaudible to anyone else. *What music, what tune?* he thought. Then, recollecting himself, and realizing that someone had to salvage this moment, he stepped forward and spoke.

"Admit the truth, Max," he began, and Max flinched. "There's a woman at the back of this—and I made Max invite me because of her. Charlotte—I've missed you." He kissed her cheek and put his arm around the place where her waist had formerly been. "I haven't seen you in months, and I told Max I had to see you before the baby was born. You're looking magnificent, has he told you that?"

"Fat," said Charlotte, rosy with pleasure and relief. "Don't try to be gallant. I look mountainous."

"You look beautiful," Rowland said, meaning it. "And what's more, it's definitely a girl this time. A daughter. A Miss Max."

"You're sure?" Charlotte laughed. "How can you tell?"

"Because you're carrying the baby low. And according to my Irish grandmother, that's always the sign of a girl."

"What nonsense, Rowland. You don't even remember your Irish grandmother."

"Wait and see in two months."

Rowland released Charlotte and looked around the room. He spied Danny, lurking shyly behind a chair. Rowland, sure the three-year-old could be relied upon to create a diversion, held out his arms to him. With a whoop of pleasure Danny hurtled forward, clamped himself to Rowland's knees, and then whooped again as Rowland hoisted him aloft.

After that, as he had hoped, it was easy. The dogs came back to life, and barked; Charlotte began to fuss with the tea things; Max had to recall, at length, the tiresome new-age caravansary that had delayed them approaching the village, and the boys—hearing Rowland's and their father's voices—had to race back downstairs, their motive part affection and part avarice, for Rowland, a great favorite with them, never arrived without bringing gifts.

In the midst of this melee, Genevieve Hunter was introduced, and Rowland briefly took her cool, narrow hand. She made some English remark—afterward he remembered that—some conventional, meaningless English greeting, uttered in a low, American-accented voice.

Rowland, who knew of her English schooling, her English stepmother, was thrown by the greeting nonetheless; he had been expecting—what? Greater force, perhaps; vivacity, he told himself afterward; possibly even wit, for her writing could be witty, and her writing style, sharply individual, was crisp.

Instead, he was granted just one look from the long-lidded, cool gray eyes; one touch from that thin hand; he had the sensation that he was erased from her memory before her hand withdrew from his.

He was, though he would not have admitted it, disappointed. Also faintly perturbed—for what reason he could not have said. Max, as shortly became evident, felt no such uncertainties. He was ebullient with glee, could not wait for an excuse to get Rowland to himself. Only twenty minutes after their arrival he was racing up the stairs, followed more slowly by Rowland.

"Must wash, must change," Max shouted back down the stairs, hauling Rowland into his dressing room. He shut the door.

"Well?" he said with triumph. "What do you think? Our little plot worked. We pulled it off, didn't we? Women are so easy to deceive."

"You think so?"

"I know so. A couple of tricky moments, with Lindsay, as expected—but you took care of that. A masterstroke—I'll admit it, Rowland, I could learn from you. You really were consummately cool. Never turned a hair. Great presence of mind . . ."

"Thanks, Max. It comes with practice."

"And Gini—you liked her? She came up to spec?"

"It's difficult to like someone on the strength of one handshake and one sentence, Max."

Rowland turned away to inspect the pictures on the walls—rows of photographs from Max's school days: a rugby team, a cricket team; then Oxford, Max and himself alongside the Oxford motorbike—he was touched by this. Max sank into a chair with an air of disappointment.

"Well, I did warn you," he said. "She's reserved. Difficult. I told you—every assignment she's been offered since Bosnia . . . if you decide you do want her to work on this story, you'll have to get her interest somehow."

"We've been over all that."

"I know. But you've got only two days, Rowland. All right, it's a good story—it might be a *very* good story. The drugs angle might interest her. On the other hand, she's been offered a number of good stories these past two months since she's back from Bosnia. And she's turned them all down flat."

"Even so." Rowland bent to another photograph.

"I'm all for the indirect approach—I buy that. Assess her. Give her a chance to get to know you socially first—fine. Make her like you, even. But I know Lindsay, and I know what she'll have been saying about you. If you do decide to use Gini, you're going to have your work cut out for you."

He paused, looking at Rowland speculatively. Rowland, examining a photograph of Max in full cricket regalia, made no response.

"I mean, face facts, Rowland. Now that you've actually seen her, perhaps you'll understand. You still think a two-day-charm offensive's going to work?"

"I imagine it can't do any harm."

"Well, I wish you luck. I told you, it was a nightmare, hiring her. There she is—she and Lindsay—both at the *News*, both dying to leave it, because that bloody awful Nicholas Jenkins is taking it so far downmarket, nothing but sex, sex, sex. Incidentally, have you *seen* his circulation figures?"

"Another fifty-two thousand? Yes, I have."

"Bloody man. And it was a good paper once. Anyway, where was I? Ah, yes. Poaching Lindsay and Gini. Well, Lindsay was simplicity itself. Stated her terms—we had the entire deal sewn up over lunch. A very good lunch, actually, at Tante Claire. Best Meursault I've ever had in my life. Two bottles. It was *fun*. Whereas Gini . . ." He made a face. "She played me off against the *Times*. For months."

"So? You've used precisely that technique in the past. So have I. Everyone does."

"I know. But I just didn't expect it, that's all. Not from a woman who looks like that. Charlotte thinks she looks like a Crivelli Madonna."

Rowland was silent.

"—And I told her, that certainly wouldn't be most men's response. It wasn't mine, and I speak as the most happily married man I know. I mean, you must have noticed—there's something about the mouth. And her figure—put it like this: it didn't *immediately* bring Madonnas to mind."

"Oh, for God's sake, Max." Rowland gave a gesture of annoyance. "She's a journalist. An exceptionally good journalist. Can't you just leave it at that?"

"No, I can't," Max replied with spirit. He eyed Rowland narrowly. "And I have to say, that's rich, coming from you. Since when were you indifferent to women? There's a new one every week."

"Maybe so. That wasn't always the case. As you very well know, Max."

There was a brief silence. This answer brought them perilously close to an area of Rowland's private life he would never, perhaps could never, discuss. There, Max was afraid to trespass. The last time he had dared to raise the subject of Esther had been at least four years before—and he could still remember Rowland's biting anger when he had done so.

"I do know," he said now. "But it was six *years* ago, Rowland. And you've broken a lot of hearts since."

"Not my intention." Rowland turned his back.

"You use these women, Rowland," Max persisted. "You may not see it that way, but it's what you do. I know you loved Esther, but can't you exorcise her some other way?"

"What would you recommend?" Rowland swung around, white-faced. "Drink? Work? I've tried those remedies. Mind your own business, Max."

"You can't grieve forever, Rowland. Not even you can do that." Max spoke quietly. Rowland began on some angry reply, then bit the words back. He averted his face, and Max, having dared this much, said no more. He lit a cigarette and watched his friend thoughtfully. He considered certain comments his wife had made on the subject of Rowland; he considered her matchmaking plans for this weekend. Had he been right to curtail them? Charlotte had accused him of getting cold feet, and Max had agreed. "Yes, I am," he had replied. "Rowland's love life is a mine field. I should never have let you even consider this. Lindsay? I must have been mad. We should leave well enough alone."

Charlotte, an apostle for married bliss, had marshaled her counterarguments with skill. Rowland, in her view, needed rescuing from himself: he was a handsome, kind, intelligent, good man who would one day make an exemplary husband and father; the course of his life, unfortunately, had taken a wrong turn since the events in Washington, D.C. of six years before.

"He's eaten up with guilt and grief and remorse," Charlotte had cried. "And women throw themselves at him. All those stupid girls, rushing about, ironing his shirts, cooking dinner for him, ministering unto him. Rowland's so *blind*. He doesn't even realize they're in love with him—and when he does, he runs a mile. What Rowland needs is a *wife*, Max. Someone kindhearted. Someone mature. Someone with a sense of humor. . . ."

"The love of a good woman?" Max put in, and groaned.

"Precisely," Charlotte replied with force. "And since Rowland's far

too obstinate ever to admit that himself, he needs guidance. A helping hand. If he could just get to know Lindsay a little better—"

"No," Max had interrupted. "No, Charlotte. It's playing with fire— and it's Lindsay who would end up in the burn unit. Forget it."

Charlotte, after further resistance, had finally backed down. Now, looking at his friend, Max wavered; Charlotte's instincts could be surprisingly sharp: what if his wife had been right all along?

"Tell me, Rowland," he began cautiously. "Don't you ever think about marrying, settling down?"

"No," Rowland replied.

"I don't see how you can be so certain." Max persevered. "I might have said that before I met Charlotte. Then I changed my mind. Rapidly, if you remember . . . ."

"I do remember." Rowland glanced back at him and gave a smile. "I was standing next to you when you were introduced, if you recall. She silenced you. I knew you were in trouble right away."

"I was deciding to marry her," Max said with dignity. "I admit my repartee wasn't too startling, but I was making silent plans. Of course"—he eyed Rowland in a speculative way—"it doesn't always happen that way. It might be a more gradual process. A woman might be just a friend, a colleague, and then the relationship—well, it might develop in an unexpected way. . . ."

He looked at Rowland hopefully, but Rowland had already lost interest. He had returned to his inspection of the photographs on the wall. He had unbent a little though, Max thought. Encouraged, he leaned forward.

"What happened to that last girl of yours," he ventured in a casual way. "The French one? Is she still around?"

"Sylvie? No. I haven't seen her in weeks."

"It's over, then?" Max looked thoughtful. "*Decisively* over? You mean—she doesn't write, or phone?"

"Decisively over." Rowland's voice was dry. "Which didn't prevent her calling me thirty-two times last week. Or was it thirty-three?" He paused, half smiling, looking back at Max, then he frowned. "Extraordinary. She seemed so independent. I don't understand women, Max. I don't understand them at all."

"Who does?" Max replied with delicacy, and waited. The expression on Rowland's face became one of gloom.

"I mean—I try, Max. I make the situation perfectly clear. No commitments, either side. They always agree. They tell me they don't want involvements either. They're modern women. . . ." He sighed. "For some reason they always stress that, just how modern they are. And then . . ."

"Yes?"

"They're never very modern the next morning, however modern they claimed to be the night before."

This statement, made with an air of profound bewilderment, both amused and touched Max. "For that," he said tartly, "you have only yourself to blame. Presumably you do something to them in the interim to effect this remarkable change. It doesn't take a *great* deal of imagination, Rowland, to work out what that might be. *My* advice—"

"I don't want to hear your advice." Rowland, as Max could have predicted, moved sharply to the door. "I've had enough of this conversation. I'm going to have a bath."

"Sure. Sure. Change the subject." Max made an irritated waving gesture of the hand. "You always do. It's a pity you won't listen to a man of my wisdom and experience, especially now."

Rowland paused. "Especially now? Why especially now?"

"Well, there is this weekend to consider. There's Lindsay. There's Gini. I'm sure you'll handle them both perfectly. You're the expert when it comes to female psychology, as you've just been explaining. So I'm sure it will be clear sailing."

Rowland hesitated, his hand on the door. Then, with a sigh, he turned around.

"I might have known it." He looked at Max closely. "You brought me up here for a reason, didn't you? There's something you haven't told me—something I need to know?"

"I was biding my time." Max gave a small smile. "I wanted you to meet Gini first. Now that you've met her, I'd better explain." There was a brief silence. Without comment, Rowland pulled out a chair and sat astride it. He waited.

"I didn't want to say this before," Max began somewhat evasively, "because I know how prejudiced you can be. You will jump to conclusions. You can be censorious, Rowland, and—"

"Get to the point, Max."

"Genevieve Hunter. Her trip to Bosnia. You want to know why I was so reluctant to send her? It wasn't just because she's a woman."

"Then what was the reason?"

"She lives with Pascal Lamartine."

This admission was met with silence, then a frown. Max shifted in his seat.

"You didn't know?"

"You know perfectly well I didn't know. And you were very careful not to tell me. Why?"

"Because I knew you'd disapprove. I guessed you couldn't have heard the gossip when you said you wanted to use her."

"I never listen to gossip. And you're right—I would have disapproved."

"Yes, well, not everyone shares your desire to separate their personal and their working lives," Max said waspishly. "She—"

"I make that distinction now," Rowland said quietly. "I try to make it. And I know just how hard it can be. I learned that six years ago. Come on, Max—I'm in no position to be censorious. You know that perfectly well. . . ."

"Maybe so. Point taken." Max, embarrassed by the gentle reproof in his tone, shifted his gaze. "But it was more complicated than that, Rowland. You see, I'd virtually decided not to send Gini to Bosnia. I had my doubts about sending a woman to cover that war, whatever her experience. Her relationship with Lamartine counted against her—that kind of involvement, in a war zone? I thought it could be counterproductive, unwise. On the other hand, I did want Lamartine's photographs—very badly indeed. Everyone was after him. If you remember, it was over three years since he'd last covered a war. He'd had that period out, being—well, a paparazzo is really the only term. Now, God knows why he did that—I've certainly never dared ask. Massive divorce bills, or so I've heard. Massive demands from the not-too-pleasant ex-wife. Whatever the reason, the moment word got out that he was returning to war coverage, going to Bosnia, every single one of our rivals was chasing him. And I was determined to clinch the deal." He paused, and looked back at Rowland, who was listening intently.

"I thought it would be a question of money, and autonomy, allowing him a major say in what he covered, when, and where. I was wrong. He had a third demand; non-negotiable. Genevieve Hunter went with him. They had to go as a team. And if I wouldn't agree to that, then another paper would. That was the deal."

This admission was met with a lengthy silence. Rowland's frown had deepened.

"Now, listen, Rowland, I want you to be clear about this. She didn't put him up to it. Well, I suppose I can't say that with absolute certainty—I have only Lamartine's word for it. But he isn't a liar, and he wouldn't let himself be used. Nor would she use him, Rowland. She has her faults, as you'll discover if you work with her, but lack of scruples isn't one of them. Quite the reverse."

He paused. Rowland still remained silent. Max gave a shrug.

"So, now you know the truth. If I'm perfectly honest, if Lamartine hadn't held a gun to my head like that, I'd have refused. But, as it was, he gave me very little option. And he was very persuasive on her behalf."

Rowland gave him a sharp glance. "He's a persuasive man?"

"Very. I like him, and I admire him, and I respect his judgment. If you met him, I'm sure you'd agree. All right, he was speaking as a man who was in love. He was partisan, and he admitted that. But he was fighting to get her a chance, a chance he felt she had earned."

"And his confidence in her wasn't misplaced," Rowland interjected. "As subsequent events proved."

"Well, yes." Max hesitated again. "She was impressive. The work she did was very fine. So the ends justified the means. It's just—"

He broke off; Rowland did not prompt him, and his silence gave Max a twinge of uncertainty. In the same situation, would Rowland have acted as he had?

He thought he knew the answer to that question. Rowland, who, in the workplace, was curiously indifferent to gender, was more likely than Max to send a woman to a battle zone; but Rowland confronted with Lamartine's demands was another matter. He would not have liked pressure of that kind, and—had he suspected collusion—neither Lamartine nor Gini would ever have worked for him again.

In which case, Max thought with a return of self-confidence, Rowland's scruples would have lost him first-class photographs and first-class reporting. One of Rowland's little problems, he told himself, was a certain moral inflexibility, a refusal to compromise. To recall that his gifted friend had an Achilles heel restored Max's humor at once. He rose.

"Anyway," he said, "for good or ill, that's what happened. I thought you should know, but all this is in confidence, needless to say. Gini thinks she won that assignment on her own merits alone, and if she discovered what Lamartine had done, if she even knew I had a private meeting with him—all hell would break loose. So not one word to her."

"Of course." Rowland also rose. "Trappist silence. You can rely on me. You probably made the right decision, from a professional point of view. Except—" He paused in the doorway. "Were there repercussions of a more personal kind? Why didn't Lamartine come back from Bosnia with her? Wasn't that the deal?"

"Yes. It was." Max, who had expected Rowland to pick up on this, gave him an anxious look. "Then Lamartine suggested he stay on, and I agreed. I assumed that was purely a work decision. Now I'm not so sure. I get the feeling they may have quarreled, even split up—though I gather Gini's admitted nothing to Lindsay. And I was shocked when I saw her tonight. She looks ill. Even shell-shocked, wouldn't you say?"

"Her manner's odd, certainly. I'm reserving judgment."

"That's unusual, for you."

Rowland made no reply to this comment. He opened the door to the landing.

"I just hope I'm wrong, that's all," Max continued, glancing in the direction of Gini's room. He lowered his voice. "I like Lamartine. I like her. If anything has gone wrong between them, I'd feel partly to blame."

"Not your responsibility, Max," Rowland said, his manner suddenly brisk. He gave Max a smile of sudden warmth, then headed off to his room down the corridor, leaving Max to wonder: how exactly *would* Rowland have dealt with Lamartine? He would ask him over the course of the weekend, Max resolved, but as it happened, the weekend took an unexpected turn, so the question was neither answered nor asked.

Downstairs, Lindsay was sitting alone, staring thoughtfully into the fire, when Danny toddled into the room, looking anxious, and clutching a painting of a blue bristly animal.

"Where's Rowland?" he said.

"Upstairs, I think, Danny. He and your daddy went up to wash and change."

"Look." He flourished the picture. "Dog. I made it for Rowland."

"It's a magnificent dog, Danny. I like it very much."

"Short legs," Danny said in a critical tone, surveying his handiwork.

"Some dogs do have short legs. That's fine."

"Could be a hedgehog," Danny said craftily, turning it upside down. "I like hedgehogs. I like them *best*."

"*That's* what's so clever, Danny. It could be a hedgehog *or* a dog. In fact, it could be a hedge*dog*."

Danny thought this was hilarious. He fell over laughing and kicked his legs in the air. Lindsay was just remembering how wonderfully reassuring small children were, because they liked the feeblest jokes, when something else occurred to her. She remembered the cake. She frowned.

"Did you know Rowland was coming, Danny?" she asked, feeling instantly guilty and mean.

"Yes. Mummy said at breakfast. She said it was a secret, a nice secret.

But if I ate up all my egg, she'd tell me. So I did. I ate it *all* up, even the yucky white bits."

Danny's eyes rounded. He became bright red. He looked at Lindsay anxiously.

"It's not a secret now, is it?" he whispered. "He's here now. He brought me a ray gun. He ate his cake."

"No, it's not a secret now, Danny." Lindsay gave him a kiss. "Besides, I won't breathe a word."

"Promise?"

"Promise. Zip the lips. Sure."

Danny loved zip the lips. He zipped his own, several times, then toddled off upstairs. Lindsay remained. She glared at the fire. Skunk, she thought: laughing up his sleeve at her throughout their meeting that morning. Lying, devious, manipulative, two-faced skunk! How long had he been planning this? What was he up to?

Charlotte stuck her head around the door, looking pink and flustered.

"Oh, there you are, Lindsay. I'm—I thought I'd just go and have a chat with Max. And change. Gini's gone to read. We're having guests for drinks at seven-thirty. They'll stay only an hour. Then we'll eat. I've made a huge steak and kidney pie. I hope it's all right. I'm afraid you and Gini are sharing the end bathroom with Rowland, so if you want a bath . . ."

"I'd love a bath."

"Well, turf Rowland out. Don't let him hog all the hot water. And ignore the boys. Rowland brought them all ray guns. It sounds like World War Three up there."

She disappeared, and Lindsay went upstairs. Martian noises emanated from the boys' attic bedroom. Gini's door was shut. The bathroom door was shut: the gushings and rumblings of ancient plumbing proclaimed Rowland's occupancy. What in hell was the man doing—running a bath, or filling a swimming pool? Did he have to whistle while he did it? Lindsay glowered at the door, then retreated to her own room.

She looked at the clothes she had packed. She had planned to wear a rather dull dress, which she had brought mainly because it happened to be pressed and clean. Suddenly, she didn't feel like it. She felt like wearing that very short Donna Karan skirt, that very short, *tight* skirt, made of the softest leather, a skirt that proclaimed to the world that Lindsay had excellent legs.

Cursing the low priority the English gave to bathrooms in old country houses, she lurked by her door, waiting. Surely even Rowland McGuire must have finished bathing by now?

The whistling had given way to operatic snatches. Rowland sang "La donna è mobile" with gusto, out of tune. Lindsay waited until the various arias had ended; she heard the bathroom door open at last. She counted to ten, then darted out.

She collided with a half-naked Rowland, and reeled back. Six feet five inches of tanned muscle blocked her path. Rowland's wild hair was wet and black and tamed and sleek. It dripped water onto his powerful shoulders; water ran down his muscled chest. He was wearing a white towel around his waist, and nothing else.

"Do you have to parade around like Tarzan?" Lindsay snapped, trying to avert her eyes from biceps, pectorals, and narrow waist and hips. "You're half naked."

"Ah, you object to the towel? I'll remove it, if you prefer."

His hands dropped to his waist. From the attic came the stuttering burst of ray-gun fire. Lindsay fled. She dived into the bathroom, slammed the door, and bolted it. She was standing in thick fog; she swore at the steaming billowy air, paddled her way forward blindly, then stopped. He'd had the grace, she noted, to clean the tub, but like all men when bathing, had left the room half flooded and the towels in a sodden heap.

She sat down by the vast iron monster of a bathtub, and stared at its clawed feet. The room smelled deliciously of Rowland's aftershave. Its scent made Lindsay feel angry, nostalgic—and weak.

CHAPTER 5

Rowland was not good at cocktail parties, which he disliked. He was not gifted at small talk, and he did not suffer fools gladly. Deficient in these necessary requirements, he avoided such occasions whenever possible, and when trapped, as now, preferred to retreat to the edge.

He talked briefly to an Oxford don, and to a painter who lived in the next village, both of whom he had met before and liked. The don, a close friend of Rowland's former Oxford tutor, sought to persuade him, as he had done before, that he was wasting his abilities and his honors degree, and should return to academic life.

"Too cloistered," Rowland said.

"Scholarship can be narrow, I grant you," replied the don, who was elderly, and an authority on Wittgenstein. "The corollary is that it's deep."

"Even so. I like journalism. It suits me. Wrongs can be righted."

"Often?"

"Sometimes. Besides, I like a patchwork life."

"Do you still climb?" the don asked, and when Rowland said that yes, he still did, the old man's face lit up. They talked mountains for a while, most enjoyably, and rock types, and the Cairngorms and the Skye Ridge. Then Charlotte came up, and led the old man away, and Rowland was able to shift a few paces backward toward the bookshelves. There, for a while, he was left in blessed peace.

Rowland thought how much he liked this house, which was very old and rambling, which smelled of woodsmoke and cooking, and which seemed to him to enshrine the settled pleasures of family life. He watched Charlotte, who was wearing an old fisherman's sweater and a long, embroidered Rajasthani skirt as she moved among her guests. She was the calmest and most maternal woman he knew, and sometimes Rowland envied Max for marrying her. Very occasionally, it would occur to Rowland, who lived alone and liked to live alone, that Max had outstripped him in the years since Oxford. Rowland's own circumstances were little changed since leaving Balliol: Max had four sons, a happy marriage. Max was anchored; above and beyond his work he had meaning and purpose in his life. He himself was without religion, family, or strong political creed; he was neither Irish nor truly English; he was an outsider, a spectator, and likely to remain so for the rest of his life.

The thought drew his eyes to Genevieve Hunter, also an outsider, he suspected, neither quite American nor quite English: his first impression of her, which remained, was of a woman adrift.

She seemed intent, he thought, on camouflaging herself. She had been wearing gray, indeterminate clothes when he arrived. She was wearing something different, but also gray and indeterminate, now. Twice she had left the room to make a telephone call, and twice returned, almost immediately, with a tense white face. He considered the information about her that Max had given him earlier, and it seemed to him that it raised more questions than it answered. He moved forward a few paces. She had a low voice, and he found himself curious to overhear the little she said.

She had been trapped now, for some time, by one of the other local guests, an American woman in her early forties to whom Rowland had been introduced earlier, and from whom he had immediately, and not very courteously, escaped. The woman's name was Susan something—Susan Landis, that was it. Her husband, an officer at some nearby U.S. air base, a tall loud-voiced man, was now boasting about his golf handicap to Lindsay.

Mrs. Landis was overdressed in English terms for an occasion such as this. She was the only woman present wearing heavy makeup, high-heeled shoes, and a tailored suit. She was nervous, socially ill at ease, and she had latched on to Gini as the only other American present. Gini, Rowland noted, had been making a stiff but polite attempt to draw her out.

Scraps of their conversation drifted across to Rowland. Susan Landis was extolling the delights of the Cotswolds; she found old Elizabethan houses quaint. She and her husband lived only a few miles away, and were settling into the area very well. Everyone was just so friendly and hospitable, why, if she and her husband accepted all the invitations they received, they'd be out every night. And her daughter—she had a daughter called Wilhemina, or Mina for short—she just adored it here, had made so many friends—was at the Cheltenham Academy, such a fine, exclusive school, and—imagine—was staying overnight in this very village with a school friend, in the manor, had Gini seen the manor? Well, it was historic; it had cost the school friend's mother—a *very* well-known interior designer—the better part of a million, or so people said.

"What is just so wonderful about being here," she was now saying, "is that it's so *safe*. I mean, can you imagine, Gini, bringing up a teenage girl in New York City these days—any big American city, come to that? Whereas here, all these darling little villages—I always know where Mina is. No hooliganism, no drugs, no muggers—" She hesitated. "I guess I shouldn't say this, but you know I haven't seen a black face since we moved here? Except around the base, that is . . . "

"Really?"

Rowland saw Gini raise her cool gray eyes to Mrs. Landis's face.

"Well, my boyfriend's due here any moment. He's black. So that should even things out a little. Excuse me, will you? There's a telephone call I'm trying to make."

It was perfectly done. For a second, even Rowland was convinced. Mrs. Landis blushed crimson. Gini left the room. Very shortly afterward, the Landises left.

"Don't, Rowland." Charlotte had materialized at his side. "I know what you're thinking."

"I imagine you would. Why on earth do you allow them in your house?"

"He's a horror, I admit." Charlotte shrugged. "She isn't half as bad as she seems. She's bullied and lonely and desperate to make friends. The bloody snobby English around here snicker about her clothes and her house."

"How about her views on race?"

"Oh, come on, Rowland. They agree with *those*. One of the penalties of living in Gloucestershire. So stop standing there in the corner, making superficial judgments on my guests. Come and cheer Lindsay up. She's been fielding Robert Landis for hours. First we had golf, then the virtues of Newt Gingrich, then he remembered who she was and wanted to know what the little ladies would be wearing this year."

"You're exaggerating."

"Only a bit. Lindsay told him breasts were small last year, but this year they were going to be *big*." Charlotte linked her arm through his. "Come on, Rowland, only ten more minutes, then it's steak and kidney pie. I made it specially for you."

Rowland hesitated. Lindsay, who had been strenuously avoiding him since he walked in, had just given him a cold glance and turned her back. She was looking very fetching in a short, tight black leather skirt and black flats. She wore a white shirt with a high collar. With her short, curly hair and her slim figure, she looked boyish, like a medieval page, Rowland thought.

He consented to be led across. Charlotte immediately left them. Lindsay said: "I had an excellent bath, thanks, Rowland. One and a half inches of lukewarm water. And all the towels were wet."

"I'm sorry. I'm not very house-trained," Rowland said.

"You don't look sorry." Lindsay raised her face and inspected his. "You look amused and unrepentant."

"Not true," Rowland replied lazily. "I do repent. I repent in my heart. It just doesn't always show on my face. My standards have slipped. That happens to men who live alone."

"Then it doesn't apply in your case," Lindsay said smartly. "If rumor can be believed, you don't spend much time alone."

"None of those rumors is true," said Rowland with feeling. "People spread these wicked lies about me. I'm a man who's much misunderstood."

"Are you trying to be charming?"

"Certainly not. Have you had a chance to look at that file yet?"

The question, for some reason Rowland could not fathom, was a mistake.

"No, I damn well haven't," Lindsay replied, and stalked off without a backward look.

Women, Rowland thought. He added a few adjectives to that noun, which cheered him up. Then, since Charlotte had left the room, and Max was deep in conversation, he seized his opportunity and escaped.

Passing Max's study off the hall, he heard Gini, arguing with a telephone operator by the sound of it, and repeating a string of numbers in a weary voice. Charlotte bumped into him at the foot of the stairs; from the top came the sound of ray guns and whoops. She gave him an exhausted look.

"Would you, Rowland? Just for five minutes? It's because they know you're here. They want one of your gory stories. Could you frighten them to sleep?"

Rowland was a traditionalist when it came to stories. "Once upon a time," he began.

He was sitting cross-legged on the floor of the boys' large attic bedroom. Teddy bears flanked his tall frame; above his head, model airplanes were strung from the rafters; a procession of plastic dinosaurs was arranged at his feet.

Max and Charlotte, orderly in unexpected ways, had named their children alphabetically. Alex, at eight the eldest, was in the top bunk to Rowland's left, with Ben, the next son, beneath him. Colin, who was just six, and Danny, were on his right. All the boys had laid their ray guns reverently on the ends of their bunks, and Colin, who had the most nervous temperament of the four, was clutching a stuffed penguin very tight.

"Once upon a time," Rowland continued, "on the far west coast of Ireland, where I grew up, lived a leprechaun called Leaf. He had bright green skin, orange eyes, and a tail—"

"Leprechauns don't have tails," Alex interrupted.

"This leprechaun did," Rowland said. "He had a tail one millimeter long, and he lived with his mother in a mousehole in the wall of my grandfather's farm. They were both as happy as the day is long, but *unfortunately*—" Here Rowland, who had lowered his voice to a chilly whisper, paused.

"Did he have an enemy, Rowland?" Ben asked with a shiver of delight. "Was he horrible?"

"He most certainly was," Rowland confirmed. "His name was Groilach. He was a black-hearted hobgoblin, and he lived in the peat bogs by the loch. He drank frogs' blood for breakfast, he had scaly skin, and he was covered in slime."

"Yuck." Ben screwed up his nose. "I bet he smelled really foul. I fell in a peat bog once, in Scotland—d'you remember, Alex? I stank. I stank for *days*."

"He smelled appalling," Rowland agreed, improvising obligingly. "Think of all the nastiest smells in the world. Boiled cabbage, for instance, and—"

"Danny's farts!" Alex shouted, and all four convulsed.

"Groilach smelled even worse. As well as an evil heart, he had a huge appetite, and he'd been after Leaf the leprechaun for years. Leprechauns, you see, were his favorite food of all . . . "

Rowland talked on quietly, until he could see the boys were lulled. First Danny fell asleep, then Alex, then Ben. Only Colin remained awake, hanging on every word.

"He didn't eat Leaf, did he, Rowland?" Colin whispered, stealing out a hand from under the bedclothes, and holding Rowland fast.

"Well, and of course he didn't," Rowland replied, knowing it was now time for his story to take a different course. "Not a chance. Leaf was good-hearted and brave, so he was bound to triumph in the end. Besides, he had a sword. And to tell you the truth, he wasn't that worried about Groilach."

"Why not, Rowland?"

"Because he had other things on his mind. He'd heard of this princess, you see. A very beautiful and very sad princess, a leprechaun princess who had eyes like sapphires and pale golden hair. She'd been imprisoned by a spell a long time ago. The spell kept her in this tower, which was a hundred feet high, and made of glass. She wept tears like crystals every day, because she longed to be rescued. . . ."

Colin was sleeping now. Gently, Rowland released his hand. He rose and stretched his legs. The room was peaceful and still, the only sound the quiet breathing of the boys. For some reason, a residue of sadness from his story remained with Rowland, and he felt reluctant to leave.

His story had brought his childhood back; he could see in his mind's eye the farm buildings he had described, where he himself had lived until he was around eight, Alex's age.

He moved across to the window and eased the curtains aside. The moon was high; the trees and hedges were already white with hoarfrost; he looked out at a silver world. On the far side of the orchard he watched a shape detach itself from the shadows of a hedgerow; he watched the dog-fox move delicately across the grass. It circled the henhouse, lifted its snout, sniffed the air, then stiffened as, from the front of the house, came the noise of people, and cars.

The last of the local guests must be leaving. Soon one of Charlotte's wonderful dinners would be served. Rowland listened to the cars crunch their way down the drive. He watched the dog-fox trot back to the hedgerow, then move off across the fields toward the hills. For a moment, straining his eyes to follow the fox's movements, Rowland thought he saw lights move, high up behind the house. This puzzled him slightly, for he had walked that way many times, and he knew there were no villages up there, and no roads, just open wolds.

Voices drifted up from the kitchen below. Rowland let the curtains fall and left the room quietly. Ducking his head beneath the beams, he made his way down the narrow, twisting stairs.

It was some while, during dinner, before his feelings of nostalgia, of separation, finally passed. Gradually though, he was drawn back into the present, warmed by wine, by conversation, by good food. It was then he noticed that he was not the only person at this convivial table to be abstracted. Genevieve Hunter's attention, he observed, was also elsewhere. She took little part in the conversation, and spoke seldom. When she did participate, the effort involved was palpable.

She was seated opposite him. Covertly, Rowland examined her. She had very short, pale, silvery hair, a pale complexion, and the expression in her gray eyes remained unreadable. She reminded him of someone, and at first he could not place the resemblance. Then it came to him. It was no one he knew: she resembled the princess of his own fairy tale that evening. Like that creature, she looked spellbound, as if someone or something had imprisoned her, as if she were looking out at the world through glass walls.

By the time Mina and Cassandra finally reached the barn, it was bitterly cold. The huge barn doors were open, and its interior was lit with strobes. People were already dancing inside, and the field around was rutted with the wheel tracks of the travelers' trailers, ancient buses, and vans. Campfires illumined little patches of ground and intensified the blackness beyond.

The field nearest the barn was a seething mass of moving shapes. Ragged children ran back and forth in packs; dogs barked; some of the travelers were dancing outside, pumping their arms and stamping to the strange loops and electronic chatter of the music; others cooked food, or just sat in huddles near their fires, on bright blankets and quilts they had laid out on the ground.

Mina shrank back, but Cassandra caught hold of her and pulled her into the throng. The music grew louder, beating in on Mina's ears; she felt assaulted by smells and sound. There was a rich drift of marijuana, of sweat and unwashed clothes; cooking fumes, car exhausts, burning wood, mud, and icy air. Outside the barn doors, a man dressed in a scarlet embroidered Afghan coat was juggling with colored balls. Beyond him, inside the barn itself, lights danced and bounced on the walls. The strobe flashes dazzled Mina's eyes. She clutched Cassandra's arm and watched her face speed up, like jerky frames of old film, so her expressions were fragmented, and the scorpion on her forehead appeared to move.

Cassandra's eyes, black, then bright, were searching the crowd. Somewhere here, Cassandra said, somewhere in the midst of the tossing hair and jerking arms they would find Star.

"He's tall," Cassandra shouted through the din of the music. "He looks like an angel. He has long black hair. He'll be wearing a red scarf."

She began to push her way through the dancers, holding Mina tight by the arm. And as they fought their way through, Mina began to feel it, the pulse of the music, and the electricity of the crowd. It was benign, not threatening, and heady too. She could feel the rhythm of synthesizer guitars start to beat in her veins; the random snatches of words incorporated into the music opened up the corners of her mind. She liked the weird, high-pitched helium voices. She chanted the words; she wanted to dance too; she wanted to get inside the sound.

She moved her feet, then her arms; she sucked in deep breaths of the smoky, acrid air. She was parted from Cassandra, then tossed out to her again into a little space on the edge of the crowd.

"You see? Isn't it great?" Cassandra's face came and went. The scorpion on her forehead came and went. She had lit a joint; its end glowed then was dark. "Here."

She passed it across; Mina sucked in the wonderful sweetness. It was instant lift: she could move on the music; the lights buoyed her; she felt she could touch the rafters fifty feet above her head—one more little suck and she might reach out her hand and touch the sky.

Cassandra was smiling; her face was making flashes of encouragement and understanding.

"You see—just wait. Come and find Star."

She turned her head the wrong way, into the music, into the strobe, and Mina, for whom time was braking, realized that Cassandra couldn't sense him the way she herself could. She tried to shape the words and tell Cassandra: she knew even without looking that Star was already beside them. He had come out of nowhere; without even turning her head she knew he was there.

She turned around to look at him and knew at once that she trusted him. At first, because he was so startlingly beautiful, he was like an apparition. She stared at the flash of his eyes; the strobe made his smile like lightning. Then he took her hand, and Cassandra's hand, and she felt it immediately, just as Cass had described it—the jolt of his power.

He greeted Cassandra, then turned to Mina and gave her a long, unwavering stare.

"And this is Mina," he said. "Your American friend. Welcome, Mina. I've been told all about you. Are you happy tonight, Mina? Are you flying yet?"

"A little," Mina said. "Yes, I am."

"Good." He pressed her hand, then released it.

"I can help. I've brought you both wings."

It was like watching a conjuror magicking cards out of air. A moment before, his hand had been empty. Now he extended it slowly, uncurling his fingers, and there, flashing in the strobe light, were two little pills. One was pink, bright pink, the color of cotton candy; the other was smooth and white as a pearl.

"A White Dove and a pink jewel," he said slowly. "Star's special gifts to two very special girls. Now, which shall it be? Is Mina a dove girl or a jewel girl?"

"Which is stronger?" Cassandra asked.

"Oh, they're both powerful. I brought them back myself, from across the sea."

"From Amsterdam?"

"Maybe. Who knows?" The music gave a twist, and Star gave a smile. "Pink for Cassandra, I think," he said, "and white for Mina. Pink like a fine Burmese ruby, and white like a nun's veil."

"No." The strobe lit Cassandra's face with little flashes of mutiny. Mina, who could not stop looking at Star, could sense something new in the air, something edgy like jealousy, or resentment.

"No," Cassandra said again, her voice rising. "I've seen those pink ones before. I want the white one, Star."

"You're sure? So be it."

He gave another tiny magic movement of his hands. In his left hand the pink pill remained, and he offered it to Mina, who took it and swallowed it without hesitation. In his right hand was the white pill, which Cassandra snatched from him. She swallowed it, then began to fumble in her pockets. Star seemed to be waiting, Mina couldn't be sure, for some dancers moved close to her, and the air flashed light and dark, but she thought that Cassandra handed him some money, so the magic pills weren't really a gift after all.

But the space was very whirly by then and the stone floor of the barn was starting to move. Before she could say anything, Star put one strong arm around her waist and began to move her away. She looked back

once over her shoulder and saw Cassandra's face in the distance, as still
and pale as the moon.

Star led her outside to a quiet place, where the music was muted. He
spread a quilt on the ground for her, a bright patchwork quilt, and Mina
sat down. Star snapped his fingers, and a small dog appeared from
nowhere. It crept onto the quilt beside Mina. Mina stroked its odd,
bristling gray fur; the dog seemed very thin, timid, and docile. Her name
was Dancer, Star said. Mina stroked Dancer's delicate pointed muzzle;
the dog crept closer and began to lick her hand. Mina felt a rushing
powerful exhilaration; she felt she loved this little dog intensely; she felt
some god had just reached down from the sky and made everything
right in the world.

Star sat beside her, and Mina looked at his face. She was astonished
that Star should single her out in this way, and she was even more astonished when she realized that for a while at least, he meant to stay.

"You have a hawk on your cheekbone." He touched her face very
lightly with his fingertips. "Your eyelids are gold. You're beautiful, Mina."

Mina stared at him. No one, not even her parents, had ever said such
a thing before.

"I'm not," she replied. "Cass is, but not me. Look—" She lifted her
face to the firelight. "I have freckles, and red hair."

"Cassandra is an ordinary girl. There are thousands of Cassandras. I
like your skin and your freckles and your hair, Mina. In the firelight, it's
flames and red gold."

Mina continued to stare at him. She was trying to place his voice,
which wasn't English, wasn't American, wasn't German or French accented. It seemed to be unidentifiable and uniquely Star's own.

"Are you afraid?" he said suddenly, watching her eyes. "I'd know if
you were, and I don't think you are."

"No. I'm not afraid. I feel—" Mina hesitated, trying to describe what
was happening to her, and something was happening to her, she could
feel it stealing its way along her veins.

"I feel quiet. Calm. It's like—there's a door opening, and on the other
side of the door there's my home."

The answer seemed to please him. He looked at her intently for a few
moments more, then he lay back on the quilt beside her, cupped his
hands behind his head, and looked up at the night sky.

Mina looked up too. The stars were very bright. She thought she
could see the Plow and Orion, the Pole Star, the Milky Way. She
thought of Cassandra, and where she might be—dancing, perhaps—then
she forgot Cassandra. A child ran by them; she looked around this im-

provised encampment. Beyond the fires and the dancers, some new vehicles were pulling into the field. She watched them distantly, a small fleet of new, expensive cars. Their lights flickered, their doors opened, and they disgorged their passengers, all male, all suited; the men were shouting to each other; they bunched and spread out, laughing and swearing, making for the barn. Mina turned to Star.

"Who are they?"

"City people. They come here to score from the travelers. And me." He sounded bored. "They pay well. They're fools."

"Are you a traveler?" Mina asked.

"No. I fit in everywhere and nowhere. I belong to no one and nothing. I come and go as I please."

"Isn't that lonely?"

"Not now. I've found you, Mina. And I've been looking for you for a long time."

He gave her a glittering look. "Let it happen, Mina," he said, then he lay back down on the ground again, his eyes fixed on the sky and his hand grasping hers.

"Lie down beside me," he said. "Pretend we're two figures on a tomb. Lie absolutely still. Watch the sky."

Mina did so. The sky was now brilliantly colored, striated, and moving very fast. She could see endless patterns, shapes twisting and turning and reinventing themselves.

"Do you know what you want in life, Mina?" Star asked.

"No, I don't. I don't even know who I am," she replied.

"I'll give you what you want, and I'll show you who you are," he said, not moving. "Hold my hand. Feel the power."

Mina obeyed him. They lay side by side in silence, for hours, for centuries. Mina felt her body be discarded. She felt the strength of her own soul. Even Star's little dog knew something extraordinary, something momentous, was happening.

After a while she became restive; she whined, then licked Mina's hand; a few millennia later she lifted her gray muzzle skyward, and howled.

CHAPTER 6

Charlotte was pleased with the way her dinner had gone. They had eaten by candlelight, at the long table in the kitchen. The pastry had risen perfectly, the steak and kidney pie had been excellent. Gini ate very little, but poor, neglected, half-starved Rowland, who had no one to cook for him—or no one serious to cook for him—had wolfed down two helpings. Had Rowland been one of her own children, Charlotte could not have been more pleased. At ten-thirty, when the others had been shooed through to the sitting room, she and Max found themselves briefly alone in the kitchen. A restful marital quietness filled the air. Charlotte was making coffee; Max, she suddenly realized, was fiddling with some port decanted earlier; it was one of his most precious ports, a Fonseca '69.

"Max," she said. "You're not actually going to give them that? Is that wise?"

"Almost certainly not. I'm going to risk it though." He caught her eye. "At dinner—you noticed the frisson?"

"I did. It was maybe a one-sided frisson, but it was there."

"It can't hurt to cultivate it."

"Max. You told me not to match-make. You said I shouldn't interfere. . . ."

"I know." He kissed her neck.

"Rowland will *talk* if you give him that. He'll talk all night, and all tomorrow as well."

"I like Rowland when he talks. So do you."

"Will Lindsay though?" Charlotte gave him a glance. "And don't think I didn't see you earlier, Max, before the cocktail guests arrived, whispering in Lindsay's ear."

"I was not whispering. I was just *mentioning* things in a casual sort of way."

"You mentioned Rowland's girls, didn't you? Max, look me in the eye!"

"Just in passing. It can't hurt her to know. It is *true*, after all." He held the port to the light appreciatively. "What's more, you remember what you said about the perversity of women? You were right. The instant I told her, I spotted it. A distinct gleam in the eye." He paused. "Why are women that way, incidentally? Why is your sex so weird? Rowland's reputation ought to make any sensible woman run a mile—"

"Max, go and give them that damn Fonseca. One glass only might be prudent. Oh—and make Gini's a double."

"You don't serve doubles of port," Max said fondly, "as you well know."

"Then give her a damn big glass. I may love her dearly, but she's tried calling Pascal six times this evening, and she's driving me mad."

This plot was foiled. Gini, along with Charlotte, refused the Fonseca. Rowland made a brief eloquent speech as to its glories when he was only halfway through his glass. Lindsay, to whom alcohol was alcohol, useful when nervous, drank her glass unwisely, very fast.

At eleven forty-five the telephone rang. Gini, who had been talking to Rowland in a desultory fashion, half rose from her chair. Color washed into her face and throat; Rowland moved away. As Charlotte went to take the call in Max's den, Rowland took down a book from Max's shelves and began reading. Gini waited on the edge of her chair.

When Charlotte returned, she found she could not meet Gini's eyes.

"Lindsay, it's that blasted Markov man," she said quickly. "He says he has to talk to you. He's calling on his car phone. From Paris."

Lindsay rose, sighing. She trotted through to Max's study and picked up the telephone.

"Will you listen to this?" Markov said without preamble. "I mean, will you just check this *out*? Is this poetry? Is this insight? Yes or no?" He held the phone close to his car's stereo speakers. The recording, which Lindsay could hear only too well, was an old one. It was "My Foolish Heart."

"Markov," Lindsay said with force, Fonseca coursing through her veins. "Who gave you this number? Louise? It's midnight, Markov. It was a lousy record the first time I heard it. It's still a lousy record now."

"You mean it doesn't *speak* to you? What are you, insensitive? How're things at Maxopolis? What's going down?"

"Markov, get off this fucking line."

"Lindy, I'm in Paris. This is Paris I'm calling from."

"I don't give a shit if it's Outer Mongolia. Stop hounding me. And don't call me Lindy—it drives me insane."

"You want to know something seriously interesting? You want to know who I eyeballed at the airport just now?"

"No, I don't."

"In the VIP lounge? Like, I'm coming *in*, and they're about to fly *out*? You want to know this, Lindy, believe me, you do."

"Oh, all right. Who? You've got ten seconds."

"Lindy, you're getting a tad boring, you know that? All right. Only Maria Cazarès. And Jean Lazare. Together—very *much* together. Like he has his arm around her, like she's crying and shaking, and he's trying to kiss her hair."

"You're sure about this?"

"Darling, I have twenty-twenty, remember, and I *wasn't* wearing shades. They were thirty feet away from me. I was *quivering*, Lindy. I overheard some *very* interesting things."

"Markov, wait a second—"

"Sweetling, I have like fifteen million people I have to call right now. I mean, we're talking Chernobyl here in information terms. I have to spread the word."

"Markov, wait! This is important. Who've you told already?"

"No one. I called you first."

"Dinner Monday?" Lindsay was thinking fast. "Maxim's? Le Tour Eiffel? Grand Vefour? Where d'you really yearn to do a shoot, Markov? Name it, it's yours."

"Hyderabad. Five-day shoot. Quest and Evangelista. Three spreads. Full color. In the Sunday. Sixteen thousand. You can swing that?"

"You got it."

"Plus Grand Vefour, Monday."

"Jesus, Markov. Oh, all right."

"My lips are sealed, sweetling. I adore you. Ciao."

Lindsay hastened back to the sitting room, face aglow. A yawning Charlotte and a silent Gini were already leaving.

"Time for bed," Charlotte said. Lindsay waited a few seconds, until the door closed behind them, then started talking very fast.

"Hyderabad?" Max said some minutes later. "Are you insane, Lindsay? No way. The Sunday will never buy that. I wouldn't even ask."

"Sixteen thousand?" Rowland said. "The port must have gone to your head. Markov's flaky. He'll be hitting the phones right now."

"He won't. We understand each other. Besides, it's less than his ad rate."

"It's extortion. He wouldn't prize that out of *Vogue*."

Lindsay abandoned Rowland, a lost cause. She turned to Max, who was pacing up and down.

"Max, just lean on the Sunday—please. I can't offer Markov color, but the Sunday can. Besides, Jancy's been dying to use him. She'll leap at the chance. He's *hot*, Max, the hottest there is. And Quest—you just wait, she's extraordinary. She's going to be *huge*—"

Rowland groaned; Lindsay ignored him.

"Come on, Max. It's such a little little favor. I just need you to lean on Jancy's editor. Dammit, Max, he was at Oxford with you and Rowland and the rest of the male world. *Network* for me for once, Max. Use your legendary powers of persuasion. . . . Shut up a minute, Rowland, I haven't finished. Please, Max—it's a circulation booster. Just one little word in his ear, Max. Is it so much to ask?"

Lindsay had her arms around Max's waist. Max's glasses were winking and blinking; he was on the edge of giving way.

"It's damn well pointless," said Rowland, who seemed to take exception to such wiles. "So he saw them at the airport together. So what? Maybe it's mildly interesting, from my point of view. It's not headline news."

"You don't know Markov. I do. This was just the aperitif, Rowland. Just let me talk to Markov. I *know* there'll be more."

"Here's a better idea." Rowland gave her a cold green glance. "How about *I* talk to Markov? Because he certainly won't jerk *me* around."

"Forget it, Rowland. Markov wouldn't give you the time of day."

"Oh, you think so? Why?"

"Because he doesn't *know* you. He wouldn't like you. He's tricky to handle, and you're one hundred percent guaranteed to rub him the wrong way."

"Well, I wouldn't be suckered the way you're being suckered, that's for sure. Max, talk to this woman, will you?"

"Not a chance," Max said, suppressing a smile and backing away. "I'm staying out of this, children."

"Just make her see reason, Max, that's all I ask."

Max hesitated. He looked from Rowland to the small, flushed figure of Lindsay. She had adopted a pugilistic stance; she looked both like a pretty woman and like an angry young boy. Rowland, in contrast, could sound heated while contriving to look extraordinarily cool. He was leaning against the mantelpiece, a glass of Fonseca in his hand, his entire attitude one of insolent male arrogance. Max sighed.

"It can't do any harm to propose the idea, Rowland," he said in a pacifying tone. "Lindsay's right—Markov is temperamental. He's also extremely well informed. And he and Lindsay have a special relationship. Markov adores her. She has him eating out of her hand."

"A special relationship? With Markov?" Rowland's face registered disbelief. "Well, now I've heard everything—"

"Maybe," Max cut in in the tones of Solomon, "maybe it would be an idea if you *both* saw him. Together."

This U.N. approach was a mistake. Rowland raised suffering eyes to the ceiling, and Lindsay, seeing this, began speaking very fast.

"If you *imagine*, Max," she began, "that for one *second* I'd sit down in the Grand Vefour with that stupid, knuckle-headed, obstinate, arrogant Irishman over there . . . If you think I'd let him loose on Markov, you must be insane. He's about as subtle as a bear in boxing gloves. He's a *throwback*, Max, to some very very primitive time. Climb back in your tree, Rowland, why don't you? And never, ever, under any circumstances ask me for my help again!"

"Done," Rowland replied. "No problem there. I prefer to work with professionals anyway. Temper tantrums aren't my scene."

He took a small, well-timed sip of Fonseca as he said this. Lindsay did not reply. She seemed, Max thought, to be practicing some odd form of rhythmic breathing. They both watched her breathe in and out, precisely ten times.

"Rowland," she said at last, her voice now sweetly calm. "You do not understand the fashion world. I know it's very very hard for you to admit that, but I think that when the effects of the port have worn off, even you will realize that it's true. You need me to check that file out, and you need me to talk to Markov, and you need my expertise, I'm afraid, because without it, Rowland, you're flying without radar, in fog, over mountains. You're flying *blind*. When you realize that, come the morning maybe, I shall expect you to apologize. I shall expect you to *grovel*, Rowland, for several hours. 'Night, Max." She stood on tiptoe and kissed his cheek. "Lovely dinner. Sleep well."

She left the room, closing the door quietly. There was a silence. Rowland put down the port.

"If you laugh, Max," he said. "If you so much as smile, I warn you . . ."

"Did I laugh? Smile? Did I say one single word?"

"Wipe that goddamn smug expression off your face, Max." Rowland sank his head in his hands. "What happened?" he said in irritable tones. "What the fuck happened? *When* did it happen? I blame the port, Max. I should never have touched it. Up until then it was going so *well.*"

Upstairs, Lindsay fairly skipped into her room. She sauntered along to the bathroom in bra and underpants. She washed joyfully and sang a few songs. She nipped back to bed, shivering with cold, pulled the eider-down up around her shoulders, angled the bedside light, and opened Rowland's green file. For a while she found it hard to concentrate. Rowland's maddening face kept swimming between her and the pages. She considered his astonishing hair and eyes; she dwelt on the sublime moment when she had wiped the conceit and arrogance off that extraordinary face with those few well-chosen words.

Once or twice she thought she heard sounds from Gini's room next door. She thought she heard movement, and then, becoming more alert, thought she heard sounds of weeping. But she couldn't be sure, and these sixteenth-century walls were thick. She listened intently, then decided she must have been mistaken; she could hear only silence now.

She returned, with better concentration, to the file, and read for an hour. When she was still only halfway through, a memory came back to her, and she felt a small pulse of excitement. There was one very obvious and central gap in the story of Maria Cazarès and Jean Lazare—it might, just might, be a gap that she could fill.

Downstairs, Max was tiring—it was past one in the morning—and Rowland was sunk in gloom.

"If you're working out ways to grovel," Max said, rising, "you can do it alone. I'll give the dogs a quick run, then I'm off to bed."

"I'll come with you." Rowland hauled himself from the chair.

They donned overcoats and boots and set off with the dogs on a circuit of the orchard. Rowland's hearing was keen. After only a few yards he stopped and listened.

"What's that noise?"

"What noise? I can't hear a damn thing. Just the wind. Come on, Rowland, it's bloody cold."

"Listen." Rowland did not move. "Music. I can hear music. It's coming from up there in the hills."

Max listened, and after a while he heard it too, distant but just discernible, a weird pulsing whooping sound.

"Probably a party," he said. "A late-night party. What the hell? Come *on*, Rowland, for God's sake. I'm freezing."

"A party?" Rowland still did not move. "Max, there's no village up there. There's not even a house. There's nothing, just fields, trees, the odd barn."

"Well, maybe it's an outdoor party. Who cares?"

"In January? In sub-zero temperatures? Max, come on."

"Look," said Max with force. "I don't give a damn if it's a satanic ritual. They can get on with it as far as I'm concerned. I'm walking around this orchard, then I'm going to bed. I advise you to do the same."

They walked on a little farther, the dogs racing back and forth among the trees. They had picked up the fox scent, Rowland thought, and remembered the lights he had glimpsed earlier. He paused.

"I might just investigate. Walk up that way. Clear my head. I don't feel like sleeping just now."

"You never do," Max replied grumpily. "It's one of the many things wrong with you. Your unnerving energy, at dawn. I'm off to bed. I'll leave the door unlocked. Bolt it when you come in."

Max returned to the house, the dogs snuffling at his heels.

Rowland crossed the orchard and opened the gate into the fields.

He liked walking, especially at night, and especially alone. Silence, he thought, and the night air, would clear his mind. He might never have admitted it to Lindsay, but some of her remarks had struck home. A bear in boxing gloves? Some Neanderthal throwback? Was that how he seemed? Was that, worse, how he *was*? He shook himself impatiently and lengthened his stride. There was a good path here, he remembered, once he had crossed the first two fields.

As he walked, all the events of that long evening reassembled in his mind. One minute he was thinking of Lindsay's remarks, the next of the odd, silent, and disconcerting Genevieve Hunter. Then he was swooping back to his own childhood, and the farm he had described to Max's boys. Why *there*? he thought. Why go back *there*? And for an instant he saw a different place, one unsuited to the simplicities of fairy stories, an ugly, cramped, damp homestead where generations of his father's family had scraped an existence. It had four damp, tiny rooms, no hot water, no bath, an outside lavatory. There was a yard, a cowshed, three sties, and four fields. Rowland loved it and also hated it. There, his parents toiled; they rarely spoke to each other. The rooms smelled of resignation and delusions and hopelessness. Sometimes, when his father had been drinking, silent hostilities would flare into violence, outright war.

Why did he alter and sentimentalize that world for the benefit of Max's sons, Rowland thought now, walking faster. Why return to that place, in fictional form, when it was one he avoided at all other times? His mother, forty when her only child was born, had been dead a decade; his father, crushed beneath a borrowed tractor, had died when Rowland was seven and a half years old. He had not set foot in Ireland, let alone his childhood home, in almost thirty years—so why return there now?

There was a mystery, of course, a family romance. Why had his mother, the least impulsive of women, married a man eight years her junior, without a penny to his name, a feckless, sweet-natured, heavy-drinking Irishman who could barely read, though he could talk like an angel if he chose? She had been a thirty-eight-year-old English spinster with a two-room flat in a cheap area of Birmingham, and a job teaching literature in a grim inner-city school, a job she had embraced with zeal and come to loathe. She met his father when he was briefly in England, working for a builder, trying to scrape some cash together, and had come around to fix some gutters.

What happened? Was it sexual attraction? Was she secretly desperate for a child? She was a conventional, even narrow-minded, middle-class woman. Why would she, of all women, fall for an Irish manual laborer, however handsome, however gifted with charm?

And his father, why had he succumbed? Had he had his eye on the proceeds from the sale of his new wife's little flat, the two thousand pounds that kept his farm solvent for a while? Could he have loved this tight-lipped, humorless woman—or had she been different once, before Rowland was born, before she made the decision to focus all her silent, bitter energy on the rearing of her child?

Christ, Rowland thought, and tried to push the memories down. He stopped abruptly, staring across the windswept hills. He could not recall his father's face anymore, time had blurred its detail, but he could still hear his voice, and he could still see, almost thirty years later, the precise shape and texture of his father's large, dirty, callused hands. They were dexterous. Gazing out across an English landscape, Rowland watched a dead man twist wires, assemble snares.

Long gone: he bent, picked up a shard of limestone, then threw it down. For his father's funeral, there was a wake, that was expected. His mother might be foreign, but she did her duty to the last. When it was over, his mother started packing very fast. Three suitcases. She was wearing black; a black coat, black shoes, black nylons, a new incongruous black and white polka dot scarf. He could feel the room trembling with anticipation, perhaps happiness. She buttoned on his mackintosh, belted it. She said, "Rowland, the ferry's booked. We're going back to England. We're going home."

Not the stuff of fairy tales. No happy endings. Rowland raised his eyes to the sky. Just for an instant, borne on the wind and a tide of rising unhappiness, he could hear another voice, Esther's voice: such an ordinary sentence—*I'm just going out to the grocery store. We're out of milk. I'll be back in twenty minutes.*

Forty minutes later he'd heard the sirens. One hour later the squad car pulled up outside the door. Two hours later he was in the morgue, making the identification. Six years later a part of him still waited for her return.

"God help me," Rowland said aloud. The wind touched him, and he swung around. He was alone, of course. He stared into the darkness, and into the wind. Too many graveyard memories. With a gesture of sudden anger he turned, and, increasing his pace, made for the first crest of hills.

Rowland paused, looking back the way he had come. Max's house and village were now invisible. To his west lay Cheltenham; he could see its city lights staining the sky. To the south was the air base where that man Landis was senior officer; he could see the runways clearly, lit by arc lights; he could make out the shapes of huts and hangars. To his north and east there were no lights, just stone walls, bare fields, clumps of thorn trees bent and twisted by the wind. The isolation, and the absence of human beings, had calmed and revived him. He could still hear the music, but his desire to investigate had left him. He would walk on, he decided, for another few miles, then return to Max's home.

There was a good track here, traversing rising ground. He followed it for about a mile farther, then paused once more in the shelter of some thorns. He felt refreshed and invigorated. He leaned back against a dry-stone wall, letting the past wash away from him. He looked up at the constellations and tried to identify them; he shifted his feet, glanced down, and saw the girl.

With a low exclamation he bent down. Until he touched her, he was almost sure he had imagined her, that she was a trick of moonlight and shadow, an accidental resemblance, a composite of dead branches and white stones.

Then he touched her, and understood: this was no illusion, the woman was real. Her legs and feet were bare, and she was dressed in dark clothes. He pushed some brambles aside, touched a cold hand; the woman did not move.

She was huddled against the side of the ditch, and her face was obscured. With practiced hands he felt her neck, then her spine. When he was sure there was no injury there, he risked moving her. Very gently, he turned her toward him, into the recovery position, on her right side.

Her body was limp and unresisting. As he moved her, moonlight struck her face, and Rowland froze. She was very young, little more than a child. Her eyelids had some metallic paint on them; there was mud on her face, and her lips were blackish. He felt for a pulse on her neck but could not find one. He reached for her wrist, and as he did so, he saw that the backs of her fingers were tattooed with the word HATE, one letter to each finger, and that the fingers were already beginning to stiffen into claws.

He felt a cold anger, then a flood of pity. He checked again for a pulse, although he knew he would not find one, not in a girl who must already have been dead several hours. He laid her gently back down, took off his overcoat, and covered her. Then he rose and ran back the way he had come, two miles to Max's, to a phone.

By two-fifteen he had called the police, roused Max, told him where the girl was, and was on his way back across the fields.

It seemed right that someone should stay with her, so he stood beside her body, staring out across the hills. He tried to puzzle out how someone so young, dressed in this way, should end up in this remote place, when it was so late, and so cold.

Shock had slowed his thinking, and it was several minutes before he made the connection between the lights, the music he had heard, and the girl. He swung around, realizing for the first time that the music had stopped. The only sound he could now hear was his own breathing, and the wind as it moved the branches of the thorns.

But if the music explained the girl's presence, it did not explain her death. He knelt beside her huddled shape, trying to work out how she came to be here, and dead, when she seemed physically uninjured and unharmed.

He looked down at her bloodless face, and then, with a cold sense of recognition, he understood. No needle tracks, so it was unlikely to be heroin. What then—pills? Crack?

He straightened up, listening to the sudden clamor of voices from six years before: a gunshot wound to the neck; Esther dying on the sidewalk one bright summer's afternoon.

So many different kinds of victims. The girl's eyes were open, as Esther's had been open; with sightless fixity she gazed up at the sky.

Rowland averted his face. His hands had begun shaking. From the valley below came shouts; he glimpsed the beams of flashlights. The boy who took Esther's purse, then shot her, had been hooked on crack since the age of twelve; he was poor, black, semiliterate, and fatherless. A born victim.

This girl was wearing a gold bracelet. Her clothes, if odd, were expensive. There were no indications here of deprivation. She had a choice, Rowland thought angrily; then, regretting his anger, and pitying her, he bent again and covered her face with his coat. The wind was stronger now, and it had begun to rain.

CHAPTER 7

Gini slept for three hours. She woke at six, and at once rose. She drew back the curtains; outside it was still dark. She washed and pulled on some clothes quickly, then padded down the stairs.

In the kitchen the dogs greeted her, whimpering, and thumping their tails. No one else was up, not even the children; the whole house was quiet. She boiled some water on the peculiar Aga stove that Charlotte swore by, and made herself some instant coffee. Her hands were unsteady, and her heart was beating very fast. It was now three days since she had last spoken to Pascal. It was six-thirty here, seven-thirty in Sarajevo.

She padded through to Max's study, which he had said she should use, closed the door, and stared at the telephones. In this room Max had installed all the hi-tech paraphernalia of the modern world. There was a Macintosh, a plain-paper fax machine, a laptop which he used when traveling, and two separate phone lines. Both phones had answering machines, and Pascal had both numbers. Max must have switched them to answer mode before he went to bed; two unwinking red lights met her gaze. During the night no one had called for Max, or for her.

She sat down and began punching in the number. She got through to the hotel on the third try. It rang for a long time. She could see the hotel lobby as she waited, see the press of journalists and TV crews and cameramen who would already be assembling there at this hour. She could see the stairs, and the elevators that rarely worked; she could see the room she and Pascal had shared. It was ugly, brown and orange; it had a 1970s picture window with antiblast tape on the glass.

"Lie beside me. Let me hold you," Pascal had said the day they returned from the hospital in Mostar. She had done as he bid. She lay in his arms, trembling. Tomorrow she would have to file her account of this particular incident. She could hear words in her head, and they all sounded hollow. She stared across the room at the window. Outside, the light was failing. She was beyond exhaustion, also afraid to close her eyes.

"Tell me what you saw. Tell me what you thought." Pascal stroked her hair very gently. It was still long, still uncut. He pushed it back from her face and made her turn toward him. "Darling, you have to do that. If you shut it away inside yourself, you'll never be free of it. Gini, please believe me. I know."

"You know what I saw." She found it hard to shape the words. "You saw it too."

"No." He took her hand quietly in his. "In that situation, no two people see exactly the same thing."

She allowed herself to look at him then. She could see the fatigue in his much-loved face; she could see regret and resignation but also strength in his eyes. Whatever I have seen, she thought, he has seen worse—many, many times.

"Gini, it isn't a cure, I'm not saying that." His hand tightened around hers. "There is no cure. You know that. You live with me. Once that door's unlocked, you can never close it again. There's a divide, Gini, between people who've been through that doorway and those who have not. I warned you of this before."

"I know you did."

"But for us there's no divide." He drew her toward him. "Gini, don't create one. Tell me, darling. Let me see what you saw."

So Gini tried. She tracked it, that former municipal building, on the outskirts of Mostar, a place surrounded by the shells of buildings, a place that had, for the past two months, housed the city's improvised hospital wards.

They had been in the long room reserved for the seriously injured. At one end were the soldiers, at the other, civilians. There were only a few children in this ward, and Gini, entering it, had been relieved. She had been interviewing a nurse, then one of the local doctors, who had been up all night operating on patients without benefit of anesthetic. She was joined by one of the volunteer doctors, a Frenchman Pascal knew from Médecins sans Frontières. With him had come a much-needed supply of painkillers and antibiotics. Gini helped him unpack these, then allowed him to lead her over to the end bed. He introduced her to the ten-year-old boy who lay there, for whom he had brought a chocolate bar. Both the boy's parents had been killed two weeks before. The boy's leg had been amputated at the knee; his right arm had sustained a minor shrapnel wound. By his bed crouched his seven-year-old sister, who refused to be parted from him. She was physically unhurt, but had spoken to no one except her brother for fourteen days.

Gini sat by the boy and talked to him, the French doctor translating. The pain and compassion she felt were so deep, they felt as eloquent as any language. The conversation faltered to an end; she hoped, passionately hoped, that this boy, with his thin face and dark, watchful eyes, would understand the concern for him she felt, even if that concern was useless and could bring him no ease.

Throughout the conversation the boy's sister never once raised her head. She shivered continually; she clutched her brother's hand. The doctor, seeing Gini's expression, intervened. He said a few words, then drew her back down the length of the ward, and into a corridor beyond. In the distance, somewhere, as always, guns boomed. The doctor was thin, bearded, about five years younger than she was. He looked at her closely.

"How long have you been here?"

"Three months. Nearly four."

"Then listen to me. That boy will survive. So will his sister. Now that we have penicillin, his wound will heal."

Gini looked back over her shoulder. Pascal, his face grim, was moving toward the boy's end of the ward. She said: "Survive? He has no parents. No home. He's ten years old. You saw his eyes."

She covered her face with her hands. The young doctor continued to watch her quietly.

"Nonetheless. He'll survive. You cannot get emotionally involved— you do realize that, don't you?" He hesitated. "I never ask their circumstances. I prefer not to know their names. I just make sure they get bandages, medication, because otherwise, they'll die. That's my function. Your function—"

"Mine?" Gini jerked up to look at him. She was crying, and no longer cared who saw the tears. "My function? What in God's name is my function? I feel useless—*worse* than useless. I feel like a *voyeur*."

"That's predictable. It will pass." He glanced away, some sound outside catching his attention. There was the noise of running footsteps, a shout, then quiet. Moving away from the window, the doctor took her arm.

"You have a function," he said. "Ask Pascal. You elicit sympathy. Indignation." He gave her a cool glance. "Then people write checks.

Politicians feel pressured. And over here"—he glanced around again, frowning—"we get the mercy flights. The relief doctors. The supplies. *That's* your function. To write. So do it. Describe this godforsaken place. *Make* people see it. Describe that child."

"It's not enough." Gini began to turn away. "It's inadequate. You know that."

"You have a better suggestion? Can you nurse? You have a medical degree?"

He continued speaking, Gini thought for a fraction of a second after that, though she could not hear his words. Swinging back toward him, she saw his face change as the air went dark. Something warm, moving fast, brushed her skin, broke them apart, picked them up as if they were weightless, and tossed them to the ground. There was a long, slow, wallowing sound, then that deep, sucking exhalation she had come to fear. She could hear the crush of masonry falling, then silence, then running footsteps, then screams.

Thirty seconds? Sixty seconds? She groped her way across the corridor, crawled to the entrance to the ward. Dust billowed, curled into her throat and eyes, then slowly began to thin and settle. One section of the ward was missing. The three beds at the far end of it were missing. The boy she had been with not five minutes earlier was gone, and so was his sister. For one long, silent moment of stupefaction and agony, she thought: *and so is Pascal.*

She helped to clear that fallen masonry, clawing at the powdery stone; she knew enough by now to know there was very little hope, and Pascal, safe, uninjured, working beside her, also knew this. When it was clear to them both that no miracle had occurred, he rose, drew her to her feet, and led her away.

Lying on that bed in the hotel room, back in Sarajevo, she tried to spell this out to him. She wanted to say: *why?* Why did the two doctors survive, and the nurse, and the other patients, and you and I? Why could that boy not have been spared, the boy and his sister? In the end, that was all she could say: one last, long, impotent *why.*

Pascal waited until she had finished speaking. His arms tightened around her. He wiped the tears from her cheeks and kissed her closed eyes.

"Why? Because it's random," he said at last, quietly. "Because it's always random and arbitrary. An old woman will be spared, a young child will die. A soldier who raped two women the previous day will survive, and some innocent bystander will not. Gini, don't try to find shape and meaning in this. There is none."

"There's no God." With a sudden furious gesture she rose from the bed and turned away. "No God. Cannot be. I see that now."

"Not one that I would want to worship. No." Pascal watched her in silence. She began to weep bitterly, burying her face in her hands.

"I want that boy *back*," Pascal heard her say. She choked on her words. "I want—that doctor said he'd survive. Pascal . . ." She raised her face and swung around to look at him. "How can you bear this? How *can* you? How can you look at these things, year after year? I thought—if I steeled myself—I could—" She broke off and bent her head. "I can't—I think . . . I can't *hope* anymore."

At that, Pascal rose and again took her in his arms. He waited until the storm of weeping ceased, and she grew calmer.

"I love you," he said, lifting her face to his.

"I love you, and I know that you love me. That boy—was loved. You will remember him. I will remember him. Isn't there some hope there?"

His voice, and his face, were grave. Gini, looking up, met the steadiness of his gaze. Unbidden and unexpected, and for the first time in weeks, a physical longing for him stabbed up through her body. It was like a cut from a knife, and it made her ashamed. Fighting it, she rested her face against his chest and listened to the beat of his heart.

"I know what you're thinking," Pascal said, and he was right: he did know a great deal of what she was thinking, though not perhaps all. "It's so fragile—yes? And love is no protection. Death could always be around the next corner, not five minutes away?"

"Yes. That. And—"

"No justice." He kissed her bent head, then sighed. "Oh, Gini, don't you see? This is what I was trying to warn you about. I knew this would happen to you. And it's the hardest thing of all. . . ."

The number was still ringing in Sarajevo. They picked up finally on the twentieth ring. She was lucky this time, for often she obtained one of the desk clerks who spoke poor English. This time it was the nineteen-year-old, the one who prided himself on his grasp of idiom, acquired from years of watching American gangster films.

He said Pascal had checked out; he'd returned that morning at four and left again half an hour later. For two hours the previous evening he had been trying to reach her, but the lines had been bad again. But he had received some of her messages, it seemed, and he would call her, without fail, in the next twenty-four hours.

Gini's hands were shaking. She replaced the receiver and buried her face in her hands. She knew what that message really meant, and why it had been made to sound reassuring. It meant Pascal had some lead. It meant he had set off somewhere more dangerous than Sarajevo, before light came. There was usually a lull in military activities in the early morning; there was less likelihood of snipers, or of a sudden bombardment, in the few hours before dawn.

She could feel the fear mounting, this terrible disabling panic that always seemed to attack her when she was least prepared. She made herself get up and leave the room. She made herself be active. Returning to the kitchen, she washed the few dishes Charlotte had left in the sink, then pulled on a coat and took the dogs for a short run.

She walked around the garden, and the orchard, her footsteps leaving prints in the frosted grass. She looked up at the fields and the bare hills beyond, and tried to tell herself that this state of mind and state of heart would pass. The random would not occur. Pascal would be safe, and soon, surely soon, he would return. They might even come here, as Charlotte had suggested. They could walk in the hills in the warmth of a summer evening. Just a few months, and this landscape would be transformed. The trees would be in leaf; there would be flowers in bloom. She would love Pascal, and he would love her, and they would be able to talk or be silent, and once again they would both be secure.

Except . . . She turned back to the house and let herself into the silent kitchen. She sat down at the table and stared unseeingly at the wall. Except: she would rather not have remembered, but she could not forget the conversation with Helen, Pascal's ex-wife, that had taken place in London shortly before Christmas, four weeks before.

She had met Helen, a thin, brisk, dark-haired Englishwoman, on two occasions before that, both with Pascal. This conversation, over a lunch that had been Helen's suggestion, had been the first the two women had ever had alone.

Helen had remarried earlier that year. Her new husband, whom she referred to as her good, safe Englishman, was a widower with three teenage children away at boarding school. He had inherited and ran a successful textile manufacturing company that had recently taken over a French silk-weaving business with headquarters in Paris and factories in Lyon. The modernization of this once-famous company now took up much of his time, Helen explained. As a result, she and Ralph had decided to postpone their search for the perfect English country house, and were going to spend the next six months at Ralph's Paris apartment; this plan had benefits for everyone concerned.

Gini listened to all this numbly. Helen described the interior decorating she had embarked on in Paris. Not a stupid woman, she made no comment about Gini's lack of animation, or on her appearance, which Gini knew was unimpressive, although she had tried very hard.

"It means, of course," Helen went on, "that Marianne will be able to stay on for another six months at her French school. She's been a little difficult about the move to England. I told Ralph—she adores him already, I knew she would—we don't want to bombard her with too much change. To stay on in her old school, with her friends, just for a while . . . All in all it seemed the most practical plan. Pascal thought it was sensible too. . . ."

"Oh." Gini looked up. "I didn't know that."

"Yes, well. He and I discussed it briefly. Before the two of you left for Yugoslavia . . . Bosnia. Whatever one's supposed to call it now. I expect he just forgot to mention it. You must both have had other things on your mind."

She looked closely at Gini, who did not reply. She gestured to the waiter to bring more coffee.

"Do you mind if I speak frankly?" she said in an abrupt way, then hesitated. "This isn't very easy to broach. I want you to know, what I'm going to say isn't motivated by ill feeling or jealousy. It might have been once, but not now."

"No, please. I understand."

"I was married to Pascal for five years. We lived together before that. It may not have been a successful marriage, but I do know Pascal. I know him very well."

Gini said nothing. She fixed her eyes on the chic scarlet cashmere sweater Helen was wearing; on the single string of pearls. Helen was around forty. She looked a decade younger, radiant, in charge of her life, on top of the world.

"Do you intend always working together, alongside each other? That might be one solution, I suppose."

"No, we don't," Gini replied. "Not always, obviously. We had thought—when we can . . ."

"I don't like the term workaholic," Helen went on. "The word's overused. It implies an addiction, obviously—but I never felt Pascal was *addicted* to his work. That would suggest passivity, a lack of willpower on his part—and no one would ever accuse Pascal of that, least of all me." She gave a tight smile. "I'm sorry. I used to be a translator, as you know. I'm fussy about words."

She paused thoughtfully, then frowned.

"I always thought Pascal was *dedicated* to his work, in an intense, almost priestly way. As if it were his vocation—you understand what I mean?"

"Yes, I do. And it costs him a great deal."

"Perhaps." Helen pushed this suggestion aside. "For my part, I found that very hard to live with. Not at first, maybe. There was a certain glamour, you know. Pascal was becoming famous. I liked the drama of it all, sending letters off to remote places, trying to get a call through to some war zone. I gave several interviews, did you know that?" Her eyes flicked toward Gini's. "People were intrigued by how it felt to be his wife. How I coped . . ." She made a face. "Of course Pascal didn't approve. He was furious when I showed him the pictures. He always refused interviews. He's never been interested in being a celebrity. Fame never interested him at all."

Gini said nothing. She wished Helen had never mentioned war zones in that particular way. She could feel Bosnia very close, just the other side of this restaurant wall; another few minutes and she'd start to hear its sounds; all that desolation and pain would come swooping back to her. This was not normal, she told herself. She had to regain perspective. She forced herself to pay close attention to Helen's words.

"Even before Marianne was born," she went on, "there were difficulties. Pascal was away for months at a time. I had to go to parties, dinners, on my own. Of course, I've always been very independent, I didn't really *mind*. . . . " She gave a small frown.

"Perhaps, if Pascal had earned more money than he did then, it might have been better. We could have had a larger apartment. I could have entertained. It's awfully easy to get left out, you know, if one's a woman living alone. I did say to Pascal, he could have earned more—it would have been so easy. Advertising agencies were clamoring to use him. I used to tease him; I'd say, surely you can fit them in, darling, before the next war. . . ."

She laughed, and glanced at Gini.

"I can see. You don't approve. Maybe you're more high-minded than I was. I really couldn't see that it would do the least harm. Anyway, that's beside the point. On the whole, we managed very well. It was different once Marianne was born."

She paused, and her face became set.

"I had to manage, Gini, I had to manage entirely alone. Of course, our marriage was a little shaky by then. Even so, if Marianne was ill, if there was any problem at home, small or large, I had to cope with it. Ninety percent of the time Pascal was away. He was on a plane, in an airport, in some damn flea-bitten hotel in the back of beyond, where the switchboard didn't work half the time, and if it did work, Pascal was never there. . . . I coped. Not always very well. Sometimes, when he got back from Afghanistan, Cambodia, Mozambique, wherever, I'd try to explain. He'd never tell me what he'd been through in those places. He wouldn't talk about it at all. And I didn't really want to know. I mean, whatever horror he'd been through—there was nothing *I* could do. Of course, I knew it wasn't tactful to start complaining about *my* little problems. I knew they'd seem petty to him. But I couldn't stop myself. There'd be scenes, tears, pleas, recriminations, on my part. None of it made the slightest difference. He'd calm me down, then go off and catch the next plane."

She paused, looking closely at Gini. "After a while it made me angry. Really terribly angry. I felt this *fury* all the time. If he'd had another woman, I think I could have coped better; at least that would have been commonplace, predictable. But my rival wasn't a woman, it was his *work*. From my point of view"—her mouth tightened—"it became unacceptable. An absentee husband is one thing. An absentee father is another. Pascal adored Marianne, of course. When he was actually there, he was wonderful with her. But he simply couldn't understand that devotion wasn't enough. Has he changed, would you say?"

The question was sudden. Gini flushed scarlet.

"It's very hard for him, obviously," she began. "He's trying to balance the things that matter most to him. Even in Sarajevo he thought about Marianne all the time. He wrote constantly, he telephoned. When he gets back, he—"

"That wasn't really what I meant, as I think you know," Helen said. "I wasn't thinking of Marianne. I was thinking of you."

Gini lowered her gaze. "We don't have children," she said in a quiet voice. "So it's different for me."

"Of course." Helen looked at her, her expression doubtful. "Anyway, it's not my business. I don't want to interfere. Do you know when he's coming back from Sarajevo?"

"No, not exactly. The situation changes every day. But soon. In a couple of weeks, probably."

"Well, he'll be back for Marianne's birthday in January. That we *can* count upon," Helen said, a slight edge in her voice. "There's a fixed date anyway."

"He'll be home before that," Gini said quickly. "He'll come back for Christmas, I know."

Helen said nothing. Looking at her face, Gini could tell she doubted the accuracy of that prediction—and of course, as it turned out, Helen was proved right. Pascal had not returned for Christmas. Indeed, his ex-wife knew him well.

"I'll get the bill." Helen had turned to wave at the waiter. "No. My treat. I insist. I'll hope to see you again soon. Perhaps in Paris, for Marianne's birthday? I'd like you to meet Ralph. I always think that these things are much simpler if they're handled openly. There's no reason why we can't all be friends now." She hesitated, and then to Gini's great surprise reached across the table and pressed her hand.

"I like you, Gini. I didn't expect to, but I do. I hope you know—Pascal deserves some happiness in his life. God knows he never found it with me. When I last saw him—he did seem so altered, so much better in every way. No bitterness, no anger—I could see how good you've been for him, and I was glad. It's just—"

"What?"

"My dear, you don't look terribly well, you know."

"I'm fine. I picked up some bug in Sarajevo. I'm fine now."

"Good." Helen smiled. "Well, tell Pascal to take care of you. Don't let him get too obsessive—after all, you are supposed to be living together now! Crack the whip a little, Gini, the next time he calls. It may not have worked in my case, but I'm sure it would in yours." She rose. "I must go. I'm catching the four o'clock Paris flight. Ralph is meeting me, so I mustn't miss it." She gave Gini a tiny conspiratorial glance. "I have a plane to catch now."

Gini returned to her apartment. She could not like Helen, and she was unsure if she could trust her, but she had heard very genuine feeling break through her pointed words. For an hour, two hours, Gini paced up and down. The telephone did not ring. Eventually, giving in to temptation, she went into the bathroom and used the pregnancy testing kit she had purchased earlier that day. It was simple enough: if you were pregnant, the strip turned pink; if you were not pregnant, it turned blue.

It took fifteen minutes to react. She sat there, watching it. She wondered what Pascal would say if he knew the truth, if she told him that she wanted it to turn pink, wanted it with her whole soul. What would he say if she confessed that the desire to have his child had taken hold of her the day of that hospital shelling, and that the desire, still acute, was with her still?

She covered her face with her hands. She had no need to imagine a reaction to an emotion she did not intend to admit: she knew what the reaction would be. She had seen it in that brown and orange hotel room, when she had explained that she had just missed her period; concern, then anxiety, then something very close to despair.

"You are still taking the pill? I don't understand."

"Yes. I am. I think it's just overwork. Tiredness."

"Gini, are you sure? You couldn't have missed a day or two by accident?"

"No. I checked. Don't worry, it's just the stress—it's happened to me before."

He tried to embrace her then; he began insisting she see a doctor for a checkup. When she had done so, and it was confirmed that she was not pregnant, Gini found herself unable to meet his eyes. She was afraid to see the relief in them. She stared at the ground.

"Suppose I had been," she said in a low voice. "What then, Pascal?"

"Darling, I don't know. . . . " He put his arms around her. "We're only halfway through our time here. This was something you so much wanted to do—this work. Your career matters very much to you. You said you didn't want children. A mistake like that, coming at a time when we're both working all hours, always on the move, in danger to some extent—"

"A mistake?"

"Well, it would have been a mistake in one sense, darling, you know that. This is something we've never considered—the last thing we'd planned, coming now, in the midst of all this mayhem."

Gini turned away wordlessly. She could hear the anxiety in his voice; she thought she could detect an undertone of impatience, imperfectly concealed.

He was right, she told herself; his reaction was sensible, pragmatic, responsible. She thought: he does not want another child; he does not want a child with me.

The pain was very great. Despite the pain, and the rationality of his arguments, the desire remained. She still wanted his baby, and she continued to clutch at the hope that she might be pregnant long after leaving Bosnia. She knew, of course, when that desire began. She could date it to the day, the hour. After Mostar. She had watched too many children die; now her body dictated—she wanted to feel a child grow within her; she wanted Pascal to watch this child be born.

The fifteen minutes had eventually passed. In that bathroom she had looked at a test-tube device, at a sample strip that reminded her of school chemistry lessons, years before. Its verdict filled her with desolation: as both feared and expected, the strip was turning blue.

Charlotte was the first of the family to surface. She came down to the kitchen yawning, wrapped in a deep blue woolen dressing gown, complaining she had been awakened by sirens.

Gini averted her face from the swell of her stomach; Charlotte, fussing over the dogs, did not notice her reddened eyes.

"I don't understand." She waved a scrap of paper. "Max left me a note—he didn't want to wake me, and I was dead to the world. But there's been some kind of accident. He and Rowland had the police out last night, after we went to bed. But why aren't they back? Where can they be? Why haven't they called?"

"I'll make some tea." Gini rose. "Don't worry, Charlotte. There's probably some simple explanation. It can't be too serious. Max would have awakened you if it were."

"No, he wouldn't. He's protective. Of me—and this daughter of ours here." She patted her stomach. "She's kicking away now. Here . . ." She held out her hand. "Feel, Gini. Isn't it extraordinary? So small, and all that power?"

Gini allowed her hand to be taken. She rested her palm on the curve of Charlotte's belly. Its hardness astonished her. At first she felt nothing, then she sensed a tremor, then movement. There was a bumping beneath her hand, as if tiny hands or feet resented this confinement and pushed against the womb's walls. Then there was stillness, then movement again, rippling out beneath her fingertips in one long, fluent curve.

"She's turned over." Charlotte smiled. "Now she'll sleep. That's the usual routine."

"She?" Gini withdrew her hand. Envy, and a longing so intense it stifled her, gripped her heart. She turned quickly away to the stove.

"I believe Rowland." Charlotte gave a low laugh. "I know he was teasing me, but I still trust him. Rowland's so odd—he might well have magic powers."

She stopped speaking abruptly and swung around.

Gini, turning, heard the sound of pounding footsteps, a voice calling frantically. A woman was running across the terrace outside. Without knocking, she flung open the kitchen door. It was only when she began speaking, and Gini heard her accent, that she realized this white-faced, disheveled woman was the smart, overdressed Susan Landis, whom she had met and disliked the night before.

"Please," she said. "Oh, God, Charlotte—please, you've got to help me. I've been calling and calling—I just went up to the manor. There's police everywhere. . . ."

She swayed, grasped a chair back, and made a choking sound.

"Please help me. Something terrible has happened. Cassandra's dead—and Mina's disappeared. She's such a good girl—she's only fifteen. Charlotte—please. I can't make the police understand. Mina's gone!"

At nine-thirty Rowland was sitting in a small interview room in the main Cheltenham police station. The room was tiny and smelled of stale nicotine. He had been sitting there since six-thirty that morning. He had not eaten, washed, shaved, or slept. Max, who had driven him there, was in the interview room next door. It was he who had made the preliminary identification of Cassandra Morley's body. Now, presumably, he was doing what Rowland had been doing for the past three hours, going over the events of the night before.

Rowland had given a statement, been questioned on the statement. What time, when, how: why had he been up there, alone, at that time of night? Why had he moved the body?

"Because I didn't know she was dead," Rowland had replied. "She was lying awkwardly. I checked for neck and spinal injuries, then I moved her. Then—"

"Are you a doctor? You have medical qualifications?"

"No. But I've had some paramedical training."

"You have? Why?"

"Look, I climb. In Scotland. I've climbed in the Alps. I know how to check for those kinds of injuries. It was automatic to do that. I suppose—I was also looking for other obvious signs . . . a head wound—I don't know."

"Did you attempt resuscitation?"

"No. There was no pulse—"

"You're sure?"

"For God's sake!" Rowland lost his temper. "Rigor mortis had set in. It was—what? Minus five degrees? By the time I found her, she'd been dead several hours."

And so it went on. An interview with one officer, then a second. The gradual and unpleasant realization that because of the circumstances, because he was a man, he might not be believed. Eventually their interviewing tactics changed and their tone became less hostile—presumably because they had received an interim medical report, and Max had corroborated his story. But Rowland was left with a sick sense of their distrust. He felt guilty by gender, a feeling he had never experienced before.

The statement was taken down, revised, amplified, then taken away to be typed. From outside the interview room came constant noise. Some of the travelers from the barn were being brought in, presumably questioned, perhaps busted for possession: Rowland had no way of knowing, and no one was likely to inform him. Around nine someone brought him tea he didn't want, and half an hour later the more senior detective returned. He was a middle-aged man who had already mentioned the fact that he had two teenage daughters. He looked as weary and sickened as Rowland felt. Passing his hand across his face, he sat down and gave Rowland the statement to sign.

"One thing." He indicated its first paragraph. "Your emergency call is logged at two-eleven A.M. What time was it when you got back to the body?"

"Around two-thirty. Maybe two thirty-five."

"And you noticed the music had stopped—when?"

"Maybe five minutes later. I'm not sure. I wasn't really thinking about it, not to begin with. Is it important?"

"It helps." He gave a sigh. "By the time our cars got up to that barn, the travelers were already packing up. The ringleaders had already left— or so the others claim. Usually those affairs go on all night. I'd like to know why they broke up early, that's all."

"There are ringleaders, then?"

"Oh, sure. The travelers will feed you any amount of crap. Claim they were just following ley lines, took tarot readings, make out they just all happened to congregate in that one place at one time. In this case, a girl's dead. So they're prepared to be that bit more cooperative. Nothing to get excited about. They know who the suppliers are—but they won't name names."

"Was it drugs?" Rowland looked at him. "Is that what killed her?"

"We'll have to wait for the autopsy report, obviously. It's probable, I'd say. We've had stuff flooding into the area recently—Ecstasy, heroin, cocaine, amphetamines. People think rural areas are safe. They think drugs are a big-city problem. They're wrong. I try to explain to my daughters—they listen. Then they laugh the second I leave the room. You have children?"

"No."

"Wait until you do. It's as easy to score around here as it would be in London. Pubs, clubs, discos, parties, raves—grass, Ecstasy, over the course of an evening, it's cheaper than beer. Sometimes they're buying garbage, sometimes they're getting something very pure. It's a kind of Russian roulette, and the kids like that. Adds to the thrill, maybe. Who knows?" He tapped the statement. "If you're happy with it, sign. I expect you'd like to get out of here."

Rowland signed.

"This is the second death of this kind in four weeks," the man went on as Rowland rose. "The last one was a girl too. It was just before Christmas. She was Dutch, a runaway. She was fourteen years old, good family, plenty of money, no problems there. She hadn't been home in nine months. Her parents identified the body Christmas Day. It wasn't the best Christmas I've ever known."

"She was Dutch?" Rowland said. "From where?"

"Amsterdam, I believe. Needle tracks on both arms. The amphetamines she'd taken didn't mix too well with the heroin. And the heroin was unusually pure. The dealers introduce high purity consignments from time to time—when they need new clients, and need to hook them fast."

He opened the door. "Thank you for your help. Your friend should be through soon. You can wait out there."

Rowland returned to the lobby. He felt angry and dispirited and on edge. He had been too late to save Cassandra Morley, and the information he had given was unlikely to be of great assistance. He sat down beneath a poster warning of the perils of drunk driving, and resigned himself to waiting for Max.

There was no sign now of the travelers. The lobby was deserted except for the constable on duty at the desk, and a plump, belligerent young man with a South London accent who was wearing an expensive suit and a loud shirt: the two were having an altercation that had clearly begun some time before.

As Rowland entered, the man raised his voice.

"Look," he said. "Can I get this through your head? I'm here to report a stolen vehicle, not answer damn stupid sodding questions. It's a top-of-the-range five series BMW. Silver. Leather upholstery. Alloy wheels. We're talking almost thirty thousand quid. . . ."

"I have those details. I have the registration number. Are you the owner of the vehicle, sir?"

"No. I'm not. For crying out loud. My name's Mitchell—you've got that? You can spell that okay? The car belongs to a lady friend of mine. I just had it for the weekend. Is that a crime now? Anything else you'd like to know? My blood group, maybe? My mother's birth date? I mean, if that's what it takes to get some action around here—"

"Was the car locked when you left it, sir?"

"Yes. No. Look—I'm not sure. I already told you . . ."

"You're not sure? Had you been drinking, sir?"

"No. I goddamn well hadn't been drinking. What is this? I already told you. I was driving back to London, from here, and—and I got taken short. I needed to take a leak. L-e-a-k—you've got that?"

The constable made a note of this information, his face impassive. Rowland listened with closer attention. This was a war of attrition, and he knew who would win.

"So I get out to take a quick piss, okay?" Mitchell went on. "I've driven off the main road. I'm on this track, in the middle of nowhere. Up ahead of me is this barn. I can see lights, hear music—so I think I'll check it out, see what's going on. What do I find? The place is crawling with hippies. I take one look—I've left the car maybe two, three minutes—and what do I find when I get back? The sodding car's gone. So I do the obvious. I go back. I ask around. I make some *inquiries*—like have any of you deadbeats seen a thirty-thousand-quid BMW recently? I get nowhere. There's all these bleeding kids milling around. I give up, start walking back down the track, and what do I find? They've pinched my sodding wallet as well. No money. No plastic. Put it this way—it didn't improve my mood. So, what I'd like to know now is—are you going to report this vehicle as stolen, or piss around—"

The constable made a note. He said: "Time, sir? This would have been when exactly?"

Rowland, watching with keen interest now, knew the question was not idle. Mitchell sensed it as well. His manner at once became evasive.

"Time? I'm not sure. Midnight—maybe a bit before."

"It's past nine now, sir."

"So?"

"Why didn't you report the matter earlier?"

"Because I was stuck miles up some sodding track, in the dark. Because I had to damn well walk miles, because when I got here, when I *finally* got here, a whole lot of jerks kept me hanging around—"

Mitchell stopped. During this last peroration, the constable had picked up a telephone and said a few words. Replacing the receiver, he emerged from behind his counter and took Mitchell by the arm.

"If you'd come through here. One of the detective sergeants would like a word."

Mitchell began protesting loudly. Rowland saw him eye the door, as if wondering whether to bolt for it. Clearly, he thought better of it. He disappeared into an adjoining room. Through the closed door his voice could be heard for a while, blustering. Then he fell silent. Rowland thought: they're telling him about the girl.

He leaned back against the wall and stared dully at the posters. Mitchell had been lying, that was obvious. He wondered whether he would prove to know anything useful, but his mind would not fix on that question, or any other. He felt a deepening black despondency, and he knew where this would lead his thoughts next if he did not guard against it: back to Washington, D.C., to a street near Dupont Circle, and to a different kind of drug killing that had happened six years before.

He passed his hand across his face and tried to force his thoughts elsewhere. Some five minutes later Max emerged. He looked gray-skinned and exhausted. Pulling on an old Barbour shooting jacket, he took Rowland by the arm.

"Let's get out of here," he said. "Come on, Rowland. I need to think. I need some air."

Max's first action, when they returned to his Land-Rover, was to try to call Charlotte on his car phone. Both numbers were busy. He tried several times, then gave up.

"Let's get home." He glanced at Rowland. "Look, would you mind driving? I'm feeling—I feel like hell."

When they were in the car, neither spoke for a while. Max lit a cigarette.

"You don't mind?"

"No. I don't mind. In fact, you can give me one."

"You don't smoke. You haven't smoked for years."

"Come on, Max. Just give me one, okay?"

Rowland drew on the cigarette, which Max gave him without further comment. Instantly, the nicotine steadied him; it was as familiar, and welcome, as it had ever been before.

"The thing is," Max began in an abrupt way a few miles farther on, "I've never seen a dead body before. Not even a stranger's, let alone someone so young, someone I knew. Pathetic, isn't it?"

"No. And it's not unusual now." Rowland kept his eyes on the road ahead. "Your parents are still alive. So are Charlotte's. Besides—these days death gets tidied away. It takes place in a hospital, behind a screen. Don't feel guilty, Max. What are you supposed to do? Take it in your stride?"

"I've led a sheltered life," Max replied. "I suppose that's what I'm saying. Just now. . . . I rather despise myself for that. You wouldn't understand. It doesn't apply to you."

Rowland said nothing. He was thinking of his father, then of his mother dealing with her death as grimly as she had dealt with her life, in a North London hospital cancer ward. He thought of the two climbing accidents he had witnessed in the Cairngorms, of the drug murders he had covered in Washington. He did not think, would not allow himself to think, of a summer's day in the chill of a Washington police morgue. *If you could just make the identification, Mr. McGuire. She's . . . you're prepared?*

"Do you know what they told me?" Max still had his eyes on the road. "They said they've had drugs flooding into this area recently."

"They told me that as well."

"Jesus Christ, Rowland. Ten years from now, it could be my children buying that stuff. Ten years? It's even less—Alex is eight. Cassandra was just sixteen years old."

"I know."

"When we bought this place, we thought—" Max gestured angrily at passing fields. "We thought, bring them up in the country, keep them away from London. Give them an old-fashioned upbringing—dogs, walks, a village school, fresh air . . . We thought it was *safe*. We thought—I suppose we thought values were different here."

"Nowhere's safe now, Max. You know that."

"There's too much money around here. Large estates, private schools, second homes. Too many rich children, too many careless parents. Cassandra Morley's damn mother was never there half the time. Her father swans around Europe with a new wife half his age."

"Come on, Max. There's plenty of victims from very different worlds. Visit a few housing projects sometime. Rich, poor—it doesn't make any difference these days."

"I know that. Of course I know that—" Max hesitated. He gestured out the window.

"You see that track there? That leads up to that barn. Some of the travelers are still up there, the police said. They'll keep them there another twenty-four hours. Maybe less, because I gather they're not being too communicative. I want to cover this story."

"So do I."

"I want to get someone up there. You could do it, of course." Max gave him a speculative glance. "Except you're an editor, not a reporter now. You have to get back to London tomorrow night, and we really need someone who could stay down here a couple of days. Someone who could talk to the travelers, talk to Cassandra Morley's school friends, find out what they know. Someone young, someone whom they might open up to."

"I know what you're thinking, Max. I'd say no."

"Why? She's a good reporter. She's on the spot. She's here right now. You were keen enough to use her yesterday."

"That was yesterday," Rowland replied curtly. "This is now. Come on, Max, you're not blind. You saw her last night. She's operating on autopilot half the time."

"She can snap out of it, presumably. Charlotte thinks she has broken up with Pascal."

"Max, the reasons are irrelevant. She looks ill. She's like a bloody sleepwalker. I don't intend to use her on the Lazare story or any other, I'll tell you that now."

Max said nothing. He was used to Rowland's instant prejudices, and to his sometimes precipitate judgments, and on this occasion, felt he might share them. He shrugged.

"Let's get back to the house anyway. I need to talk to Charlotte. Then we can decide. Right here, then left . . ."

Rowland accelerated past the manor, where several police cars were parked, and turned into Max's drive. It was only as they entered the house that he remembered Lindsay, and the argument the previous evening. Today he was due to apologize to her, or grovel, as she had put it. He could hear women's voices coming from the kitchen: neither apology nor groveling seemed relevant now.

Entering the kitchen, it was at once obvious to him and to Max that something had happened in their absence. The atmosphere was tense. Charlotte was white-faced, Lindsay looked as if she might have been crying. Gini was standing at some distance from the others, her back to the room. When Max and Rowland entered, she did not look around.

Before Max could even begin speaking, Charlotte was in his arms. She began spilling out her story, how Susan Landis had arrived, and then her husband, how the police had finally stirred themselves and made inquiries.

"Max, it's not just Cassandra," she finished. "It's Mina Landis too. She was *with* Cassandra last night. They both went up to that barn."

"Mina did? Then where is she now?"

"That's the point, Max, no one knows. She's disappeared. She's not at home, she's not at the manor, she's not with the travelers, she's not at the barn. Robert Landis just telephoned again. Apparently, the travelers are now claiming she left the place last night. In a car. With some man."

Charlotte was close to tears. Max put his arms around her and drew her quietly aside.

"Darling, don't," Rowland heard him say. "You mustn't. Think of the baby."

Rowland turned away. The closeness of Max and Charlotte at such moments always moved him, and left him at the same time with a sense of exclusion, of bleakness. It was as if they spoke a private language, a married language, not one he had ever spoken, he thought, not one he was ever likely to learn. He noted that Lindsay, too, turned away at the same moment and began busying herself with the kettle at the stove. One of the dogs whined. Max and Charlotte continued to speak to each other in lowered voices.

Rowland leaned up against the window and stared out across the garden. A clock ticked; he felt a leaden exhaustion. Lindsay was making coffee; Max and Charlotte continued speaking, Max holding her closely to him, then persuading her to sit down. Genevieve Hunter, Rowland thought, looked ill; her face was white with strain. She was now watching Max and Charlotte. Max's concern for his wife seemed to cause her some unaccountable pain.

"May I say something?" she began abruptly, interrupting Charlotte and speaking in a brusque, ill-judged tone. "We're all wasting time. In the first place, Robert Landis wants Max to call him. He's with the police in Cheltenham now."

"Look, Gini, just leave it, okay?" Lindsay banged down the kettle and swung around. "Don't let's have another row. Just let Charlotte explain in her way. Give her time. She's seven months pregnant, in case you hadn't noticed."

"It would be hard not to notice," Gini snapped. Charlotte gave her a look of reproach and surprise. Max frowned.

"Look, Gini," he began quietly. "You don't quite seem to understand the situation. And remarks like that don't help. So, if you wouldn't mind . . . "

"Fine." The warning went unheeded; Gini's mouth tightened. "But all this speculation is pointless. It's been going on for an hour now—more."

"Gini, it's not just speculation." Charlotte took Max's hand. "Lindsay and I were just trying to understand what could have happened. Mina could have been abducted. She could be dead too. There's a hundred possibilities and they're all horrible."

"Abducted? That's not what the witnesses say." Gini turned back to Max. "Max, will you listen to me? The witnesses who spoke to Landis and the police were specific. Mina wasn't drugged. She wasn't unconscious. She wasn't dragged into some car by some B-movie villain. Unless they're lying, what happened is very clear."

She hesitated; Charlotte had begun to cry. Max bent over her, and Rowland, seeing Gini's face become pinched and obstinate, felt the first strong stirrings of dislike. His hostility was shared by everyone present, and he could see she sensed that. Color came and went in her face. Ignoring the others completely, she addressed herself again to Max—an exclusion that enraged Rowland even more.

"Max, it's *obvious* what happened. A fifteen-year-old girl lied to her parents. She went up to that barn in the certain knowledge that it was the last thing they'd let her do. She probably smoked some grass—she was seen smoking—"

"Her mother says she wouldn't *do* that, Gini," Charlotte began. "Marijuana? I keep telling you—it's not possible. She didn't even touch cigarettes. Susan Landis said so."

"Oh, for God's sake." Gini gave a gesture of exasperation. "And you believe that? Her mother would be the last to know. Max, *listen*. The witnesses are definite. She left around midnight in a car with a man. All right, they claim they can't describe the car or the man—but the point is, they say she left with him *willingly*. Thanks to the lies she told, no one realized she was missing. So whoever was driving that car had a ten-hour start. If Mina's going to be found, it won't help to indulge her parents' fantasies about what a sweet, obedient child she was. Fifteen-year-old girls *don't* behave the way their parents hope. If they did, no one would be dead now." Her voice had risen and her tone had sharpened. Rowland's temper snapped.

"For God's sake," he began in a voice cold with anger. "What in hell's the matter with you? Other people have feelings, even if you don't. You don't sound too damn charitable, you know—"

"Charitable? I'm trying to be realistic."

"Then think before you speak. A young girl is dead. I found her body. Max and I have been up all damn night. Charlotte's trying to help. This was someone she and Max knew. . . ."

"I know that. And she's dead. None of us can help Cassandra Morley now. We'd help Mina Landis more effectively if we didn't stand here weeping and wasting time."

"Oh, for Christ's sake." Rowland gave her a look of contempt. "Why in hell don't you just keep quiet and stay out of it? Judging from your behavior yesterday, that's what you usually prefer to do."

There was a silence. Genevieve Hunter took a step back as if he had hit her. Blood rushed into her face. She looked at him, then looked blindly around the room. Then, bending her head and averting her face, she fumbled for a coat thrown over a chair, picked it up, and pushed past Rowland to the door. Lindsay began to move forward with a low exclamation of distress.

"Gini, wait—where are you going?"

"I'm going for a walk. I need some fresh air."

The door slammed behind her. There was another, longer, silence. Rowland watched her walk rapidly across the garden and out of sight. Lindsay, with a glance at Charlotte, gave a sigh.

"Rowland, you shouldn't have said that. Gini hasn't been well. She didn't mean—"

"I don't give a damn. Someone had to say it. Let her go for her walk. If she walks the whole way back to London, I won't grieve. Max—let me call John Lane. Or Chris Huxley. One of them should be available. If he left London now, he'd be here in an hour and a half."

"Use the phone in my study. I'll come with you. I'd better speak to Landis."

Max followed Rowland from the room. In the kitchen, Charlotte and Lindsay exchanged glances. Lindsay crossed the room and sat down next to her.

"Oh, Lindsay." Charlotte gave a sigh. "I wish I'd never invited her. That may not be too charitable either. But I do."

"I don't blame you. Charlotte, don't get upset. She's being impossible, she's been impossible all morning. This is the worst I've ever seen her."

"She was up at six." Charlotte gave her a worried glance. "I heard her moving around. Then I went back to sleep. Lindsay, she claimed she'd slept well, but I'm sure she hadn't. And she'd been trying to call Pascal again."

"She didn't get him?"

"No." Charlotte hesitated, then met Lindsay's eyes. "Is it over, Lindsay? Has she said anything? I think it *is* over. As soon as I saw her yesterday, I knew."

"I'm not sure. It's what I'm beginning to believe. Why would he stay away so long? First he was staying for two weeks, then it was four. Then he was coming back for Christmas. . . . Charlotte, it was going to be their first Christmas together. She bought a tree, she bought all these presents for him—I can't tell you how happy she was. Like the old Gini used to be."

"And then he didn't come?"

"No." Lindsay gave her a troubled look. "I didn't find out until afterward. I assumed he was there as planned. But he wasn't. She spent the whole Christmas holiday alone."

"Alone? But what about her stepmother?"

"She's away. Gini claimed she'd spent the time with some friends

I've never heard of. I know she was lying. She can't stand being pitied, Charlotte."

"I know." Charlotte shook her head sadly. "Well, Rowland didn't pity her anyway. Lindsay—I wish he hadn't said that. I know he was upset, and I know he'd had no sleep, but Rowland can be so harsh."

"It might do her some good. You never know." Lindsay frowned, glanced at Charlotte. "You know what she said, when she mentioned fifteen-year-old girls?"

"How they could behave? Yes. I may not want to remember, but I do."

"Well, there were reasons for that, Charlotte. Very personal reasons. I'm sure she identifies with Mina. Do you know how old she was when she first met Pascal?"

Charlotte did not; and Lindsay then told her. She described their first meeting in Beirut, and their six-week affair. She described the intervention of Gini's father. She was aware that in telling this story she was breaking Gini's confidence, and as she came to the end of it felt ashamed.

Charlotte listened quietly and with mounting dismay. "Fifteen?" she said. "She had an affair with Pascal *then*?"

"She lied to him about her age." Lindsay sighed. "Now do you understand? It isn't just that she loves Pascal now. It isn't just that she's been living with him this past year. It's deeper than that, Charlotte. It goes back such a long way."

"I don't want to hear any more."

Charlotte rose, her kind face clouded with unhappiness. She gave a helpless gesture.

"I *hate* this, Lindsay. Poor Cassandra, and Mina. Gini. Love affairs. Lies. All this anger and misery. Us having dinner last night, and all the time Cassandra was up there, lying in some field. It's so terrible. So ugly. And it makes me so afraid."

She began picking up mugs and plates from the table, as if to restore order to the room would be to restore order to the world.

"I'm going to take the boys out," she said abruptly. "I can't expect them to play upstairs all day. I'll take them around to a friend in the village. Then I'm going to see Susan Landis. She shouldn't be alone."

"Charlotte . . ." Lindsay began on a warning note.

"I know. I know." Charlotte was again close to tears. "But you have a child, Lindsay. You must understand. And I have to do *something*. I can't bear it here, Lindsay. It doesn't feel like home."

CHAPTER 8

For an hour after Charlotte left, Lindsay tried to occupy herself. Max and Rowland remained closeted in Max's study. She could just hear the sound of their voices, the sound of telephones. She felt excluded and useless. Gini had not come back.

She could not settle. She tidied the kitchen, went outside and walked around. She went as far as the gate to the fields, hoping she might see Gini returning, and intercept her, try to talk some sense into her, but there was no sign of her anywhere, and it was bitterly cold.

She returned to the house, picked up Rowland's file, and tried to concentrate on the rest of the press cuttings, but their subject seemed frivolous and remote: not for the first time in her life, Lindsay thought how much she loathed the fashion world. Not her actual work, not her actual job, but its milieu, its atmosphere, its bitchery and waywardness, its reckless obsession with the new. A young girl was dead, she thought, and closed the file impatiently; beside that fact, what did any of this matter? A truly trivial pursuit, she thought, unsmiling, and one on which she had spent seventeen years. The idea unnerved her: it was one thing to pursue this work when it provided a home and income for Tom, but in another year, two years, Tom would be going to university, leaving home. What will I do *then*, Lindsay thought, will I go on, measuring out my life with the collections every year?

She could feel fear, and a sense of hopelessness, just inches away. Such feelings were better not indulged, she knew, and they were selfish, inappropriate now. How death changes things, she thought. She had just seen Charlotte fighting a sudden awareness of the fragility of life, of the bulwarks of family and marriage; now she felt that too. Activity, she told herself—that was the cure. She could be useful, at least, even if excluded. She would make Max and Rowland some sandwiches, walk the dogs. Keep the home fires burning, she said to herself wryly, and walked through to the hall.

"Max . . ." she began, then stopped. Max's study door was ajar. He and Rowland were talking. She could hear their conversation only too well.

"Forget it, Max," Rowland was saying in a cold, angry voice. "I told you. Try John Lane again. Use Huxley."

"Look—I can't damn well get them. No reply from Lane. Huxley's calling back at four. He's in bloody *Norfolk*. That's no use. I need someone here right now."

"Then let's think of someone else. And let's make it a man, for God's sake. I've had enough of female histrionics. First Lindsay, now her."

"Think about this, Rowland. You're overreacting. Why? She's gone for a walk. Maybe that'll give her time to think."

"Does she think? I see no evidence. Neither of them *thinks*, Max. They just lose their tempers, flounce out, turn every issue into some damn personal conflict. They're a pain in the ass."

"All right. All right. I could try Nick, I suppose."

"Call him now. If you can't get him, I'll go up to that damn barn myself. The police won't keep those travelers there forever. We're wasting time."

"You call Landis. Use the other line. Get an update—they could have word on the car she left in. Then call the news desk again. Oh, and tell Landis we need a picture of Mina, a recent one."

There was silence, then sounds of dialing. Miserable and angry, Lindsay turned away.

She returned to the kitchen and began to make sandwiches. Fifteen minutes later she heard the sound of rapid footsteps, then Gini entered, kicking off her muddy boots by the door.

Lindsay stared at her in astonishment. Gini looked transformed. The cold air had brought color to her face, but beyond that it was as if a different woman had just entered. There was new light in her eyes, new determination in her face. She moved in her old way, every line of her body indicating energy and purpose. Lindsay, dumbfounded, stared at her, unable to break her gaze. The transformation was sudden, and for a second it made her unaccountably uneasy: she had forgotten just how lovely a face Gini had; she had forgotten how her vitality could light a room.

"Where's Max?" Gini began without preamble.

"In there. With Rowland." Lindsay hesitated. "Running you down, Gini, if you want to know the truth. Listen—"

"I don't give a damn, okay? I need to talk to him. I've been up to that barn. I went to see the travelers."

"That's where you've been?"

"Of course. What's more, they talked to me. I took them some cigarettes, some scotch. That helped."

"You bribed them?"

"Lindsay, it's *currency*, that's all. Very useful currency. I used it in Sarajevo all the time. Plus grass. The most useful currency of all. Max!"

She broke off. As she called his name, Max and Rowland had entered, still in argument. It was apparent to all four people in the kitchen that the word "bitch," just uttered by Rowland, did not refer to Max's dogs. Both men, seeing Gini, fell silent. She ignored their expressions and the comment just overheard.

"Max," she began. "I've been up to that barn, and I've talked to the travelers. Mina Landis *was* there last night, and she did leave with a man. She left shortly before midnight in a stolen car. A brand-new five series BMW. Silver. The man driving it is called Star—"

"A silver BMW?" Roland glanced at Max. "I know about that car. Go on."

"No one knows where this Star comes from, or where he hangs out. No one knows where they were headed—I gather it could be anywhere. Star gets around. This last week he was in Amsterdam—or so he claimed."

"Amsterdam?" Rowland said sharply.

"Yes. And he came back well supplied. Grass. Amphetamines. Betablockers. And something new called White Doves. They must have been something special, because they were triple the price of all his other stock. And he was very sparing with them. He had only a few."

She stopped, sensing the new and sudden tension in the room.

"Have I said something? Am I missing something here?"

"Never mind that for the moment," Max said quickly. "What else? Did you get a description?"

"Of Star? Sure. Age—early to mid-twenties. Tall—around six feet two or three. Clean shaven. Black hair, worn long, down to his shoulders. Blue-black eyes, strong features—they say exceptionally good-looking, at least the women do. Dresses like one of the travelers. Old tweed coat, black clothes, always wears a red scarf. Could be British or American or European. No one knows."

There was a silence. Rowland, who had been watching Gini closely as she spoke, glanced toward Max; Max nodded.

"In that case," Rowland began, "we have a lead—a strong lead. Max, you call Landis. I'll call the police. Then I'll head off for Cheltenham. A man called Mitchell reported that BMW as stolen this morning. The police were interviewing him. With luck, he'll still be there."

He turned toward Max's study, and then, as if it were an afterthought, glanced back at Gini.

"You want to come?"

"Yes. Why not," Gini replied. In the corner, unnoticed, forgotten, Lindsay sighed and turned away.

Mitchell had been continuing to help the police with their inquiries all day. At least, that was the police term for a sullen silence interspersed with bursts of uninformative vituperation. This shadowboxing had just come to an end. Mitchell had been released for the moment, but he knew what he was facing: a night in a cheap hotel until the credit card company got its act together and provided replacement plastic; weeks of continuing hassle from the cops. This prospect made him very jumpy. There was still some chemical fry-up going on in his brain. He left the station in a truculent state, whereupon these two journalists descended upon him. At that, his mood lifted. The blond-haired woman reporter was attractive; the man with her paid for a whiskey, and it gave Mitchell's battered ego a boost to be approached by the press.

Mitchell downed the first whiskey fast. When the second was in front of him, and just as he was about to reach for it, the male journalist, McGuire, he'd said his name was, placed one large hand on top of the glass.

Mitchell gave them a look, trying to get the measure of them. McGuire was tall and strongly built; he needed a shave. He had the coldest green eyes Mitchell had ever seen, and he looked like trouble. The American woman, Gini Hunter, on the other hand, was a bit thin, but pretty. She had an astonishingly sexy mouth, and sweet, trusting gray eyes. Definitely the more sympathetic of the two, a pushover, Mitchell thought; he decided to ignore the man, address her. "Come on, give me a break," he said. "I feel like hell. I've told you all I know."

The hand on the whiskey glass did not move. Gini sighed.

"Oh, damn. And I was so sure you'd be able to help us. Ah, well. Rowland, let him have that whiskey. He's doing his best."

"You think so? Well, I don't buy his story at all. It's lies from start to finish. Just a variation on the crap he fed the police earlier. Definitely not worth another whiskey. And this is a double too."

"Oh, come on, Rowland." She gave Mitchell a complicit look, as if apologizing for her partner's approach. "You're not lying to us, are you?" she said. "I don't blame you for being cautious. I would be too, in your situation. But after all, even if you were buying, I'm sure it wasn't anything too heinous. Was it grass? Speed, maybe?"

"For Christ's sake, Gini," the man said in a rough tone. "When will you learn? He's a goddamn *pusher*. That's what the police think. They told me just now."

Mitchell stared at him in alarm. This was news to him, unwelcome news. He felt himself starting to sweat. He gazed around the bar, trying to wipe the chemical haze from his brain.

"Listen," he said, turning back to Gini. "Let's get one thing clear. Maybe I *was* buying—I might admit that. But not selling—no way. And I know nothing about that dead girl. I never fucking well laid eyes on her. That's God's own truth, okay?"

The obscenity was a mistake. The second it slipped out, McGuire's face hardened. He turned to the woman beside him. "The hell with this. I've got better things to do."

He rose, and, taking the whiskey with him, began to move away.

"Wait, Rowland." Gini gave Mitchell a sympathetic look. "Don't take any notice of him," she said, lowering her voice slightly. "I believe you. I know you wouldn't lie, not about something as serious as this. That poor girl's dead, after all."

Mitchell, whom nobody had believed all day, felt an overwhelming flood of gratitude. He felt a sudden lurching need to confide in this woman.

"Listen," he began, leaning forward, "I'll tell you this—the dead girl, he'll be behind it, and she's not the first he's harmed. There was a French girl last winter—he slit her face open with a razor. There was another girl after that, a Dutch girl, rich parents, good school. Anneke, her name was. She went with him for a bit. He . . . passed her around, if you get my meaning. She was supposed to be his girlfriend, but that's what he did. Well, I asked him about her, I asked him yesterday, and she's dead. I'm telling you, he's a fucking maniac. Look—look here. . . ."

He leaned forward into the light.

"Look what he did to my nose. Yesterday. He fucking *bit* me! Suddenly, for no reason at all. Now I'll have to get a blood test. I've probably got AIDS. I'm probably dying . . . I don't mind telling you, I can't take much more of this. I've had no sleep. He gave me this stuff yesterday, forty quid it cost, said it was new, a White Dove he called it—well, Christ knows what it was. It really blew my mind. You see my hands? They're still shaking. All the lights in here, they keep moving up and down."

McGuire had returned to the table, and had sat down, but Mitchell, launched now, scarcely noticed. He kept looking at the woman, who was listening intently with an expression of shock and concern.

"Rowland, please let him have that drink," she said in an indignant tone. "You can see he isn't feeling well. I *told* you he'd help us."

With a shrug, the man passed the whiskey across. Gini gave Mitchell some potato chips and a sandwich. Mitchell, who was ravenously hungry, wolfed them down. The two reporters then had a brief conversation in lowered voices. The woman appeared to be proposing something; the man seemed to resist her ideas. Eventually, with a shrug, she turned back to Mitchell.

"Listen," she said. "Rowland thinks I shouldn't tell you this. I think he's wrong. The thing is—the man you're describing, I think I know who he is. I think he could be the very man I'm trying to nail."

"Leave it out, Gini," said her companion, but she ignored him. Mitchell, listening closely now, began to preen.

"Seriously?" he said. "In that case, I certainly could help you. I mean, like, why not, yes? I don't owe him any favors. You get him locked up, we'll all cheer."

Gini looked impressed, then suddenly doubtful. "You're sure?" she said. "I don't want to put you in any danger."

"You think I'm afraid of this guy? No way." Mitchell preened a bit more. "I mean, you protect your sources, right?"

"Of course. Total anonymity." She had produced a tape recorder out of nowhere. Mitchell, now mesmerized by her eyes, barely noticed when she flicked its switch to record.

"Tell me," she said, hanging on Mitchell's every word, "this supplier of yours—he was your supplier, right?—do people call him Star?"

Mitchell nodded. Leaning forward, he started talking, in detail, and very fast.

An hour later, as it grew dark, Gini waited in Max's borrowed Land-Rover. Rowland was inside the police station, talking to the same detec-

tive from that morning. Gini watched shoppers laden with packages going home. She watched Mitchell leave the pub and weave his way along
the road. Fifteen minutes passed, then Rowland returned.

"They still haven't located the BMW," he said, climbing into the driver's
seat. He switched on the ignition and revved the engine. "I passed on what
Mitchell told us—for what it's worth." He hesitated, then glanced toward
her. "You were good with Mitchell, very good indeed."

She shrugged. "We did a good routine. Not original, but tried and
true. And we were lucky with the timing. I just wish he could have told
us more. This Star's real name, for example." She gave a half-smile. "An
address. That might have helped. Something concrete."

"I can follow up on the Dutch girl. Anneke. Her father's a diamond
merchant. I got the details from the police just now." Rowland's tone
was flat. He was staring through the windshield at the parking lot.

"What else?" Gini glanced at him. "There's something more."

"They completed the post mortem. An hour ago. Cassandra's death
was drug-related. They won't know exactly what she took until they
complete the toxicology reports."

"How long?"

"They say three days minimum. It could be much more."

He released the brake and let in the gears without further comment.
They reversed out of the parking lot and into a complicated maze of
streets. The shops were closing, and the traffic was heavy. Neither spoke;
finally, they cleared the outskirts of the city and turned off on quieter
country roads. For a while Rowland concentrated on their route, with
which he was not familiar; these winding roads had to be taken with
some caution in the dark. Before him, the tarmac dipped and curved.
They had entered a section of beech woods; trees arched overhead, creat-
ing a tunnel. Rowland slowed. When they reached a straighter, more
open section, he glanced once more toward Gini, who—unusually for a
woman, he thought—had remained silent all this while.

Her face was obscured from him by darkness. The Land-Rover was
drafty, and it was cold. She was sitting huddled in her coat, her bare
hands clasped in her lap; around her throat was a shamrock-green
woolen scarf. Above it Rowland could just glimpse the pale curve of the
nape of her neck. Her hair, longer at the front and the sides, was
cropped very short at the back. It was an odd, ragged haircut, like that
of a very young boy, and for some reason it touched him. It gave her an
air of vulnerability he had not noticed before; it looked as if she had cut
it herself—and with a pair of blunt scissors too.

Rowland wondered if that was the case, and if so, why. He wondered if she had indeed broken up with the celebrated Pascal Lamartine, as Max had suggested. He wondered if her silence meant that she was retreating again, like the princess in his story, behind that glass wall.

He decided it was time to speak, to make some kind of overture.

"Anyway," he said. "We did get some hard information—or you did. The police ought to be able to locate Mina now. It's a distinctive car. They're distinctive people. A man that good-looking, dressed in that way. A very young girl, with red hair . . . If they're still together, of course."

"Oh, I think they're together," she replied. "I'm sure they are."

"Any particular reason?" He glanced toward her curiously. There was no sign of any glassy resistance, he noted. She had spoken in a normal way, with an odd air of certitude.

"No strong reason. Instinct, mainly. And what Mitchell said too. There seems to be a pattern to this Star's behavior. The French girl last winter; she was replaced by Anneke; now Mina. He takes them over, and he holds on to them. For a while. He likes young girls—and Mina looks much younger than her age apparently. According to Charlotte, she looks about twelve."

"Go on."

"He seems to be drawn to girls from affluent backgrounds. From apparently happy homes. Then there's nationality—the girl he cut with a razor was French; Anneke was Dutch; Mina's American. Maybe he likes uprooting people from their homes and families. Maybe it gives him a sense of power."

"That's interesting. And?"

"And it made me wonder just how far away he'd take Mina. After all, they had that ten-hour start."

"I know. They left at midnight, in a fast car. It's two to three hours at most from here to the Channel ports. They could have taken the tunnel, or a ferry or a hovercraft. Max is checking the schedules. There're certainly early morning departures. They could have been across the Channel, in France, by dawn."

"And then they could go anywhere. Amsterdam, for instance."

"Precisely. Or Belgium or Italy or France or Germany. On the other hand, they might never have left England at all."

Gini shivered. She drew her coat more tightly around her. "He's dangerous," she said. "It makes me very afraid for Mina."

"He's certainly dangerous," Rowland said in a grim way. "And what he peddles is dangerous as well."

There was a silence. Rowland downshifted, then went up through the gears. Eventually he said in an abrupt way:

"Look. I owe you an apology. When Max and I got back to the house this morning . . . What I said about being uncharitable. It was rude. I'm sorry I spoke in that way."

"I'm glad you spoke in that way. You shouldn't apologize. You were right. If you were harsh, it was deserved." She paused. "In fact, if anyone should apologize, it's I. I'm ashamed of the way I spoke. I'm ashamed of the way I've been behaving. That's not relevant to you—but I'd like you to know."

She made this admission with obvious difficulty in a quiet voice. Having made it, she relapsed into silence. Rowland, who was beginning to find her reserve unnerving, steeled himself.

"I also wanted to say," he began stiffly, "that I know your work. I've always admired it, and the pieces you wrote from Sarajevo were very fine."

"Thank you." She made a small flinching movement. "I—I don't talk about Sarajevo. I've made that a rule."

"Can't you take praise?" Rowland replied somewhat sharply.

She turned and gave him one long, steady look, then turned away. "No," she said quietly. "Not on that subject. I would never feel the praise was deserved."

"Why not?"

Rowland glanced at her again; she did not immediately reply. He had wondered—uncharitably, he thought—if she might have been fishing for further compliments. Then he caught the glitter of tears in her eyes and knew the suspicion was a cheap one.

"Tell me," he said more gently. "Explain. I'd like to hear."

"What I wrote wasn't adequate." She kept her face averted, but he could sense a sudden agitation. "What I saw there—I doubt I conveyed a thousandth part of it. Maybe that's always true in that kind of situation. But, foolishly, it wasn't something I'd foreseen. Words—I don't trust words very much anymore. When did words ever change anything?"

"Maybe not often, and maybe not for long." Rowland hesitated. He could sense that she would respect him not at all for a glib answer. "On the other hand," he continued slowly, "what does silence achieve? The right words, the right newspaper stories, can effect change."

"The pen is mightier than the sword?" She gave him a small glance. "My father used to quote that. I believed it once. I don't believe it anymore."

"I met your father once," Rowland said. "In Washington. When I was posted there. I worked there for a couple of years."

That caught her attention. She turned to look at him, her hands tightening in her lap. For an instant, glancing away from the road, he saw anxiety in her face.

"How long ago?"

"A while. About seven years. I spoke to him only briefly. It was in a bar called O'Brien's—a lot of the *Post* journalists used to use it."

"Yes. Well, it would have been a bar. If not that one, some other. He drinks. As you'll certainly know."

Her tone was sharply defensive; Rowland slowed.

"I did know that. Did he always drink?"

"He's an alcoholic. Before he became an alcoholic he was a heavy drinker, the kind of heavy drinker who claims he can kick it anytime. I don't know exactly when he crossed the boundary between the two, if there ever was a boundary."

"Did he drink when you were a child?"

"I don't remember. I've never really lived with my father. I've lived in England with my stepmother since I was five, six years old."

Her manner was growing more incommunicative by the second; Rowland could sense the barriers rise. They drove on for several minutes in silence. After a while he saw her hands move in her lap. She said: "He's in a clinic in Arizona now. In a twelve-step program. He's been there before. It may work this time. Was he very drunk when you met him? I hope—I'd like to think he wasn't. People forget. They have such short memories. Once upon a time—he was a fine journalist, once. . . ."

Rowland could hear, and was touched by, the plea. He had a brief memory of a celebrated man, a Pulitzer Prize–winner who was now a florid, loud-voiced, overweight Harvard boor. He had been protected by a shrinking group of acolytes; shortly before Rowland had left, he had lurched to his feet, then slumped to the floor.

"Not that drunk," he replied mildly. "Nothing that noticeable . . ."

"Was he talking about Vietnam?" She gave him a sharp, pained glance. "Why?"

"It's one of the stages. That's all."

Rowland, who could hear desolation beneath the irony in her tone, decided to lie. "No, no, that subject never came up." He reached a junction, slowed, then turned left. "Besides, if it had, I'd have been interested. I've read your father's Vietnam book. And I admired it. His early work was very powerful."

"Oh, I'm glad you think that." For the first time, Rowland heard her voice lift with an unfeigned delight. Disliking himself as he did it, he slid in the next question fast, and—as he had hoped—caught her off guard.

"—And he must have influenced you, presumably? Was it your father's influence that took you to Bosnia? Or Pascal Lamartine's?"

"I wanted to make my father proud of me. When I was still a child, I
always thought, if I could become—" She stopped, her hands twisting in
her lap, head bowed. "Perhaps, if I'd been a boy. A son. It might have
been different. As it is—it's men who make wars, and men are better at
writing about them. There have been women who've reported wars, of
course, and done it well. But not many." She hesitated, regaining control, and her voice became dry. "So now I'm not sure what to blame for
my failure. My sex or my character. On the whole, I think it's my character, don't you?"

Rowland did not reply. There were several aspects of that answer that
interested him, not least its resolute avoidance of any mention of Pascal
Lamartine. Why did she think of her work in Bosnia as a failure, he
wondered. With each sentence she spoke, he was revising his opinion of
her, first this way, then the other. He liked her final question, and the
way in which it was voiced. It had taken him by surprise.

Slowing the car, he glanced toward her, then, coming to a sudden decision, drew onto the side of the road.

Stopping the car, he turned to look at her.

"May I ask you something? Do you know why you're here?"

"What—here at Max's, this weekend?" She looked at him uncertainly,
moonlight sharpening the planes of her face, then gave a slight smile.

"Yes. I realize, Rowland. I'm not a fool. I'm here because Max and
Charlotte feel sorry for me. Because Lindsay's been nagging them, I
imagine, and telling them I'm on the edge of a nervous breakdown. I'm
here as an act of kindness—which I haven't repaid too well."

"Is Lindsay's diagnosis correct?"

"About the nervous breakdown?" She met his gaze, then frowned and
looked away. "No. I think perhaps I was close. At Christmas. Christmas
wasn't a very good time. I'm better now." She hesitated. "Meantime, of
course, I've been behaving badly, as you pointed out this morning. I've
been irritating people. I've been irritating you—and I do know that. I
can feel myself doing it." She gave another half-smile. "You know what
Lindsay says? She says I give her compassion fatigue."

Rowland, amused, returned her smile. He wondered what it was that
had occurred at Christmas. He had caught the pain in her voice as she
said the word, though she attempted to disguise it.

"She's right, of course. I have been selfish, and self-indulgent. I'm going to reform." She was beginning to speak more quickly now, still
keeping her face averted. "So, I did want to say, I should be working, I

realize that now. When I got back from Bosnia I couldn't write. I turned down several stories."

"Did you? Yes, I think Max might have mentioned that."

"But when we were talking to Mitchell earlier, when I went up to that barn . . . I could feel the story taking hold. I'd forgotten how that could feel, that sense of purpose and drive. But now—I would like to find Star. I'd like to find Mina, above all. So if I could help in any way—if you or Max wanted someone to talk to Cassandra and Mina's friends, per-haps—I could do that. I'd like to do that. It's—I am here, after all. . . ."

Her suggestion faltered away. Rowland realized that as she made it, she lost confidence. She expected him to demur, or refuse. Something, he thought, or someone, had damaged her confidence very badly.

"Why does it interest you so much?" he asked.

"Because of Mina." She let her hair fall forward, obscuring her face. "I used to know a girl like her."

"You did? And was she equally unwise?"

"Possibly. But she was luckier."

She shivered, then seemed to realize for the first time that the car was no longer moving.

"Anyway—we should get back. Why did you stop?"

"Because I wanted to tell you why you were here this weekend. It wasn't an act of charity. You're wrong."

"Am I?" She turned to look at him.

"Yes. You're here because I asked Max to invite you. I persuaded him to set up this weekend. I wanted to meet you. And I wanted you to work for me."

"You did?" She colored. "I don't understand. Why couldn't you ask me in the usual way? Why all this subterfuge? Oh, I see . . ." Under-standing suddenly flooded her face. "You thought I'd refuse? Or you thought Lindsay might have prejudiced me against you."

"That did cross my mind."

"But it's not just that?" She looked at him closely. "It's something more. You wanted to assess me—to see if I came up to scratch—this neurotic woman who was being such a bore."

"I wouldn't put it in those terms. You'd been covering a war—a par-ticularly ugly war. Obviously that had affected you. I'd think less of you had it not affected you. But I had to be sure."

"You don't have to be tactful. I don't particularly like tact. You don't seem to be a very tactful man. I'd rather you were straight with me." She paused. "Oh, I see. I begin to see. There's a connection, isn't there, be-tween your story and this one—a connection you hadn't foreseen? It's something to do with drugs, with White Doves, with Amsterdam. That's why you and Max reacted that way earlier."

She stopped. The excitement and wry amusement that had raced across her face disappeared. "Ah, well," she said in a resigned way, and leaned back in the seat. Rowland watched the moonlight move across her face.

He said: "Would you let me explain?"

"Now? Here?"

"We might as well. Before we go back to Max's. There'll be fewer interruptions, and besides, it won't take long. Are you cold?"

"A little."

"I'll leave the engine running, and the heater." He paused, then cut the lights. He waited until his eyes had accustomed themselves to the darkness. He gestured to a track, silver in the moonlight, which led up across the fields.

"You see that track? It's another route to that barn. But this story, as you've gathered, doesn't begin there. It doesn't begin with Cassandra's dying, or even a man called Star. Until today I'd never heard of Star. It begins . . ."

He paused; he knew that if he were entirely truthful, he would have to say that for him, it had begun years before, in Washington—but such feelings, which he intended not to reveal, were irrelevant now.

"It begins in Amsterdam. Last year . . ."

"Last autumn," Rowland said, "I'd been working on a series of drug investigations. Shortly before I joined the paper, I was given a new lead. I was advised to take a closer look at a relatively small drug-manufacturing outfit based in Amsterdam. Up until then I'd primarily been concerned with heroin and cocaine, the new smuggling routes, the involvement of the Mafia in Russia, and so on. Those investigations are still continuing; this story was one I wanted to pursue. The outfit in Amsterdam had a specialty, you see: designer drugs, the drugs of the future, some people say—although they're already very successful, of course, in this brave new world of ours."

He glanced toward her as he said this, perhaps to see if she had picked up that last reference. Then, frowning, looking out across the fields and in profile to her, he continued.

His manner of speaking, succinct and dry, interested her; once or twice she would have said that he experienced stronger emotions than he betrayed, and she thought she could sense a buried anger, which he kept under tight control.

"The outfit in Amsterdam," he continued, "was the brainchild of two young men. One was an American who'd operated for years on the fringes of the narcotics-smuggling world, a supplier and a user as well. The other, his partner, was a gifted young Dutch chemist. Both men had had some success manufacturing and selling MDMA, otherwise known as Ecstasy, and variations upon it. By last year, however, they had sensed that the market for Ecstasy had peaked—the teenagers in the clubs who were their prime market were getting leery. There had been Ecstasy deaths, there was a growing realization that the drug wasn't the sexual panacea it had seemed, and the market was being flooded with impure imitations, some of which were little more than aspirin, or chalk, and some of which were lethal. Fashion plays a large part in the youth drug market. Teenagers who won't go near a syringe, who wouldn't risk mainlining, are perfectly willing to take pills or capsules—but they're always on the lookout for something new, something that gives a better turn-on, a bigger thrill.

"The Dutch chemist wanted a new product." Rowland glanced toward her. "Commercially, the man is sharp. So he knew precisely what he was looking for. Something that was, if possible, more addictive than Ecstasy, something that gave a rush, and then immense energy, like speed, and above all a product that provided an even stronger sexual thrill than Ecstasy had produced—and without its sexual downside."

"It had a sexual downside?"

"Of course. In some instances, it aroused but it made erection difficult for the male. All hard drugs have an adverse effect sexually, either short- or long-term—and needless to say, the Dutch chemist was well aware of that. He was also aware that if he could formulate a product that boosted sexual performance, it was likely to make him a rich man. A very rich man."

"And he succeeded?" Gini asked.

"Yes. He succeeded—or so he claims. He was helped by the fact that he found an investor, someone prepared to back his experiments. Considering the size of the Dutch operation, that investor was generous. He provided two hundred and fifty thousand Swiss francs of funding, straight out of a numbered account in Zurich. It was handed over to the American partner in the Amsterdam Hilton, in April last year. Six months later, the Dutch chemist had perfected his product, and he was ready to start marketing it. I think you must know what he called it."

"White Dove?"

"White Dove. Indeed."

There was a brief silence. Gini looked at Rowland curiously. "You're very well informed," she began. "Who's been feeding you this information?"

"I have a contact in the U.S. Drug Enforcement Agency. The Dutch chemist and his American partner have been under surveillance for almost a year. Amsterdam is a major conduit in the trafficking routes for heroin and cocaine. It's not unusual for the DEA to have operatives in place there."

"No." Gini looked at him uncertainly, noting his sudden reserve. "But it might be a little unusual for them to feed so much information to a British journalist."

"I told you—I worked in Washington for several years." He was now curt. "I have contacts there that go back a long way." He paused. "I'll come back to the question of the funding, and the identity of the investor, in a moment, if I may. Meanwhile, here's what happened last autumn. The chemist had his new product—for which his hopes were high. The next move was to start feeding it out to clients—and that was the American's task. He began in the usual way: friends in the rock music business were supplied. He passed some out to contacts in gay clubs. He gave some to photographers and models he knew. Word spread fast. Musicians discovered they could record all day, all night, and all the next day as well. Models discovered it killed their appetites stone dead. The word was, with White Doves you felt confident, happy, and inspired. You didn't require sleep. Or food. The appetite for sex, needless to say, was not impaired."

"It delivered?"

"So it was claimed. According to the American, it induced a craving, and when that craving was indulged—well, the earth moved. Six, seven, eight times a night—according to him. He's prone to exaggeration, of course. On the other hand, they tripled their prices in two months, and the clients still kept beating a path to their door. So I imagine there was some truth in his claims."

Rowland, whose tone had been dry, gave a shrug. Gini sighed.

"That's predictable. A drug that makes people thin, happy, and sexually successful? That just about covers every twentieth-century need."

"We live in a secular world." Rowland, who had never felt greatly in tune with that world, and who sensed from her tone that she was not either, turned back to look at her.

"You understand, don't you, the kind of money that can be involved? Eventually, of course, White Doves will be copied. Other manufacturing outfits will obtain the drug, break it down, replicate it. But that takes time. What the Dutchman and the American want to do now is step up production—fast. They intend—again according to the American—to make their killing inside two years. He's estimating they'll clear a cool eight to ten million, at which point he's planning to retire. He may do just that. Or the DEA, or the Dutch police, or his own heroin habit may slow him down. Meantime—if White Doves actually cause killings of a rather different kind, neither he nor his Dutch partner will lose too much sleep. As far as they're concerned, an element of risk can enhance their product. They're not worried about the Cassandra Morleys of this world."

There was a silence. As he had spoken, Gini had watched his anger grow, although it was perceptible only in his eyes.

"We can't know what caused Cassandra's death until they complete those toxicology reports," she said quietly. "All right, she was seen with Star last night, and he was in possession of White Doves. That may be suggestive, but it's not proof. It's circumstantial at best. Meantime, Mitchell definitely *did* take one. And he lived to tell the tale."

"I agree. And Mitchell is—what? Five feet ten? And heavily built. I'd say he weighed at least fifteen stone, two hundred pounds. Whereas Cassandra Morley was slender, less than half his size. It could simply be a question of body size and dosage. There could be other factors—food, water intake, alcohol intake." He paused. "I don't want to jump to any conclusions either. But I think you can see why this story interests me—why I wanted to pursue it before any of this weekend's events happened."

"Yes, I can."

"Gini—" He turned to look at her. "The right journalism can help to change things. Maybe it's only a small alteration—to prevent one more teenager like Cassandra from dying, to close down one outlet for drugs while millions of others survive, to prevent a man like Star from peddling his products, even if it's only for a while. But it is still change, and change for the better. Whatever you felt in Bosnia, however much your faith in your work was impaired—you must see that, surely?"

Had she not done so, Gini thought, she would have been swayed by him now. For the first time, he allowed his feelings to manifest themselves. Just for an instant, a certain impetuosity and an idealism in his manner reminded her of Pascal.

"I do see that," she replied quietly.

"In that case—" He paused, as if coming to some sudden decision. "In that case, work with me on it, as I wanted you to do."

His directness surprised her, as did the swiftness with which the decision was made.

"You're sure?" She looked at him closely. "Last night, this morning—would you have offered me this story then?"

"No."

"But you do now?"

"Yes, I do."

"Then I accept. I want to work on this. I want to work on it now."

Her reply pleased him, she thought. He made no comment, however, but turned away from her and restarted the car.

"In that case," he said, "there's some other things you should know."

"Such as who provided that funding? Who came up with a quarter of a million Swiss francs from a numbered Zurich account?"

"Sure." He smiled and pulled out onto the road.

"Who was it? Someone with known drug connections?"

"No. The reverse. But it is someone you'll have heard of. Someone whose involvement puzzles me a good deal."

"Who was it?"

"A Frenchman." Rowland steered them fast around a sharp bend. "A very rich, and a very influential Frenchman. His name's Jean Lazare."

He gave her the rest of the information as they drove back, speaking as succinctly as he had done before. Gini, listening with close attention, admired his ability to impart all the necessary facts, in the correct order, and his scrupulous avoidance of bias. He spoke what he incontrovertibly knew, and nothing more. Used to working in a milieu in which her first task was almost always to try to sift fact from the accretions of supposition and surmise, quarrying for some truth that was often deeply buried beneath layers of misquotations, unsubstantiated allegations, and willful misrepresentation, she was grateful for this. McGuire was unexpectedly punctilious, and punctiliousness was not a quality she despised.

He finished giving her the requisite information as they reached Max's drive. He steered the Land-Rover around to the back and pulled into the stable yard.

"Before we go in"—Gini turned to him—"I want to be sure I have this correct. It was Lazare's chief aide who delivered that money?"

"Yes. His name is Christian Bertrand. Sorbonne. Harvard Business School. A high-flyer. He's worked for Cazarès and Lazare for several years."

"And he returned to Amsterdam this week to collect a supply of White Doves? Six White Doves? Why so few?"

"I don't know," Rowland said. "Of course, as Lindsay never ceases to remind me, it's the Paris collections next week. The Cazarès show is on Wednesday. Perhaps those White Doves were what Lazare needed to get himself through the collection and its aftermath. That's certainly what the American is claiming. . . . On the other hand, it seems out of character. Lazare isn't a weak man. He's supposed to have this iron will, this iron control."

"You mean you thought the drugs might be destined for someone else?"

"That crossed my mind. Maria Cazarès seems the likelier candidate. There are rumors about her volatility, her health. She's the linchpin of a billion-franc industry, of a company that Lazare was said to be trying to sell off last year. If he were still interested in selling, Cazarès herself has to function, and has to be seen to function. It's of key importance that she actually appears, in apparent health, at the end of her show. If she didn't do so, if the current rumors about her health, her design capabilities, proliferated, what would that do to the price of that company? It would fall. Now, if a small supply of White Doves not only ensured that she appeared, but ensured that she did so radiant with confidence—you do see?"

"Yes. I do."

"Anyway . . ." Rowland reached for the handle of his door. "That's all speculation at this stage. We should concentrate first on this lead. Locate Mina. Locate Star. Talk to Mina and Cassandra's friends. Talk to that Dutch girl Anneke's family—"

"And talk to your DEA contact," Gini said quickly. "If I'm to go to Amsterdam, I should certainly talk to him."

She broke off, sensing Rowland's sudden unease. He left his door unopened; there was a brief silence; wind buffeted the car.

"No," he said eventually. "I'm afraid that's not possible. That's—out of bounds."

Gini stared at him in astonishment. "Out of bounds? Why? Rowland, all the information you've been getting has come from that one source. I *have* to talk to him. There have been developments—he might know something about Star."

"I'm sorry. No. Any contact made with the DEA is made through me. Those are their terms, not mine, and I have to accept that. I'm a passenger here. They have my assurance, my word, that my investigations will do nothing to prejudice theirs."

"But I *wouldn't* prejudice them. I've been in this kind of situation before. I understand the drill, Rowland—"

"No."

"That's it? Just no? I have to accept that?"

"If you want to work with me—yes, you do."

His tone was courteous and unyielding. Gini, who had been about to argue further, decided to wait; she would return to the attack at a more propitious time. She glanced once more at Rowland; his green and steady gaze was disconcerting, she found. She looked away, across the cobbled yard. From one of the barn roofs an owl took flight. She watched the white beat of its wings, then climbed down from the car.

Without speaking, Rowland led the way across the yard and through the gardens. When they came to a flight of steps, he politely held out his hand and guided her up them. Although it was so cold, his hand felt warm to the touch. Gini glanced at him fleetingly, wondering if his silence indicated some displeasure, but his face gave no indication of any emotion at all.

"Watch your step, it's icy here," he said as she stumbled at the top of the stairs.

There was ice on the flagstones of the terrace also. Gini made her way across them carefully, then paused for a moment, looking up at the night sky, bright with stars.

"You never see stars in London anymore," she said. "The lights of the city block them out. Aren't they magnificent? I used to be able to recognize some of the constellations, but now I've forgotten them. Orion . . ."

"Those stars there."

"And the Pole Star? The Plow?" She tilted her head backward.

Rowland, who had not been looking at the sky, now glanced upward again.

He pointed out each sequence of patterns in turn. There was the Plow, there the Great and Little Bear, there Cassiopeia, and there the Pole Star, so useful in navigation. Looking up at this last star, Gini shivered, and Rowland, with an air of courteous concern, took her arm and guided her across the slippery flagstones, to the door.

Lindsay was sitting in the kitchen when she heard the spurt of gravel as the Land-Rover turned into Max's drive.

She had been reading a story to Colin and Danny. In pajamas and robes, they were now curled slumberously on either side of her, fighting sleep. Max was in his study telephoning; Charlotte was upstairs supervising Alex and Ben's bath. Lindsay closed the book. It was eight o'clock. Rowland and Gini had been gone several hours.

"Bed, you two," she said. "You're both half asleep. No, no arguments. Off you go."

Danny gave her a wet smack of a kiss; he and Colin left obediently, hand in hand. Lindsay rose and paced the room. Ten minutes passed. What on earth were Gini and Rowland doing? Were they sitting talking in the dark?

Max had said, over tea, his manner very casual, that he was just wondering if Lindsay might be persuaded to give Rowland a lift back to London the next day. He himself, he said, had decided to return a little later than usual, on Monday morning, by train. If Gini was going to work on the Cassandra Morley story, she would want to stay on a day or two, to interview Cassandra's and Mina's friends. Max then began to discuss train timetables. Lindsay, thinking his manner was shifty and evasive, quickly realized the reason: Max thought this proposal would not please Rowland McGuire.

"Why can't he take the train with you?" she asked.

"He just can't, that's all. I—he doesn't like trains."

"Why on earth not?"

"He's—funny about them," Max said, polishing his eyeglasses.

"He's funny about a lot of things, if you ask me."

"Come on, Lindsay. You can stand his company for a couple of hours, surely?"

"Oh, very well," Lindsay said. "I've got something to tell him anyway."

"You have?" Max looked interested.

"Yes. He gave me that file to look at, you remember? The one on Lazare? I've finished going through it, and I noticed something strange. I—"

"Damn. The phone's ringing. It'll be the news desk. Or Landis. Tell me later, Lindsay."

Max disappeared. He had reappeared, several times, while Lindsay was reading to his sons, but had shown no inclination to question her further. Lindsay, nursing her discovery, was disappointed. Max was not interested in anything she had to say, she thought glumly. Rowland probably would not be interested either. She beat a tattoo on the kitchen table. Twenty minutes after hearing the Land-Rover, she heard footsteps on the terrace at last.

Rowland and Gini entered on a blast of cold night air. Lindsay looked at them circumspectly. Rowland was helping Gini off with her coat; he made some remark Lindsay could not catch, and Gini smiled.

"Did you see Mitchell?" Lindsay began, determined not to be invisible.

"What?" Rowland was now removing his own overcoat. "Oh, yes, we did. And very useful it proved. Where's Max?"

"So what do you think, Rowland?" Gini was saying. "One day here? One day should do it. Then I could go on to Amsterdam."

"One day should certainly be enough. I doubt the school friends will have much to contribute—but they might. They could have heard about Star—it's possible that either Cassandra or Mina had met him before."

He stopped. Max had just entered the room, waving a piece of paper. Insofar as Max could ever look excited, he looked excited now.

"Breakthrough," he said. "They've found the car. The police just called."

"The BMW? Where?"

"Somewhere interesting." Max's glance intersected with Rowland's. "In Paris, would you believe?"

"Paris? They're sure?"

"It's confirmed. It had been abandoned in the Pantin district, close to the *periphérique*. A humble *policier* found it around three hours ago."

Max broke off; a telephone had begun ringing. Hearing Charlotte answer it upstairs, he turned back to Rowland.

"Yes, Paris," he continued. "And given your previous information, Rowland, that's an interesting choice of destination, wouldn't you say?"

Lindsay, resigned to invisibility again, had been watching Rowland. He was slow to reply. The reason, she realized, was that his attention was on Gini. She was standing very still, her hands frozen in the act of removing her green scarf. She was listening to the murmur of Charlotte's voice in the distance; her eyes were unnaturally bright, her face was tense and pale. She began to move as she heard Charlotte's footsteps above. She was already running toward Max's office as Charlotte shouted down the stairs: "Gini," she called. "Quickly—he's been trying to get through for hours. The line's awful, but you can just hear him. Gini, quickly—it's Pascal."

Part Two

EUROPE

CHAPTER 9

The church bells woke Mina. They made their way into the dream she was having. At first, still inside the dream, she thought they were cowbells, and she was high in the mountains somewhere. Then they became sleigh bells, and she was flying across the snow under a fur rug, with Star by her side. Then the dream began to slip away, and she understood they were church bells, somewhere outside this Paris room. She stirred, opened her eyes, and began to remember. She remembered the room, the mattress on which she was lying, and the clean patchwork quilt that covered her, a quilt covered with navy-blue stars and scarlet hexagons.

She sat up, rubbed her eyes, then smiled: Star had said he was going out, that was it, and she should rest: well, now he had returned.

He was sitting opposite her on a small wooden chair, and he was watching her wake.

"What time is it, Star?"

"Time for the second Mass. Eight o'clock."

"Mass? You mean it's *Sunday*?"

"It's Sunday. You were exhausted. It was a long drive. We had to find this place. You've been sleeping for hours and hours. You want some breakfast? There's a café I know near here."

"I am hungry. Maybe the pink jewel made me extra sleepy. I would like breakfast."

"There's a bathroom on the landing. You can use that. Look—I

149

bought you a present while I was out. It's a scarf. A blue scarf. It matches your eyes."

He magicked the scarf out of his pocket; he magicked it into his hand. Mina saw that it was silk, and a most beautiful color, the color of a kingfisher's wing. She gave a small cry of delight. Star rose and put it gently in her hand.

"Cover your hair with it," he said. "Just for now. We have to be careful, Mina. Even here."

Mina looked at him hesitantly.

"I will be able to call them soon, won't I, Star? I don't want them to worry. My mother—Star, if it's Sunday now—she'll just be frantic. I have to tell her I'm safe. It's all right—I won't say where we are. . . ."

"Sure you can call them." He smiled, and the room lit with his smile. "If you hadn't been sleeping—you can call them from the café. It has a phone booth. Come on, little Mina." He took her hands in his. "This is an adventure, remember? Our adventure. Later this morning—" He broke off, and Mina saw his face change.

"Later this morning, what?" she said, watching his eyes alter and darken.

"Later this morning I have an appointment, that's all. I have to go out to the airport. Charles de Gaulle. While we're there—you can decide. There's hundreds of flights to London. One every hour—more. If you want, I'll put you straight on a plane. You can be back home this afternoon."

"I could?" Mina looked at him uncertainly. "Star, I don't have any money for airfare. I don't have any money at all. I gave all the money I had to Cassandra."

"No problem." He gave another of his conjuror's movements, and there was money, fistfuls of it, in his hands.

"Francs, dollars, pounds—more than enough for a flight to England. Just say the word, Mina, and we can both leave. We can go anyplace in the world."

"I couldn't let you pay my fare." Mina frowned. "I'd have to pay you back, Star."

"Let's not fight about it. Who knows? Maybe we'll get out to the airport and you won't want to go. Hurry up—it's a fine day. We can sit in the café and watch the sun shine on Paris. Paris is one of the four most beautiful cities in the world."

He made this pronouncement very seriously. Mina was impressed.

"Which are the other three?" she asked.

"Venice, New Orleans, and Hong Kong. One day I'll take you to them. Maybe."

"You know all those places?" Mina said, but he turned away as if suddenly bored.

"Sure," he replied. "I've been around."

Mina could tell she was dismissed. She was learning about Star, and one thing she'd learned was that his moods changed very suddenly. One moment he gave her this fierce attention, so it felt as if his blue-black eyes read her mind like a printout; the next moment, something happened: he blanked off, and his face closed.

She went out onto the landing, found the bathroom, washed, and combed her hair. It was a primitive bathroom, but then, this house was old. They were right at the top of it, on the attic floor, and the house itself was at the summit of a hill. Opening the window, she could see a dazzling roofscape, domes and slates and chimneys and spires. Star said this was a friend's pad; he said they were in the student quarter; he said they were on the Left Bank, which was the best part of Paris, and they were near the Sorbonne.

Mina took her new blue scarf, which was so fine, like a scrap of summer sky, and tied it carefully over her red hair. She fixed it the way the traveler women fixed theirs, gypsy fashion, so it fastened at the back and came low on her forehead, just above her brows. It looked pretty, and she smiled at her reflection. She had washed off that silly hawk transfer, but she'd left the last of the gold paint on her eyelids, and she was still wearing Cassandra's old black clothes. A skirt that was long and loose, halfway down her calves; an Indian shirt Cassandra bought in a thrift shop; a heavy jacket, also black, with black embroidery, that Cassandra's mother had brought back from somewhere abroad. She looked so different now, so much older—and she felt older, too, as if in one day and two nights she'd come of age and traveled around the world.

She could not wait to tell Cassandra what had happened, where she had been. She could imagine the scene at school; she could hear her own voice: *Yes, we left at midnight, we drove all through the night. When we came to Paris, it still wasn't dawn. We stayed at a friend's place. Star has friends everywhere, he told me. He's always traveling, Cass. I could have stayed there with him. He asked me to stay. He said—if we wanted, we could go right around the world.* . . . She checked herself. Star was calling to her. She thought of her mother then, and her father, and the doubts resurfaced. She felt jittery, a little anxious and afraid.

Star took her to the café he knew, and they sat in the window. She began to feel calmer as she watched Paris go past.

"You've never been here, then?" Star said, watching her. She was eating chocolate croissants and drinking café au lait. He reached across and flicked a tiny piece of pastry that was stuck to her chin.

"No. Never. I always wanted to come. We've been all over—but always these really dull places. Air-base towns. Germany was worst. I hated Germany. My mother did too. We were stuck right out in the middle of nowhere, this horrible little place, all closed in with pine forests. Daddy was off working all the time. Or playing golf. He's a golf fanatic. He has an eight handicap, so I guess he's good at it, but Mommy and I nearly went crazy. We had cabin fever. Mommy says that's what it's called—"

She stopped. She must remember not to gabble and gush, she told herself. She could see Star didn't like it, because it made his face close. Maybe she was boring him. He looked away; he began to fidget and tapped his fingers on the table, and she could tell—something was getting to him, because normally Star was so still.

"I'll be back in a moment," he said in an abrupt way, and rose. Mina watched him thread his way past the tables and disappear in the direction of the men's room. She sat there trying to finish the croissant, trying to watch Paris, but the delight had gone from the streets outside and the croissant suddenly tasted stale.

He was away a long time, ten minutes or more. When he came back though, she could tell at once that his good mood was restored. He sat down opposite her, fastening his shirt cuffs. His hands smelled of soap. He smiled at her with the special smile that made her feel they both had all the time in the world.

"In Germany . . ." He leaned forward and touched her hand. "Was that when the quarrels started? You remember you told me in the car?"

"Maybe." Mina frowned. "I was only thirteen when we left there. We were there three whole years. It could have been earlier, and I didn't notice, or I pretended it wasn't happening. We were in Hawaii before Germany, and that was better. I'm not sure. I guess—they must have been happy sometime. When I was small. They really loved each other when they got married. Mommy told me. She said Daddy just swept her right off her feet, and—"

She stopped, fighting sudden tears.

Star watched her with that still, intent gaze he had. Then he took her hand in his. He said: "Mina. Love comes and goes. You have to learn that."

"It doesn't stay?" She looked away. "In books it does. In movies."

"It might stay." He lit a cigarette, drew on it, and exhaled. Mina watched him through the smoke's blue coils.

"Everyone wants it to stay, for sure. That makes people strive too hard. They get anxious and stressed out. What you should do is just wait. Let it come. Hope it lasts. Just a little bit of love is worth having. There's a whole lot of hate in this world."

Mina continued to watch him closely. She thought his answer sounded wise, though it was not quite the answer she had been hoping for.

"Star," she asked, "if it happens, when it happens—how can you know?"

In answer, he gripped her wrist hard, so hard it hurt her, and jerked her forward in her chair so she was leaning right across the table, and he was leaning right across the table, and his beautiful face was just inches from her own. "Look me in the eyes," he said. "Go on. Look. Look properly, Mina. Let yourself see . . ."

Mina looked into his eyes the way he told her. The iris was very dark, almost black, and flecked with blue. She could see herself in his eyes, a tiny Mina, and then she lost herself and saw only his gaze, so the room vanished and it was like looking down into the ocean. She watched waves move; she watched this slow, hypnotic, deepening sea, and she trembled a little, then sighed.

Star's grip became gentle. He stroked her hand. He said: "Now you know me. And I know you. I need you so bad, Mina. The first second I saw you, I knew."

Mina gave a gasp. Star released her hand. He rose.

"Come on," he said as if this were a normal moment, as if he had just said nothing special. "Come on. We have to get out to the airport. It's time to go."

Mina pushed back her chair and reached for her jacket, a series of small, flurried movements. Star was already moving toward the door, and she ran after him, and caught his hand.

"Star," she began. "My phone call. You said I could call my parents from here."

"The phone's out of order. I checked just now." He took her arm, drew her out into the street, and hailed a taxi. "Come on. You can call from the airport. There's a hundred phones there."

But when they reached the airport, he seemed to have forgotten this promise too. He walked along the concourse, up escalators and down them, his pace very fast. Mina had to run to keep up with him. The place was crowded, and she was jostled on all sides. She could hear a confusing tumult of foreign voices, foreign tongues, loudspeaker announcements.

She paused just for a second in front of one of the flight boards and watched the numbers flicker back and forth. There were flights to England, just the way he said. The ten o'clock flight had left, the eleven o'clock was being called. There was another at midday.

"Come on. It's this way." Star came back for her and caught her arm again, and led her on. He was walking faster and faster, and when Mina looked up at him, she could see that he seemed angry, terribly angry for no reason at all.

"What did I do? Star—" She plucked at his arm. "What did I say?"

He stopped and stared at her blankly.

"What? Nothing. I'm in a hurry, that's all. There's a flight coming in. I don't want to miss it. Through here . . . Wait. Hold my coat. That's better. Now, don't say anything, and stay by my side."

He bundled the old tweed overcoat into her arms. Without the overcoat, she realized, he looked quite different, nothing like a traveler at all. He must have showered and changed earlier, she realized, and—how odd that she hadn't noticed, but she always looked at his face not his clothes—he now looked different, like a student perhaps, one of the Sorbonne students, in a black sweatshirt, a black jacket, and clean black jeans.

"Your scarf," she said. "Star, you're not wearing your red scarf. . . ."

"Shut up," he said. "I told you. Don't talk. Through here."

He led her across to a door at the side of the concourse, and then into a corridor. Mina ran along beside him, clutching his coat. Suddenly her mind was filled with questions. What had happened to the lovely silver car? She remembered his parking it in a side street somewhere—but where was it now? Where had Star been all that time she'd been sleeping—she must have slept, she realized, for at least sixteen hours. And where was his little dog, who had sat in Mina's lap all the way on that long trip? Dancer, who had been hidden under a blanket with Mina when they passed through customs, and who had been there—Mina was sure she had been there—when Mina fell asleep in that attic room.

"Where's Dancer?" she burst out, still running to keep up with him. "Star, what's happened to Dancer? You said she went everywhere with you."

"She's not with me now." He stopped so suddenly that Mina cannoned against him. There was now no doubting the anger; his face was black with it, and Mina recoiled.

"She's at a friend's. You ask one more question, and—"

She saw him fight to regain self-control.

"And I'll leave you here," he finished. "I'll just walk away and leave you. I hate questions. I hate women who ask questions. I thought you understood that."

"I do. Star . . ."

"Then do what I tell you. When I tell you. There's a reason. You understand? Now. Stand there."

Mina did as she was bid. The corridor they were in now was quieter, at the side of the main terminal, she thought. Star moved away from her and waited. After a few minutes a man appeared, an airport employee, a janitor perhaps, wearing a uniform. He seemed to know Star, and Star seemed to know him. They spoke briefly in lowered voices. The man looked over his shoulder. Star made one of his conjuring movements. Mina wasn't certain, but she thought some money changed hands.

The man produced a key and opened a door, an unmarked door. Star beckoned to her, and the man ushered them through. The man himself did not follow them. He closed the door behind them. Mina looked around her. They were standing in a quiet airport lounge, carefully furnished in muted shades. There were groups of armchairs, a thick carpet, tables stacked with the latest magazines.

"Where are we?" she whispered.

"It's a VIP lounge," he said in a low voice. "You know what that is? When important people are flying out, or in, they come through here. No press allowed."

"Are we allowed?"

"No. But we're not doing any harm. Just quietly watching, waiting. That's all."

He drew her to one side, behind a tall potted palm. Mina felt a thrill of excitement, an illicit tingling of the nerves. There were other people waiting, she saw, quite a few of them, and beyond, at some distance, there was a group of airport personnel. No one seemed to have noticed them. The airport people were fussing over papers and forms, and telephoning; the others, several men, a couple of women, all elegantly dressed, were facing the window beyond. Mina craned her neck: the window was glass, floor to ceiling. It overlooked a runway. She could just see an airplane taxiing in, a small private plane, she thought, with a logo she did not recognize on its side. Star saw it too, and as soon as he saw it, Mina felt his body go rigid.

"Don't move," he said out of the corner of his mouth. "Watch. Don't move."

So Mina watched. She felt a sense of gathering disappointment. After this mysterious buildup, very little occurred. The plane outside taxied to a halt. She could just see its forward door being opened, then the men and women waiting moved toward the window, obscuring her view. She caught scraps and murmurs of reaction from them, but they were all speaking French, and Mina's French was poor.

She could sense a certain tension, and an excitement, in the watching group, as if they were expecting the unpredictable, but nothing special happened at all. Whoever was on the plane must have descended from it and made their way up to this lounge from an entrance below, because suddenly the group by the windows began a flurry of new movement toward the far entrance doors.

One man, drawing aside, began speaking rapidly into a mobile telephone. Another opened a black attaché case and quickly extracted some files. They assembled themselves on either side of the entrance doors in a formal greeting party. An immaculately coiffed older woman in an exquisite suit stood to the immediate right of the doors. Next to her, one step back, stood the man Mina thought seemed the most senior. He was wearing a black overcoat, tortoiseshell-framed tinted eyeglasses, and a dark suit with the finest, narrowest pinstripes. The rest of the group, deferring to these two, stood a little behind them and to the side.

Then the doors beyond opened, and the arrival began. Mina had a clear view now: she could see that the awaited party consisted of a man and a woman. The man was about fifty, she thought, and even at this distance he radiated pace and power. His hair gleamed, black as a bird's wing. She could see that he was relatively short, formally dressed. His skin was tanned, and Mina thought that he might be Italian, or Spanish, and that he moved like a king.

He began speaking as he came through the doors, and it was almost funny the way the others all scurried to attention and scraped and bowed. Then the man made an imperious gesture of the hand, and the clamor of voices ceased, and the scurrying ceased, and the man stepped aside to let the woman with him go past.

She was tiny, Mina saw, very slender and very little taller than Mina herself, and she moved with grace, like a dancer. Her hair, too, was jet black, and almost covered with an expensive silk scarf. She was wearing dark glasses so large, Mina could scarcely see her face. She could just glimpse her lips, which were pale, without makeup. She was wearing a fur coat, a most beautiful dark fur coat that reached to midcalf. Her hands were gloved. Gold gleamed at her wrists, and Mina watched it glitter as she began greeting people. She touched someone here, reached up to kiss someone there, and Mina could see that this procedure both surprised and pleased them, because as the woman and her male companion passed down the line, those behind her glanced at one another, raised their eyebrows, and nodded to each other, as if in congratulation. She could feel it suddenly, an elation as sharp as scent in the air. Then she could smell an actual perfume, a burst of spring flowers, then the woman and her solicitous guardian-companion were moving forward, moving forward, with the others closing ranks behind them. There were little eruptions of words and laughter, so the air in the room felt buoyant, then a door swung open and they were gone.

The silence afterward was as tense as a wire; Star never once moved. He had not taken his eyes off the woman and the man from the second they entered until the second they were gone. He remained, statue-still, staring after them. His face was set, expressionless, and pale.

Mina did not dare to speak. She could see that he might still be angry, or he might be feeling pain, but either way there was something dreadfully wrong.

After a long while Mina plucked at his sleeve again. "Star," she whispered. "Is that why we came here? To see them?"

"What?" He turned to look at her, then seemed to recollect who she was and where they were.

"Yes," he said. "That's why we're here. That's who I came to see. I have plans for them—that woman and that man."

"Plans?" Mina looked at him hesitantly. The glitter in his eyes frightened her. "What kind of plans? I don't understand."

"You will. Three days from now. On Wednesday. You know how long I've waited for that day to come around? Twenty-five *years*, that's how long."

"But why—who are they, Star?"

"They're my enemies."

"What, that man and that woman?" Mina backed away a little because his eyes were now making her very scared. "Why, Star, why? Do you know them? Who *are* they?"

Star did not answer the first two of those questions for several days. He answered the third there and then.

"They're famous," he said. "Very famous. *World* famous." To Mina's horror, his face suddenly convulsed; she thought for one horrible moment that he was about to hit her.

"The woman is Maria Cazarès," he said. "And the man with her is known as Jean Lazare."

Maria Cazarès cared about cars. In Paris, Lazare kept four on permanent call. Telephoning from the villa outside Fez that morning, he had instructed them to send the car he had purchased for Maria's birthday two years before. It had been hand-built for a member of the Krupp family in 1937. They possessed later Rolls-Royces, but Maria found their detailing less stringent—she preferred a prewar Rolls.

To travel in the back of this vehicle was to be cocooned from the world. Glass panels protected them from their driver; tinted glass screened them from the gaze of passersby. Lazare leaned back against the thick leather seats, upholstered in the finest hand-stitched Connolly hide. The only sound was the faint and reassuring whisper of the car's wheels. The air smelled of Maria's scent, of jonquils and narcissus, of the most delicate spring flowers. It was the first, and still the most celebrated of the Cazarès perfumes, L'Aurore. Lazare closed his eyes briefly. He had not slept the previous night. He was no longer young; recently, he had been discovering just what it did to a man to sleep only fitfully, and to wake always tired.

He felt Maria stir beside him and opened his eyes. She was pressing her face to the window glass, staring out at the passing streets. Her small, gloved hands clenched and unclenched in her lap. She suddenly swung around.

"Jean, tell him to turn off. I want to see Mathilde. It's days since I saw her. I want to see her now."

"Darling, no." Lazare reached across and took her hand. "You called her four times from Morocco. It's Sunday. It's still early. You'll wear her out, darling. You forget—she's not young anymore."

"I miss her. I wish she lived with us still. You shouldn't have sent her away, Jean."

"Darling, I didn't." He sighed. "She *retired*. I bought her that nice apartment, she has her own maid. . . ."

"She was *my* maid. She was like a mother to me. She understands me. And now you've banished her."

"Banished? Darling, you know that's foolish." Lazare, who had indeed never liked Mathilde Duval, a severe, hard-faced peasant woman from Provence, controlled his temper. Mathilde had looked after Maria for more than twenty years; she was possessive, secretive, a man-hater who worshiped at Maria's shrine—but he had not banished her. Encouraged her retirement at most—but then, Mathilde had been worn out by the stress of the last five years.

"Listen," he went on. "You can see her tomorrow, darling. When you feel stronger. When you've had time to rest." He paused, trying to think of some means of distraction. "Forget Mathilde for the moment, darling—why don't you show me the things you bought?"

To his relief, the distraction worked—Maria's attention span was now short. At once, and with an eager smile, she opened the leather satchel she had brought back from Morocco, which one of the aides, as instructed, had placed beside her in the car. One by one she began to examine the small, pretty items it contained. She knew what they were, for she had purchased them herself, but even so she held up each object with a gasp of surprise and delight, as if this satchel were a party grab bag and she were a child.

The visit to the Morocco house had been Maria's sudden whim. It came to her at nine at night the previous Friday; they left two hours later by private jet. But Maria had been restless and tearful the entire way. They no sooner arrived in Fez than she wanted to return.

Lazare, anticipating this, had made arrangements. The Jeep was prepared and waiting. After a little food, which Maria would not touch, they were driven out into the desert. There they would watch as the mountains, invisible in the darkness when they set out, emerged in that exquisite light, rose and azure, that composed a desert dawn. This sight, which had delighted her in the past, diverted her only briefly. Lazare took her hand.

"Darling, look," he said. "You see that peak there? You see the snow, Maria? Look how the light makes it gold."

"It's cold, Jean. I want to go home."

"Darling, just a few minutes more. Stand close to me. Wrap your fur tighter. I'll put my arm around you—there. Think, darling, don't you remember the collection in 'eighty-five? We came here then, Maria. We stood in the very place we're standing now. You were so worried about that collection—no inspiration, no ideas, you said—not one! Then we watched the light—and it came to you. Those colors. You remember? We drove straight home, and you began drawing, pages and pages of drawings, the most wonderful drawings. So light, so delicate—and the colors, Maria, you must remember the colors. That year you made clothes for goddesses. No one who saw them will ever forget them. People talk about them still."

"That was then. This is now. I was happy then. I'm not happy now."

"Darling, you *are*. We both are." He embraced her, and she trembled.

"Jean, I need my present. Can I have my present now? You promised me. You said in the morning. It's morning now."

"Very well," he had replied.

Then they drove back to the villa, very fast. He sent the servants away. He took her into her favorite place, a secluded inner courtyard. In its enclosure there was a formal Moorish garden with jasmine plants and orange trees. There was a small fountain, its water tumbling into a stone cistern lined with tiles of lapis and gold. The only sound was the murmur of the water. Lazare seated her on a stone bench by the fountain, and then, with his usual care and ceremony, he placed the small white box with its silver cord ties in her hand.

She began to tear at the wrappings eagerly. She opened the tiny box with its folded scrap of gold *faille*.

"What is it, Jean? Oh, what can it be?"

She looked up at him, her lovely face rosy with anticipation. Her wide, dark eyes fixed themselves on his. Her lips were parted: that look, so trusting, so innocent, so childlike, had always cut his heart.

"Don't tell me—let me guess! It's something tiny, and very beautiful. Is it a ring, Jean? Or a shell? An emerald? A scarab? A pretty stone—you remember those lovely stones we found that time in Thailand? Yes, it's small, and hard—I think it's a stone."

Lazare smiled. It touched him, and had always touched him, that Maria's delight in the beautiful was so hectic and so catholic. Was there another woman in the world, he wondered, who could be equally entranced by a priceless diamond as by a lovely but worthless shell or stone?

"None of those things, darling," he replied. "This is very tiny, indeed—and a little magical. Would you believe me if I told you you held a bird in your hands?"

"A bird, Jean?" She stared at him.

"Yes, my darling. You have a little dove in your hands, a little White Dove—that's what they're called. You take it—you see, I have a glass of water here, all ready for you. You must take it with water, darling, never wine—and then, you'll see. This little dove is very powerful. It will give you a new set of wings."

"You're sure?" She kept her eyes fixed on his. "You promise me, Jean? Last time . . ."

"I know, darling. No mistakes now. I swear to you. Try."

She opened the scrap of gold *faille*. She inspected the tiny white pill solemnly, then took the glass of water from him. She swallowed the tablet like an obedient child taking proferred medicine from a concerned parent. Five minutes passed, perhaps ten; Lazare watched her face and listened to the water tumble from the fountain. Some while later, she pressed one of her tiny hands against her breast and gave a cry. Then, very shortly afterward, it began: a day and a night of fevered activity: a drive to the souk, her arms spilling over with small purchases; a swim in the pool; a desire to dance, a desire to lie down, a desire to talk as she had not talked to him in many years, a shifting, endless, fragmented day and night.

Seated beside her in the antique Rolls, Lazare could still feel on his skin the now-unaccustomed caress of her lips and her hands. For him it had been an agony; for Maria it had been twenty-four hours, more, of unadulterated happiness. Or so she had said, many times. The happiness, he judged, was wearing off now.

"This looked so pretty yesterday."

She was holding up for his inspection a bracelet she had purchased in the souk the previous day. It was made of silver, with coral and turquoise beads. It was old, and indeed pretty, and would once have comprised part of an Arab girl's dowry. It was exactly similar to twenty or thirty other bracelets Maria had purchased in that same souk before. "And this."

She held up a tiny bell of pierced brass, then tossed it down. "Jean . . ." She clasped his hand. "When we get home, I want to sleep. I want to sleep for a year and a day, like a princess in a fairy tale. I want to sleep in the blue room, Jean, with those white sheets you had sent from London."

"Darling, whichever room you want. Rest. Don't worry. It's all arranged."

"You will stay with me and talk to me? Just till I fall asleep? You won't leave me alone?"

"No. It's Sunday, darling. I'll stay with you all day if you like."

"Sunday. I love Sundays." She sighed. "I shall lie there and talk to you and listen to the bells."

She leaned back against the leather seat and closed her eyes. Jean looked at her face, which he had loved for so long. Her forehead was smooth and still almost unlined. Her long black lashes made a crescent above the curve of her cheeks, and her cheeks were still rosy with faint color. Desire for her washed up through his body, and he was as helpless to resist it as he had always been. Leaning across, he kissed her mouth gently. Her lips parted beneath his with a sweet familiarity. He undid the silk cord fastenings of her coat and slipped his hand beneath the fur. He began to stroke the softness of her once-lovely breasts; he felt with his fingertips for the pulse of her heart.

She moved against him in response, locking her arms around his neck. He began to kiss her closed eyes and her thick hair. Then, abruptly, she stiffened and began to push him away. He drew back at once, and lifted one of her small hands, and kissed it. He could not meet her eyes.

"Jean, don't. Darling, please don't cry." She began kissing his face, trying to force him to look at her. "Please don't. I can't bear to see you sad. I feel so much better, truly I do. If I can just rest, and maybe—" She hesitated. "Maybe just one more little White Dove, Jean. You said you brought me more. You said they'd be good for me, darling, and they were."

"When we get home."

He drew back from her, settled himself beside her, averted his face, and held her hand. She waited patiently then, because her trust in him was absolute, and she believed that although he had no compunction about lying to others, to her he never lied.

This house, about twelve miles outside Paris, lying in gentle country between the city and the palace of Versailles, was the first Lazare had bought her. Eighteenth-century, pre-Revolution, its every detail had been restored to his specifications with exacting care. Once upon a time Lazare had returned there with a sense of joy and triumph; now those feelings were impaired. It was just another house, albeit perfect of its kind. Lazare found its layout blurred with the details of his other properties, so much so that sometimes he would stand on the stairs, look around him at the corridors, the gilding, the mirrors, and think: *which way from here?*

Today, as she requested, they went upstairs to the blue room with the white-lace-edged sheets from London, and the bed Marie Antoinette had once owned, and the small, priceless, uncomfortable Louis XIV chairs. It was a woman's room, a restful room, its various soft hues calming to the eye. Lazare sent the maid away. He brought out the small white parcel from his pocket; Maria took the pill eagerly. She drank a little of the water he offered her, but she would not drink it all.

"Darling," he said. "You must take water. You must take more food. Shall I ask them to send something now?"

"No, Jean. Later. Oh, my lovely bed! It's so pretty, and so comfortable."

"It was made for a queen."

"Not a happy queen. Not a very nice queen. Still, never mind, it's mine now."

She moved across the room. She kicked off her shoes, tossed the fur on the floor. She lay down on the blue bed with its blue canopy, then she patted its blue counterpane. "Sit beside me, Jean. The way you promised. Talk to me, darling. Talk me to sleep. You're the only one who can."

He went to sit beside her. She lay back, closed her eyes. Very gently and skillfully, he unpinned her hair. He spread it out across the whiteness of the pillows. He stroked her hair, black as the wings of a raven, and her forehead, which was as pale as ivory, and he began to tell her about their past.

Maria loved all his stories, but this story, *their* story, was her favorite. He began it in the old house, which she still remembered, with those balconies that looked like lace but were forged out of iron. He reminded her of how it had been then when both of them were poor, and he was so proud, so difficult, so obstinate, and so wrong.

He said: "It was a terrible time, darling—do you remember? I lived with the truth daily, and it was destroying me. It ate me alive. Then—"

"But then it was all right." She stirred a little and clasped his hand. "It was all right in the end. Because I showed you the way."

"You did." He leaned across and kissed her forehead. "You did. And that was brave."

He hesitated then, because this part of their story was hard for him. Perhaps she would not notice, he thought, if he moved on, left out these particular incidents.

Maria seemed almost asleep. Perhaps this White Dove was calming her; perhaps reactions could differ day by day.

"Two years after that," he went on, "we made the journey. We took a train, then a plane—"

"No. Don't skip." She had opened her eyes. "I hate it when you skip. Tell me the best part. Tell me the first time."

"That wasn't the only best part, surely, darling?"

"No. No—but it was one of them. It's the one I like to remember best. Please, Jean."

"Very well." He sighed. "It was in your room. You remember that room?"

"I do."

"I had been drinking. I couldn't make myself drunk, although I tried very hard. I walked. Round and round the city. It was night by then. I came back to the old quarter. I walked around and around the grave-yard—you remember that graveyard, with those great monuments like houses? Where you used to play as a child?"

"I remember. I think I remember."

"I went there, to think of you. There was jazz playing in the distance. A blues number, with saxophones. The rhythms nearly drove me insane. I was very desperate."

"You needn't have been desperate. It was simple. I told you all along."

"I wouldn't listen. I didn't dare. So—that night—I felt powerful, and I felt damned. I was at the crossroads of my life. I felt I could live forever, or kill myself then and there. I felt I had to speak to you. I was so afraid of you. One word from you and I'd have done anything, everything."

"I gave you the word."

She opened her eyes and turned her gaze upon his face. She had begun to tremble again, and her eyes were unfocused, a little glazed.

"You do remember?" She caught at his arm. "Tell me you remember. What was the word?"

"*Maintenant.*"

He said it quietly, using the old accent they had both once shared. He turned his face away as he said it, because of the pain that word *now* recalled. He could see the room where she said the word, which was shadowy, and he could hear the sounds from outside, the distant and mournful drift of the blues. He could hear the shriek of the freight-train whistle, and the rush and rattle of its wheels.

Sound carried in the still of the night, and those freight trains were long: thirty boxcars, forty sometimes. He had heard that sound go past, and watched her face, so pale and so small, looking up at him from the shadows. *Now,* she had said, almost angrily, in a fierce and peremptory tone, as if she could stand these evasions no longer and was determined to cut through all the pretenses and defenses he had erected before.

Now, she had said, and he had listened to the freight cars, looked at the crucifix that hung on the wall, and understood that he could fight no longer: all his resistance had gone.

He had gathered her up into his arms then, with a deep sigh, and kissed her for the first time in the new way, like a lover as well as a protector and a friend.

"And that was how it began," he said now in the quiet of the blue room. "I knew then what the consequence would be. We both knew. We began something that couldn't end."

She had begun to move beside him as he spoke, he realized, although the movements were slight, and it was a while before he became aware of them, he was so tightly locked in the past. She stirred, moved onto her side, plucked again at his sleeve.

"Touch me, Jean. Please. Touch me like last night. I want to try again."

"Darling, no. You want to sleep. You said so. . . ."

"I did want to sleep. I don't now."

She sat up and tossed back her thick hair. Her fingers began to pluck at the buttons of her blouse. Her face was flushed and her movements hectic. She managed to undo only two of the buttons, then the silk of the blouse tore.

"It doesn't matter. Leave it. . . . I don't care. Jean, please touch me. Stroke my breasts. Kiss me, darling. Please kiss me now."

He could feel the exhaustion deepening as he turned to her, and he could sense his own foreboding, a sapping certainty that this would turn out ill. He began to stroke her back, and then her breasts, as she asked. He tried not to feel or see how terribly thin she had become, but it was impossible. He could feel every disk in her spine, each rib; her breasts, always small, were now those of a pubescent child.

He closed his eyes and buried his face against her neck, fighting the exhaustion, and the shame.

"Darling, no," he said again gently. "You should rest, and be calm."

"I don't want to rest." Her voice had risen on that high, imperious note he had come to dread. "I want you to make love to me. Is that so much to ask? *Why* won't you? *Why* can't you? I know you love me. I know you want me. So what's wrong? Jean, you're not fifty yet. Are you too old?"

That taunt was a new one. She saw the anger come into his face and gave a small cry of triumph.

"That's it. That's it. You're too old. You can't do it anymore."

"You're wrong." He rose and looked down at her coldly. "When I have the inclination, I can perform."

"So perform now. Prove it. I don't believe you."

"Very well. Since you ask me so charmingly."

"Jean—"

"Lie still, damn you."

He undid his belt, loosened his trousers, left his clothes on. When he thrust up inside her, she gave one long, shuddering cry, then began to writhe in his arms. He pressed her down hard with his full weight and trapped her arms. As he moved inside her, he felt and saw nothing. His mind was completely dark. His one intent was to succeed as quickly as possible, to kill pain with pleasure, even if the pleasure was a brief thing that would not last.

Climax eluded him; he thrust on, and then she began to speak and move under him—and this made it worse. She talked a new whore language and made new whore moves—and that, of course, was not what he wanted; that he could purchase—and when desperate these last few years sometimes had purchased—anytime.

He put his hand across her mouth to silence her. He could feel despair just the other side of some screen in his mind, but he refused to look at it. Last night had been a failure. He had to succeed now.

She was murmuring under his hand. He closed his mind to her insinuating words. He summoned back from his memory the lost Maria of their past. He felt the modesty of her hands and saw the trust of her eyes. That Maria he worshiped; to love her had been his only religion, the guiding principle of his entire life. He fixed his mind on this Maria, and even now she did not fail him: just to imagine her was enough. Kissing her breasts, he shuddered and came. The ejaculation felt violent. The instant it was over, he pulled out of her with a gesture of disgust, hating himself, hating the woman his lost Maria had become.

He had not satisfied her, as he had once been able to do so easily. She caught hold of his hand and pressed it hard between her thighs. She closed her eyes and rubbed against him in a frantic way. It took her more than five minutes to achieve satisfaction, but her pleasure seemed intense; she at once released his hand.

"Go to sleep." He jerked away from her, rose, and began to fasten his clothing. "Go to sleep. You can surely sleep now."

She made no reply, but lay still, her eyes closed. Lazare sat down on one of the small, uncomfortable, priceless chairs. He felt he hated the chair, the Marie Antoinette bed, all the past years of acquisitions and accumulation. The houses, the cars, the planes, the paintings: he loathed them. He had acquired them believing they could assuage loss, but now he looked down into the emptiness at the heart of his life and felt sick with fear.

He sat there, in hard-faced desperation, for an hour. Maria never moved once during that time. He was afraid to speak or move himself in case she was only pretending to be asleep, but he longed to escape from this room. He wanted to go out into the park and walk beneath the avenues of sweet chestnut. He wanted to breathe clean air, and think, and be alone.

These pills had been his last hope, the last component in a Faustian pact he had made. Now he saw them for the disaster they were. Never mind what happened on the day of the collection, never mind if Maria failed to appear, never mind if her imagination remained barren, never mind if he had to endure another five years as infernal as the last five— he would destroy the remaining White Doves and purchase no more.

The business would suffer eventually—but he no longer cared. He could keep it operating, and by the same means. He would simply continue to employ, at inflated salaries, the two anonymous gifted young men who tried to imitate the inimitable, and who had produced pastiche Cazarèses these past five years. If they could just survive these coming collections, he would reactivate the negotiations begun a year before. In due course he would sell the company, and then he and Maria would— would what? He realized suddenly that he could see no future for them unless some doctor somewhere, some magician he had not already consulted, could find a cure.

On the bed across the room, Maria stirred. She sat up, pushed back her hair, and regarded him calmly.

"Jean," she said, "where is my paper? Where are my pencils? My special pens?"

"They're over there, darling," he replied wearily. "On the table, where they always are."

To his astonishment, she said nothing further, but crossed to the table, drew the paper toward her, and began sketching. She was still half naked. He rose, fetched a robe, and draped it around her. She shrugged him aside irritably.

"Don't fuss over me, Jean. Turn the light on. Go away."

He switched on the lamp beside her and moved a few paces away, watching her with painful concern. It was the first time she had attempted to draw in more than a year. How long would it be before she tore up the papers, tossed them aside—an hour? Half an hour?

For the moment she seemed completely absorbed. He moved to the far side of the room, where she need not be aware of his presence, and sat down. There were books on a table next to him. He picked up one of them and began to turn its pages quietly, though the content did not register with him at all. In this way, her pencil strokes and the ticking of a small elaborate gilded clock the only sounds, one hour passed, and then two.

Late in the afternoon he rose and moved to the windows. He looked out at the dark. Behind him he heard a sudden movement; the scattering of papers; one long, high, thin cry of utter despair.

He crossed to her quickly and crouched down, encircling her with his arms. Her drawings were tossed down on the floor all around him. At first, trying to soothe her with his embrace, he scarcely noticed them. Gradually first one, then another, swam into his vision. He tensed, then bent down to pick them up. He looked carefully at the washes of color, the quickly sketched lines. To an outsider they would have been almost meaningless, and perhaps unimpressive, but these sketches were a private language he and Maria shared. He could read assurance in a stroke of the pen, and it was assurance he read now.

He looked up at her, his face blank with astonishment and with the effort of suppressing hope. He thought: they work, those White Doves do work, after all.

Maria's head was buried in her arms. She was weeping bitterly, her body racked with sobs.

"Darling, don't cry," he said in a low voice. "These are beautiful—the most beautiful drawings you've done for years. You see? I always told you, darling. . . ."

She was not listening. She lifted her face; tears spilled from her eyes.

"I want my baby back," she said. "Jean—please. I want my son. I have to see him. I need him. Jean, it's breaking my heart."

He felt the pain knife through him, as he always did when she began on this plea. Putting his arms around her again, he explained quietly and gently, as he always did, that this was the one thing he could not give her.

"The baby's *dead*, Maria," he said. "Darling, you have to accept that. The doctors explained—"

"You're lying. The doctors know nothing. You took him away, Jean. You *banished* him, the same way you banished Mathilde. You were ashamed of my baby." She buried her face in her hands. "I want to see him. I want to see him *now*."

Lazare fought to control himself. This refrain had first begun at the time of her operation, five years before. Once she realized she could no longer have children, something snapped in her heart and her brain. Before that he had always believed she had accepted her loss and left her grief behind. Then it had resurfaced; this past year and particularly these past few months, wild scenes of pain and accusation had become more frequent. She was now half choking with tears. He found the grief and the intransigence unbearable. In a sudden rage he swung around and slammed his fist down hard on the table. The lamp fell and the pens scattered.

"Stop this," he shouted. "For the love of God, stop this. The baby's *dead*, Maria—he's been dead for over twenty-five *years*. I can take you to his grave. I can take you to the church where the funeral was held."

"What funeral? I never went to a funeral."

"Maria—you were too ill. I went. I organized everything. I can tell you the name of the priest. I have the death certificate. Do you want me to fetch it? Do you want me to make you read it? Dear God, how many times do I have to prove this to you?"

She was still not listening to him. The tears had stopped, and her face had set in an obstinate mask. She lowered her eyes, then gave him a side-long glance he found almost sly. Bending down, she began to pick up her papers and pencils and pens.

"Go away," she said in a flat, sullen tone. "I don't love you when you shout at me. You're lying. I won't listen. Go away."

He left her then, in a fury with himself and with her. When he returned, an hour later, Maria was sleeping deeply, and the new maid was just leaving her. With an apologetic look, she informed him that Mademoiselle Cazarès had been telephoning; she had summoned Mathilde.

Lazare was beyond caring: let the damned woman come, he thought, and turned to examine the scattered drawings left on the table.

During his absence, he saw, Maria had not been sketching clothes. She had covered page after page with random hieroglyphs, random words. Interspersed with these, and drawn with the utmost delicacy, were little pictures from their past. A crucifix, a cradle, and row upon row of vaulted graves.

One drawing in particular caught his attention: on the largest of the tombs, she had printed the name of her son, Christophe, and his age at death, which was three months. Perhaps she was at last beginning to accept what he told her, he thought, forcing back the tears that started to his eyes as he read this boy's name.

Other details of this drawing puzzled him, however. There seemed to him to be a meaning in it which he could not grasp. To the right of Christophe's tomb, Maria had drawn a sun; to the left, a crescent moon. Above his grave, drawn as boldly as if it were some biblical sign, there was a large multipointed star. The rest of the drawing was in black and white: as if to emphasize the star, and proclaim its significance, Maria had colored it gold.

CHAPTER 10

Approaching Notting Hill Gate that Sunday evening, Lindsay was beset with nerves. She signaled right, turned left, and narrowly missed a post. She stole a glance at Rowland, who sat beside her, his long legs stretched out as far as the confines of her small car permitted. He looked unperturbed.

She slammed on the brakes outside her own house and peered up at its façade. The couple who lived on the lower floor appeared to be out, but lights burned at the windows of her own apartment: Tom might be home, and Louise would certainly be in, she thought with a sinking heart.

"I'll just run up and find that photograph and my article," she said. "I can't explain properly about Lazare until you see that picture. So I'll just grab it, then I'll run you home—where did you say you lived?"

"In Spitalfields," said Rowland. "It's in the East End. It's miles away. Why don't I just take the tube? Anyway, you can't park here, you're blocking the street."

"Nonsense," said Lindsay, who was only half listening, and whose knowledge of London's East End was vague in the extreme. "It'll take us—what? Fifteen minutes? I told you—this is *exciting*, Rowland, wait until I explain."

"What about our lunch tomorrow? Why can't you explain then?"

"Because this could be important—urgent. Besides, I'm—I'm not going to have time for lunch tomorrow, I realize now. It's too much of a rush. I have to pack for Paris, and— Look, Rowland, just wait in the car, will you? Then if someone wants to get past, you can move it."

She leapt out before Rowland could argue further, ran inside, and began charging up the four flights of stairs. Halfway there, she paused; she realized she might have sounded rude, inhospitable. Too bad, she decided. She had had the entire journey from Max's house to make up her mind, and she was determined on two things: first, she was going to see Rowland McGuire's home at all costs, and second, Rowland McGuire was not, under any circumstances, to encounter Louise.

She flung open the door of her apartment to a rich smell of frying onions and hamburgers. She could see Tom at the kitchen stove, and a sink piled high with unwashed dishes. She could see Louise on the living room sofa, her feet up. She was dressed to kill, and drinking a glass of wine.

"Hi, Mum," said Tom.

"Where is he?" said Louise.

"He's outside in the car, I *told* you," Lindsay said, hugging Tom, then moving through the room at top speed. "I told you when I called. I just need to pick up a couple of things, then I'm giving him a quick lift home."

"Darling, how dreadfully rude. What can you be thinking of?" Louise, who was fast on her feet when she wanted to be, was already at the window. "Look. The poor man's parked the car for you. Goodness—he's *devastating*, darling. Why didn't you say? And now he's standing down there like a lost soul—and it's freezing cold."

"Louise . . ."

"Coooeee . . ." Louise was leaning out the window and waving her glass. "Hello, Rowland," she called in siren tones. "Lindsay can't find those papers. Come up and have a glass of wine."

"Please, God, don't do this to me," Lindsay muttered under her breath. Louise closed the window and turned around. "What was that, darling?"

"I was praying," Lindsay said. "I was praying my life might change. I was praying *you* might change. Never mind. . . ."

"Answered prayers are always the most dangerous, as Truman Capote put it," said Louise. "Or *was* it Capote? It sounds Catholic. A bit Jesuitical. Maybe it was Graham Greene?"

She was reaching for the buzzer to open the front door.

Lindsay gave her one last desperate look, her fair, sleek, impossible mother, and fled into her bedroom. She went on praying that she'd find what she was looking for *quickly*: she tugged drawers open; she scattered files. *Vogue*, she thought. English *Vogue*, and an article that was one of the first she'd ever written, when she was starting out and still working freelance. Was it 1978, or 1979? Had she filed it under "Free-lance" or under "*Vogue*"?

"Darling, what a *noise* you're making in there," Louise called. "There's no need to hurry. I've introduced myself. Tom's introduced himself. Goodness! It does smell awfully *oniony* in here. Tom, open the kitchen window. Can you cook, Rowland? No? And a very good thing too. It's a woman's province, in my opinion, but then, Lindsay has these advanced ideas. Poor Tom manages very well. Sit here beside me, Row-land—just toss those magazines on the floor. I hope you like the Chardonnay—Australian, of course, madly cheap but quite fun. Now, tell me, have you known Lindsay long?"

Lindsay dropped a stack of files. Dear God, she thought; even Louise, a fast worker, was not usually this unsubtle. Deciding she could not bear to overhear any more, she kicked the door shut. From beyond it, as she searched, came the interchange between Louise and Rowland, a blessedly indistinguishable stream of words. Rowland was being forthcoming, she thought, as she caught his lower tones. Damn; the article was *not* filed under "*Vogue*"; it must be in "Freelance," then—and it was that file she had dropped. Its contents were now scattered all over the floor. With a moan of exasperation she sank to her knees and began scrabbling among the papers. They were back to front, upside down. It took her almost ten minutes to find the article and its accompanying photograph. The instant she saw it, she knew she had been right. She felt a surge of triumph and excitement. Clutching the papers to her chest, she opened the door.

". . . and so you've never been married, Rowland?" she heard. "A handsome man like you? What's wrong with modern girls? Why, in my day you'd have been snapped up, Rowland, long ago."

"Evasive tactics," she heard Rowland reply. "I have them down to a fine art."

"Nonsense!" Louise cried. "You just haven't found the right woman yet. I can always tell—you're a romantic, Rowland, I'm sure."

"You're right," Rowland said astonishingly. "Louise, you see into the secrets of my heart."

"Without her glasses," Tom put in, "which she's too vain to wear, she can't see the wall opposite. So I doubt—"

"Now, Tom, don't advertise my frailties." Louise gave a gusty sigh. "Though it is true, Rowland. I have to admit it. I am getting older, and I am getting rather frail."

"Never," said Rowland in firm and gallant tones.

"Now, Rowland. No flattery. You're a sweet man, but the truth is,

I'm not getting any younger, and without Lindsay I couldn't manage at all. I feel I'm a terrible *burden* to her, though she never complains."

"It wouldn't occur to her, I'm sure."

"Yes, well, I *depend* on her," Louise said, her voice sharpening, as if she objected to something in Rowland's tone. "It's a case of whither she goes, I go. Like Ruth. In the Bible. You know."

Lindsay, who had remained frozen in her bedroom doorway throughout this not-unfamiliar recital, could stand it no longer. Usually, it took Louise several weeks to work through this repertoire; why on earth had she accelerated to this degree?

She entered the living room, face set. She wondered if Rowland had noticed that the room, though large and pleasant, looked as if it had recently been struck by a hurricane. Would he notice what two days of Louise and Tom could do to a room, and if he noticed, would he care?

Tom was sitting opposite Rowland and Louise, amid a pile of books on Ingmar Bergman. He was wearing no shoes, and had holes in his socks. On his lap was a tray on which was a giant-size squeezy bottle of ketchup, and a plate piled high with burgers, french fries, and onions. Louise and Rowland, meanwhile, looked distinctly pally. Louise's blue eyes were fixed on Rowland, and Rowland's face wore a relaxed, easy smile. Tom met Lindsay's gaze with an expression of profound sympathy. He even remembered, loyally, to attempt to rise.

"Don't get up, Tom," Lindsay said rather wildly as Rowland beat him to it. "Rowland, I've found the article."

"And we should go, alas." Rowland had already put down his wineglass and was now extending his hand, with extreme courtesy, to Louise.

"Louise, it's been a pleasure to meet you. Tom, I'll send over those books I mentioned."

Louise was busy mouthing the words *wonderful man*, and making sure Rowland saw her do it. With surprising difficulty, considering how nimbly she'd nipped across to the window earlier, she allowed Rowland to help her up from the sofa. She gave him a brave grimace, then a brave sigh. "No, no, it's nothing . . ." She waved Rowland aside. "Just this little pain I get in my spine. Rowland, I'm so glad to have met you. Of course, I felt as if I knew you already. Lindsay talks about you all the time."

"Yeah. She bad-mouths you," Tom put in, loyal and truthful to the last.

"Does she indeed?" Rowland said with a cool green glance in Lindsay's direction. "Ah, well. The hostilities are over, Tom. We're at the peace negotiation stage now, isn't that right, Lindsay?"

Rowland contrived to make this process sound curiously erotic. Lindsay, who found his glance and his tone were affecting her body in a number of inexplicable ways, averted her gaze. Louise made an odd chirruping noise that possibly indicated parental indulgence and possibly indicated rage.

Lindsay had to admit that Rowland was both decisive and manful when he chose. Before Louise could launch her next salvo, he had Lindsay by the arm, had steered her through the door and led her down the stairs.

"She does that," Lindsay said, getting into her car, which Rowland had parked perfectly, in a tiny space, with two inches to spare. She began hauling on the steering wheel. "I'm sorry, Rowland. She does it to everyone. She does it all the time."

"I could see that," he replied, unperturbed. "Hard left, Lindsay. Take it slowly. Well done."

Scarlet with exertion and shame, Lindsay finally extricated them and set off up the street.

"East?" she said. "If I just keep going east, will you direct me from there?"

"You're going north at present, Lindsay. Make a right, here."

Lindsay obeyed. They bowled along for a considerable distance in silence. Lindsay had a slight run-in with a blind taxi driver, and a brief altercation with a battered Ford Cortina, occupied by four youthful comedians. The comedians overtook her on the inside; they appeared to object to her lane procedure at the last traffic circle. As they barreled past four arms were extended from the Cortina's windows simultaneously, and four fingers were stabbed up at the air.

Lindsay hit the horn as the Ford disappeared into the distance. She glanced toward Rowland, who was still looking calm.

"You're a pleasure to drive, Rowland. I can't stand backseat drivers. People will tell me when to brake, or signal; it drives me mad. Gini's impossible. Nervous as a cat. The whole way down to Max's, she kept her eyes closed."

"I don't blame her," Rowland said in easy tones. "You're a terrible driver. You're one of the worst drivers I've ever encountered in my life. Your only rival, as far as I'm concerned, was a one-eyed taxi driver who once drove me in Istanbul. He was smoking hashish at the time. He had something of your style."

Lindsay decided to take this as a pleasantry. "I drive perfectly well," she said firmly. "A bit fast, maybe. I don't like hanging around."

"Most women make poor drivers anyway," Rowland went on. "They lack spatial awareness. Tests have been done. It's been scientifically proved."

"What nonsense."

"It's true. It's why there are so few women architects. It's why women make such mediocre chess players."

"I play brilliant chess. I taught Tom."

"Who wins when you play Tom now?"

"Well, he does. But that proves nothing. Tom's exceptional."

"I thought he might be. I liked Tom."

"Did you?" Lindsay swerved joyfully. "Oh, I'm so glad. I don't expect he said very much—not with Louise there."

"No. He didn't. That was why I liked him. He has good taste in films. Remind me to give you some books for him. Also—" He glanced toward her. "He doesn't miss much, I'd guess."

"Tom doesn't miss *anything*," Lindsay said with pride. "Left or right here?"

"Left," said Rowland. "Oh, well, never mind. We can approach it this way. Go past that factory, turn in here, that's it. . . . Now turn left by the Hawksmoor church. Isn't it a wonderful church? It's my favorite in the whole of London. I can lie in bed and look at its spire."

Lindsay, who had never heard of Hawksmoor, turned sharply left where indicated. She was just thinking what an extraordinary neighborhood Rowland lived in, one of the slummiest and roughest she had ever seen in this city, when her eyes took in the street and the house he was indicating. She gasped, slammed on the brakes, and came to an abrupt halt with one wheel on the pavement.

"My God. What an incredible street. What incredible houses . . ."

Rowland was looking fondly at the row of brick façades. The houses were terraced, with fanlights and tall sash windows. Small flights of steps led up to their doors.

"They're 1730, or thereabouts," he said. "They were built for the Huguenots, who came here when they were driven out of France. They were famous as merchants and silk weavers. It's always been a refugee area. After the French left, it became a Jewish quarter. Now it's predominantly Bengali. I rescued this house. It was falling down when I bought it."

"It's beautiful, Rowland."

"Isn't it? It's still a bit primitive inside. I've had it twelve years. Friends used it when I was in Washington. I've never really gotten around to furnishing it exactly. . . . Oh, my God. Quick. Start the car!"

Lindsay, who was already climbing out as he said this, looked around in bewilderment. A short way up the street, she saw, there was a long, low white Mercedes convertible. From it had just emerged a tall, thin, and very beautiful young woman. For one second, in the dim streetlight, Lindsay thought it was Gini. This girl had the same figure, the same cropped blond hair, the same wide mouth, the same air of determination. But Gini would not be wearing spray-on silver trousers, a cropped black T-shirt, and a black leather motorcycle jacket; she would not be wearing startlingly scarlet lipstick, and she would not be provoking this reaction in Rowland, who—now out of the car—looked poised to flee.

"You sheet," the girl yelled, reaching Rowland, and striking him hard in the chest. "You peeg. I call. I weep. I write you letters from my 'eart. I seet in my car. I wait. I weep some more—beeg tears, look. 'Ow can you do zis to me? *Merde, je m'en fiche, tu comprends?*" She continued screaming in her own language, her mouth distorted with woe, tears plopping onto the leather jacket. Periodically, she struck Rowland, and periodically Rowland said, *"Sylvie . . ."*

In mid-Racinian recitative, Sylvie turned her attack from Rowland to Lindsay's new, shiny Volkswagen. Swirling around with impressive speed, she raised her fist and brought it down hard on the hood. A dent appeared.

"Now, just wait a minute," said Lindsay, advancing.

"Beech," screamed Sylvie. "Inglish beech. You steal my man. I show you what I think of beeches. And their stupid cars."

She kicked the Volkswagen's bumper. Another dent appeared.

"What the hell? That's *it*," Lindsay said. She made a grab for Sylvie but missed as Sylvie was hoisted into the air.

"Out. Go away. Go home." Rowland was shouting in a voice audible at least three blocks away. "Now. That's it. It's *over*."

He had Sylvie in a firm grip several feet above the ground. Her legs kicked furiously. She was clawing and spitting like a tomcat. Even Lindsay was impressed, and Lindsay had a fierce temper of her own.

"I die." Sylvie suddenly went limp. "I keel myself. I cut my neck. Right now."

"No. You don't," said Rowland, frog-marching her along the sidewalk to her car. "You have remarkable powers of self-preservation, Sylvie."

"I keel that beech, then, before I go."

"That bitch is my wife, Sylvie," Rowland said, depositing her next to her car somewhat violently. "We got married yesterday. It was a whirlwind romance. Now, go home."

"Ta femme? Hypocrite! Menteur! C'est impossible!"

"Not impossible. Would you like to see the ring?"

He spoke with absolute green-eyed conviction. Sylvie gave an eldritch wail. She uttered a stream of French insults, slapped Rowland's face extremely hard, leapt into her Mercedes, and screeched away.

Rowland turned to Lindsay, who was still standing, mouth agape, by her poor wounded car. Without speaking, his expression unreadable, he took her by the arm, led her up the steps, and opened his front door. He switched on the light. On the doormat inside, and trailing from the letterbox, was an assortment of women's panties.

Lindsay bent and picked them up. There were black lace ones, pink lace ones, white lace ones. She looked at Rowland.

"Sylvie's?" she asked.

"They're her style," Rowland replied. "Posting them through the letterbox is her style as well."

"Bloody *hell*," said Lindsay, and they both began to laugh.

They laughed all the way up the staircase, which was uncarpeted, and along a corridor, and into the first floor reception room. Lindsay, who felt weak from laughing, sank down in the room's only chair.

"Oh, my God," she said at last. "She was *extraordinary*, Rowland."

"Not extraordinary enough," he replied.

"Does this kind of thing happen to you often?"

"Variations upon it, yes. Two or three times a year. God knows why."

Lindsay did a rapid calculation: Max had said that none of the women lasted longer than three months. "Three months is the all-time *record*," he'd said. "For most of them one month's more the mark."

Lindsay wondered whether Sylvie was a one-monther or a three-monther, then she checked herself. This was none of her business, after all.

Rowland, she realized, was moving around the room very fast. Having displayed such impressive equilibrium earlier, he was now looking agitated. He was closing the wooden shutters to the tall windows, switching on lamps. For the first time, Lindsay began to take in the oddness of the room. It was perfectly proportioned, and it was paneled; there was a beautiful old fireplace next to her that showed evidence of recent fires. It was also the barest, the most monastic room she had ever been in. Apart from the chair in which she sat, a table piled high with books, and shelves overflowing with books on the far wall, it was almost completely empty. There were no radiators and it was bitterly cold.

"I wonder," said Rowland, looking distinctly ill at ease now. "Is it a bit chilly in here?"

"It's polar, actually, Rowland. I'm getting frostbite."

"The fire. I'll light the fire. That should help."

He began piling kindling, paper, and logs in the fireplace. He contrived to light the fire with one match, something Lindsay could never do.

He rose, and backed away. "A drink," he said. "Yes, you'd like a drink, I expect. I do have whiskey. On the other hand, you're driving—"

"It's all right, Rowland," Lindsay said, taking pity on him. "I'm not planning on staying, I promise you. Relax. This is work. I'm going to show you this article, then I'm out of here. Meantime, one small whiskey would be excellent—and it wouldn't do any harm."

"Fine. Fine." Rowland still looked anxious. "Right. I'll just get the whiskey, then. It's in the kitchen, I think."

He disappeared at a rapid pace. Lindsay listened to his feet clattering down the bare staircase. She rose and began to walk around the room. There was one other element, which she had not noticed immediately. The entire wall behind the chair on which she had been sitting was covered with black and white photographs. Mountains. Peak after jagged peak. Lindsay, who feared and disliked mountains, bent to peer at them more closely. They were annotated, she saw, in Rowland's clear and beautiful handwriting. Each peak was identified, and beside it was a date, and further notes. Some of the notes referred to weather conditions, others, presumably, to routes, but they were in an incomprehensible jargon, packed with words like "arête" and "corrie," which Lindsay did not understand. Max had said Rowland climbed, and Lindsay had envisaged modest rockfaces. Surely he had not climbed these?

Rowland returned a few minutes later with two glasses, a bottle of scotch, a small jug of water, and a saucer containing salted peanuts.

Seeing Lindsay bent toward one of the photographs, his manner at once warmed.

"That's Sgurr Na Guillean." He indicated a fearsome peak, crested with snow. "In the Cuillins, on Skye. I traversed the ridge there last month. The weather was extraordinary—completely clear for two whole days. I spent Christmas night bivouacked just there."

He pointed at a sheet of sheer snow, with a vertigo-inducing drop below it. It looked to Lindsay like the most inhospitable place in the world.

"On a ledge, and roped, obviously, in case the weather changed."

"Christmas night?" Lindsay said in a faint voice. "Were you alone, Rowland?"

"Yes. Which probably wasn't wise, on Skye in winter. I usually climb with friends. But at Christmas—you know. Most people want to be with their families. And besides, I like to climb alone."

Lindsay said nothing. She could feel the pace of her mind accelerating, going into overdrive. She tried to engage the brakes of good sense, and they failed.

Rowland handed her the whiskey, and passed her the saucer of peanuts. Lindsay could tell he was proud of finding these, which he offered with touching courtesy. Looking at the peanuts—there were ten of them—she knew she was one inch away from tears.

Afterward, she always knew it was at this precise second that she fell in love with Rowland McGuire. But she could never decide what provoked that debacle. Was it the thought of him alone on a mountain on Christmas Day, or was it because the damn peanuts were so stale?

Rowland found two upright chairs, which he placed side by side at the table. He swept the books to the floor, and Lindsay placed on the table the green file he had given her, and the article she had brought from her home. They both sat down, and Lindsay tossed back her whiskey too fast.

"Now," she began, intensely aware of Rowland's proximity, "I'm going to help you, Rowland, just as I promised, despite the fact that you neither apologized nor groveled."

"I forgot. I promise I will."

"So pay attention. You're about to enter a world you don't understand."

"I'm paying attention," said Rowland with suspicious meekness. "I'm hanging on every word."

"Right. We mentioned all the mysteries about Lazare and Maria Cazarès—you remember? Where they came from, how he first made his fortune, whether they are lovers, the nature of their relationship now, and so on. What would you say was the *central* mystery, the single most important one?"

"Where each of them came from. If that could be answered, some of the other questions might be answered as well."

"I agree. Now I'm going to test you—you say you've read this file of yours. What's the authorized version of their origins?"

"The PR version? It's quite a good tale. Maria Cazarès was born in a tiny village in Spain and orphaned when she was still a small child. She then went to live with some relative, an aunt or possibly a cousin, also Spanish by origin but then living in France. This aunt—whom no one ever met or interviewed, incidentally, was a very skilled embroideress, who had worked for Balenciaga for many, many years. This elderly, unmarried woman took Maria in—and taught her to sew. From an early age Maria proved very talented. After the aunt retired from Balenciaga's workshops, she found it hard to live on her pension, and so she began a small private dressmaking business, with Maria as her assistant. The aunt then conveniently died, and Maria continued this work on her own. Slowly she began to make a name for herself among the stylish women of Paris, and plucky little thing that she was, she carried on sewing in her freezing atelier until she had enough money to open a small shop. One day, who should pass that shop, and be at once mesmerized by the clothes in its windows, but a rich young man, origins unknown, called Jean Lazare. Lazare, instantly recognizing Maria's genius, befriended her. He invested in her business, and guided her from then on. In 1976, after remarkably few setbacks, he launched her—Cazarès gave her first couture show."

Lindsay gave him an admiring look.

"Word perfect, Rowland. And do you buy that story?"

"I quite like it. It's familiar. There's a touch of Little Nell, a whiff of *La Dame aux Camelias* and *La Bohème.* . . ."

"But do you buy it, Rowland?"

"No. I suspect the Spain/Balenciaga link is a red herring. I think it's invention from beginning to end."

"It diverts all the attention to Maria Cazarès, I agree. And it leaves unanswered a whole lot of other questions—if Lazare is not French, for instance, and he's never managed to sound pure French, then where is he from? Corsica? A former French colony like Algeria? Could he be Portuguese, or Spanish? All those have been suggested, but if any of it is true, why not admit it? What has he got to hide? He's hinted in the past that his family might have had links with Corsica, and that he had a poor upbringing. In which case, how did he acquire the fortune that he needed to set Cazarès up as a couture house? Answer: no one knows."

"But you think you've found some clue?"

"I think I've found more than a clue, Rowland."

"You do?" Rowland was now looking at her closely. "Well, it must be something major. You look different, you know. There's a strange *glow* about you."

"I expect it's the firelight," Lindsay said hastily. "And then, I *am* excited. I suspected I was right all weekend."

"You kept very quiet about it."

"Yes, well, I didn't want to interfere. There was a crisis—you and Gini and Max had work to do. I wasn't sure if you'd still be interested."

"I am still interested," he said. "Very interested. So, are you going to explain?"

"Yes, I will." Lindsay wrenched her eyes back to the file. Rowland moved his chair a little closer. Firelight flickered against the paneled walls.

"Your researchers did a good job, Rowland," she said slowly. "There are clippings in this file that I've never seen. I didn't begin working in fashion until 1978, and it was 1984 before I first attended the Paris collections. So I was especially interested in the coverage here of Cazarès's early shows—the clothes that first made her name, the clothes that began the legend. Going through the pictures of that early work, I came across this. It stopped me in my tracks. It's an evening dress by Maria Cazarès, from her very first collection in 1976. As photographed for American *Harper's Bazaar*."

She drew out the clipping she referred to, which was in full color and from the original magazine. Rowland leaned across to inspect it.

"No one else could have made that dress, Rowland," Lindsay went on. "Not Lacroix now, not even Saint Laurent in the past. It could *only* be a Cazarès. You can read her signature in every detail. This dress is part of her St. Petersburg collection—that's how it's remembered now. Look at the cut and fullness of the skirt—isn't it the most wonderful color? That rich, dark, seaweedy green. Look at the detailing on the hem—that narrow band of black silk velvet. Look at the gold and green brocade of the sleeves, and the shape of the overjacket. You see how its curves are emphasized by the fur trimming? Look at the way the bodice and armholes are tailored, so the shoulders seem narrowed—"

She stopped; Rowland had just yawned.

"Rowland, please—just *try*. This is important. If you can't read the signature, you won't understand. Now, tell me what you see here."

"I don't like that turban thing the model's wearing. It looks absurd."

"Rowland, forget the turban. Look at the *dress*. Try to see its component parts. Try to read its language. Try to see the *story* this dress is telling. Isn't it romantic? Doesn't it make you think of St. Petersburg balls? Think . . ." She cast around desperately. "Think of *War and Peace*, Rowland. The ballroom scenes in that. Think of Natasha's night-time sleigh-ride through the snow."

A glint of comprehension began to appear in Rowland's eyes.

"Yes, maybe . . ." he said, frowning. "I begin to see . . . You've read *War and Peace*, then?"

Lindsay sighed. "I may not have read classics at Oxford," she said in patient tones, "but I'm not completely uneducated, Rowland. Of course I've read *War and Peace*. As a matter of fact, I read a lot. I read all the time."

Rowland looked at her with new interest. "Do you?" he said. "What are you reading now?"

Lindsay lowered her eyes. On her bedside table she kept the books she intended to read and the books she usually ended up reading, side by side. At the top of the pile at the moment was a fat airport romance, six hundred pages of love and heartbreak, which soothed her at the end of a hard day. Its author's style might lack grace, but the plot was deft and the characters dramatic. Their emotions were violent; last Thursday, on page 345, the hero had died; tired Lindsay had cried.

"John Updike," she said. "The last of the Rabbit ones, you know."

Rowland's face lit up the instant she mentioned the name. He began speaking; Lindsay, resolving to start that novel that very night, interrupted fast.

"Rowland, I know you'd prefer to discuss books, but now's not the time. Please, I need you to concentrate on this."

Rowland apologized. He bent over the photograph of a ball gown designed two decades earlier, and stared at it with fierce concentration. He seemed determined to deconstruct its female codes. Lindsay, amused, watched him apply his intellect to it.

"It has both male *and* female elements," he said at last. "The dress itself couldn't be more feminine. But Cazarès has married it with a man's waistcoat—with the kind of garment a Cossack might wear."

"That's excellent." Lindsay shot him a look of approval. "You're learning. That's the essence of the Cazarès style—the union of apparent opposites. Male and female, rough and smooth, exotic and austere, chaste and impure. That's her grammar, if you like. Now—keep concentrating. Look at this second photograph here."

Feeling nervous, she drew out the article she had brought from her own files and laid it in front of him. The picture accompanying her interview was full-page. It showed a regal, white-haired, and still-beautiful woman standing in a resplendent drawing room. Draped across the chair next to her was a dress, a long dress, with an accompanying overjacket trimmed with fur.

"It's the same dress," Rowland said almost at once. "Same dress. Same jacket. They're identical."

"Indeed they are," Lindsay said on a note of quiet triumph. "And that's odd. Very odd indeed. Almost inexplicable."

"Why? I don't understand. Explain."

"Because the first dress I showed you was made in 1976. And this one here was made exactly ten years earlier. The 1976 dress is a Cazarès—that's indisputable. This 1966 dress, though identical, as you say, was made by an unknown girl, an amateur seamstress, whose name was Marie-Thérèse."

She had Rowland's full attention now. She watched him take in the implications of this. She watched him begin to seek an explanation.

"It becomes stranger, Rowland," she went on. "I know what you're thinking. You're wondering if perhaps Maria Cazarès and this Marie-Thérèse could be one and the same? You're wondering if this 1966 dress could date from her unknown period, pre-Lazare, pre-fame, when she was allegedly working away in that freezing atelier the PR people love to describe."

"You're right. That's exactly what I'm thinking."

"Then think again. Because this dress *wasn't* made in a freezing atelier. It wasn't even made in Paris. It was made in America."

"America?"

"Yes, Rowland. In New Orleans."

"Shall I go on, Rowland?" Lindsay said hesitantly a short while later. Ten minutes had passed, during which her account had been interrupted by a reaction on Rowland's part that she did not understand. He was now standing with his back to her, having risen to put another log on the fire. He appeared to have forgotten that she was there, and was standing staring down into the flames.

"I'd like you to hear the story as I was told it," she continued. "It's a good story—at least I like it. It's a love story of a kind."

"Of course." Rowland turned. "I want to hear it."

"Is something wrong, Rowland?"

"No, no. It's just—when you asked if I knew that city. I was remembering the last time I was there, that's all."

"Did you know it well? Was this when you were working in the States?"

"Fairly well. I went there a few times. I had a friend in Washington." He hesitated. "Her brother was a lecturer in law at Tulane. We went there to visit him a few times."

"Tulane?"

"It's the university in New Orleans. It has one of the best law faculties in America. Never mind. That's hardly relevant. Go on."

As he spoke, he returned to the table and sat down. Lindsay, who had no intention of questioning him further, could not tell whether his memories of this place were happy or unhappy; perhaps both, she decided. Just for an instant she had glimpsed a very different Rowland McGuire from the one she thought she was beginning to know. She sensed he had no wish to reveal this aspect of himself, and was angered by his own brief lack of control. He picked up the bottle, and when Lindsay shook her head, poured some whiskey into his own glass. He lifted the liquid against the light, examined it, and then turned back to her with an attempt at his usual manner.

"So tell me this love story of yours, Lindsay. Go on."

"You're sure? It's getting late. I could leave you my article if you'd prefer. You can read the story there. Almost all of it. Everything except the end—which I was asked not to use."

"No, no. I dislike unfinished stories. Stories should have a clear beginning, a middle, and an end." He smiled. "Besides, I'd rather hear it from you."

"Very well." Lindsay's heart gave a skip. She picked up the photograph of the tall, white-haired, patrician woman with the lovely dress beside her. She could remember that interview so well: it had been her first major freelance commission. She had been twenty, proud of hitting on the idea for the piece, proud of placing it with *Vogue*, and—when she reached the house where the interview was to take place—very nervous indeed.

It had been a house in Belgravia, a tall, white-pillared building, its doors opened by a butler, the first butler Lindsay had ever seen outside films. She followed him up a wide staircase and into a huge drawing room with three long windows overlooking the garden square outside. It was autumn; a fire was lit, yet the room was filled with spring flowers. The former Letitia Lafitte Grant, now Lady Roseborough, had risen as she entered, and Lindsay, confronted with this figure of legendary elegance, had quailed.

Then her hands had been clasped, and Letitia had begun speaking in that warm southern voice, so Lindsay's courage returned.

"Come have some tea, my dear. You've come here to ask me about my clothes? We'll have us such fun—there's things I'm going to show you that I haven't looked at in a million years. . . ." She had pronounced it *ye-ahs*. Lindsay, in the quiet of this room with Rowland now, could hear Letitia's slow drawl as she herself recounted a story heard long before.

"The woman in this picture," she explained, "was called Letitia Lafitte Grant, at least that was her name when this dress was made for her. She came from a very old Louisiana family, and had married into an even older and even richer one. Her family had heritage and the Grants had oil. When Letitia married, she went to live in their house, a very beautiful antebellum mansion on the north bank of the Mississippi, between Baton Rouge and New Orleans. She was a famous southern hostess, a famous beauty, a famous horsewoman, and a famous collector of couture. She was also, I think, a generous woman—a woman with a very kind heart."

Lindsay paused. "I went to interview her because of her legendary elegance. She was the kind of woman who could look wonderful in anything. She could make an ensemble out of a borrowed man's shirt, one of her husband's tweed jackets, an old pair of jeans. She loved couture clothes, went to the Paris collections twice a year for over twenty years, and had kept her entire wardrobe in a state of perfect preservation. She died about three years after I interviewed her. Her couture collection is in the Metropolitan Museum in New York now.

"The idea of the interview was that she would show me her collection—the Schiaparellis, the early Chanel, the Balenciagas—and she did show me all of those. I had asked her to select one of her favorite dresses for the photograph, and that's the dress she chose, draped over that chair."

"It was a surprising choice?" Rowland asked; he was listening intently now. "You expected her to select a dress by some famous name?"

"Yes. I did. She explained that she had chosen it because this dress reminded her of a happy period in her life, when her children were almost grown-up and before her first husband's final illness began. And because it reminded her of an extraordinary young girl, the girl who had made it, Marie-Thérèse.

"Letitia told me that it was a very New Orleans story," Lindsay went on. "She said I had to imagine a city very different from the one New Orleans later became. When there were fewer tourists, when it was still possible to feel the city's past. She said I had to imagine the heat, and those beautiful houses in the French Quarter, with their wrought iron balconies, and their atmosphere of decay. She said I had to imagine the city's opposites, its mix of riches and poverty, its mix of races and nationalities—French, Spanish, Caribbean—its mix of religions and superstitions and tongues. She said I had to imagine a city unlike any other in America, where the extraordinary was an everyday occurrence. She made me see her New Orleans, Rowland, and then she told me the story of Marie-Thérèse.

"Letitia had made the girl's acquaintance some years before this dress was made. Marie-Thérèse was then about fourteen, and was attending a convent school in the French Quarter, where one of Letitia's maids had also been at school. On the maid's recommendation, Marie-Thérèse was given some work for the Grant household, embroidering linen and so on. She had been taught her skills by the nuns at her convent, several of whom were French, and Marie-Thérèse, who was of French descent herself but born in New Orleans, was said to be their ablest pupil. When Letitia saw the work she had done, it was so exquisite that she asked to meet the girl. She was at once struck by her. She was quiet, almost excessively modest, not beautiful, but arresting—Letitia described her as *jolie-laide*. She had a very pale skin—magnolia pale, Letitia called it—a childlike manner, and jet-black hair. Letitia was eager to give her more work—mainly because she knew that this girl's circumstances were very poor."

Lindsay paused, and glanced across at Rowland. "Marie-Thérèse had a brother, and they had been orphaned, it seemed. The brother had abandoned school when he was thirteen and his sister just nine. He had become sole provider for his sister from then on."

There was a silence. The fire hissed as a log shifted.

Rowland slowly raised his eyes to meet Lindsay's gaze. "There was a brother? An elder brother?"

"Yes, and according to Letitia, a very protective brother too. An ill-educated, sensitive, proud, and touchy young man."

"Interesting. Go on."

"As a result of that meeting, Letitia took a great liking to the girl. Periodically, she would come out from the city to visit Letitia; Letitia never went to the girl's own home. Over the next two years, Letitia gave her work whenever she could, and whenever the girl, who was still at school, felt able to take it on. Gradually she was entrusted with other tasks besides embroidery. She made some blouses for Letitia, then a beautiful shawl. She was allowed to make alterations to some of Letitia's clothes, and Letitia could see how they fascinated her. She would tell the girl stories of her own visits to the couture houses, of the fittings she went to, and the perfectionism that was insisted upon. She explained about *toiles*, how each garment was assembled and hand sewn. One day she gave Marie-Thérèse one of her oldest and favorite garments, a prewar Chanel suit that had been accidentally torn, and was, she thought, beyond repair. The girl took it away and returned with it in perfect condition. When Letitia examined it, she realized that the girl had taken the entire jacket apart and restitched the whole thing. Marie-Thérèse was trembling with excitement; usually she spoke very little, but that day she could not stop talking about what she had learned. Do you know what she said to Letitia? I quoted it. She said, '*Madame*, I could always see the art, but now I understand the science of clothes.'

"From then onward," Lindsay went on, "Letitia took an even greater interest in the girl. She encouraged her to talk about her circumstances, her home, and her brother. And she was perturbed by what she heard.

Marie-Thérèse and her brother's home consisted of two rooms in a poor part of the Vieux Carré, almost next door to the convent and its school. The rooms were rented to them by the nuns, whose order owned several run-down properties in that part of New Orleans. It was known as the Maison Sancta Maria, because it had a small statue of the Virgin Mary set into a niche in the garden walls. The renting of these rooms was an act of charity on the nuns' part—and also something more. They believed, as did her brother, that Marie-Thérèse had a vocation. They were pressing her to become a novice once her schooling was over. Marie-Thérèse had accepted this. She told Letitia she intended to take the veil.

"This concerned Letitia, who was not Roman Catholic. She suggested the girl should think very seriously before taking such a step. She said she herself was more than prepared to offer an alternative: Marie-Thérèse could join the Grant household; she could be trained for domestic service, or ways might be found to make use of her sewing skills. To Letitia's surprise, the girl refused, though with charm and modesty. She explained she was always guided by her brother, who would never countenance such a step. She said that she could not consider any course of action that would separate her from her brother, who was everything to her—her guardian, protector, and friend. Letitia pointed out gently that although the brother worked for the nuns, helping to maintain their gardens, to become a nun would certainly involve separation from him. Marie-Thérèse listened politely but seemed not to understand."

Lindsay turned to look at Rowland.

"I was never told their surname," she said, "but the brother's Christian name was Jean-Paul. That's very easily abbreviated to Jean, of course. Just as a Marie-Thérèse, who lived in the Maison Sancta Maria, might well, if she were later to alter her name, opt to be plain Maria—especially if she wished to disguise her nationality, wouldn't you say?"

"Yes, I would," Rowland replied. "But I don't want to force a connection too soon." He hesitated.

"I like this story of yours, Lindsay. But I'm not sure that I see the love story yet."

"You will. It was as a result of that conversation," Lindsay continued, "that Letitia's St. Petersburg dress was made. Every year for Mardi Gras, the Grants gave a ball—it was a great event in the Louisiana calendar, and each ball had a theme. They had held an Ottoman ball, a Venetian ball. In 1966 the theme was to be Russian, and Letitia decided that instead of having her dress made in Paris, as she usually did, she would have it made by Marie-Thérèse. Her motives were not purely charitable. If the dress proved a failure, it would not matter greatly—

Letitia had roomfuls of clothes. But if it was the success she hoped, she knew her friends would all want to use this marvelous girl. Then, perhaps, Marie-Thérèse would see that there truly was an alternative life to the cloister."

"And did Letitia succeed?"

"No. The plan backfired. The dress was glorious, a succès fou. All her friends were indeed eager to know the name of the girl who had made it. But neither they nor Letitia ever had the opportunity of employing her. After the night of the Mardi Gras ball, Letitia saw Marie-Thérèse only once more."

Lindsay paused, frowning into the fire across the room. Then, with a sigh, she turned back to Rowland.

"When Letitia reached that part of her story," she said, "I saw her face change. I thought she was about to tell me that something dreadful had happened, perhaps that there had been an accident, that Marie-Thérèse had died. But I was wrong. That wasn't what happened at all. She told me the end of the story on condition I would not print it. It wasn't death that intervened, Rowland. It was the brother—Jean-Paul."

"I see. And Letitia had never met the brother?"

"No. She knew he worked all the hours God made—in the nuns' gardens, in a menial capacity in various New Orleans bars and hotels. Once or twice, at her husband's suggestion, and because his sister claimed he was a gifted mechanic, he had been allowed to help service the Grant cars—they included a number of prewar Rolls-Royces, for which Letitia's husband had a passion."

"And Lazare now collects similar cars."

"Precisely. These jobs had never developed into anything more permanent. The regular staff disliked the boy; they found him arrogant, hypersensitive, always imagining slights that weren't there. He had a violent temper; no one wanted to work alongside him. When the brother arrived on her doorstep the day after her Mardi Gras ball, Letitia found she could understand that reaction. She took an immediate dislike to the boy."

Lindsay hesitated. "She pitied him to some extent, I think. He was only nineteen, and Letitia could see that he'd made a pathetic attempt to appear well dressed. But from the moment he entered her house, he was aggressive and rude. He told her, in a haughty way, that his sister did not need her patronage, that he had always supported her financially and always would if need be. He said he would not tolerate interference in Marie-Thérèse's life from a Protestant family who could never understand a Catholic girl. He spoke at length, and with great emphasis, of his sister's modesty, purity, and religious devotion. He said he would allow Marie-Thérèse to do no more work for Letitia, and that their meetings would cease—all she was doing was poisoning the mind of his sister, tempting her with worldly things. Marie-Thérèse was destined to become a bride of Christ, he said, and this had always been apparent to him, from her earliest years. It was what their dead mother would have wished for her, and he meant to ensure that wish was fulfilled. He recited this speech, which was clearly prepared, with few interruptions from Letitia. Then he stormed out. As with his sister, Letitia saw him only once again."

"How extraordinary. How strange . . ." Rowland said into the silence that followed. "Poor Letitia. So what happened next, Lindsay? Tell me the end."

"Several years passed. Letitia had been offended, and she made no further attempts to see Marie-Thérèse. Occasionally she would hear of her through the maid who had first introduced her, but there was little information, and gradually she lost interest. She had other more important things on her mind: her husband's illness had manifested itself, though it had not yet been diagnosed. It was three years later, in 1969, that she heard from her maid that there had been some crisis: Marie-Thérèse had completed her schooling by then, and had begun instruction at the convent. But she had never completed her novitiate, claiming a loss of faith. This, and other factors, the maid said, had eventually led to a quarrel between the nuns and Marie-Thérèse. She and her brother were about to be evicted, put out on the streets. They had very little money, and no home.

"The maid, convent-educated like Marie-Thérèse, was also a modest girl. When she first heard this story, Letitia sensed that there was some other reason for this eviction that the girl could not bring herself to name. She blushed deeply, and became vague and incoherent when questioned. She said Marie-Thérèse had betrayed the trust the nuns had always shown in her, and that she was seeing no one because of her shame.

"Letitia's husband was very ill at this time. She did not press the matter. Then, in January 1970, her husband was in remission and Mardi Gras was approaching. There would be no ball that year, but Letitia's thoughts returned to Marie-Thérèse. She sent for the maid and questioned her. With great reluctance the maid was eventually persuaded to give an address where Marie-Thérèse and her brother were now said to be living. She said she'd heard that they were desperately poor, and that Marie-Thérèse had been ill, but she would divulge nothing more.

"A few days later," Lindsay went on, "Letitia decided to set off on an errand of mercy." She paused. "I think you can probably guess, Rowland, what she discovered. But oddly enough, it was not something she herself had ever foreseen, and so she was profoundly shocked, even appalled. It took her a long time to find the house, which was dirty and dilapidated, a rooming house in an area to the north of the French Quarter, an area most whites shunned. When she finally reached the house, the front door was open; there were no doorbells, and no name plates. There was an elderly man sitting on the stoop, drinking bourbon. He said that Marie-Thérèse and her husband lived there, in a back room on the top floor. Letitia could hear a baby crying as she mounted the stairs. At first she assumed the noise was coming from one of the other lodgers' rooms. Then she realized, as she reached the top of the stairs. The door to Marie-Thérèse's room was open, as if someone had only just returned—she crossed to the doorway and stopped, without speaking. Marie-Thérèse was huddled in a bed on the far side of the room. She was nursing a tiny baby, trying to persuade it to feed. Bending over her, and with his arm around her shoulders, was her brother, Jean-Paul. Letitia said that she knew instantly, knew beyond any shadow of a doubt, that he was the father of this child.

"She was on the point of leaving before they even realized she was there. Then something stopped her: she could hear from the way in which the baby was crying that it was ill—Letitia had four children of her own. She could see that Marie-Thérèse was painfully thin and looked sickly. She could see tenderness and fear in the way Jean-Paul spoke to mother and child, and she was ashamed of her own immediate reaction. She was on the point of speaking, of suggesting they send for a doctor—her own doctor, if necessary. Then Jean-Paul looked up and saw her. His expression was so terrible that she found she dared not speak. Instead, she put down the basket of fruits she had brought with her, knowing the gift was absolutely inappropriate now. She was watched, in silence, by Jean-Paul, whose face was rigid with anger and scorn. She took out all the money she had with her and placed it in the basket. Then she turned, and left without a word.

"And that was almost the very end of the story," Lindsay said, meeting Rowland's troubled gaze. "Letitia never saw brother or sister again. For some six months after that, she continued to send money to them by mail. It was never acknowledged; she never knew if it was received. Later that year she heard from her maid that brother and sister had left New Orleans. But when she asked about the baby, the maid denied all knowledge of it, so Letitia became concerned. She wondered if the baby could have died. She worried that it might have been adopted, or fostered, or put in a home. She made many inquiries, all fruitless, and finally went to the convent, where she was received by the Mother Superior. This woman confirmed that Marie-Thérèse had had a child—a male child. She would say nothing as to the question of the child's father, and she denied all knowledge of the child's present whereabouts. Marie-Thérèse was unmarried. Dead or alive, she said, the child of such a union could not be her concern.

"Letitia was very angry, but she had come to a dead end and could discover nothing more. Later the same year, her own husband died. Letitia left Louisiana to visit friends in Europe. Some time after that she met her second husband and moved to London. She had returned, she told me, to Louisiana from time to time, but she never felt at peace there again. She never heard any more of the extraordinary girl and her brother. All that was left of the entire episode was the dress in this photograph here. A dress that must now be somewhere in the Metropolitan Museum—packed away, carefully protected in acid-free tissue paper."

She met Rowland's eyes, then looked quickly away. She turned her gaze toward the fire, the shutters, the paneling, the photographs of mountains with their annotated routes. Rowland said nothing, but she could sense he was affected by this story, as she had been the first time she heard it. His head was bent to the two photographs of Russian dresses. With a sigh, Lindsay rose.

"So you see, it was a love story," she said. "A love story of an unusual kind."

"Most are—to those involved," he replied.

Lindsay continued to stare at those mountains; a log shifted in the fire.

"I'm certain it's the story of Cazarès and Lazare," she said at last. "Rowland, I'm sure."

"I am too. I probably shouldn't be. There's no proof beyond the dresses. But I have instincts too, Lindsay—as much as you do. I can hear the truth in it." He hesitated, then looked up to meet her gaze. "But you have to understand, Lindsay—I'm sure you do. Even if I could prove every last word of it, it's a story I could never use in their lifetime. Max wouldn't countenance it. Neither would I. It's their affair. It's intensely private—and a child is involved. . . . What are you doing?"

"Getting my coat. I do understand. I knew you'd say that. I knew it could only be background. I ought to go home now."

"Why? It's only nine—we could go out for a meal, I thought. I'm very glad you told me all this. There's a hundred and one things I want to ask you."

Lindsay stopped in front of those mountain photographs. She looked at their noted routes. She breathed in and out ten times, then put down her coat with a smile.

"Aren't we married, Rowland?" she said. "I seem to recall we were married yesterday, after a whirlwind romance. . . . So, shouldn't we act married? Why don't I cook you a meal?"

CHAPTER 11

"This is a bad idea," Rowland said, clattering down the bare stairs behind her. "Lindsay, I'm warning you. I told you I wasn't house trained. There won't be any food."

"Of course there will," she replied over her shoulder. "Through here? Every kitchen has food in it, Rowland, even yours."

It had not escaped Lindsay's notice that her proposal to cook had caused Rowland deep unease. In the gospel according to Max, of course, Rowland's one-monthers and three-monthers always insisted on ministering to him.

"Listen, Rowland," she said firmly, removing from the back of the kitchen door a frilly apron Rowland would certainly never have purchased. "Let's get one thing clear. This is *work*. We're colleagues. With luck we might end up friends. I do not have designs on you. I'm not moving in on you. I hate people who do that. I've had innumerable lovers who tried to do just that to me—and they're all ex-lovers now."

"Really?" Rowland said, recovering his poise, leaning back against the door and raising an eyebrow. "Innumerable, eh?"

"You don't need chapter and verse." Lindsay began opening cupboards. "I'm just telling you, the techniques are roughly the same. In my case they start telling me what wine to buy. Then they criticize my clothes. Then they tell me how to bring up my son. Then they complain about the hours I work. At which point"—she glanced back at him with a smile—"I usually let Louise loose on them."

"If they're that easily detached, they probably weren't worth bothering with in the first place," Rowland remarked.

Lindsay, mildly thrilled by this statement, ignored it, and made a great show of going through cabinets in search of food. The exchange seemed to have been useful, she thought; Rowland now appeared much more relaxed, in a good humor, even quietly amused. He found a bottle of wine and uncorked it. He set two places at the table.

"So, Sylvie wasn't serious, then?" Lindsay managed to interject. Rowland looked genuinely astonished, then a little embittered.

"Serious? I thought you'd heard the gossip. I never get seriously involved. Didn't your informants make that clear?"

Lindsay decided it was safer to say no more. She concentrated her attention on Rowland's kitchen, which, though primitive, had charm. The refrigerator might be antique, and the gas stove looked prewar, but the room had a beautiful York stone floor, and a splendid built-in breakfront—at present, unfortunately, still painted its original Victorian brown.

Blue, Lindsay thought; that wonderful flat, washed-out Swedish blue; or perhaps an off cream. Then you could put lots of blue and white plates on it, and a huge jug of wild flowers. You could have a rush mat on the floor . . . really, all the room needed was repainting, and *things.* . . .

"So tell me. I'm going to cross-examine you now," Rowland said, sitting down at the pine table—it was nice, that pine table—and running his hands through his astonishing hair. "First, why has no one else made this connection before? Those two dresses are identical. Your piece appeared in *Vogue,* after all."

"Timing, mainly," Lindsay answered, staring at Rowland's small store of edibles and wondering how on earth you could make a meal from these ingredients. "My article didn't appear until spring 1979, three years *after* the Cazarès St. Petersburg collection. It ran in an English magazine, and that particular 1976 Cazarès dress was featured only in an American publication. Unless you put the two photographs side by side, you'd never make the connection. At most, you'd note a resemblance and pass on."

Inside the cabinet there were two shelves. On the bottom one were the items Rowland had evidently purchased: five cans of tomato soup, several cans of tuna fish, an unopened package of instant five-minute rice, some breakfast cereal, marmalade, and jam. On the upper shelf were articles evidently purchased by Sylvie and perhaps by her predecessors—

some of it looked dusty, sad, as if neglected for months, or even years. There was a large bottle of very expensive virgin olive oil, a jar of sun-dried tomatoes, a can of pâté de foie gras, some raspberry vinegar, some green peppercorns, and a little pot of musty Provençal mixed herbs.

"You don't have any eggs, do you, Rowland? Sorry, what did you just say?"

"Letitia," he said, fetching eggs, then sitting down again, apparently now happy to let Lindsay get on with it, as she much preferred. "All right, so no one else spotted the similarity, but she must have. She bought couture. Surely she must have noticed that the hot new Paris designer had produced a dress identical to the one made for her ten years before?"

"No. Because she gave up all that after her first husband died. She stopped going to the collections. She stopped buying couture. She would have heard of Cazarès by the time I interviewed her, obviously. But she wouldn't have seen the *Harper's Bazaar* picture of that actual dress. I keep telling you, Rowland. It's an American publication. If she'd known, she'd certainly have told me. I'm certain she had no idea. . . . Rowland, don't *watch* me when I cook. It puts me off."

"Sorry. I wasn't really watching you. I was thinking. Staring into space. Are you going to scramble those eggs? I like scrambled eggs."

"Yes, I am," said Lindsay, breaking eggs into a bowl. "It's going to be a hodgepodge. A Tom sort of meal. And it's going to be damn difficult scrambling eggs in this thing. They'll stick. The bottom of the pan's all wobbly. Don't watch."

Obligingly, Rowland averted his eyes.

"The dates fit," he went on in a thoughtful way, "the ages fit. Lazare's—what? Almost fifty? And Cazarès never reveals her age, but she must be in her forties, even if she looks younger. If she was sixteen or seventeen in 1966, that would make her around forty-five or forty-six now. Possible?"

"Yes. Insofar as you can tell from one glimpse on a runway twice a year. When she's heavily made up, and darts away again as quickly as possible."

"It would explain a good deal," Rowland went on. "The accent Lazare has, for a start; a New Orleans French accent is very strange. Presumably Cazarès managed to eradicate hers—but then, she was better educated than her brother. More important, it explains the pathological secrecy, of course. The deliberate laying of false trails. Can you imagine it, Lindsay, if it's true? All those years pretending they were not related, desperately hiding that one central truth from the world?"

"No, I can't," Lindsay said. "But I know it would be horrible—

corroding. And they weren't just disguising the fact that they were re-lated. They were lovers as well as brother and sister. If the rumors can be believed, they're lovers still."

She broke off from stirring eggs to turn the bread toasting under the grill.

Rowland made no comment.

"That child haunts me," she continued, her face troubled. "I could see he haunted Letitia as well. What do you think became of him? Did he die, get put in some home? I think perhaps he did die. Perhaps he was handicapped in some way."

"The child of a brother and sister? I know."

"Think, Rowland, if he'd lived, he'd be in his twenties now. Grown-up. Older than Tom. And they could never acknowledge him, never even see him. I think that would be so desperately hard. . . . What is it, Rowland?"

"Nothing." He had turned to look at her, suddenly intent; then he shook his head. "All of this is speculation anyway. It's not even easy to check it out. There's no surname. It's too vague."

"If you did have a surname"—Lindsay was now spooning eggs onto toast—"would you be able to run checks then?"

"Oh, you could run some even without a name. You could start with the Grants, with that convent and its school. With a name, you'd cer-tainly get a lot further. You could then trace the births of Marie-Thérèse and her brother. You should be able to trace the birth of her child—and discover whether or not he died. It's conceivable you could trace them to France, through immigration records. That might provide an early ad-dress. That might give you a lead on how or where Lazare first made his money, even when they changed their names. But it would take a long time, it might lead nowhere, and besides, I told you, Lindsay. This is background and it has to stay background."

Lindsay said nothing. It had occurred to her that there might be a quick way of discovering that surname, and an ingenious way too, but she did not intend to mention it to Rowland, in case she was wrong.

They sat down to eat their meal. It was a kind of picnic, Lindsay thought. They had toast and scrambled eggs, then toast and pâté. Then Rowland, who was still hungry—it seemed unfair that a man could im-bibe so many calories and remain whiplash lean—ate cornflakes for des-sert. He made coffee—and at some point during this odd meal, which began companionably enough, Lindsay could sense that just as he had done earlier, he was retreating into some private world of his own.

"I'm sorry," he said at last, catching her eye. "I'm getting locked back into this Lazare story. That happens to me. I'm not good at switching off. And there's one detail that's bothering me."

"About the story I told you?"

"Indirectly, perhaps. It's more than that though."

"You can't tell me why you're interested in Lazare?"

"Lindsay, no. I'm sorry. When it's over, I'll explain."

"But Gini knows? She's going to work on it with you?"

"That's certainly the plan."

"So it does relate to what happened at Max's? And it does relate in some way to Amsterdam?"

"Lindsay, don't ask." He rose. "Look, it's past ten now. I ought to call Gini—I said I would. She was going to see Susan Landis this evening, and some of Cassandra and Mina's friends. It's getting late. Would you mind if I just called her briefly? I won't be five minutes."

He was fifteen. He returned, looking thoughtful and distracted.

"So, any progress?"

"No, unfortunately. Gini saw a group of girls from that Cheltenham school. One claimed Cassandra had mentioned Star a few times. But that's all. None of them was much help. There have been no sightings of Mina—if there had been, Gini or Max or the newsroom would have called. We're running the story of Cassandra's death and Mina's disappearance tomorrow. With photographs of both of them. That might bring something in. Meantime, Gini's going off to Amsterdam in the morning, and you're off to Paris."

He stopped speaking abruptly. Then: "Let me get your coat—and I'll just quickly find those books I promised Tom."

Five minutes later Lindsay was in her car, a book on Bergman, another on Fellini, and a tome on the French nouvelle vague on the passenger seat beside her. It was a long, slow, cold drive home, with many misturnings and doubling-backs. She had been thanked with warmth and courtesy. She still felt dismissed and dispatched.

What had the evening achieved? She had cooked perfect scrambled eggs in an impossible saucepan. She had provided Rowland with information that might be fascinating but was of little practical use. He didn't even trust her enough to explain the exact nature of the story he was working on. The story he and Gini were working on.

"I hate the world," she told Tom, who was still up and watching a late movie.

A small bump on the sofa, which in the dim light Lindsay had mistaken for cushions, uncurled itself and sat up. It proved to be Tom's quiet, sweet-faced, and somewhat formidable girlfriend. Her name was Katya. Tom put his arm around her.

"Never mind," he said in a kind way, eyes still fixed on the screen. "The world doesn't hate *you*. Nor do I."

"Nor me," said Katya. "Hi."

Lindsay felt cheered. She went to bed, tossed the fat airport novel on the floor, kicked it under the wardrobe, and read Updike for two hours. At one in the morning she got out of bed, retrieved the fat novel, and turned to the end. The hero was a veritable Lazarus, it seemed. He came back to abundant life on page 502, seduced the heroine again on page 503, quarreled with her magnificently on page 510, and after an eight-page sexual marathon, led her altarward on the penultimate page.

Like Rowland, Lindsay was a traditionalist when it came to stories: she had a weakness for triumphal love. Comforted by this rousing ending, she returned to bed and slept well.

Rowland, meanwhile, lay in his bed on the top floor of his Huguenot house with its view of Hawksmoor's spire. Across the street, as he had first observed shortly after Lindsay's departure, a white Mercedes convertible was parked. He had no inclination to check whether it remained there, but lay on his back, wakeful, watching the time go past.

He thought back through the story Lindsay had recounted. He thought of her, and of Gini, then Cassandra, who was dead, and Mina, who was still missing, and finally of a young man with dark hair, a young man in his twenties, a young man of undisclosed nationality, Mitchell's candy man, Star.

At three he fell into a light sleep; he dreamed of a shadowy Esther, and a shadowy New Orleans. Although he retained a clear sense of direction, he was dazed. They walked together along Decatur, up Dumaine, along Bourbon to Canal. Esther was trying to tell him something, but he could not hear the words.

He awoke with a start and lay there, fighting the restlessness such dreams always caused. Hours inched by; he felt the peculiar turmoil of exhaustion and sleeplessness; he felt under siege from the demands of the present and the past.

At five, abandoning the possibility of sleep, he rose, went downstairs to his cold kitchen, and made coffee. Sitting there at the table, he finally submitted, and let the past back into his mind. It was not such a very long history: he had met Esther, a DEA operative, within a month of his taking that assignment in Washington, D.C. Until then, he had spent most of his free time on the fringes of Georgetown, in the company of fellow English journalists. It was a close-knit, gossipy, expatriate community, inward-looking, dependent on American contacts for work yet treating Americans, Rowland found, with a curious, faintly derisive patronage; this patronage, he noted—and it angered him—modulated in private, and after drinks, into scorn. The clannishness, the clubbiness, was already beginning to pall, and Rowland was already finding that he was gravitating more and more to the company of American journalists, when a friend at the *Post* introduced him to Esther.

On the occasion he first met her, in a fashionable downtown restaurant, she drew his eye for several reasons: she was unusually tall; she was beautiful; she was formally and exquisitely dressed—and she was the only black woman in the room. Rowland, the outsider, the displaced person, the man who never felt English, or Irish, who had never had the sensation he belonged, shook her hand. She gave him a long, cool, quantifying look: Rowland felt an immediate, and astonishing sense of recognition, the signaling of like to like; it was followed by a rare exhilaration, then some ruthlessness on his part. The friend who had introduced them was ditched, unceremoniously, within the hour. Moving on with her somewhere, anywhere, the place was immaterial, they ended up at three in the morning at a street near his house. Esther was a Smith graduate; she had a law degree from Harvard; her great-great-grandmother had been a slave. These facts mattered very much, and not at all.

"Come home with me," Rowland said.

She gave him one long, still, grave, considering look.

"I just might do that," she replied.

A week later they rented an apartment together near Dupont Circle. A month after that, Rowland proposed; Esther, more cautious than he, refused.

"Very well," Rowland said. "I shall repeat the suggestion a year from now. In the meantime, I'll just make myself indispensable."

"You're indispensable now," she replied dryly. "As I suspect you know."

A year passed; during that year Rowland's newspaper decided to send him to France. Rowland rejected this assignment, and subsequently resigned. To his surprise, he found it was an easy decision: Esther's work tied her to Washington; his did not, but he found that he had plenty of free-lance work there from both British and American papers. His English friends doubted the wisdom of this move, and Max—visiting from

London—castigated him for it. Their demurrals made Rowland impatient; he did not doubt his own abilities; he knew he could alter the course of his career; he intended, and needed, to be with Esther: the choice was effortless, and no sacrifice was involved.

"Marry me," Rowland said to her—and being meticulous about such things, he reiterated his proposal exactly one year later, to the hour.

"I just might do that," Esther replied.

A date was arranged; the week before, they were due to visit her brother again, in New Orleans. Her brother, host to them on several previous occasions, had promised to be Rowland's best man. At the last minute Rowland was forced to cancel that visit to cover an urgent story. He was writing up his copy, was near to completing it, when Esther announced she was just going out to the grocery store.

He had glanced around quickly from his desk; Esther had smiled, waved a hand at him, and told him to hurry up and finish writing. Now, sitting in his kitchen, his coffee cold and undrunk, Rowland looked at that tiny, frozen frame: the last time he had seen her alive. Had he not changed the date of their visit, she would still have been alive; they would have been married, might have had—would surely have had—children. My fault, he thought as he always thought at this point. My fault, and I didn't even say good-bye.

The boy who killed her, a crack addict just sixteen years old, stopped her on the way back from the store. Two blocks from their house. He demanded her purse—and, according to the witnesses, Esther at once gave it to him. For no known or comprehensible reason, the boy shot her anyway. He raised his gun and fired into her neck at point-blank range. Esther fell; she bled to death on the sidewalk. Mindful perhaps of AIDS statistics, the little clutch of bystanders who gathered around her did nothing; no one administered first aid.

That fact, which had made him so bitterly angry at the time, still made him so now, six years later. It would, almost certainly, have made little difference—or so Rowland was subsequently informed. Still, it remained for him an act of iniquity: even if those witnesses could not have saved her, surely one of them at least could have held her, cradled her, talked to her as she died?

He found the manner of her death unbearable, and sometimes he believed that his own inability to abandon mourning was connected not simply to her death, but to the *way* in which she died. It was as if he had to compensate for that act of omission and for his own act of omission in not saying good-bye. The futility of this task, of which he was aware, did not deter him. Max had told him once, sharply, to stop doing penance. Rowland, hearing the accuracy of the remark, turned away in silence. He felt penance had been imposed upon him: choice was not involved.

Now he never spoke of Esther to anyone, under any circumstances. He preserved his grief with this privacy, and when—with the passing of time—he sensed that this grief was less intense, it made him ashamed.

Grief, he was beginning to discover, could not be activated at will, no, not even predawn, alone in a cold house, in an empty room. Esther was beginning to slip away from him. He could still recapture the sound of her voice, and sometimes the exact quality of her gaze, but her image was more shadowy than before. He could sense her, escaping his grasp, edging away from him into that netherworld the dead occupy, while more vivid figures, living figures, moved to the fore.

Was this release, or betrayal? Could you betray the dead? Once he would have answered that last question in the affirmative; now he was unsure.

He waited another hour, and then—at seven—called Gini, who was still in the country with Charlotte, but preparing to catch an early flight to Amsterdam. There she was going to see Anneke's parents, who might or might not have information about Star.

"Ask if he could be American," Rowland said. "Ask if he could have American connections."

"Why? Rowland, I'm not hopeful they'll know anything anyway."

"Never mind. Just ask."

When he had hung up, he felt angry with himself. He was doing what he most despised, breaking every rule in his own book. He was seeing connections where none existed—but then, that was not surprising, he told himself. For several reasons, among them lack of sleep, his judgment was impaired.

"Is there any chance this Star could be American?" Gini asked. "Or could have American connections? Did your daughter Anneke ever mention making American friends?"

Across the room from her, Erica van der Leyden shook her head. "No. Apart from the note Anneke left, she never mentioned this man. I don't recall her having any American friends. We lead a quiet life. Anneke was at school all day. When she came home, she had homework to do. If she was out, it was always with friends I knew. My husband and I never allowed her to wander around Amsterdam on her own, going to cafés, that sort of thing. Anneke had a strict upbringing. My husband and I are old-fashioned."

"Of course," Gini said politely, wondering whether there was any point in continuing. She had been here, in this lovely, tranquil, exquisitely furnished room for nearly an hour. To enter it was like stepping into one of the Dutch interior paintings she had always loved. A Delft-tiled wood-burning stove stood in the corner; tall windows overlooked one of the loveliest canals in Amsterdam. Erica van der Leyden was as civilized and as understated in appearance as the room; she spoke perfect English; she was about thirty-six, dressed in conservative clothes, low-heeled shoes, a well-cut skirt, a sweater, and pearls.

Only her hands revealed the grief she experienced and the tension she felt. She could not keep them still. Every time she had to speak her dead daughter's name, her hands clenched. Gini pitied her deeply. She could see that Erica van der Leyden was a woman fighting desperately to stay calm, a woman hanging on by the slenderest of threads.

There was only one discordant element in this room, and that was the teenage girl now slouched in a chair to Gini's right. She had been introduced as Fricke, Anneke's elder sister, and was about sixteen. She was not prepossessing, and Gini suspected she both knew that, and chose to emphasize it. She was overweight, with heavy eyeglasses, and long, fair, greasy hair. She was wearing jeans and a turtleneck sweater, and she, too—to judge from the few sullen remarks she had so far made—spoke excellent English.

Her mother had already made two attempts to persuade her to leave the room. Neither had been successful, for all that strict upbringing. Rising to her feet now, Erica van der Leyden made a third.

"Fricke, I'm sure you must have some studying to do."

"I've already done it."

"Then if you would leave us alone, please, for just a short while. You can see—this isn't easy for Miss Hunter or for me." She hesitated, then said something more sharply, in Dutch. Fricke gave her another sullen stare and did not move.

"Why shouldn't I stay? I'm Anneke's sister. I don't suppose it occurs to anyone I might have something useful to say."

The rudeness, and the fact that she spoke in English so Gini could not mistake the rudeness, seemed to please her. Erica van der Leyden flushed, and Gini quickly intervened.

"No, please. Don't ask Fricke to leave on my account. It's true. She might well remember something—something that seems unimportant perhaps."

Fricke made a small grimace that might have implied satisfaction, or scorn. Her mother gave a resigned gesture of the hands and returned to her chair. She gave Gini a bewildered, helpless look. Gini could feel this interview slipping away from her. She leaned forward.

"Perhaps, Mrs. van der Leyden, if you could describe Anneke to me. I know it must be painful, but under the circumstances . . ."

"Of course." Her hands twisted in her lap. "Another young girl is dead. A third is missing. My heart goes out to their parents. I wish I could assist, but—"

"If you could just tell me the kind of things Anneke liked, that might help. Did she like to go to the movies, or dance? Did she like music?"

"Well, she liked music, I suppose—modern music, as most girls of her age do. She was interested in clothes. She used to buy fashion magazines, didn't she, Fricke? We had some arguments, as mothers and daughters do, about hair, and makeup and clothes—but nothing serious. Anneke was a very sweet girl, not as clever as Fricke, of course, but imaginative. Gregarious. She had lots of friends. She had pen pals too, all over the world. She loved receiving letters and cards. And then she was quite good at languages. She liked to travel. We had all been to Italy, and Spain, and to Switzerland to ski. She made a school trip to Paris last year, and another, the year before, to London, which was a great excitement. She took ballet classes. She was good at dancing, very graceful. . . ."

It was the very ordinariness of what she was describing that undermined her: Gini saw the realization come into her face—that the girl she was describing might be any young girl from a reasonably privileged and educated background. Her own inability to convey her daughter's uniqueness—that was what made her suddenly choke on her words. Tears rose to her eyes. With a gesture of apology she rose and turned away.

Gini expected Fricke to go to her mother then, and attempt to comfort her, but the girl did not move. She continued to sprawl, exactly as before, watching with an air of surly condescension. Gini stood.

"Mrs. van der Leyden," she said. "This is distressing you. I'm sorry. Perhaps it would be better if I left now?"

"No. Please. You've come a long way. I said I would see you. Perhaps—there's a photograph of Anneke I would like to show you. I'll get it. If you would excuse me one moment . . ."

She left the room. In the heavy silence that followed, Gini returned to her chair. She picked up the note Anneke's mother had produced earlier, the note that Anneke had left behind. It was dated the second of April, the previous year. On an attached sheet of paper, for Gini's benefit, was a neatly inscribed translation. It read:

Dear Mother and Father,

Yesterday I met a new friend, called Star. He is a wonderful man, and very kind. I'm going with him to England for just a few days. I'll be back Friday. I'll call from England. Don't worry.

Lots of love,
Anneke

Nine months later she was dead. Her parents never saw her alive again. It was the stuff of every parent's nightmares, and the note's insouciance, its naïveté, chilled Gini to the bone.

"She actually believes all that, you know."

Fricke spoke so suddenly that Gini started.

"I'm sorry?"

"My mother." Fricke rose. "She actually believes all that rubbish she said now. Pen pals. Ballet lessons." She gave Gini a measuring look. "I suppose you believed it too."

"Not necessarily." Gini returned that look coldly. "Your mother was trying to help me. She may be mistaken in what she said."

"Oh, yeah? She's mistaken all right. My father too. They didn't understand Anneke. They didn't know her at all."

"Look, do you have something to tell me?"

"I might have."

"Then why don't you get on with it and stop wasting my time?"

The girl flushed, then gave a shrug and turned away. Gini waited. Her instinct was not to prompt and not to plead—and it seemed to be correct, for it was Fricke who was the first to give way.

"I can't talk to you here." She hesitated. "You know the Leidseplein? It's a big square, near the Vondel Park."

"I know it. I've been to Amsterdam before."

"There's a café there, on the north corner. It's called the Rembrandt. I'll meet you there in half an hour. I have a violin lesson then. I'll skip it. She'll never know. . . ."

"Fricke—"

The girl was already moving toward the door. She gave Gini one last, sneering glance.

"If you're there, fine. If you're not—who cares . . . You reporters are all crap anyway. When Anneke first disappeared, they were all on the doorstep, they phoned all the time. Now that she's dead—what happens? Nothing. They've all gone on to the next fucking tragedy."

She brought out the two expletives with some care. Gini did not react to them or to her comments, and this seemed to disappoint her. She left the room.

Gini remained only a short while longer with Mrs. van der Leyden. Yes, she learned, Anneke had kept a diary and address book, but she had taken them to England, and they had never been found; the police had already been through all her other personal papers, which had provided no information, and which were now packed away. No, there had never been any hint of serious unhappiness or disturbance on Anneke's part. She was a contented, well-adjusted girl with nice friends from good families.

This portrait did not convince Gini, and she knew it did not truly convince Anneke's mother either; that was why she stressed its accuracy so desperately and at such length. She continued to speak in this way as she led Gini down the stairs and across the hall. There, her hand on the front door, she abruptly stopped. "Sometimes she would have these little moods, of course," she went on, pleading in her eyes. "As all teenagers do, as Fricke does. It's nothing. It passes. It's part of growing up. She knew how much we loved her. She loved her family in return."

Gini could hear the agonized unspoken questions, and read them in her eyes. They were the same questions Mina's parents had not dared to voice to her the previous night: What didn't we see, how did we fail her, where did we go wrong?

"Please. Take the photograph. Keep it. It's yours."

Erica van der Leyden pressed the picture of Anneke into Gini's hands. Her face crumpled, became lax with grief.

"I *loved* her," she said with sudden passion. "I loved her so much. If you don't have children, you can't understand. I love my husband, of course—we've been married many years, and I would never tell him this. . . . But the way I love him, it's nothing, *nothing* compared to the way I love my daughters. Is that terrible? I don't care. It's true. If I had to sacrifice him for them, I wouldn't hesitate, not for one second. Him, myself, this house, everything we possess—it's all meaningless, I'd abandon it all tomorrow, I'd *kill* to bring her back—"

"Please," Gini began.

"—that's what it means to be a mother. No man on earth can ever feel like that. Such desperate desperate love. Oh, dear merciful God . . ."

She was shuddering from head to foot. She covered her face with her hands, then suddenly gripped Gini hard, forcing her to look up at her face.

"Tell me Anneke knew that. If I could just believe she knew that . . ."

"I'm absolutely certain she knew it," Gini said quietly. "Mrs. van der Leyden, I'm sure she knew. . . ."

It was an inadequate reply, but it seemed to console Anneke's mother—temporarily, at least.

"Perhaps you're right," she said. "I pray to God you're right."

Leaving the house, Gini walked away fast, and stood by the canal, holding tight against the railings of the bridge. She was trembling with the force of Erica van der Leyden's emotion. It had passed from Anneke's mother into her; she felt as if it were in her lungs and heart and blood. It was fearsome, and she feared it most because it had not simply been transferred from Anneke's mother to herself—something within her had risen up to meet it, to recognize it. I have been *claimed*, Gini thought, beginning to pace the bridge, breathing in great gusts of the cold air; and because she knew that this had always lain in wait for her, that it was her female birthright, this moment was one she never forgot.

She crossed to the far side of the canal and looked back. Anneke's mother was drawing the blinds against the gathering dusk. Gini knew she had crossed a divide. For a moment she felt physically weak, weighted down by a disabling passion and concern. The next instant she experienced its very opposite, a heady strength so powerful, so affirmative, she felt light with joy.

She had been ready for this initiation into womanhood, she thought. She had been preparing for it since arriving in Sarajevo, but how curious, how unlikely, that this revelation should be effected in a strange city, in the bourgeois hall of a bourgeois house, by a woman she had never previously met.

This was how it felt to be a mother; this was the nature of that condition; she could feel its vulnerability and its power flow in her veins. She felt a sudden and overwhelming flood of gratitude to the woman who, having lost a child, had given her this gift.

Was the conduit grief, or love? Both, she thought, and, turning, quickening her pace, made her way toward the Leidseplein, and its cafés and its lights.

In the summer months the Rembrandt café would have been filled, no doubt, with students, backpackers, the international army of the young. Now, in January, its interior was almost deserted. Those few customers there were all foreign and elderly, perhaps retired couples taking low-price mid-winter breaks.

Gini chose a prominent table by the windows and ordered coffee. She waited, calming herself, forcing her mind back to her work, though she knew from this moment on, she worked with new purpose and a deeper determination, and that her work would be informed by the emotion she had seen in Erica van der Leyden's face. Two young girls had died; Mina

Landis would not make a third, she would not let that happen—and as she let that thought settle in her mind, she felt it was not some empty assertion or boast: she was *armed* now, and injury to another daughter, another child, was something she could actually prevent.

She needed assistance, however; she needed some new lead. Unless Fricke proved helpful, she could see that this visit, even if far from a wasted journey for her, was one that would produce little hard information. She needed a signpost; someone had to show her which road to take next.

She had already seen the police inspector who had handled Anneke's case; he also had spoken perfect English, and been eager to assist. But nine months of inquiries, it seemed, had thrown up virtually nothing.

"Your police have the advantage over us," he said. "They have a description at least. To tell you the truth, I'm surprised Star actually exists. I'd decided Anneke van der Leyden invented the name. It wouldn't have surprised me. With girls her age, nothing does."

A dead end, Gini thought. The previous day, at Max's, before Rowland left with Lindsay for London, she had tried to persuade him once more to let her talk to his DEA contact here. She had been expecting a refusal, and a flat refusal was precisely what she got.

"Then just give me a place name, Rowland," she had said, walking out to the drive with him. "A café. A bar. Somewhere this Dutch chemist goes, where his American partner hangs out."

"No. I will not. I've already explained. I get information on condition I do nothing to prejudice a DEA investigation that's been in place for months."

"I'm *not* going to prejudice it, for God's sake. What do you think I'm going to do, Rowland? March up to these guys, order a crate of White Doves, flash my press card, and demand Star's real name or else?"

"The answer's no. It has to be no. I gave my word, my professional assurance."

"Oh, very well. It seems to me that finding Mina is rather more urgent than some DEA shadow play that's been going on for months. Still, you're the boss."

He was not amused by that. He gave her one long, cold, green look.

"Shall I just make something crystal clear? You step out of line on this, Gini, you embarrass my source, and I'll take you off this story. You won't work for me again—ever. Understood?"

"Understood," Gini had replied with an irritable shrug. She had been about to turn away, go back into the house, but something in Rowland's manner made her pause. He seemed to be waiting for some further response. Gini hesitated; she knew her manner had been graceless; she still did not find it easy to accept instructions from men—she had worked with too many men in the past whose editorial dictates she despised, and Rowland McGuire's tone, that cold, flat statement of terms, had made her hackles rise at once.

He was still waiting: standing in the driveway, his hands thrust into the pockets of his overcoat, the wind lifting his dark hair away from his forehead, his green eyes—he had the clearest green eyes she had ever seen—still resting on her face. She could feel his disapproval—and he seemed to regret that, as if he had expected better of her. This was not just intransigency, male obstinacy, she realized, feeling guilty. Rowland was waiting for her to admit that his seniority to her was not the issue; he was waiting to see if she had the honesty to admit that he was right.

"I'm sorry," she said, turning to him with a gesture of apology. "Really. I do understand the priorities here. I give you my word, Rowland. I won't do anything to prejudice your source."

"It could be dangerous if you did," he said, and something in his tone confused Gini.

"Dangerous? You mean to me?"

"No. Of course not. At least I hope not. To my source, obviously."

"You mean—if his cover was blown? Rowland, I'd never do that."

"I did explain. The DEA didn't put an operative into Amsterdam just to report on the activities of a small-time Dutch chemist, however lethal or successful his product. Amsterdam is a major conduit for heroin and cocaine. At a conservative estimate, five billion dollars worth of those drugs passed through that city in the last twelve months. With those sums of money involved, the stakes are extremely high. So are the risks for any operative on the ground. I imagine I don't need to explain that."

Gini flushed. "No. Of course not. You're right to rein me in. I'm sorry I spoke as I did. I realize—I'm rushing it, going too fast. I do that. I get obsessional. It's been remarked on before. I'm nearly cured. . . ."

He had looked at her then with slightly more warmth. He began to walk away toward Lindsay's car, then turned back.

"Just as a matter of interest—who remarked on your impetuosity? Was it Max?"

"No. My father—for years. And Pascal's certainly touched on it more than once."

She knew he picked up the wryness of her tone, but he made no further comment. He gave her one last odd, assessing look, then climbed into Lindsay's car for the drive back to London.

An unusual man, Gini thought now; an interesting man—and a man who was every bit as capable of impetuosity as she was. Lindsay had described him, on the trip down, as arrogant. Gini wondered if she had since revised that view—with which she herself would not have agreed. In the short time she had known Rowland McGuire, she had already clashed with him twice. She did not like to recall that moment when he had rounded on her in Max's kitchen and accused her of lack of charity. He was the only person present on that occasion who had had the courage to say what they all thought, and she admired that. Not arrogant, she thought, but uncompromising—and though she might not admit it to him, she owed Rowland a debt for that angry remark. It had shocked and shamed her out of the slough of despair and aimlessness and misery in which she had been drowning for months; but she was grateful for it. Rowland McGuire had put her back on course. Thanks to him, she had rediscovered how it felt to be herself.

She must call him, she thought, as well as Pascal, when she returned to her hotel. Meanwhile—she looked at her watch—it was nearly four, and Fricke was late.

She opened her bag and took out the picture of Anneke. It was a studio portrait, her mother had said, taken to celebrate her fourteenth birthday. Her last birthday; within a year of this picture's being taken, Anneke was dead.

A pretty, elfin-faced girl stared back at her. She had short flaxen hair, like her mother, cut in a neat bob. She was wearing an old-fashioned dress, which made her look younger than her years. Like Mina, she could have been taken for a twelve-year-old. She was thin, flat-chested, and her smile looked forced, as if cameras made her self-conscious.

"She hated that picture," a voice said.

Gini looked up to see Fricke by her side, clutching a violin case. She made a grimace, then sat down, poured herself some coffee, and immediately—with a defiant glance at Gini—lit a cigarette.

"It doesn't even look like her. They dolled her up." She gave Gini another of her slow, measuring looks. "So. This girl who's missing now—Mina, right? You have a picture of her?"

"Not with me. No."

"Does she have dark hair by any chance? Black hair?"

"No. She has red hair. Why?"

"Because he likes dark hair. Anneke told me. She dyed her hair black to please Star. You didn't know that?"

"No."

"Well, she did. He cut it off, cropped it, so it was really really short, like yours. Then she dyed it black for him. She liked it. It looked cool, she said."

"I see." Gini returned the measuring look. "So, is this what you wanted to tell me? That you and Anneke were in touch after she left? And your parents don't know this?"

"No one knows." She gave Gini a mutinous glance, then pushed back her hair. "Tell them if you like. I don't give a shit."

"I don't want to run telling tales." Gini paused, trying to assess her. "But why tell me?"

"You came all the way from England." She blew out a cloud of smoke, then shrugged. "Maybe I was touched by that. Maybe I thought you had a brain in your head, better than most of those creeps who tried to interview my mother. I was watching. I thought you were pretty smart. On the other hand . . . Maybe I just felt like it. Anneke's dead now. Why not?"

"And that makes a difference? Had you promised her you'd say nothing?"

"Yeah. She called twice when my parents were out. The first time was about three days after she left. The second was about two weeks after that. She made me swear I wouldn't tell—and there was nothing to tell anyway. None of it was heavy—she just wanted to chat. She didn't tell me where she was. She said she'd be coming back. . . . And I believed her. I thought she really was okay, the way she said—"

She began to cry suddenly, as suddenly as her mother had. Tears dripped down her nose and misted her glasses. She took them off and began to rub them furiously with a paper napkin. Gini watched her quietly: without her glasses, without that expression of sneering defiance on her face, Fricke looked young, vulnerable—and afraid, Gini thought.

"Is that the problem, Fricke?" she said gently when the girl's fit of sobbing had stopped. "Have you been feeling guilty about this?"

It was the wrong approach. "Who said I felt guilty?" Fricke snapped. "Why should I? I told you—she didn't say one fucking thing that would have helped anyone find her. Get off my back . . ."

"Fine," Gini said, and decided to try another tack, since sympathy evidently made the girl feel angry and cornered. "Then let's stick to some facts. Let's start with you—who taught you your slang, Fricke? Were they American or British, because someone did."

"I don't know what you're talking about. Everyone Dutch speaks good English. I've been learning it since I was six."

"Come on, Fricke. You didn't learn four-letter words in a classroom. You use them in a very idiomatic way. You scarcely pause to think."

"So? It's a crime, is it, to have English friends, American friends?" She gave Gini another scornful look. "All year Amsterdam's full of foreigners, people my age. Sure I talk to them. I meet them all around the place. . . ."

"Where all around the place?"

"Just all *around*. In cafés. Art galleries. Here in the Leidseplein."

"Oh, come on, Fricke. Let's stop fencing around. You covered for Anneke, didn't you? All the time your mother was explaining how careful she was, how she always knew where Anneke was, I was trying to figure out how Anneke got around the restrictions. It didn't take a great leap of imagination. You did it together, didn't you? Gave each other alibis? Backed each other up?"

"So what? Everyone does. So we skipped jail once or twice . . ."

"Sure. And your sister ended up dead. Who introduced her to Star, Fricke? Was it you? One of your American or English friends?"

"No, it fucking wasn't. I never met him. I never saw him in my life. . . ." Her voice rose. "You're getting this all wrong. You're just like my parents. You think Anneke was my sweet little kid sister. Listen, she went on the pill when she was twelve. It was Anneke the boys all chased, it was Anneke who was screwing around, not me. And last January she got thrown over by this boy she really liked. It really cut her up. My mother thinks she was so happy—well, she wasn't. She used to cry, she'd come to my room every night, and we'd talk, and she'd cry some more. . . . That's why she went to Star, because he *understood*."

"What?" Gini said. She had known that if she kept the pressure up, Fricke would eventually make a slip. She had just done so, and she still hadn't realized. She was staring at Gini blankly.

"She went *to* Star, that's what you just said. Not—went off *with* him, *to* him."

"I made a mistake."

"No. I don't think so, Fricke. Your English is too good. I know why you phrased it that way. Anneke already knew Star, didn't she? She didn't meet him the day before she left, the way she wrote in that note. She'd planned to leave." Gini sighed. "Oh, come on, Fricke, you're sixteen, you're intelligent. Why do you think I'm pressuring you like this? Your sister's dead. Another girl in England is dead. Mina is with Star right now, and she's at risk. I want Star found, and I want him stopped. You want that too—surely you do? So why the hell can't you trust me and give me your help?"

There was a long silence. Gini was not sure, even then, if she had made the right approach. Outright appeals, antagonism, sympathy—nothing she said seemed to reach this girl. She was still looking at Gini with a mutinous hostility, as if Gini were irrevocably on the other side of some impassable wall between the young and the adult.

Gini could sense the impasse. Feeling suddenly tired and dispirited, she signaled to the waiter to bring more coffee. There was an irony here, beneath the surface of this difficult conversation. Gini wondered if Fricke would believe her if she tried to explain how close she herself felt to Anneke, to Mina. She thought of herself, a few weeks short of her sixteenth birthday, cutting school, taking a plane to Beirut to join her father, the last futile attempt she had made to make her father notice her, take some interest in her life.

"I want to be a journalist too, Daddy," she had said. "I thought—if I came here. Watched you. I could *learn*. And I wanted to see you, of course."

He hadn't even replied. He'd just sat there in his hotel room, sipping his bourbon. When she mentioned journalism, there was an immediate flicker of derision in his eyes; he laughed suddenly—a snort of laughter. Gini had never forgiven that.

Her father had been her god: since she scarcely knew him, rarely saw him, it had been easy to imagine him as such. In Beirut, day by day, watching him sit sweating in the bar of the Hotel Ledoyen, doing next to no work, rehearsing his endless anecdotes about Vietnam, his Pulitzer, to a crowd of sycophants, she had discovered how misplaced her idolatry had been. She turned back to Fricke, to her cold, hostile stare. The girl was already on her third cigarette.

"I can understand some of this, Fricke," she began. "I can remember how it feels to be your age, Anneke's age. I can remember—oh, the confusion, the pain, the clash of loyalties. I can remember all that."

"Oh, yeah?" The girl gave a small smile. Her certainty that Gini could not, that the experiences of her sister and herself were unique, unprecedented, infuriated Gini. Then she remembered: that blind teenage arrogance, that conviction that no one, ever, could have experienced emotions so complex and intense, she too had felt that.

She gave another sigh and looked away. She thought of the day on which she had first met Pascal, of his introduction in the Ledoyen bar, of her father continuing to hold court, her own embarrassment—it was midmorning, and her father was at the three-bourbon stage already, the anecdotes getting too protracted, too boastful—and then her gradual realization that this tall, silent young Frenchman, standing on the edge of a group of men twenty strong, was watching her father in silence, with an expression of undisguised contempt.

He had left the bar shortly afterward; she had followed him, furious, intent on challenging him. The challenge had escalated into confrontation, almost a fight. The conflict in Beirut was still localized then. Pascal Lamartine had caught hold of her arm and dragged her out into the white heat of the street.

"Take a look at your father's unimportant little war, then," he had said, his face tight with anger. "You won't find it in a hotel bar any more than he will. It's just down this street."

There had been another car bomb. Lamartine had his cameras out at once. She stood amid the wreckage, tilting walls, rubble, screams, and lamentation: a child's feet protruded from the masonry right in front of her. It was the first time she had ever seen, and smelled, death and grief.

She froze, then tried to help. There was a man, and they were trying to lift him onto an improvised stretcher, a length of corrugated metal. An Arab woman spat at her, and she stumbled back. She had blood on her hands and blood on her face. Then, out of the confusion of people and noise and movement, Lamartine had come back. She could see shock, contrition, anxiety on his extraordinary face. She felt his arms lock around her, and then he was drawing her away, around a corner, down a street. They stopped in a hot, narrow street near the harbor. He had a room there over a bar. He drew her into the shade of a doorway, began to speak in an agitated way, then stopped.

She had looked at his face, his fierce, intelligent face, his gray eyes. She watched his gaze become steady, then intent. She knew then, as he knew, what had to happen next. Less than fifteen minutes after leaving the scene of the bomb, she was in his room, in his arms, making love for the first time, with a man she had only just met, scarcely spoken to, but felt she had known all her life.

Could she tell Fricke this, or some of this? Would it make any difference if she did? Could she say, trust me, Fricke, I know how it feels to be wildly in love for the first time in your life. I know how it feels to toss caution aside and gamble everything on one glorious risk. It can work out, Fricke—it did, eventually, years later, in my case. I still love the man concerned; we met again. I am with him now—those fifteen-year-old instincts of mine may have been unwise, but in my case they were correct.

She leaned forward, some of those sentences on her lips; then she drew back. No. In the first place, Fricke would not believe her; in the second, it would be irresponsible. Such instincts had been deadly in Anneke's case.

The silence had continued for some five minutes now. Fricke was frowning into space, fiddling with her cigarette. Her thoughts, Gini realized, had been following a completely different track. She now turned back, pushed aside her lank hair, and gave Gini a cautious look.

"What you told my mother this afternoon—" She hesitated. "That was true? It was definitely Star who got Anneke onto drugs?"

"Yes, it was. I interviewed someone in England, a man who sees Star pretty often. He met your sister twice with Star. She was on heroin by then, and Star was supplying it. He used to help her give herself a fix."

"You didn't say that to my mother."

"No." Gini sighed. "And you can understand why, I think."

"I guess so."

Gini looked away. She could hear Mitchell's voice. According to him, Star was charging twenty pounds for Anneke when Mitchell first met her. Some months later, when he next saw her, the price had dropped by half, so it took twice as many men to buy the same fix. Star had said he was teaching Anneke the laws of supply and demand, that this was economics, a graduate course. "Get this straight," Mitchell had said with an air of self-righteousness. "She gave me a dose the first time, and by the second—*no way*. She was filthy. She had lice. She was a junkie—okay? She had those dead eyes junkies get, like all they can think about is smack, get me smack. She was a zombie. . . . And Star thought that was pretty amusing. That's what he gets off on. A power trip."

None of this could be said, of course, or even intimated. Gini turned back to Fricke; they looked at each other. Perhaps something in her face communicated—afterward Gini was still unsure—but where persuasion had failed, silence was effective: Fricke suddenly began to talk.

"She met him in France," she said. "On that school trip my mother mentioned. February last year, about two months before she ran away with him. They ran into each other in Paris—I don't know where, in some art gallery, or a museum café maybe. But he must have been a quick worker, because those school trips are really tightly supervised, curfews, teachers crawling all over the place. He couldn't have had more than fifteen, twenty minutes before the next patrol. That was enough. He gave her an address. Anneke was writing to him after that. She told me—she'd met this really wild guy, she'd written to him, and he was writing back."

"She was writing to France?"

"I don't know. Anneke said he moved around a lot. She got secretive after she met him. She'd just throw out these little hints. She never told me what they were planning, that she was going to run off with him. I would have done something then if I'd known. I'm not a fool. I would have gone to my father—"

She hesitated once more, eyeing Gini. Then, as if she had come to a sudden decision, she reached down into her shoulder bag and drew out a book.

"Here." She slid it across the table. "It's Anneke's address book. The first time she called me—that's *why* she called. Because she was worried about this book."

Gini stared at the girl, who had blushed crimson. Carefully, she opened the book; it was a small loose-leaf binder crammed with names, numbers, and addresses.

"Where was this, Fricke?"

"In this special hiding place she had. Under a loose floorboard in her closet. She kept her diary there. Her supply of birth control pills. Grass sometimes. She'd taken Star's letters and the diary, but she'd forgotten this. You were going to ask, weren't you? It was going to be your next question, I could tell."

"Yes. It was."

"Take it. You keep it. Show it to the police. I don't care anymore. I hid it for her, because she was afraid they'd find it—she knew they'd search her room. And then, when she still didn't come back—I went through it. I've been through it a thousand times."

"His address must be in here? That's why she was so worried, why she called, why she asked you to hide it?"

"Yes." Fricke drew in an unsteady breath. She lit another cigarette. "Except it *isn't* in there—or I can't find it. There's no entry for Star. There's a thousand names and addresses in there. All her pen pals, France, Germany, Italy, England, Belgium, America, Africa . . . she'd been into that since she was nine. She got seven, eight letters at least every week. You find him, if you can—but I'm telling you, it's impossible. It's like looking for one pebble on a beach."

Gini reopened the notebook. It was a typical teenage girl's book, untidy, covered with doodles and scribblings, and crossings-out. It was partly typed and partly handwritten; it was a mess.

"Fricke—I'm very grateful. But I can't read Dutch."

"You don't need to. He wasn't Dutch, he wasn't based in the Netherlands. You can read the foreign addresses—look, that one there, that's in France, and there's one in San Francisco. You *might* find something. You're a journalist. I thought . . ."

Fricke, so hostile a short while before, was now looking at her with pleading, as if Gini and her putative skills were her last hope. Gini, who was not optimistic, did not want to disappoint her or raise those hopes.

"I'll try, Fricke. I promise you that. I'll go through this tonight. If necessary, the police here can look at it." She added, "You do realize, don't you, Fricke—for your sake as well as theirs, you're going to have to tell your parents this?"

"I know." Fricke lowered her eyes and fiddled with the cigarette. "You think they'll be angry?"

"No. I don't. I think they'll understand. They love you very much, Fricke."

"I know they do. Oh, shit . . ."

She began crying again. Gini waited quietly until this new fit of tears ceased. She took out the props of her trade, her tape recorder, her notebook, and as she had hoped, they seemed to give Fricke new confidence.

"You want to interview me? You really think I can help? I told you—Anneke said very little."

"That doesn't necessarily matter. If you can remember what she said, Fricke—the little details, the ones that seemed unimportant, irrelevant at the time. Those are the ones that often help the most."

"I've got a good memory. Pretty good, anyway."

For ten minutes after that Gini took her carefully through the sequence of events: the first meeting in Paris, the correspondence, Star's arrival in Amsterdam, their departure, the two subsequent telephone calls Anneke had made, the long silence that came after them, the months of waiting, and then the news of her death. As Fricke spoke, Gini could feel some memory, some echo of this, inching its way forward from the back of her mind: school trips—it was connected to that; someone, somewhere, recently had mentioned something similar, but Gini could not recall who or when.

"So you think Star came to Amsterdam to get her, Fricke, is that right?"

"Yes. I'm sure he wasn't here before that. She told me he was coming. She said she was going to see him—she was so excited. And that was the day before she left."

"He must have had a very powerful influence over her to make her do something so risky."

"He had. It was like—like he *summoned* her, came to claim her. He told her he'd been looking for her all his life, and the second he saw her, he knew she was the one. Like it was destiny, or fate."

"And she believed that—why? Because she was fourteen and it made her feel—special, singled out?"

"I guess so. She said—when she phoned—she said he was *powerful*. She kept talking about that. He read the tarot cards for her. He said he could show her who she was."

"I see." Gini lowered her eyes to her notebook. Again she had the sensation that Anneke was so close to herself. That intoxicating sense of self-discovery, she could remember that so well. With Pascal, in Beirut, and now. She always felt that when she was with him, she knew who she was. But if Anneke's story was, in some respects, a mirror image of her own, its outcome had been very different. Anneke had been unlucky, undiscerning, and certainly foolish—though Gini would never condemn her for that. She had fallen in love with a man who was dangerous, even evil: from the moment Mitchell had started his story, she had never doubted that.

"Go on, Fricke," she said, looking up. "All this helps me, and it may help Mina too. You must have asked Anneke a lot of questions. You were talking on the telephone—what? Ten minutes each time, more? Think, Fricke."

"She said he asked about *us* a lot. He'd get her to describe our parents, me. He wanted to know about—oh, ordinary things. Family things. What we did at Christmas, where we went on vacation, how my parents first met."

"Did he talk to her about his own family, where he came from?"

"No, never. Anneke said he hated women who asked questions, she'd learned that. And every time she asked, he got angry, really angry. So she thought maybe he'd had something horrible happen when he was a child. Like maybe he'd been abused, or fostered out, or put in a home, something like that. But that was just guesswork. He never said one word about his parents, where he grew up."

"And the anger—she used that word?"

"Yes. The first time she called. She said he was really hard to handle, because one minute he'd be really quiet and sweet, and the next, for no reason, he'd go completely crazy. Freak out. Start screaming at her."

"Rapid mood swings?"

"I know." Fricke met her eyes. "Afterward, when she didn't call again, I got afraid. I thought maybe he was *on* something. But Anneke said he was clean. She said she could handle the moods, she was the only one who could. He told her she had the soothing gift—that's what he called it. He'd make her lie down next to him and stroke his forehead some special way. She was proud of that."

Gini made no comment. She was listening to the alarm bells in her head. *On* something, or more than that? Out of the shadows around Star she could see a word emerging—*sociopath*.

"Anything else, Fricke? How did they spend their time? They traveled around, but Anneke wouldn't say where." She flicked back through her notes. "They listened to music, smoked a little grass . . . what else?"

There was one other activity that was an obvious addition to that list, and Gini knew she was going to have to ask about it eventually. She waited. Fricke was frowning, trying to think.

"He had this thing about being clean," she said at last, surprising Gini. "That's it. Because Anneke was laughing about it. She said when he spent time with the travelers he'd let himself go, but the second they left them, he was a fanatic for washing. He'd take baths, three, four times a day. Shower, go to bed, get up in the middle of the night and shower again. She said that. What else? He read. He read a lot. She mentioned that."

"Did she say what kind of books?"

"Yes. She said he liked war books. Books about weaponry."

"*Weaponry?*" Something cold moved along Gini's spine. "Fricke— you're sure? Tarot cards and books on weapons? That doesn't seem to fit."

"That's what she said. She was boasting, telling me how clever he was. Like he had this fantastic memory. He had this book with hundreds of pictures of guns, different kinds of guns, some catalogue thing, and they used to play this game. She'd test him. She'd cover up the name and the details so he could see just the picture, and then he'd identify them. Every single one. And not just that, he knew their—what would you call it?"

"Technical specifications?"

"Yeah—that. Their size, the kind of ammunition they used, how many rounds they could fire in what time. He knew all that. No mistakes. He was word perfect, every time."

More alarm bells, much louder now. Gini bent over her notebook, anxious lest Fricke read the reaction in her face.

"But he didn't actually *have* a gun, Anneke never said that? He just liked looking at pictures of them, right?"

"Oh, no. He didn't have a gun. It wasn't serious. Just like a party trick."

"Fine. Fricke, this is very helpful. It gives me a profile. A shape. And I know Anneke met him in Paris—that's a strong lead. I have this address book. I'm just wondering . . . When Anneke was due to meet him here, when he came to Amsterdam for her—she didn't mention where she was meeting him?"

"No."

"Suppose she'd been selecting the meeting place, where might she have chosen?"

Fricke deliberated for a few minutes. "The Antica," she said finally. "It's a coffee house. They sell grass there. It's licensed. Anneke used to go there with the boy who broke up with her. It's cool—it's got a good atmosphere. She might suggest that. Or she might just suggest they meet on some street."

"Is the Antica easy to find?"

"Sure. It's near the Singel Canal. It's well known. Ask anyone. It won't help. The police already took Anneke's picture there a thousand times."

"A thousand and one won't hurt." Gini smiled. For the first and only time, Fricke returned her smile. Then she looked at her watch.

"Look. I have to get back. My mother worries—if I'm late, she'll call my violin teacher."

"Just one more question, Fricke. I think you probably know what it is."

The girl had risen; she stopped, then sighed.

"Yeah. Sure. Did Anneke mention sex, right?"

"Was she sleeping with him, Fricke? I was told she was, but I'm not sure. Something about this man puzzles me. Sex seems too obvious, too simple."

"It puzzles me too." Fricke met her eyes. "I mean, usually, Anneke would say straight out. If she was screwing a boy, she'd tell me. It was no big deal. She'd say, hey—we did it last night, and it was really good, or not. But with Star . . . she never mentioned sex. Not once. I assumed—well, I assumed that was what they did most of the time. Listened to music. Smoked a little grass. Made love. She was crazy about him, obsessed, so I couldn't understand. So in the end, the second time she called, I asked her. I said, and so you're having sex, right?"

"And how did she answer?"

"She didn't answer." Fricke's face contracted. "She started crying. And then she hung up."

CHAPTER 12

The Antica coffee house was in an old section of Amsterdam, in a narrow street lined with bookshops and small art galleries. Inside, it consisted of one large, pleasant room lined with paneled booths; on a rack, newspapers in several different languages were available to patrons; at several tables, people were playing chess. The atmosphere, cosmopolitan and faintly bohemian, reminded Gini of the older cafés in Greenwich Village in New York, except that the air smelled strongly of marijuana, and grass was openly on sale at the bar, along with drinks and cigarettes.

Seating herself at the bar, and arming herself with a *Herald Tribune* from the rack, she ordered coffee and bided her time. The *Tribune* had run the story of Mina's disappearance, and Cassandra's death, as a small item on page three, rather as Gini had expected. Missing-girl stories took time to build. If the girls concerned were in their teens, editors assumed they were runaways, and there were too many runaways to make headlines. It would be days, she judged, possibly weeks, before Mina's story became front-page tabloid news—unless her father used his position and influence to make waves, of course.

Folding the paper, she looked around the café. It was now five in the afternoon, and the Antica was in a pre-evening lull. It was less than half full, and the clientele was mixed, in terms of age, gender, and nationality. Most of the customers had the air of habitués; there were several student types, two older men playing chess, a quiet girl reading a book, a louder group of men in the far corner, arguing in German. She turned back, and kept her eye on the bar staff, wondering whom to approach.

They appeared to be working shifts; shortly after she arrived, the first two, who had been Dutch and Australian, departed. They were replaced by two Americans, one a tall, blond young man in his late twenties, the other a slightly older woman with dark hair and a warm laugh. Both were wearing a uniform of white shirt, red vest, and black pants. Both dealt with the other bar customers in a bewildering range of tongues, Dutch phrases, Italian, French. Catching her eye, the woman smiled.

"More coffee?"

"Thanks. I'm admiring your language abilities. . . . Oh, and some cigarettes . . ."

"You're sure cigarettes?"

"Yeah." Gini strengthened her own accent. "You have Gitanes?"

"We sure do. And as for the languages . . . Don't be too impressed. I can say 'The men's room is on the right' in about ten languages. Not too useful, huh?"

She leaned up against the bar and looked at Gini.

"You're new here, right? I haven't seen you before. Your first time in Amsterdam?"

"Yes, it is. I'm just passing through. I don't know the city too well. . . ."

"It's a great city. Freedom city—right, Lance?" She grinned across at her partner. "Lance is a surfer. From L.A. A wave freak. But even he thinks it's cool."

"So what's a surfer doing in Amsterdam? It's a bit low on beaches."

"Making loot. Seeing the world. Same way I am. You?"

"No such luck. I had a job waiting tables in London. I just got fired. I came here to see a friend, and I think I've missed him. I've had it with Europe. I'm thinking of going home."

"I know the feeling. Stick it out. I was pounding the sidewalks for weeks before I got this job."

"You were? How long have you been here?"

"A couple of months. Came late last fall. Lance here holds the all-time record. He's been here six months."

"He has? Hey, I don't suppose either of you could help me? It's just, this friend I'm looking for—I'm pretty sure he said he came here. You might know him, maybe? Know where I might find him? Tall, long dark hair, really good-looking."

"I like it. Tell me more."

"Mid-twenties. People call him Star."

"What—just Star?" She frowned, then shook her head. "Nope. No bells ringing. Hey, Lance, you know a guy comes in here, name of Star? A hunk, dark? Sounds like the man of my dreams?"

Lance grinned, and approached, polishing glasses.

"Star? What, the cokehead? Sure I know him. Comes in from time to time. Haven't seen him in a week though—more. No way is he the man of your dreams, Sandra. I mean, we are talking like *seriously* out to lunch." He rolled his eyes and clutched his temples, then abruptly stopped this clowning.

"Bad news," he said. "Not your type, Sandra. Not your type at all."

"A cokehead?" Gini said. "Oh, come on . . ."

Lance shrugged and moved away to serve another customer. Sandra laughed.

"Take no notice. Lance is a health nut. You take Tylenol, he thinks you're into substance abuse. Still, I guess you're out of luck."

"Story of my life. What do I owe you?"

She paid, and waited a short while, until Sandra had moved off to clear some tables. She had one more try with Lance, but got nowhere. Lance said Star showed up every month or so, or had recently. He didn't know where Star might stay, didn't know any friends of Star's, but he did know this really great brasserie that Gini would love.

"How about it?" He leaned across the bar. "I'm free at nine. You have the most fantastic eyes. Anyone ever tell you that?"

"It's been mentioned. In similar situations. Sorry, Lance. Another time."

"No worries. Stay away from the cokehead. See you around."

With a wave of the hand to Sandra, Gini left. She returned to her hotel. It was large, international, and anonymous. She felt she could move around it blindfolded; she might have been anywhere in the world; the room made her feel rootless and displaced.

This was the danger period, she knew—when she slowed down. She stood there, fighting the loneliness that kicked in the second the door closed. It was six-thirty. She tried calling Rowland—it would be five-thirty in London—but his secretary had just left and he was not answering. She tried the features desk, then news: the copy editor she spoke to there said McGuire was somewhere in the building and he would pass on the message, but some kind of crisis had blown up, so it might be a while before Rowland called back.

"What kind of crisis?" Gini asked.

"Have you ever seen McGuire when he's angry?"

"No. Not really."

"Well, it's that kind. Scorched-earth time. So watch out."

Gini next tried Pascal, but tonight was one of the bad nights. She redialed a score of times, but she could not get through. She had given Pascal the number here when she called him the previous day; if he was able to call her, he would. Maybe it was better not to reach him at this exact moment anyway. Each time they spoke, Gini was finding it harder and harder not to say—*Pascal, please come home.* Tonight the phrase might easily slip past her guard. No, wait, she told herself: it was Marianne's birthday next week. Maybe Helen would be proved right, maybe he would return for that: a fine thing, she thought angrily—she was now reduced to taking comfort from the predictions of Pascal's ex-wife.

She rang room service and ordered some food. Then she took out Anneke's address book, set it down on the dressing table, where the light was brightest, and began going through it line by line.

It was a wearying task. Anneke had a tiny handwriting; these pages were crammed with insertions, crossings-out, arrows to changes of numbers, scribblings, and doodles of hearts and flowers and faces. At first she hoped Anneke might have used these hearts as a sign to indicate boys she favored; gradually she realized they were random. She could imagine Anneke on the telephone, pen in hand, this book in front of her as she embarked on protracted teenage telephone talks, doodling as she spoke, scattering these untidy pages with a myriad of tiny misleading signs, with graffiti that made Gini's eyes ache.

After an hour she gave up and ate her room service dinner. She had some coffee, and thought longingly of a hot bath, a mindless TV movie, an early night. Then, remembering Fricke and feeling guilty, she returned to the book. She had already flagged the pages that contained French addresses. Now, taking out her own notebook, she copied them out. There were eighteen of them, some typed, some handwritten. From those she extracted the seven with Paris addresses and stared at her list. All seven were the addresses of girls, presumably pen pals of Anneke's: Lisette, Chantal, Suzanne, Marie, Christine, Mathilde, Lucile.

This was not helpful. It *must* be here, she thought, perhaps disguised, perhaps coded. Why else would Anneke have been so protective of this book? Why else ask Fricke to hide it? On the other hand, although Anneke might have met Star in Paris, there was no way of knowing whether she also wrote to him there. Fricke had said he moved around. Maybe Paris was misleading, she thought, yet Mitchell's BMW had been abandoned there too. She stared at the seven girls' names in her list, and suddenly her memory unlocked.

The French Connection, she thought. Maybe it was *not* a false trail: not only Anneke but also *Cassandra* had made school trips to Paris the preceding year—one of the friends Gini had talked to had mentioned it in passing. Supposing Cassandra, like Anneke, had met Star there? That would mean that all three girls associated with Star before Mina were linked to France. The first girl, the one whose face Star had cut with a razor—she had been French, according to Mitchell. And she and Rowland had neglected that girl, she realized: they had concentrated on the two who were dead. But this French girl had been Anneke's immediate predecessor in Star's affections—if affections they could be called. Could it be, was it possible, that when Anneke was writing to Star, Star, who constantly moved around, she wrote to him care of that girl at her Paris address?

But what was her name? Gini could not remember. I must have asked Mitchell, she thought, rising quickly and taking out Mitchell's interview tape. Surely I asked him?

For a moment, rewinding then advancing the tape, she was afraid the question had *not* been asked. It had been a very difficult interview to keep on course: Mitchell had been spaced out, and kept sidetracking. . . . She stopped. She had found it, just a brief exchange, before Mitchell had veered off on some other subject. And it was not she who had asked the vital question, but Rowland McGuire. The interjection was his, and the sound of his voice, here in this hotel room, startled Gini. She replayed the section twice:

—*And the French girl, the one he cut up with a razor. What happened to her?*

—*Search me. God only knows. Went home? Took off somewhere? Look, I need another drink.*

—*You're not getting one. Concentrate. Can you remember her name? Any details? For God's sake—he cut her face open. What were you doing then? Standing around watching? You couldn't have stopped him?*

—*Look, it happened fast—all right? Sure, I was shocked. I'm not an animal. . . .*

—*No, but you are a coward. It makes me sick, listening to this. . . .*

—*All right, all right—cool it, okay? I don't want any trouble. Christ, Gini, what is it with this guy? I'm trying to help. . . .*

—*He's angry, that's all. He gets like that. . . .*

—*Well, tell him to fucking well back off. He lays one finger on me, and I'm back in that police station, making a complaint. A formal complaint . . .*

—*You think so? Listen, Mitchell, by the time I'd finished with you, you wouldn't be able to walk across to the station, let alone talk when you got there. You smile once more, and I'll knock your teeth down your throat. . . .*

—Okay, okay—I'm nervous, that's all. I smile when I get nervous. I told you—I'm not feeling so good. I'm thinking. I'm trying to remember. She was a pretty girl. She'd known him some time, I think. What was her name? Something beginning with 'C'? Cecile? Claire? No—I've got it. Chantal, that was it. Brown hair. Brown eyes. About eighteen. That's it. . . .

The anger in Rowland's voice had been perfectly genuine, Gini thought. He had exaggerated the threat, yes, and had produced the required effect; they had both slipped into the good cop/bad cop routine with ease, without prior discussion, and it had worked. But Rowland's loathing for Mitchell, his banked anger, had been almost palpable. She had felt it radiating in the bar as Mitchell talked; she had watched it darken his face, and she could hear it again now. Indeed impetuous, not as controlled as he liked to pretend, she thought—and his anger had obtained a vital name, *Chantal.*

She felt a quick dart of excitement, rose, and turned back to Anneke's address book. She riffled quickly through the pages, found the entry for Chantal again, and there, staring her in the face, but faint, right on the edge of the page so it was easy to miss, was the sign she had been looking for.

Her telephone was ringing. Gini half rose, turned back, stared at the entry. There, next to the address for Chantal, an address that was typed, was a tiny asterisk: an asterisk or a *star*, she thought with a sense of triumph. The telephone was still ringing. She crossed and picked it up.

It was Rowland McGuire, though he did not pause to identify himself. His voice was icy with anger.

"How many bars and cafés did you try before the Antica?" he said. "How many did you try after it? You'd like to put up a billboard, advertise on TV, perhaps? Maybe you'd be good enough to explain what in hell you thought you were doing? You gave me your *word* on this."

He continued to speak. Gini stared at the wall as Rowland McGuire, gifted at invective, proceeded to take her apart stitch by stitch. She felt confused, then humiliated—and furious with herself. She knew there was no point in even trying to interrupt at this stage, and she was thinking hard.

Someone must have called him direct from the Antica very shortly after she had left. It could have been only one of two people. She had assumed his contact in Amsterdam was a man, and Rowland, she realized now, had played along with that foolish assumption. He might have been misleading her; he might not. Whichever of the two it was, she thought, they were good.

"Sandra?" Gini said as he paused for the first time. "Or is your contact Lance?"

She expected she would receive no reply to that question, and she did not.

"That wasn't your concern before—and it certainly isn't now. I spelled this out to you, not once, but twice. You gave me your word, and I *trusted* you. . . . Apart from the fact that you lied, it was unprofessional behavior of the worst sort."

"Rowland. I can explain . . ."

"Sure you can explain. In London. Meanwhile, you're off this story as of an hour ago, you understand?"

"Rowland, will you *listen*? I went *only* to the Antica. I didn't go anywhere else. . . ."

"You expect me to believe that? Out of God knows how many bars and cafés in Amsterdam, you happen to pick the one where your appearance is guaranteed to cause maximum trouble? Don't waste my time and my intelligence. I suggest you get the first plane out in the morning. Better still, get one tonight."

"I went there because it's where *Anneke* used to go." Gini's temper snapped. "Nothing to do with your damn contact, Rowland. What is this? I had a *lead*, and I followed it up. Do you want this story, or don't you?"

"Yes. I want this story. I want this story more than you're ever likely to understand."

"Fine. I want it too. I want to find Star. I want to find Mina. And I'll do that a whole lot quicker without you breathing down my neck."

"This is sensitive. You knew it was sensitive. If you had a lead, you could have called me. But no, you just went chasing off. You do understand what you've done, don't you? You've compromised me. You've ignored my explicit instructions. You've put someone I know at risk. As a result, you've not only prejudiced *this* story, you've prejudiced others."

"The hell I have!" Gini's voice rose. "I don't know what your precious source has been saying to you—"

"My precious source, as you put it, has given me a very clear and accurate account. Don't try and damn well shift the blame. I know exactly what you did, and exactly what you said. Maybe those tabloid techniques suited the last paper you worked on—but they don't suit me." He broke off. "Look, I don't have the time or the inclination for this. I didn't expect to have to go through the rule book to someone with your experience. If I have the time, you can explain in London. Which gives you a while to come up with a better excuse."

"I'm not coming back to London," Gini interrupted furiously. "I'm going to follow up this story *my* way, at my pace. Which will give *you* time, Rowland, to work on your apology."

"What did you just say?"

"You heard. The hell with this—who in God's name do you think you are? Do this. Do that. Call back every five seconds. *No one* works like that."

There was a silence. When he next spoke, Rowland's voice was very cool and dangerously polite.

"Perhaps I didn't make myself clear. You seem to have some problem in understanding what I say. You're off this story—you've got that? And I very much doubt, given the circumstances, that you'll work for me again. I had my doubts about you, and the way in which you operate—"

"What?" Something in his tone made Gini tense. "What do you mean—the way I operate?"

"I thought—I was fool enough to think—I was a good judge of character. I see now . . ." His voice was becoming angry again. "All those apologies of yours, that sob story you gave me in the car about how you'd lost confidence—it didn't mean a damn thing. Dear God—I should have *known*. I blame myself. You used me to get this story the same way you used Pascal Lamartine to get you to Bosnia. *Why* did you do that? It wasn't necessary. I told you—"

"What did you just say?" Gini had gone very cold. "I used Pascal? How dare you say that? No way is that true."

"Oh, it isn't? Fine. My mistake. Look, I have to go. Just get that plane."

"No. *You* wait. Don't you dare hang up. You're going to explain that, Rowland, and explain now. And don't damn well tell me what to do and where to go."

"Goddamn it, I'm your *editor*. I put you on this story—God only knows why—and I can take you off it anytime I choose."

"Don't pull rank on me—Lindsay was right about you. She said you were arrogant. Sitting in London, passing judgment, leaping to conclusions . . . You know *nothing* about my going to Bosnia. Why don't you check? Ask Max . . ."

"Oh, I've already asked Max. You *knew* Max would never agree to send you to Bosnia, didn't you? You tried everything, even played him off against the *Times*, and when that didn't work, you sent your boyfriend in to clinch the deal."

"I did what? That's not true—I don't know what you're talking about." Gini fought to control her voice; she had begun to tremble, and she could sense it, some vile revelation, very close. "You've been listening to lies—someone's cheap lies—"

"No, I haven't." His voice rose. "I don't damned well listen to gossip and rumor. Lamartine made a deal with Max. I know that for a fact. Max wanted Lamartine's photographs—and when Lamartine made your presence a *condition* of working for us, Max gave in. He'd *never* have sent you out there otherwise. And judging from your present behavior, Max was right. You're erratic, and untrustworthy, and—"

"Pascal wouldn't do that!" She heard her own protest echo into the telephone. Her voice had risen, and was unsteady. Tears had sprung to her eyes. "How can you say that? How dare you say that? You know nothing about me. Nothing about Pascal. Pascal would *never* make conditions of that kind. Unlike you, he's a professional."

That stung him; there was a sharp intake of breath.

"Yes. Well, no doubt you were persuasive when you put him up to it. You were persuasive with me. I'll say this for you, Gini, you put on a good act."

"You bastard. You lying, sanctimonious bastard. I—"

She stopped. She was listening to the dial tone. At the second adjective McGuire had hung up.

Gini replaced the receiver. She was trembling from head to foot. It could not be true, she told herself. Pascal would never deceive her like that.

Then, the next second, she knew it could be true. She could remember the afternoon he had set off for his private meeting with Max. She could remember his quiet elation when he returned, and the negligent way in which he had said that it had been a good meeting, but nothing was finalized yet. He and Max had been circumspect. Her terms had finally been met four days later, Pascal's signed and sealed two days after that. She could not decide which she minded more, the fact that Pascal could, out of love, misinterpret her own wishes so disastrously, that he could lie and then continue to lie for more than six months—or the fact that, as Rowland McGuire had been quick to point out, she had overestimated her own worth.

Her own abilities, her experience, her years of fighting to get just such an assignment, had counted for nothing. She'd been sent out there as Pascal's *girl*, as a price paid with reluctance to secure his services. She felt the most acute and painful humiliation. How many other people were privy to this? Had they all known, the other reporters, the editors in features and news, the assistants, the secretaries? Had they all been as scornful as McGuire? Had they all been gossiping, and laughing behind her back?

Her first impulse was to reach for the telephone, to call Pascal, demand the truth. But as she reached for the machine, humiliation and shame receded and anger flooded back. She felt rage against Max, bland, amusing Max, who had said one thing and thought another. She felt the most bitter rage against Rowland McGuire, who jumped to the wrong conclusions, put two and two together and made six, who had been prejudiced against her, she now saw, from the very beginning, and who had just addressed her with such contempt.

He might think she was just going to drop this story, crawl meekly back to London and hide her head: well, he was wrong. Every major lead on this story with the exception of Mitchell had come from her. It was she who had persuaded Mitchell to talk, she who had won Fricke's confidence, and she who had the Paris lead now. She thought of Erica van der Leyden that afternoon—the way in which Anneke's mother had clasped her hands. That female exchange was far greater validation than any Rowland McGuire could provide; she had no intention of stopping now. Think, act, *move,* she said to herself. A quick future image of McGuire sprang into her mind. She saw him contrite; she saw him take back everything he had just said. But this little glimpse of a possible future disturbed her, and she pushed it aside at once. She had spent too much of her past life seeking her father's approval; she did not intend seeking McGuire's.

She loathed him, she told herself. She did not care one jot how the man reacted. She had nothing to prove to him; she was her own arbiter, proving her worth and her ability to no one but herself.

Without further hesitation she called the front desk and told them to book her on the next flight to Paris. There was one in forty-five minutes. If she hurried, she could catch it. This hotel, part of a large group, also had a branch in Paris. "Fax through a reservation for me, will you?" Gini said. But there she met her first hitch. Unfortunately, that would not be possible, the clerk explained. They had already had this problem earlier: not only their sister hotel, but every other major hotel in Paris was fully booked.

"You see," said the clerk, "it's the collections. They start tomorrow, and of course—"

"Forget it," Gini said. "I'll fix it myself."

She dialed the St. Vincent hotel in Paris, where she knew Lindsay and her staff would be occupying several rooms and suites for the duration of the collections. She could not get Lindsay, who was out. After being transferred from phone to phone, and at the point when she was about to hang up, she finally reached Lindsay's assistant, Pixie: Pixie, who was usually so ebullient and efficient, but who now sounded frantic, inattentive, and distressed. Gini could hear telephones ringing in the background; the noise of people and conversations and running feet. She began to explain her predicament, then stopped.

She realized Pixie was crying.

"I'll try," Pixie was saying. "I'll do my best, but I can't promise. Hang on—I'm coming. I'm sorry, Gini—Max is on the other line. I'm trying to find Lindsay; she's out with Markov, and she doesn't even know yet. It only just came through on the wires. It's pandemonium here. I don't know why I'm reacting this way. After all, I never knew her. But I felt as if I did, and—"

"What's happened, Pixie?"

"You mean you don't know? I thought that must be why you were calling—"

"What's happened?"

"It's Maria Cazarès. She's dead."

CHAPTER 13

Gini raced for the airport. She caught her plane with five minutes to spare, and it was not until it was airborne that she had time to think. Pixie had known no further details, not how Cazarès died, or where, just that she was dead, had died earlier that day and that it was natural causes—or that seemed to be the case.

"I'll do my best about the room," she had finished, "but you can imagine, Gini, right?"

Gini could imagine only too well. She could imagine what might or might not have caused this sudden death; she could imagine the immediate consequences. A second circus would be coming to town. From America, from Britain, from all over Europe: when legends die, the jackals move in.

Her flight left on time; every ten minutes Gini checked her watch. Half an hour to landing, twenty minutes to landing. She had only hand luggage. With luck, she could be in a taxi and at the St. Vincent within thirty minutes of clearing customs.

Then the problems began. They were stacked over Charles de Gaulle airport. When she finally reached the taxi stand, there was a long line. The trip from the airport was slow, the center of Paris gridlocked with traffic. She ran up the steps of the St. Vincent, into its huge marble-floored lobby. There she stopped dead.

Rowland McGuire had been luckier, it seemed. He rose to his feet as she entered. As she attempted to walk straight past him, he blocked her path. He then took her arm.

"What kept you?" he said.

Gini gave him a furious look; she struggled to free herself.

"Don't you touch me," she began. "Just get out of my way."

"Let's not waste time," he said, tightening his grip and propelling her toward the elevator. "I suggest we go straight up to our room."

"What did you just say?"

"Our room. It has three phone lines and two faxes. It's a suite. One bed and one couch. Since I'm a gentleman, I'll take the couch."

"Let go of my arm, damn you."

"—Besides, neither of us will be getting much sleep. The French press has a head start, and I intend to catch up. Press eight."

"Go to hell."

"Along the corridor. First door on the right. That's it. You like it? It's the last available room of its kind in Paris. It's cost the *Correspondent* six thousand francs above rates. When in doubt, bribe. Now . . ." He closed the door. "I would like you to listen to me."

"Let me out of this room." Gini rounded on him, her face white with anger and distress. "You think I'd work with you now? After what you said to me? Just get out of my way. I don't want to work with you, I don't want to be in the same *room* with you."

"Maybe. But you're going to hear me out."

"The hell I am. I remember what you said. You damn near accused me of being a whore."

"I never used that word."

"Don't lie. It's what you meant."

"Possibly. My phrasing was more tactful, I think."

Gini smacked him hard across the face. She had to reach up to do it, but she hit him with her full strength. The blow left a mark across his cheek. Tears had sprung to her eyes. She drew back, shaking, fighting to control her voice.

"You think I work like that? You think I operate that way? Well, I don't. I never have—never. I *despise* women who do that. I fought for *years* to get an assignment like that. I *care* about the stories I work on. I tried to cure myself of that in Bosnia because I thought I couldn't do my work and care—but I'm *not* cured. And now I don't want to be. I'm going to find Mina Landis—and I don't need your help. I'm going to find her because—"

She broke off with an angry gesture of the hands. ". . . because I talked to Anneke's mother, and . . . she wept. You wouldn't understand. But I care, Rowland, I care very much about that."

Her voice had risen, and the emotion she felt was so strong, she could scarcely speak. Furious that Rowland McGuire, of all people, should see her like this, she began to push past him.

"Just get out of my way, Rowland. I have nothing else to say to you. Let me out of this room."

"No," he said in a perfectly level voice. "I won't do that. I'm not even sure I *could* do that."

"What?" Gini said, and then she stopped. Suddenly she began to see Rowland McGuire, really see him. It was as if a camera changed focus, from long shot to close-up. One minute he was faceless, blurred, just a tall shape between her and the door; the next, she could see the man himself. He was wearing an overcoat, one of his usual old tweed suits, a white shirt with the top button undone, and a green tie with the knot loose. Earlier, manhandling her into the elevator, he had seemed dourly amused; he did not seem amused now, or angry, or resentful of the fact that she had just slapped his face.

She could see the mark her palm had left across his cheekbone, a red weal that emphasized his pallor and the set determination in his face. He was regarding her with absolute seriousness, his green eyes resting unwaveringly on her face. His hands were by his sides, he appeared simultaneously relaxed and intent. She glanced down, weighing her chances of pushing past him, then looked up, met that intent green stare—and sensed the danger at once.

They were standing very close to each other, their eyes locked. At that moment, when she was least expecting it, out of antagonism, haste, and furious anger, she felt something arc between them that was none of these things, a sexual message so sharp she gave an involuntary intake of breath.

She felt it pulse through her own mind, she saw it reflect the same instant in his face. She saw a deeper concentration come into his eyes, and then a surprise—as if he had expected this, foreseen this, as little as she had. In the same moment, again with unspoken accord, they each stepped back.

Gini looked at the door, which was shut but unlocked. Rowland McGuire had moved to one side, so to leave would have been simple. She took a step toward the door, then hesitated. Rowland put a hand on her arm, then instantly withdrew it. Gini realized her anger had gone. There was still noise, turmoil, in her head, but it was of a different kind.

"How did you know I was coming here?" she asked in a quieter voice.

"I called your hotel in Amsterdam. They told me you'd left for Paris. I called about fifteen minutes after you left." His eyes never left her face. "I called from my car, on the way to the airport. I was already on my way here. Someone had to cover this. I had fired you. I was the only other person with the necessary background. I was going to apologize. Ask you to join me here. I wanted—" He hesitated. "The hotel told me you'd had difficulty obtaining a room in Paris. I guessed you'd have tried to contact Lindsay, so I called here. It wasn't difficult to track you down. I knew which flight you'd taken. So, I got here. Found the room. Made some calls. Waited."

"When did you hear about Maria Cazarès?"

"For certain? About five minutes after we spoke. I first heard the rumor about an hour before from a journalist friend here. He phoned back to confirm just after I hung up on you. Confirmation came through on the wires about five minutes after that."

"So you'd heard a rumor she might be dead before we spoke?"

"Yes. I had. Plus I'd had two very difficult conversations with my source in Amsterdam. That was the timing. It isn't an excuse."

There was a silence. Gini could sense an emotion that was at variance with the calm precision of his speech. She hesitated.

"What made you want to apologize?"

"I realized how badly I'd behaved."

He paused, his face suddenly troubled. Gini, who had known the instant she asked the question that it would have been safer unvoiced, prayed he would not answer it more fully. She was about to interrupt him, when he spoke.

"I want you to know," he went on in a deliberate way, "I am ashamed of what I said. Not only because I was wrong—on two counts. Also, because I lost my temper and I said things there's no reason you should forgive." He hesitated, and she could sense his struggle. "Despite what people say about me, I very rarely lose control to that degree. I now see, of course, why I did."

Gini admired him then. His gaze did not waver as he made this admission—and no woman could have misunderstood what he meant. His meaning was absolutely clear in his expression and tone. It might be an understated declaration, but a declaration it was. It was characteristic of him, she suspected, to phrase it in such a way, so she could ignore this revelation, or, with equal directness to his, respond.

She stared at him, unable to break his gaze. She knew that if he spoke again, if he tried to make his statement more explicit, she would be free.

She could walk past him then, go out that door. She waited; he did not speak—but the silence in the room did.

She could feel the danger acutely now, the threat of the next, the threat of the unforeseen, the possibility just around the corner of her as-yet-unmade response. She could feel time picking up speed. The second or two it took her to make her reply was freight-train fast, freight-train loud. She had a brief and confused sensation that she, and he, were passengers here. One wrong word, one wrong gesture, and they'd both be getting on a train there was no getting off.

"It wasn't true, what you said," she said. "About the Antica. About Pascal . . ."

And she thought, for an instant, she was safe. She had bypassed his declaration, and she saw his mouth tighten as he registered that. She had used Pascal's name, which should under these circumstances, have made her entirely secure; instead, the use of his name had a very opposite effect. Rather than carrying a charmed strength, it was suddenly weak: with it came a tide of uncertainties and unhappiness, all those months of loneliness and misery, of waking alone, and sleeping alone, and walking alone through London streets. It was no protection at all from this acute and unexpected sexual awareness, an awareness that sent a charge through every nerve in her body so she could scarcely think for a need to be touched.

"Don't," she began, and she was still telling herself, as he moved, that she would be safe if he did not touch her. "Don't. It's all right. It's my pride that's hurt, that's all."

He did not argue with that lie; he said nothing at all. He took her hand and drew her against him gently. He looked down at the tears on her face, then held her still against him in a gentle embrace. After so many weeks of abstinence, the shock of a man's body, and a man's embrace, was intense. She let her face rest against the muscles of his chest; she listened to the beating of his heart. She felt a sense of protection, and then of need. The body could be starved of affection as much as the mind, and for a short while just to be held, and be held by a man, gave her relief. She felt as if she had been struggling so long, fighting herself for so long, and now—suddenly—she was released.

Then it began to steal upon her, the realization that this was not just any man, and not a neutral embrace. It was a particular man, strong, a little taller than Pascal, a man whose body, touch, manner of holding, was new to her. She realized that her breasts were pressed against his chest, that he was becoming aroused, that one of his hands rested in the small of her back, exerting no pressure as yet.

Behind her in this room which she had scarcely looked at when she
entered it less than ten minutes before, a telephone had begun ringing.
She had a confused sense that it might be for either of them, and that if it
was for her, someone was trying to reach another woman, leading some
previous life. She let it ring, and Rowland let it ring, five times, six.

He rested his hand against her throat, then lifted her face to his. She
met his steady green, intelligent gaze: a man who could indeed be impetuous, a man who was more than prepared, when he judged it necessary, to take risks. She felt him stir against her, and a tremor of response
ran through her own body. Even then, when she knew they could both
sense consequences, repercussions, when the noise of them was so loud
in her head that she could scarcely think, even then he was scrupulous,
and he gave her a choice.

"This story is breaking," he said, "and that call might be urgent. Do
you want to answer it?"

Gini looked up at this semi-stranger. Want for him surged up through
her body with an astonishing force.

"No, I don't," she said.

"Neither do I," he replied, and with that acknowledgment past, he
did not hesitate. With the noise of the ringing telephone blindingly loud,
and his composure suddenly gone, he pulled her against him. He kissed
her hair, then her eyes, then her mouth. It was urgent, and very swift:
Gini opened her mouth to his; she cried out as his hands touched her
breasts. At some point the telephone stopped ringing; at some point
Rowland locked the door, but afterward neither of them could have said
when, or at which point.

A while later Gini rose from the bed and went into the bathroom. She
felt blind; blinded by its darkness, still blind when she switched on the
light. It had the predictable luxury of such hotels. It was lined with marble. Rowland's belongings—a brush, a comb, a shaving kit—had been
thrown down carelessly on a shelf. Above the basin was one mirror, behind her on the opposite wall was another. Gini looked at a room that
would not stay still, in which reflections doubled back and the veins of
the marble seemed to pulse. She made herself focus; she looked into the
mirror; she looked at herself.

Sex was like pain, she thought. If you were without it for a time, you
forgot how all-powerful it was. It was sex she could see in this mirror
now: its imprint could be seen on her mouth, which was swollen; on her
skin, which was flushed, and on her body, where his hands had touched

and gripped. She ached with the pleasure of being fucked; her thighs were wet; she smelled of sex, leaked sex, and she could still feel the little aftershocks of sex, the residual tremors of sexual delight that came to her as she remembered how he had done first this, and then that.

This, then, was what she was. These specifics measured out her betrayal. For all her certainties, all her past vows, she had still arrived here, in a situation she had never envisaged, and would have claimed was beyond the bounds of possibility. She had made the choice, and to compound her own faithlessness, the sexual pleasure had been intense.

Why had she had that fixed, stupid, adolescent certainty that only Pascal could give her this? Why had she convinced herself that love altered the very nature of this act and gave it a resonance and intensity it otherwise lacked? What a very female mistake, she thought: what a woman's error; how many men would claim that? That belief was unfounded; she could read its untruth in her reflected face, and feel its untruth in her womb. In betraying her lover, she had learned a most bitter and unwelcome truth about herself.

She ran some water in the basin and washed herself. She returned to the bedroom. Faint light came through the closed curtains. Rowland McGuire was lying on his back, his head cradled in his hands. He turned as she entered; Gini crossed, and knelt down beside him. Naked, he was very beautiful. The hard lines of his body still gleamed with sweat. She rested her face against his shoulder and pressed her mouth against his skin, which tasted of salt. He placed his arm around her quietly and drew her closer, his hand resting against the jut of her hip.

The intimacy and peace were also unexpected. Neither spoke for a while. Gini felt the remembrance of his kisses and embraces wash through her body. She was the first to speak.

"Once, Rowland," she said. "It has to be that way. It was just this one time. Nothing happened before it, and nothing must happen after it. It was accident, chance."

"A mistake?"

"No." She met his eyes steadily. "No, I would never say that. But it's something neither of us meant to happen, or even wanted to happen. And then it did happen. If we never think of it again, never speak of it . . ."

"Treat it as a momentary aberration?" He was watching her intently.

"No. I'm not sure. . . ." Gini flinched. "Maybe. How would you define that word—exactly define it?"

"I can give you a dictionary definition. It's a straying from the path, a deviation from type."

"That, then," she said, grasping at the word. "A straying. Something neither of us would have thought of, or allowed, or planned in normal circumstances."

"Were these circumstances so abnormal?" He removed his hand and sat up.

"Yes. I think they were."

"A room. A man and a woman? An unexpected choice? Is that so abnormal?"

"It felt that way." She turned away from his gaze. "I love Pascal. Rowland, none of this alters that."

He gave her a sharp, questioning look but said nothing. He rose, reached for his clothes, and began to dress.

Gini sat up, watching him, pleating the sheets in her hand. She wondered if he thought her naïve, or disingenuous; he judged her as a self-deceiver, perhaps. And at that, a memory came back to her, an incident from her past she disliked to recall.

"I was warned of this once," she began in an agitated way. Rowland turned to look at her, in the act of fastening his belt.

"A man warned me. His name doesn't matter, and he's dead now, in any case. He told me—these things happen, and they get under every guard. Duty, ethics, vows—even love. He said nothing was an adequate defense against—"

"Against what?"

"All of this." Gini gestured sadly to the bed. "Sexual desire. Sexual attraction. Suddenly wanting someone so badly, you can't think. He warned me how powerful that could be. I was angry. I told him he was wrong." She rose. "That was a year ago. He was killed a few days afterward. I now see he was right."

"Was this man your lover?"

"No. Absolutely not. I was working on a story about him, that's all. I was with Pascal. I don't sleep around, Rowland, all right?"

"I didn't think that. I wasn't suggesting that. . . ." He hesitated, then buckled the belt, reached for his tie and jacket.

"We'll do as you suggest," he went on, his manner becoming brusque. "This never happened. It was a dream. A hallucination. A departure from the prescribed plot."

"I'll describe it to Pascal that way, shall I?" Gini said, averting her face.

"Do you tell Pascal all your dreams, all your imaginings?"

"No. Of course not."

"Then I wouldn't mention this one."

"Lie, you mean?"

"Lie by omission. Yes."

Gini hesitated, looking at him. He had turned away from her so she could not see his face.

"Do you lie, Rowland? Do you lie well?"

"Very well. When necessary. Yes."

"Would you lie to me?"

"Of course. Without hesitation. And you'd never suspect." He turned back to look at her, and then, to her surprise, he crossed back to her, took the blouse she was still holding out of her hand, and drew her into his arms.

"I'll say this just once," he began quietly, resting his hand against her hair and drawing her face against his chest. "I give you my word—I'll never tell anyone what happened tonight. I'll never discuss it, under any circumstances—not with any other woman, not with a man. And if this is something you want erased from the record—it's erased. It's without consequences. From now on I'll treat you exactly as I did before this happened, and you will treat me the same way. And no one will ever suspect."

"Can you do that?"

"Yes. I'm good at disguising my feelings. I learned as a child. I've had plenty of practice since."

"Feelings aren't involved." Gini broke away from him. "This has nothing to do with emotion. It's sex—"

"Even simpler, then. I've always found sex very easy to forget."

He moved away from her and began to pick up objects that had been scattered about the room earlier: a wallet, keys. His composure hurt Gini, as did the tone of his replies, and she despised herself for this. It was a very female perversity, she thought, to start objecting when a man granted her her wish, and she had no intention of giving in to that impulse. Without further comment she began slowly to dress.

Rowland had moved across to one of the fax machines and was reading various messages. Gini was unsure when those messages had come through: before, during, after? She could not have said.

"The Cazarès offices have closed down for the night. Apparently."

He looked up from the page. "I doubt that. They may not be taking calls, but they'll be working. Preparing the authorized version of Maria Cazarès's death. Lazare is holding a press conference at eleven o'clock."

Gini hesitated, then tried to match her tone to his. "Nothing more on the circumstances of her death?"

"No. Heart failure—cardiac arrest was the first rumor. There's been no advance on that. And there's still evasiveness as to exactly when she died, and where. Not at one of her own properties—that was the initial rumor. I have some inquiries out about that. She was taken by ambulance to a private Catholic hospital, the St. Étienne. She's been treated there before, apparently. It would be useful to know from where, and when, the ambulance picked her up."

"If our suppositions were correct, she'd been taking White Doves for—what? Two days? Three?"

"Probably three. But they're still suppositions. And likely to remain that way, I suspect, as far as the doctors and clinic are concerned anyway."

"Won't there be a post mortem?"

"I don't know. I imagine it depends on Lazare, and the degree of his influence. The security shutters came down very quickly on this."

"And the collections? She was due to appear Wednesday. Her show is on Wednesday. Will they cancel that?"

"Presumably. Either way, they'll announce it tomorrow, at the press conference. . . . We can see if Lindsay knows anything later. I've left word. She must still be out with Markov. They were supposed to be at the Grand Vefour, but they must have changed the reservation. It's conceivable Lindsay hasn't even heard yet. Anyway"—he turned back as Gini picked up her coat—"shall we try your Chantal? It's possible Star could be there, I suppose. Mina too. The rue St. Séverin, isn't it?"

"Yes. It's close to the St. Séverin church. In the Latin Quarter. About fifteen minutes from here." Gini glanced at her watch. "It's eleven-fifteen now, Rowland."

"I know. Late to be making a call." He shrugged. "It gives us the advantage of surprise anyway."

"It'll probably be another false lead. This man Star seems to have a gift for disappearing."

Gini stopped. She had reached Rowland's side; they were both now standing in the doorway; she watched him undo the bolt, and she had a sudden hopeless sense that she could not keep up this pretense.

She wondered if Rowland also felt this; he gave no sign of it. He was about to open the door, but turned to look at her. She could see strain in his face then; she saw his eyes rest on her mouth. He hesitated. "I want to kiss you again," he said. "I suppose you realize that?"

"Rowland—don't. We have to stop this. We have to stop it now. You said—"

"I know what I said." He hesitated again, then slowly lifted his hand, rested it against the nape of her neck. "Just tell me one thing—before we go." He frowned. "Your hair—you cut it yourself? When? Why did you do that?"

"It was when I came back from Sarajevo. I don't know why exactly."

Gini paused; he did not prompt her, but waited for an answer just as he had that afternoon in the drive outside Max's house. "I was unhappy. I wanted to change myself. So I took the easy way out, the woman's way out. I changed my appearance instead. I just hacked it off with some nail scissors. My hair was long before. Why?" She raised her eyes to his. "Does it look horrible?"

"No. It does not. It makes you look—I like it. I noticed it when we were in England, driving back from meeting Mitchell, and . . . it's not important. We should go."

It was important, of course. Gini knew that, and she knew Rowland knew too.

"I like you, Rowland," she said as he was about to open the door. "I want you to know that."

"Why?"

"You're astute. Very quick. I like you for the things you don't say."

"And your silence was the first thing I liked about you. . . ." There was a pause, then he took her arm, and his tone altered. "We should hurry. The rue St. Séverin. We should have been there two hours ago. What happened to those two hours?"

"There was a hitch in the story. A kink in the plot line. We neglected our work," she replied as they stepped into the elevator. "Press ground, Rowland."

The lobby was full of journalists. Seeing some Englishmen he knew, Rowland disappeared into their group. He listened attentively, then spoke, his voice quiet, his manner confidential.

"What were you doing back there?" Gini asked as he joined her in the cab outside.

"Obtaining information. Spreading misinformation. Reverting to type." He smiled. "What's the first rule of journalism, Gini?"

"Oh, I know that. My father told me often enough. It's the one you forgot earlier. Check—then double-check."

"That's the second rule." Rowland gave her a sharp glance. "We *both* forgot the first rule."

"Which is?"

"Always be ahead of the pack."

The rue St. Séverin was tiny and very narrow. It was dominated by its church. The church's gargoyles reared up across the sidewalk, almost touching the buildings opposite. Facing the church was a stretch of Algerian and Moroccan restaurants, advertising couscous and kebabs. As the clock in the tower above them struck, Star drew Mina into the dark doorway of the church.

"It's eleven-thirty," he said. "Wait here, and don't move. I'll be ten minutes, fifteen at most."

"Can't I come in with you, Star?"

"No. You can't. Keep your scarf on. Stand out of the light." He grasped her hands and fixed her with his beautiful eyes. "I need you, Mina. You promise me you'll wait?"

He crossed the narrow street and disappeared into a doorway between the restaurants opposite. Mina stared at the building he had entered. It looked as if there might be small apartments above the restaurants; the windows were less than fifteen feet from where she stood. They were lit but not curtained; she could see the flickers of a television set, the shadow of a moving figure, nothing else.

Cautiously, she looked along the street. The restaurants would have phone booths, she thought. If she were quick, if Star was really away fifteen minutes, she could try to call England. She had no money, but she could call collect, though she wasn't sure how to do that from France. She took a step forward, then her nerve failed her. No. Star was sure to come back, sure to catch her; better wait.

She looked at her watch. He had been gone only a couple of minutes. He had been promising her, all day yesterday, all day today, that he would let her make the call, and then, when it came to the point, something else would intervene. He would say no, he had to wait for a friend, or they had to go out and meet someone, but he would never explain whom they were seeing or why. Whom was he seeing now, for instance? Whom had he been seeing this afternoon? Some horrible, shuffling, muttering old woman dressed in black who lived in this huge, horrible, musty apartment, full of knickknacks and crucifixes, and horrible gaudy pictures of Christ.

Mina had had to sit in a corner while Star and this old woman muttered to each other in French, and while the old woman kept stroking Star's hand and fawning over him as if he were some kind of god. The old woman kept talking about Maria: it was the only word Mina understood—Maria this, Maria that. Star had given Mina some grass to smoke before they left for the old woman's apartment, and it had been powerful, but it hadn't given her a lift. It had made her feel sick, and trapped, going round and round like some squirrel in a cage, so her thoughts wouldn't fix. When they got to the old woman's apartment, it was airless and hot, and Star had sat her down right next to a radiator, which made her feel worse.

In the end, right in the middle of one of the old woman's endless weird crooning speeches, Mina had known she was about to pass out, or be sick. Star showed her through to a bathroom in an irritable way, and she could sense that whatever the old woman was telling him was making him angry.

"Stupid fucking old bitch," he said when they were back in the air, back in the street. "She doesn't know if it's tomorrow or last week. She's fucking up my timing. Now I'll have to drag all the way over here tomorrow."

"Why, Star?" she asked before she could stop herself, but for once he answered.

"Because I was supposed to meet someone there," he said. "A friend. She should have been there, and she wasn't, because that fucking old bitch can't tell Monday from Tuesday. Never mind. I have time." He stopped. "You see that pharmacy there? Go in and get the hair dye. Here . . ." He pressed some money into her palm. "Hurry up. I can't do it. A man buying hair dye, they'd remember that. You do it. Hurry up."

Mina took the money. She wondered if there might be a telephone in there, but of course there was not. She found the package of dye and paid for it. She wondered if the friend Star was supposed to have been meeting was that woman she'd seen at the airport, the one he'd said was Maria Cazarès. When she'd been coming back from the bathroom in the old woman's apartment, she'd seen into a bedroom, a bedroom like a shrine, with a big bed with a pink silk eiderdown and photographs of Maria Cazarès everywhere, hundreds of them, on tables, on chests, on the walls. Except no, she thought now: Maria Cazarès wasn't Star's friend, she was his enemy, he had said.

She was getting cold now. Star had been gone more than five minutes. She edged out of the doorway and crossed the narrow street, ready to dart back if need be. Smells of food grilling assaulted her, and she pressed closer to a restaurant window, realizing how hungry she was. Star never seemed to want to eat. It was hours since they had eaten. In a mirror to the side of the restaurant doors, she suddenly saw a girl, very close; the girl startled her and then she realized the girl was herself. She stared at her reflection. With a glance over her shoulder she eased back her blue scarf and then grimaced. Tears came to her eyes: Star had cut her hair himself. Then she had applied the dye. He'd let her look at herself in a hand mirror, just very quickly, when it was dry, and he had seemed so pleased, he'd kept saying how pretty she looked.

She didn't look pretty, Mina thought. She looked ugly. The dye had not taken well, so her hair was now a crude rusty black. It stuck out in jagged tufts all around her face. She looked like a refugee, an outcast. . . . She shrank away from the glass and darted back across the street. She replaced the scarf and tied it tight. What if she'd been seen? They'd been seen this afternoon, a few minutes after leaving that old woman's house. Not by a *policier*—Star never walked near uniformed police, but cut away the second he spotted them. No, they had been seen by a man in an ordinary suit, in an ordinary unmarked Citroën. He stopped, picked up a mobile telephone, started speaking, then got out.

But they were already running by then. Around corners, into shops, out again, through a whole maze of narrow streets. When they finally stopped, Mina could scarcely breathe, and Star was white to the lips.

"You saw him?" He caught hold of her arm. "Christ, they're everywhere. Police, plainclothes police. In cars. On the street. He saw your hair—I saw him look at your hair. We have to get back. We have to change the way you look."

He put his arms around her and hugged her tight. "Mina. If they catch us here, you know what they'll do to me? They'll put me in prison. They'll lock me up."

Mina tried to tell him that she wouldn't let them do that; she'd explain that she'd chosen to come with him. But Star wasn't listening. He raced her back to their attic room and then he made her dye her hair. He sat there in the corner of the room while she did it, he wouldn't even let her use the bathroom, in case the dye left traces, and one of the other lodgers saw it and suspected. So she had to apply the dye with a basin while Star sat surrounded by all the red curls and tresses he'd cut off. They were on the table, on the floor, but he didn't seem to see them. He was reading the tarot, slapping down the cards: the tower, the lovers, the hanged man, the queen of diamonds, the king of cups. His beautiful face darkened. Mina could tell he didn't like what the cards told him, and the next thing she knew, he'd swept them all on the floor, then picked up the chair and thrown it across the room. It hit the wall, and smashed.

"Hurry up." He threw himself down on the bed and lay back, staring up at the ceiling. His fists clenched and unclenched. "Dry your hair, Mina. Come here. Talk to me. Stroke my forehead."

Mina did as she was bid. She crept up close to him and stroked his hair, then his face.

"Can't you tell me what's wrong, Star?" she said timidly.

"The cards were bad." He reached up and grasped her hand. "I didn't like the cards. Go on, Mina. You make me feel better. You're the only one who can. You have the soothing gift. Stroke me very gently. Like that."

Mina continued to do so. She felt proud, but also a little afraid of what Star might do next. She felt cold, with her still-damp hair, and she could see little rivulets of black dye dripping down onto her arms and her shirt.

After a while, a long while, she felt him tense, and she knew what was coming next. He gripped her wrist and opened his eyes, and stared at her, one long, unblinking stare. He looked into her and through her, his beautiful face set like a mask, not one muscle moving. Then he pulled her hand down, away from his forehead. He rested it on his chest, then moved it lower and pressed it against his crotch.

Mina knew what he wanted her to do now, because he'd shown her the previous day. She had to stroke his thighs and his groin while she murmured his name over and over. When he closed his eyes, that was the signal: then she had to unzip his jeans and free his penis, which Star called his cock. The word embarrassed her and made her blush, because apart from Star and Cassandra, no one else she knew ever used that word. Fortunately, she did not have to use it herself; she just had to stroke him, holding his penis in her hand. She was to continue saying his name while she did so; she had to breathe quietly, and lie very still; he would tell her when to stop.

When he first asked, pleaded with her to do this, Mina had thought that perhaps this was how sex could begin sometimes. She had always expected it to begin with kisses, but perhaps this was a prelude to making love which some men liked. She told herself that she knew what would happen next. It would be the way Cassandra whispered, the way it had so clearly been explained in biology class. Star would become aroused, then blood would engorge his penis, then he would have what her teacher called an erection and Cassandra called a hard-on—and then he would certainly kiss her, and then they would make love.

Behind all this mist of confusion and words, Mina thought she was prepared for this. She did not want to go on being a virgin, but she wanted the loss of her virginity to be special—not some rushed fumbling of the kind Cassandra had described, but a glorious occurrence she would never forget: she wanted it to be her gift to a man she loved—and she loved Star. As soon as he first began talking to her, she had known that at once.

No diagrams or descriptions, however, had prepared her for this. She knew she was flurried and nervous, and was perhaps making some technical mistake, but when she unzipped his jeans and took Star in her hand, even when she began to stroke him, nothing happened at all. Star's eyes remained closed, but he did not protest, or correct her, so gradually she lost her fear. She stroked his beautiful, taut flat stomach, then laced her fingers in his dark pubic hair. Timidly, she ran her index finger along the length of his penis: its large size surprised her, and so did the extreme tenderness of this skin. She traced a vein, then held this lovely thing in her hand. She might have liked to bend forward and kiss it, because she felt overwhelmed with love for Star, and with these secrets of his body, but she did not quite dare. She continued to stroke, and once she felt a tiny quiver of life pass through this soft flesh, but then it lay inert once more, cupped in her hand, and she began to feel desperate.

"They spring up," Cassandra had said. "They spring up and stick out—like a shelf. I like it when that happens. It makes you feel so powerful, Mina. It's great."

What was she doing wrong? Mina tried to blink back the tears. She knew what was wrong. Star did not love her; he was not even attracted to her; she was stupid and plain and clumsy; she did not inspire want.

"Star," she whispered when she could bear it no longer. "Star, is something wrong? Isn't this what you want?"

He rose up in the bed in one fast, fluid movement. He drew back his arm and hit her hard across the face. He hit her with the flat of his hand and his full strength. The blow was so powerful, it knocked her back against the wall and off the bed.

She crouched on the floor, too afraid to cry, and then Star caught hold of her and dragged her up. He was shaking with rage and his eyes had that glittery look she was coming to dread.

"Nothing's wrong," he said, shaking her. "Nothing—you've got that? You think I want sex?" He shook her again. "You think I want to fuck? Well, I don't. I don't want any of that—that's what ordinary men want."

Mina began crying then. The tears choked her, and her head hurt, and she was desperate to make him understand.

"But I love you, Star," she whispered. "I love you so much. I thought you might want to make love to me. If you wanted to, I would. . . ."

"Have you? Ever?" He shook her a third time, and when she said no, he suddenly embraced her very tight, locked her in his arms and rocked her back and forth.

"That's good," he said. "That's good, Mina. You have to understand—we're special. This is special. We're not like everyone else. We commune, Mina. We fuck with our eyes, with our minds, with our souls, Mina. That's what we do. That's what I want."

Mina stopped crying and stared at him. She looked at his face, which was extraordinary, burning with conviction, and she thought what he said was extraordinary, the most strange and wonderful thing any man could say—and then a horrible little doubt crept in at the back of her mind: had he ever said that before, to anyone else?

Almost at once, though, that doubt slipped away. Star was so kind and so tender to her after that. He took her in his arms and kissed her face, and told her she was the best and the sweetest thing that had ever happened to him in his life; he told her she was his salvation, and Mina believed the blaze in his eyes and his voice. Since then there had been no outbursts of rage, just the occasional hints, like the rumblings of a volcano, the suggestion that even when controlled, some terrible fury she did not understand seethed beneath.

He has been *hurt*, she thought now, edging back into the darkness of the church doorway, so badly hurt that nothing could soothe him for long, not the strokings and whisperings of his name, not even the game he liked to play with that gun catalogue, though his expertise there could always restore his humor for an hour at least.

She lifted her watch to her face and stared at the hands. Star had been gone almost twenty minutes. She felt suddenly afraid that he wouldn't come back, that he'd tired of her, decided just to abandon her there. She looked up at the lighted window opposite but could see no one. A taxi was just pulling in at the end of the street. She shrank back into the shadows, imprisoned there by fear and love, by an anguish of uncertainty—by the most potent combination of weapons any man can use against a woman, of course, but Mina did not understand that. Less than a minute later she gave a low cry of relief: the door opposite had opened, and Star was across the narrow street in an instant.

Mina began to move forward, into the light spilling from the restaurants, and then she stopped. Two people had climbed out of the taxi, a man and a woman. They were now moving along the street. They were checking the numbers of doors, and they were speaking English: Mina caught the man's deeper tones, then the woman's low voice.

Star, usually so cautious, seemed unaware of this. He had come to a halt just in front of her, and was staring at her as if she were invisible, as if he looked at a wall. Tears were streaming down his face.

"Star, quickly. These people are English," she whispered, catching hold of him. "Come out of the light."

He still did not move; he seemed not to hear her. The man and the woman were closer now, about thirty feet away. Frightened, Mina backed into the shadows of the church doorway, pulling Star after her. He had begun to make a noise, a terrible noise, a low, moaning noise. Mina fumbled with the handle of the door behind her and opened it.

"Don't, Star, don't," she whispered, and tried to cover his mouth with her hand. Shaking, she half pushed, half pulled him into the church and swung the door shut. It was dimly lit and empty. Candles flickered in some distant recess. Star slumped back against the closed door, then slumped to the ground. He crouched there, silent now, then buried his face in his arms. Mina stood absolutely still, listening, torn between Star and the footsteps outside, which had been coming closer but had now stopped.

"It's the house over there," the man said. Mina could hear him clearly. "The one with the lace curtains. Someone's in—there's lights, there's a television on. . . ."

Mina froze, pressing her ear to the door panels.

"Shall we both try?" It was the woman's voice. "It's late. We don't want to alarm them."

"You try first. A woman is less intimidating. Be careful what you say. If she's there, I'll come over—let's play it like that. I'll wait here in the doorway, out of sight."

The woman seemed to hesitate. "Is something wrong, Rowland?"

"No. Nothing. Go on . . ."

Mina heard the woman's footsteps cross the street. Her male companion moved back so he was just on the other side of the church door. Mina held her breath. Then, to her astonishment, she heard the man give way to some unexplained emotion. He made some quick violent movement; Mina thought he struck the wall beside the door with his fist; she heard him say *Christ* once, in a low voice, then again, even more quietly, then she heard the sound of knocking from across the street. Then silence. Then voices, the woman's and a girl's, speaking rapidly in French.

The conversation was brief; a door slammed. The woman's footsteps approached.

"No Chantal?"

"She claims not. Hasn't lived there in months. Doesn't know where she does live now. And doesn't take kindly to a stranger turning up on her doorstep at this time of night."

"Was she lying?"

"Maybe. I couldn't tell. She slammed the door in my face."

"Damn. Now what do we do? Maybe we should go back to the hotel. I need to think."

"You need to *sleep*. You look exhausted."

"I'm fine." He cut the woman off in a curt way. "Come on. This is hopeless. We can't force our way in there. We'll have to give this information to the police. You realize Chantal could be there despite what she said. So could Star. So could Mina Landis, come to that."

"Rowland, I know. Damn, we've done the wrong thing. We shouldn't have come here like this. If they were there, or if that woman knows them, we've just alerted them. That was stupid. *Stupid*. We're not thinking clearly."

"I'm aware of that. Let's get back to the St. Vincent . . ."

The footsteps moved off. Slowly Mina began to breathe again, began to move again. She looked down at Star. She thought he had heard none of this. He was still crouching at her feet, his hands still covered his face.

Mina knelt down beside him and put her arms around him. His face was wet. Gently she began to coax him and whisper to him; she tried to persuade him to lift his head.

"Star," she said, "please don't. What's happened? What's wrong? Don't cry—I can't bear to see you cry. Look at me, Star. We can't stay here. Someone's looking for me. They mentioned the police. We have to leave."

"She's dead." He raised his face. "Maria Cazarès is dead. She died this afternoon. This evening. I just saw it on the television. She died hours ago, and I didn't know. I didn't sense." He made a horrible choking sound in his throat. "The cards *lied*. They should have warned me. I wanted her to die. I think I did. But not like this. Not like *this*!"

His sudden violent gesture knocked Mina aside. He stood up.

"This is *your* fault. Your fault. That stupid fucking old bitch's fault. If you hadn't been sick, I'd have stayed, I'd have waited. I *knew* it was the right day. I knew she was coming—and she did. One hour, two hours after we left. After *you* made us leave, with your fucking dumb whinings and complainings, you're too fucking hot, you feel sick. . . ."

He pulled Mina up to her feet and shook her, then grasped her so her face was just inches from his own, and his blue-black eyes glared at her with that awful glittery look.

"I'd have seen her die—you realize that? I could have stood there, just the way I planned, and watched her die at my feet. With that dumb fucking Mathilde weeping and screaming and calling for a priest. Trying to find her rosary, trying to find some little sacred picture, as if a picture would save her—I could have seen all that. And I would have rejoiced. *Rejoiced*. Twenty-five years I've waited for this—and you, you—"

He stopped. His face worked. Mina was so afraid, she could not move. He lifted his hands and clasped them tight around her neck. "Shall I kill you, Mina?" he said, his voice steadier now, and the blue-black eyes looking directly into hers. "I could. I could snap your spine, just like that. Break your neck—then I could leave you here in the church. I could put your body on the altar. Lay you out, Mina, with candles at your head and candles at your feet. . . ." He paused and drew in one long, slow breath. "So, shall I kill you? Maybe I'll kiss you, Mina? What do you think?"

Mina could not speak. She tried to move her lips, and he increased the pressure on her neck, just for an instant, then he moved, bent, kissed her very hard on her closed lips.

"You're safe," he said. "I'm merciful. Anyway, I need you. I need you more than ever now. I'll have to change my plans. Adjust. I can do that. I'm resourceful. I'm quick."

He took her by the arm as if nothing had happened, led her out into the street, and took her back to the attic room. All the way there, Mina could sense his mood was changing yet again. She could feel a new electricity in the pace with which he walked, in the light in his eyes; he looked—bright, she thought, as if he gave off rays of invincibility.

"Sweet," he said. He had been laying out the tarot as soon as they entered; he was still in his long overcoat, and Mina was crouching on the bed.

"The cards are *sweet*. I knew they would be. It's okay—I can do it now. I have the means—look."

Then he took out the gun. Mina knew very little about guns except what she had learned from his catalogue games. This was small, a nickel color; he tossed it down onto the patchwork quilt between her legs.

"It's not loaded. Don't be afraid. Pick it up. Isn't it beautiful? That's what I had to collect tonight."

Mina touched the gun, then withdrew her hand. Star picked it up. He caressed it. He held its muzzle against his temple. "Bang," he said, smiling now. "One bullet in the heart. Another in the head. *Au revoir,* Jean Lazare. Simple. This fires fifteen rounds a second. Nasty ammunition. It rotates, after impact, inside the body, inside the brain. You don't survive. You get lacerated—and that's not nice, Mina, I know all about that. My life's been one long laceration, they took my heart and they tore it into little, little strips. One day, I'll tell you about that. . . ."

He talked on, and Mina watched him and the gun. She was afraid, but she was thinking hard. Star needed help, she could really see that now; he needed help from doctors, but he'd never agree to see one, she knew that.

"Wednesday morning. Two more days—less," he was saying, and Mina lay beside him, as still as a mouse. She was trying to work out how and when she could escape from this room, this house. The door was not locked, but there was a problem she could not see around. As far as she knew, as far as she had been able to judge in the three days they had been together, Star never slept.

CHAPTER 14

"Wait," Markov said to Lindsay. "I promise you. This is the place Quest always comes. And she always eats late. . . ."

"This late? It's nearly one o'clock in the morning."

"Trust me. One-fifteen—no later. You could set your watch by her. That's what she's like."

"Markov, I *know* what she's like. She doesn't *talk*, for a start. About the most I've ever heard her say is 'Hello' and 'Good night.' "

"She talks to *me*. . . . If anyone knows anything about Maria Cazarès's death, Quest will. She's Jean Lazare's favorite model. He *found* her. Come Wednesday, come the Cazarès show—"

"Which will be canceled. Come *on*, Markov."

"—she's due to be the star of the show. I'm telling you—she'll know *something*. What's the alternative? You want to sit around the hotel with a whole pack of airheads listening to *rumors* half the night? With Quest, we *mainline*, right? We tap right into the power source." He paused; his dark glasses turned in Lindsay's direction. "What's the matter with you, Lindy? You've been as jumpy as a cat all night."

"I'm upset. Shocked. That's obvious, surely? Who wouldn't be? I can't believe she's dead. It doesn't seem possible."

"And?"

"And I ought to call the hotel again. Markov, I told you. I need to talk to Rowland McGuire."

251

"Lindy. You have tried five times this evening to reach McGuire."

"He was *out*, Markov. He might be back now."

"—And *when* you call him, Lindy, there's these little signals I'm picking up. Like, serious agitation . . ."

"He's my *editor*. I need to talk to him."

"Sure." Markov gave a huge yawn. "And editors edit. They sit at a desk—in London, in his case—and they edit away. Ring, ring, fax, fax, kill those Markov pictures, I don't like waifs. . . . I mean, correct me if I'm wrong, Lindy, but I seem to remember that around fifteen seconds ago it was war. I seem to remember you were going to wipe him out."

"That was last week, Markov. I've changed my mind."

"Just your mind, Lindy? And how about McGuire? I mean, how come he's abandoned his desk, how come he's suddenly on a plane, in Paris? I'm revising my ideas of this man, Lindy. Like I had the wrong angle before, the wrong aperture, wrong shutter speed, wrong *film*. What's brought him hotfooting to Paris, Lindy, my love? Is it work? Is it a woman? Fill me in."

"Don't be so damn stupid, Markov. Of course it's not a woman. I've no idea where you get these ideas."

"Looking at you, sweetheart, that's where I get them."

"Well, if you knew McGuire better, you'd know you were wrong. It's *work*, Markov—pure and simple. And I'm not sure why he's here. His deputy is holding the fort in London. I spoke to Max, not Rowland."

Lindsay hesitated. She had finally reached Max about an hour before, and Max had been in diplomat mode. According to him, someone now needed to be in Paris urgently, and since Gini was unavailable, it had been jointly decided by Max and Rowland that Rowland should go.

"What d'you mean, Gini's unavailable?" Lindsay had said. "According to Pixie, she was flying here this evening—at least that was the plan."

"Sorry, Lindsay. You'll have to ask Rowland. My other line's ringing. I have to go."

When Max had mentioned Gini's name, Lindsay had detected some *froideur*. With a sigh, and a glance at Markov's maddening dark glasses, she rose.

"Look, Markov, let me try the hotel again. Rowland must be answering now."

"'Lindy. Lindy. Never chase them. It's a very bad idea, you know." Markov wagged a finger and gave her a look that might have been motherly.

"I'm not damn well chasing him." Lindsay hesitated, then sat down again. "Get this straight, Markov. I work with him. I need to talk to him about work. About Maria Cazarès. That's it. End of story. That's all."

"You can't lie to me, Lindy. You never could. I see it all. I see the light in the eyes, the flush in the cheek. You know Aphrodite, the goddess of love? You know she had children? You know what those children were called?"

"No, I don't. I never even knew she had children."

"Well, she did. As a result of an adulterous affair with Ares—the god of war. She had five children by him, Lindy. You know what they were called?"

"I have a feeling you're going to tell me."

"You bet I am. They were called Eros and Anteros—that's love, and reciprocal love; Harmonia—that's easy enough to understand. And then there were two others. Their names were Deimus and Phobus."

"Meaning?"

"Terror and fear."

Markov gave her one of his small, sad, flickering smiles. He lit a cigarette and inhaled deeply.

"Worth remembering, yes? The children of love. I think about that particular union from time to time. I think about the *offspring* of that union. Terror and fear."

"Are you giving me a warning, Markov?"

"Sure. Oh, sure. You won't listen, no one ever does. So, I'm just kind of sliding in a little reminder. On account of the fact that I can't stand most women, but I'm pretty fond of you. Also, you're unhappy, aren't you?"

There was a silence. Lindsay considered Markov. It did not surprise her that he should be so well acquainted with Greek myth. It would not altogether have surprised her had Markov leaned across the table and begun speaking Greek. Markov might go to extreme lengths, both in his appearance and in his manner of speech, to suggest he was a fool, a gadfly, a fashion victim: in reality, he was none of these things. Markov was astute, sensitive, gifted, and intelligent, also both resilient and brave. His long-term partner had died of AIDS two years before; Markov had nursed him through the final stages of his illness. Markov was indeed in a position to understand why terror and fear should be the offspring of love.

Watching her now, as the minutes ticked by, he was wearing his habitual disguise. Black clothes, head to foot, black sunglasses despite the fact that this restaurant allegedly favored by Quest was a small, dingy neighborhood place on a Montmartre back street, with lighting rather worse than that of most cellars. On his head, as usual, was a hat—Markov was rarely seen without one, and this, Lindsay thought, was a particularly ridiculous example, wide-brimmed, velvety, a fin-de-siècle hat, an Oscar Wilde hat. From beneath it escaped long, fair, wavy tresses. The final touches were two silver crucifix earrings and a fistful of silver rings. Markov, who hailed from Los Angeles but claimed to have been born on a jumbo jet, had been, since the death of his lover, rootless. He spent his life moving around the world, from shoot to shoot. He could make any woman he photographed look ten times more beautiful than she actually was. Some of his pictures, transcending fashion, haunted Lindsay, who considered him the best fashion photographer in the world—not a view that was widely shared, for Markov's work was too subversive, too strange for many tastes. In Lindsay's view, as man and photographer, Markov was a kind of enchanter. Looking at him now, she realized with a sense of surprise that not only was he almost certainly her closest friend, but that she wanted to talk.

"Oh, very well. You're right," she said, giving Markov a troubled look. "I like Rowland. Maybe more than like him. The other day—I went to his house. I was just talking to him, and—something happened. You know, Markov. One of those little rebellions of the heart."

"Sure. I know those. Go on."

"There is nothing more. I thought I'd cured myself—it's been years, Markov, years since that happened. I'm not a child. I'm not a fool. I'm almost thirty-nine years old. I have a son who's seventeen. I have *stretch marks*, Markov. If I go to bed with someone, I make sure the lights are turned down low."

"Oh, for God's sake, Lindy. . . ."

"It's *true*. I know it's stupid. I tell myself, it doesn't matter, there must be someone out there who doesn't care about all that. Someone who won't mind about the lines on my face, because he's not looking at my face, or my bottom, or my breasts, he's looking at *me*, at the person inside."

Lindsay stopped; she could feel distress inches away, and she despised herself for that. She gave an angry gesture. "You don't want to hear this. I can feel self-pity coming on."

"I do want to hear it. I understand."

"Well, I don't meet them, that's all. If they exist, these miraculous men, I never get an introduction. The men I meet fall into three categories: they're already married; they're liars; or they're bores. It's my *age*, Markov. Only the rejects and the walking wounded are left. At least that's what I thought. And then I met Rowland McGuire."

"The dark, tall, and handsome McGuire?" Markov smiled.

"Yes. But that's not the reason. I hope it's not the reason. . . ."

"So give me a few others."

"He's intelligent—very. I think he's kind. He's amusing. He has an edge to him."

"Very good. And the main reason?"

"Oh, all right. He's been hurt. Something's happened to him, and I don't know what it is, but I can sense it. He needs love. He *deserves* love. He needs the right woman, Markov, the right *partner*."

"Don't we all?"

Markov glanced down at his watch; Quest, late now, if she was ever coming, had still not appeared.

"So why shouldn't you be the right partner?" Markov removed his dark glasses and met her eyes. He gave her one of his quick, squirrelly looks, then replaced the glasses. "You're smart. You're kind. I like the way you look. Plenty of people like the way you look. You look—boyish, peppy, you've got these really honest eyes. You're funny—you make *me* laugh. You've got this sunny nature, you don't sulk, you don't have moods, you give a lift to the day. You're interested in other people, you're not some fucking egomaniac like most people I know. You're *generous*, Lindsay, you're not tight, you're not mean—and I'm not talking about money, right? You give. I remember. You gave a whole lot to me two years ago."

Lindsay was touched by this. She took the hand Markov held out to her and squeezed it. "Thanks, Markov. That's the nicest testimonial anyone's ever given me. Maybe you should pass it on to McGuire."

"If he's what you say he is, he wouldn't *need* a testimonial. He'd just have to use his eyes."

"No." Lindsay shook her head and looked away. "I wish that were true, but I'm afraid it isn't, Markov. Things don't work that way. And anyway, I'm not right for him."

"Why not? And don't mention stretch marks again."

"Because I'm not—oh—difficult enough, maybe. If he had me, he'd always be chasing something more. He'd want—something I could never provide."

"I see," Markov sighed, and raised his eyes to the ceiling. "You mean he's *that* type?"

"I told you he had an edge, Markov. Think, dark side of the moon."

"Sexually?" Markov said.

"Almost certainly. Emotionally as well. Intellectually too. Forget it, Markov. I've had time to think about this. I've been thinking about it for most of the day. Rowland and I—it would be like mixing wine and milk."

"It might be fun. . . ." Markov gave another of his sad, flickering smiles. "With that kind, it might be a whole lot of fun for a while."

"Excitement, sure. Also heartbreak. I don't want to know, Markov. I've been down that road once or twice."

"Me too."

"And he'd take me too far. Those would be his terms. Either that, or I'd get dropped off at the first turn. I'm nearly thirty-nine, Markov. Approaching forty! I don't *want* that now. I want—" She broke off, then smiled. "Peace. Security. Tranquillity. *Harmony,* if you like . . ."

"And McGuire wouldn't provide those?"

"Not for me. No."

"Come on, Lindy. You're not convincing yourself. You're not convincing me. I can see this little ray of hope way back there in the eyes."

"The hell you can. With those damn glasses, I doubt you can see me at all. I'll test you. Who came in about two minutes ago?"

"Quest did," Markov replied, despite the fact that he had not turned his head once during the conversation. "And the magnificent one is now at her usual table, table five, right behind me in the corner. She's just got her usual waiter to bring her usual carafe of vin ordinaire, and she's just lit the first of the many Gauloises she will smoke throughout her meal. Excuse me, *Liebling.* I have work to do. . . ."

Lindsay watched as Markov rose and crossed to the table Quest occupied, in the darkest corner of this dark bistro. Lindsay did not expect Quest to acknowledge her own presence, although they knew each other. She was correct. As Markov rose, Quest turned her beautiful blind stare in their direction, then looked away. As Markov, uninvited, sat down opposite her, and—being Markov—at once drank some of her wine, and lit one of her cigarettes for himself, Quest yawned. In her guttural voice, and in an affectionate tone, she said, "Markov, piss off."

Markov looked delighted at this reception. He leaned closer and began to talk; Quest responded, inaudibly to Lindsay. Lindsay watched her with fascination. Her real name was Russian, and unpronounceable. She had been born in Smolensk, the daughter of a steelworker and a factory hand. She had come to the West four years before; she was over six feet tall, thin, and big-boned for a model. She was Garboesque in that her build was mannish, with wide shoulders, long legs, narrow hips, and large hands and feet. She had the most haunting face Lindsay had ever seen, with gaunt high cheekbones, strong vivid brows, and huge angry eyes of a brown so dark it caused lighting difficulties in the studio, for her eyes photographed too black, too deep. It was for this reason that despite her discovery by Lazare, and despite the use Cazarès made of her as their star runway model, magazines had been slow to use her.

It was Markov who had seen her possibilities. Quest obeyed none of the rules—which had interested Markov from the first. She was solitary, gruff, profoundly indifferent to money, fame, and—it was rumored—either sex. She was without the plasticity usual in most successful models; she never attempted to act or to adapt. She simply turned up, on time, allowed herself to be dressed, coiffed, made up with an air of sublime indifference, then she stood towering in front of the camera and glowered at the lens. She had one expression only, of distrustful and magnificent contempt. Markov adored her. He said, in his more extravagant moments, that she was half man, half woman, a female for the twenty-first century. "When she's milked the decadent West of enough money," he'd said with delight, "she'll go back to Smolensk. She wants a *farm*. She wants to keep sheep and cows. Seriously. She's astonishing. She knows exactly who she is, what she wants, and how to get it. I love her. I learn from her. I worship at her shrine."

His regard was, Lindsay knew, returned. And his promise that Quest would talk to him but no one else seemed now to be confirmed. Lindsay could not hear what Quest was saying, but she was speaking rapidly, with emphasis.

Lindsay hoped she was coming up with some useful information, since the quest for Quest had used up an entire evening. She and Markov had begun by canceling the Grand Vefour—the headwaiter had not been amused. Then they had chased around Paris, visiting what Markov claimed were Quest's favorite evening haunts. Lindsay had followed Markov up and down a particularly lonely stretch of the Seine; she had shivered in the medieval streets of the Île St. Louis, and shivered again in some tiny Russian Orthodox church, where Quest—according to Markov—came every evening to pray.

"What does she pray *for*, Markov?" Lindsay had asked.

"Don't know." Markov lit a candle—for Maria Cazarès, he claimed. "Spiritual enlightenment? Cows?"

"For heaven's sake, Markov. I'm freezing. Can we go? I'm giving up on Quest. She's not going to know anything anyway."

"She will. You should get to know her better, Lindy. You'd like her. You could learn from her too."

"Learn what?" Lindsay started moving off to the door.

"How to be alone. That's valuable."

Lindsay had not replied; she eased back the huge door of the church, and the wind gusted. Behind her, pyramids of candles guttered, the gold of icons burned. Lindsay could smell incense, that tang of religion; she was not a churchgoer, and she occasionally found Markov too Californian.

"Hurry up," she said, making for the street and the city air. That church had been their penultimate port of call. Then they had come here, to this back-street restaurant, high on the hill of Montmartre, down an alleyway, with a slanting view up to the floodlit white dome of Sacré-Coeur.

The visitations, the delays, seemed to have been fruitful. Lindsay could feel the odd journey they had made, five hours plus of searching, working in her mind; she could feel Markov's earlier comments too, bubbling away like yeast. He was returning to her table now, his face bright with discoveries evidently made.

"Let's go," he said, taking Lindsay's arm. "You're not going to believe this. I'll drive you back to the hotel. We can talk in the car."

In the car, the CD kicked in as soon as he started the engine. "My Foolish Heart" had been rejected, it seemed, in favor of an old Annie Lennox number, a great Annie Lennox number: Lindsay heard that love was a stranger in an open car. She leaned forward and switched off the sound.

"That isn't a message I want to hear right now," she said.

"Why not? Great song. Great singer. Great lyrics. The essential impetuosity of *l'amour*. I feel it *speaking* to me, Lindy. . . ."

"So do I. That's the problem. Anyway, I want you to talk. Come on—what did she say?"

"She said . . . some very interesting things." Markov, who drove fast and well, and who could provide information fast and well when he chose to do so, accelerated.

"I tell you this, Lindy, despite the fact that Quest swore me to secrecy, because you're one of the four people I like in the world. And because I know you'll be careful whom you tell. If you have to, tell McGuire. But don't blab it around." He paused. "First: the Cazarès collection *isn't* canceled. It goes ahead, the day after tomorrow, Wednesday, eleven A.M., precisely as planned. Tomorrow morning Lazare is giving a press conference—and all the passes to that are being sent out now. The line will be that Wednesday's show is *un hommage*. What Maria Cazarès herself would have wanted. Moving, isn't it?"

"Actually, it is. And?"

"And now—get this—guess where Quest has been all night? At the

Cazarès workshops. Getting fitted for three very special ensembles, three *new* ensembles . . ."

"What? Tonight? It's less than two days to the show. That can't be right, Markov. All the clothes for the collection will have been finished a week ago. Lazare always insists on that. The most they'd be doing is small last-minute adaptations—trimmings, accessories. . . ."

"Sure. But I told you—these outfits are *special*. They're Maria Cazarès's last work. Her final designs. As drawn by her own pen, this last weekend. Lazare's idea. He was there, in the workshops, Lindy, *tonight,* putting the fear of God into everybody. Quest was sent for within one hour of Cazarès's being pronounced dead."

"What? I can't believe that."

"There's more. Think, Lindy—what time did I first hear? Around eight. And when you checked back with Pixie, what time did she say it came through on the wires?"

"About seven forty-five."

"Exactly. So work out just how long Lazare took to release the news. Quest was summoned at *five* this afternoon. If it's true that Cazarès had died an hour before, she died at around four. So what was happening for the next three and three-quarter hours?"

"I don't know." Lindsay gave a shiver. "They were getting the security in place, oiling up the press machine, making sure everyone put out the right story, the right way. . . ."

"Sure. That's certainly what the courtiers and minions were busy doing. But not Lazare. I'm telling you, Lindy, Cazarès is dead one hour, she's not *cold* yet, and he's there, in the workshops, raising hell. They're cutting the material for the dresses *on* the model, the way Chanel used to work, because there's no time to make *toiles*. Every tiny little detail has to be just so. Quest is standing there, getting pins stuck in her, getting slices taken off, because the cutters are so damn terrified they can't hold the scissors steady, and there's Lazare, in the middle of mayhem, people scurrying in all directions, and he won't compromise, he's going through fifteen, sixteen, seventeen samples of materials, he's got them running down to warehouses, and bringing back bales, he's got embroideresses, he's saying no, those buttons won't work, they're one eighth of an inch too big—and all the time, Lindy, *all* the time, he's in emperor mode. Like—no tears, no grief, no condolences given or accepted, just this white, set face and that voice that makes your blood run cold."

"An *hour* after she died? I *cannot* believe this, Markov. He loved her. I'm sure he loved her. *You're* sure he loved her. She was the one thing he cared about—"

"Oh, true." Markov braked at a tight corner, then accelerated again. "If you'd seen them at the airport, Lindy—I told you. Like my hair is standing on end, I've got goose pimples the length of my spine, because any second Lazare's going to spot me, and then I'm *history*, because this guy, I mean—he makes me think about crucifixes, Lindy. About stringing garlic around my neck and praying hard. I mean, all the time I'm standing there, quaking behind this palm, I'm thinking, oh, no, it's after nightfall and before dawn. . . ."

"Come on, Markov, stop exaggerating. Lazare looks fit, active, tanned."

"Not Friday night, he didn't. White, Lindy—his face was *white*. He had a desperate kind of *thirsty* look. Definitely but definitely one of the children of the damned. And then, when she started in on children, babies . . ."

"You're *sure* she said that, Markov? You couldn't have misheard?"

"I speak French, Lindy. I know the French for *baby*. And *child*. And *son*. And she kept repeating it, over and over—I want my baby back, I want my son—and he was desperate to shut her up, calm her down. . . ." Markov hesitated. His voice became quiet. "He *kissed* her, Lindy."

"You didn't mention that before."

"I know. It felt a bit blasphemous—discussing it. I shouldn't have been there. I shouldn't have seen it. I felt excited—and then I felt cheap for getting excited."

"It didn't stop you phoning me, I notice."

"I know. Sainthood eludes me. But if you'd seen the *way* he kissed her." Markov hesitated again. "It was to stop her talking, partly. But not just that. You could see—he wanted her, and he loved her. He looked like he'd *die* for her, or he thought *she* was dying, maybe, I'm not sure."

"Markov, you can't know that . . ." Lindsay began as they rounded a corner and the lights of the St. Vincent came in sight. "You're reading too much into it."

"No. I'm not." Markov stopped the car. He turned to her and removed his dark glasses. Lindsay was allowed to read the expression in his eyes.

Ashamed, knowing she had been misled by his tone, Lindsay took his hand. Markov gave a wry smile.

"I just knew, okay?" he said. "I recognized that country. I speak its language. I was there myself, just over two years ago. It's not a language you forget."

"No. You don't," replied Lindsay, who had circumnavigated similar territory herself. She leaned across and kissed Markov good night.

"Watch out for McGuire. Watch what you say to him," he called as she stepped out of his car. "I'll see you at Chanel tomorrow afternoon."

In the still-crowded lobby, Lindsay hesitated. She wanted to tell Rowland this, and she wanted to see Rowland very much, but it was now nearly two in the morning. She stared at the telephone booths, and in the end dialed his extension; he picked up on the second ring.

"No, no, come up," he said, interrupting her apology. "I'm working. Gini's here with me, working. She just got in from Amsterdam. Room 810."

Lindsay was surprised to hear this, but not that surprised. Presumably Gini had *not* been unavailable, as Max had thought: Rowland must have tracked her down; and Gini, of course, was more than capable of working through the night on a story once she had locked into it. For Gini, when at work, two A.M. was *early*, she thought, and smiled as she entered Room 810, to find Rowland at the fax machine and Gini talking fast on the telephone in French.

Both of them seemed energetic, hyped up, Lindsay thought. Rowland began explaining that there had been a provisional sighting of Mina Landis earlier that day. News of this had taken time to be relayed back, via the British police, and the *Correspondent* news desk: Gini was just trying to check the details now.

He led Lindsay to a sofa at the far end of the room; Lindsay sat down, but he did not. Lindsay began explaining what Markov had told her, and Rowland listened with close attention. Once or twice he looked back at Gini, then interjected a question. Lindsay continued her story, and it was only as she reached its end that she sensed something wrong.

The room had a careful feel. On the far side of it was a door that presumably led into a bedroom. It was shut. There was a tension beneath the surface here. She looked at Rowland in puzzlement: his demeanor seemed much as it always was. She glanced across at Gini, who was twisting the telephone cord as she spoke. She had been about to ask which floor Gini was on, whether Pixie had found her a room in this hotel, or somewhere else—and then she realized: this was a question better not asked, a topic it would be unwise to discuss.

Gini had come to the end of her conversation. She put the telephone down. She glanced at Rowland, then away, and began to explain. There *had* been a sighting of Mina Landis. It was still unconfirmed, but a girl answering her description, and a man resembling Star, had been seen by a plainclothes policeman in the sixth arrondissement. She reached for a map of Paris and laid it out on the desk.

"Here," she said. "They were seen in this street here, in the Faubourg St. Germain area. . . ." She frowned. "I know that neighborhood. It's only a few streets away from the place where Maria Cazarès died. How odd."

Rowland was already moving toward the desk.

"Do they now know where she died?" Lindsay said.

"What?" Rowland glanced back at her in a distracted way. "Oh— yes, apparently so. It was on the late TV news bulletins. She'd been visiting some elderly maid of hers—now retired. They were having tea together and she suddenly collapsed. According to the first reports, she was dying by the time the ambulance got there."

"Oh, then they've released that much . . ." Lindsay said.

"I imagine they had no choice. Some French journalist will have been handing out hundred-franc bills to the ambulance crew within half an hour of her death's being rumored, let alone announced. There were paparazzi crawling all over that hospital—that was on the news too."

Rowland bent over the desk. He angled the light. Gini, who had not looked up once during this exchange, still kept her eyes on the map. Rowland began to trace streets with his right hand; he rested his left on the back of Gini's chair, then removed it.

"You're right," he said. "It is very close. . . ."

Their hands were now, Lindsay saw, lying side by side on the map, about four inches apart. Gini remarked in a low voice that it was an expensive area of Paris, not an area where you would expect retired maids to live. Rowland agreed that this was so. He glanced at his watch and drew back. A series of utterly unremarkable movements: Lindsay rose, intent only on disguising her shock and distress.

Had her evening with Markov been less strange, she thought, had she not had that conversation with him about love and sex, she might even have been deceived by those unremarkable movements and accepted them as such. As it was, she could sense the electricity and tension they were designed to disguise; she could sense that it was Rowland and Gini's united wish that she leave—and that she do so at once.

Meanwhile, she had to pretend that Rowland's urgent desire to take Gini in his arms was not as nakedly visible to her as if the act had been performed. Luckily, neither was paying her much attention, and she could dissemble, when required, well enough. She rose, stretched, and said she must get some sleep, that there were two shows tomorrow— Chanel and Gaultier as well as the Cazarès press conference.

Gini nodded and gave her a dazed look.

Rowland, who also looked half blind, escorted her to the door. He said he would certainly try to be at that press conference; Gini said she would too, if she had time, though it was unlikely to be useful.

"Party-line stuff," she said. "Still, if Lazare himself is going to speak . . . I'll try and come with you, Rowland."

"Good night, Lindsay," Rowland said, opening the door, and closing it behind her at once. Lindsay stood for a second in the corridor; she was shaking; she pressed her hands against her face. This couldn't be true, she thought. Rowland, perhaps—but not Gini, surely not Gini?

She heard Rowland engage the lock and chain before she was two feet away. She returned to her room, paced, found herself unable to sleep. She tried very hard not to imagine what might have been said behind that locked door after she left.

Very little, in fact, was said. As the door closed, Gini bent again to the map; she did not dare to look up. She heard the lock engage; she heard Rowland approach, then stop.

For Rowland, distance was a last resort. If he remained here, two feet away, he thought, and if she did not look up, or meet his eyes, then he might be able to disguise what he felt. *Once*, she had said at a point when he had already made love to her twice. Throughout this evening, in the cab, in the rue St. Séverin, here in this room, while she telephoned and he used the fax, she had moved through his thoughts. In his mind he had continued to touch her, kiss her, make love.

Perhaps she did not feel this, he thought. He stood at that safe distance, just those two feet from the desk. His body had begun to stir the instant he locked the door. He looked at Gini's bent head, at the pale curve of her neck, at the ordinary white shirt she was wearing, the ordinary black skirt. She was extraordinarily slender; he could span her waist with his hands, yet she had full and very beautiful breasts, their areolae wide and dark. He closed his eyes, fighting the memory of his own hands, and his mouth, pressed against those breasts. He felt her hands on his skin, the soft openness of her mouth. He swore in a low voice, looked blindly around the room, half turned, then moved back to the desk.

He stood immediately behind her, then, when he could resist the impulse no longer, rested his hands against her shoulders and her throat. He felt her body become rigid with tension at once. Even then, he thought later, even then he might have been able to retain control, but she tilted her head back and met his eyes. He bent forward and kissed her mouth, and in that instant he was lost. She caught hold of his hands and drew them forward inside her blouse. She gave a moan that might have been desire or despair, then twisted up out of the chair and into his embrace.

He could read the need and the desperation he felt in her eyes, and in that moment was certain that she had been as desperate to continue something unfinished as he had been.

He began to undo her blouse as she fumbled first with the buttons of his shirt, then his belt. As he caught her to him, and her bared breasts touched his bared skin, she gave a low cry and shuddered against him.

She rested one of her hands against his thigh, then his groin. She gave a moan, clinging to him and seeking his mouth. Rowland could think of nothing but entering her again. He pulled her down beside him, murmuring her name; she lay back among scattered papers and scattered clothes, drawing his hand down between her thighs. She was very wet; his fingers could slip inside her easily; she arched back in a quick ecstasy of pleasure.

She parted her legs, frantic for him to enter her. Rowland thrust up into her deep, knowing she would come almost immediately. If he moved a very little, he thought, just once, just twice. Lifting himself on his arms, looking down at her face, he watched her astonishing eyes, watched the waves of abandonment move like light across her face. He waited, withdrew, thrust again, and began to move carefully, because they were still not familiar to each other, and he wanted her to adjust her rhythms to his. It took her a little while; at first, as he fucked, he thought she was resisting him, deliberately mistiming her response to his strokes. He thought he knew the reason for that, as he waited, moved, waited again, although this was hard for him, because he was very aroused, and his own climax was close. He used all his skills, every pleasure device, and at last he felt that odd female resistance begin to give. Her eyes opened and met his. He bent his head and kissed her breasts, moving deep inside her.

"Darling, I can't—don't fight me," he said in a low voice, and at that all her resistance melted away. She began to move with him, perfectly in time, and it was inutterably sweet. He watched her face, for that tiny second of stillness which he was beginning to know, and which meant she was just on the edge. Then he could no longer watch because the pleasure was too sharp, the desire too intense. He caught her to him as they came, and said her name. There were other things he wanted to say, and in the next moments was very close to saying, but he forced himself to leave them unspoken. He clasped her hand, trusting that the language of the body would have spoken to her instead.

Later, when they lay beside each other in bed with faint predawn light edging the curtains, she turned to him, her mouth lax with pleasure and her eyes languorous with sexual fatigue. She rested her hand on his stomach, laced her fingers in his pubic hair, and watched him stir, become erect.

An instant tremor of response ran through her body. She leaned across so her breasts brushed against his penis; she bent, and took him in her mouth, and Rowland shuddered at the touch of her tongue and lips.

"We taste of each other," she said, lifting her head, then kissing his mouth. "Of each other, and of too much sex. We said once—I said once . . ."

"It was already too late when you said that." He clasped her hand, and their fingers interlaced. "Once. Five times. Six. A hundred. Does it make a difference?"

"Maybe not. I still want you so much. I can see you, feel you wanting me. In the rue St. Séverin?"

"Yes." Rowland smiled. "And outside the church too."

"In the taxi?"

"It was particularly bad in the taxi. Here too. While I was trying to listen to Lindsay, and you were on the phone—I couldn't really hear what she was saying. . . ."

"I couldn't hear that policeman. All I could hear was you. Your hands. This."

She moved so that the lips of her sex brushed the tip of his penis. Then, slowly, her eyes holding his, she lowered herself onto him, as if she were impaling herself on his flesh. There were tears in her eyes.

Drawing her down to him, Rowland kissed her tears. He felt desire for her, and also a profound tenderness.

"Are you sad? Darling, are you?" he said against her mouth. "Don't be. I understand. It can still be once—in a sense. Just this one night . . ."

"Yes, that. One night. A time out of time, and . . ."

She could not continue. She began to tremble. Rowland came with a sense of painful release and an immediate sadness. After that she curled into the curve of his arm and fell asleep, and Rowland lay there, holding her close, listening to her breathing, counting the hours left to them and waiting for the late winter dawn.

Several times during the night the telephone had rung, and the front desk had picked up. At six-thirty, as the first thin city light stole into the room, Rowland rose and went through into the sitting room beyond. As was the hotel's practice, the messages had been placed in an envelope and slipped beneath the door. The calls had all been for Gini and there must have been several, more than he had realized, for the envelope was bulky. He placed it on Gini's desk, picked up some of the scattered papers, and looked down at the map of this city he and Gini had scanned the night before.

Where next? he thought, and tried to focus on the demands of this story, this piece of work. He looked at the objects spread out on the desk: the map, Anneke's address book, his notebooks, Gini's notebooks, a tape recorder and tapes. The objects would not connect; their links were unimportant to him. He passed his hands across his face; he felt sexually spent, jagged with exhaustion, with the speed of events. Could change, decisive change, occur overnight?

He stopped. He was lying to himself. It was not simply a matter of hours. These events did not begin when he led Gini into this room for the first time the previous night and suddenly felt a surge of acute desire for a woman he scarcely knew. *When* did it begin? How long had he been being prepared, *shaped,* for an event he did not expect?

He stared down angrily at the map on the desk, trying to fight these uncertainties. The telephone rang. Rowland picked it up.

There was a buzzing; he listened to silence, then more interference, then a humming of wires.

"Yes?" Rowland said impatiently. "Who is this?"

"It's Pascal Lamartine," said a voice, coolly enough but with edge. "Could I speak to Genevieve Hunter, please?"

Rowland took a fraction of a second too long to reply, he thought, but when he did so, he felt his tone was well judged.

"Sorry—I'm afraid you've been put through to the wrong room," he said.

"Is this Room 810?"

"Yes, it is. And Genevieve Hunter was using it yesterday, but they moved her out when I arrived. I'm her editor. I think they put her on the sixth floor, near Lindsay Drummond. You know Lindsay?"

"Yes. But the desk said—"

"Oh, the front desk's useless," Rowland said in easy tones. "They don't seem to know where anyone is. The hotel's full, the *Correspondent* has umpteen rooms. Get them to check again. It might be the sixth floor.

I think some people are up on the twelfth. Unless they moved her to another hotel, of course."

"Very well. I'll try the desk again."

"The thing is . . ." Rowland said quickly. "I'm not sure if you'll catch her. She said she'd be making an early start. Some interview, I think . . ."

"This early?" The man's tone sharpened. "It's not seven o'clock yet."

"You might catch her. I could be wrong. I can give her a message later if you like. I'm supposed to be meeting her at a press conference around eleven. Does she have your number? You want her to call you back?"

"No. No message. Damn—" Lamartine broke off; the line crackled. "She can't call me back. I have to go. Look—if you do see her, will you tell her I'll call again this afternoon? Around three or four?"

"Fine. I'll try to get that message to her . . ." Rowland began, then realized he was listening to the dial tone.

The effort of these lies had not left him unmoved. He felt a moment's self-disgust, then anxiety. Was Lamartine in Sarajevo, or elsewhere in Bosnia? Could this call mean he was planning on coming back?

In the bedroom Gini was sitting up in bed, her face white, her eyes wide and dark.

"It was Pascal, wasn't it?"

"Yes. It was." Rowland hesitated. "Did he know you were coming here?"

"No." She had begun to tremble. "He must have called the hotel in Amsterdam. He might have called Max. Once he knew I was in Paris, he'd probably guess I'd be in Lindsay's hotel. He—I couldn't reach him from Amsterdam. He isn't in Sarajevo. He's gone back to Mostar—"

"Gini, don't." She was now shivering uncontrollably. Rowland put his arms around her. "Gini, listen. It's all right. You heard what I said? I had to lie. . . ."

"I know you did. I could hear some of it. It's just—you lied so well. Oh, Christ . . ."

"Gini, *listen* to me. He accepted what I said. He's going to call back around three or four. I'll have you in another room within the hour, I promise you. It's all right—we have time. Let me call the desk. I'll ask about rooms. I'll get some coffee sent up."

Rowland reached for the telephone. Gini watched him, her eyes wide with anxiety and pain. She was shivering violently and seemed unable to move or speak.

"There," Rowland said, turning back from the telephone. "The coffee's on its way. They think they may be able to find a single room somewhere, there's some guest who may be checking out a day early. They'll call back. Gini, listen. Get up. Take a shower. Get dressed. By the next time he calls, we—"

Rowland stopped. She could not meet his eyes; she crossed her arms over her breasts. Gently, Rowland took her hand.

"Gini, don't," he said in a quiet voice. "You're making it very hard for me. If you cry—you can see how that affects me. If we can just—if we get on with our work. That is still what you want?"

"It has to be. It has to be . . ." She gave a low cry and then wrenched her hand away. "I don't *know* what I want anymore. I don't know who I am. I can't think. . . ."

She buried her face in her hands. Rowland hesitated, fighting the temptation to speak, then he finally said what he had been wanting to say for hours. Within the words a resentment was contained, he realized, an anger at Lamartine that had been building for days and which he could no longer suppress.

"Gini," he said, "I don't sleep with married women. For better or worse, I make that a rule. You're *not* married. You have a choice."

"You're wrong." She jerked her face up to meet his gaze. "I *am* married. I feel married. You don't have to wear a ring to feel that. You don't need a piece of paper, witnesses, any of those things."

"I know that."

"I know you thought it was over. I know Max thought that, and Lindsay and Charlotte—but you're all wrong. It *wasn't* over. It couldn't be. Pascal is my whole life. . . ."

Rowland drew back sharply, as if she had just struck him across the face. He rose, and stood looking down at her for a few moments in silence. There was a rap at the door to the suite. Rowland ignored it. His green eyes rested on her face.

"You're certain of that?"

"Yes. No. I'm not certain of anything. If it was true—I couldn't do this."

"I would imagine not." The green eyes had become cold. He suddenly shrugged. "That will be the coffee. I'll get it. You get up, get dressed. Then—"

"Then, *what*? We do what we said? Rowland, the lies have *already* started. You've already lied. I'll have to lie this afternoon. I *hate* this."

"We brought this upon ourselves. Now we have to extricate ourselves." He was already turning away. "It's damage control."

He left the room, pulling on a bathrobe. As he reached the door to the corridor, he was asking himself just how deep that damage was.

"I'll take that," he began as the door opened, then stopped.

Standing outside was a tall, dark-haired man dressed in black jeans and a black leather jacket. Rowland knew instantly from his expression who he was.

"Can I help you?" Rowland said, placing one hand on the doorjamb.

The man gave him a hard, cold, gray-eyed stare.

"I would like to see Gini," he said in a tight voice. "Is she asleep? Perhaps you'd tell her I'm here."

Rowland, thinking fast, gave him a blank look. He was weighing the fact that he had been taken in, that Lamartine was, if need be, as determined a deceiver as himself.

"Gini? What, you mean Genevieve? I'm sorry—didn't we just speak on the phone? I recognize your accent."

"Yes. We did."

"I assumed—hell, never mind. I can't be awake yet. Didn't I explain? There's been chaos over rooms. They shunted me in here last night. They shunted Genevieve somewhere else. The *Correspondent* has most of the sixth floor. Have you tried that?"

"Can we stop this, and stop it now?" The man's eyes glinted. "I haven't spent two days traveling to end up in some Feydeau farce. Would you move aside, please?"

Despite the politeness of his tone, Rowland could feel the anger; he knew a physical fight was very near.

"Look, I'm sorry," he said pleasantly, "but you're making a mistake. This is my room. Take it out on the front desk. I'm about to take a shower."

"I heard the shower come on," Lamartine replied less pleasantly. "I was wondering how you managed to turn it on from here."

"Did I claim I was taking a shower alone?" Rowland hesitated, gave him a rueful smile, then lowered his voice. "Look, this is a little embarrassing. I'd be grateful if you wouldn't mention it to Genevieve. Office gossip, you know. It's just—well, this is Paris, and my secretary's with me. I'm a married man. I'm sure you understand. . . ."

For a moment he thought it had worked. He saw doubt register on Lamartine's tense face, then hope, then scorn. Rowland, watching these reactions, felt a sense of dislocation. Another spin of the wheel, and this man could be himself. Lamartine was almost as tall as he was; he had a similar build, had the same color hair, was approximately the same age: the emotions he saw in Lamartine's face now would have been his own under these circumstances. Rowland felt rivalry but also kinship: we are *alike*, he thought, then tensed: Lamartine was about to hit him. He saw the preparatory move, braced himself to make the counterblow, then, as the blow never came, he saw one last facial change. Upon Lamartine's features came an expression of love and pain that only one person could have evoked. In acknowledgment of that expression and its claim, Rowland dropped his arm and quietly stepped aside.

Gini had put on a bathrobe, he saw, but her feet were bare. She was standing about fifteen feet back from the door, her eyes fixed on Lamartine's face.

"Don't lie anymore, Rowland," she said in a low voice. "I can't let you do that. It's wrong."

There was a silence like glass, then Lamartine walked into the room, passing Rowland without a glance. He came to a halt in front of Gini. He neither touched her nor raised his voice. Speaking in French, he suggested that Gini get dressed and leave at once. He would wait five minutes, and no longer than five minutes, by the elevator, in the corridor, and he would be grateful if she would hurry, since it was evident—and here he glanced at Rowland—that they had matters to discuss.

Under extreme stress, he was quick-witted, Rowland thought. At the door he paused, and their eyes met.

"Are you married?" Lamartine said sharply.

"No," Rowland replied, and before the door closed, he watched Lamartine take in the implications of this.

CHAPTER 15

"Don't speak to me—wait," Pascal said, pulling Gini into the elevator after him. They descended eight floors in silence, not touching, polite as strangers. Even so, the other passengers could sense their emotions, Gini knew; she caught their stares, their quickly averted glances. She stumbled blindly through the press of journalists already assembling in the lobby, and into the cold, damp air. She began speaking then, some incoherent plea, but Pascal would not listen. He grasped her arm and began pulling her across the street, then across the first bridge they came to, making for the Left Bank, beyond the wide, sluggish gray expanse of the Seine.

He looked almost concussed, Gini thought, her own vision blinded with tears. He seemed scarcely to see or to hear the traffic bearing down on them. Once on the Left Bank, he drew her along the quay, then into a tiny narrow street, the rue St. Julien le Pauvre. She realized then where he was taking her, where he must have spent the previous night; a small hotel in which they had stayed together twice the year before. She hung back with a low cry of pain, but his grip on her arm tightened. He led her inside the old building, up the narrow stairs, and into a room with an oblique view of the river and Notre Dame.

This was the same room they had been given on their two visits, prior to Bosnia, when they had come to Paris to see Marianne. They had made love in this bed, leaned together out of that window, back in the spring

271

last year, that time when they had both been so joyful, when the world made such sense. Entering the room, she could feel their own ghosts. She turned away, covering her face.

Pascal slammed the door. "Now. You tell me . . ." He could scarcely speak. "How long has this been going on? *Tell* me—Gini, in God's name—how long have you been lying to me? Since you left Bosnia? Before?"

"No. No—I promise you." She swung around to him with a look of pleading. "Pascal—it was last night. *Only* last night. Never before."

"You expect me to believe that?" He jerked away from her. "Your face. Your eyes. I can't look at you. You've cut your hair. You smell of him—I don't *know* you. Dear God—just keep away from me. I'd have sworn on my life you could not do this—not you."

"Pascal—"

"Just don't say anything. Wait. For God's sake, don't touch me. I could kill you. I could kill him. Just wait. I must think. I can't breathe. . . ."

He turned away from her, clenching his fists, and began to pace the room. With a low, muttered exclamation he swung the window open and leaned out toward the soft air and the soft rain. The curtains fluttered in the wind; a piece of paper on the table drifted to the floor. On it, in Pascal's handwriting, were the names of ten large Paris hotels and their telephone numbers. The St. Vincent was the last on that list. Looking at his handwriting, Gini began to cry.

"Is this how you found me? I thought you must have spoken to Max."

"Max? No." He turned around and gave her a blind look. "I can't—I've been traveling for two nights and a day. I haven't slept. I went to Amsterdam. I was going to meet you in Amsterdam. I thought—I meant it to be a surprise. Then, when I found you'd left, I came here. I got in about two this morning. I realized it was the collections—I thought you must be at Lindsay's hotel. When I found where you were—it was so late, your room wasn't answering, I decided to wait until morning . . ." He could not go on. She saw pain and incomprehension darken his face; he turned, closed the window.

"None of that matters. It's irrelevant. I—I can't think. I can't see. All I can see is that man, blocking the door. I knew he was lying. I could tell from his face. Then I saw your coat on a chair. But even then, even then—I was still thinking, no, it can't be true, I must be wrong. Except I did know. I knew immediately. I knew this morning, almost as soon as he answered the telephone. Something in his voice—" He broke off; she watched him fight to regain control. "I'll never forget it. Standing in a hotel corridor. Dying inside . . ."

"Pascal, please." She made a quick impulsive move toward him. "I can't bear to see you like this. Please. If you would just listen to me—let me try to explain . . ."

She halted; the expression on his face halted her; she let her outstretched hand fall.

"Explain?" He moved farther away. "I should have known—in this situation—anything one says, it's going to sound like a cliché, as if we're both trapped in a bad play. And yet I feel—I love you so much, Gini. And I thought you loved me."

"I do love you—"

"Please—don't." He lifted his hand. "I don't think I can bear it if you tell me that kind of lie. You've been in bed with someone else— *How* could you do that? *Why* would you do that? What in God's name made you do that? I spoke to you Sunday night, at Max's—that's less than forty-eight hours ago. You said nothing then—you never gave me the least indication—"

"There was nothing to say then, Pascal. I wasn't lying to you then. I wasn't hiding anything."

"Your letters . . ." He couldn't hear her, she thought. Every interjection she made seemed to pass him by. He was reaching into his jacket pocket now, pulling out a bundle of letters. He tossed them away from him onto the bed.

"Everything you said—I know those letters by *heart*. You know how often I've read them, and reread them? You said—*always* was one of your words. I didn't ask you to use that. You were free, and you *chose*. Gini—how could you do that? Why? I trusted you so completely. I thought— You think I could have gone off, anytime these last two months, and gone to bed with some other woman? I couldn't have done that, I couldn't have *wanted* to do that. The only woman I wanted was the woman I loved."

Gini turned away from him with a low cry of despair. She looked unseeingly around this room, this very French room, with its blue toile-de-Jouy-covered walls; nymphs and shepherdesses disported themselves among romanticized ruins; small heraldic animals punctuated these pastoral scenes. The patterns blurred before her eyes and clamored in her mind. She couldn't look at Pascal; she was afraid to look at a face she loved so much.

"It wasn't planned," she burst out. "Pascal—it may make no difference, but I want you to believe me. There was no lead-up to this, no flirtation. I wasn't persuaded or seduced—it wasn't like that at all. I can't let you think that—it isn't fair to Rowland. He didn't foresee this any more than I did. I've only just met him, I scarcely know him. We're working together, I told you that—and when I arrived last night—we were quarreling, and then—I can't remember. I think he touched my arm. Or took my hand. And then—it just happened. I weakened. It was my fault. I don't know why I did it. I've—missed you, and I've been unhappy, and lonely too. None of that is any excuse, I know that—"

She stopped. The expression on Pascal's face had finally registered through her tears.

"You only just met him? When exactly did you meet him?"

"Pascal—does it matter? Please . . ."

"No. You answer me. When?"

"Last Friday."

"Last Friday?" She saw his face blank with shock. "You mean you've known him less than three days?"

"Yes."

"I see." All the color ebbed from his face. "That's how long it took him? Dear God. I can't believe this. I can't believe it of *you*."

"Pascal—please . . ." He had begun to pace the room again. "I can't let you think of it like that. It's wrong. He didn't maneuver me toward this—not once, not at all. We were simply working together. And then it happened. . . ."

"No. You *let* it happen." He swung back to her again, his face now tight with anger. "Let's just be clear on that one point. You know as well as I do—in that situation, if it arises, there is always a moment when you choose, when you still have time to turn away. Before the kiss, before the certain sentence, before a certain glance is exchanged—you *choose*. So just spare me all the nice liberal lies, Gini, at least. Don't tell me you can love one man and screw around at the same time with another. Spare me that. We both know it's not true."

"I *don't* know that!" Her voice rose. "Pascal, it's not always that simple. You can't be so absolute."

"Oh, but I can." He met her eyes. "I am absolute. And so were you. Once."

Gini believed what he said; this, too, had been her credo. She bent her head. She was terrified he would question her further so that she would have to admit the extent of her own disloyalty. She expected questions: how, when, where, why, how often: such crudities would, she knew, have leapt to her own lips had their situations been reversed. However much they intensified the pain, they were preferable to doubts.

So she waited for the questions, and when they did not come, began to understand that they had already been answered for Pascal by her gestures, expressions, and tone of voice. Or perhaps it was simply that Pascal was proud, refusing to ask questions that disgusted him.

To her surprise, he began trying to describe to her the circumstances of his journey here. At first she thought that this was because he could not bear to speak of anything more immediate. Then she realized: this description was a form of search—it was as if he were searching for her here, in the circumstances he described. That she understood: for it was against the yardstick of the events witnessed in Bosnia that they had both once measured love. He was asking her, obliquely, if she remembered that.

He had left Mostar in a U.N. convoy, he said, hitching a lift in the back of an army truck that was evacuating women and children and the seriously injured. The trip, over rough roads, had taken several hours. On those transports, generally, the children were beyond tears; sometimes their mothers, parted from husbands and families, not knowing if they would see them again, were similarly deadened; sometimes not. He had left Sarajevo, finally, at dawn the previous day, in the belly of a transport plane. That had taken him to a remote military air base in Germany. From there a series of connecting flights had been contrived; he had reached Amsterdam finally, a few hours after she left that city, around eleven the previous night.

He had had, he said, a *film* in his head: this film had sustained him throughout his trip. He would reach her room, walk into it: these were the words they might say to each other; these were the things they might then have done. This film, revised, had still been in his mind a few hours before, when, at six forty-five, he dialed her room at the St. Vincent for the fourth time in four hours—and Rowland McGuire picked up. Reaching this point in his account, he could not continue. She saw his face change, take on an expression she had often seen before, and which, in Bosnia, she had come to think of as his pre-firing-line look.

Pascal's rivals, his ex-wife, and, indeed, even her father, had often accused him of having some adrenaline sickness, a death wish. Gini knew that to be untrue: Pascal always weighed very precisely the risks he took. It was true that he was less protective of his own safety than were most people, but he was not foolhardy. Before he made the decision to move forward into some danger, some firing line, there was that one brief, taut moment of assessment. This expression she saw on his face now, as he turned back to look at her for the first time since he began to speak. He was standing absolutely still, she saw, the light from the window slanting across the planes of his fierce, narrow, intelligent face. His gray eyes met hers steadily, and she knew he was weighing their past, what they had had—was perhaps weighing her against that morning's events. She felt a lurch of fear then, for Pascal hated compromise, and she knew he was more than capable of walking out of this room now, of ending it quietly but firmly, and then never relenting, never coming back.

She gave a low cry, half anguish and half protest; his face changed. He crossed to her, and, touching her for the first time, took her hand in his.

"Listen to me. Look at me." He turned her face to his. "Gini, we have to move beyond this. I can't—at the moment I can't see and I can't think. Something must have been so terribly wrong. Darling—you're so thin. Your hair. Your face—"

His voice became unsteady. He drew her toward him. "You've been hiding things from me—on the telephone, in your letters. I don't mean that man—nothing to do with him. Gini, why did you do that? What's *happened* to you since you left me? I thought we had no secrets from each other."

He paused, his expression bewildered, his eyes searching her face. When she did not immediately reply, he clasped both her hands tight and forced her again to look at him.

"Right. This is what we do. We leave now—yes? We leave Paris together, by the first available flight. And then we go back to London, to our apartment, or some other quiet place, where we can be alone together and we can talk. We can retrieve this, but we have to do it at once. Now. Darling, look at me. Say you'll do that."

Gini hesitated; there was a silence, and that silence, he read. He released her hands and stepped back from her at once.

"You won't do that?"

"Pascal—in a day or two, yes. I want that too—I want it more than anything else. But I can't leave now, not today, it would be wrong of me to do that. I *have* to see this story through. I told you—a young girl is missing. I—I have to find her. I have to find the man she's with. Two people have died as a result of him. I *cannot* walk away from this."

There was a silence, a silence that terrified Gini. She could feel an ocean of words welling up inside her, some huge, deafening weight of emotion that had been too long dammed up. She could feel Pascal's anger now; the tenderness and concern of a moment before had been wiped from his face.

"I see." He gave her one long, cold, appraising look. "You cannot walk away from this story—or you cannot walk away from that man? Which is it, Gini? I'd like to be clear—very clear—about this."

"It's the story," she replied quickly. "Nothing to do with Rowland McGuire. In fact, if I asked him, I'm sure *he* would leave, return to London—"

"You think so? I wouldn't agree. I would say he'd be very reluctant to leave you. I very much doubt he'd return to London so obligingly. Judging from the way he looked and behaved this morning. Judging from the expression on his face."

"Pascal—please. I'm sure you're wrong. He'll be regretting what's happened. He'll want to extricate himself."

"Do you think I'm a complete fool?" He gave her a furious glance. "You think I don't *know* what a man looks like in that situation? Don't lie to me. You'd been making love all night—I knew that the instant he opened the door. I knew when he lied so gallantly on your behalf—and when you damn well let him do it. Christ . . ." Gini flinched at his violent gesture. "He is *not* going to walk away from this. He has no wish to extricate himself—quite the opposite. He made that crystal clear as I left that damn room."

"Pascal, he did *not*. He said one word to you then . . ."

"One word was enough. What he said was irrelevant. I could see it in his face. If he'd hit me, he couldn't have made it any clearer. And you damn well knew that. You know it now. You can't meet my eyes. You're either lying to me or lying to yourself. It wasn't just some quick, meaningless fuck you both instantly regretted—was it? *Was* it?"

"I won't answer that."

"You already have." He fought to regain control, turned away, then swung back. "So don't try to foist the decision on him. It has to be your decision. Your choice." He paused. "And think hard before you make it, because you won't be revising it—tomorrow, or next week." He gave her a look that cut her to the heart, in which anger mixed with the deepest regret. "We've been here before," he went on in a tight voice. "Choose, Gini. Call it choosing between me and this story of yours if you like. There's a plane in an hour, and I shall be on it. With you or without you. Goddammit!" His control finally snapped. He slammed his fist against the wall. "You think I'm going to plead with you now? You think I'm going to try to remind you of what we were, what we meant? I will not do that. I *will* not do that. If you love me, you'll come with me. If you don't, then this whole last year, most of my past, was a mistake. So choose, Gini, choose now. I won't wait."

"How can you say that? How can you do this? Did I ever give you that choice?" She swung around to him, her voice rising in sudden accusation. "You've been away nine *weeks*, Pascal. You said it would be three, at the most four. It's *nine*. Did *I* do this to you? Did I say, if you love me, Pascal, you'll get the next flight out of Sarajevo and come back? Did I *ever* say that?"

"You're suggesting the situation is the same? Dear God, what's the matter with you? Was I involved with a woman out there? No, I was not. I was faithful to you—I couldn't have been anything else—and you damn well knew that. I left you in no doubt as to my feelings, not when I spoke to you, not when I wrote. I'm not asking you to choose between me and your work now. I'm asking you to choose which matters more to you—me, or the man who persuaded you into bed last night."

"He did not do that—I told you. And he has nothing to do with this. I'm asking for a few days, that's all—Pascal, I can't explain. In Amsterdam— I *swore* to myself I'd do this."

"You've sworn a lot of things." He gestured at the letters he had tossed aside on the bed. "You want to remind yourself of some of the things you swore to me? You've obviously forgotten them. They can't have been too deeply meant."

"That isn't true! Pascal—can't you understand? I'm not trying to excuse what I did. But you must see—while you were away my life didn't just *stop*. I was alone, week after week. I was *changed* by what I saw in Bosnia—and I couldn't tell you about that. I couldn't tell you how ill and desperate and mad I felt. I wanted you to be free, so you could work— and so I couldn't even tell you how much I longed to have you back. Do you know how hard it was *not* saying that? Week after week. I was so sure you'd come back for Christmas. I was certain—I can make up films too, Pascal, did you ever think of that? I can imagine. I had this Christmas film in my head. I saw—oh, stupid things, perhaps, our first Christmas together. In our apartment. A tree. I bought a tree. And stars. I bought you presents and wrapped them up. And then you *didn't* come."

"Gini?" He moved toward her. "Darling—what are you saying? You told me none of this. At Christmas you said it didn't matter. You said we'd have Christmas when I came back. You said—"

"I *know* what I said." She could no longer control the tears that had begun to spill down her face. "But it wasn't what I thought. What I felt. I hoped—I was so sure that you must understand. I thought—even Pascal can't stay out there forever. He must miss me. He must *want* to come back. And then—it was when I saw Helen. I had lunch with Helen, and she said—"

He had begun to move closer, was reaching for her; at the mention of his ex-wife's name, he stopped dead.

"What? You saw Helen? When? You never told me that."

"Before Christmas. I could see she thought I was stupid. She knew you better than I did. She knew you wouldn't come back for Christmas, or the New Year. She told me how it was when she was married to you. How she could never reach you. How she had to cope with Marianne all on her own—and I thought, yes, she's right, Pascal *is* dedicated, that's what he's like, and it's why I love him. Except—"

She stopped. Pascal's eyes had darkened with anger. He caught hold of her arm.

"You finish this," he said. "Go on. Except what?"

"Except it was *destroying* me, Pascal. Never knowing where you were, if you were safe. Not being able to tell you what I felt. It was tearing me apart *now*—and when she said that, when she said how it was, I thought—that's how it would be if *I* had Pascal's child. I'd be a second Helen. The baby would be a second Marianne. And you'd *still* be an absentee father, just the way she said."

"Dear God, never say that to me." He caught both arms in a painful grip and shook her hard. "Look at you . . ." He wrenched her face toward him. "I can see the marks of that man's hands on your throat. I can *smell* him on you, and you talk to me about my wife and my child? You know what that marriage was like—you know what kind of hell it was. If it hadn't been for my daughter . . ."

"Oh, I know you love Marianne. . . ." Gini fought to break his grip. "Why are you here in Paris now, Pascal? Don't lie to me. Don't tell me that you suddenly decided you had to see me. I *know* what finally brought you back—and it wasn't me at all. You're here because it's Marianne's birthday next week."

He hit her then, so hard she fell to the floor. The blow knocked her against the base of the bed, and she crouched there, shielding her face. He had never hit her before, and the blow was so unexpected and so painful that her vision went black. Pascal caught hold of her and pulled her back to her feet.

"How can you say that? How?" He was shaking with rage. "Don't you believe anything I've ever told you? That's all it takes, is it, to undo all your trust in me—one conversation with my ex-wife? That's your justification, is it, for getting into bed with a man you've known three days, and fucking him all night? Christ . . ."

He thrust her away from him. "Don't answer that. You don't need to. Don't speak to me about Marianne. I love my daughter. And just now I don't want to hear her name on your lips."

"What's that supposed to mean?"

"You know. We both know." He stopped, then drew in a breath to steady himself. "I'm sorry I hit you. I don't want it to end this way. However, it has. I'd better go. If I stay—I could hit you again. I—" He looked around the room blindly. "There was a moment—in Bosnia— when I thought . . . Never mind that. Just don't talk about Marianne in that way. You have no children. You can't understand. All that joy and guilt and remorse. Trying so hard, feeling you've never done enough. I did have to work, you know." He gave her a pained glance. "No doubt Helen left out that part of the equation. But I did have to support a child and wife. I take photographs. Of wars. You can't do that nine to five and come home for dinner every night. She did know that when she married me. When Marianne was born, we did make plans. Where I should go, when I would return. How I could ration out my life. Meet my responsibilities as a father. According to Helen, the result was fail- ure, and the failure was entirely mine, of course. I might have hoped—" He hesitated. "I might have hoped that you would see it differently. It doesn't matter. You listened to my ex-wife and you judged me. Now I understand what happened last night. I'll go. There's no point in pro- tracting this. It's painful for both of us."

"I wanted your baby." Gini gave a cry; she made a small rushing movement toward him, then stopped. "Oh, Pascal—couldn't you see? Couldn't you guess? It began in Bosnia, in Mostar maybe. Because I loved you so much, and we saw so much death." Her voice wavered and her face contracted. "I knew it was impractical. I could see you didn't want it. But it just took hold of me, and I couldn't get free. I wanted your baby so much, I couldn't think of anything else."

There was a silence. He had listened to this stumbling confession in- tently, with a pale, set face. As she came to its end, he gave a small ges- ture of the hands, an eloquent gesture, as if he were about to relinquish something he valued very much.

"I see." His face became closed. "That was what you felt. Why couldn't you bring yourself to tell me?"

"Why? Because I was too proud. Because I didn't want to have to per- suade you. Because that kind of decision has to be made by two people, not one—and it ought to be made *joyfully*. All that—"

Her voice broke. She began to speak again, and then gradually she real- ized that although she was pouring out to him her strongest feelings, emo- tions that had been dammed up for months, and although her confession seemed to move him, there was no relenting on his part, and no response.

She came to a faltering halt. He continued to look at her for a mo- ment afterward, then gave a sigh.

"I wonder if you really mean that." He glanced away, then back.

"Perhaps you do. I can't tell anymore. I wish you'd told me at the time. My reaction might have been different from the one you expected—who knows? As it is, perhaps it's just as well. Presumably you changed your mind, did you, when you had that conversation with Helen, and you suddenly realized what a very unsuitable father I'd make?" The words were coolly said; the blood rushed into Gini's face.

"No—I did not," she said. "That wasn't what I thought, not exactly. I told you. I wasn't well. I couldn't think clearly. I was afraid, terribly afraid. You have a child already. You might not have wanted a child with me."

"I would certainly have resisted making a decision in Bosnia." His voice remained cool. "A decision like that—it determines the next eighteen, twenty years of your life. It wouldn't have been wise to rush into it then, in a war zone, when we were both under stress. You always told me how important your work was to you—in fact, you've been reminding me of that just now. So I would have suggested we wait until we had returned to London, had time to think—" He bent and picked up his camera case. "As it is, of course, it's irrelevant now. Out of the question. You have all these requirements for the father of your children, and I don't measure up to them. You've made that clear."

"Pascal—please. I know what you're going to say next. Don't. I know you so well—if you say it, there'll be no going back."

"I know it's hurtful. It still has to be said." He gave her a long, steady, and regretful look, then moved toward the door. "I *have* a child, Gini. I know what that involves. If you have requirements for any future father of your children, doesn't it occur to you that *I* have requirements also? I know what I would want in any future wife, in the mother of any children I might have. This time—" He hesitated. "This time I'd want to be sure that there was love on both sides. The kind of love that didn't waver, that would endure. Responsibility, fidelity—all those things." His voice became bitter. "Above all, like most men, I would want to be totally sure that any child my wife gave birth to was actually mine." He paused. "You can be very self-absorbed, Gini. Even so, I imagine you can understand that."

The final reproach was gently made; Gini had never felt such shame. With a low cry she held out her hand to him.

"Pascal, wait. Whatever I did—I do love you. I still love you. I can't bear to hear you say these terrible things. I wish none of this had happened. I'd give anything to put the clock back. But you *could* trust me. I'd never—you could come to trust me again. Please—we could move beyond this eventually, you said we could."

"That was an hour ago. How strange." He looked at her blindly, then glanced down at his watch. "Yes, an hour. It feels like a lifetime. In that hour you've told me how passionately you wanted my child, and I'll never forget your face when you said that." He paused. "But it didn't prevent your going to bed with a virtual stranger, did it? You still let him cover up for you, and lie to my face—" His voice broke. "Is that love, Gini? It isn't any love I recognize. I would have died rather than do that to you. I—look, it's better if I just go. I can't bear any more of this. You've changed, Gini." He lifted her face up to his. "You used to be so— open. So direct. And now—you equivocate. You shift ground. You claim one truth, then deny it with your next breath. What did that to you? The war? My absence? A man you scarcely know? Tell me the truth."

Gini looked for a long time at his face.

"All three," she answered at last in a low voice.

She could see that the admission hurt him as much as it hurt her to make. His face contracted; then he turned away.

"That's honest, at least. Thank you for that." He moved to the door again, half opened it, then looked back.

"I could have kissed you then. I wanted to very much. Did you know that?"

"Yes. I did."

"Better not to weaken in that particular way." He shrugged. "If one's going to do this, better to do it cleanly, don't you think? I have to catch that plane. I'll have moved my things out of the apartment by the time you get back. Gini, good-bye."

And with that, just as she had expected, he left. The door closed quietly behind him. She heard his feet descend the staircase. Running first to the door, and then to the window, she saw him emerge from the entrance below. He crossed the narrow street, crossed the small park beyond at a fast pace. She watched his tall, determined figure as he receded into the distance. On the quay beyond the park he hailed a taxi and climbed into it. Indeed absolute; he never once looked back.

With tears blurring her vision, Gini ran to the bed. She picked up the letters she had written to him and pressed them tight against her chest. She felt cut to the heart by his words; it pained her deeply that he should have left these letters, these talismans. She stared at the walls of the room, with their remorseless patternings of ruins, of shepherds and nymphs. Shame and self-reproach and uncertainty washed through her mind. She thought: I could go after him—and then she felt it, welling inside her, a resistance, even a rebellion, that lay deep inside herself.

She was almost thirty years old. Her years of fertility were shortening month by month. That desire for a child—had Pascal understood, truly understood, when she spoke to him of that? He might; he might not. Oh, *decide,* she said to herself, beginning to pace the room, trying to force herself to think. And then it occurred to her as it had—if she were truthful—once during the previous night, that she might have conceived now, that even now, within her, infinitely small, were the beginnings of new life.

That possibility terrified her. Standing suddenly still, she realized that whatever decisions her mind came to, her body might already have made for her an irrevocable choice. Her fear deepened, and then, stealing along her veins, came a furtive exultation, an ill-advised joy; she tried to examine the idea of maternity—and maternity under these circumstances—she tried to see its implications, but they were too huge and her mind could not grapple with them. She watched herself take refuge in a certain fatalism, that woman's defense.

Wait, she said to herself, wait—because no decision could be made until she was certain, and meanwhile neither Pascal nor Rowland need be involved; she felt, obscurely, that she had forfeited that right.

With that realization, that here essentially she was alone, some equilibrium returned. Clutching Pascal's letters, she moved to the window and looked out at the Seine, at that slanting view of Notre Dame; from this partial viewpoint it resembled the bow of a great ship.

She thought of Anneke's mother, and a promise made to herself. She ran out of the room, down the stairs, and into the street. *Work*, she thought, hastening back to the St. Vincent.

Room 810 was empty. Rowland McGuire, adhering to his schedule, had already left.

CHAPTER 16

M*orte d'une Légende* read the headline on the newspaper delivered
to Lindsay's room that morning. Beneath it was the famous Beaton photograph of a laughing, short-haired young woman, her hands half obscuring her face. Lindsay began to translate the long article.

Her French was serviceable, but not extensive: she could not cope
with the lyricism, the orotundity here. She could gather that the facts repeated the authorized version of Cazarès's life. Beyond that, she could
see that Maria Cazarès was already being turned into a symbol, before
she was twenty-four hours dead.

But a symbol of what? She struggled with the vocabulary, the syntax.
Several things, it seemed: of modern womanhood, of modern women,
whom she had freed, the writer claimed, redefining their images of themselves. Of France, in that she embodied the French virtues of elegance,
discernment, and chic. By the final paragraph, the claims seemed to have
swelled, as if the male writer were drunk on his own prose. *L'éternelle
feminine,* Lindsay read, trying to construe a clutch of dense phrases. She
had the gist, she thought. Maria Cazarès, *une femme solitaire, unique, et
mysterieuse* . . . yes, yes, she understood that . . . was the something
something and the very embodiment of the eternal feminine—whatever
that was, Lindsay thought with sudden impatience. Giving up, she
tossed the paper aside.

How typical, how predictable, she thought, that having decided

Cazarès was an enigma, a female enigma, they should give the task of decoding her to a man. Lindsay, who had slept badly and still felt restless, moved to the window and looked out. It was still early; she could see the day would not be clear. The sky was low, the clouds scudding fast. Wind whipped the branches of the trees and rippled the Seine. The air was watery, gray, promising rain and then more rain: a day of half-light and mist.

This hotel room was beginning to feel confining. She made some time pass, first by telephoning home and speaking to Tom, and then by sending a second fax to her contact at the Metropolitan Museum in New York, who had not yet replied to her query of the previous day. Then, having hesitated some time, and finally having decided to risk it, she called Rowland's room, since it was now nine in the morning and need not, therefore, be too embarrassing if it was Gini who picked up the phone.

She let the number ring, but there was no answer. Then, still feeling on edge, she went down to the room the *Correspondent* was using as their headquarters. Pixie, dressed in a garment that appeared to be made of knitted string, was already there. Lindsay picked up her pass for the Cazarès press conference that morning, checked on a few other details, was about to leave, then paused.

"You made sure there were passes for Rowland and Gini?"

Pixie gave a small smile.

"Oh, sure. I had them sent up to their room last night." Then, after a delicate pause: "Clever of McGuire to get that room. I wept, pleaded, offered to sell the management my body—and I had no luck at all."

"So? Rowland has more heft than you do," Lindsay said.

Pixie's smile broadened. Lindsay knew what that smile meant: it meant gossip, speculation, the spirals of office intrigue.

"Well," Pixie said, "he's that kind of man. Not easy to refuse."

"What's that supposed to imply?"

"—Though I thought it was pretty odd. Him sharing that room with her. I mean, he'd fired her only a few hours before."

"What? Rowland fired Gini?" Lindsay shook her head. "No, Pixie. I saw them both last night. You're wrong."

"Oh, *everyone* saw them last night," Pixie said in a negligent tone. "After all, this place is stuffed to the gills with reporters, what can you expect? They were seen going out late last night. They were seen when they returned. One look at her face, apparently—there was what you might call ribaldry in the bar."

"What absolute rubbish," Lindsay said sharply. "I was with them both later. They were working, that's all."

"They were? For how long?"

"Look, Pixie, I was up in the room with them a good two hours, maybe more. We were all three of us working. And you might think about doing some work right now."

She moved to the door, hoping this lie would quell the gossip, then hesitated. "What made you think Rowland fired Gini?"

"I don't think. I know. Tony called me from London late last night. McGuire was on the telephone, in his office, with the door closed, but Tony overheard. He said you couldn't *help* overhearing, McGuire was so mad, you could have heard him in Piccadilly Circus."

Lindsay sighed: Tony was Pixie's latest boyfriend, and devoted. He worked in a very junior capacity in the features department, in an office across the corridor from Rowland McGuire's.

"Well, I'm sorry, Pixie," she said, "but for once Tony has it wrong. I told you—I was *with* them. Gini certainly has not been fired."

"Oh, she got reinstated." Pixie gave her a sidelong glance. "I mean, that was obvious to everyone in the lobby last night. But he did fire her. And he didn't mince his words. She'd screwed up in Amsterdam, Tony says, and McGuire was going wild. Then he started in on Pascal Lamartine. Tony said he'd have died if he'd been on the receiving end. Tony said that was the *worst* he'd ever heard him. Then he slammed down the phone, he'd fired her by then, several times, and then he came storming out of his office with his green eyes flashing fire. Then he left, and before he left he went suddenly quiet and—" Pixie gave a sigh. "I just wish I'd *been* there, that's all. I told you he was gorgeous. Can you imagine how *totally* gorgeous he'd be in a rage? I love tempestuous men. . . ."

"Pixie, for God's sake!"

"Well, I do. Show me the woman who doesn't. I'm just honest, that's all. Just the *thought* of McGuire in a rage makes my nipples go hard."

"That's enough, Pixie."

"It's his eyes, mainly . . ." Pixie, always irrepressible, gave a small shiver of delight. "And that black hair. And the voice. And the muscles. And the fact that he's so tall. Also I hear he's incredible in bed. I mean like *seriously* incredible, so you can hardly *walk* the next day. Walk? I can tell you, I wouldn't be walking anywhere, I'd just be lying there, waiting for more. . . ."

"Pixie, stop this right now. I'm not interested in these fantasies."

"They're not fantasies. All this is well documented. There's this girl I know . . ."

"Pixie!"

"She scores them, all right? And her top mark is twenty-five. She gives them marks for invention, stamina, intuition, size, tendresse, output, concern—"

"Intuition? Who is this girl?"

"And you know what McGuire scored? One hundred. He went right off the charts. She was *floored*. Also, and this is *corroborated*, because she checked, and it wasn't just her—also, he has these rules . . ."

"Rules?" Lindsay said faintly.

"Yes." Pixie lowered her voice to a more confidential tone. "Like— *before*, right—he always makes the situation crystal clear. It's sex, maybe friendship—and that's all. The relationship isn't going to have any future, there's going to be no commitments on either side. Those are his terms. And he sticks to them too. I mean, not even any endearments, no 'darlings,' no personal revelations of any kind. This girl said she didn't know one thing more about him when he ended it than she did the day it began. It drove her totally wild."

Pixie gave Lindsay a long, significant look. Lindsay had a brief battle with her own most vulgar instincts; the instincts won.

"How long did she—"

"Two months. I gather the all-time record is two and a half. This was some years back, just after he returned from Washington. She said he went through women like a *machine*. She said that when it began, when he spelled out his statute of limitations, as it were—well, it was fatal. She fell in love with him before he'd finished the first sentence. And then, the next morning, when she got out of bed and, like I say, she could hardly *stand*, she made herself this promise. She was determined, but determined, to be the one who changed his mind."

"Well, she clearly didn't succeed—" Lindsay said.

"She tried really hard," Pixie continued, launched now, and speaking fast. "She thought that if she managed to hide the fact that she was totally crazy about him, she had a chance. I mean, she's having the most incredible sex of her life, she figures there *must* be progress of some kind. Only there wasn't." Pixie sighed. "And the instant he realized how she felt—well, one night she was so overcome she just told him—that was it. Curtains. Kind but immovable. The end."

Lindsay had begun to move toward the door.

"She tried everything," Pixie went on, and Lindsay stopped. "She was getting so desperate, she was so madly in love, she hit on this really crazy plan. She'd get pregnant. She was sure, if she could just do that, she'd change his mind. So she stopped taking the pill and she never said a word.

Only, of course, that didn't work either. Condoms." Pixie gave Lindsay a significant look. "Always. Because he's careful as well as wild. And no way could she get around that—believe me, she's inventive, and she tried."

Lindsay had blushed crimson. She turned back from the door. "Pixie, stop this at once. We shouldn't be having this conversation."

"Why not?"

"Because we just shouldn't. I don't expect you to understand. Let's put it down to the generation gap. This is someone's private life, someone we both know and like."

"I thought you *didn't* like McGuire? You said he was arrogant."

"Never mind. Like him or dislike him, it makes no difference. That kind of gossip always ends up causing trouble, and pain. I don't want to hear any more. I don't want you passing this kind of rumor around. If there are rumors, those rumors are untrue. . . ."

"If you say so." Pixie shrugged.

"I mean it, Pixie. Just keep your speculations to yourself, and don't damned well encourage them in other people. I assume you have work to get on with—because if you haven't, there's something badly wrong."

Pixie gave her a look of astonishment.

"Everything's under control, Lindsay."

"Just make sure I get the transparencies from the Chanel and Gaultier shows by nine tonight. Make sure Markov's there, at his hotel, before you bike his invitations around to him, and remember, Pixie, any hitches, one fuckup, and you're unemployed."

Pixie had colored. "I'm good at my job," she protested. "This is going to run like clockwork."

"It had better," Lindsay said, walking out, and just managing to prevent herself from slamming the door. She knew Pixie would probably be making some face at it once it was closed—and she was, of course, fully justified. Lindsay's cheeks were still bright scarlet. She quickly left the hotel, went out into mists and soft rain, and took in deep breaths of damp air.

She was furious with herself. How could she reprimand Pixie for gossiping, when she had just been listening avidly to gossip herself? How could she then compound her own felony by picking on Pixie's work, when that work was always excellent? She had just set Pixie an appalling example, and if she had succeeded in stemming the tide of gossip about Rowland and Gini, she would not have done so for long. She glanced back at the hotel. The lobby had been seething with journalists, with TV crews. In that kind of hothouse atmosphere, gossip bred faster than germs.

She felt dirtied by her own curiosity, sickened by the kind of details people bandied around. Beyond and behind such feelings were others.

Deeply troubled, Lindsay crossed the quay and leaned over the balustrade, looking down at the Seine. Prior to the conversation with Pixie, she had been trying to convince herself that her own instincts the previous night had been wrong. Now she felt doubly unsure. One aspect of Pixie's report worried her, and that was the description of Rowland's firing Gini, and the manner in which that action was performed.

Lindsay knew just how vulnerable Gini was to criticism from those she liked or admired. It was a legacy, of course, from her father, from all those years when she had tried to prove her worth, and win his affection, and failed.

Lindsay had never dared to say this to Gini, but she had always believed that this inheritance had been a strong contributing factor in her attraction to Pascal Lamartine. Lindsay might not have heard all the details of Gini's original involvement with Pascal, for Gini was reticent, but she had heard the story of how Gini had first met him, in that press bar in Beirut, and it seemed to her there was an obvious aspect to that story to which Gini, and presumably Pascal, were totally blind.

What had ignited their affair? It was Pascal's hostility to Gini's father that had ignited it, and Gini's intuition, subsequently confirmed, that Pascal Lamartine was contemptuous of Gini's father, at whose shrine Gini had painfully worshiped for so long. At the very moment when Gini's own doubts about her father were beginning, along came a handsome, impassioned, and very romantic man who loathed and despised Sam Hunter on sight—and said so to Gini in no uncertain terms.

As one figure of authority began to crumble before her eyes, Gini replaced him with another—what if, now, Gini was about to, or was in the process of, replacing that second mentor with a third?

Lindsay began to pace back and forth, feeling more agitated now. In order to love, she thought, Gini—like many women—had not only to admire, but also to feel she could learn. She had to look up to the man she loved, admiring his gifts, his character, his intelligence, his moral worth—and believing always that he was better endowed in these respects than she was herself.

Such a female weakness, Lindsay thought, aware that it was also her own. Gini might preach equality, and imagine she practiced it, but Lindsay believed that too much equality in love would be something Gini would loathe. Nothing appealed to Gini so much as a teacher, and nothing was so likely to attract her to a man as some reprimand from him she knew was deserved.

Would a bitter dressing-down from Rowland McGuire have a deep effect on Gini? Lindsay frowned down at the gray water, knowing that—if she herself were truthful—it would certainly have influenced her. Then she realized: in Gini's case, that particular question had already been answered, and in front of her eyes.

It was Rowland McGuire's sharp and angry condemnation at Max's house, that moment when he accused Gini of behaving selfishly, that had snapped Gini out of months of illness, misery, and self-reproach. With a few sentences Rowland McGuire had been able to effect a change that in months of sympathy and argument, Lindsay had failed to achieve. Lindsay thought she could see a pattern now. She could see how, if her relationship with Pascal had been impaired, or if Pascal had, in Bosnia, failed Gini in some way, Gini might possibly end up in Rowland McGuire's arms.

And as for Rowland's motivation—well, that was obvious enough, Lindsay thought, turning angrily away. Gini was beautiful; for men, as Lindsay had watched over the years, she carried a powerful sexual allure. She could see Rowland McGuire's responding to that, McGuire, who went through women "like a machine." To him it was a matter of two months, three months, a scrupulous exercise in which his heart was not involved.

Lindsay felt indignant, then angry. In such a situation, her sympathies were always with the woman, and Gini was her closest woman friend. This anger at McGuire took root and grew as she made her way to the Cazarès headquarters for Lazare's press conference.

By the time she reached there, Lindsay had argued herself into a position where, she told herself, she felt no attraction for McGuire anymore, not even liking. Pixie's words ringing in her ears, she told herself that Rowland McGuire was an irresponsible, cold manipulator of women, a Casanova, a Valmont, the kind of man she most despised. Then, through the press of people, she saw him. One look at his face and she at once changed her mind.

It was a while before she saw him. When she reached the Cazarès building it was still half an hour before the start of the press conference, but the rabble had already arrived. The street outside and the courtyard within were crammed with vans, with the white sprouting mushrooms of satellite dishes, with the cables and impedimenta of TV crews. CNN was there, and the other major American network crews; she could see familiar faces from the BBC and ITN. The French, the Italians, the Germans, the Spanish, the Japanese—they were all out in force. Lindsay pushed through a wall of people, a babel of tongues. Inside the front lobby the crush was even worse: like the melees that attended the collections, but worse. Lindsay could feel that peculiar intensity of hysteria generated by a crowd, but here, in addition to the mad desire simply to get in, there were other, stronger emotions. There was a vicarious thrill to the drama of sudden death.

Lindsay was pushed, shoved, trodden on, nearly thrown to the floor as she approached the doors to the hall where the conference would be held. Black-suited Cazarès courtiers were trying to control the crowd, but there were too few of them; they could not hold back this surge. Jostled, Lindsay let the crowd pick her up and propel her forward. She could now see into the hall beyond, which was blindingly bright from TV lights; she could glimpse, at its far end, a black dais, a table, a lectern, microphones, cameras, and—surmounting it all—a huge blow-up of that Beaton photograph of Maria Cazarès. Lindsay was caught up, thrust into the room, carried forward by a wave of people—and then she saw Rowland McGuire.

He was standing just a few feet from her, on the eddying edge of the crowd. He was using the advantage of his height to scan over the heads of those entering to watch who came through the door. He was wearing, Lindsay saw, a black overcoat, a black suit, and a black tie, a formality of dress that made him stand out from the crowd. His face was pale and set; he never once moved his eyes from the doorway, and Lindsay knew, without a second's doubt, for whom he was searching that crowd.

He must have seen Lindsay enter, though he gave no indication of doing so, because he made one quick move, still keeping his eyes on the door. A heavy American who had pushed past Lindsay earlier now found himself thrust aside so hard, he nearly fell; Lindsay found that her arm had been gripped, and she had been drawn through the press of people to his side.

"You see that usher there?" He gestured to one of the Cazarès assistants. "He has three seats for us, center aisle, fourth row. Claim yours now. I'll join you in a minute."

"Three seats—and they're keeping them? Rowland, how on earth—?"

"Ways and means." He gave a tight smile. "Just go."

Lindsay did so. The assistant in question could not have shown more solicitude had she been the editor of American *Vogue*. Lindsay looked around her, mystified, then saw that the editors of American *Vogue* and *Harper's Bazaar* and French *Vogue* and *Paris Match* and *Hello!* were in the same row. She was greeted with raised eyebrows and little quick air kisses. Five minutes later Rowland joined her. As he sat down, he said: "Have you seen Gini this morning? Did she come back to the hotel?"

"No. I didn't know she'd gone out."

"She had some research to do." He turned, craning his neck, and looked back at the doors. "Maybe she was held up. . . ."

Lindsay said nothing. He radiated tension. She looked at his pale, averted face; she looked down at his strong, capable hands, which were half clenched, and she could sense deep perturbation. Something had obviously happened, something well beyond the scenario she had been painting. She felt ashamed at her own triviality; the last residual influences of Pixie's stories fell away.

If Gini was coming, she was too late now. They were closing the doors at the back of the room. At the front, in the pit below the dais, the phalanx of photographers and TV crews stirred.

Lindsay said gently, "Do you always wear black, Rowland, on occasions like this?"

"What?" He glanced toward her, then away.

"Most people don't bother. Not anymore. Not even for funerals, these days."

"I don't really know. I wasn't thinking about it particularly." He turned back to look at the rear doors again. "Habit, maybe. Upbringing. When I was a small child—in Ireland—people dress for death. It's a mark of respect—why?"

"No reason." Lindsay was touched. "I like it. It's old-fashioned. But it feels right—that's all."

He was not even listening. He rose and removed his overcoat, which he tossed down on the floor. As he rose, Lindsay saw women's heads turn. She glanced up: Rowland's dark, untamable hair fell across his forehead; the black suit, the white shirt, emphasized his height and his looks. Just along the row from her she heard a sharp American whisper: *Darling, who's that perfectly divine man?* Rowland had evidently sensed none of this. "Damn," he said, sitting down again as a group of somber-suited, impeccable Cazarès executives came onto the dais in front of them. "Damn. It's too late now. And I need to talk to her. . . ."

"You have a lead?" Lindsay said in a noncommittal tone: it might be a lead, she supposed, but that was not the first thing that sprang to mind.

"What? Yes. I do. And it'll have to wait now."

He turned back to look at the dais. Lindsay tensed. Jean Lazare had just entered, and as he did so, walking at a quick pace to the lectern, silence fell in the room.

The tribute he gave was brief, and he made it four times: first in French, then in English, then in Spanish, and finally in German. While he spoke the room was hushed, the only sound the soft whirr of cameras. When he ended, and only when he ended, came the flashing of scores of camera bulbs.

Lindsay could follow some but not all of the French; Rowland's comprehension, she thought, was better than her own. He listened with total concentration; once or twice he frowned. As Lazare switched to English, he appeared to continue to listen, but Lindsay was unsure if he actually did so. She was straining hard to catch every phrase, so her attention was diverted, but she could sense that although Rowland kept his eyes on Lazare, he scarcely saw him. His true attention seemed elsewhere, perhaps back in the French version of Lazare's statement.

"Yesterday afternoon," Lazare began, "as you will know, Maria Cazarès suffered a heart attack. She was at the home of her former maid, to whom she was devoted. I take comfort from the fact that when this happened, so suddenly, she was not alone, but with a friend. I should like to take this opportunity now to thank the doctors of the St. Étienne hospital, who made every effort to revive her, and who gave her every possible care. Unfortunately, their efforts were not successful. Mademoiselle Cazarès died a short while after she arrived there. I was by her side."

He paused. "I wish to announce that as would have been the wish of Maria Cazarès herself, her couture collection will be shown tomorrow, exactly as planned. It will include three designs, her last designs, drawn by her the day before she died. Maria Cazarès was born an artist, and was an artist to the end.

"Tomorrow morning, at Cazarès, there will be a spirit of joy, not sadness." He paused again, on a note that was one of command. "We will be celebrating one of the most extraordinary women of our time, and certainly the most extraordinary, gifted, and visionary woman I have ever known. She was a couturière of wit, of originality, of passion. She was a woman who, as she once said, understood both the art and the science of clothes. . . ."

As he said this, Lindsay gave Rowland a sharp glance.

"I know," he said in a quiet voice. "Quiet. Listen to the next part."

Lazare looked around the hushed room, that sea of upturned faces, then continued, his voice with its strange harsh accent perfectly level, unemotional, and controlled.

"It is not for me to write her obituary. But I should like to say this: I knew Maria Cazarès and worked closely with her for many, many years. In that time I never knew her to be other than vigilant, devoted to her professional task. This involved, as is always the case for any woman, many sacrifices. Maria Cazarès did not marry; she did not have a child.

It has been suggested in the past, by those who did not know her, and were ill informed, that this choice was easily made. That was not so. Her dedication was not achieved without both sacrifice and struggle, and in this context, only a French term will serve: like all great artists, Maria Cazarès was, in respect of her art, a *religieuse*.

"She was also"—he made his first tiny hesitation—"a woman who brought joy to people's hearts. In her private life she showed candor, understanding, grace, courage, and generosity. She had, and always retained, a childlike directness and simplicity, and she remained to the end unseduced by fame.

"In her professional life"—his voice gained strength now—"she was that rarity, a woman designing for women, while almost all the other practitioners of her art were men. She redefined the ways in which modern women chose to present themselves to the world; in changing their image, she perhaps helped to alter their conception of themselves. I leave that question to be decided by others, but I will say this: it was an education for a man to work with her, and to know her gave me insights I value greatly, into a world in which the instincts of the body and the heart are as valid and as important as the deliberations of the mind—let us use shorthand: into the female world."

He looked down—although he was speaking without notes—then raised his head, standing formally, stiffly, almost as if to attention, Lindsay thought.

"I pay my last respects now, and I will use one last French phrase. For the world, Maria Cazarès was an artist: for me she was, and always will be—the *amie de mon coeur.*"

He stopped, his dark eyes resting on the body of the hall. Lindsay felt a tightening of pity and sympathy around her heart. What must it cost him, she thought, to speak in this way, to blend truth and what was surely falsehood so seamlessly? To speak in that level, deliberate, uninflected tone? Lazare, still betraying no emotion, gave the Spanish version of this tribute, and then the German, then turned, and immediately left the stage.

Rowland was on his feet before the executives on the dais had moved. He had Lindsay by the arm, and was leading her quickly down the aisle as the crowd began to move, as murmurs began and a tide of reaction began to swell. Lindsay was surprised by his haste, then understood it: Gini was standing just inside the doors at the very back of the hall.

Lindsay just caught a glimpse of her pale face; she saw Rowland give her a sharp and questioning glance, then he drew them both out into the lobby, into the courtyard, hastening them along and stopping only when they had rounded a corner. He came to a halt in a quiet, narrow side street with a row of apartment buildings opposite, and behind them a high wall.

"You heard?" Rowland said, and Lindsay realized that not only was the question addressed solely to Gini, but that as far as either of them was concerned, she herself was not there.

"Yes." Gini was backing against the wall; she began speaking fast. "They let me in just as he was reaching the end of the French version. Such control—such extraordinary control. How could he do that? How could he speak in that way? So formally—and he wasn't even using notes. I—" She broke off, and looked at Lindsay for the first time. "Rowland told me your New Orleans story. I was thinking about it all the way through. I could hear it, under his words, inside his words. . . ."

Lindsay found she could say nothing. She was riveted by Gini's face. She had recently been hit, and hit hard. Right down the left side of her face, and across the cheekbone, there was a darkening bruise.

She was trying to conceal this, Lindsay observed, by standing so that this side of her face was turned to the wall behind her. The tactic was not succeeding. Rowland was now also looking at the bruise. Lindsay watched his face change, watched him begin on some quick, involuntary movement. Gini, her eyes on his face, lifted her hand, then let it fall.

There was a silence, a silence that seemed to Lindsay to be filled with noise, with a tension that could not be dispersed. Gini began speaking again: she seemed to believe, Lindsay thought, pitying her, that if she just kept speaking, the nature of this moment could be concealed.

"The way he described her character," she began. "Then. He said something about candor . . ."

"Candor, understanding, grace, courage, and generosity." Rowland's eyes never left Gini's face. "Those were the words."

"Yes. And *religieuse*. Something about insights that she gave him . . . It was right at the end. And he evaded the issue of time, of how long he'd known her."

"Many, many years," Rowland said. "Time was immaterial. He made that clear with his final words. Her dying made no difference. She remained the—"

"Are they issuing the text?" Gini interrupted him very fast. "I wasn't taking notes. I meant to, but I wasn't . . ."

"They'll issue it. They're probably issuing it now. We don't need it. I can remember the salient parts."

Gini gave a low sigh; her hands clenched and unclenched.

Lindsay looked from one to the other and stepped back quietly. She knew that she had no place here.

She began to detach herself as quietly, quickly, and plausibly as she could. She said that she had to meet Markov, which was true; she said she had to see him before that afternoon's Chanel show. She could, she knew, have announced that she was to embark for Mars: neither Gini nor Rowland would have noticed. They were locked into a silent communication that was as voluble as a torrent of words.

She turned and began walking quickly away. At the corner she looked back once. Gini was now standing with her back against the wall, her head bent. Rowland was directly in front of her, his arms either side of her body, his palms pressed against the wall. He was speaking with force.

As Lindsay looked back, he stopped speaking, and Gini slowly raised her head to meet his eyes. Lindsay did not wish to be a spy, or to see any more. She turned the corner, fought her way through the crowd still spilling out from Cazarès, passed for a second time through that babel of tongues, and made her escape fast. She knew what her next task was: she had to eradicate this pain, an actual pain as discernible as a headache, that seemed to have lodged itself around her heart.

How long was it since Lindsay had left them, Gini thought, ten minutes, fifteen? It could have been longer. It could have been much less. Time was refusing to obey its ordinary rules. She turned back to look at Rowland, who was now standing beside her, his face averted, his back against the wall.

He was breathing fast, as if he had been running. She could sense his anger and his agitation in the air.

"I just want to *work*, Rowland," she said, turning to him and touching his hand. "Please. I may not be capable of anything else—but I am capable of that. I just want to fix my mind on this story. I want to pull the pieces together, and I want to find Mina, above all. You agreed, Rowland, you agreed that we could do that—"

"I know."

He hesitated, then turned to look at her. Her pale face was upturned to his; he could not bear to look at the bruise. Her lovely eyes were wide with an expression of entreaty. When she looked at him in this way, Rowland felt he could refuse her nothing; he wondered if she realized that. He felt he must be utterly transparent to her: she must know.

"Please, Rowland," she went on. "I can't talk to you about this. It wouldn't be right. You don't need to be involved. I have to deal with it, come to terms with it in my time and my way. I don't think I even *could* talk about it. Too much has happened too fast. So—I just want to fix on something relatively simple, relatively clear. A series of steps: this interview, then that one. Please help me do that, Rowland. I ought to be able to do it on my own—but I can't. Not today. Not now."

Rowland would have said she was a woman who would never admit weakness; he was immeasurably touched by that confession of weakness now. At that moment he wanted nothing so much as to take her in his arms, but he could see that would be wrong, possibly unfair—and that she was trying to tell him this indirectly.

"Very well." He moved a little farther away, and Gini, watching him do so, and watching a guarded expression come upon his face, thought: he's distancing himself.

"I worked after you left." He was staring past her, along the road. "Since you forbade me to stay with you, or come with you . . ."

"Rowland. Don't."

"I had no choice. So I worked. After a fashion. I spoke to the French police. I made some other calls. I realized something that we missed last night, which was actually very obvious—but still." He glanced down at his watch. "So, I'd say we have a choice. We have two possible leads. We can either try to interview that maid whom Cazarès was visiting yesterday—though I'm pretty sure that Lazare will have her well protected from the press, under virtual guard. Or"—he turned back to look at her—"or we can talk to that girl Chantal. She's with the police now, or should be, if we hurry."

Gini stared at him. "You arranged for them to pick her up? When? This morning?"

"Yes." He gave her one of his cool, unreadable green glances. "I can work quite well in adverse circumstances."

"So I see. I'll have to learn from you. . . ." For a moment her face clouded; then she made a brisk gesture. "You're right. It's the next stage. Let's talk to Chantal."

Chantal was a small, thin, angry woman with brown urchin-cut hair and brown street-urchin eyes. Rowland and Gini first glimpsed her through the glass panels of a police interview-room door. The French plainclothes inspector who led them there was called Martigny. He was a short, dark-haired man with sharp eyes and a quiet manner. Outside

the interview room, he continued to complete the rundown on Chantal
which he had begun in his office a short while before. It was succinct,
and in many respects, Rowland thought, predictable.

She was twenty-two years old, the daughter of a French-Canadian
mother and an American father she had never known. Her mother had
two other illegitimate children from whom Chantal had been separated
at the age of eight, when she was first taken into foster care.

Her childhood, insofar as she ever had a childhood, had been spent in
a succession of foster homes, from which she had a history of abscond-
ing. At fourteen she had served her first sentence, in a juvenile detention
center in Quebec, for shoplifting. At sixteen, in Detroit, she had been arrested for car theft, and at seventeen, in New York, for prostitution and
possession. She was virtually uneducated and semiliterate, and for the
past three years she had been based in France. She was a registered
heroin user, a dropout from a methadone program. In the past year, two
charges of prostitution and drug trafficking had been brought, and subsequently dropped for lack of evidence. She was in danger of depor-
tation, since none of her papers was in order, and she was not a
woman—unsurprisingly—who was cooperative with the police.

For the past two hours, Martigny said, two of his best officers, a man
and a woman, had been questioning her. Since there was no possible
charge, she was about to be released. Her story, prized out of her by the use
of threats, was that she knew no one by the name of Star, and never had.
She couldn't explain how her name and address came to be in the possession of some dead Dutch girl. Yes, she met lots of foreigners around Paris,
and yes, she or one of her friends might hand out her address—she was
generous that way: she had a room, a nice room, and sometimes people
needed somewhere to crash. She couldn't remember this Anneke, whoever
she was; it was an offense now, was it, to hand another girl her address?

Martigny studied these two reporters who, according to his British
colleague, had been helpful to the British police. The man looked as if he
hadn't slept in a week; the woman had a bruise down the side of her face
that suggested she'd been recently hit. There was a tension between them
that might have been professional, or emotional, or sexual.

Martigny shrugged such considerations aside. Chantal spoke fluent
English and French, he went on; they could try questioning her in either
language, and he was prepared to allow them twenty minutes. Time
made no difference: if he gave them all day, they would not persuade
this woman to talk.

He left them there; the woman officer remained by the door as the interview began. Rowland and Gini faced Chantal across a narrow table

scarred with cigarette burns. She sat opposite them, chain-smoking, biting her nails, averting her gaze, yawning, tapping the tabletop with her thin fingers and occasionally darting in their direction small brown glances of derision and hate.

The scar on her face was one of the ugliest Gini had ever seen. It ran from the outer corner of her left eye to the corner of her mouth. It had healed badly, into a long curving cicatrix that had left the skin puckered and inflamed. It gave her a deeply disconcerting quality, as if two women, not one, faced them across the table. Once pretty, and still pretty when she turned her face aside, she seemed to accept this inflicted ugliness with defiance. Whenever she answered one of Rowland's questions—he was speaking to her quietly, in excellent French—she turned her scarred side toward him, Gini noted. Her mounting nervousness and impatience were very apparent; Gini wondered if she needed a fix.

Gini felt very calm, curiously so, as if marooned on a flat sea, beyond the breath of any emotion at all. This had the effect of heightening her surroundings, so she saw the girl, and her reactions, with an intense precision. She felt that if she could just continue to do so, she need not remember or think about anything else.

Her silence—she had not spoken once since they entered—seemed to be irritating Chantal. At first the girl had ignored her, fixing her eyes on Rowland's handsome face, and answering him rudely, but also boldly. Perhaps this was the way she addressed her johns, Gini thought, this odd mixture of flirtation and contempt. She seemed eager to place Rowland in the same category as the rest of the male sex—an importuner who might require only answers now, but who, given the chance, would make a more basic, and sexual request.

All of Rowland's patient questions were being blocked. Chantal's eyes flicked in Gini's direction again. She yawned, lit another cigarette, then interrupted him suddenly, in English.

"So why's *she* here?" She gestured at Gini. "She have a voice, or what?"

"We work together. I did explain," Rowland replied in a level voice. The girl's accent, speaking English, betrayed her hybrid origins: it was not Canadian, not American, or British or European, but somewhere between all four. Gini saw Rowland register this.

"What's happened to your face?" Chantal turned to look at Gini. "You walk into a door? Someone's fist?" She gave an insolent smile and jerked a thumb at Rowland. "His?"

"What's happened to *your* face, Chantal," Gini replied, and felt Rowland tense.

Chantal gave Gini a considering look. "Go fuck yourself." She drew on the cigarette. "That's my business, all right?" She pursed her lips, then turned back to Rowland. She gave him a long, blatantly sexual stare. "Why don't you tell her to fuck off," she said to him. "And that tight-assed bitch at the door. If you and me were alone, who knows—I might open up then . . ." She passed her tongue across her lips as she said this, and leaned forward, so the threadbare sweater she was wearing was drawn tight across the outline of her small breasts.

She had perhaps hoped to embarrass Rowland, certainly to disconcert him. When her moves produced no effect whatsoever, she seemed disconcerted herself. She glanced away, looked down, seemed almost to shrink back into herself. She hunched her shoulders and folded her arms across her chest. She suddenly looked much less sure of herself, even vulnerable. That body language was telling: watching it—the attempt at sexual appeal, the insecurity when it was rejected—Gini saw a possible approach. She leaned forward.

"I know how you got that scar anyway," she said. "A man named Star did that to you with a razor, in England last year. I feel I know Star quite well by now. He's unstable. He has a cocaine habit, and he has mood swings—rapid ones. When that happens, he's capable of using a razor on a woman, and disfiguring her—or worse. Why is that, Chantal? Does he hate women? Does he have some sexual problem with women, perhaps?" Chantal had tensed. She bent her head and began to pick at her nails. Gini glanced at Rowland, who nodded.

"You know what I think he told you, Chantal?" Gini kept her eyes on the girl's bent head. "I think he told you that you had—the soothing gift. That's what he says to women, isn't it? He told Anneke that. I expect it's what he's telling Mina Landis right now. And I'm sure she'll believe him. After all, she's only fifteen years old. She's a great deal more gullible than you are because, unlike you, she's led a very sheltered life. Yet even you believed him, didn't you, Chantal? You went right on believing you could control him—until the day he cut your face."

Chantal's head jerked up. She gave Gini a venomous look. "Look—I don't *know* him, you stupid bitch. How many fucking times do I have to say it?"

"Oh, you know him, Chantal." Gini sighed. "And you know how he lies too. He didn't tell you the truth about the other girls, did he? Did you know he had Mina here with him in Paris? Because he does, they were seen together yesterday. Has he admitted that to you? Or does he spin you some different line—that Mina's like Anneke, like all the other little girls—disposable? Whereas you—you are the constant in his life? Is that what he told you, Chantal?"

It was instinct, a house of cards put together on the spur of the moment, but as soon as the words were out, Gini knew she was on the right track: Chantal's face went white. There was just one small convulsive movement of the hand, hastily covered up. She flicked the butt into the brimming ashtray in front of her and lit the last of her cigarettes.

"Fuck you. I'm getting sick of this. I'll say this one last time. I don't know Star. Never did. I don't recognize your description—nothing. So get the fuck off my back."

"Let me show you their photographs."

Gini reached into her bag. She took out the pictures of Mina and Anneke and handed them to Rowland, who silently passed them across. Chantal jerked her head away.

"Look at them, Chantal," Gini said in a quiet voice. "I think you never met either of them—but you knew about them, didn't you? You knew about them and you wondered what they looked like. Didn't you? Wondered what made Star interested in them, when he had you?" She paused. "Look at them and you'll see. Two different girls—yet in one respect they're alike. They both look younger than their age. They both look like children. . . . Is that when it started to go wrong for you, Chantal? When you started to look too much like a woman? Was that it?"

She stopped. Rowland had quietly laid his hand on her arm in warning. Chantal bent her head to the pictures. She was now chalk white, and beginning to shake.

"How old were you when you looked that innocent, Chantal? Eight? Nine? Ten?"

"You fucking cunt." Chantal scraped back her chair and rose unsteadily to her feet. "Listen"—she swung around to the impassive policewoman—"get her out of here. Get me out. You can't fucking keep me here. I have rights . . ." She was trembling violently.

Rowland said quietly, "Gini—she needs a fix."

"I know that. I could see that when we walked in. Chantal, show me your arms. Show me what else he did to you . . ."

Gini rose as she said this. Neither Rowland nor the policewoman moved. There was a silence; then, to Rowland's astonishment, Chantal allowed her hands to be taken and the thin sleeves of her pullover to be gently eased back. The needle tracks ran the length of both arms, like barbed wire, from elbow to wrist.

Without speaking, Gini drew the sleeves down again. Chantal's hands flexed and she began to bite her lip. She was beginning to sweat, and the trembling in her limbs had increased. Gini looked at Rowland, and one look was enough of a hint.

He came around the table and said in a low voice: "If we get you home—will that help?"

Chantal shot a quick look at the policewoman, who was careful to appear deaf; she gave a nod.

Rowland put his arm around her and began to draw her toward the door. "Let us take you back. The police are finished with you. We'll get a cab. That will be quicker, okay?"

When they were outside the station, Gini turned to the girl. All the blood had drained from her face; her forehead was clammy with sweat.

"You're late?" Gini said. "How late?"

"Over an hour. Nearly two. Those pigs do that . . ."

Gini pitied her then. All the defiance and bravado had gone. She could not focus her eyes; they had that look Mitchell had described, that dead-eyed yet frantic look of animal need. She swayed. Farther up the street Rowland had succeeded in flagging down a cab. He climbed into it and the car accelerated toward them, then came to a halt. Chantal surfaced, just momentarily, from her glassy state, and gave Gini one quick, sharp street look.

"You and him?"

"He has been, yes."

"I thought so. I can always tell." She swayed again. "Just get me back to my room."

She half fell, half slid into the rear seat beside Rowland. She lay back with her eyes closed. The tremblings intensified and became a series of spasmodic jerks. Gini held her hand and averted her face.

The room on rue St. Séverin was a terrible place. In a space twelve feet square was crammed a double bed, a table and chairs, boxes, piles of clothes, a huge television set. It smelled of poverty and an attempt to make a home without means; from the restaurants below, cooking smells drifted up. Two women lived here, Gini realized, Chantal and— presumably—the older woman who had answered the door to her the previous night. The remains of a breakfast lay on the table: two cups, two plates, some croissants and jam. On top of the unmade bed were two bundled nightdresses, one blue, one pink. The room was very cold, and smelled damp. An effort had been made to keep it clean. The dishes in the sink were neatly stacked. There was a cat-litter tray on the floor, and in a corner, half hidden behind a pile of cheap paperbacks, was a thin black cat. Curled up in a ball, on the bed, was a thin, timid lurcher dog. Gini bent to it and stroked its gray bristling fur. Then she turned to the windows. Through the net curtains she could just see the outline of the church. It was still raining; the thin light was already beginning to fade. She stared at the curtains and the church, because she could not bear to watch what was happening with Rowland behind her. "Help me," Chantal was saying. "You have to help me. I'm spilling it. I can't hold my hand steady . . . Christ. I burnt my hand."

Gini glanced back, feeling sick. Chantal had made the solution; Gini could see the small plastic bag of white powder, the blue of the gas jet, the little square of aluminum foil. One moment Chantal had the syringe in her shaking hand; the next it had dropped. Gini saw it roll across the floor and come to rest by the cat tray. She averted her eyes.

She heard Rowland pick it up, then the suck as it was filled.

"The mirror . . ." Chantal said. "I have to stand in front of the mirror. Otherwise I fuck up."

Gini heard Rowland move aside. There was silence. Rowland said, "Oh, Jesus Christ . . ."

Gini swung around. Chantal was facing the mirror, the syringe raised to her face. For an instant she couldn't understand what was happening, then she realized. Chantal was injecting the heroin solution into her eye. She was holding her lower lid down with one hand while she inserted the needle with the other. The clear liquid in the syringe turned pink. Gini turned away, covering her face, and beginning to tremble. Rowland moved behind her; she felt his arms come around her shoulders. She twisted back to look at his grim, pale face.

"That can happen," he said in a low voice. "They do that. When their veins are badly shot. Wait. She'll be all right in a minute. Then she'll probably sleep."

"All right?" Gini stared at him. "She won't be all right. How many hours before she needs another fix?"

"You think we're going to cure her—here and now? Come on, Gini. If we hadn't brought her here she'd have managed it some other way. And she'd have been in an even worse state."

He stopped. Chantal gave a deep sigh. Gini, turning, saw that the trembling had stopped and a very faint color had returned to her face. She began speaking then, fast, in a low voice, addressing Rowland as if they were alone in the room.

"Look. I need to sleep, all right? I'll be fine. My friend Jeanne will be back. I will kick this—in the end I will. She's helping me. I'm careful. I'm careful what I buy. I don't share needles. When Jeanne gets here—I'll be all right."

She swayed back against the sink and closed her eyes.

"You were pretty polite to me. I liked that. So—I'll tell you. Star— I've known him half my life. He's like me—a cross. Too many breeds, too many countries, too many homes, too many beatings and—so I'm fucked up, and he's fucked up. That's why. We're both really fucked around in our heads. . . ."

She dropped the syringe. Neither Rowland nor Gini spoke.

"And I don't know where he is. I swear to you—somewhere in Paris, but I don't know where. I saw him last night. He told me he was alone, but he—he lies a lot, and if that girl is with him, he'll hide her. That's what he does. You don't need to worry too much. She's probably okay. He'll just give her some grass, talk to her—maybe a few pills. That's okay—he always has good stuff. He won't fuck her or rape her, you don't need to worry about that. . . ." She gave a low laugh, then stopped and opened her eyes. She was focusing now, better than before; she raised her hand to her cheek.

"Only—you'd better know this, because what she said—" She gestured at Gini. "She was right. He can get angry. He gets these bad angers, really bad, like trips. And last night—I got him a gun. He wanted a gun, he's been wanting one for months, and he had the money and I had the contacts, so I fixed it for him. He collected it last night, just before you came knocking at the door." She turned her face toward Gini. "It was you, right?"

"Yes, it was." She felt Rowland tense, as she did. "What kind of gun, Chantal?"

"I don't know. Just a gun. He told me he wanted it—I got it. He showed me some pictures, made me write down the name."

"A handgun?" Rowland said.

"Yes. Small. Some special ammunition stuff. It's no use looking. I wrote the name down on a piece of paper. I threw it away weeks ago. It was German—no, maybe Italian."

"Why would he want a gun?" Rowland moved toward her. Her eyes had closed again.

"I don't know. He likes guns. Always did. He gets off on them, just looking at pictures of them. It was expensive—I know that. Nearly four thousand francs . . . Serious. That's what he said. It was a serious gun. Only then"—she swayed again—"only then—I don't know. The TV was on in the corner while we talked—and then he suddenly got this look on his face. There's a look he gets—in the eyes. He had it before he did this to me. . . ." She touched the scar on her face. "So maybe, it's not so good for that girl. I don't know. Look—I have to lie down."

She stumbled across the room to the bed and lay down, eyes tightly shut. Rowland looked at Gini, then bent over the bed.

"Chantal. Just try to stay awake. Can you hear me? Does he have a name, a name other than Star? What was he called when you first met him?"

He broke off and stepped back. There was the sound of footsteps running up the stairs, then the door was thrown back. The woman Gini had spoken to the previous evening came into the room, her face pale with fear. She stopped, looked at them both, then pushed past them and knelt down by the bed.

She took Chantal in her arms and began to stroke her hair, talking to her all the while in a low, crooning voice. When she swung back to look at them, there was no mistaking the love and the anger in her face. "How long did they keep her there? Those animals?"

She spoke in French, and Rowland answered her in the same language: "About an hour, maybe more," he said.

The woman burst into a stream of angry accusations, directed at the police, them, the world.

"Jeanne, wait." Chantal attempted to sit up, then fell back. "He's okay. He helped me. I can't talk. They need to know about Star. Just tell them his name, explain, all right?"

She closed her eyes again and seemed to drift off into some state close to sleep. The woman called Jeanne rose. In heavily accented English she spat out her explanation.

Star was to blame for all this. It was he who first got Chantal on to heroin, he who ruined her face. And Star was just one of his names—the latest he'd selected and the one he now liked the best. He had numerous surnames she could offer them, she said with scorn in her voice: Lamont, Lacroix, Newman, D'Amico, Rivière, Adams, Dumas—they could take their pick. When it came to first names they had a choice of two. He occasionally used the English version of his name, but he preferred the French. This past year he'd been claiming it was his true name, the name on his birth certificate—she doubted he had such a thing, but for what it was worth, the name was Christophe.

CHAPTER 17

Outside, in the damp air and the gathering dusk, standing in the doorway of the St. Séverin church with the gargoyles arching above their heads, Rowland said, "I need a drink. You need a drink. Don't argue."

He walked her, fast, toward the Sorbonne, then turned off the boulevard St. Michel into a quiet street and into a small, old-fashioned bistro, almost empty; they were given a booth with high-backed seats, so they were enclosed as if in the cabin of a ship. There was a red and white checked tablecloth, with a white paper one placed diagonally over it: two knives and forks, two ordinary glasses for wine. Rowland ordered brandies, and when Gini hesitated, made her drink. He watched her; for the first time that day, some of the tension left her body, and faint color returned to her face.

Her face seemed so lovely to him, he found he had to turn away, study the menu, consult with her, with the short, plump *patron*, anything to wrench his attention away from her mouth, from the mauve bruising across her cheekbone, and from the flare of her eyes, her wide-spaced, expressive, and very beautiful eyes which seemed to him to ask an unspoken question yet fear his possible response.

He ordered the food. Work, he thought: if he could just keep the conversation on their work. He began speaking, and she began speaking—both at once.

Rowland smiled, hesitated, then leaned back.

"You first."

"Nothing—I was just going to say—you were very good with Chantal. She liked you—insofar as she's capable of liking a man. Did you realize that?"

"No." Rowland shrugged. "It seemed to me I was getting nowhere with her. Every question blocked."

"No. You're wrong. You were patient, and quiet—and polite. She was grateful for that. Maybe it doesn't happen to her too often. Maybe—" Her eyes flickered up to his face.

"Maybe what?"

"Maybe she liked your appearance. I imagine you're used to that."

Rowland leaned forward.

"Shall I tell you what made her decide to talk? It wasn't me or what I said. It wasn't even because she needed a fix desperately. I was watching her, and I know precisely the second when she decided."

"When we showed her the photographs?"

"No." Rowland looked at her, touched that she did not realize. "No. You used a particular phrase. It touched an immediate chord. Maybe you hit on something Star had actually said to her, maybe not—either way, it went straight to the heart." He paused. "You asked her if she believed she was the constant in his life."

Color washed into her cheeks. "Are you sure?"

"I'm absolutely sure. In any interview, any conversation like that, there's always one moment when the questioner breaks through. That was it. What made you hit on that phrase?"

"I don't know. It just came to me. We knew she was different from the other girls—she was older, for one thing. She'd known Star for some time, Mitchell said that. And I just began to wonder—if that was how she saw her role in Star's life. It's something women like. . . ."

"Is it?"

"Of course." She looked away. "Women are more monogamous than men. So they find ways of excusing their men when they stray. Being told they're somehow in a different category, believing they're in a different category, a more permanent, a more serious category—that's one of women's protective mechanisms. I've seen it often enough." She hesitated, and a reticence Rowland was beginning to realize was very characteristic of her masked her face.

"Anyway"—she took a sip of her brandy—"I'm sure of one thing."

"Anneke was *not* writing to Star care of Chantal? I agree. I also thought that."

"In which case—we're back to the beginning again. We have a clutch of false surnames, a first name that may or may not be genuine. We know Star has a gun, which makes things worse. But we don't know why he wanted the gun and we still have no idea where he is."

"No. We know more than that. We know something interesting, and curious too. . . ." Rowland fell silent as the owner of the restaurant returned and began to ply them with food: freshly baked bread, salads, *pommes frites,* and two omelettes the man said were made with wild mushrooms, and his own hens' freshly laid eggs.

Rowland smiled at this very French perfectionism; he waited until the proprietor left them, then leaned forward. As if trying to appear hungry, Gini began to eat.

"We know more than we thought," Rowland went on. "This was staring us in the face yesterday. Think. Maria Cazarès died yesterday afternoon, at the apartment of her retired maid. Right?"

"The apartment in the Faubourg St. Germain area, sure. We discussed that. I know the district. I even know the street . . ."

"You do?"

"Yes." She hesitated. "Pascal Lamartine's ex-wife lives on that street now. It's her new husband's apartment. I went there twice, last year, to pick up Pascal's daughter, Marianne. It's a very fashionable neighborhood."

She looked away, then continued to eat. She had set herself a test, Rowland thought, to see whether she could mention Lamartine's name without any show of emotion—and she had almost succeeded, though not quite. Better not to inquire, he thought, better to let it pass, although he noted the fact that while Lamartine's ex-wife had remarried, Lamartine had not.

"We also know," he went on, "that it was close to that apartment, yesterday afternoon, that there was a sighting of Mina Landis and Star."

"Yes. At about two P.M. We also discussed that."

"But what we didn't discuss was whether that was coincidence—or something more. At that point, we got—distracted, as I remember."

"Rowland—"

"Very well. But we did." He looked at her seriously. "In fact, the maid's name wasn't mentioned on those TV news bulletins. It was mentioned in the newspapers this morning, however. Her name is Mathilde Duval. Does that help? Now do you begin to see?"

"Oh my God." She dropped her fork with a little clatter, and stared at him. "Anneke's address book. Those seven girls' names I wrote out. There was a Mathilde."

"Exactly. A Mathilde Duval, at the address, the *same* address, where

Maria Cazarès died yesterday afternoon. I think *that's* where Anneke was writing to Star, not care of Chantal. Maybe he also gave her Chantal's address, as a backup, a fail-safe, I don't know—but there's definitely a connection between Star and Mathilde Duval."

"Who isn't a girl at all. Who's an elderly woman—damn, how stupid I am."

"—And since the conversation with Chantal, I'm *certain* there's a connection. I brought Anneke's address book with me. Look at this."

He drew it out of his overcoat pocket, then passed it across the table. Gini turned to the entry for Mathilde Duval. The entire page was scattered with little hieroglyphs and scribbles. Very faint, next to Mathilde's name, was a tiny crucifix shape.

"Christopher," Rowland said. "Christophe. It means Christ-bearing. Anneke knew Star's other name, which might be his real name, and she made a little sign for it, next to the address to which she wrote to him. I'm certain of it, Gini. And you see what this suggests?"

"That if Star knew Maria Cazarès's maid, he could also have known Maria Cazarès herself? Rowland—you think so?"

"I do. I think he was visiting the maid yesterday, and that's when he and Mina were seen—probably when they were leaving. And within two hours of his leaving, Maria Cazarès was there too. There's some connection here between Star and Maria Cazarès, between Star and Jean Lazare. First, Star is obtaining White Doves from the same source as Lazare. Second, he chooses to be in Paris, where they are both based. Third, he has some connection with a maid to whom Cazarès was devoted, whom she visited frequently. And that connection is of some duration, Gini. If we're correct, and Anneke *was* writing to Star care of Mathilde, we can even date it. Their connection *must* go back to last March at least." He paused. "Now, all these details could just be coincidences, but I think not."

Gini was watching him and listening intently. He could see her mind start to race.

"Rowland—you don't think? It couldn't be—"

"That Star is the missing child in Lindsay's New Orleans story? I'm ashamed to say it did occur to me, yes. Almost as soon as Lindsay told me the story. So, for what it's worth, I got in touch with the *Correspondent*'s Miami stringer yesterday. He's gone to New Orleans to do some checking. It's also why I wanted you to ask Anneke's mother if Star could have been American, or had American connections."

"And has the stringer come up with anything?"

"Not so far, no. He's in search of a last name, mainly. He was going to try that convent, and the Grants. But it's nearly thirty years ago, and I'm not optimistic that he'll have much success."

"You said—ashamed? Rowland, there *is* some connection, you admit that. And Star is around the right age. He's black-haired, like Cazarès and Lazare. He has the right kind of past history—foster homes, children's homes—or so Chantal said."

"I know. He has vaguely the right qualifications—and so have thousands of other men. No, Gini. It's too neatly convenient, and it's too damn far-fetched."

"Far-fetched things do happen. Open any newspaper any day of the week—they're *full* of far-fetched stories. Besides, is it that unlikely? Suppose Star *was* their child, and suppose he was fostered out or put in a home shortly after birth—he would have the right to be given his parents' names when he reached a certain age. He could have tried to trace them." She paused, then shook her head. "No. You're right. It doesn't stand up. How could he have traced them? Lazare and Cazarès have been very careful to cover their tracks."

"I agree." Rowland shrugged. "Even so—I thought it was at least worth instigating some inquiries. But I don't seriously believe that *is* the connection between Lazare and Cazarès and Star. I wouldn't even have considered it, but at the time—I'd had two nights with very little sleep. I was thinking of Cassandra, and I couldn't forget the way I found her, how she looked. . . ." He glanced away. "For that, and other reasons, my judgment was impaired, and I'm well aware of that."

"What other reasons?"

"Work. Pressures of work. I'm still coming to terms with a relatively new job—a desk job, which is something I've never done before, something Max talked me into." He hesitated, then turned back to face her. "Coming to terms with other changes in my life. And resisting them, of course."

For a moment he thought she had picked up his inference; then he realized she had not. But something he had said had made her suddenly thoughtful. She picked up her fork again, then put it down. She had eaten only half her food. She pushed it aside with a gesture of apology, then seemed to forget it. She raised her eyes to his.

"Do people resist change? You think they do? Why, Rowland? Because they're afraid?"

"Perhaps it's fear. Change can be for the bad as well as the good," he said in a guarded way. "So they cling to the known. Avoid the possible abyss."

"Do you think—do people resist change in others, or just in themselves?"

He could see the importance of this question to her: "Yes, I do," he said quietly. "In themselves, and in others. Both."

"Why? *Why* do they do that?"

"Gini, for a hundred reasons—you know that. Because of the unpredictability of change. Because change can seem like betrayal, a treachery to people's former selves." He broke off, and Gini could see that he had suddenly brought himself up close to some experience painful to him. She saw the decision not to discuss it, or impart it, mask his face. "It's pointless to resist," he went on, after a while, in a quiet voice. "If the change involved is deep—not frivolous, superficial—I'm not sure that it even *can* be resisted. It will happen, like it or not. And sometimes"—he looked away again—"sometimes, if the change is very rapid, by the time you acknowledge it's happened, it's too late."

There was a silence. She bent her head. She moved her knife one inch, then moved it back.

"And you think it can be rapid?" she said.

"Oh, I think it can be astonishingly fast. I think it can happen in the middle of a sentence, halfway through a meal, walking along a street. I think it can happen between falling asleep and waking the next morning." His voice became dry. "No doubt it's been approaching for some while, creeping up on you in a stealthy way—until finally you permit yourself to admit capture. Then it's irremediable, of course."

"You're sure?"

Rowland could see that she was following a train of thought separate from his own. He had just spoken to her with a frankness he had not used in six years, and yet she had missed his meaning. He wondered if that was intentional, then saw it was not. He considered being more overt, then rejected that option as a form of trespass.

"Is it? Is it irremediable?" She was now leaning toward him, her eyes bright, her face tense with entreaty.

Rowland sighed: "I would say so," he replied. "Gini—that particular clock can't be wound back."

He sensed her draw away; he saw her begin to reach for her scarf and her coat. He signaled for the bill. She had recovered her composure and was trying to appear businesslike. Rowland watched her tie the shamrock-green scarf around her throat. He reached across the table, touched her hand, then withdrew his.

"So what do you want to do now, Gini? Go on? Stop? Rest?"

"Go on." She picked up her bag. "We'll go to Mathilde's next. Okay?"

"It's what I would suggest. If you'd prefer to go back to the hotel—they did find a room for you. . . . I could go to Mathilde's. You look tired, Gini."

"No. I'm not. I told you. I want to work. Rowland—we have to go on with this. We *are* making progress. And Star has that gun. I want to find Mina." She frowned, her face becoming set. "I'm determined to do that." She rose. "Let's both go to Mathilde's. Fight our way past Lazare's guards if they're there."

She smiled as she said this. Rowland followed her out of the restaurant. In the street outside, she glanced up at the sky. Her hair was still damp from the rain, and so was his. The last light of the afternoon had faded. A student rode past on a bicycle; from a house opposite, a child called to his mother. In the distance, muted, they could hear the roar of the city's rush hour traffic.

"How dark it is," she said.

It was after five when they reached the rue de Rennes. It was, Rowland thought, a dull if expensive street, high bourgeois, one of those citadels of the rich to be found in any large city, the Paris equivalent of Mayfair, or Park Avenue: a wide boulevard lined with trees and flanked on both sides by ornate ten-story turn-of-the-century apartment buildings. Their ranked windows glittered with lights. There were few passersby; Gini, walking beside him, came to an abrupt halt.

"It's that building across there. It's the one next to Helen's."

"Helen's?"

"Helen Lamartine-that-was. These apartments are huge, Rowland. . . ." She hesitated, and he could see how tense she had suddenly become.

"There's no point in our both going up."

"You want me to go?"

"I'd rather you did. I'll give you ten minutes—then I'll wait around the corner. There's a café there, just up on the right. You can't miss it."

"Very well. In any case, Lazare's thorough. I doubt I'll be as long as ten minutes."

He was right. Gini waited, shivering. She turned up the collar of her coat and paced. She stared hard at the sidewalk, the trees, the porticos of these buildings, fixing on their details and refusing to allow the past back. Rowland returned six minutes later.

"As we thought. There's some damn woman from the Cazarès press office standing guard. She gave me her card and told me to call their offices tomorrow if I had any queries. She was extremely charming. Then she shut the door in my face."

"She did?" Gini looked at him in a curious way, a speculative way. "What sort of age was she?"

"Age? God knows. Forty? Forty-five? What difference does it make?"

"It might make a difference." Her voice was dry. "You have certain advantages, Rowland, and you tend to underestimate them."

He was already beginning to walk away. "What are you talking about?"

Gini looked at his tall figure, at his extraordinary eyes, at his hair. She linked her arm through his.

"Just around this corner, Rowland," she said, "next to that café I mentioned, there's a flower shop. One of the best in Paris. Filled with the most exquisite roses, lilies, narcissus . . ."

"So? What of it?"

"You may work for a very reputable newspaper, Rowland, and you may be very good at your job, but even you can learn. Come with me." She smiled. "You remember what you said to me on the telephone in Amsterdam? Well, let me just show you a few *tabloid* techniques."

It was not yet six in the evening, and Mathilde Duval, a woman of entrenched habits, was already preparing for bed. Juliette de Nerval, appointed her guardian and protector by Jean Lazare himself, watched this process with some pity, and a great deal of revulsion.

She did not know Mathilde Duval's exact age, but she looked eighty at least. She was, of course, of peasant stock, and peasant women, particularly from the south, aged quickly—so she might be younger. Whatever her true age, Mathilde was the embodiment of everything Juliette most feared. Whatever it took, she told herself, watching the old woman, she herself was never going to end up like this.

Mathilde was no more than five feet tall, if that, and bent as a witch. Heavy black clothes, head to foot; thinning hair scraped back against her scalp; a bristle of hairs on her chin; a face etched with deep lines, not just beneath the eyes and around the mouth, but everywhere. Her hands were twisted with arthritis; her ankles were swollen; she was virtually blind; she moved around this ghastly apartment at a snail's pace, fingering a rosary, touching little sacred pictures, and muttering to herself.

The temperature in the apartment was about ninety degrees. Although the old woman was forever fussing, and dusting, and brushing, it smelled. It smelled of mothballs, which Juliette had forgotten existed; it smelled of burnt cooking oil, and dust, and clothes that weren't quite clean. Occasionally—she was beginning to suspect Mathilde might be incontinent—it smelled powerfully of urine. Then the old woman would disappear into one of the bathrooms for a long time, emerging fresher.

Juliette knew that even if the old woman fell, or called for help from that bathroom, she would find it very difficult to go to her aid. She pitied, but her skin crawled.

At seven she was off duty. Meanwhile, she couldn't breathe, and she felt sick.

The old woman's preparations for bed seemed endless. First there had been the meal, then some hot milk, then the bed in her room had to be turned down and a hot water bottle put in to warm the sheets. Then she prayed—on her knees, by the bed. Then she went into the room next to hers, that dreadful shrine to her beloved Maria, and insisted on turning that bed down, as if Maria were going to be sleeping there, as if she were waiting for a woman she knew to be dead.

That particular part of her nightly ritual had made Juliette shiver; she began to have a horrible feeling that she and the old woman were watched, that they were not alone here, that some revenant stealthily and silently approached.

She had backed out of the pink room fast as Mathilde began to light a series of votive night-lights under the photographs of Maria Cazarès. Their flames flickered. In their wavering light the walls and the pictures seemed to move. The bed, with its monstrous fat pink silk eiderdown, looked as if it might stir. Juliette, who would have said she did not believe in ghosts, sensed them now. She could feel presences in the corners of this room, the caress of a cold hand on her spine. She fled. Back in the sitting room, trembling, she smoked several cigarettes.

The old woman was washing now. Juliette listened to the noise of running water, the thrum of pipes. She tried not to watch the time. She stood in the middle of this room, with its mass of crowded furniture, trying not to see the crucifixes, the saints' pictures, and the portrayals of Christ. Above the mantelpiece there was a huge depiction of Him: greenish-pink; He was indicating a large hole in His heart region, within which burned a light.

Juliette averted her eyes. None of the windows would open. She wished she could leave. She even wished that English journalist—that quite extraordinarily *handsome* English journalist—would come back. Anything to get her out of this place. Another hour, she told herself; less. Then she could go home, have a bath, a large drink, and talk to her husband—if he was there, of course. They could talk about Stockholm, to which city her husband, a diplomat, was shortly to be posted. Only another month, Juliette thought, and she couldn't wait to leave Paris, leave Cazarès. She'd worked there nearly ten years, and she'd realized—suddenly, about six months ago—that she no longer relished her responsibilities or enjoyed her position. The spirit of Cazarès had gone, she thought, and had been gone for a while, perhaps as long as five years; she had just been slow to realize it. Lazare had disguised the alteration, of course; with unflagging energy—an energy she suspected ate him away—he herded them all on, never relaxing his standards, never acknowledging their collective pretense. He knew the heart had gone out of the whole enterprise; he knew they were trying to breathe life into the dead, but his cold refusal to acknowledge that fact in the smallest degree drove them all on. No one dared to question, or express doubt or dissent.

Juliette moved around the room restlessly. It occurred to her suddenly that Maria Cazarès almost certainly died in this very room—at that thought, she froze. Where? On the sofa? In that chair over there where Mathilde said she permitted only her beloved Maria to sit? On that rug, in front of the fireplace? Juliette shrank back from the rug, and with trembling hands lit another cigarette.

So many lies, she thought; that was what her job amounted to now. She was paid a handsome salary to disseminate untruths. No, there was no truth in these foolish rumors that Maria Cazarès was unwell. No, certainly, no extra staff were employed to assist with designs: every last item of the couture and the ready-to-wear was designed by Maria Cazarès herself. . . . Even the press conference today: much of Lazare's speech, which had moved her to tears, had been either a direct lie or a careful evasion of the truth.

Maria Cazarès had *not* died at the St. Étienne hospital; she, Juliette, had spoken to the ambulance people, to the doctor who admitted her, and they had been definite. Cazarès was probably dead by the time poor, frantic, half-senile Mathilde had managed to telephone; she was certainly dead by the time the paramedics entered this apartment, and none of their attempts at resuscitation had met with any success. So she had not died at the St. Étienne with Jean Lazare at her side. Juliette did not know why he made that claim—unless it was something he wished to believe himself.

She had spent the previous night trying to plug gaps, and putting out to the press the story Lazare favored, in the manner and at the time that he chose.

The doctor at the St. Étienne, now rehearsed, had been available for interview. Lazare was skillful, Juliette thought. He understood how to give information to the press so they noticed less what he withheld. And what he was chiefly withholding, of course, was Mathilde—though why he should do so, Juliette could not conceive. This mumbling, half-senile old woman was unlikely to tell any reporter anything useful or scandalous. She was Maria's devoted maid; they had been taking tea together; Maria had suffered a sudden and massive heart attack—where were the secrets there?

Throughout the day Juliette had fended off only a few reporters; some Frenchmen that morning, a seedy cameraman from some British tabloid, and a rather more intelligent Italian paparazzo that afternoon. The paparazzo had wanted a picture of the room in which Cazarès collapsed; Juliette thought he had not expected to get it via the front door, and had not been greatly dismayed when he failed. After that, nothing—until the English journalist from a respectable paper, a paper Juliette would not have expected to take the least interest in this furor, had turned up.

It had been unpleasant, endless—and a fairly pointless exercise to boot. She listened, hearing a door open—and then realized, to her great relief, that the old woman had finished washing at last and was now shuffling along the corridor to her bed. Juliette heard the creaking of floorboards, then further mutterings: more prayers, she thought, and looked at the clock. This last hour of duty seemed the longest hour of her life.

Tomorrow morning, at ten-thirty, further duties remained to be performed. A limousine was to be sent to collect Madame Duval and bring her to Cazarès; she was then to be settled backstage for the duration of the show. This was tradition. Mathilde Duval had always attended the collections, had done so for twenty years—more. In the past it was she who arrived there with Maria Cazarès, she who stayed by her side throughout, soothing her nerves, talking to her, keeping her calm, tucked away in a little private back room until the moment Maria dreaded arrived, the moment she had to face the audience, the cameras, the applause.

The fact that Maria was dead altered nothing, Lazare said. It would have been Maria's wish for Mathilde to be present, and present she would be. Juliette shivered again and edged toward the doorway. She could hear the muttered praying continue. Through the open door opposite, she could see into that terrible pink shrine of a room. She turned back to the sitting room, frowning now. Was there something to conceal here? She had assumed she was here purely as a result of Lazare's almost pathological secrecy concerning Maria. But what if there were a serious reason for his insistence Mathilde be kept away from the press? Was it Mathilde he was worried about—or was it this place itself?

This idea had not occurred to her before. The instant it did, she began to look around her with closer attention. She moved to the mantelpiece and inspected the ugly objects crowded there, then to a table on which were perched more photographs of Maria, all of them fairly recent, she judged. She edged between small rickety tables, toward the far end of the room, which was dominated by a huge, very ugly secretary piled with knickknacks and papers, like every other surface here. There were pens, and bits of string, and scissors and sticks of sealing wax, and bottles of ink. The old woman had spilled some ink, she saw. A little pool of it, now dried, blotched one of the sheets of paper. It looked as if she had been trying to write a letter. Juliette bent over the page: the old woman's writing was as crabbed as she would have expected; she could read only the opening words: *Mon bien-aimé Christophe. Il faut que je te voie, c'est urgent . . . Je suis navrée' tu me manques . . .*

Who was Christophe? she wondered. Some grandchild, perhaps? The rest of the letter, unfinished, was obscured by the spillage of ink, as if the old woman had been writing, knocked over the ink bottle, then abandoned the effort. Poor thing, Juliette thought. She straightened a few items on the desk, feeling guilty for her own curiosity. There was a small pile of tiny boxes, she saw, thrust behind the pile of papers. Their wrappings were scattered beside them, and those wrappings could have come only from Cazarès: she recognized the silver cord, the gold *faille*, the signature white silk scraps.

Perhaps Maria had brought some presents for the old woman yesterday, she thought, and given them to her before they took tea, before she collapsed. How sad. Whatever these three little boxes had contained, they were empty now. Perhaps little pieces of jewelry, some small token of affection. If so, she knew Mathilde would not let them out of her sight.

She crossed the room and looked along the corridor. The muttered prayers had ceased. She tiptoed to the door of the old woman's room and peeped in. She was lying there, breathing steadily, eyes open and staring into space. She looked as if she were waiting for something, or someone. Juliette crept away. She was just telling herself that she was letting her imagination run away with her, when the doorbell rang, startling her.

She went to the front door, peered through the peephole, hesitated, then felt a sudden rush of elation: that handsome English journalist had come back.

She unbolted the door and opened it at once. This Rowland McGuire, whose card was in her pocket right now, had a half-amused, half-reckless look on his face—an expression Juliette decided she liked. In his arms, spilling out of his arms—and this she liked even more—was one of the most exquisite bouquets she had ever seen in her life.

"For you," he said. "I was just wondering—when you come off duty—might I buy you a drink?"

He had the most devastating green eyes she had ever seen, and also the most devastating smile.

She hesitated for half a second; it was almost seven anyway. Then she returned the smile.

"I admire persistence," she said. "And after today a drink would be excellent. I'll just get my coat."

From the window of Helen's penthouse apartment, Pascal had a clear view of the street below. Standing in the darkened room in which Marianne was now sleeping, he watched Rowland McGuire leave the building next door and descend its wide portico steps. He was with a tall, elegant, middle-aged woman. Pascal caught a glimpse of her high-heeled shoes, her pale blond hair; she looked as if she were making some adverse comment on the weather; she drew her long fur coat more tightly around her. McGuire said something to her, at which she smiled; they disappeared, side by side, along the street.

Pascal rested his face against the cold dark glass. Behind him, Marianne's breathing had become peaceful. The room was quiet, filled with the stuffed toy animals Marianne loved. The book from which he had been reading to her lay beside her bed, next to the tiny night-light in the shape of an owl with folded wings, which Pascal, knowing she feared the dark, had bought for her on one of his trips. From where? London? New York? Madrid? Rome? He had no recollection. He could no more remember this small event than he had been able to concentrate on the words in the story he had been reading aloud. Before he began reading, when he had been standing here at the window, as he was now, he had suddenly realized who they were, the man and the woman opposite, the tall man and the slender woman who kept her face carefully averted from this building as she spoke.

To see them made his heart ice; he had continued to stand there, unable to move. He had watched McGuire leave Gini there, cross the street, and enter the apartment building next door. Just at the second when Pascal had decided to go down, go out, speak to Gini, McGuire had returned. They had walked away, and near the corner Gini had taken his arm. The gesture had been companionable; its easy working familiarity, as if they were not lovers but merely colleagues, cut Pascal to the heart. Here, too, he thought, he had been usurped. Now, turning away from the window, he told himself that it was fortunate he had not taken that plane, fortunate he had seen this, fortunate he had resisted that impulse to go down and speak to her. Gini was obviously continuing her work with McGuire despite a scene that morning that had left him scarcely able to function, to think. He loathed, and also despised, protracted endings. Yes, he had decided to remain in Paris, but everything that needed to be said had already been said—there was no going back.

He looked down at his sleeping child, his heart welling with love for her; he bent and kissed her forehead, then left the room. He returned to Helen's opulent living room, where she was sitting quietly, reading a book.

"That took a while." She looked up with a smile, saw his expression, and closed her book. Pascal picked up his overcoat.

"Yes. I read the whole story twice. Then we talked. I think she's nervous about the dentist tomorrow."

"Oh, she'll be fine. It's only a filling. You're taking her. That makes it a treat." Helen rose. Pascal wondered if she would ever lose this knack she had of making the positive negative, of making what might have been a compliment a reproach. Since Helen's remarriage, their relationship had been easier, but even now she could never resist such sly digs.

"Have a drink." She had moved to the sideboard. "Come on, Pascal. Ralph won't be back for an hour at least. You can stand my company for ten minutes, surely? And you look as if you need one."

"All right. A whiskey—neat. Thanks."

He began to move around the room in an aimless way as Helen poured the drinks. Helen's second husband, he thought, had been able to give her everything she had always wanted, all the material things he himself had failed to provide. Looking at the room, with its expensive furniture, wall-to-wall carpeting, predictable paintings, costly upholstery and curtains, it seemed to him both soulless and curiously bogus— like a stage set for some thirties drawing-room comedy. According to Helen, it had been redecorated at her behest, by one of the top interior designers in Paris. Her husband, Ralph, it seemed, had had simpler tastes, but Helen had converted him, of course.

Pascal sat down on a sofa covered in a Bennison floral chintz. He rested his arm on a riot of faded roses and accepted his drink. Helen pushed several little silver dishes toward him, little dishes containing pistachios, black olives. They were arranged on a huge glass coffee table on which rested a vase of lilies and several piles of coffee-table books. Picture books about houses and china and rugs and paintings and furniture—about things you could *buy*. Were the books consulted? Pascal wondered. He could scarcely believe they were read.

Helen was wearing a flattering wine-red woolen dress. Her dark hair was cut in a new style that suited her. Her jewelry was discreet. She was looking well, he thought; she was looking poised, rich, attractive. She looked like the wife of a man of means—which was, he supposed vaguely, how she had always wanted to look.

How could he have been married to her for five years and known her so little, he thought. And the idea of his own mistaken conception of her deepened his depression. Helen liked material things—it was as simple, as basic, as that. Pascal, indifferent to possessions—interested in art, for instance, but perfectly content to travel to a museum or gallery to view it, and with no desire to acquire it himself—had assumed that Helen felt the same way. Surely, when he had first met her, she had been concerned with things other than acquisition? He could remember talking to her about politics, plays, books, films—and being certain at the time that she was as genuinely interested in them as he was himself. But perhaps she had not been. Perhaps he had simply failed to see her, or to understand her from the first. Perhaps the same was also true of Gini. I am a photographer, Pascal thought; it is my job, my life, to *see*—and yet I've been blind. He swallowed half the whiskey in one gulp, and, ignoring Helen's little pout of displeasure, lit a cigarette.

Helen had been watching him closely. "What's wrong, Pascal? Because something is. You arrived with a face like thunder. I can see the storm clouds right now." She paused, eyeing him in a meditative way. "You've quarreled with Gini—is that it?"

"Just leave it, okay, Helen? I'm tired, and I'm not in the mood for one of your interrogation sessions—all right?"

"As you like." She shrugged. "It's perfectly obvious, nonetheless. You should learn to talk to people about your problems, Pascal. It's not good to bottle things up the way you do."

"Oh, for God's sake. Who says I have a problem?" He rose, paced the room, and then, with a cold glance in her direction poured himself a second drink.

"When you have a problem," Helen said in a sweet voice, "you glower, then you pace. Deny it all you like. And in your present mood, I wouldn't advise another drink."

"Why not?" He turned to give her a cold stare. "Maybe I feel like getting drunk for once in my life."

"It's your funeral. Just don't get drunk here." She gave another irritable shrug. "How much longer are you staying in Paris?"

"I'll stay until Marianne's birthday next Monday. I'd like to see her on her birthday. If you don't object."

"No, Pascal. I don't object. You can come to her birthday party. I told you. There's no reason now for any hostility. We can all be friends. Ralph and you, Gini and me. We can be civilized."

"Sure." He gave her another cold look. "We can have nice civilized meals together. A little civilized lunch, perhaps?"

"Oh, I see." She caught the inference at once. "That's the problem, is it? I've sinned. I've actually dared to go out and have a normal lunch and a normal conversation with another woman. Oh, sorry, Pascal. My mistake."

"Not any other woman. Gini. And I know precisely what you said at your 'normal' lunch, so don't bother denying it. You were making trouble, as usual."

"As a matter of fact, that's not true." She turned and gave him a smile. "I took Gini out to lunch because I thought I could get to know her better. Since she's going to be helping to look after my daughter when Marianne stays with you, I thought that was quite a reasonable course to take."

"And that was necessary when you'd already met Gini twice? Don't lie to me. I know you too well. I damn well know why you talked to Gini the way you did."

"For heaven's sake. I simply thought I'd try to get to know her better. And I may as well say it, Pascal—when I saw her I was shocked."

"Shocked? Why? No doubt your female intuition went into overdrive. It usually does."

"You don't need intuition to see when a person's ill—miserable, deeply distressed. I was *appalled* by the state she was in." She turned angrily, to top up her drink, then rounded on him again, her face tight with indignation.

"As it happens, I was also touched by her loyalty to you, and her efforts to disguise how unhappy, how obviously unwell she was. So don't bloody well preach at me, Pascal. You're so *blind*. That hadn't happened to her overnight. She'd obviously been that way for *months*. So why didn't you notice when you were in Bosnia together? Why, in your usual way, didn't you come home when you said you were coming? She thought you'd be back for Christmas. I damn near wept. . . ."

"I don't have to account to you for my movements. Gini *agreed* I should stay on. There were aspects of that war I still hadn't covered. And Gini understood that a great deal better than you ever did."

"Did she indeed?" Her mouth tightened. "Dear God, Pascal—you haven't changed one bit. I begin to think you never will. Don't you ever get sick of your everlasting wars? Doesn't it ever occur to you that you can't spend your entire life sacrificing everyone, including yourself, to this obsession of yours? I thought you'd learned. I thought you'd begun to see that you can't always put work first, second, and third, and everything else a poor fourth. Obviously not. I might have known it. The three years when you *didn't* photograph wars taught you nothing. The second you got to Bosnia, you reverted."

"Yes, well, you, of course, wouldn't begin to understand that." He slammed down his glass on the table. "To you, my work never mattered. All it did was pay the goddamned rent. It would have been so much nicer, of course, if you'd married an ordinary businessman who worked regular hours for a great deal of money and came running home to you at six o'clock every fucking night. To you my work was always an inconvenience—a tiresome irrelevance, some eccentricity on my part. We've been over that a million bloody times, and I don't intend to go over it again."

"Don't imagine I want you to. It makes you angry and defensive—and boring—if you want to know. One can get awfully tired of crusades, Pascal. I certainly did. Take care that Gini doesn't." She looked at him sharply. "You have quarreled, haven't you, Pascal?"

"As a matter of fact, it's over." His face darkened. "No doubt that delights you. Go on. Here's your perfect opportunity. You were always expert at hitting someone when he's down."

"I gave as good as I got," she said. Then: "Look, Pascal, I'm sorry if you and Gini have argued. No doubt you'll make up. This time. And the time after that. You'll make up because you love her a great deal more than you ever loved me." As if gathering her courage, she added:

"She's not *right* for you, Pascal."

She spoke the words just as he reached for the door. Her timing, Pascal thought furiously, had always been good. He turned and gave her a look of contempt.

"You imagine I'm interested in your opinions of Gini? Keep them to yourself."

"As you wish." Her face became set. "But I'm damn well going to say this, Pascal—and you're going to listen for once. What you do *not* need, Pascal, is a woman who's highly sensitive, highly intelligent, whose emotions are very close to the skin—and Gini *is* like that, as even you'd admit." She gave him a cool glance. "In fact, if you want me to be perfectly frank, what you need, Pascal, is someone older, with no interest in a career, and someone with whom you yourself are not passionately in love. You need an *undemanding* wife. Your life makes too many demands. Your work does. Your character does. And too many demands cause strife."

"Oh, fine." He gave her a look of pure dislike. "So I need someone stupid, someone insensitive? Someone I don't love? That's my ideal wife? Point me in the direction of this paragon of dullness. I can't wait."

The reply made Helen laugh; then her face became serious. "I didn't say you couldn't love her, Pascal. I said not being passionately *in* love with her would be an advantage." She hesitated. "Do you imagine I'm passionately in love with Ralph?"

"I haven't considered the matter. Frankly, I couldn't care less."

"Well, I'm not. I love him in a quiet, companionable way—"

"Oh, I'm sure you do. And would you still feel that kind of affection if he were less rich?"

She flushed, hesitated, then, to Pascal's surprise, gave him a rueful look. "Very possibly not. I'm a realist. We have different priorities, you and I, Pascal—we always did. I don't believe it's such a terrible sin to want nice clothes, a nice apartment. And it's not just for my own sake. Ralph is in a position to give Marianne so much. A lovely house in England, ponies, the best schools—with your consent, of course. It will be stable, and it will be privileged. Put your hand on your heart—could you ever have given her that?"

There was a silence then—a long silence during which Helen had time to regret the tone she had used and to appreciate that she might just have made a strategic mistake. Pascal's anger seemed to have gone; his eyes rested on her face; she could sense—and it perturbed her—both disapproval and regret.

"I give her my love," he said at last. "Isn't love the best gift?"

He had spoken very quietly. Helen turned away with a small gesture of distress.

"Yes, well," she said quickly. "You're right. I wouldn't argue with that—who would? Don't make me feel small, Pascal."

"That wasn't my intention."

"No. Maybe not. Oh, dammit—you could always do this. And I thought I was cured. . . ." To his surprise he saw she was suddenly close to tears. She brushed them aside angrily, then steadied her voice. "I shouldn't have said that about Marianne. It was cheap. And as for

Gini—" She hesitated. "I do *try* to be impartial. I do genuinely like her. I do want it to turn out well for you both. I don't want Gini to end up as unhappy as I was. I don't want you to end up miserable and embittered and alone. I'd like this particular fairy tale to have a happy ending . . . in my better moments I do want that."

She looked at him with a wan smile.

"And some of what I said—it wasn't that wide of the mark, was it?"

"No." He shrugged. "Your analysis of my defects—that was accurate, at least. Helen, look—I should go."

"Don't forget tomorrow." She moved toward him. "You have to collect Marianne, and stay with her, and bring her back. You have to provide fatherly moral support—at which you're excellent when you choose."

Pascal gave her a shrewd look in which she detected a glint of amusement, but he made no comment.

"Fine," he said. "I'll see you in the morning. I'll collect Marianne around nine-thirty. Good night."

Pascal had arranged to borrow a friend's apartment in Montparnasse. He stood at its windows, looking down over Paris, thinking back over Helen's words. He could sense desperation very close. Angrily, he opened a bottle of whiskey, poured a large glass, and tossed it back.

He waited, furious with himself. The alcohol refused to kick in. He remained stone-cold sober, and with a cold sobriety he examined his own behavior, the patterns of his life.

He could see now, with a painful clarity, that if Gini had erred, he had erred also. He should not have allowed his obsession with his work to keep him in Bosnia so long; he should have understood the depth of her distress. It had, of course, been convenient for him to be reassured by her letters and telephone calls, to tell himself that since she was coping so well, so much better than he had anticipated, it was acceptable to remain another week, and then a week after that. Working, he had little sensation of time passing. He measured it in terms of the pictures he obtained. To put his personal life on hold, to concentrate entirely on documenting events that would eventually become part of history—indeed, as Helen had said, he had reverted to that state of being too easily and too immediately. He now deeply regretted that. Yet beyond that failing lay another—deeper and less easy to assess. He should have seen Gini's desire for a child; he should have understood its source. In the play and flex of their relationship, it was necessary that he be tempered by her qualities as she was tempered by his. Her reaction to the events they had witnessed, a reaction he could sense but not analyze too effectively, seemed to him peculiarly female; trying to define it, he thought of it as watery, as springing up from the ground, as carrying all before it, as subject to currents, as *flowing*, so that between those she encountered—that boy in Mostar, for instance—and herself, there was and could be no divide: something Pascal could not define, an outflowing of spirit perhaps, passed from these people and rushed into Gini herself.

This was not his way of operating. He had in the past always depended on those virtues which, he supposed, he thought of as male: a capacity for detachment, rationality, the negation of emotion as a tactic for survival. You could not weep and take effective photographs; indignation and anger were of no help when deciding on the technicalities of focus, film, and shutter speed under fire, or under stress. He had, and he knew this, dehumanized himself for at least the duration of his assignments. It was a strategy that had always served him well. Now, reexamining it, it filled him with doubts.

None of this in the end truly mattered, he thought, rising, and beginning to pace. He could unravel his past actions and hers a thousand ways; he could not explain her infidelity, and he doubted very much that Gini could herself. It was an action so out of character and so utterly unforeseen by them both that it still left him feeling concussed with pain and uncertainty, half blind and half deaf.

It did not, of course, prevent his loving her, or even diminish the love he felt for her; if anything, and with an evil ingenuity, the doubts the action engendered made the love more agonizingly intense. Was this event small, or large? He paced again, back and forth, until finally some hope returned, and he could again foresee some future life, many years hence, in which his continued closeness to Gini and hers to him had rendered that infidelity an event of minor importance, and one which had brought them closer, made them more rich in their love, not less.

Instantly gripped by the old conviction, unable anymore to tolerate the patterns he saw in his own life, he reached for the telephone and dialed her hotel. Gini was now in Room 615. She picked up on the third ring.

Their conversation was brief. No apologies, no recriminations, no interrogations on either side. Pascal was afraid of the damage of too many words; also he could hear pain, but possibly alteration, even obstinacy in her voice.

He suggested they meet now. She quietly refused. He suggested she meet him the following morning, and explained his appointment with Marianne. He suggested they meet immediately after that. She refused these proposals as well. They both needed time, she said, then apologized for this cliché. There was a pause; she would be working the following morning, she said.

Pascal looked at the void that had opened up in his life.

"I love you," he said.

He said the words first in English, then repeated them in French.

He expected, or at least hoped, that this must effect a translation. It did not. She gave a small gasp he was unable to interpret, then replaced the receiver.

The following morning, setting off to collect Marianne, Pascal, who had finally forced himself to sleep, was making plans. As soon as Marianne was safely delivered home, he would go straight to Gini's hotel; if Gini was not there he would track her down. Not another day would go by without resolving this.

Reaching the rue de Rennes, he was astonished to find that no search for Gini would be necessary. Turning the corner, he saw her waiting on the sidewalk opposite Helen's apartment building, standing in the same place he had glimpsed her the night before. When she caught sight of him, she ducked back into a doorway. He followed.

To see her was like a blow direct to the heart. It did not occur to him for one second that she could have any purpose here except to see him—but that supposition proved wrong.

She claimed she was there to watch an apartment; she was there to work, and she would prefer it if he would leave. Another man might have argued, but Pascal, who could read her eyes, did not. He turned away, collected Marianne, and left with her, hand in hand.

As Pascal and his daughter rounded the far corner and passed out of sight, Gini watched their departure from the doorway of the apartment building opposite.

Her vision blurred. She retreated a little farther back. When she was calmer, she examined her watch.

It was nine thirty-five when Pascal disappeared around the corner. At nine-forty she finally saw Star for the first time.

He drew up opposite in a large black Mercedes sedan, parked in a restricted zone, and climbed out. He looked up and down the boulevard. Just prior to entering Mathilde Duval's apartment building, he consulted his watch.

CHAPTER 18

At ten on that Wednesday morning, Rowland still believed that this story might take weeks, at best days, to unravel. By ten-thirty he saw just how wrong he was. The countdown had already begun; by the time he realized that, it was just thirty minutes before the start of the Cazarès couture show, and he feared he was too late.

At ten that morning he was on the telephone, still trying to locate Gini, who was not in her room—he had already been down twice to check—who was not in the restaurant, or the lobby, and who was not replying when she was paged. This desk clerk, the third to whom he had spoken, said he wasn't certain, but he thought he had seen her go out.

"When?" Rowland said. "What time?"

Eight, maybe eight-thirty, the desk clerk said, sounding harassed.

Rowland slammed down the telephone. He stared at the wall. He was at once certain that only one person could explain this sudden disappearance: it had to be Pascal Lamartine. It couldn't be work: if it had been work, Gini would have informed him of where she was going, and why. So it had to be Lamartine. He began pacing, then stopped: of course—he saw it now. They must have contacted each other the previous night. Had Lamartine telephoned—perhaps even seen Gini then? Rowland watched the hours he had spent alone, since last seeing Gini, open up. Hour upon hour, and every minute of those hours, was suddenly filled with doubts.

During the time he had spent in conversation with Juliette de Nerval, Gini, as agreed, had returned to her new room here. Rowland, hastening back, had had a brief conversation with her in the doorway of that room, shortly before nine o'clock. Rowland had known he might have gained admittance to that room, and he had wanted admittance—passionately. Watching her pale face, and her wide, dark eyes, Rowland had thought that one touch, one word, might make her relent. Fighting the desire he felt, respecting something in her eyes, sensing that this issue might be forced on another occasion but not now, he had finally withdrawn, and spent much of the night arguing with himself as to whether that restraint had been correct.

At four in the morning some pole in his mind had steadied him, and he had finally, briefly, slept. Now the compass of his mind oscillated violently. North, south, east, west: he rewrote those hours spent alone, plotted them one way, then another. One moment he felt absolutely certain that his final route, and Gini's, must take a certain course; the next, distrusting instinct, he lost faith.

He moved back to the telephone, picked up a notebook, examined a fax sent by his stringer from New Orleans overnight, which seemed to confirm that as far as work was concerned, anyway, his intuition could be relied upon. He thought of telephoning his source in Amsterdam, Sandra Lucas, who had been Esther's closest friend and a good friend to him when he'd needed one, in another country, in another life. When Esther was suddenly gone and he was alone. He began to dial the code for the Netherlands; he replaced the receiver. He dialed the first digit of the extension to Gini's room, and someone began banging at the door to his suite. He swung around at once, certain Gini had come back.

When he opened the door with Gini's name on his lips, Lindsay saw disappointment tighten his face. She forced herself to ignore it. She was in a state of nervous agitation anyway, partly because of the fax she now held in her hand, partly because she was anxious not to be late for the Cazarès show, and partly because, despite all her resolve, she still found it difficult to be unaffected by encounters with Rowland McGuire.

She came into the room fast, looking at her watch and waving the fax at him. She explained the necessary details very quickly. It was probably of no use to him anyway, but for what it was worth, she now knew the surname of Marie-Thérèse, and her brother, Jean-Paul.

"All couture clothes are labeled, Rowland," she said. "Just like other clothes—though the labels are more prestigious, of course. Marie-Thérèse had handled couture clothes. She respected them. She learned from their every little detail. I just *knew* that when she made that dress for Letitia, she'd label it. It was the first real dress she ever made. I knew she'd want to *sign* it. Somewhere on that dress—if I could find the dress, if the dress still existed—I'd find her signature, her *name*. And I have. The curator at the Metropolitan checked for me. The dress was there: Letitia had stipulated it be kept. And there *was* a label—with the name hand embroidered. Here's the name, Rowland—on this fax."

Rowland had read, and was now rereading the fax. She saw him frown, then shake his head.

"What's the matter, Rowland?" She hesitated. "I have to go. I'll be late for Cazarès. . . . Does the name mean something to you?"

"That was very clever. Thank you, Lindsay." He gave a half-smile. "In a hundred years, I'd never have thought of that. . . ."

"Well, you're a man. And not the kind of man who's very interested in labels on clothes." She looked away; she wished Rowland had not smiled at her like that. It was too direct, too devoid of nuance. I am the invisible woman, Lindsay thought, and with more excuses about time, and Markov, she left.

Rowland continued to look at the fax. The name Marie-Thérèse had so proudly sewed onto a dress nearly thirty years before was familiar to him: Rivière—one of the aliases chosen by Star. He could see, obviously he could see, the implications of this: Star might indeed be that lost New Orleans child. But Rowland still did not believe it.

At that moment the telephone rang. It proved to be the hotel's assistant manager speaking in an agitated way. Rowland could just hear the sound of a woman's crying; he stiffened. "Forgive me, Monsieur McGuire," the man said. "But could you come down to my office? We need your assistance."

"Is it urgent?" Rowland began. The man interrupted him.

"Yes, Monsieur McGuire," he said quietly. "I fear it is."

Mina thought the night would never end. She thought her opportunity would never come.

At first, for hour after hour, Star was so *up*: she could feel him soaring and when she looked at his eyes, the pupils were pinpricks, they blazed with blue-black light.

He read the tarot twice. He bathed twice, and showered once, locking her in the bedroom while he did this. When he came back from the shower, it was around two in the morning—Mina couldn't be certain, because her watch had stopped. She kept shaking it and holding it to her ear and watching the hands, but they didn't move. Star saw none of this.

He was laying out clothes on a chair: a black suit, a brand-new white shirt still in its plastic wrapping, a necktie, black socks, black shoes. He polished the shoes three times, then he stood in front of the mirror and looked at himself. He acted the way some women acted in front of a mirror, Mina thought. He held his hair back, then let it flow around his face and shoulders; he turned this way, then that. He smiled at himself in the glass, and Mina, crouched on the bed, thought he looked more beautiful than ever, and utterly insane. He flirted with his own reflection, lowered his thick black lashes over his beautiful eyes, and gave himself a lingering look.

"I could have been a movie star," he said in a matter-of-fact tone. "A really major star—don't you think?"

"Yes, I do," Mina said in a small voice. "I guess you still could . . ."

Star turned, and frowned.

"Oh, no," he said almost kindly. "That's not on the agenda. I know what my future will be. I have it all mapped out."

Then he told her exactly what he was going to do the next morning, and when.

"You see," he said, "the Cazarès collection will last one hour. It begins at eleven and ends at noon. I'll be there, out front, watching it. It's not easy to get in, of course. Invitation only, and those invitations are very carefully checked. There's security, muscle—everywhere. But I can get around that. Maria's been helping me. I had a practice run last fall. It worked like a dream. It will work again, Mina, I know that. The cards know that. . . ."

A dreamy look of pleasure drifted across his face.

"Oh, yes, I'll be there. Just one of the students they admit. In my jeans, with my red scarf, standing with the other students, way back, where you can't see shit. I'll be invisible—until the moment comes. I won't be invisible then, of course. They'll all be watching, all those famous people. All those rich people. Jean Lazare will come out to take his bow, and then . . ." He picked up the gun and caressed it. "Imagine, Mina. I might even get filmed doing it—that would be good. I'd be on every network in the world. Prime time, Mina. The whole world will watch me fire that shot," He smiled back at his own reflection in the mirror. "I want to look good then, I want to look like—an angel of death."

He moved back to the bed, took out some grass and some pills, and began to arrange them in a pattern on the quilt. Mina watched him, too terrified to speak.

Star selected two pills and swallowed them down: one was a White

Dove, the other was speed, he said. This action made Mina even more afraid: it was the first time she had ever seen Star take drugs. He drank several glasses of water, then took her hand in his.

"You're afraid. Don't be." He kissed her forehead. "I'll be coming back for you, Mina—didn't you realize that? When it's all over, I'll come back here, and I'll wash, and fix myself up. There might be blood, you see, and . . ." His vision glazed; he sighed, then shook himself. "So I'll take a shower, then I'll put on my black suit, that new shirt over there, and then, Mina, we're going places, you and I, because I'll be free, you see. Free for the first time in my life."

Mina made a little murmuring sound of agreement, and it seemed to suffice. Minutes later he became restless again. He disappeared into the bathroom, locking her in the bedroom as he left. When he returned, and lay down beside her, she could see that he'd washed yet again, but he hadn't washed well enough: there were traces of some odd white powder around his nostrils and upper lip.

He said he had another pink jewel for her, and Mina tensed. She knew why he was going to make her take that: because it would make her dreamy and dopey, and then it would make her sleep. For hours.

Mina took the pill from him and put it into her mouth. She knew she had to distract him, so she asked him to show her the gun again—and it worked. It took only a second as he rose from the bed. She just had time to spit the pill into her hand, then let her arm hang down over the side of the bed. She pushed the pill under the mattress, and Star never noticed a thing.

He smoked some grass—that very strong grass that made her feel sick, then he made her smoke it too, and when he saw she wasn't inhaling, his eyes got that glittery look. He made her inhale, twisting her left arm up behind her back so the pain was excruciating. He made her smoke almost an entire joint, and she hadn't eaten all day, and she could feel it start to twist about in her head and make her fears very large— huge physical things, like great birds that came swooping down at her, then drove her over some precipice and into a pit.

She lay beside him, trying to fight these birds off. Beside her, Star was busy; he was doing something she did not want to watch. She could hear him undo his zipper. She could hear his hands move, feel body movements, hear the alteration in his breath. She could sense stealth, and also desperation. Finally, when she could bear it no longer, and the birds had retreated for a while, she opened her eyes cautiously and looked down, under her lids.

He was erect now. He knew, it seemed, how to arouse himself. As she watched, she saw him take up the gun again and felt a dart of pure fear; then she saw that the gun was to be part of this ritual. He stroked his penis with the barrel of the gun; his flesh quivered. Mina shut her eyes tight. There were more furtive movements, then his body jerked sharply: *Christ,* he said, *Christ . . .*

Mina wanted to be sick. She was shaking with fear and disgust and pity and love. She thought, I must wait; I must wait.

It was dawn when her chance came. She could hear the birds outside begin singing; she watched a thin gray light begin to edge the curtains. It must be seven-thirty, perhaps nearing eight. Star's eyes were closed, his breathing regular. She inched toward the edge of the bed; just as she was about to rise, his hand shot out and gripped her wrist.

"Star," she said in a whisper. "I don't feel too good. It's that grass. I have to be sick. . . ."

She thought he might insist on coming with her to the bathroom, but he did not. He turned and gave her a long, still look with his blue-black eyes. He looked into her and through her, and Mina thought: he *knows*; he knows I'm going to betray him.

He couldn't have known, though, because he let her go. She padded out to the little bathroom; she was still dressed, but her feet were bare. She didn't dare to take her shoes—then he would certainly suspect.

In the bathroom she felt the waves of nausea pick her up and toss her forward and back. She was sweating badly; she was terrified she might pass out. She vomited several times, and began to feel a little better. She stole a look over her shoulder, then turned on all the faucets in the bath: almost at once, and just as she had hoped, the pipes began to rattle and cough. She hoped the plumbing was noisy enough to drown the sound of her escape.

She fled down the stairs, expecting him to shout, grab her from behind at any second. She fought with the bolts and the locks on the front door, and when it opened, half fell into the street. She began running, at random, first this way, then that, until she was in a maze of small streets and was sure at last that he could not be pursuing her. She leaned against a wall, tears streaming down her face. She fought to control her own breathing, but she couldn't seem to get enough air. She took great gulps of cold air, then she realized she was about to be sick again, so she bent over the gutter and coughed up bile.

A woman was passing with a little dog on a leash; the woman gave her a look of disgust and averted her face.

All Mina could think about then was calling home. She could hear her father's voice. But when she finally found a telephone, she couldn't make the operator understand: she tried again and again, wasting time.

Then another idea came to her that had been there at the back of her mind all along. That man and woman she had overheard in the rue St. Séverin: she knew the man's name because the woman had used it. She knew the name of their hotel—the St. Vincent. Mina was sure she also knew who they were: she'd figured it out during the night. They were private detectives hired by her father. For all she knew, her father might be with them in Paris right now, looking for her, searching for her.

Mina had no idea where she was, or where the St. Vincent was.

She kept stopping passersby to ask them, but when they saw her clothes and her bare feet and her dyed hair, and when they smelled the vomit and saw the tears, their faces closed up. They didn't want to know; they'd start turning away, and when she tried to catch hold of them and plead, they'd get angry and shake her off.

She could have gone to a policeman, of course. She saw two as she staggered then ran the last few yards of a street called the boulevard St. Michel; they were standing in the wide, busy street beyond, which was filled with traffic. She looked at the river beyond that. A bus hissed past her, very close. Mina jumped back, terrified. No, she thought, not the police. She didn't want Star to be harmed, arrested; she wanted him to be stopped and helped. She wanted him to be taken to a doctor, to some quiet, soothing, hospital place.

No, not the police, she thought, and scurried across the street to the bridge, weaving between the hooting cars. Even then, when she was on the bridge, she didn't see it. A woman she stopped, a woman kinder than the rest, turned and pointed it out.

"*Mais, il est là,*" she said. "*En face, vous voyez . . .*"

And then, seeing Mina had not understood even this simple statement, she took her by the shoulders and pointed. And Mina saw it—a huge gray castle of a place: the St. Vincent; the name was written in curly bronze writing, huge letters, just above its entrance.

It all took so long, Mina thought. Every second seemed a minute, every minute an hour. Even when she was finally safe in some assistant manager's office, even when the man called Rowland finally appeared, she could not seem to make him understand.

"Oh, *hurry,*" she cried, "you must hurry. He's going in as a student, that's what he plans. He has his admission ticket, he showed it to me.

And he's ill. He didn't hurt me, you mustn't think that. But he needs a doctor, and—"

She knew what the problem was: it was herself. She could not stop shaking or crying. The man called Rowland was kind: she could see he was trying to calm her and trying to understand, but all the information she had to give him was tangled up in her head.

The manager man seemed less angry now and sent for some water. The Englishman helped her into a chair and took her hand in his.

"Sip the water slowly," he said. "Take your time, Mina. . . ."

"There is no time—" She sprang to her feet. "We have to be quick. It's *today*. It's this *morning*. He has the gun, and the ammunition. Look, *look* . . ."

That was the moment, she thought later, when the Englishman began to understand; when she pulled out the gun catalogue which she had taken when Star was washing the previous night.

She pulled it out, unrolled it, flourished it in his face. Her hands were trembling and her voice was unsteady, but he was beginning to understand: she watched the realization dawn in his eyes:

"This is what he's going to use . . ." She stabbed her fingers at the picture of a gun. "He'll wait—until this Lazare man takes his bow—that's what he said. Then he's— He won't really do it, I'm sure he won't. It's just that he's *sick*. He says he'll move down the aisle from the back, and— He doesn't hate them, Maria and Jean Lazare. He says he does, but he wept when she died. It was the night she died that he bought this. . . ."

Rowland looked down at the gun she was indicating to him. Seconds slipped by as he reshaped the confusion of her sentences, and the details of Star's scenario finally slipped into place. The Cazarès collection was due to begin in under half an hour. The gun concerned was a black Beretta 93R, firing fifteen 9mm rounds per magazine. The ammunition to which she was pointing was a blue GECO hollow bullet. It contained a plastic core, which displaced when fired, so that as the bullet hit its target, it commenced a tumbling trajectory specifically designed to cause maximum tissue damage. With this ammunition, even a poor marksman could effect certain death.

"Mina," he said quietly. "These gun magazines. How many of them did Star buy? Just one—or more than that?"

"Five." She did not understand the importance of the question, Rowland could see. Her answer was little more than a whisper. "Five. He showed me how they slot in the handle. He laid them out for me, all five of them on the bed."

Rowland turned to look at the assistant manager. His face was now ashen. His eyes flicked to the clock on the wall: its second hand ticked. Less than half an hour, Rowland thought; an auditorium filled with the rich and famous, with television cameras, with the assembled world press. *Star:* why had he not understood the implications of that chosen name?

Reaching in his pocket, pulling out a card, he thought: an automatic weapon, five magazines each containing fifteen rounds, seventy-five bullets in total. . . . He had a brief grim vision of possible carnage. He pressed the card into the manager's trembling hands.

"Call that number," he said. "Now. At once. Get me Luc Martigny. Get the police."

The Mercedes that Star had been driving was a very expensive car. It was a 540i. Gini glanced into its pale leather interior. It was presumably stolen; moving out of sight of any windows above, she noted its license plates.

For one moment, as the car had first pulled up and she watched the young man emerge from it, she had not realized it was Star. The man getting out of this vehicle had been wearing a black suit, a white shirt and tie; he did have long black hair, but it was drawn back from his face and tied at the nape of his neck. He resembled some young, successful executive from one of the less straitlaced professions: he could have been in advertising, or have been a record producer—something like that. Then, as he closed the car door, she saw him full-face and her doubts disappeared. Star—movie-star good looks, just as the travelers had described him.

Her hunch had been that if Star did visit Mathilde Duval regularly, he must—sooner or later—turn up. Well, she had been right, but the timing surprised her. Juliette de Nerval had told Roland that Madame Duval was to be collected by limousine at ten-thirty that morning, taken to the Cazarès show, and brought back. So why was he here now?

Mathilde Duval's apartment—again according to Rowland—was on the top floor of this building. Gini glanced up at its ranked windows, then frowned at the Mercedes. To park the car so flagrantly in a restricted zone suggested Star did not intend to stay long. She felt alarm then: Madame Duval was elderly and infirm—and she lived alone. Gini hesitated, then ran up the portico steps.

Her way was barred by massive locked doors. Peering through their glass panes, she could see through into a large marble-floored lobby dominated by a magnificent bronze-colored cage elevator. The lobby and the elevator were identical to those in Helen's building. As in Helen's building, there was no sign of a concierge guarding the lobby, which was deserted and silent. Gini wondered if this building was occupied mainly by those rich enough to own several homes, and whether, as in Helen's building, the majority of the apartments here were often left empty for months at a time. She pressed her face against the glass. She could see the cables and counterweights; the elevator itself was on another floor.

She looked at the battery of bells and intercoms set into the wall next to her. She pressed two of those bells, for the other two apartments on the tenth floor, and obtained no reply. She began trying bells on lower floors; with her sixth attempt she was lucky. A woman answered, sounding impatient. Using a strong American accent, and speaking in what she hoped was convincingly poor French, Gini explained rapidly that she was staying with friends here. They'd given her the key to their apartment, but not the pass key to the front door.

"Oh, quelle bêtise—ces idiots . . ." The woman embarked on a brief diatribe as to the annoyance of this situation, which happened on the average of four times a week. Then, after a few more wan pleas from Gini, she did what no inhabitant of an American city would have done—pressed the buzzer. Gini pushed back the doors and went in.

She moved toward the elevator shaft and looked up, feeling a prickle of fear run the length of her spine. The floor indicator arrow was pointing at ten; she could just see the base of the elevator high above her. She could hear nothing at all.

Suddenly, she froze. The elevator had whirred into life. She watched the cables, the counterweights begin to move. Star was coming down.

Wait, she thought; act like a resident. Just stand by the elevator—what could be more natural? Wait, and see if he comes down alone.

He did not come down alone. A woman who could have been only Mathilde Duval was standing next to him, supported by his arm. As the cage came to a rest, and Gini could see the old woman through the bars, she felt her heart flood with pity and fear for her. She was tiny and obviously frail. She was dressed with evident painstaking care, in an all-black outfit that might have been fashionable forty years before. She was wearing new black gloves, and her hands were trembling: Gini could not tell if this was caused by infirmity or fear. As Star reached for the doors, the old woman lifted her face and Gini tensed: Mathilde Duval, she realized, had acute glaucoma: her eyes were blue-white, milky, almost opaque.

"Bonjour, madame. Monsieur," Gini said as the gates opened. She gave the old woman a nod of polite greeting. Mathilde Duval did not respond or even turn her head. Virtually blind, Gini thought—also deaf.

She could feel Star's eyes boring into her. Her mind was still flashing with uncertainty: speak, or remain silent? Do nothing now, or intervene?

Mathilde Duval herself made intervention imperative. As she stepped out into the lobby, she staggered and almost fell. Star's arm tightened around her. He hauled her back onto her feet and tried to hasten her progress.

The old woman crept forward a few more steps, then came to a halt. She pressed her hand against her chest.

"Un moment, Christophe," Gini heard her say. "Tu marches trop vite pour moi . . . Souviens-toi, je suis vieille maintenant."

Star ignored the plea. He looked as if he would drag her out of the lobby if necessary. Gini heard him give a low curse. He began to tug at the woman's arm. Gini stepped forward.

"Madame Duval?" she said. "Vous êtes malade? Je peux vous aider? Un moment, monsieur . . ."

Mathilde Duval's lips were blue; she was breathing with difficulty. Gini looked up, met Star's unwavering gaze. She began on a new plea: there was a bench, perhaps if Madame Duval sat down for a little while? She saw Star hesitate before he complied. He looked at the woman's lips, and then helped Gini to assist her to the bench. Gini sat down beside her; Star drew back.

Taking Madame Duval's hand in hers, Gini began making further suggestions—anything that might buy her time. Perhaps a doctor should be called? Perhaps it was unwise for Madame Duval to venture outside on such a day, when it was beginning to rain, and bitterly cold. . . . The suggestions bought her about thirty seconds. Star's eyes never left her face once.

"You're not French. You're American, right?" He was reaching into his pocket. He took out a small container of pills.

"Oh, yes, I am." Gini gave him a quick glance. "I didn't realize—listen, she really doesn't look too well. Her lips are blue, and—"

"Do you live in this building?"

He was taking one tiny pill from the container, his eyes still intent on her face. His voice, Gini thought, his odd, low, attractive yet unidentifiable voice was just as described.

"What? Oh, yes—I do."

It seemed the safe answer. She could hardly claim to be visiting, yet recognize Madame Duval. Star seemed to accept the reply anyway.

"She has angina," he said in even tones. "She's eighty-five years old. She just needs one of these pills. She dissolves them under her tongue. They're magic. In a couple of minutes she'll be fine."

He slipped the tiny pill between Madame Duval's lips as he said this. She gave a sightless little smile of gratitude, her milky eyes turned to a space two feet to the side of him. Star straightened.

He said: "Show me your key."

"I'm sorry?" Gini looked up at him. His face betrayed no emotion whatsoever.

"Your key. You live here, so I guess you have a key, right?"

"Oh, for heaven's sake ..." Gini rose. "What is this? Of course I have a key. I live on the sixth floor. Look, I really think we should call a doctor. ..."

"I agree." He smiled. "Let's go right up to your apartment and call one now. I'll come with you."

Gini felt fear, and she knew her fear and her indecision showed in her face.

Then, he did not hesitate. He gave a small frown and put his hand in the pocket of his black suit.

"Oh, shit," he said in a mild way. "The cards said to expect the unexpected. This morning. That's what they said. I guess they were right."

He spoke in a distant, unemotional tone. He gave a small sigh, then a shrug, and took out a gun. He lifted it with steady hands and an expression of slight irritation on his face. Gini looked at the gun, which was now pointing directly at her chest, from a range of three feet.

"Look, please ..." she began. "I don't understand. I just wanted to help Madame Duval. ..."

Star was not listening. He frowned.

"Can you drive?" he said.

Gini was trying to obey all the rules. Avoid eye contact; speak reasonably; do not show fear.

"Yes, I can drive, but—listen—"

She stopped. She realized she had just made a foolish admission and Star had noticed her reaction; he was extremely quick.

"That's okay." He sounded almost kind. "You gave me the right answer. If you'd said you couldn't drive, I'd have had to shoot you now. I don't really want to do that yet. It could make a noise; a mess. It could fuck up my plans. ... I have to cover every eventuality, you see. I have to be flexible, resourceful. I was born that way—so that's cool. Now, walk out to that Mercedes outside. It's not locked. Get in the driver's seat. I'll get in back with Madame Duval."

He gave another small frown; he looked, Gini thought, like someone planning some normal daily routine, faintly irritated when perceiving some potential minor hitch.

"Are you smart?" he asked. He released the safety catch on the gun with a small click. Gini stared at the gun; she swallowed.

"I'm not rash, if that's what you mean. . . ."

"Fine. Then don't do anything dumb—will you? I mean—don't start screaming or trying to run away. When I give you the keys, start the engine and drive—drive really well. Otherwise, I'll fire. Then Madame Duval won't be troubled by her angina anymore."

The old woman seemed to catch the sound of her own name. Some color had returned to her face, and for the first time, she looked up. She lifted her blue-white eyes and smiled. Gini helped her to rise; Madame Duval began to murmur. Crossing the lobby at a snail's pace, she told her dear Christophe that he was a good, kind boy to be so patient.

As they reached the sidewalk, Gini looked along the street. It was deserted. Her hands had begun to shake. She opened the driver's door and slid into the seat. She looked at the seat, then the floor by the pedals, and gave a low moan.

Star and Madame Duval settled themselves behind her. The old woman took out a rosary. Gini, who did not dare to look around, could hear the click of the beads. Her mouth was dry with fear; as she had climbed into the car she had noticed something: there was a sticky brownish substance splashed on the leather of the seat; there was a pool of it, still wet, by her feet.

"Yeah. It's blood." Star had leaned forward. He was just touching the barrel of the gun against the back of her neck. "You know how many people I've killed this morning? Three. The third was the chauffeur. It's his blood on the seat. His body's in the trunk right now. Start the engine, drive to the end of this boulevard, then make a right."

Gini wondered if she could flood the engine. She depressed the accelerator hard, and pumped, before she turned the ignition key. Star laughed.

"That won't work. Not with a Mercedes. You ever drive one before? They're the best. My father likes the best. Mercedes. Rolls-Royces. He has four—did you know that?"

The engine purred into life. Gini hesitated, then pulled out carefully and drove along the boulevard. Behind her, the rosary beads continued to click.

"She's not praying for you. Or me," Star said in a conversational way. "She's praying for my mother. My mother's dead. She died very suddenly Monday afternoon. Took too many little pills, I think. That's what Mathilde says. She was writing a letter to me, and she'd taken three of her special little pills—which was a pretty dumb thing to do, of course. So she never finished the letter. She collapsed. Went into convulsions. It took a while, Mathilde says. Not too pretty. But then, I guess death never is."

When Gini did not reply, he seemed irritated. Glancing up into the rearview mirror, she saw him frown again.

"My mother was a very famous woman," he said in an insistent tone. "World famous. You'll know her name. Maria Cazarès." He paused. "Make a left at the next intersection. Who are you? Police—some kind of police? A private eye? Did Mina's father hire you, maybe?"

"No. I'm a journalist," Gini said, trying to keep her voice steady. "I've—been investigating Mina's disappearance." Where was little Mina now, she thought wildly. What had he done with her?

"Oh, yeah? And Cassandra's death? Too bad about that. I saw it in the paper. Mina doesn't know, of course," he said. "A journalist. That's nice. You write for American papers?"

"Sometimes. But I live in London. So I work for a British newspaper there. The *Correspondent*."

"Oh, I know that paper!" He sounded pleased. "That's an important paper, right? Like the *Times*?"

"Yes. You could say that."

"Hey. That's good. Make a right here." He was smiling at her now, in the rearview mirror. His smile made Gini's blood run cold. "You know, just for a minute back there in the lobby—I was puzzled. Because the cards told me to expect the unexpected, like I said—but they said it would be something good, something useful. . . ." He frowned again. "You know the real reason I didn't shoot you back there? Nothing to do with the driving. I lied a little then. It was because I was waiting. I mean, obviously, you were the surprise—and at first it didn't seem too positive. It looked like you might really fuck up all my plans. But I trusted the cards, you see? And I was right to trust the cards. Because you're an accident, sure, but you're also exactly what I need. Slow up. Make a left here."

Gini could scarcely hold the steering wheel. She knew she was sweating with tension and hoped he could not see that. She could still feel the barrel of the gun on the back of her neck. He was moving the barrel up and down in a kind of caress. Gini was very afraid of guns. In Bosnia and elsewhere she had seen at close quarters what modern weapons could do. She tried to make her voice calm.

"Why am I what you need?" she said.

"Why?" He sounded astonished. "You can't guess? Because you can write my story, of course. You can *explain*. I'll give you an exclusive if you like. You can syndicate it—worldwide. That's what happens, right?"

"Yes. That does happen. On big stories. Occasionally."

"Oh, this will be a very big story." He sighed. "When this story breaks, I'm going to be famous. A celebrity. People will know my name, here, right across Europe, in America. You're going to help make me a star."

Gini was beginning to understand. She could see where he was taking her now, in every sense. They were now just off the rue du Faubourg St. Honoré; she could see the famous *hôtel particulier* that was the Cazarès headquarters. She could see the building immediately adjacent to its courtyard, where the collection would be shown. She could see the satellite dishes, the TV crews, the crowd of fashionably dressed people waiting for admittance, milling back and forth on the sidewalk. She hesitated, then said quietly, "A star? Star is one of the names you use, isn't it? Sometimes you call yourself Star?"

"That's right. You can call me that if you like—you know, when we're just talking, when you interview me. But when you write the story up, you have to use my real name, the name on my birth certificate: Christophe Rivière. Slow—slow down. Make a right. Stop in front of those mews gates."

Gini did as he commanded. She looked at the tall iron gates with the name *Cazarès* on a brass plaque attached to them. Beyond the gates was a narrow courtyard, and a line of twenty garages that once would have been stables and carriage houses for the great house behind which they were set. Star lifted a small electronic device, and the gates opened. He told her to drive to the end garage, where, with the same device, he opened a steel plate door. She drove in, stopped, and switched off the engine.

The lockup was small. There was just room for Star to help Madame Duval out. He drew the old woman to one side of the entrance and instantly returned.

Gini was sitting very still, staring in front of her. She knew what he was going to do. He was going to lock the doors. He was going to close and lock the doors and leave her here with a dead man in the trunk.

"Please," she began in a low voice as he returned to her open window. "Please don't lock me in here."

"It won't be for long," he said in reassuring tones. "I'll come back for you. Give me the car keys. Right, now, listen. There's no car phone—I ripped it out. You can't move the car. The doors are two-inch steel plate—high spec. No one's going to hear you if you shout or hammer on the doors, because the other Cazarès cars are all out, lined up in the rue

St. Honoré, waiting to collect the big names when the show is over. So no one's coming back here for an hour and a half, at least—except me, of course. I won't be long. Just wait until I do what I have to do. It's something I've wanted to do for a long time, something I've been planning for a long time. Over a year now. Ever since I realized . . ."

He hesitated for the first time. The barrel of the gun wavered fractionally. Gini saw an expression of anxiety come into his beautiful eyes.

"And if I'm a bit stressed out then—don't let that frighten you, okay? It's just something that happens to me. I get this headache, right in back behind my eyes. I'll show you what to do. You just have to kind of stroke me. Then it goes away. Also, I have some pills, some special pills. I might take one of them, maybe—to celebrate, you know?" He smiled. "I might give you one. We'll see. Now—you have a watch? I'll be back around eleven-twenty, eleven-thirty at the latest. What's your name?"

"Genevieve. People call me Gini. Star—please . . ." Gini wondered if she threw the door open very quickly, whether it would take him by surprise; knock the gun from his hand. She was afraid to risk it; the gun was two inches from her face. "Look—why don't you let me come with you? I'd write a better story that way."

He looked uncertain, and for a moment Gini thought her suggestion had worked. Then he shook his head. In the same low, terrifyingly reasonable voice, he explained.

"No, I can't do that," he said. "At Cazarès, they have these people on the doors, front and back. Really heavy security. I can get in with Mathilde, that's all fixed. But they wouldn't let you in, Gini. They don't know you, you see? Eleven-twenty—okay? Time means everything to free men."

He had closed the doors before she was out of the car. As she reached them, she heard a lock and bolts engage. The garage was now pitch black. She felt in the dark for the outline of the car, and her hand rested on what she knew was the trunk. She froze, listening. She could hear movement, she was sure she could hear movement from inside that trunk. A shifting, stealthy sound. She backed away with a moan of fear. Then she flung herself at the doors and pulled at them. They did not budge an inch. From the car came a trickling sound.

Gini crouched down close to the doors. She could hear Star leading Madame Duval away. He was telling her, with an impatient edge to his voice, to hurry just a little. She wouldn't want to be late, would she, he suggested, for her dear Maria's great day?

Gini waited. She heard the footsteps depart. She knew what she had to do, but it took minutes to steel herself. She had to open the trunk of the car; she had to do that.

Eventually, with shaking hands, she did so. As the trunk opened, a courtesy light came on and she could see inside the compartment clearly. She immediately wished it had not. She gave a stifled cry and jerked back. The thing in the trunk moved. She pressed her hands over her mouth. It was very hard not to scream, and even harder not to slam the lid shut.

CHAPTER 19

"What's going on?" Markov said, swinging around and trying to peer through the press of people crowding them from the rear.

Lindsay had tight hold of his arm. They had nearly reached the entrance doors to the great salon where Cazarès's last collection would be shown. All around them was the decorum of classical architecture—the lovely roofs, windows, and entablature of seventeenth-century design at its most graceful; all around them was chaos—the thrustings and yellings and hysteria of the crowd. Up ahead Lindsay could see dark-suited executives and muscular security men. In front of them and behind them was an angry surge of humanity, hell-bent on getting through the doors. Ahead of her now she could glimpse three celebrated fashion editors; the head buyer for Bloomingdale's; a French film star, long a patron of Cazarès and famed for her enigmatic beauty and chic; a rock star of international renown, together with his fifth wife, then a herd of indeterminate shoulders and heads and backs and waving arms. White invitation cards flashed. It never ceased to amaze her that everyone, famous or unknown, powerful or humble, rich or poor, elderly or young, was put through this. Markov said that all the couturiers cultivated these fights for admittance, fostered the panic, and intentionally humiliated those they sought to impress. "They want the adrenaline pumping," he said. "And the fear—that you could be the Queen of

England and you *still* might not get in. They want us all down on our knees, Lindy, pleading to be one of the Elect. That way our critical faculties get shafted before we're inside the door. They've abrogated our power. It stinks."

Lindsay agreed with this, yet she still resigned herself to the process. She had now been trapped in this manipulated hysteria for the past thirty-five minutes. Her body was sore with being pummeled and pushed. Her head already ached. She could hardly breathe—and when she got inside the salon and finally made it to the sanctum of the front row, she still wouldn't be able to breathe, for heat and bodies and scent. But she wouldn't mind. Her own status would have been confirmed by precisely the same people who had been humiliating her and everyone else—and that she valued, or always had in the past. Now, thinking of comments Rowland McGuire had made on this process, she despised herself.

Even so, she could feel the panic rising, the sensation that the frantic crowd behind might at any moment trample her underfoot. Just let me get *in*, let me get seated, she thought.

"Well, what do you know? It's the fuzz." Markov was still craning his neck. He removed his dark glasses briefly in order to obtain a better look. "Storm troopers yet. It's the GIGN, Lindy—look."

Lindsay risked the briefest glance around and was astonished. Through the gaps in the swelling crowd behind her she could see the familiar and menacing black vans pulling up, blocking the street beyond the courtyard. Arguments had broken out; attempts were being made to move the clustering Cazarès Mercedes and the TV crew trucks. A siren whooped, then stopped. The black doors at the back of the GIGN vans were opening, disgorging helmeted black-garbed men. Someone behind her gave her a violent shove.

Lindsay almost fell, then recovered her balance. She clung to Markov.

"What on earth . . . I thought they used them only for riots— antiterrorist stuff?"

"Don't argue with them, that's for sure." Markov gave a little smile. "Seriously bad news. *Not* renowned for their sense of humor. And positively bristling with arms. Quite delectable though—don't you think, Lindy? All that black leather? Those wicked fascist boots?"

"What are they doing? And stop showing off . . ."

Markov, here today in his capacity as a celebrity, gave another small smile. He always played to the crowd, and his comments had been made in a loud voice.

"I rather think," he said more quietly, "that they're *filtering* people out. They're making for the animal pen right now. No, don't look—we're nearly inside."

They surged through to the entrance doors. Beyond, Lindsay could see rows of gold chairs, banks of cameras, the glitter of lights. Black-dressed female Cazarès minions were patrolling the sanctum, spraying scent from cut-glass bottles. She smelled spring, the scent of narcissus and hyacinth: *L'Aurore*. She glanced back one last time. The animal pen was a small area, chain-link-fenced, off to the side of the courtyard. It was crammed with the young, the poor, and the impassioned: art students, fashion students, fans; a few might possess admission tickets, most would not. Every year, at every collection, some of them would manage using guile, deception, theft, forgery, or sometimes force, to get in. Lindsay found their desperation frightening. It was like her own, but she felt—irrationally—that it was worse.

And Markov was right, she saw; it was these people who seemed the focus of the attentions of the black-garbed special police. She could just see a tall, dark, long-haired young man being yanked to the side. He was screaming abuse, being pulled by the hair. As she was propelled forward through the entrance doors, he gave a sudden scream of pain; then his yells stopped.

It was past eleven; even at Cazarès, where events were usually organized with near-military precision, the collection would begin late. The salon was still less than half full, its space a bewilderment of color and movement, of air kisses and embraces and shrieks. The usual arguments were breaking out about seating; the usual accusations and miniaturized fights. At Chanel yesterday, two exquisitely dressed women had come to blows; they had hit each other with their identical quilted, gold-chained Chanel bags. Both Markov and Lindsay had enjoyed this.

It was as always—and yet it was not as always. Once she was seated, and as the great room began to fill, Lindsay realized there were police inside as well as outside—not GIGN, but plainclothes police. They were moving along the back rows, and they had a dog handler with them. She stared in astonishment and craned her neck. It was difficult to see exactly what was going on because the seating was tiered and the lights dazzled her eyes, but there was obviously a serious security alert. She could feel a new tension in the room, a buzz of rumor and alarm. It spread from the photographers clustered around the end of the runway up and through the room. She caught little whispered clutches of words and sudden nervous glances: *bomb, terrorist threat, sniffer dogs.*

"Well, they don't like the hoi polloi," Markov said, pointing. "Watch the back row, Lindy. That's the second one they've yanked out."

Lindsay narrowed her eyes, shading them from the lights, and watched another young man being hustled away. He was tall, with long, dark hair, dressed in black jeans; he was wearing a red bandanna around his neck.

The collection finally began half an hour late. By then, the activities in the back row had almost ceased. The room was settling, and expectation was in the air. Attention was returning to the runway. Gradually, the room hushed. Lindsay glanced up at that back row once more. Whatever had been the cause for alarm, precautions were still being taken. At the very back of the ranked tiers, and at intervals down the central aisle that led to the photographers' pit, were police operatives. A solid line of flak-jacketed black-helmeted men ringed the rear tier. She gave a small shiver, then glanced down at her program. Maria Cazarès's last three designs would punctuate the show. One would be the first shown; one would mark its midpoint; the third would be the collection's finale.

Lazare, who had always come out just before Maria Cazarès herself and stood next to her while she took her bow, would on this occasion appear last of all, and, of course, alone.

The lights dimmed; there was a sudden and glorious burst of Bach. Lindsay and Markov lifted their faces to the runway. Just before the first model appeared—Quest, swinging along at top speed, glaring at audience and cameras with her customary disdain, half-veiled, hatted, dressed in a magnificent confection of eye-blindingly assertive fuchsia-violet—just before this Lindsay thought she glimpsed the figure of Rowland McGuire. She caught sight of him for an instant, standing in an aisle on the far side, talking to a man who might have been police. Then the music and the movement and the loveliness of this Cazarès dress distracted her attention. A small sigh of collective delight rose from the room. When Lindsay next remembered to look across at the aisle, Rowland was nowhere in sight.

She focused on clothes, and the details of the clothes. She made her customary quick sketches and notes. She felt excitement, nostalgia, sadness, and elation begin to fill the air.

Afterward, when it was all over, both she and Markov would have to admit until the very end that they had heard and sensed nothing.

Quest knew; one or two of the other models knew; the *directrice* backstage knew; the police knew. But this was theater, and the show went on—as Lazare and Maria Cazarès would have wished.

Jean Lazare first saw the young man by Mathilde Duval's side at eleven-ten. He was first brought to Lazare's attention by Juliette de Nerval, who explained that he was Madame Duval's great-nephew, and that the old woman, tearful and nervous, had telephoned her early that morning, insisting that she could not face this sad occasion alone, and saying that her beloved great-nephew had traveled up from the country especially to assist her at this time of trial. Without him Mathilde would not attend, so Juliette had given her reluctant consent. She hoped, she said, eyeing Lazare nervously, that she had been correct.

Lazare gave the young man a long, considering, and cold look that finally, to Juliette's puzzlement, became one of amusement. Yes, yes, he said, moving away; of course her decision had been correct. Perhaps someone would show the young man and Madame Duval to her usual room, and her usual seat?

Juliette, flustered by the sudden security alert, had hastened to do this. Both Madame Duval and the young man were, at present, in the corner of the huge, chaotic room in which the models made their lightning changes. They were facing an eddying sea of makeup artists, hairdressers, dressers, and models. They were hemmed in by racks of clothes, by scurrying assistants. The air was rank with scent and abrasive with hair lacquer. Madame Duval, her handsome great-nephew's hand supporting her elbow, looked dazed and faint.

Juliette managed to persuade them both back down the maze of corridors behind this dressing room, to the small, quiet room where Madame Duval had always stayed with Maria Cazarès. She settled them there, made sure Madame Duval was comfortable, and that the video screen showing the runway was well positioned for her. She made sure that tea, coffee, canapés, and drinks were available—not that Madame Duval ever touched any of them—and then rushed away to another part of the building, and the next crisis with these impossible, alarmist, and very stupid police.

At eleven twenty-five Madame Duval's great-nephew was brought to Jean Lazare's attention a second time. On this occasion it was Lazare's senior aide, Christian Bertrand, who raised the subject. Lazare was, as expected, in the dressing room, the one calm person in a surging ocean of chaos. He was standing next to Quest, a model Bertrand disliked, who was looking astonishingly beautiful in an astonishingly beautiful dress. Fuchsia-violet: worn with a collar of amethysts three inches deep. Lazare was personally adjusting the veil to Quest's romance of a hat. He wanted it lower by two millimeters. He turned away from Quest only when he had achieved this.

"Monsieur Lazare." Christian Bertrand spoke in a low voice. "I'm sorry to interrupt you with this, at such a moment . . ."

"Yes?"

"—But in view of the situation, the security out front. I was told, Monsieur Lazare, to take every precaution, and—the young man with Madame Duval. He appears to have left her alone, sir. And no one knows where he is."

"I know where he is." Lazare gave Bertrand one of his black-ice looks. "He is in my office, waiting for me. I shall join him shortly. Attend to more urgent matters than Madame Duval's nephew, if you would be so good. The collection begins in"—he checked his watch—"three and a half minutes. If it begins one half minute after that, consider yourself relieved of your post."

"Yes, Monsieur Lazare."

Bertrand backed away. The towering figure of Quest, three inches taller than Bertrand in high heels, moved past him. From here, just backstage, the noise of the audience was muted, soft, as seductive as the sound of sea in a shell. The models were ready, the minions were ready, everyone was ready. Bach burst forth, trumpets proclaimed elation, confidence, magic, and success. Quest mounted the steps, braced herself, moved forward, and disappeared out to the runway beyond. Waves of reaction mounted and broke. Bertrand looked at his watch. It was eleven-thirty precisely. He began to make his way back to his office, where he would watch the show on closed-circuit television. As he left the dressing room, he saw to his surprise that Jean Lazare, who always remained there supervising each last tiny detail of each outfit, was also leaving. Lazare turned in the direction of his own office, near the exit, at the end of a long corridor. This departure from tradition seemed to please him; he left the room, Bertrand noted, with an expression of relief on his face.

Lazare's office here, like his office in the main Cazarès building, was austere. It was also, as were all his workplaces, soundproofed. Entering the room and closing the padded door behind him, he wondered if the young man who was claiming to be Madame Duval's great-nephew had realized this.

He was seated, much as Lazare had expected, in a chair facing Lazare's large, plain, black desk. His eyes were fixed on the twenty-four-inch video monitor with its view of the runway and a beautiful, arrogant, fuchsia-dressed Quest. As Lazare entered, he glanced around, and then rose politely to his feet. He was, Lazare thought, disconcerted. He had not expected Lazare to be here now, and he had not expected it to be this easy, perhaps.

Lazare looked at the young man, who was taller than he was by six inches at least. He noted the black suit—he, too, was wearing black—and the carefully pressed white shirt. The shoes were newly polished, the tie was discreet. The young man, who had a beautiful face, began on some quick apology and explanation for his presence. Lazare cut him off.

"I know why you're here," he said. With a sigh he moved to a side table, poured himself a drink. He offered one to the young man, who refused with a quick shake of the head. Lazare could see that he was almost certainly on something: his pupils were narrowed to pinpricks; he radiated a peculiar tension, like light. White Doves? Lazare thought, then reconsidered: no, probably not. It could be cocaine, or speed—and if so, the young man had better be careful. His judgment would be impaired, his reflexes slowed.

He took his brandy glass with him to the desk, sat down, and looked at the young man. He wondered if he would be cold or impassioned, slow or quick. He might relish drama, Lazare thought—he looked the type. At this he felt impatience, weariness, and a certain contempt.

"Do you know who I am?" the young man demanded with that desire to take the initiative Lazare found tiresome in the young.

"I imagine you are not Madame Duval's great-nephew," he replied. He took a sip of the brandy. "I also imagine you're going to tell me who you truly are. Make it brief."

The young man did not like that reply. Indeed, a taste for dramatics, Lazare thought, watching him: his response was to remove a gun from his pocket and place it, under his hand, on the desk.

Lazare glanced down at the gun, which he recognized as a Beretta. The safety catch was off.

"Continue," he said.

"You have security in here?" The young man jerked his gaze away, tensing. "You have an alarm system—something like that?"

"Of course." Lazare indicated a small panel built into the surface of his desk. "I could activate that. I could also activate a small button set into the floor by my feet. You needn't worry. I have no intention of activating either. Besides—unless you are a very poor shot—I'd be dead or dying before assistance arrived—so there isn't a great deal of point to it."

He was still disconcerting the man—even alarming him, he realized, and this was not what he wanted. He saw his eyes swivel and the color come and go in his face. With a quiet gesture Lazare pushed his chair back from the desk. He sighed.

"I'm now beyond reach of either alarm. You prefer that?"

"Sure I do. Stay like that."

"Tell me who you are," Lazare said. "I should tell you, I already know the part you played in Maria Cazarès's death. It was you who told her about that chemist in Amsterdam, was it not? Your friend who could provide the one pill that would restore her happiness and enable her to work? Maria told me—oh, nearly a year ago now—that some friend had discovered this man. She told me it was another designer. I didn't believe her—but that didn't matter. I even believed in the man and his experiments for a while, which was why I was persuaded to help fund them. I wanted to believe, of course."

"You did?" The young man stared at him. "Why?"

"Because we had tried everything else. Innumerable doctors, clinics, methods of treatment. I had spent five years exploring the further reaches of medicine, with the help of some arcane and semilegal practitioners as well as some of the finest doctors in Europe. I was—desperate." He paused. "And when one is desperate, one will try anything. Is that not so?"

The man made a small convulsive gesture of the hand. Lazare frowned.

"There's one thing I don't understand, however. When you planted the idea in Maria's mind that this chemist and these pills would be her salvation—did you realize they were lethal then?"

"They're not lethal." He gave Lazare a look of derision. "She was so fucking dumb. You were so dumb. You let her get hold of too many at once—and she took them. Four in one day, one from you, then three at Mathilde's. No food. No water. She was sick already, very thin"—he gave a shrug—"so, what do you know? Cardiac arrest." He paused. "But you're smart, I'll give you that. I didn't want the pills to kill her. Quite the reverse."

"You wanted them to ensure she was well enough to attend her collection today, is that it? I see. Of course." Lazare gave a small frown. "You wanted her out on the runway."

"Oh, I wanted you *both* out on the runway." The young man gave a complacent smile. "You—no problem. But I could see she was cracking up fast. I could see that way back last year. I didn't want that. I didn't want her fucking up my plans. She *had* to appear. The White Doves should have fixed that. . . ." His eyes narrowed. "It's odd, isn't it? You're a careful man, a detail man—everyone says that about you. Every article I've ever read, that's what it says. Yet you let her overdose. Why was that?"

A tiny flicker of emotion passed across Lazare's impassive face. The young man was not so unintelligent, he thought.

"Let's just say . . ." He gave a sigh. "I made it difficult for Maria, but not impossible. The pills were in a drawer in my desk. She knew which drawer and which desk. She knew that drawer was locked, and she knew I kept the key. In the end—and, of course, I couldn't be certain what the result would be—I left her the choice. If she wanted to break into my desk, if she wanted to increase the dosage, when I had very clearly told her what that dosage should be—that was her choice. You see . . ." He looked away from the young man and let his eyes rest on the blank wall opposite.

"You see, I had come to the end. I could not go on any longer. I would never have expected to say that. I am not a man who gives up easily, or who likes to give up. But I had reached that point. Perhaps Maria had also. Death can be merciful, you know. There comes a point when it is very good simply to draw a line, close the accounts, close the book. . . . You're too young, perhaps, to understand that."

Lazare half rose, then, seeing this movement increased the young man's agitation, sat down again. He looked at his watch. He glanced up at the TV screen.

"So. I think I know what you told Maria. I think I know who you managed to persuade her you were. Mathilde Duval has told me certain details too. I now know how you first met her, and how you insinuated yourself, first into Madame Duval's life, and then Maria's. It wouldn't have been difficult, an old, half-blind, near-senile woman; another woman who was desperately sick. Convince me. That may be rather more difficult, I think."

The young man rose, still holding the gun. He stepped back one pace from the desk and fixed his eyes on Lazare. Lazare wondered how many times he had rehearsed this moment, how often he had scripted it. Many times, he thought, watching him dispassionately—and in front of mirrors too, he would have guessed. The young man struck an attitude, as if performing for a camera, an invisible audience.

"I'm your son," he said.

Lazare continued to watch him, silently and without reaction. The man's mouth tightened and his eyes began to take on a fixed and glittery look.

"I'm your son. Maria Cazarès was my mother. My name is Christophe Rivière. Your name was Rivière once. I was born in New Orleans in December 1969. You made her abandon me there. You made her put me in an orphanage, waiting for someone to adopt me—only no one ever did. I've seen my birth certificate—Maria showed me. She told me—how unwilling she was, how she wept and pleaded with you, but you wouldn't fucking listen. You fucking wrapped me up and disposed of me like I was trash."

"I see." Lazare folded his hands. His quiet tones halted the rising torrent of words. The man stared at him, white-faced. "Maria showed you your birth certificate. Did she also show you the certificate for your death?"

The young man drew back his lips in a quick sneer.

"Oh, sure. She showed me that. And she knew it was fucking well faked. There *was* no certificate—not until years later. It was *years* before you first produced that. By that time you were fucking rich enough to buy anything you wanted. A back-dated certificate? An infant death? No problem. How much did it cost you? Five hundred dollars? A thousand?"

"Five thousand," Lazare said.

He spoke in the same quiet voice as before. The boy's face became a blur of rage and excitement. He was beginning to tremble violently; the barrel of the gun wavered to the ceiling, then back.

"I *knew* it," he began on a rising note, "I fucking *knew* it. You fucking asshole, you bastard . . ."

"Hold the gun steady," Lazare said. "If you wave it around like that, it could easily go off. I'm not armed. Look . . ." He reached inside his jacket, and fear flared in the young man's eyes. "I simply want to take out my wallet. You see?" He laid the black leather wallet on the desk. "And now I want to take out a photograph, which I would like you to inspect."

He took out a small colored snapshot as he said this and slid it across his desk. The boy snatched it up, then threw it down.

"Who's that? Some fucking sick kid. Some spastic kid . . ."

"*That* is my son." Lazare felt such anger then, he wanted to rise, strike out, smash his fist in this young man's face. He waited, letting that anger subside, then continued in a cold, flat voice.

"That is my son. His name was Christophe Rivière—just as you say. He was born with cerebral palsy. Do you know what that is? It is one of the cruelest diseases that can afflict children. It does not necessarily affect the intelligence, but it does cripple the muscles of the body—as you can see from that photograph. It is progressive, and the deterioration cannot be reversed. My money—when I acquired it—bought my son the best possible care. Prior to that he was in a Catholic orphanage for sick children in New Orleans, and then he was in a very fine clinic in New York State. I visited him four times a year, every year of his life. He finally died, shortly before his twelfth birthday, in 1980."

He looked down at the photograph, then quietly returned it to the wallet and replaced the wallet inside his jacket. The young man never moved once.

Lazare hesitated, then made the smallest gesture of the hand.

"I loved my son intensely. I was always fiercely proud of him. I could never express to you—or to anyone else—how much I admired his courage. The decision to leave him behind in America was the hardest decision I ever made in my life. When I set out to acquire a fortune, I did so for his sake. His welfare—and the welfare of his mother—have always been the controlling factors in my life." He gave a sigh, and his voice hardened. "I can see you don't believe me. As you like. For reasons that need not concern you, I chose to shield Maria from this. I see no reason to shield you. You are a fantasist. You are not my son. My son, much as I might wish it, is not likely to return from the dead."

He braced himself then as he said these words, because he could see their effect. The young man's face worked, and his hands shook. He was trembling uncontrollably. Lazare could see a terrible combination of emotions work their way through him: rage and disbelief and fear and grief. He expected him to fire then, and felt a grudging respect when he did not.

Lazare bent his head and passed his hand across his face. All the energy released in him by the arrival of this young man had now gone. He felt an absolute weariness of body and soul, a lethargy and an indifference so deep that he was surprised that his obstinate body continued to function, that his lungs circulated oxygen, that his heart beat.

He thought of his son, whom he had loved with such intensity, his son's continued suffering, making that love poignant from the first. If he could have rewritten his own life, he knew that he would have ensured that Christophe spent his brief life with Maria and himself no matter if Maria, weaker than himself, cracked under the demands of that pain. But he could not rewrite his life.

The decision had been made at a time when he was young, torn between love, shame, and guilt—and the guilt had been so corrosive, so intense. For Maria too, of course. He glanced up at the young man facing him. Could she really have believed his claims? Perhaps she had, with a part of her poor fractured mind at least, though Lazare noted she had still been careful in what she revealed. The boy obviously had no inkling that the parents he was claiming were brother and sister—or perhaps Maria had simply forgotten that fact, displaced it, as she did anything that caused her pain: perhaps.

His own great weakness, he thought, had been his inflexibility. Once decided upon a course of action, he had always judged it weak to countenance change. In trying to protect Maria, he had denied himself closeness to his son—yet that closeness, he now saw, was what he had most craved in life.

He looked up at the tall, strong, and handsome young man facing him now. How ironic, he thought: he is as desperate for a father as I am desperate for a son. Does he not realize that—if miracles happened, and he were my child, I would not be able to speak for joy—I would rise and embrace him, my life would be utterly altered, and I might even believe that there was, after all, a God?

"So tell me"—he raised his head—"tell me why you've come here today. Tell me what you want."

Stammering, boasting, the boy did. He was deeply deranged, Lazare thought; he seemed to have no conception of how impossible his plan was. All that seemed to concern him was that this execution—which he called a killing—should be public. He wanted it to be seen, witnessed, photographed, even filmed. That interested Lazare briefly. Listening to the young man's tirade, he considered the seductions of fame—to which, as he had mentioned in his final public tribute to her, Maria had been as indifferent as he himself was.

The boy had the fame sickness, he could see it now. It was there in his pale face, glittering eyes, and wild gestures. His own desire was to become famous, world famous, with the firing of one or two shots. Parricide was to be his route to celebrity, his stage the runway, his audience the world's press. Lazare sighed. He himself considered all fame deeply treacherous; yet with fame, this boy clearly believed he would find his lost identity, he would know who he was.

Lazare did not intend to die in such a way; nor was he, he realized, prepared to wait. He glanced up at the TV screen: the model Quest was advancing down the runway in one of Cazarès's last designs, a black suit trimmed with sable. A long black sable scarf trailed over her arm, and down to the floor. As she turned, she gave it a practiced kick.

The collection had reached its midpoint. The suit was in every respect exquisite, though Lazare had never shared Maria's taste for furs. He frowned, then stood.

"I will not cooperate," he said.

The young man stared at him. He flourished the gun.

"You have to. You walk out of this room when I say. You walk along the corridor, through the dressing room, and out onto the runway—with me. Then I do it."

"Thanks to your incompetence, my salon is filled with armed police."

"So much the better."

"Do you want a bloodbath?" Lazare gave him a long, cool look. "Well, perhaps you do. You will not get it with my assistance. This is Maria's last collection, and it will be shown in the same manner as all her other collections. Perfectly. With discipline. One thing you should understand . . ." Lazare met his eyes. "I have never obeyed an order from anyone in my life. Around here I give the orders."

"Not now you don't." The young man gave a smile. He waved the gun again.

Lazare returned the smile and began to walk toward the boy, around his desk. He watched the gun waver and the young man step back. He saw him glance toward the door, and he saw him begin to panic. He realized he would have to say the right thing, exactly the right thing, and that he would have to be quick.

Should he tell this young madman that he wanted to die, was prepared to die, and that if the young man would not oblige him now, he'd find other means himself? But no, he thought, watching him: the young man wanted more than the pleasure of firing the shot—and to admit to desiring it would be certain to make him delay, even abandon, his attempt.

Lazare looked lovingly at the gun. Anger might provoke him, he thought, because he could feel the young man's fury, even smell it.

Anger, insult . . . he gave a small shrug. Whatever it took.

"How stupid you are," he said, sharpening his voice. "You can't make me do anything. What are you going to do if I won't leave this room with you? What can you do? Fire? Your hands are shaking. You haven't the guts. You can't go through with it, can you? And if you did—you'd miss. Have you actually handled a firearm before? No. I thought not."

He pushed past the boy, who made no attempt to stop him. He moved toward the door slowly; the boy still did nothing. Lazare turned. He was trembling now, holding the gun at the wrong angle, his arm extended, the barrel wavering. His face was blanched of color, distorted with emotion. Lazare almost pitied him; he gave him a look of contempt.

"My son had great courage," he said. "I loved that courage in him. In all the years I knew him, I felt respect, admiration, humility because of that."

"*I'm* your son. *I'm* Christophe. Just stop fucking lying. . . . Maria recognized me—my *mother* knew who I was."

"Maria was not sane." Lazare looked at him coldly. "By the end she was very nearly as crazy as you are. You're afraid, aren't you? You can't even hold a gun steady, let alone fire it. Unlike my son, you're a coward when it comes to the test. A coward and a boaster and a fool. A nobody."

With this, he turned his back. As he reached for the door handle, he thought he had failed, even then, and that he would, after all, have to endure the next few hours: the meaningless applause, the emotion, the accolades, and the emptiness after that. It was a pity, he thought with a flicker of amusement, because if ever there was a way of ensuring that Maria Cazarès's last collection was never forgotten, it was this. Still, it did not really matter. He could go, later this evening, to any of his houses; all were equipped with a pharmacopoeia of Maria's sleeping pills and painkillers, several of which, taken in the right quantity, preferably with alcohol, would prove as efficacious as a bullet.

He turned the handle, and pain exploded in his back. The room resonated with noise, so as he fell, he thought that perhaps the young man, the nameless young man, had fired more than once. He slumped against the wall and heard himself make a strange liquid noise.

He watched the dying process with an acuity that surprised him: here were its stages, the flowering of blood on his white shirtfront; the warm gush of blood from the groin, so he thought he had lost control of his bladder and felt a second's fastidious distaste. The words that became blood in his mouth, and then the vision loss as the room rushed toward him, then darkened, then ebbed.

He was aware, dimly, that the young man was frenzied now. He had begun screaming something, words that might have been love or abuse. He was touching him now, Lazare thought; he could feel his hands clasping his chest, then his neck and face. All he would achieve, Lazare thought as his grip on consciousness slackened, would be to daub himself with blood.

Lazare tried to sit up. He felt affection for this young man now, and gratitude. He wanted him to know that the room was soundproofed, so with luck the shots would not have been heard. He wanted to tell him that if he left quietly, by the rear staff entrance, the collection would proceed and he might even escape—for a while at least. He wanted to tell him something else too, something infinitely rich, which he could feel welling in his mind and heart, some priceless secret of life. Its exact nature, however, eluded him.

Star, bent over him, clutching at him, saw his face contort as Lazare tried to speak. He began to kiss his father's dying face. He watched his lips start to form a word, or words, and clung to him, waiting for this final message, which he knew had to be recognition, and love.

Lazare's lips moved; he coughed slightly; from his mouth came a gush of bright arterial blood. Star waited. Nothing happened. Lazare did not slump. His eyes did not close. It wasn't like the movies, Star thought, shaking him. He waited some more. The room spun and jumped. Gradually, he realized that there would be no words, no final gesture, and that Jean Lazare was dead.

He wept, then he stood, then he paced. *Bad, bad, bad,* he thought. He could feel his mind slipping, none of the gears would mesh. He felt outrage and anguish. Accelerating forward from the back of his brain with vast and rushing momentum came another idea: he had been robbed.

This made him shake, then laugh, then weep. He bent down over his father's body, and then—even though he didn't much like its design—he stole his watch. He buckled it around his own wrist. He took Jean Lazare's black overcoat from the coatstand and put on Jean Lazare's black leather gloves. The gloves were too tight, but they hid the blood on his hands. The overcoat was too short and too small, but he found that by slinging it over his shoulder it could be made to cover the blood on his shirtfront. He inserted a new magazine into his gun, thrust it into his pocket, and opened the door.

He could hear the tides of the audience in the distance, and see poor, half-blind, half-deaf Mathilde in the room across the corridor, milky eyes turned to the television screen. The passageway was deserted. He crossed into the room opposite, picked up a white silk cushion, pressed the barrel of the gun into it, and fired twice into the back of Mathilde's neck. Point-blank. She died better than his father. She slumped forward in her chair at once. No noise from the gun, just this huge white open silence, a great sky of silence. He could feel it again now—invincibility, very close.

He left the room, turned left, and walked out through the rear staff exit doors. They led out into a small alleyway, at the end of which were gates, and a security guard in a small glass and wood sentry box.

He could see no police at this entrance. From here, the mews, the garage, and *fame* were less than a four-minute walk away.

He could feel his own cunning coming back, seeping along his veins. He stopped at the sentry box and smiled at the guard, who recognized him from earlier that morning, he thought. *Just testing*; he asked directions to the nearest pharmacy—Madame Duval was a little overcome. Then this struck him, under the circumstances, as funny; he gave a snort of laughter. What she needed, he went on, leaning against the open window of the sentry box, was this special tisane. He watched the security man, who said—a little too fast—that yes, old women could be like that, fixed in their ways, and there was a pharmacy—a very good pharmacy—nearby, just two streets away on the left.

Star looked at him; he could feel God in his skull. If the man hadn't stressed the excellence of the pharmacy, he thought, he might have let him live. As it was, he had a twitchy rabbity look Star did not like. He took out the gun and fired two bursts straight in the man's face. He watched it splinter and pulp and spray, then he reloaded, stuffed the gun back in his pocket, and jogged the few hundred yards to the mews.

No sirens, no shouts, no sound of running feet. Easy, easy, easy, Star thought: it was just so fucking *easy* to be great. He opened the gates to the mews and jogged the last few yards to the end garage. He listened, but he could hear nothing at all except the calm of this God in his head. He was about to open the garage doors, then he thought: a little reward.

He took out the container of White Doves. Six remained. One—taken with speed the previous night while Mina lay beside him, pretending not to be afraid, pretending not to be awake, pretending she wasn't going to betray him like everyone else—one taken then had produced a confidence swoop. Also other interesting and gratifying effects.

He tipped one pill into the palm of his hand. He added a second, then swallowed them. Water, he thought: must take some water—but that was okay. He could drink water, do the interview—at Mathilde's place.

"Gini," he said, calling her name through the doors in a low voice. "Gini, it's okay. It's me. I'm sorry I'm late."

CHAPTER 20

"Sweet," Star said as the garage doors lifted. He was standing directly in front of Gini, blocking her escape. She stood looking at him, transfixed. He was covered in blood. There was blood on his shirtfront, on his hands, under his nails, on his neck, on his face. The front of his hair was wet with blood, and caught in his hair, in one loose lock at the front, were some small sharp white fragments. Bone; tiny fragments of bone, Gini thought. She clamped her hands across her mouth. He stood there, drenched in blood, tossing down an overcoat, a pair of black gloves, a wide smile on his face.

She slumped back against the garage wall, shaking.

How many more people had he killed? Just Jean Lazare; just the driver of this car—or, as he had claimed, more than that? The driver of this car had been *young*, she thought, insofar as she could tell the age of a man left with only half a face. She had taken off her green scarf and pressed it against the terrible wounds. She knew what was going to happen, because she had watched similar things happen in Bosnia; nothing could have saved him, and it was useless to try to stanch the blood. Nevertheless, she did try. It had taken him over an hour to hemorrhage to death.

Now she, too, was bloodstained. She was wearing a sweater and a thick coat, but shock was making her bitterly cold. She could not stop shivering—and Star, when he finally noticed, seemed pleased by this.

"It's okay. It's okay," he said. "I was shaking too. Just a little bit. Just before—just before I did it, you know. Don't be ashamed, Gini—it's all right."

"I can't drive . . ." She backed away from him, then held out her hands. "Look. I can't drive with my hands like this . . ."

He hit her across the face hard and without warning. Gini staggered and half fell. When she looked back at him, she saw the look Chantal had described. White skin, glittering eyes, something horrible, something that deeply repelled her, about his mouth.

"You fucking drive. You fucking drive and you fucking drive now." He caught hold of the lapels of her coat and slammed her back against the car door. He was about to add the threat, the *otherwise*, and then did not. He had seen her fear, smelled her acquiescence. That made Gini ashamed, and shame made her angry. She did what he told her to do, as slowly as possible, and it seemed to her that he was deaf, unaware of danger. She could hear the swoop of sirens in the distance now; he, it seemed, could not.

He sat upright in the seat next to her, holding the gun pointed toward her stomach as they approached the mews gates. Gini took as long as she dared to turn out; she kept praying for police cars, for running feet. He directed her then through a maze of little alleyways and back routes, and she kept praying they would come to some barricade, but they did not. The noise of the sirens was very loud, then more distant. He still seemed unaware of them. She felt he was watching something, some private horror film of his own, yet he remained alert, directing her first left, then straight, then right.

Once, when she thought he was not looking, when his eyes seemed fixed but sightless, she risked switching on the lights to full beam in an effort to attract attention. He noticed at once.

"Don't do that," he said. "Just don't fucking fool around. Switch them off. I'm going to give you—the story of your life. You want that, don't you? Make a right."

Gini realized where they were going then. He was taking her by a more direct route than he had used earlier that day, but he was taking her back to Mathilde's street, Mathilde's apartment. Her mind was working better now; fear and anger were giving time an extraordinary clarity and precision. With precision, she saw that if she went up to that apartment with him, he would—sooner or later—kill her. That course of action had to be prevented, but she could see no way to avoid it. If she refused, he'd shoot her in the car, or in the street, or in the lobby, or in the lift.

"Star," she said eventually, reducing her speed slightly, "did you hear the sirens back there?"

"No. Why?"

"Well—I'm just thinking. Are we going back to Mathilde's?"

"Yes."

"Do you think that's such a good idea? We're sure to have been seen. They could be following us right now—and if we stay in that apartment too long . . . You could get trapped, Star. You know what happens. They surround the building, cut you off, so there's no possible escape."

"Oh, but I don't want to escape." He gave her a white smile. "You didn't realize that?"

"No. No. I guess I didn't. But, Star . . ."

"Look—I'm not dumb, all right?" She heard another of those unpredictable flashes of anger. "No one *ever* escapes. Today, tomorrow, next week—they close in and they finish you off. Meantime, you're my hostage—this is a hostage situation, right? So you know what they do, I know what they do. They evacuate the building. They surround the building. They put their best fucking snipers up on the roofs. They move into the apartments opposite, and next door and underneath. They install their listening devices so they know what room you're in. They make a telephone connection. They get some smooth fuck, some asshole shrink, to talk to you on the phone. They start in on their psycho-profiles, right? And meantime, they're oh-so-nice, oh-so-fucking-cooperative. You tell them you want a car, a plane, a helicopter—some shit like that—and they never miss a beat. They say, sure, Star, no problem—anything else we can get you? You'd like a yacht, maybe? Concorde? How about we fix you up on the Orient Express?"

He laughed. "You think I'm dumb enough to buy all that? I've watched the movies a million times. . . . Make a left here . . . and I *know* what they do. They let you sweat. They wait for the tension to get to you. They wear you down. They figure, sooner or later you're going to need to sleep, you're going to start to *crack*. And then, when they figure they've got the timing right, they send them in. And those guys—SWAT, the SAS, the GIGN—they're good. Thirty seconds—less—and you're out of there, Gini. And me—you know what's happened to me? The same as happens to all the other poor fucks: I'm dead, like some fucking rat in a fucking hole. . . ." He gave a long, slow sigh. "Well, I don't plan on dying like that. Never did."

Gini listened to this long recitation in silence. Its accuracy chilled her. She gripped the steering wheel hard. They had just turned into the far end of the rue de Rennes. Three blocks ahead was Mathilde Duval's apartment building. She slowed.

"But you do plan on dying?" she said quietly. "Is that it?"

"Maybe." He shot her a secretive look, then smiled. "That worries you, doesn't it?"

"Sure. You die—I die. I have this feeling you just pronounced my death sentence." She felt some nerve return and glanced at him. "Though I don't see how I get to write your story if I'm dead."

"You'll find out. Soon enough." He gave another secretive smile. "Just don't ask questions—okay? I don't like women who ask fucking questions all the time. I—what the fuck are you doing?"

Gini had just seen the pedestrians ahead of her—seen them, and recognized them. Walking slowly, forty yards in front, still about twenty yards short of Madame Duval's building: Pascal and Marianne.

They were hand in hand. Pascal had his camera case slung over his shoulder. He was bending toward Marianne slightly, listening to her. Marianne was skipping along, chattering, her face lifted to her father's. Gini hit the accelerator pedal. Star jabbed the gun hard in her crotch.

"There's some people there. Star . . ."

"Brake. Brake now."

"Star—they'll see. You're covered in blood. They'll—"

"Stop. Right here. I'll fire on the count of three. One. Two . . ."

Gini stopped. They were right outside Madame Duval's building. Pascal and Marianne were about ten yards behind the car, on the sidewalk, on her side of the car, so she could see them advance in her side mirror.

"Star, wait . . ." Another few seconds and they would have passed the car, passed the Duval building, turned into Helen's building. They were still talking, laughing, they might notice nothing. "Star—you don't want trouble now. Just—"

He had reached across, snatched the keys out of the ignition, and was already out of the door. Gini kept her eyes fixed on the wing mirror. She could hear Marianne's high, childlike voice. Her tiny triangular-shaped face was still lifted to her father's. She was wearing navy woolen tights, a navy and red plaid pleated skirt, a navy reefer jacket. Her dark hair had been newly cut with bangs, in a bob. Her gray eyes, so like her father's, were still raised to his. She is just nine years old, Gini thought. Star was closing the passenger door, walking around to the sidewalk; just another few seconds. They still might not notice him. Provided she stayed in the car, provided Pascal did not see her, if she didn't move and Star didn't speak—please God, Gini thought.

One yard; half a yard. Go on, she thought—walk on by.

"*Mais regarde, Papa—cet homme-là* . . ." Pascal's reaction speed,

honed from years in war zones, was very swift. Even before Marianne's
footsteps faltered, before she began on that high puzzled remark, Pascal
had halted, turned, scooped Marianne into his arms. He was starting to
turn, starting to move away as Star got to her door, opened it, and said:
"Okay, Gini—get out."

Gini did not move. She could see Star's white face bent toward her,
leaning into the car. She could see the gun—and she thought that he was
blind as well as deaf. He hadn't heard the sirens, he couldn't see Pascal
or Marianne, if she could just give them another fifteen seconds,
twenty—that would be enough. She stared at the gun, waited to hear the
retreating footsteps. There was no sound of footsteps, just a terrible
white and endless silence. Then Star began to scream. His scream jolted
her heart, echoed along the street.

"Out of the fucking car, out, *now*. You get out or I blow your fucking
head off—out, out!"

She slid out fast: speed, not delay, might be the answer. She twisted
out of the car and up, almost into Star's arms, and he was yanking her
arm up behind her back, jabbing the gun in her neck. From the corner of
her eye she could see Pascal, four feet to her left, clasping Marianne in
his arms, one arm locked around the child's waist, one hand, fingers
spread, pressing her face against his shoulder. One tiny flashing frame of
film: she saw his face, white, intent, poised, the pre-firing-line look. Had
Star seen them? Was he aware they were there?

"Please, Star," she began, moving between them, holding his eyes,
lifting her free hand to his face. "Just take me inside. I want to be inside,
with you. . . ."

Something was happening to his face, to his eyes. Something was
kicking in, something that gave him a new, concentrated, rapacious look.
His arm was curling around her shoulder now, his grip becoming gen-
tler. He began to draw her toward the portico steps, holding the gun,
rubbing the gun against her throat. Up the steps, all eight of them; under
the cover of the canopy. He fumbled with his left hand, drew the keys
out of his pocket, handed them to her.

"You open the door. Open the fucking door. Get the elevator
quick . . ."

It's all right, Gini thought. No one was moving, no one was near: it
was just her and Star and this key; the world had narrowed to this tiny,
fraught space. Her hands shook; she couldn't stop her hands shaking.
They were shaking so badly, she couldn't insert the key into the lock. It
scratched and jittered against the metal.

"Let me help you, Gini," said a cool voice from right behind her, and she felt Pascal's hand close over hers.

He guided the key at once into its slot.

Pascal could feel the shutters clicking in his mind. A series of fast, power-driven shots. The distinctive car, being driven erratically, accelerating fast, then braking sharply, just those few feet in front of them. One part of his mind was still listening to Marianne, and the birthday party she would be having, and the magician who could produce rabbits from hats, then he was also seeing the man get out from the passenger seat, and seeing the blood, then the glint of metal. And it was still—just—all right, because he had Marianne in his arms, was starting to turn, there was a doorway behind them less than five feet away, and the man, crazed, moving jerkily, like a marionette, did not seem even aware of their presence on the sidewalk. So there was still time to turn, shield Marianne, walk, not run, he thought—and then he heard Gini's name and he did not turn or move away—which was simultaneously the one right thing in the world to do then, and the most terrible mistake.

She bought him time. He watched her do that in a moment that lasted less than ten seconds but felt a century long. She shielded them with her body, then she walked up the portico steps with the man and she bought him time to set Marianne back down on the sidewalk, push her back into the doorway beyond.

"Don't move," he said. "Wait until I'm in that building, with Gini and that man, and the door is closed. Then run back to Maman. Tell her to call the police—at once. Tell her what you saw. Where I am. You understand, Marianne?"

She lifted her face to his, her eyes wide and fixed on his. He felt a second's terror that she would cry, or argue, or cling to him. Then he saw her features become set and still and determined. She nodded, and Pascal, seeing for the first time how much she was his daughter, felt a sudden tight and agonizing love for her. He pressed her hand in his, ran soundlessly back along the sidewalk and up the steps. More tiny, quick flashes of information as his hand closed over Gini's and he helped her insert the key in the lock. The gun was a Beretta, a 93R, he saw, and the man holding it was unused to firearms, hyped, but with a delayed reaction speed. Pascal watched his white face and jittery eyes. He thought he wasn't really aware of Pascal, hadn't taken him in until they were all three in the lobby with the entrance doors shut. Then, in the middle of that black and white chessboard floor, with the elevator behind him, Gini clasped in front of him, and the gun still thrusting at her neck, jabbing under her chin, he seemed to see Pascal for the first time. *Slow the film down,* Pascal thought, because he could see the man had some movie racing in front of his eyes, looping, too many frames per second, so he'd get sense, then a gap, sense, then a gap.

Pascal met his eyes and smiled at him as if they were old acquaintances. Shouldering his camera bag, he said, "You want me to get the elevator? Which floor?"

The simplicity of the question seemed to help the man.

"Just get the gates," he said.

Pascal did so, moving slowly, without threat. The man backed inside, still clutching Gini, still jabbing the gun at her throat. Pascal made to close the doors on them, then, at the last moment, held them and inserted his foot in the space.

He was trying to read Gini's expression, trying to pick up some tiny hint. He could make no violent move, and no threat. Gini's eyes, wide with fear, had been fixed on him. As he held the door, he saw her face become tight with meaning. He saw her look very deliberately at his camera case.

"Can I help?" Pascal said, trying to read this message. "I work with Gini, you see, and"—he frowned, then understood—"I'm a photographer . . ."

"You are?" The man was staring at him, his eyes glazed, then alert. He made a small twitchy movement.

"That's cameras?" He jerked his head at Pascal's case. "You have cameras in there?"

There was, just perceptibly, something that might have been excitement, even awe, in his voice.

"Sure. Cameras. Lenses. Film. Color. Monochrome . . ."

"Well, what d'you know? Now, how about that?"

The man gave a small shiver. He kept the gun under Gini's chin, and his eyes on Pascal.

"This is Pascal Lamartine," Gini said in a low voice. "He and I—we work together. . . ."

"Look, why don't I come up with you?" Pascal stepped into the elevator. He stood well back, by the gate. "Which floor?"

He watched the man's face carefully. He had expected some reaction when he moved through the gates, but there was none. The man seemed to be reacting to his name; as soon as Gini used it, he registered racing disbelief, then glazed incomprehension, then—as they traveled upward, and he seemed to get a fix on the name, a curious elation and relief.

Not in the elevator, Pascal was thinking, and not in the tenth floor lobby either. These spaces were too confined, and the man was still holding Gini too tight. In the apartment, he thought as the man tossed him some keys and told him to open the door; yes, here, Pascal thought as they entered a large, overfurnished room: here—when he finally moves away, if he relaxes, loses concentration. . . .

"I know you, Pascal . . ." The man's face now wore an expression of almost messianic triumph. He had had the sense to position himself with his back to the fireplace wall, with Gini still in front of him, the gun still at her neck.

"I know you. I've followed your work. I have pictures of yours. Those ones of Caroline of Monaco you took? Remember those? I clipped those. And that American movie star—Sonia Swan? Those were great. I clipped those too. You work for all my favorite magazines—*Paris Match*, *People* . . ." He frowned. "I haven't seen your stuff so much recently. . . ."

"No. I've been doing other things recently. You know how it is."

"Sure. Sure. I do. I mean, it must have been tough, getting in so close to all those celebrities, getting past the security, the dogs. Taking the pictures the world wasn't meant to see . . . I loved that. I mean, that bitch Sonia Swan, no better than a hooker. You showed us what she *really* was." He was quivering with excitement. Pascal thought: how ironic. The three years of his own life he most despised, the three years of his life that shamed him still—and yet they were the three years that were useful now. He looked at this man, and thought: a specific kind of insanity; a fan; a fanatic.

"I still have pictures of yours I clipped." He gave a high-pitched laugh. "I've got them here. I keep some of my things here, in my mother's room across the hall. We could look at them later, maybe? They're in this suitcase, under the bed. . . ." He paused again, then regained control. He gave another small, twitchy movement.

"So, listen, Pascal—you're smart, right? This is what I want you to do. I want you to go through this apartment, every room, and close the shades and the drapes. Put the lights on and leave them on. Then go in the kitchen and get me some water. Bottled water, okay, out of the fridge. Mathilde keeps it there for me. Bring the sealed bottle and a glass. And don't stop being smart, Pascal, because—"

"No. No. Sure. I understand."

Pascal moved to the windows of this room. He was calculating time. Five minutes? Ten? Would they use sirens, or opt for the silent approach?

He moved fast around the apartment, learning its geography. One long central corridor, windowless; on either side of it, two large rooms; on the right, two bedrooms, each with its own bathroom; on the left, the sitting room they had first entered, then a dining room beyond that; finally, at the end of the corridor, a large, old-fashioned kitchen. It had almost exactly the same layout, though smaller, as Helen's apartment—and as he realized this, his hopes rose.

He entered the kitchen, and they were dashed. Like Helen's apartment, this, too, had a service door that led out to the fire escape stairs. Pascal stared at this door angrily: he had been counting on it. It was blocked by a huge, immovable refrigerator. He unlatched each window, as he had done in all the rooms, though he doubted it would be helpful. The windows looked long unused; they had been painted in. He leaned hard against the one above the sink; it did not budge an inch.

He looked around the room, then quietly began opening drawers. He finally found the kind of implement he was looking for: a long, thin, very sharp boning knife. He slipped it inside his jacket pocket without great optimism. A knife was a close-range weapon; a gun was not.

He was returning with the water—why water?—when he heard from the room beyond a sound that made his heart stop. A low moan, then a muffled cry from Gini. "No, please ..." he heard. "Star, no—listen, please, not yet. We have to talk. You want me to do the interview. I have a tape recorder in my bag, and tapes, and—"

Pascal reached the door five seconds too late. There might have been an opportunity, but it had gone. Whatever Star had been doing, he had heard Pascal's footsteps and had stopped. Pascal halted in the doorway, white-faced.

He could read the scenario, and it made him deeply afraid. Gini had been forced to her knees in front of Star. She was trembling violently. Star's belt was undone. He held the gun nuzzling against her temple with his right hand. His left hand was grasping Gini by the back of the neck. On his face was an expression of arousal and urgency that was naked. As Pascal entered, he jerked Gini back up to her feet.

"Put the water down. Get back over there. Now." He waited until Pascal had done this. "Okay. We do the interview. Pascal can take some pictures. Yeah. That could be good. I have to tell you the whole story, and . . ." His eyes glazed sightly, then focused again.

"I did have a whole lot of things I wanted to say. But I don't know. I might keep it brief. I—there's other things I might want to do. You know, before . . ."

He stopped. His head jerked around like an animal's. He became instantly alert. He listened, and Gini listened, and Pascal listened—to the whoops of many sirens.

They came closer, became deafeningly loud, then stopped.

Star gave a long, slow sigh. He drew Gini back against his body, and Pascal, watching Gini's face with horror, knew why he had done that. He watched the blood drain from her face. She closed her eyes; her fists clenched. Star's right hand held the gun to her throat; he moved his left hand so it rested on her breast.

He had listened to the sirens. Now he seemed to listen to the silence.

"I guess the audience just arrived," he said.

At eleven-thirty, as fuchsia-dressed Quest swung out along the runway, Rowland moved up the aisle of the salon to its exit doors. He looked at the rows of pale faces, at the line of operatives circling the rear tier, and every instinct in his body said *wrong*. This scenario was too neat, too convenient, whatever Mina had been told. He left the building at once. This was a piece of *theater*, he thought—and wherever its director was, he was not, had never intended to be, out front.

Leaving the building, his sense of being an extra in someone else's production increased. The arrival of the GIGN had, inevitably, intensified the interest of the press. Outside the courtyard of the Cazarès building, a huge mob of reporters and photographers and TV crews were engaged in a series of running battles with the police. They would spill across the barricades at one point, then be forced back, then advance again. Rowland cut around behind them and turned into a series of side streets. He passed a mews with locked gates, where the fleet of Cazarès Mercedes were presumably garaged, then found his way to the rear staff entrance.

It could not be long, he thought, before this gate came under press siege as well, but for the moment it was quiet. The surly guard on the gate did not take his appearance well; he informed Rowland that only authorized personnel were admitted here, and only authorized personnel *had* been admitted. Reaching for a telephone, he told Rowland to leave, and leave *now*, before he called his security backup. Rowland left: he could think of only two other places where Star might have gone—Mathilde Duval's, or Chantal's. But Mathilde Duval would be at Cazarès's now, watching the collection from the rear room Juliette de Nerval had described to him. Chantal's, then, he thought. Less than ten minutes later he was getting out of a cab in the rue St. Séverin. He paused by the church, then crossed the street. The entrance door was open. He paused in the doorway, looking up the flight of stairs that led to Chantal's apartment. The door above was also open. He tensed.

He knew what had happened, what must have happened, before he pushed the door back. He could see the blood smeared on the wall opposite; he could hear frantic scratchings and the yowling of the cat.

The cat had been shut up in one of the cupboards under the sink. The cat, for some reason, had been spared; Chantal and Jeanne and their small, thin gray dog had not. Jeanne had tried to put up a fight. She was sprawled at the base of the blood-spattered wall; Chantal, who might never have known what was happening, had been shot while in bed. The bed was soaked in blood; there was blood on the floor, the net curtains, the walls. It could only have been Star who had done this, and he had signed his handiwork in blood: there was a crude blood star on one wall, above Jeanne's body; there was a second blood sign by Chantal, a daubed crucifix of blood, just above the bed. Next to the dog's body was a pile of clothes—black jeans, a red scarf, the student uniform Star had told Mina he would wear to Cazarès's. Rowland averted his eyes from the bodies. The sink, the surrounding worktops, and floor were all stained with watery blood; he thought—this was *planned*; he came here and he did this, and then he changed and washed.

A sense of incomprehension and outrage fought with shock. Wrapping a handkerchief around his hand, Rowland called Luc Martigny, then— the noise was unbearable—opened the cabinet door and released the cat. It streaked past him, down the stairs. Rowland backed out of the room; these silent sprawled bodies were sending out signals to him, they were telling him a story, and it was not simply a murder story, the atrocities here were more complex. He fumbled his way back down the stairs and waited in the doorway below for the police. He tried to steady his own breathing; he tried to listen to the memories in his head, Chantal the day before, Mina that morning, both women in very different languages explaining to him that although Star had these *angers*, he posed no sexual threat. "Please," Mina had said, "please, he's not really bad. He didn't hurt me. He didn't do anything to hurt me—please understand."

Rowland stared hard at the black outline of the St. Séverin church. A light rain had begun to fall; he heard the approaching sirens, was dimly aware that Martigny and fellow officers were entering the building. He listened to their footsteps on the stairs, the muffled exclamations that escaped even these professionals. He could feel a deepening premonition and fear, a growing alarm. Where was Gini? He watched the church gargoyles arch above his head.

Martigny remained only a few minutes in Chantal's apartment—Rowland registered that. When he returned, he took Rowland by the arm and led him across to a police car.

"I'll explain in the car," he said. Rowland listened in silence as they raced through the crowded streets. The air flashed blue and white with alarm; the sirens were at once outside him and inside his head.

"It isn't just those two women back there," Martigny began in a terse voice. "It's *five* dead. Lazare himself; that maid Madame Duval, and a security guard on the rear gates—"

"And?" Rowland said.

"And now we know where this Star is. The call came in about five minutes ago. He's at Mathilde Duval's apartment. And I'm afraid he's not alone. Your colleague—Genevieve Hunter—is with him. No, wait, listen. At gunpoint, as a hostage. But she isn't alone. There's a photographer with her, a man you may know—Pascal Lamartine." Martigny hesitated. Rowland did not speak.

"The presence of another man . . . that improves the situation, perhaps." Martigny glanced at him. "Of course—it is serious. Obviously so. Five people dead. Those women back there . . ." He hesitated again; Rowland met his gaze.

"He'd raped them, hadn't he?"

"Yes. I'm afraid he had. Maybe before death, maybe after . . ." Martigny's expression became closed. "Meanwhile—we need your help."

When they reached the rue de Rennes, a grim-faced Martigny disappeared. He returned to Rowland to revise his roll call of the dead.

"Not five, six," he said. "They've just towed the Mercedes. Believe me, you don't want to see what's in its trunk."

He lit a cigarette, drew on it deeply. He and Rowland stood side by side in the rain, looking along the boulevard. They were still evacuating buildings, still bringing in the *matériel* for a siege. Crime-scene tapes fluttered; police cars, black vans, clustered; the street rang to the sound of booted feet.

Rowland raised his eyes slowly up the façade of Madame Duval's building. On its roof, and the roof opposite, he saw black shapes as police snipers moved into place.

"It's that apartment up there," Martigny said. "The one with the closed blinds."

"I know which it is," Rowland said.

"We'll make a telephone connection in about ten minutes. He hasn't ripped out the lines apparently, which helps. We don't want to start talking too soon, and when we do talk to him, we have to do it the right way. We need your help—English, French? Possible approaches we could use? You know more about him than anyone else does. . . ."

"Sure. Of course."

"Look." Martigny took his arm. "I told you. She's not alone with him. That helps."

"You think so? Since around eight o'clock this morning, he's killed six people."

"Even so. In this situation, you can never predict. She'll probably be all right. They'll both be all right. He needs them alive—they're his ticket out. Listen—have a cigarette. . . ."

Rowland shook his head. He kept his eyes on the building opposite.

Martigny was not a fool. "All right. Okay," he said, "he probably doesn't need both of them—I admit that."

"You know damn well he doesn't." Rowland turned on him angrily. "Two makes it *worse*, not better. He loves an audience. He'll kill one of them and keep the other alive—for a while."

"He'll keep the *woman* alive," Martigny said. "We both know that. That's obvious enough—the woman is physically weaker, easier to intimidate."

He paused. He met this Englishman's cold green gaze, and he knew exactly what was passing through his mind, since it was also passing through his own.

"Don't," he said quietly. "It doesn't help to imagine the worst—not in this situation. Wait. Within the next half hour we'll be talking to them, we'll have the listening devices in place, we'll have the plans to the apartment, we'll know exactly where he's standing—if he blinks, we'll know." He shrugged. "Near enough anyway. . . . Come on through here. This van. They're setting up the tapes and the telephone link."

Rowland followed him slowly. As they had spoken, another three vans and five cars had turned up. The first TV crews were arriving, the first clutch of cameramen. He stepped over cables and wires; he watched another posse of GIGN don helmets and flak jackets. He had seen it in a hundred movies, a hundred news reports—and at that he felt the same sense of foreboding he had experienced earlier. It was like a movie, he thought, because Star intended it that way, and because Star was still, in every sense, calling the shots.

"Don't you see?" he said to the quiet, dark-suited psychologist who would make the first telephone contact and who was sitting opposite him now. "Don't you see? This is what he wants. Maximum coverage— prime-time reports. He's *scripting* this. This is his movie. This is when he finally gets to be a star, when he's been a nothing, a nobody, for most of his life."

"Flattery?" the psychologist asked.

"Perhaps. Certainly no overt criticism. And he doesn't like questions, the Dutch girl said that. But the mood swings are very rapid—and he's almost certainly on drugs. Possibly cocaine, possibly something else . . ." Rowland stopped. He was desperate, and angry, and out of those emotions an idea came to him. He thought of dead Cassandra, dead Maria Cazarès.

"There is one possibility . . ." he said, then shook his head. "No. It's too dangerous."

The psychologist and Martigny exchanged glances.

"Monsieur McGuire," said the psychologist, putting on headphones. "In this situation, everything is dangerous."

"Open the suitcase, Pascal," Star said. "Stay back there by the table and open the suitcase. That's great."

Pascal opened the suitcase, which had been, as Star said, under the pink bed in the pink room, the room filled with pictures of a woman Pascal recognized as the couturière Maria Cazarès.

He glanced up. Star was still jittery, but also careful. He was positioned fifteen feet away, still with Gini in front of him, still with the gun jabbing her neck. On a small table next to him was Gini's tape recorder and microphone. A tape had been inserted.

It was recording now. Pascal knew, and Gini knew—he could read the knowledge in her face—that this tape was not helping them. This tape was Star's route to notoriety, to immortality—not any interview Gini might write. Pascal, piecing these events together, could see that whatever Star might have said to Gini earlier, he had never intended her to write up this scene afterward: transcribe his words now, possibly, better still, record them so the world could later hear his voice—but not survive to give her own account any more than Pascal would survive any photographs he might take.

They were useful to him now, Pascal thought, but when the pictures had been taken and the recording had been made, he would kill them. Pascal knew that with absolute certainty; he also knew which of them he would kill first.

The suitcase was crammed with notebooks and press clippings and photographs. They were in disarray. With extreme care he began taking them out and laying them on the table in front of him.

"Don't muddle them up, okay?" Star said sharply. "They're in order—all right? On the top there's all the stuff about my mother and father—and the notes I wrote, after I realized, when it all started to make
sense. . . ."

His mother and father, apparently, were Maria Cazarès and Jean
Lazare. Pascal piled the notebooks in one place, the dog-eared cuttings
next to them.

Beneath them, he saw, were bundles of tattered miscellaneous papers
and other press clippings. There was a collection on Monaco's royal
family, including his own stolen pictures of Princess Caroline to which
Star had referred; there was a section on the Kennedy family, one on an
English duke with a Canadian wife, one on an Australian-American
press magnate, and several on various American movie stars. He laid
each of these out in neat piles. Beneath them, at the bottom of the case,
was a collection of pornographic pictures, much-handled and of extreme
violence. Pascal closed the lid of the case on them. Star made a peculiar
wiggling movement, gestured toward the secondary piles of press clippings, then smiled.

"Those were my false starts, all right? That duke—the movie star—I
always knew there was something different about me, that I wasn't just
anybody, you know? I tried tracing my mother—as soon as I was old
enough, and they'd let me, I tried. But, of course, Maria had covered her
tracks. You know what they tried to make me believe?" His voice was
filled with derision. "They tried to make me believe my mother was this
hooker, this two-bit fucking hooker, now deceased. Well, I wasn't about
to buy *that*. In Quebec I saw this fucking social worker bitch, and she
brought out all these papers, a birth certificate—there wasn't even a father's name on the fucking thing—and she said I couldn't meet my
mother because my mother was dead, got beaten up good by one of her
johns, some shit like that. . . . And the way she looked at me, with this
kind of fucking pity on her face. I wanted to kill her right then, I just
wanted to snap her fucking neck, because she was feeding me all these
fucking lies. And then I saw—she was just part of the conspiracy, that's
all. So I let her live. Smug fucking dumb lying bitch . . ."

He shuddered, and Gini flinched.

"After that—I had to find them, my parents, right? And they'd made
it really hard for me—so I followed a few false leads, and then I got
lucky; just like that. I met Mathilde. I was in Paris, I'd just come here
from Amsterdam and I was down on my luck, the cards weren't good, I
had no money—and this friend of mine, Chantal, we'd had a fight, so I
had no place to go—and then I met Mathilde. A few blocks from here.

She was in this little park, feeding pigeons—and I got talking to her. I just wanted a meal. A place to sleep. I wasn't feeling too well—I get these pains in my head. So she brought me back here and she cooked me this food—and Mathilde was all right. I liked Mathilde. She was lonely, and she started talking—about Maria. And I knew who Maria was, of course, because I'd read about her in the magazines, and so—slowly, I began to see. A week later, maybe less, maybe a day later, I don't remember—but Mathilde told me how Maria had lost her baby son, way back, in New Orleans—and then, *light,* I mean, *I saw.* Everything fit. The dates fit. I'd been in New Orleans one time, for a while. My hair—it's black, like hers, like that pig Lazare's. Yeah—my hair, and my eyes . . . I look like my mother. Don't I?"

"I can certainly see a resemblance," Pascal said.

He kept his eyes on Star. His attention seemed intermittent now, his gaze wandering like his words. He'd look at Pascal, then Gini, then the gun, then he'd stare off into space. Pascal had the sensation that this conversation was familiar, that it had been repeated many times, and that mostly it was a conversation Star was having with himself.

Cautiously, Pascal moved around the table so the distance between them was slightly reduced. Star did not react. He had begun to touch Gini again. In a clumsy and ill-coordinated way, he began to squeeze her breast.

Gini flinched. "Star—let me just check the tape. . . ."

She kept her eyes fixed on Pascal's face. She could see his reaction to this mauling from Star; his expression was murderous. She tried to signal him with her eyes—don't move, don't protest. "Star—the first tape's about to run out. It's okay—I have plenty more. Let me insert a new one. . . ."

"No. We don't need it. It's over. That's it. . . ."

"No, Star—it can't be. I—there's so many things I want to ask you. People will want to know how Maria reacted when you told her who you were—because you must have told her, Star, surely?"

"Yeah. I told her."

"They'll want to know what she said. And then they'll want to know what happened next. . . ." She kept her eyes on Pascal and frowned. "They'll want to know why you decided to kill Jean Lazare—and what happened when you did. . . ."

Pascal did not move a muscle. He could see she was trying to give him information and buy time as well. Was the blood still daubed on Star's face and hands Lazare's?

"People will want to know the facts, Star," she went on. "Pascal's a good judge—you think they'd be interested, don't you, Pascal?"

"Sure." Pascal kept his voice even. "It's the details that make the difference."

"Why I killed him?" Star laughed. "How I killed him? How I would have fucking killed her if I'd had half a chance? Sure, I'll explain that. . . ."

He flourished the gun, then jabbed it back in Gini's neck. His reaction delay was now lengthening, Pascal thought. It had taken him nearly fifteen seconds to answer Gini's question, yet he was clearly unaware of the time lapse, of Pascal's own interjection. His mind was *shorting*, Pascal thought.

He was now allowing Gini to bend to the recorder and change the tapes. Pascal watched for an opportunity. None came. About twenty seconds after Gini pressed record, he pulled her back in front of him and began speaking again.

"You know what? He *pleaded* with me. . . ." His voice rose.

"The great Jean Lazare. The emperor himself, down on his fucking knees, begging, offering me anything I wanted, if only I wouldn't shoot. I liked that. Let me tell you—I *enjoyed* that. My fucking father, crawling on his knees to me. I've waited so long for that."

It had been, Pascal saw, the wrong approach, an unwise, perhaps even fatal choice of topic. Star was excited again. There seemed to be a direct line in his head between the humiliation he was describing and sex.

He stopped speaking, pulled Gini roughly back against him, and began to run his hands up and down her body. He rubbed himself against her back, his gaze never once leaving Pascal as he did this. He smiled, and his eyes took on a fixed, glittering look.

"Don't try it, Pascal. The safety catch is off. The gun's *cocked*. You know anything about guns? This is a fifteen-round magazine. Nasty bullets. You can really get off on these bullets. You can really spray them around. . . . She'd be dead, and you'd be dead, before you'd moved two fucking feet. . . ." His voice rose. "You don't like that, Pascal? It upsets you, huh? Makes you feel a bit inadequate, a bit *impotent*, maybe? Well, too bad. I had *years* of that. Years of being pissed on and dismissed and ordered around and locked up. Years crawling to those cocksuckers, in the homes, at night, jerking those fucking bastards off—you know how fucking old I was? Five years old the first time, up the ass, in my mouth, I had ten, twelve fucking *years* of that, treated like I was shit, like I was some fucking nobody—"

Pascal froze. Gini gave a low moan and clamped her hand across her mouth. Pascal started to move; he knew Star was about to start shooting; he watched his face contort. The telephone rang. Star was jamming the gun at Gini's mouth—then suddenly, five rings in, he seemed to hear the phone and stopped. A shudder ran through his body; he drew back; his face became blank and tight, then he seemed to relax. He jabbed the gun in Gini's ribs.

"Get back over there. With him. The far side of the table, where I can see you both. Neither of you move. I have to take this call. . . ." He shivered, then laughed. "I have to talk to my shrink."

He watched Gini stumble across the room. He waited until they had both reached the far side of the table, twenty feet back. Keeping his eyes and the gun trained on them both, he picked up the receiver and cradled it on his shoulder. He listened, smiling. Pascal could just hear the voice of the man addressing him, a quiet, even voice.

Pascal drew Gini tightly into his arms. Whoever the man on the telephone was, he prayed to God he was good, and he prayed he would realize that they had to be quick.

He locked his arms around Gini. He kissed her tears, kissed her upturned face, tried to still the tremors of fear in her body. When Star began speaking so the sound of his own voice was drowned, he pressed his mouth against her ear and her hair and began to whisper, so she could only just hear him. He felt her body go rigid in his arms. He knew, and she knew, he thought, that this might be their last conversation. So little time, and so much to be said.

"Gini. We haven't got very long . . ."

"I know. I thought he was going to fire then."

"He was. He's right on the edge. But he wants those photographs—and there's something I could try. . . ." He waited until Star began speaking again, then continued whispering. Gini listened, her eyes fixed on his. She could feel his lips against her skin and her hair. His suggestion terrified her.

"No." She pressed her lips to his face. "No, Pascal—please, he'll kill you. He wants to kill you first. We should wait—keep him talking."

"We have to try. You can see how unstable he is. The police will try to tire him, wind him down. We don't have time for that. . . ."

He stopped as Star laughed, listened, then began speaking again. Pascal looked down at Gini's blanched face. How long did they have? Ten minutes, fifteen?

"Pascal." Her hand closed over his. "Why didn't you run? Out in the street, with Marianne. You had time—you could have gotten away—oh, Christ. . . ."

She stopped. She already knew the answer in any case, and had she doubted it, she could read it in the tenderness that flooded his face.

"The question didn't arise," he said simply; she heard his voice catch. "Gini—nothing is altered. I love you so much. You know that." As he said this, he bent and kissed her mouth, turning her away so she was shielded from Star's view. Her mouth opened under his, and her eyes closed. He could feel the love and the desperation to communicate love in her embrace.

He kissed her deeply, thinking it might be the last time he would ever do this. He listened to the language of her response. He looked down and could read the alteration, the new resolve in her face.

Star's voice rose; he laughed again. Pascal drew back a little; he said, against her throat, his words only just audible to her: "The pink bedroom, Gini. In there. I want him in the room that upsets him the most. The room with the least light."

In the communications van, Rowland adjusted his headphones. The police psychologist, who had introduced himself to Star by his first name only, Lucien, had been talking to him now for almost five minutes. Rowland could see exactly what the man was doing—trying to calm and extract information at the same time, trying to delay, trying, more specifically, to establish a relationship of dependency and trust. It was Rowland's impression—and the psychologist's, he suspected—that Star knew precisely why he was doing this.

Star was being too cooperative, Rowland thought—but his cooperative replies—they had both switched from French to English—were being made in an increasingly insolent, mocking tone of voice.

"Food?" Star said now, and laughed. "Oh, hey—yes. I mean food would be really good. There's a larder here, and a fridge, and they're both stuffed with food, so I guess, if I wanted, I could stay on here for days—even weeks. I mean, I wouldn't *starve*, right? And neither would Gini or Pascal. We'd *share*. But when you say food, I guess you have something pretty special in mind, yes? You know what I really like? Langoustines. There's a restaurant in St. Germain, *L'Age d'Or*, it's called—it does langoustines this really special way. Now, if you got some of those sent in . . . Not immediately. Maybe in an hour. If you called me back in an hour. No—half an hour. No—twenty minutes. No, let's take a rain check on it, okay?"

The psychologist glanced at Martigny and frowned.

"Of course. That can be arranged," he said, still in the same calm voice.

"And the car," Star laughed. "Don't forget the car. I'll be needing that. I want Jean Lazare's 1938 Rolls to take me out to the airport. But I don't want it yet. I'm enjoying myself too much. Then—let me just run down the list again . . ."

He began to enumerate the list of absurd demands already made; the psychologist switched his microphone to mute. He glanced at Martigny, then at Rowland, then shook his head.

Martigny turned and spoke to the GIGN officer next to him; Star's voice continued. When there was silence in the van once more, the psychologist switched off the mute button. Rowland watched the tapes revolve. His sense of powerlessness and fear increased by the second.

"Meantime," Star paused, "it's too bad—but we've got the shades closed, and the drapes, so we can't see out, and, of course, your snipers can't see in. . . ." He giggled. "So you'll have to tell me—this is causing a stir, right? You've got the press there now? The camera crews? No—don't bother answering. I mean, you're a straight guy, I can tell that, but you just might lie. That's okay. Tell them I'll be making a personal appearance, on the balcony out front, later tonight. Meantime, I'll get Gini to take a look—don't shoot or anything, will you? Gini—you want to do that? The far window. What? CNN? And—all the others? That's great. Really great. You can go back to Pascal. Slowly. That's it. Smart girl. It's okay. Don't cry. Pascal—you want to kiss her again? Don't mind me. Go right ahead. You can fuck her if you like. You first. Me next . . . Only kidding. It's these little pills I take, you see. They give me this—lust for life. I might just take a top-up right now. . . . Oh, *excellent*. Oh, these are seriously good. . . . Look, Pascal—I hate to say this to a Frenchman, you know—but your technique, it's not so good. It's too gentle. You know what really turns women on? Rough stuff. They really really like it when you smack them around."

Rowland bowed his head. The psychologist interrupted.

"Christophe," he said. "Christophe? Can I make a suggestion? Wouldn't it be easier, better all around, if you could make a gesture of goodwill? In return for arranging the car, say, you release one of your hostages. . . ."

"Gini?" Star laughed again. "You want Gini, right? I'm not so sure. She and I—we get along. I'd need to think about that."

The psychologist made a small sign to Martigny; one finger held up.

"Then what I suggest is this. I call you back in exactly twenty minutes, okay? That gives you time to consider my proposals. You may think of some other things you need. There might be someone you'd like to talk to, and if there is, we can arrange that."

"I don't think so." Star giggled again. "Not too likely. They're all dead."

"Fine. Twenty minutes. I'll call you then. At precisely two o'clock."

He cut the connection and turned back to Martigny and the GIGN officer.

"Can you be ready to go in before that? Say fifteen minutes from now?"

The other two men had a brief muttered conference.

"Half an hour would be better," Martigny said. "Forty-five minutes would be better still."

"I wouldn't advise that."

"You don't think you can persuade him to release Genevieve Hunter?"

"He has no intention of releasing either of them. Or using the car, or the plane. You heard him. He's excited. He's playing games."

Rowland watched the decision be made. He watched the GIGN officer leave; he heard movement outside the van, the shouldering of weapons, the sound of footsteps moving off.

The psychologist passed his hand across his forehead. Martigny, sitting down, lit a cigarette.

All three men sat in silence. They watched the second hand of the clocks move forward; they watched the banks of tapes. They listened to the quiet relayed voice of the movement tracker, then a burst of static. Rowland froze: he had just heard Gini's voice.

Martigny gave a sigh. "At last. They have the listening devices in place. When they go in—they'll go in front and rear simultaneously. Thirty seconds before they go in, the telephone will ring. Fifteen seconds after that we kill every light in that apartment. Then . . ."

He did not need to continue. Rowland knew, in essence, what happened next. They would rappel down from the roof. Diversionary noise and blinding light; GIGN operatives, helmeted, in full body armor, each man with night sights and each man audio-linked. In theory their training enabled them to enter a strange room in darkness, at top speed, yet still distinguish who were the hostages and who was not. Rapidly, using automatic weapons, they would take Star out—and only Star. Sometimes this technique was successful, sometimes not.

Both Pascal Lamartine and Star, he thought, were of similar height; both had dark hair; one man was holding a weapon, the other was not.

He fixed his eyes on the clock face set into the side of the van above the banked tapes and equipment. The reception from the apartment was intermittent—like listening to a badly tuned radio station. Suddenly, after a burst of static, he heard Lamartine's voice; he sounded cool, even relaxed.

"Not in here," he said. "In your mother's room—the pink room.

There's a wall of her pictures in there. If you stood back against that . . . I can try some long shots. It's just—"

"What? What's the problem?"

"For covers, I need a head shot. I'd need just one good close-up."

"Covers?"

"Sure. *Time. Newsweek. Paris Match.* I need monochrome and color—monochrome for newspapers, color for magazines."

"I don't like that room. It's my mother's room. I don't want—"

"Fine. Okay. We'll do it here. It's not as good—"

"No. No. We'll go in there—just don't try anything, okay, or I fucking fire, and she . . ."

The voices faded again. Inside the communications van there was absolute silence.

"What in God's name does he think he's doing?" Rowland burst out. Martigny gripped Rowland's arm. The psychologist shook his head.

"I wouldn't have recommended that room. Or any mention of the mother."

"Or cameras." Rowland rose. "Cameras least of all. He loves cameras. He loves publicity—you saw that. He's perfectly capable of killing Gini on camera. It's the worst thing Lamartine could possibly do. Call Star again. Call him now. You have to stop this."

Both Martigny and the psychologist looked at the clock. Five minutes had passed.

Martigny began flicking switches, speaking into a microphone; the tapes clicked, began to whirr.

In Madame Duval's apartment the telephone began ringing. All three men adjusted their headphones and listened. In the apartment, no one picked up.

"Let it ring," Star said. "Let it ring, and get on with it. Hurry up . . ."

Pascal was reading him, trying to read the room. On entering it, as he had anticipated, Star's unease had immediately increased. Watching him, Pascal had the impression that Star was still watching some private movie, and that it was unspooling before his gaze very fast. The faster the movie, the slower his reaction speed seemed to be. He was now backed up against the wall Pascal had indicated, his body framed by pictures of Maria Cazarès. He was clutching Gini in front of him, the gun wedged against her neck. The lighting in here was even dimmer than in the sitting room beyond. Pascal raised one of his cameras and looked through the viewfinder. He focused on Star's curious eyes. He could not rush this; he had to wait for Star's eyes to adjust to this poor lighting, for the pupils to dilate.

Fixed to this camera was a device he rarely used, known as a ring flash. When fired, it produced an intense burst of blinding light. Fired straight into the eyes at close range, that light might gain him fifteen, twenty, thirty seconds of advantage—which might or might not be enough. It was certainly not enough while Gini remained in this position with a gun to the neck.

He lowered the camera. Star's eyes were now fixed on the huge pink bed behind Pascal. Pascal sighed. In a calm, regretful voice, he said: "It's no good like that. Gini's too tall. I'm not getting your face. . . ."

"Fuck you. How about like this?"

With one quick violent movement he shoved Gini down on her knees, holding the gun to the side of her head.

"No"—Pascal met his eyes—"I won't take that picture. And no one would print it if I did."

"Fuck you both. I—what was that?"

Star had begun to shiver. His eyes swiveled around the room. Gini gave a low moan of fear. Pascal, who had also heard the noise—a slithering sound—gave Star a blank look.

"What? I can't hear anything. . . ."

"You can—there!" Star's face became rigid. "Something's moving. I can hear something—stirring. It's over there—by the bed."

Pascal knew perfectly well that the sound was above them, and came, almost certainly, from the roof. He half raised the camera, took a step forward. Star was pressed against the wall now, his face distorted with fear. He was beginning to make a low choking sound in his throat. Pascal felt time freeze, then speed up. He thought: one more sound and he'll start firing.

"She's come back. . . . My mother's come back. She—I should have washed. I wanted to wash. She can smell the blood on me. She's here. . . ." His eyes jittered away, turned back to Gini, turned back to the bed.

"You . . ." He gave Gini a kick. "Check the bed. Pull that cover back—the pink one. It's moving—Christ, it's fucking moving. . . ."

Now, Pascal thought as Gini rolled out of Star's reach and sprang to her feet. As she moved to the bed, and reached for the cover, Pascal lunged forward fast, two feet, three feet. Star was still pressed back against the wall, white to the lips. He was trembling from head to foot, the gun wavering back and forth. He opened his mouth in a silent scream. From above them came a long bumping, slithering movement. Gini was twitching the pink bedcover aside. In a low voice she said, *Oh my God,* and one split second before Star pulled the trigger, Pascal fired the flash.

The room exploded with light and noise. The room was splitting apart. Pascal dived. He felt his right shoulder crunch into Star's rib cage. He had started firing before Pascal hit him, and he went on firing as he fell. Pascal was blinded by the noise, the bursts of fire, the horrible abattoir screaming from Star's mouth. As he fell, Pascal kicked his gun arm and Star gave a scream of pain. There was a burst of fire, an explosion of glass. Metal spun through the air as the gun flew out of Star's hand, then Star's fist was smashing into his mouth.

He tried to shout to Gini—he couldn't see Gini, and she might have been hit—then Star slammed into him again, grabbing at his throat, digging his fingers into the artery in his neck. Ten seconds of that pressure and he'd lose consciousness: Pascal jerked his knee hard up into Star's crotch, felt him sag and grunt with pain, and the grip of his fingers relaxed. He got in one more good punch, low in the throat, and Star reeled, then grabbed. They crashed back against the pictures on the wall, slammed into a chair, into one of the small fragile tables with which this apartment was filled, then crashed to the floor. Pascal fell awkwardly, one leg twisted behind him—and that second's disadvantage was all it took. In an instant Star was on his feet again. He kicked out viciously, and pain shot down Pascal's arm, across his ribs. He almost blacked out, started to rise, watched the room spin and tilt, then a woman's voice, a voice he hardly recognized, said: "You kick him again, and you're dead."

Pascal thought: merciful God, poor Gini. He was trying to push himself to his feet, pain shooting through his arm. He knew the arm, his right arm, was broken, and the film was slowing, he could see with a hideous slow-motion clarity what was going to happen next. Star had become still, and suddenly intent. A slow smile lit his face.

"Sweet . . ." he said. "Go on, then—shoot. You can't touch me, the cards told me. You fire and you'll miss."

She *would* miss—through a mist of pain, Pascal could see that: Gini, who hated and feared guns, who did not even know how to hold a gun like this.

The Beretta needed a two-handed grip. She was holding it, Pascal saw, in the worst possible way, a woman's way, backed up against the end of the bed, the gun in one hand, her arm fully extended, so the weight of the gun and her terror made the barrel waver and shake. He could see she was rigid with fear, her eyes fixed, her face white. When Star took one slow step forward, she flinched. From somewhere very distant, Pascal heard sounds, footsteps, low commands, new urgency. He thought distantly—fine, but they're too late. He tried to haul himself to his feet, and Star took one more step forward. He radiated confidence now, it came off him like heat.

"You dumb fucking cunt," he said in a low voice. "You know what I'm going to do? What I was about to do earlier. And your fucking boyfriend there can fucking watch. Find out how it fucking feels—both of you. Because when I come, I'm going to blow your fucking brains out. Get down on your knees, cunt, give me that fucking gun, bitch. . . ."

Backed against the bed, Gini watched the centuries it took him to walk ten feet. She could see all this *detail*, the smashed room, Pascal's smashed arm, the blood streaking his white face. He was still trying to rise, and Star was approaching with that wet, ugly smile on his extraordinary face.

She understood: she could hear what the small voice in her head was saying: Pascal could not reach her in time, no one was going to burst through the doors or the windows in time, so it was just her and this approaching shape, and this heavy instrument in her hand, which might be nearly out of ammunition, so if she fired, she had to be very careful not to miss.

Star was still moving, words were still spilling out of his mouth, and then as he moved, he made just one little mistake. As he stepped past Pascal, he aimed one final kick at his legs—and then it was easy. As she curled her finger around the trigger, she was back on a bridge in Amsterdam, and soaring right through her body was a current of astonishing force. All that latent female power, in Anneke's mother, in herself. The power blacked out the panic and the pity, so when he was four feet away from her, she fired.

The gun kicked like a live thing, and she kept on firing, and she could see she must have missed, though he was so huge a target and so close, because he was still coming at her, so she held the gun closer, clutched it with two hands, and as he reached for her, she fired straight at the bloodstains on his chest.

What happened then was horrible. He reeled back, his eyes opened wide with surprise, and his body began to dance as she kept firing, little jerking spasmodic movements, like a marionette. She waited for him to stop this terrible puppet dance, and come at her again. She pulled the trigger again, and nothing happened, just a series of little clicks, so she waited for him to stop dancing and grab her, and as she waited, she thought: I've failed, and now Pascal and I, we're both dead.

She began to turn to Pascal, then Star made a retching, gargling noise. She stared at him. He jerked forward onto his knees and clutched at himself, as if something live, some animal, were inside him, moving around his body, in his stomach first, then his chest, then his throat. He fixed his eyes on her face and opened his mouth wide to say something, but the words seemed to clot in his throat.

She could see Pascal rising, feel him reach her side at last, and quietly take the gun from her hand. She thought he threw it down; but she couldn't take her eyes from Star's face. She waited for the words, watched his lips form them, then he vomited, and a great gush of blood spewed out of his mouth. He fell forward, facedown, arms outspread, and Gini continued to stare at him. She was waiting for him to get up.

Pascal was drawing her into his arms. It was dark, no light, the telephone was ringing, and she could hear the smash and crash of glass.

"Gini, don't look," Pascal was saying. "Just stand still. Let me hold you."

"Did I kill him?" she said.

Several times over, Pascal thought, but he did not say this. He drew her to one side. The room was filled with shouts. He pressed her back against the wall, shielded her with his body, and let the aftermath take its course.

They put the power back on eventually. Gini looked back once as black-clad men hustled them out.

Dead Star was lying on a pile of smashed wood and china and glass, arms outflung, fists clenched. By his left hand was a small headless china figurine, and a crucifix; by his right was a torn photograph of Maria Cazarès. In the fight, various objects had fallen from his pockets: one was a packet of much-used tarot cards; another was the container with Star's last three unused White Doves.

CHAPTER 21

Rowland stood waiting in the street. Brightness had begun to fade from the air; a thin rain had begun to fall. The incipient darkness was pooled with the artificial brilliance of arc lamps. He frowned into their rainbow dazzle, then, moving into the shadows by the police vans, took up his vantage point. From here, despite the crowds of reporters and police operatives, he had a clear view of Madame Duval's building and its portico steps. He knew that Gini was safe, but he wanted to see with his own eyes that she was safe. That, he felt, was the next and necessary step.

Waiting in that cool, quiet hinterland that lies beyond shock and violent emotion, he could watch the unraveling of his own predicament as if he watched on film the sequences of some other man's life. He was thinking, in a distanced way, about the nature of heroism—in which quality he believed, although he knew that belief to be old-fashioned, and to most minds suspect. He admired courage, whether spiritual or physical. Perhaps it even required a certain small measure of courage on his own part now to acknowledge that since Gini was safe, he himself owed Pascal Lamartine a debt.

"They'll be down in a few minutes." Martigny had materialized at his elbow, stamping his feet in the cold and drawing on a cigarette. He exhaled, gave Rowland a sidelong glance.

"Women. They're so unpredictable. You know—when we were listening, when we thought she wasn't going to fire?"

"Yes."

"Well, something must have got to her. She pumped twelve bullets into him. When they get him to the morgue—I wouldn't like to do the autopsy."

"I imagine not."

"Skin, and inside . . ." He shrugged, and tossed the stub of his cigarette into the gutter. "And I thought it was all over. I wonder, was it fear, you think?"

"Or anger."

"I guess."

He moved off a few paces, then turned back.

"You look— You want a drink? I can get you something. Some cognac? A whiskey?"

"No thanks."

"You can't talk to her." Martigny gave him a kind glance. "You do realize that? They both have to go for medical checks. Then debriefing. Lamartine's a hospital case. Cracked ribs and his arm's badly fractured. She—it depends how deeply she's in shock. You won't be seeing her before tomorrow morning at the earliest. You understand that?"

"I do. Yes."

"Meantime, I owe you. So if you want to stick with me when we start going through that apartment . . ." Martigny jerked his thumb at the mob of reporters beyond the barriers. "I'd rather you got the full story. Those bastards have been getting in my way all day. They're about to discover just how uncooperative my department can be. So, what d'you need? Six hours? Eight? Overnight? Let them chase their own tails until we hold a press conference tomorrow morning, because I certainly won't be holding one tonight."

They exchanged glances. Rowland gave a wintry smile.

"Overnight would be more than generous. I'd certainly like to see that apartment. I have to get on to my news desk, get copy through to them."

"No problem. There's a load of his papers up there. Notes, letters, some weird kind of diary he kept. Plus there's your colleague's tapes, of course. All evidence, naturally."

"Naturally."

"Not for release to the press until a much later stage. So, should any journalist happen on some of that evidence—in the melee, when my back was turned . . . I'd have to launch an inquiry, of course."

"Without doubt."

"Though the trouble with such inquiries is—they tend to get nowhere. Too much paperwork . . . You know how it is."

"I'm grateful."

"No need." Martigny shivered, and drew his overcoat around him. "You want to join me for a meal later? My wife will cook us something."

"I'd like that." Rowland gave him a glance. "And then we could always share that brandy."

Martigny laughed. He slapped Rowland on the shoulder, then made a gesture which was expressive and deeply French.

"They're bringing them out now. I'll leave you alone until they've gone."

"Is it that damn obvious?" Rowland averted his face.

Martigny gave Rowland one last glance of quiet and half-amused sympathy, then moved away. An astute man, Rowland thought, and also a tactful one. The next instant, tensing, he forgot him. There was movement by the portico, shouts from reporters, a sudden blaze of TV lights.

A police car had drawn up at the foot of the steps. Gini and Pascal Lamartine were ushered out fast, flanked by police. Rowland caught a glimpse of a woman's white face; Lamartine's left arm was around her shoulders; her fair head was bent. Lamartine paused as she ducked into the waiting car first. For one brief instant Rowland could clearly see his face. Etched upon it was an expression of love and of concern that spoke to Rowland across the distance that separated them: it said *married*. It marked a boundary that Rowland was not prepared to cross.

Or so he told himself then, frowning into the fine rain, forcing himself to remain in the shadows, invisible; the honorable thing to do. Rowland watched the car pull away fast. Sirens curled through the damp air. His own decision—made then, made earlier?—angered him, but he accepted its ethics even as he felt the first cut of sharp and bitter regret.

It was then, as the car rounded a corner and disappeared, that he began to plan his own disengagement from Gini. It would have to be contrived, he told himself, so that it caused the least guilt, and the fewest repercussions—at least in her case. He would have to lie to her. In a distant way, he wondered whether, when the moment came, he would be able to do so effectively. Could he lie as well as he had claimed to her he could, he wondered. Could he lie so well that she would never suspect?

"Ready?" Martigny called to him.

Rowland nodded, and crossed to his side. They were bringing out the stretcher and bodybag as he and Martigny reached the lobby. A glint of light on black plastic; some difficulty in maneuvering this load out of the elevator cage. Rowland thought: an ignominious departure. He averted his eyes.

Upstairs, confronted with that pink shrine of a bedroom, he paused. He had imagined this room, as it was described to him by Juliette de Nerval. He had imagined it again as he waited in that police van. Yet it was not as his mind's eye had seen it. He had not foreseen this much blood, this much debris. He passed his hand across his eyes: this room, his own life—both seemed to him fantastically unreal.

He looked at the wreckage steadily, then Martigny beckoned to him and they went into the sitting room. Martigny quietly drew him aside and thrust a pile of press clippings and handwritten papers into his hands.

My Biography, Star had written in a small, neat hand:

> *They tried to tell me my mother was this hooker, and my father one of her johns. After she died, when I was around two years old, I was fostered out to this sister of hers, who was married to some GI Joe, & lived near Baton Rouge, Louisiana. I guess they didn't like me, because they got rid of me pretty soon, and when I was around four I got dumped in the first of the homes. This version of events is one big lie. Now I know the truth, which feels real good. So let me explain: this is who I am. . . .*

Rowland felt pity: he could identify with this. Wouldn't we all like the answer to that question, he thought; wouldn't we all like to say with certainty—*this is who I am*. He sheafed through the papers, seeing the handwriting deteriorate further on as Star explained a quest that had gone murderously wrong. He switched on Gini's tape recorder, then quickly switched it off again as he heard her voice. All the components he needed for an immediate story were here. He had learned self-discipline, and so patiently, and with no outward sign of disquiet, he retired to a corner of the room and set himself to work.

They finally allowed Gini to leave the hospital the next morning. At seven, when Pascal was sedated and sleeping, a car was provided to take her back to her hotel. Gini climbed into it meekly, then gladly sensing the driver's indifference, persuaded him to drop her off. She was desperate to be alone, just to walk and breathe and think, so she made her way back slowly, by a circuitous route, breathing in the cool damp air, watching the eastern sky lighten, listening to the echo of her own footsteps along the still, almost deserted streets.

She walked down to the Seine and stood on the quay for a while, watching the slide of the water, watching the events of the past days, and the past night. She watched the questions she had seen in Pascal's eyes, the questions he was too wise to voice. She watched the police ask questions, to which her patient replies felt correct but not right. She watched the consultant explain, gesturing at shadows on X rays, that this was a compound fracture, necessitating a complex operation, in which steel pins would have to be inserted in the arm, here and here and here. She watched herself, alone with the consultant now, in a small anteroom: "He must be able to use his hands," she said to the man. "It's his right arm that is broken. He's a photographer. A very fine photographer. He has to be able to work quickly. He has to be deft. You do understand?"

The man—eminent in his profession—said in a kind way that he did understand, that he already knew this.

His reassurances seemed to come at her from a great distance. She could feel sense fragmenting. She felt that this man was not hearing her, or not fully understanding her, so she brushed aside his remarks about postsurgical therapy, patient cooperation, and a period of healing that would take, at the very least, six months.

She reiterated her fears, and her arguments, until suddenly midsentence, she realized she was not asking this eminent man to cure any injury Star had inflicted; she was asking him to cure *all* the injuries, especially those she had inflicted herself.

Those words, as such, were not said, but she felt that the doctor sensed something of her meaning; he read, maybe, the pain and the guilt and the distress she felt. He chose—and it was perhaps a wise choice—to ascribe her reaction entirely to shock. Gini, who knew this to be untrue, did not argue. She consented to the prescribed interlude of quiet and rest. She was led to a small room; she lay down on a narrow hospital bed. In order to hasten the departure of the nurse assigned to her, she pretended to sleep, and lay there with closed eyes, watching with mortification and sick despair reenactment after reenactment of her own shame, of her betrayal not just of Pascal, but also of herself.

Fatigue and misery and self-reproach made her grip on these events begin to slacken eventually. For the first half hour, all she could see, fearfully repeated, were her own actions, that night at the St. Vincent. Yes, it was true; she had done these unimaginable things, and said these unimaginable things, but as they danced before her eyes, as she made herself reexamine them, they began to seem not more real, but less. Her tired mind rebelled. She began to feel that it was not she who had acted in this way, but some other Gini, a woman who had sprung up unheralded from nowhere, a succubus, a dream woman, a mirror woman who had stepped out from the glass and for a few hours reversed the rules of life, so north became south, and right, left.

Grasping at this idea, and despising herself for doing so, she fell into a restless, feverish sleep. And in the sleep, up from her unconscious, came a man who might have been Rowland McGuire, who spoke with his accent but did not have his face. This man rearranged all these actions in yet another form; he consoled, and with a promissory air, said no, she was reading the sentences all the wrong way; if she would only let him rearrange the words in a different order, she would understand. With a conjuror's hands he took the words "shame" and "self-betrayal," and they spelled out "love" and "hope." She watched all those bright vowels and consonants sparkle in the air, and just when they were suggesting to her that a right might lie beyond a wrong, she awoke, crying out.

Now, looking down at a gray city river, the dream eddied into her mind, then slipped out of reach. She felt a terrible despondency, a conviction that she could understand those events no better than she could understand that impulse which had come to her out of the air and had made it possible, just hours before, to pull a trigger, fire a weapon, end a life. Turning away from the flux and current of the water, she fixed her eyes on the loveliness of the particular buildings in front of her as their outlines emerged in the strengthening light. If understanding and reason failed her, she thought, beginning to walk again, then duty and precept and principle would have to suffice.

I have no choice, she said to herself; I have no choice; I have made my promises, I am almost a wife.

She increased her pace, repeating this litany to herself. She loved Pascal, and with repetition, this litany gathered strength. By the time she reached the hotel, she was convinced this strength was more than sufficient to carry her through any parting from Rowland McGuire—and a parting, a final and absolute one, she also planned and scripted as she walked.

But confronted with him later that day, across the nervous and narrow expanse of her hotel room, she could see only the banalities and untruths of that carefully prepared script. One look at his face told her: that speech had been contrived for a different and lesser man, some man she had allowed her mind to invent. It would be unpardonable to speak it now, an insult to him, and also to herself.

She was afraid to look at him, and terrified of what would happen if he touched her. So she edged away from him as he stood awkwardly by the door, wearing an overcoat, booked on a London flight. She turned her face to the window with its view of Paris lights. Her carefully stacked arguments fell apart in her mind. I have no choice, she repeated silently and fiercely to herself—but even that sentence, so reassuring, so clearly true a few hours earlier, now failed her. Choice entered the room with him; his physical proximity made every certainty shift.

She turned finally to look at him. He was frowning. He glanced back at the door as if regretting he had come here, then he began speaking. Gini could scarcely hear his words, let alone make sense of them, though their sense was clear enough. She knew at once, instinctively and with absolute certainty, that he, too, had planned some careful exodus speech, and was duly beginning upon it.

It would have been easier for them both had he been able to continue with it. But the increasing strain was evident, in his gestures and tone, in his pale, tense face. He negotiated, by sheer force of will, just three sentences. Then abruptly, with a sudden angry gesture, he stopped.

That occasion was not the first on which Rowland had seen Gini that day, and their previous encounters had given him, he realized now, a misplaced confidence. They had met first that morning, in the doorway of this same room, when their conversation had been brief: stiff inquiries on Rowland's part as to her welfare, and Lamartine's; equally stiff reassurances on Gini's part. Rowland's mind burned with the unsaid, but a night spent working, filing copy, had left him convinced that he possessed the resolve to act. That afternoon, when to his surprise Gini insisted on working with him, filing more copy on a story that even blasé Max admitted to be a scoop, he had remained obstinately convinced he had the willpower to negotiate this.

He had sat next to Gini, editing her copy on screen. He watched her words scroll; he watched the cursor move; he watched words delete and paragraphs shift. He was aware of the ironies of the procedure, aware that his skills as an editor would shortly be required in a rather different context. He thought as he worked: if I put it in this way, if I use this particular phrase, if I'm careful to delete that emotion; he glanced at her set profile, then quickly away. It seemed to him that any script he concocted would involve not only the deletion of truth, but also of himself.

He felt capable of effecting his plan, nonetheless. He experienced some indecision after Gini left, when briefly his own feelings rebelled, and he twice postponed his London flight. But he was sure by the time he finally came down to this room to say good-bye that he had such weaknesses under control. It might well be that during this brief interview he had to make Gini think ill of him, but he was prepared for that. Being proud by nature, it was not easy for him to envisage losing her respect, but if such a reaction facilitated her disengagement from him, it was a price he was determined should be met.

Yet something began to fail him almost at once.

He allowed himself, finally, to look at her. She was standing by the window with her face averted. He let his eyes rest on the light of her hair, the pale curve of her throat, the soft grayish dress she was wearing. The longing he felt for her then was intense. It was not physical desire, though he knew perfectly well that surge would overwhelm him immediately if he were unwise enough to move forward, or touch her. It was a longing beyond explanation, and certainly the other side of reason, a longing for the joy she alone could now gift. He knew how insubstantial this power was: he knew it was compounded of a thousand frail elements, much intuition, some instinct, some irrational hope, yet it was tensile, as irresistible as steel cables, a winch. He could feel it winding him in, winding him in, through a silence that first whispered, then spoke. He knew she listened to the language of that silence as intuitively as he did. She turned slowly back to meet his gaze, and he was one inch away from the complete certainty that she not only knew, but felt as he did.

She gave a small distressed gesture of the hands, displacing air. He watched her face alter, soften, and then flood with regret.

"Don't." She moved across to him and took his hand in hers. "You were going to make a speech—weren't you?"

"I was."

"Please don't. I can imagine it. I was going to make a speech too. A similar one, I think. None of it would have been true—it might have made things easier, but it wouldn't have been true. I was going to be—oh, hard. Brittle. Dismissive. Light. Maybe a little cheap. I thought cheap might help. . . ." She paused and gave a half-smile. "And you?"

"Brusque. Shabby. Stereotypically male. I've had some practice at that."

She smiled again, then, her eyes filling with tears, shook her head.

"I'm glad you stopped. I'd have hated that. It would have meant I was wrong about you—that you were less than I thought." She hesitated, then looked up at him with an expression half doubtful, half pleading.

"May I say something else instead? It's brief, I promise you—and I probably shouldn't say it, but . . ."

"Tell me."

"I could love you, Rowland . . ." She gave a small gasp, or sigh, as she said this, as if the words shocked her as much as they did him. She jerked her face away as if ashamed, then turned back, clasping his hands. "Oh, God—I think that's true. I think I knew that—but I don't know why. When I walked into that room here with you, when you began talking—it was before you touched me, I'm sure of that. I think it's why I went to bed with you—but that might just be an excuse. Except no. No . . ." She shook her head angrily. "It isn't an excuse—that's how it was. Something *came* at me, out of the air, I hadn't foreseen it, I promise you that. It wasn't a matter of strategy, decisions . . . I just . . . I could see all the possible consequences very clearly. I could *hear* them, Rowland, shouting away in my head—all the lies, the misery, the betrayal of trust, the hurt to someone I loved—someone I still love. Oh, God . . ." Her face contorted. "I could see—all those consequences, all those barriers—and I *still* did it. I'm not proud of that, but I can't be ashamed of it either. I could—I could sense something, there in the room with us, and it felt *bright*, Rowland, good, like hope, like a promise— no, not like a promise, like a glimpse, just a glimpse of another future, and I . . . oh, God. I shouldn't be saying this—"

She broke off, her eyes filling with tears, and bent her head. She had begun to tremble as she spoke. Rowland was deeply moved; everything she attempted to describe, in all its flimsiness and strength, he, too, had felt. He said her name and drew her into his arms. "Darling," he began. "I understand. I know exactly what you mean. Listen to me, Gini."

"No. No." She drew back from him a little, then clung to him again. "No—you must listen, Rowland. Please listen. Don't touch me—I have to finish this. I have to make a choice, I know that. I've known for days. I've been thinking and thinking—I've thought of nothing else. I *have* to decide. And I've chosen, Rowland—I've already chosen. I'm going to stay with Pascal. Rowland, he loves me—I have to do that."

"No, you don't." He caught her to him again and forced her to meet his eyes. "You don't have to decide—not yet. You shouldn't even be trying to decide, not now. You should wait—think. Gini, listen—you think that was nothing to me, what happened here between us? You say you *could* love me? Why do you say that—why? You know it's much closer, much stronger than that. . . ."

"No. No—and I mean what I say. I don't *trust* that kind of love, Rowland. I don't trust being *in* love—it's too—it feels like being drunk—or drugged. It makes me—I can't *think* when I feel that way. I feel *blind*—I'm sure I must *look* blind. Rowland, look at me. . . ."

Rowland looked. Her face was alight with contradictions, with pain, and with delight. Her eyes, bright with tears, dazzled him.

"You think I can look at you now . . ." he began in an unsteady voice. "Darling—I feel blind too—but I also feel—Gini, will you for God's sake listen to me. . . ."

"No. I know what you're going to say. I can feel it *here.* . . ." Color flooded into her face. She pressed her hand against her heart. "You feel as if you can see better. As if you see *more.* I know. I feel that too. But, Rowland, you can't *trust* that. It isn't the first time I've felt it. And it doesn't *last,* you know that as well as I do—we're both old enough. It's there—and then it dwindles away. So I have to *listen,* Rowland, to all those other voices. Trust. Honor—if I have any left. All the promises I made to Pascal. The things I said. The things I *swore.* I can't go back on them. I do love him. I love him very much. I owe him—so many things, I can't explain . . ."

"You don't need to explain." He jerked away from her, his face darkening. "I *know* why you're saying this. He saved your life yesterday. That's the reason for this. If that hadn't happened, this might have been different."

There was absolute silence. Gini stared at his face. It was taut with strain. Suddenly, with an oddly formal gesture, he released her hands and stepped back.

"I didn't mean to do this. I didn't mean—above all—to say that. I intended to leave here and keep my feelings to myself. That was what I planned." He hesitated. "I can see how much Pascal Lamartine loves you. I don't doubt you also love him. I feel I owe him a debt for what he did yesterday. But I find I can't . . . Too much is at stake." He gave a quick, angry shrug. "I want you to be very clear. I'm old-fashioned—Lindsay said that. And so—if you would have me, I'd marry you. And if you're still going to dismiss me, you can do it knowing that."

His manner had become more formal by the second; his final statements, made in a way that was almost harsh, were as devoid of emotion as he could make them—and the more effective for that. Gini's eyes filled with tears.

"*How* can you say that, how? Rowland—stop. You scarcely know me—"

"I know you enough."

"That can't be true. You shouldn't say such things. It isn't fair to me. It isn't fair to yourself."

"Isn't it?" He gave her a hard look. "Why not? I can see the alternative only too clearly. I love you, Gini. I know what it would be like, walking out now, not seeing you, not hearing your voice. That half-life. Dear God—I can see that so *well* . . ."

"It needn't *be* like that . . ." She covered her face with her hands. "Rowland, you know I'm right. Those feelings don't *last*. You may feel like that now—I may . . . But if we're determined, if we ignore them, avoid meeting—we'll forget. All this, *all* this—it will become weaker and weaker, and finally absurd, and then one day we'll both look back, and we'll think—Thank heaven I was sensible. What a fool I was—how could I ever have imagined—"

She stopped. She watched his face, lit by concern, become still and set. He took her hand in his.

"You think we're imagining this?" he said quietly. "If so, thank God for imagination. I trust it beyond reason. Are you telling me you don't?"

There was a silence then while he waited for her reply. Outside the room, a church bell tolled the hour, traffic passed, voices from other lives floated upward from the street. Gini looked at her imaginings, and his. She could see a possible future, just as he did. It was hazy, a little misted, like the light of a spring morning in which the loveliness of the day to come is glimpsed. She watched her life fork, north, south, right, left. The vision she now saw was very like the bright panorama Pascal had first opened up to her eyes. Both men seemed able to dismantle some defense in her mind, flooding it with illumination and promise. She was unsure if their ability to do this was innate, or if she herself gifted it to them. To discover that another man besides Pascal, and so soon after Pascal, could achieve this, confused her. It made her distrust joy, and it also made her distrust herself.

Besides such insubstantiality, duty and loyalty and the settled daili-ness of established love seemed so sure, and so commendable. It was a question of *discipline*, she told herself, of honoring vows made, and re-maining true, therefore, to Pascal and to herself. She looked one last time at the other Gini, the mirror woman who was so much more pre-pared to flout rules and take risks, and she rejected her, canceled her out.

She felt an immediate diminution, an intense stab of loss. This she ig-nored; if she felt unaccountably less now, she told herself, she would feel more, she would feel enfranchised, in due course.

"You have to catch a plane. I have to go to the hospital," she said.

"I see." Rowland at once released her and stepped back. "That's your final decision?"

"Yes, Rowland. It is."

She saw the reply glance like a blow across his face. He half turned in a blinded way, then turned back. He glanced down at his watch, checked the airline ticket in the pocket of his coat, braced himself, and then said in a stiff, abrupt way the one thing she feared most.

"We had unprotected sex," he began awkwardly. "I'm sorry, but I have to say this. I broke one of my own inviolable rules in that respect. If there were any possibility that you could become pregnant—I couldn't walk away from that. You do understand?"

"I'm on the pill, Rowland," she replied, and looked down. She stared at the carpet, at the patterns that separated them. She watched him approach. He stood for a while, looking down at her without speaking. Then, very gently, he lifted her face and inspected it.

"You're not telling me the truth," he said in a quiet voice. "I understand why—but don't lie to me, Gini, not about something as important as this. Look at me. I want you to make me a promise. All right, I'll go now. But when you know for certain, either way, then you send me a telegram, or you make one telephone call. Just tell me, Yes, I am—or no, I'm not. You promise me you'll do that?"

"Yes. I do."

He took her hands in his. "If the answer is no, very well, I'll obey your wishes. I'll stay away. I'll get on with the rest of my life. But if the answer is yes, I don't care where you are in the world, or whom you're with, I'm on the next plane. And you won't find it so easy to persuade me to leave then. Are you clear about that?" ·

He watched her face change, and her eyes flood with assent. At that point, curiously certain that he would eventually be recalled, he had intended to leave, and even turned to go. But she made some inarticulate sound, or gave some inarticulate gesture, and then—being human, being male, and far less resolved than he wished to appear—he gave way and kissed her on the mouth. Sensing her response, he might have stayed even then, especially then, but she took him by the hand, led him firmly to the door, and closed it quietly but firmly on him before either of them could risk further speech.

CHAPTER 22

Leaving that Paris hotel, Rowland had felt blind. He felt blind in the elevator, blind to the airplane, blind to the customs formalities in London. It was with a sense of surprise that he found himself, sometime later, in his own house. Disconcerted, he looked around his living room, a room that had always given him pleasure: for the first time it seemed to him cold, alien, and bare.

For two weeks after that he functioned on automatic, certain a summons from Gini must come. He anticipated, and feared, the mail each morning; he tensed at each telephone call. In February, late one Friday afternoon, the telegram finally arrived. It consisted of a one-word negative, followed by her name. He knew why she had been so terse—had he himself not even suggested it?—but the brevity of the message and its finality caused him great pain.

He sat for a long while, holding the scrap of paper, watching the future he had unconsciously been planning for those past two weeks shrivel before his gaze. Then, angry at himself, he called an airline and made a reservation on that evening's last flight to Scotland. Packing his climbing equipment later, catching a cab out to the airport, he felt almost calm. He knew the cure for this, he told himself; he had taught himself how to live without love before.

He climbed in the Cairngorms that weekend, in ideal weather and dangerous snow conditions, and he climbed alone. Once or twice, tempted, he took unjustifiable risks; he felt a defiant and bitter amusement when nothing untoward occurred.

He returned to London, to his house with its view of Hawksmoor's spire. He worked—this, too, had proved effective in the past—twice as hard. With the assistance of his DEA contact, Sandra Lucas, he knew that he would be able to tie up the last loose ends of his Amsterdam drug story: the Dutch chemist and his American partner were about to be raided; they would not be making the fortune they had so blithely anticipated; they would not be pushing White Doves much longer.

"It's tonight," Sandra Lucas said one morning in March, calling from a safe phone in Amsterdam.

"And then?" Rowland replied.

"And then they both go down, Rowland. We have Mina Landis's evidence. We have the toxicology reports on Cassandra Morley. Manslaughter is the best they can hope for, even in Holland. They'll both go down—and for a very long time." There was a silence. She gave a sigh. "I know it's not enough, Rowland. It's never enough. But the American has shifted quite a lot of heroin in his time. He'll certainly talk. He may give us some links in that chain. . . ." An awkwardness came into her voice. "I wanted to ask you something—this crusade of yours . . ."

"It isn't a crusade. It's news."

"—Are you still doing it for Esther?"

Rowland did not reply.

"Okay. If you won't answer that, then just tell me this—you still think of her?"

"Sometimes. Not so much recently."

"Good. I'm glad." Her voice became brisker. "She'd never have wanted this, you know. She was a realist. She'd have wanted you to let her go."

Was that what the dead required of the living—to be forgotten, to be relegated? Rowland doubted it. Nevertheless, the comment affected him, and perhaps chimed with feelings of his own. At the end of March he finally decided, late at night, and alone in his house, that it was now time to acknowledge that he had changed, that he had already begun the process of letting the past go.

He gathered together all the reminders of Esther that he had kept so carefully all these years. They were few: some letters she had written him when she, or he, had been working away; letters friends had written to him after her death; photographs taken by him, of her, in the Washington apartment they had shared, and finally, photographs of them together, taken by Esther's lawyer brother, on one of their visits to New Orleans. Quietly, Rowland reread the letters for the last time, then consigned them to the fire in his living room. He watched them blaze up, then slowly added the photographs one by one. He looked for a long time at the last of these pictures, himself and Esther, caught in a shaft of sunlight, walking along hand in hand. The street, he thought, was Canal; it was midafternoon; Esther was laughing; she had just been presented by Rowland with a flower, and she had tucked it into her hair. The flower was white, a white carnation: its crisp curled petals bloomed against the blackness of her skin. Rowland hesitated, then consigned this photograph, too, to the fire. He had intended to complete this ritual with one last item—Gini's brief and negative telegram.

He picked it up from the table where it lay in readiness, leaned toward the flames—and then found he no longer had the will to burn it. He folded it up again and replaced it in his wallet. It was a small weakness, he told himself; in no way did it alter his determination to put her out of his mind.

His conscious mind, of course; that determination did not prevent her returning to him at night, in his dreams. It was from one such dream, tranquil and resonant with the illusory promises of dreams, that Max roused him, at three o'clock one morning, to announce that Charlotte had just given birth to their first daughter. In April, Rowland received an invitation to the christening of this child, to be held the following month.

May; Rowland accepted. He was touched by the request, and touched by Max's obvious joy and pride. "We'd like you to be the godfather," Max said in his office one day over a sandwich lunch. "Charlotte insists. You predicted it would be a girl, after all."

"Delighted. An honor." Rowland smiled.

"Charlotte's asking Tom to be the other godfather. . . ."

"A very good choice. I like Tom."

"Godmothers—we're not sure yet. One of Charlotte's sisters, probably . . ." Max gave Rowland a small sidelong glance. "And then we thought, Lindsay perhaps . . ."

Rowland merely nodded. His attention rarely left work for long these days, as Max had noted, and now it had already returned to the story on Max's desk, which they would run the next day.

Written by Gini, and faxed in by her directly to Max, it detailed the raid made that week on the Amsterdam drug manufacturing outfit, and the subsequent arrest of the Dutch chemist and the American pusher behind it. The story seemed of greater interest to Rowland than the details of Max's daughter's christening and the identity of her godmothers.

Noting this, Max sighed and, as soon as Rowland had left his office, telephoned his wife, who—an obstinate romantic—still cherished hopes on Lindsay's behalf.

Charlotte questioned Max for a while, with vivacity. Max, who felt he knew Rowland better than his wife did, and who knew he was in a better position to judge Rowland's present state of mind, heard her out patiently. He then began the gentle process of making Charlotte face facts. Finally opting for a racing analogy, he informed her that the odds against Lindsay were—at very best—one hundred to one.

"Darling, listen to reason," he said. "I promise you, I *know*. Lindsay is a total long shot."

Charlotte made dismissive noises. It was not unknown, she reminded him, for total long shots to romp home.

Lindsay, who gambled rarely and always incautiously, might have agreed with her. She had spent the past months trying to subdue such instincts, but did not always succeed. She was not assisted by the fact that the months since Paris had given her time to consider, and time to make certain observations of her own.

She observed that Gini, to whom she spoke regularly on the telephone, had remained with Pascal in France. She observed that Gini's voice lifted with optimism and delight as she discussed, first, the success of the operation on Pascal's fractured arm, and then his slow but gradual progress since. She observed that neither Gini nor Pascal seemed eager to return to London, and were planning to remain in Paris until late May at least. She observed that Rowland McGuire now worked longer hours than anyone else in the *Correspondent* building, even longer than Max. She observed—with Pixie's assistance—that McGuire had become curiously impervious to the seductions of seductive women: his latest research assistant—or so Pixie claimed—a young woman so flagrantly nubile, Lindsay had hated her on sight, was rumored to have flung herself at McGuire shamelessly; she had been firmly and impolitely repulsed.

In her better moments, Lindsay could disregard such observations. In her weaker ones, unfortunately, Markov seemed to contrive to pop up. He had appointed himself love's agent provocateur. "How's it *going*, Lindy, my love?" he caroled down the telephone from that location in Hyderabad. "Any *progress*?" he demanded from somewhere in the Mojave Desert. "What *is* this?" he shrieked from a mobile outside an abandoned Australian silver mine, where he was photographing ball gowns. "Are you a *woman*, Lindy? What's your heart pumping, darling—water, or blood? Get to it. I fly back tomorrow. I'm taking you to dinner. And believe me, I shall expect *action*. I shall expect a *full* report."

"Well?" he said the next night in a wildly fashionable restaurant. "Fill me in, sweetheart. *Full intercourse*—or are we still at the tiresome courtship stage?"

He adjusted the brim of his hat, sighed, and lit a cigarette.

"Neither," Lindsay said. "Rumor has it, he's now a monk."

Markov brightened. "*That's* promising. Abstinence is bound to increase your chances. Especially in his case. Now, did you try drinks-after-work?"

"Yes, I did. Will you give it a rest, Markov? He didn't want a drink. He also didn't want lunch, or dinner at my flat. He didn't even bite on the movie idea—and I thought that was bound to work. Three hours of Eisenstein, plus Tom, so he'd feel safe. I was *sure* that would tempt him, but no."

"You're not *trying*, Lindy. You have to be *bolder*. Act, or you'll always regret it. Swallow your pride, darling. Stamp on your principles. Leap in where angels fear to tread."

Lindsay considered this. "How?" she said.

Markov looked thoughtful. "Shared interests," he announced at last. "Tell him you want to learn to climb. Buy one of those terrible anorak things. Stride across the hills with him. Clutch his manly arm occasionally. Carry his pitons—"

"Give me a *break*, Markov. I'd look like hell in an anorak. I get vertigo on my front steps."

"Okay, okay. Let's think. *Churches*. You said he liked churches."

"I said he liked *one* church, Markov. It's right across his street."

"Like one, like them all. Stop making difficulties. I feel this one, Lindy, I can see it panning out. A weekend in the country. Somewhere like Norfolk. Norfolk has very good churches. I went there once. You do a bit of preparation, obviously, before you go. Read some books. Then you talk about buttresses. You make *sensitive* comments about rood screens, sweetling."

"Rood screens? I can't stand this. Pour me another drink."

"Okay. Let's think."

Light came to Markov's face. "That's it. *Books!* I've hit on it. You said he reads. You said he reads all the time. Tolstoy. Updike. Proust. Heavy-brigade stuff—you mentioned that. Darling, it's *simple*, I see it now. A poetry reading. Or, you borrow his Tolstoy, then say, 'How about we go out to dinner, Rowland, and you talk me through *Anna Karenina, War and Peace?*' Tutor into lover. No man can resist it, Lindy."

"Last week," Lindsay said in a small voice with dignity, "I borrowed a novel from him. It was there on his desk. I *knew* he'd been reading it, and I thought . . . Anyway. I borrowed it. I took it back, two days later—and it was a long novel, Markov. I thought he'd be impressed I was so quick. I gave it back, and I made a speech. It was a good speech too, straight out of all the best cribs. It was astute. It was *sensitive*, Markov, so damn sensitive, I nearly wept—"

"What novel?"

"Never mind. It was French. During my speech he took three phone calls and sent four faxes. I was wearing a new dress too. I'd had my hair cut."

"*Nada?*"

"Oh, he was *kind*. He did listen a bit . . ." Lindsay gave a shaky sigh. "The kindness hurt most of all, I think. I mean, he doesn't *dislike* me, I can see that. But he's not remotely interested. Whereas—I can't sleep at night for thinking of him. I go over and over everything he says to me—just in case it might suggest he'd actually noticed me. I'm so damn inventive, it's *pathetic*, Markov. He says, 'Good morning, Lindsay'—and I think, maybe there's a double meaning in that."

Markov removed his dark glasses. He looked at her small, tense, boyish frame, at her short, curly hair, and at her pale, wide-eyed face. She was about to cry, or perhaps laugh; he could not have said which.

"—If I see him, it feels like spring. If I don't, there's no point to the day. I contrive all these meetings—anything just to spend three minutes in his office. I'm so *ashamed*, Markov. I know I'm making a fool of myself, a woman my age chasing a man like him. But it's as if he's locked in somewhere, and sometimes I think I might be able to give him a key. So it's much worse than it was before. The harder I try—I think it's because I can see he's not happy, and I'd so like to—Oh, shit. I'm going to cry. I'm sorry about this. You see, the trouble is . . . Oh, *hell*. Now my mascara will run. I've had too much wine, I think."

Markov pressed her hand and made encouraging noises. After a moment, the brief tears stopped.

"Right," he said forcefully. "I've had enough of this. As of now we stop pissing around. This is serious—so we switch to red alert. Full mobilization. We activate the Stealth bomber, Lindy my love. And we fly right in, over that fucker's radar defenses."

"Stealth bombers?" Lindsay gave a sniff.

He gave her a cunning look. "Trust me, I have a plan. Never been known to fail. Especially with a man of his character."

"You don't know anything about his character. Neither do I, I realize. You don't know him. He's an *enigma,* Markov."

"Crap. Women always think that about the men they love. And the amount you've told me, sweetheart, I know this guy like he's my brother. I know him upside down, and inside out, like I *invented* him, Lindy. And this man has a weakness, *Liebling,* an Achilles heel."

"He has?"

Lindsay, knowing she never learned, that she was cursed to be eternally optimistic, drank some more wine fast. Markov looked sublimely confident. She felt new hope.

"Gallantry," Markov said, thoughtful now. "He has these protective instincts toward women. Sweet, that—"

"He has a broken heart," Lindsay said bitterly. "At least, that's what I suspect."

Markov brushed this minor problem aside.

"Darling," he said, "in this world, even the best of hearts mend eventually. It's just a matter of time. I'm not saying he's going to be a pushover—I never underestimate the opposition. It'll take a while, I can see that. But first he has to notice you, spend some time with you. . . ." He frowned, then added in a casual voice, "When's that christening you mentioned? At Maxopolis? It's in two weeks' time, in May, right? And *he's* going to be there, and *you're* going to be there." A triumphant smile appeared on his face.

"What is it, Markov?"

"Oh, my God, why didn't I think of this before? I mean, it's just so perfect, this cannot fail, this—"

"What *is* it, damn it?"

Markov grinned broadly.

"Remember fairy tales?" he said. "Then think, *damsel in distress.*"

CHAPTER 23

The heart could mend, Gini thought. She raised herself on one elbow and looked down at Pascal's face. He was sleeping deeply still, but then, it was early, only just six o'clock. His dark hair was rumpled, falling across his forehead. Sleep eased the intensity of his features, and one by one she enumerated these accidents of nature she so loved: this the brows, this the cheekbones, this the mouth. A ray of sunlight moved against his face; he stirred, then returned to sleep. Gini leaned over him, watching him with a jealous delight. If she kissed him, she wondered, just very lightly, would he wake?

She decided against it. She wanted this morning to be perfect, and she had preparations to make. Very quietly, she eased herself from the bed and stood by the balustrade looking down at their wonderful tall studio room, and its great north window, and its curtains edged with light.

They had been back in London two days. No one knew yet that they had returned. They had been right to keep their arrival a secret, she thought. Most of their friends would be away this weekend at the christening of Max and Charlotte's daughter. She and Pascal had been away for so long, over three months, that people were unlikely to call anyway. Even so, this secrecy gave them a few days' more protection from intrusion. They were alone, and it felt intoxicating, as if they possessed this city. She gave a quick impulsive gesture of exultation, hugging her happiness to herself. A *May day*, she thought; a beautiful May day in which the sun would shine without fail, and the new leaves would move in the lightest of breezes beneath the arch of their window. A May day; a heart mended; yes, happily ever after—a new life.

She crept down the stairs to the room below and began quietly to tidy it. Today had to be perfect, so she threw away yesterday's newspapers, and neatly stacked the books she had been reading the previous afternoon, and folded a sweater Pascal had tossed down the night before. Then, on an impulse, she unshook the folds again and pressed her face against the wool; it smelled just discernibly of his skin and his hair, and at this time she felt inexpressibly happy. She thought: I was right; all my predictions were correct, and—refolding the sweater—she told herself that although occasionally he still infiltrated her dreams, she had cured herself of Rowland McGuire. She and Pascal had been close, very close, to disaster, but they had inched away from it, and escaped.

The escape had not been an easy one; there had been times in Paris when she had despaired, as had Pascal. But something—God, luck, perseverance—had been there to assist them. And now, today, she could feel her own good fortune: she might not have merited it, but fortune was hers and it had been lavishly dispensed.

Twice blessed, she thought, and gave a little pirouette of impromptu joy. Then she pulled the sweater on over her thin white nightdress because she wanted to feel Pascal against her skin. She padded out to the kitchen and began her preparations dreamily, laying a tray—maybe she should put a flower on that tray? Absurd, she thought; but these details mattered because she wanted them both to remember them always. So: perfect tray, perfect breakfast; and a perfect beginning to this, a perfect day.

"What a day . . ." someone remarked as Rowland opened the back door to Max's house and stepped out into the freshness of the May morning.

Rowland halted, annoyed. It was not seven yet; he had not expected anyone else to be up. He had certainly not expected to encounter anyone else in Max's garden, and the accents and intonation of that particular voice filled him with foreboding. He glared to left and right. No one was visible.

"Perfect," he replied in a discouraging tone.

"A perfect day for a *walk*," said the voice, which now appeared to come from behind a clipped yew. "Mind if I join you?"

Rowland did mind. He minded very much. He accelerated in the opposite direction, around a hedge, and along a laburnum tunnel. Just when he was congratulating himself on the success of this maneuver, Markov—the risible figure of Markov—materialized at his side.

"*What* a good idea," Markov said in faintly satiric tones. "A walk before breakfast on an English spring morning. The wind in one's face. A stride across the hills. Or maybe a gentle *meander* along the river valley . . ."

Rowland gave Markov one quick, assessing glance. He had not the least idea why Max and Charlotte had been insane enough to invite Markov to the christening of their daughter, although he assumed Lindsay had had a hand in the invitation. He regretted his presence in their house, and he regretted it even more here. He looked Markov up and down. The intolerable man was, as he had been the previous evening, wearing foolish clothes. His trousers appeared to be made of black velvet. His jacket—no, Rowland could not bring himself to look at the jacket. He was wearing earrings, and had set a black baseball cap back to front on his long flaxen curls. As usual—he had not removed them once during dinner the previous night—he was wearing dark glasses. *Reflective* dark glasses.

Rowland scowled at his own mirrored face. He glanced down at Markov's very white high-top designer sneakers. His lip curled. With luck, he thought, Markov, the heavy smoker, would be out of breath before they left the orchard.

"Not the valley," he replied with great courtesy. "I'm going up there." He pointed in the direction of the hills. "Do join me, by all means. Only I should warn you. It's steep. And it's likely to be muddy."

"No worries." Markov waved a languid hand. "I guess I'll manage to plow my way through. I love walking. Back home—I'm from California, did I mention that?"

"I guessed."

"—Back home, you know where I go? You've heard of Yosemite?"

"I've climbed in Yosemite actually. Several times."

"Wow. Cosmic coincidence! I go there every month. I get back from location, no matter where, and I *trek*. Out into the wilderness. Beyond the reach of man. It kind of irrigates my mind. I guess you'll understand that. . . ."

Rowland shuddered, and lengthened his stride.

Reaching the bottom of the steepest hill behind Max's property, he began to lope up its narrow and indeed muddy path. To his intense irritation, Markov kept up. Rowland accelerated again; he waited for complaints, or pants, or sighs; none came. Markov was right on his heels, like some appalling hound of God.

"I would have thought," Rowland said tightly some way farther on, "that a country christening wasn't really your style. Or walks, for that matter."

"In that case," said Markov, putting on a spurt, "you'd be oh so but completely one hundred percent wrong. I wouldn't have missed this occasion for *anything*."

Rowland gave him a glance of pure dislike. Markov, who was tall, lean, and wirily built, had now somehow contrived to get in front of him. He bounded ahead, his ghastly sneakers flashing white as he negotiated boulders and rabbit holes. Rowland slowed, but this technique did not work either. Markov, blessedly lost from sight just minutes before, suddenly popped up from behind a thorn thicket. With a wide, authoritative smile, he once more took his place at Rowland's tweed-jacketed elbow and matched him stride for stride.

"Of course, the real reason, the serious reason I'm here is Lindsay," Markov went on in a reflective way. "Because I really admire her and like her, and right now she needs her friends. So—moral-support time. I guess she hasn't told you? No—there's no way she would. Poor Lindsay. She really needs help and advice—but can she ask for it? No. Too much pride, of course."

He cast a little glance at Rowland McGuire as he made this pronouncement. Rowland's handsome face gave no sign of any reaction, and Markov felt a grudging admiration. Just as devastating as Lindsay had claimed, he thought, and no pushover. This would require rather more labor than he had anticipated; Rowland's scorn was almost palpable. It was there in the contemptuous flash of his green eyes, and in the set of his lips. Markov decided to be more impressive; wave the wand, he thought—oh, and better modify the speech.

Dispensing with his usual verbal mannerisms—so much camouflage, in any case—Markov talked on. He wondered how long it would take this McGuire man to realize that his companion was not a fool. Five minutes. Ten? It took fifteen. Five minutes on the subject of Scotland, where luckily Markov had been often on shoots; five minutes on the subject of Dostoevsky—here Markov knew he excelled—and five minutes of complete silence. It was the silence that clinched it, Markov felt. Rowland McGuire accelerated the last five hundred yards to the crest of the hill at a pace even Markov could not quite match, but he then waited for him there, a slight smile on his face.

"Okay," Rowland said as Markov reached his side. "You walk well. You talk well. Why are you here?"

"I'm not hitting on you," Markov replied with some impudence. "Just in case it like crossed your mind."

"It didn't. I'm sure you rarely waste your time."

" 'I wasted time, and now doth time waste *me*,' " Markov quoted smartly. "Not my style. You're right."

He leaned up against a wall, drew out a pack of Marlboros, and lit one. He turned his reflective glasses to the valley a long way below them. "Great view from here."

They were not far from the place where Rowland had discovered Cassandra Morley's body. Rowland, thinking of that night, and other events subsequent to it, made no reply. He, too, leaned against the wall, and with a closed expression turned his face to the valley below. After a while Markov, reading the alteration in him, silently passed him a cigarette. McGuire, who—as far as he knew—did not smoke, accepted it without comment. They leaned back in the sunshine, tobacco smoke curling into the air. Neither spoke. The silence lengthened and became almost companionable.

"Well, what do you know?" Markov said at last. "You're not what I expected at all. Seriously, I quite like you. And I thought you'd be a prick."

"Oh, really?" McGuire colored. "And who gave you that impression? Lindsay, I suppose."

"Lindsay—a bit. Other people too. I asked around. After you killed those pictures of mine. Remember that?"

"Ah, yes."

"Not that anyone had a bad word to say—exactly. I mean Lindsay's always singing your praises. How much she admires your judgment. Your editorial skills."

"Lindsay?" Rowland looked genuinely astonished. "I can't believe that. She never stops telling me how to do my job."

"Oh, that's just her way." Markov gave an airy gesture. "It means nothing. Just Lindsay being defensive. Or teasing you maybe. She might do that. She found you insensitive, I think, and she did mention you were pretty *arrogant*—but then, other people said that."

McGuire's color deepened. He shrugged. "Well, maybe so. It's one of my faults. I have plenty of others, no doubt."

"Yeah, sure. Don't we all? And then, of course, you have a reputation as a womanizer, did you know that?"

McGuire's color deepened even further. He shot Markov an angry glance.

"I can't see that's any of your business." Then: "Lindsay said that?"

"Lindsay? No. Someone else. Lindsay wouldn't bad-mouth you that way. One, she's discreet, actually rather seriously discreet, and two—I told you, she likes you. You know, up to a point. Apart from the arrogance, that is. Not that she gives you much thought, except when I'm prompting her. She has other things on her mind right now. Too bad. You've noticed the change in her, I guess?"

"Change? Change? Since when? No—I haven't."

"Oh, well, she hides it, at work, I suppose. And then, you haven't been at the *Correspondent* that long, have you? It's about what, six or seven months?"

"About that. Yes."

"Oh, well, it happened just after you arrived, so I guess you wouldn't really notice the difference. How tense she is. Like really strung out. I mean, I know she wouldn't break down, or cry—not at work, not in front of someone like you. . . . But I've known her for years. I'm gay. She trusts me. So when she sees me, she really opens up."

There was a silence. McGuire seemed to be weighing this. He frowned out across the valley, the wind lifting his hair from his face. Once or twice he glanced back at Markov, as if about to speak, and then remained silent. Markov was glad of his mirrored glasses; McGuire's glance, cool and assessing, disconcerted even him. The obvious response of most people at this point would, of course, have been to ask exactly what was wrong with Lindsay. McGuire's refusal to do the obvious interested Markov; he awarded him a few more points, and waited. Eventually, Rowland said: "I suppose, now that you mention it, I have noticed some alteration. As you say, she doesn't take me into her confidence, but—she has been *quieter* just this last couple of weeks."

It was two weeks since their dinner. Markov made no comment.

"And then—I did notice yesterday. She's looking pale . . ."

Pale and *interesting*, thought Markov, who had supervised the makeup himself. In Markov's view there were two types of men in the world; one knew when women were wearing makeup, the other did not. McGuire almost certainly fell into the latter category, he had guessed. He now congratulated himself.

"I hope she's not ill in any way? Is there some problem at home—with her mother, with Tom?"

The question was asked in polite and neutral tones; it was accompanied by another penetrating green glance. Markov, unsettled by that glance, hopped down from the wall on which he had half perched, and moved off toward the path.

"No, no—all fine on the home front," he said in an evasive way, and waited for further prompts. None came. Silently Markov cursed.

"So, what I was thinking was . . ." he began as they turned back down the path with unspoken assent, "the thing *is*—I'm off on location next week. First Haiti. Then Tangier. Then somewhere kind of . . . re-mote. In the African bush. So I won't be back for over a month. . . ."

"Haiti? You choose odd locations for your fashion pictures."

"Don't I *just*," replied Markov, repressing a small smile. "I guess I like to shake up people's expectations. Give them a surprise."

"Yes. I can imagine you might like that."

"The point being—I'm away, Lindsay loses her number-one confidant, right? So I'm looking around. I'm *casting*. I need a stand-in—just for four weeks. I had thought you'd do—I mean, you work in the same office, you seem to get along okay. I mean, she's not going to pour her heart out to you the way she does to me, obviously, but you could help in other ways. Take her for a meal now and then. Maybe the odd trip to the theater, the movies. Nothing heavy. Just so she could get away from that monster of a mother of hers. So she had a chance to go out once in a while instead of just sitting alone, getting more and more miserable every night. I mean, the main trouble is, she's been badly hurt, and when that happens to women, all their self-confidence goes, you know? Some jerk throws them over—after three years, would you believe—and *wham* suddenly the women, they've got this fixed idea in their heads—they're hideous, they're dumb, no one likes them, no one wants to talk to them—massive hemorrhaging of self-esteem. . . ."

Markov paused. He had promised Lindsay, under oath, that he would tell no direct lies, but allow McGuire to make certain assumptions. He glanced at McGuire; surely this message had gotten through? Or would he need more narrative tricks?

"I find this hard to believe." Rowland was frowning, looking puzzled. "Lindsay always seems so confident, so assured. She's very good at her job, she's highly successful, I wouldn't have thought—"

"Oh, you know women—"

"No, actually, I'm not sure I do."

"All the same. Unfortunately. Success? What does it mean? Nothing. *Nada.* Complete zilch. I mean it's *okay*, up to a point—but it's not what they *really* want, right?"

"What *do* women want?" Rowland asked with a sidelong glance.

"Love, of course," Markov said, ignoring the glance, which might have been amused. "Love, love, love. The holiness of the heart's affections. All that."

"Very wise."

"You think so? Perhaps. It's fine until it goes wrong. When that happens, a man just picks himself up, gets on with his life—I speak from the sidelines here, of course. . . ."

"That's certainly what people say."

"Whereas a *woman*—oh, no. Terminal angst. And when they've been lied to, of course, lied to for over three years, promised marriage, the whole bit, and then that turns out not to be in the cards, because, guess what, the bastard's *already* married, with a very rich wife he can't leave, and three beautiful, vulnerable little kids—and when the woman concerned, she's had no inkling of this, and she's been lied to and lied to, and it turns out he's been boasting about her so all his friends know, know, I mean, these really *intimate* details . . ."

Markov stopped. That surely had to be enough. McGuire was now looking concerned. He felt pleased with himself. The lie indirect. Perhaps it needed one final tiny gloss.

"And of course," he went on, "when the woman *still* loves the man concerned—then it's worse. It makes me really angry, as a matter of fact." He shot Rowland a quick glance. "I don't like to see a good woman wasted. I mean, the way I look at it—from the sidelines, all right—Lindsay's got everything going for her. She's pretty. She's smart. She's kind. She's generous. She's good. She's a great mother—and she ought to make some man a great wife."

"I'm sure she will. In due course."

"Maybe. I have my doubts. Because there's a few problems. One of them being—as far as Lindsay's concerned—other men don't exist."

Rowland, as Markov had hoped, looked faintly encouraged by this. "That's why," Markov went on, pressing home this advantage, "I approached you. I mean, I had reservations at first. Mr. Lothario, right? The last thing Lindsay needs right now is some other guy taking advantage of the state she's in, making some cheap pass—"

"If that's a warning," Rowland said with edge, "I can assure you it's unnecessary. It's not my practice to take advantage of women. Particularly unhappy women. Despite what you may have heard."

"My opinion too. Now that I've met you, that is." Markov flashed a smile. "Besides, it's just for a few weeks. Escort duties. At most a shoulder to cry on. Someone to give her reassurance and advice."

This was met with further silence. They walked on, descending the final slope and approaching the entrance to Max's orchard. McGuire paused at the gate, frowning again. Apple blossoms drifted from the trees, and lay like confetti at their feet.

"Look," he said in an abrupt way. "If Lindsay truly needs that kind of help, then I'd be glad to provide it. Of course I'd be delighted to take her out for a meal, take her to the theater. I told you—I like Lindsay. But advice? Reassurance? A shoulder to cry on? I'm not sure I'm the best candidate. I always try to avoid getting involved in other people's personal problems. Particularly those of women. I've found—"

"Yes?"

"—I've found I just end up making them worse. I'm not sure why that is."

"I can't imagine," Markov said with the smallest of glances at Rowland's magnificent physique.

"But if Lindsay just needs an escort occasionally, someone to listen, of course I'd do that. . . ."

"And it is only for a few weeks," Markov put in. "You'll be my understudy. Then, when I get back from Tangier . . ." There was a slight pause.

"Or," Rowland said evenly, "the remote part of the African bush . . ."

"Right. Right. Up the Zambezi someplace . . ."

Markov, feeling triumphant—this was not so very difficult after all—threw open the orchard gate.

"It just seems slightly *odd* that no one mentioned this to me before," Rowland said in a thoughtful way. "And no one did. Not Max. Not Charlotte."

"Did Max even know?" Markov cried on a rhetorical note. "Did Charlotte know? My impression is *not*. Lindsay's secretive. She doesn't open her heart to many people. Virtually no one in fact."

"—And then, Lindsay herself gave me a rather different impression. This would have been back in January. She very kindly cooked dinner for me then, at my house. And I could have *sworn* she mentioned—"

"Other men?" Markov cut in fast. "A succession of other men? Oh, she does that. It's a cover-up, of course. I can't believe that took *you* in. You can't be that slow, surely?"

"Maybe it's that insensitivity of mine," McGuire said politely with a half-smile. "It blinded me, I suppose. How stupid of me. Well, well, well."

He followed Markov into the garden. Markov decided silence was now the best response. He was sweating with the effort of those fast final lies, and something in McGuire's tone confused him. The man's self-possession faintly irritated him, and also faintly alarmed him.

"Look," he said as they approached the house. "Maybe I should have kept my mouth shut? Maybe this is a bad idea of mine. But I mean, how many single men are there to ask. . . ."

"Very few. We're a vanishing breed."

"I can't ask Max. He hasn't the time. He's got a wife. Kids. It had to be someone Lindsay knows, and trusts."

"Not at all." McGuire laid one large strong hand briefly on Markov's shoulder. He gave him a warm smile. "It will be an honor to be your understudy."

"You won't say anything to Lindsay? I mean, if she knew I'd spoken to you, she'd have cardiac arrest. . . ."

"You can rely on me," Rowland replied. "I shall perform my role to the very best of my abilities. Until you come back, that is."

Markov sighed. This, of course, was not the scenario he intended. But there was nothing more he could do. From now on it was up to Lindsay. Allowing Rowland to precede him into the house, Markov looked up at the brilliant sky and the whirling blossoms. His lips moved. He could on occasion be superstitious, even pagan: since it was now in their laps, he was offering up a little prayer to the gods.

Pascal had been dreaming about loss. These dreams had first begun in the early years, when he first covered wars. They had recurred, in various forms, ever since. Sometimes the dreams were replays of actual events he had witnessed but thought forgotten. He would see a tiny child crouched over the dead body of a parent, or a mother prostrate over the grave of her soldier son, and waking, he would recall the exact place where he had witnessed that incident—in Mozambique, or Bosnia, or Afghanistan. His unconscious mind had selected one random image out of millions, and he would think, on waking—*why that particular grief?*

At other times, and this made him more uneasy, the dream of searching and losing was a vague, shadowy thing. It would lead him through some remembered war zone, into the streets near his home; frantic, he would be searching for his daughter one moment, for Gini the next, and sometimes for a phantom presence that he would suspect, on waking, was himself. The search was always accompanied by acute anxiety and mounting fear. He woke, always, startled, dry-mouthed, and drenched in sweat.

Nearly twenty years of wars: he had learned how to deal with such nightmares. So, this morning, he applied the learned techniques. He waited quietly, until the pounding of his heart slowed. He concentrated on the details of his immediate environment, this bed, this room. Sometimes he might begin on a silent recital, a multiplication table, the list of his appointments for that day.

This morning the dream lingered longer than was usual. It clung with a cobwebby tenacity to the corners of his mind. He began to recite silently some lines of poetry taught to him by his father. Still the dream clung, leaving him with a paralyzing sense of misery. He persevered, and slowly the room began to reassert itself. The details of the dream shimmered, surged back, and then were gone. He had remembered that he was back in London again, that he was with Gini, that his arm was mended now and his fingers once again deft and strong. He sat up, listening, touching the sheets beside him, which felt cool. He could hear the sound of Gini's movements below, the quietness of footsteps, the opening and closing of a door.

He felt an immediate, bounteous, and immeasurable relief: his first instinct was to call out to her, but he waited, then lay back and closed his eyes. For a few moments he wanted to listen to this relief, to the sound of hope, because it had not been easy to achieve, and there had been moments, those past weeks in Paris, when he had feared it would never return.

While he remained in the hospital, spending night after long night alone, he had believed that they could remake their life together, and reaffirm their love, because this was what they both passionately desired. Their difficulties could be surmounted. It was, he had told himself then, a question of determination, of *will*.

Released from the hospital finally, and reunited with Gini in that borrowed apartment belonging to friends, he had embarked—in a way he knew was very characteristic of him—on a *program* of reconciliation. At first he trusted in words. They would *talk* their way around every obstacle and past every evasion. Every one of those difficult topics: his work, her work, the nature of fidelity, the possibility of a child. He would resist the jealousy he still felt; they would both resist indulging in accusation; they would *talk* themselves back to truth, and they would become not less, but more than before.

Almost at once, however, they both sensed these conversations were leading them astray. However much they fought it, their words took on a dry, therapeutic tone, as if they were discussing the marital problems of two strangers. The more clinically truthful their language, the more strained these conversations became: Pascal felt they spoke across a chasm—and it was a chasm good intentions could not bridge.

What they needed, Pascal felt, was some fiercer link. They did not need some careful, engineered construct, but some invisible power that could arc between them. But to search for this power, to coax it back to flickering life, made them both fearful. Once upon a time, as they were both bitterly aware, this electricity had simply *been* there. Words had not been needed then to galvanize them; the current of communication had flowed from the simplest glance, or touch.

Now, even the touching was tentative. It could be unsure, or ill timed, or fumbled, or overassertive; all its former immediacies seemed to have been lost. For weeks Pascal felt watched. True intimacy was impossible, for he felt that a third person shared these rooms with them; his presence intruded into their conversations and interrupted their attempts at making love. Pascal tried to exorcise this man, then, realizing Gini was also attempting to do the same, felt the jealousy come surging back. Did she compare kisses? Had he touched her there, and in this way—and when he did so, *if* he did so, what had been her response?

He longed to know, and loathed himself for this. He would permit himself to ask no such vulgar questions, and he would not allude to his feelings, he was too proud to do that. He knew they affected what he came to think of as his performance—and how he loathed *that* term, though it was apt—and he could see the pained efforts Gini made to reassure him. The loving embraces, the strokings, the soothing words, her apparent fear that he no longer desired her—how he hated all that. She kissed him now as if she doubted her right to do so. Pascal, wanting her desperately but fearful of failure and comparison, would jerk away from her touch. This was torture to him. Pascal, an absolutist, hated all lies; until then he had never understood just how much the body could lie. He had assumed, naively, that untruth and evasion required speech.

It was six weeks before he could bring himself to make love to her. When he finally did, it was after a violent argument, during the course of which they had both drunk too much wine, perhaps because they had both begun to believe that antagonism might succeed where care and patience had failed. A short-circuit device; fucking her, Pascal thought—we both intended to incite precisely this.

The act had not been the reunion he had planned; it had been angry, unsatisfactory, and brief. Afterward, Gini wept—and for the first time in his life he turned away from those tears with a cold repugnance he had never expected to possess.

"*You* did this," he said to her. "It was you who brought us to this." He slammed out, and walked furiously and mindlessly through the dark Paris streets.

The next day, a reconciliation; both were contrite. Then more arguments, and reconciliations again. Pascal began to grow desperate: this cycle was only too familiar to him. He could not believe that with a woman he so loved, he was experiencing again the remorseless downward spiral of disaffection he had been through with his ex-wife.

Perhaps, he thought, as the ugly month of February became March, perhaps if he could only *act* love better, he would be released, and would be able to express the love he knew was there, locked somewhere inside himself. It had sprung to his lips unaided facing Star in Madame Duval's apartment; looking at death fifteen feet away, it had been impossible to disguise: it had simply *been* there, and he had sensed in Gini its unhesitating and immediate response.

If the love could well up then, why not now? What was wrong? And he then began to believe that conscious action and careful speech would achieve nothing. They needed some near divine intervention for which he had no apposite term. Willpower was no use to them; love could not be willed. With fear, he began to believe that love was as mysterious as the welling-up of water in the desert: in essence, it was a *gift*.

If so, the gift proved elusive. He redoubled his efforts, as she did. Their mutual politeness pained them both. In long discussions late into the night, they planned new kinds of futures together: these visions—civilized, caring, egalitarian—convinced neither of them very much, he felt. He promised that he would either abandon war coverage altogether or restrict such work to a few months every year. She countered that this was unacceptable; she would not allow him to give up this work, this vocation, for her sake. Pascal listened to her arguments, remembered the comments of his ex-wife, and made his own private resolves: this mistake he could at least avoid again. Others also: one day he found the contraceptive pills she had begun taking again the previous month, and threw them away. They quarreled violently over this—and yet that action, that quarrel, proved a turning point. Pascal made love to her that night, and for weeks afterward, with a new and fixed determination: this act he intended to have consequences: *Conception*. Then, and only then, would she be repossessed.

This determination, they both found, altered the tenor of a familiar act. Pascal abandoned endearments and gentleness. He could sense some resistance in her, and so he set about fucking her into submission, then out the other side of submission. When this had finally been achieved, he knew that they were alone at last, and that he had found a route back.

For such a change, of course, you could not set a precise time or date, but some change they had both recognized: it was there when they fell asleep exhausted, and there again in the morning when they woke. It grew, day by day, after that; it came stealing back to them, not through the medium of words at first, but through glance and through touch. He had sensed a new calm, a cessation of striving, then the ghost of an old contentment, and finally, one evening, just there, unsummoned, an assured peace.

He rose now, suddenly eager to be with her, and quickly pulled on some clothes. He went barefoot down the stairs, and in the room below paused. He could sense something in the air of this room, some alteration in it, the eddyings of some unseen force.

He moved forward slowly and silently and looked into the kitchen beyond. Gini had not heard his footsteps; she was concentrating on some task with an eagerness that touched him to the heart. On the blue tray in front of her she was arranging a plate, a cup and saucer, and a glass. The glass was a champagne glass. Pascal frowned. He watched her take a flower from a vase on the windowsill, and cut its stem, and then arrange the flower on the tray. Its exact placing seemed to preoccupy her. She laid it first on the plate, then on the blue napkin, and finally next to the glass. She was wearing a nightdress, surmounted by one of his sweaters that was several sizes too large for her. The garments gave her the unstudied grace of a young girl; her head was bent over her arrangement; her hair, longer now, almost reaching to her shoulders, was tousled from sleep.

He felt suddenly the most profound love for her. It washed through his body with astonishing force; he felt it settle like an ache about the heart. The emotion was of such suddenness and intensity that for an instant he felt blinded, as if, newly emerged from some dark underworld, he stared directly at the sun. He lifted his hand involuntarily, as if to shield his eyes—and that small movement caught her attention. She looked up and gave a small cry of surprise.

He half knew already, he later thought. He stood looking at her for a few more moments in silence. Her face looked soft, a little sleepy, as if she had just recently awakened from more pleasant dreams than his own. Her lovely eyes—he had startled her—had widened. She made one quick gesture, as if she would have hidden the tray if she could; then her expression changed.

Watching her face, he began to know. He felt the knowledge, and the elation that came with it, begin to pulse along his veins. Her face had an almost secretive look, a very female look that was simultaneously triumphant and afraid. He felt such tenderness for her then that he could not speak; he took her hand, then drew her quietly into his arms.

He held her very close, and they stood for some time in this way, without speaking, their bodies interlocked. Gini could feel the beating of his heart; she listened to what she had so nearly lost, and what she had regained. Women, possibly, doubt less than men. That morning, she found all her doubts and prevarications had flooded away.

Her body spoke, and in accents of such joy that she had no desire to listen to any last cautious whisperings in the mind. She had silenced those whispers in any case, she believed; silenced them weeks before. Now her own grip on contentment was sure—and if Pascal's was, or had been, more tenuous, she would cure him. That cure was now within her gift; she felt its power.

Today she could do anything: she could make water spring from dry rock; touch a mountain and make it move. Remake a marriage? Heal a breach of trust? Easy. Easy. She could do it with one finger, one flick of her wrist, one word. Never in her life had she felt so female, and never in her life—no, never—had she felt this power. Such bounty: taking Pascal's hand, she waited; it passed through her palm and fingers; it passed from her hand to his.

Pascal said: "When did you know?"

"At once, I think. The next day. The next hour. But I had to be sure. So I waited. I saw the doctor yesterday."

"Yesterday? You should have told me."

"I had to wait. I meant it to be perfect. I was going to wake you, and then . . ." She caught his hand and pressed it against her stomach. "Do you think it's a girl? Or a boy? I think it's a boy. Your son. And you know how old he is? I know exactly. Six weeks, two days, and—oh, about five hours. I *know* you remember. . . ."

"I think I do." Pascal smiled.

"The Monday. By moonlight. We'll have a moonlight child. We—" She stopped, seeing his tears. "Oh, tell me—please tell me. You did want this? You are happy? You will love him? Or her? And me . . . You will love me and trust me now? Always? I will, always. Oh, please, answer me, Pascal."

Pascal drew her against him and pressed her face against his heart. Just for an instant, there and then gone, he felt some vestigial sadness, almost a weariness, as if his morning's dream had returned. It clouded the edge of his vision momentarily, this product of the disparities between them, in years, in experience. Fortunately the sensation was brief; wisely, he concealed it.

"Which question first?" he asked gently, kissing her. "My darling, this may take some time. . . ."

Lindsay always wept at weddings, and of course at funerals. At christenings, she discovered, she wept too. First she wept because the words of the service were so beautiful; then she wept because Max and Charlotte's baby was sleeping so peacefully; then she wept again because holy water woke it, and on waking, the angelic baby bawled.

As she was leaving the group by the church after the ceremony, making her way along a narrow pathway bordered by gravestones and the foam of May wildflowers, Markov caught up with her.

"Good," he whispered. "But don't overdo it. Your mascara's running again. We want *discreet* sentiment. Wipe your eyes."

"Oh, piss off, Markov," Lindsay said. "This isn't acting. Go away."

Markov went. Lindsay rubbed her eyes with a tissue, then skulked off to a corner, under some trees.

She watched the rest of the large christening party linger by the church for a few last photographs. Various friends and neighbors, whom she knew; Tom, persuaded into a suit for once, with his girlfriend Katya on his arm; Charlotte cradling her lovely baby; and Max, beaming at everyone, Max looking absurdly tall, thin, elbowy, and proud. For some reason Max's elbowiness made her want to weep again. She sobbed quietly into her sodden Kleenex. From the church came wails from Max's sons: "*More* pictures? Do we have to?"

"Shut up, Alex. Stand still."

"What's all the fuss about? It's only a stupid girl. . . ."

Lindsay smiled. She fixed her eyes on the tombstones in front of her and began to read the epitaphs: 1714, 1648, 1829. Much-loved wife, dearly beloved husband of, widow of, daughter of . . . The epitaphs calmed her; she dried her eyes.

The group by the church was leaving now. Only a few of the guests lingered, as the rest set off for the party at Max's and the christening champagne. She could see the tall figure of Rowland McGuire, on the edge of the group as always. He was in conversation with a young girl Lindsay knew to be Mina Landis. Her parents were divorcing—or so Charlotte said; she and her mother were returning to America soon. The girl was slightly built, and seemed painfully shy; Rowland seemed to be making an effort to draw her out, but his kindness was receiving little reward. The girl hung her head, and seemed to make monosyllabic replies; shortly afterward she was claimed by her mother and swept away. Rowland lingered, looking up at the church, unaware he was observed.

Lindsay thought: I could go over to him and join him. I could put Markov's advice into practice right now. I could ask him about buttresses and pillars. I could look at that famous Norman doorway with him. We could look at saints and angels together—and he could explain their symbolism, no doubt. But she turned away. She did not have the heart for the deception, and she could not bear the spectacle of Rowland, being kind.

None of this is going to work, she thought miserably; *none* of it. She waited until Rowland McGuire had disappeared back into the church— why? To examine its architecture? To pray?—and then she returned to the path. She picked some cow parsley—Queen Anne's lace, Charlotte called it, a much prettier name—as she walked. She went down the old, worn steps, out through the lych-gate, and into the lane.

In the distance, some guests, the last stragglers, had reached the entrance to Max's driveway. She saw the floaty pastels of the women's dresses, heard a shout, then laughter from the men. Rowland McGuire said: "You cried."

She turned around to find him at her shoulder, frowning into the sun, very nearly a foot taller than she was, impossibly handsome, unreadable, maybe amused, maybe sad.

"Yes, I did," she replied a little irritably, walking on, Rowland keeping pace with her. "I'm sentimental. I like babies. . . ."

"I can see that."

"I also like puppies. Kittens. Foals. Lambs. The last time my cat had a litter—there were eight kittens—I cried all morning. It isn't a virtue. I do know that. No one else cried back there."

"Charlotte did."

"Charlotte has cause."

They walked on a short distance in silence. Lindsay tried to think of memorable remarks, and failed. For the first hundred yards she felt self-conscious and tongue-tied, an intellectual pygmy; for the second hundred yards she felt happy—he had *chosen* to walk with her, after all. By the time they reached Max's drive—that cursed optimism of hers—full-blown elation had taken hold. He was *there*, she thought, drinking in the sunshine, and the air, and the scent of new-mown grass.

"I like your dress," Rowland said into the silence, in somewhat cautious tones.

Lindsay tripped; she turned to stare at him.

"What did you say?"

"Your dress. It's—I can't stand fussy dresses. I like that. It's . . ." he searched around for an adjective.

Lindsay looked down at her dress, cream linen, midcalf, high-necked, short-sleeved. She was aware that it looked good—well, *quite* good—against her tan.

"Plain?" she offered, smiling. "Modest? Elegant? Restrained? Matronly? Dull? Cream?"

"Most certainly not matronly. It suits you. It makes you look . . ."

Apparently the appropriate adjective failed him again. Lindsay could see how hard he was trying, and she felt a rush of pure affection for him. With a naturalness which surprised her, she took his arm.

"Come on, Rowland. I can see you find compliments difficult. It doesn't matter. Let's get some wine. There's champagne, and a wonderful cake. It has three tiers, and a stork with a baby in a bundle in its beak. . . ."

"Does it indeed?"

"God—what a glorious day!"

Lindsay lifted her face to the sky. Rowland watched her do this but made no comment. He escorted her through the gardens to the rear lawn, where formal Max, who liked ceremonies, had organized a resplendent marquee. Lindsay, among friends, began to enjoy herself, although every so often Markov would materialize at her elbow and remind her, in a sepulchral whisper, to look tragic.

"Jesus," he hissed, toward evening, when the party was winding down. "You're supposed to have a broken heart. Go off somewhere on your own. Linger in the distance, looking kind of *pensive*. Don't argue. And give me that damn champagne."

Lindsay obeyed him. It was actually quite natural to do so, because all afternoon Rowland McGuire's polite attentions had been marked. He had ensured, for over three hours, that she was plied with canapés and cake, and that her glass was filled. He had ensured that, when trapped, she was extricated, and when stranded, she was not alone. As a result, Lindsay felt somewhat tipsy, but pleasantly and not dangerously so. She felt a benign dreaminess that might have been due to the attention as much as the champagne.

She wandered off from the remaining crowd of adults and children to the far end of the garden, where there was a lopsided summerhouse, constructed several years before by Max for his sons, and—thanks to Max's inexpert joinery skills—now half falling down. It had a pleasing dilapidated air, and was canopied with a strangulation of roses and vines.

Lindsay sat down on the rickety bench beneath it and breathed in the scents of flowers. The light was just beginning to fade, becoming mauve on the flanks of the far hills. She could hear voices, and was glad they were distant and muted, and glad she was alone.

She closed her eyes and listened to these unfamiliar and welcome country sounds: birdsong and birds' wings, from the field just beyond the hedgerow, the soft, velvety breathing of cows. In one more month, she thought, I shall be thirty-nine years old. She sighed contentedly; this fate, which had previously struck her as terrible, now did not seem so terrible at all.

"Are you all right?" said a voice. "I've been looking for you."

Lindsay opened her eyes. There, outlined against the light, was the tall, dark-suited figure of Rowland McGuire.

"I'm fine," said Lindsay, forgetting to act the tragic heroine. "I'm glorying in all this." She gave a broad, encompassing gesture of the arm. "The smell of grass and flowers. The shade. The birds. The cows."

"I'm interrupting you."

"No, no—not at all."

Rowland looked unreassured. He hesitated and then sat down next to her. He crossed his long legs, then uncrossed them again, then frowned in the direction of the fields.

He might have been calculating their exact acreage, Lindsay thought after a silence had fallen and endured for several minutes.

"Your friend Markov," Rowland ventured, after a while. "He's an interesting man. Not what I expected at all."

"You were prejudiced, I imagine. People are. He plays to their prejudices—you know, the dark glasses, those foolish clothes."

"I suppose," Rowland said with a certain weight and a sideways glance, "that it was arrogance on my part. . . ."

"Possibly. A little," Lindsay said with a smile. "You can be arrogant occasionally, Rowland."

"I know," he replied with a certain amusement and possibly some gloom.

"You should let people surprise you."

"You think so?"

"Yes, I do. I've always liked the unexpected. Things coming at you, out of left field . . ." Lindsay, catching his eye, suddenly remembered her role. She gave a small sigh and folded her hands together. "Even when"—she went on, aiming at a pensive tone of voice, dignified but bravely sad—"even when the surprises are painful. Yes, even then. After all, in life, there're always lessons to be learned."

There was a silence; a long silence. Lindsay did not dare to look at Rowland. She felt almost sure she had overdone that last remark. Unconvincing, she thought, *and* fatuous. She rose.

"I was just wondering . . ." Rowland, who looked vastly amused by something, also rose. "I gather Tom and his girlfriend aren't going back to London with you tomorrow?"

"No. They're going on to friends."

"I suppose it wouldn't be possible for you to give me a lift back, would it? I came down with Max, you see. . . ."

"You won't criticize my driving?"

"I wouldn't dream of it."

"Fine, then. Very well."

Two hours, Lindsay was thinking as she made this crisp reply. Three if she drove slowly, if the traffic was bad. Why had she never noticed how glorious Max's garden was? It looked like Eden. She began to walk back toward the voices, and the fluttering pink and white draperies of Max's rented marquee. Rowland appeared to be intent on escorting her this short distance. Lindsay began to pray for traffic jams, for a ten-mile tie-up, for a punctured tire, a broken fan belt. In the distance she could just glimpse Markov, half concealed behind a bush, much the worse for drink, making faces at her. She began to pray that Rowland would not notice this odd behavior, and this prayer seemed to be answered. Giving a violent gesture, Markov toppled over into the bush with a crashing of branches. Lindsay stole a glance at Rowland; but no—God was merciful—he was looking the other way.

As they reached the French doors that led into Max's drawing room, the telephone began ringing. Rowland excused himself, went inside, and presumably took the call, for the ringing stopped and a long silence ensued.

Lindsay lifted her face to the sun contentedly.

A few minutes later, his features expressionless, Rowland emerged.

"Did they want Max?" Lindsay asked. "He's still up by the marquee, I think."

"No. The call was for me. I've been expecting it, I suppose."

"Good news? Bad news?" Lindsay looked at him curiously. "Are you all right, Rowland?"

"I'm fine. Shall we join the others?"

He guided her around to the terrace. As they reached the steps, he sighed, then smiled and took her arm.

About the Author

Sally Beauman was born in England and graduated from Girton College, Cambridge. She began her career in journalism at *New York* magazine; she was the youngest woman ever to be appointed editor of *Queen* magazine, was an associate editor of the *Daily Telegraph* magazine, and has written for *The New Yorker*. She has published two works of nonfiction and three previous novels, *Destiny, Dark Angel,* and *Lovers and Liars.*

Sally Beauman lives with her family in London and Gloucestershire.